INTO THE WILDERNESS

Also by Sara Donati

INTO THE WILDERNESS
DAWN ON A DISTANT SHORE

LAKE IN THE CLOUDS

Sara Donati

BANTAM BOOKS

New York   Toronto   London   Sydney   Auckland

LAKE IN THE CLOUDS
A Bantam Book

PUBLISHING HISTORY
Bantam hardcover edition published August 2002
Bantam mass market edition/May 2003

Published by Bantam Dell
A Division of Random House, Inc.
New York, New York

Library of Congress Catalog Card Number: 2002018217

ISBN 0-553-58279-8

Manufactured in the United States of America
Published simultaneously in Canada

OPM   10   9   8   7   6   5

For Jill Grinberg

Lake in the Clouds

White-tailed Deer

Chipmunks

Kingston

Lake Ontario

Utica

Lake in the Clouds

Hidden Wolf Mountain

Spinners

Barn

Many Doves

Strawberry Fields

School

Little Muddy

steep climb

Ruick residence

Mill works and overseers residence

Scranton

marshy

School ruins

Half-Moon Lake

Todd's residence

Gabriel Oak's cabin

Church

Gathercole residence

Sacandaga R.

marsh

Trading Post Tavern

Hench residence/ Smithy

laboratory

Paradise

Abandoned Middleton Place

Wilde's orchard and residence

POCONO MOUNTAINS

Bethlehem

Primary Characters

Elizabeth Middleton Bonner (also known as Bone-in-Her-Back), a schoolteacher

Nathaniel Bonner (also known as Wolf-Running-Fast or Between-Two-Lives), a hunter and trapper; Elizabeth's husband

Dan'l Bonner (known also as Hawkeye), Nathaniel's father

Luke or Luc (Nathaniel's first son by an early alliance), resident in Scotland

Hannah (also known as Walks-Ahead), Nathaniel's daughter by his first wife

Mathilde (or Lily, called Two-Sparrows by the Kahnyen'kehàka) and Daniel (called Little-Fox by the Kahnyen'kehàka), Elizabeth and Nathaniel's twins

Selah Voyager, an escaped slave

Many-Doves, a Mohawk woman who lives at Lake in the Clouds; Nathaniel's sister-in-law by his first marriage

Runs-from-Bears, of the Mohawk Turtle clan; the husband of Many-Doves

Blue-Jay, their eldest son; Kateri, their daughter; and Sawatis, their youngest son

Strong-Words, once known as Otter, brother of Many-Doves, living to the west where he has married into a Seneca longhouse

Strikes-the-Sky, Seneca, friend of Strong-Words

Curiosity Freeman, a freed slave, Richard Todd's housekeeper

Galileo Freeman, a freed slave, the manager of Todd's holdings, and Curiosity's husband

Daisy, their daughter, and her husband, Joshua Hench, blacksmith, living in Paradise; their four children, Sarah, Solange, Lucy, Emmanuel

Almanzo, their son, living in New-York City, employed at the African Free School

Richard Todd, a physician
and landholder
Katherine (Kitty)
Witherspoon Middleton
Todd, his wife
Ethan Middleton, Kitty Todd's
son by her first husband
The widow Kuick, born
Lucy Simple, originally of
Boston. Owner of the mill
and the land around it,
bordering on Hidden Wolf
Isaiah Kuick, her unmarried
son and heir
Ambrose Dye, her overseer
The slaves at the mill:
Ezekiel, Levi, Shadrach,
Malachi, Moses, Reuben,
and Cookie
Jemima Southern, a servant
to the widow Kuick along
with Becca Kaes and Dolly
Smythe
Mr. George Gathercole,
minister; Rose, his wife;
Mary, their daughter
Anna Hauptmann McGarrity,
owner and proprietor of the
trading post
Axel Metzler, her father and
proprietor of the tavern
Jed McGarrity, hunter,
trapper, and village
constable
Liam Kirby, a bounty hunter
from New-York City,
formerly of Paradise
Cornelius Bump, assistant to
Dr. Todd
Gabriel Oak, formerly
village clerk

Grievous Mudge, a schooner
captain on Lake Champlain
Sary Emory, his widowed
sister and housekeeper
Baldwin O'Brien, circuit
judge, formerly tax
collector

In New-York City

Elizabeth's cousin Amanda
Spencer and her husband,
William Spencer, Viscount
Durbeyfield, resident in
New-York City; their son,
Peter
Mrs. Douglas, their housekeeper
Harold Bly, innkeeper of the
Bull's Head, and his wife,
Virginia Bly
Meriwether Lewis, President
Thomas Jefferson's secretary
DeWitt Clinton, senator
Dr. Valentine Simon, founder
of the Kine-Pox Institution
and his colleagues and
assistants: Dr. Paul Savard,
Dr. Karl Scofield

At Red Rock

Splitting Moon, daughter of
Made-of-Bones of the Wolf
longhouse of the
Kahnyen'kehàka at Good
Pasture
Elijah, escaped from slavery
July 1794
Renhahserotha' (New-Light),
their son
The Runaways at Red Rock

LAKE IN
THE CLOUDS

New-York Daily Advertiser
April 6, 1802

RUN AWAY FOR THE SECOND TIME a slight built, dark-skinned Negro named DEMETRIUS, the property of the Honourable Henry Cook, Esquire. A very likely young fellow, about 20 years old, has a remarkable swing in his walk, with a surprising knack of gaining the good graces of almost every body who will listen to his bewitching and deceitful tongue, which seldom speaks the truth. From his ingenuity he is capable of doing almost any sort of business and for some years past has been chiefly employed as a cobbler, a stone mason, and a miller as occasion required, one of which trades, I imagine, he will, in the character of a free man, profess. Whoever delivers said valuable Negro to his rightful owner shall receive a reward, besides all reasonable charges.

THE BOUNTY HUNTER MICAH COBB has tracked, captured, and brought to Justice many escaped Negroes, among them Virginia's violent and savage Captain of the Swamp and his band of maroon Thieves and Murderers. Likewise can he return to you runaway or stolen property. "Both thy bondmen and thy bondmaids shall be of the heathen that are round about you ... And ye shall take them as an inheritance for your children after you, to inherit them for a possession; they shall be your bondmen for ever." Lev.25 Rates upon inquiry at the Bull's Head on the Bowery.

RUNAWAY from the Subscriber. William Braun, an indented apprentice, uncommon tall and fair, speaks a broken English. All persons, especially masters of vessels bound for German-speaking ports, are forbid harboring said William upon penalty of law. Whoever will return the runaway to the Subscriber will have Five Dollars Reward. James Burroway, printer, Beaver Street.

FOR SALE a Negro woman, in every respect suitable for a farmer—she is 25 years old, and will be sold with or without a girl four years old and a boy two. Jas. Minthorn, Park Ave.

RUN AWAY a middle-sized high yellow Negro woman, named CONNY. She is about 35 years of age, has some scars on her back, and has a very impertinent countenance. She is fond of liquor, and is apt to sing indecent and sailor songs when so taken. With her a MULATTO man named MOSES, about 40 years old, near 6 feet high, has lost an eyetooth, has a scar or two on some part of his face, and plays on the violin. As I have whipped him twice for his bad behaviour, scars may be seen upon his body. He may try to earn his living as a cooper, having learned that trade on my farm. Reward. Albert vanderPoole, Long-Island.

RUNAWAY from the merchant Hubert Vaark of Pearl Street, a house slave named RUTH, a dark-complexioned wench of loose morals, far gone with child. Artful in her ways, quiet spoken and cunning. Took with her when she left a silver salt box and a carving knife with an ivory handle. It is supposed she may be endeavoring to get to Canada where she and her child might pass for Free. Whoever takes up said Negress, and delivers her to her owner shall receive a bountiful prize, besides all reasonable charges; and if any persons harbour her from just rewards for such wicked behavior as she has shewn, they may expect to be prosecuted to the full extent of the laws of God and man. "Neither shalt thou desire thy neighbour's wife, neither shalt thou covet thy neighbour's house, his field, or his bondman, or his bondwoman, his ox, or his ass, or any thing that is thy neighbour's." Deut. 5:21.

HEREBY BE IT KNOWN that Meg Mather, lawful wife of the subscriber, has eloped from her husband in the company of a Frenchman known as Andre Seville. She took with her the subscriber's infant son, a French Negro slave girl called Marie, and a mantel clock. A reward will be paid for return of the boy, the slave, and the clock, but a husband so maligned by such shameless and sinful behavior is glad to be free, and will give no reward, nor will he allow the wanton back into his home. He therefore warns all persons from trusting her on his account. He will pay no debts of her contracting. Jonah Mather, Butcher. Boston Post Road.

NEGROES TAKEN UP. Committed as runaway to the gaol of this county, two African negro men. They have told so many different stories in what part of the state or continent their owner lives, and speak such broken language, it is impossible to say where they belong. One of them says his name is JAMES, about 40 years old, 5 feet in height, well made, holes in his ears, and has lost one of his fore teeth. The other is called PETER, about 30, 5 feet 4 inches. Both have remarkable small feet. The above negroes were taken up about the first of March, and are now hired out according to law. James Lewis, Sheriff.

A WARNING to all Free and Manumitted Negroes. Captain Matthew Tinker has again brought his ship MARIA to the North River. Captain Tinker has three times been charged with the kidnapping of Free Blacks from the city streets. His custom is to remove them from this State to the South, where they are sold into Slavery never to be seen again.

Captain Tinker operates in malicious and knowing violation of the Gradual Manumission Act of 1799. BEWARE. Libertas.

RAN-AWAY from Nathan Pierson, on Long-Island a negro man named TITE, about 5 feet high, thick set, about 20 years old, very likely; had on when he went away a light-coloured homespun coat, spotted calico trowsers, large smooth plated Buckles. He plays on the fife. Whoever will take up said negro and confine in the gaol in New-London, shall have TEN DOLLARS reward, and all necessary charges, paid by NEZER SLOO, Gaoler.

FOR SALE. The TIME of two indented girls, one MULATTO, one IRISH, strong, upwards of three years left to serve, who can do any kind of house or dairy work, brought up in this family. Inquire of Isaac Whetstone, Park Street.

Hereby let it be known that the New-York City Almshouse currently houses more orphaned infants than can be adequately cared for. Honest and God fearing couples with room enough to take on a foster child may apply to MR THOMAS EDDY. Compensation as determined by the City Council is fifty cents per month per infant less than two years of age.

City of New-York
in the State of New-York
MARGUERITE MATHUSINE SOLANGE
HURON DU ROCHER

You are hereby notified, pursuant to a 2d Pluribus Subpoena directed to you, and now in the hands of the Sheriff, that you be and appear before the honorable Justices of the Supreme Court in this city to be held at the Tweed Street Court House on the first Monday in July next, to answer the libel of your husband, Tiberius Maximus Huron du Rocher, praying for a divorce from the bonds of matrimony. James Lewis, Sheriff.

RAN AWAY from the Subscriber, Annie Fletcher, an indented servant. She is about five foot tall, dark hair, uncommon light eyes, missing the second finger on her left hand. All persons, especially masters of vessels, are forbid harboring said Annie upon penalty of law. Whoever will return the slovenly and ungrateful wretch to the Subscriber will have one cent reward. Elisha Hunt, Sailmaker

Two Dollars Reward. Lost, a young half-grown female DOG of the Newfoundland breed. Yellow and white, with curly hair. Whoever returns said DOG to the Subscriber shall have the above named reward. Francis Loud, Orange Street.

TEN DOLLARS REWARD. Deserted on the night of 3d inst. from the Rendezvous at Fort Gandervoort, Charles Hook, a soldier in the Infantry of the United States. He is 27 years of age, five foot six inches tall, blue eyes, black hair, dark complexion. Wearing a plain green coat and blue nankeen trowsers edged with red and a round hat in which he wears a pidgeon feather dyed blue. Whoever may apprehend and return said Deserter to this Rendezvous or any military post in these United States shall receive the above reward and reasonable costs paid. A. L. Hayes, Lieutenant

THE NEW-YORK DISPENSARY hereby makes it known that public donations have made it possible to offer KINE POX Vaccinations against the dreaded Small-Pox to the City's Poor, at no cost. A SAFE and PAINLESS procedure recommended especially for children. Inquiries to Dr. Valentine SI-MON at the Dispensary or Almshouse

PART I

Spring 1802

Chapter I

In the spring of Elizabeth Middleton Bonner's thirty-eighth year, when she believed herself to be settled, secure, and well beyond adventure, Selah Voyager came to Paradise.

It was the screaming of the osprey that brought the women face to face, just past dawn on a Sunday morning. Elizabeth and her stepdaughter Hannah were skirting the marsh at the far end of Half-Moon Lake when the birds started up, making so much noise chasing each other in great diving swoops that the two of them stopped right there to watch. Weary as she was, Elizabeth was glad of the excuse to rest.

On the edge of New-York's endless forests the winter gave way reluctantly to warm weather, but when the osprey came back to the lake it was a certainty that the last of the ice would soon be gone. And there were other signs as well, all around them: a red-winged blackbird perched on a cattail; wood frogs hidden among the rushes, their queer duck-clack call echoing over the water; reeds flushed with new green. Elizabeth was looking over the lake and taking comfort in what the day had to offer when Hannah caught sight of a clutch of small white flowers in first blossom. Bloodroot gave up a deep scarlet dye, and it was highly prized.

Elizabeth said, "Can't it wait?" And knew it could not; Hannah simply could not walk away from such a useful growing thing. That she had gone a night without rest was immaterial:

she could have run up the mountain and trotted back down again without stopping, or needing to.

With an apologetic look, Hannah pulled a small spade from her basket and knelt down to lift the plant. And froze, as still and attentive as a deer who comes upon a hunter in an unexpected place.

Almost directly before her was a pair of shoes, sitting atop a low oak stump in the early morning sun, as if put there to dry after a walk through the bush. Roughly cobbled and worn down to almost nothing, with scratched blue buckles. Elizabeth had never seen such shoes on anybody in Paradise.

A stranger on the mountain then, and not far off.

The thing to do would be to walk on. It was foolish to even consider confronting a stranger (a trespasser, Elizabeth reminded herself) on the mountain, no matter how curious the footwear such a person might wear. Not with the solemn charge entrusted to her this morning; not as weary as she was. The men would see to it. With the osprey still screeching and wheeling over the lake, Elizabeth was staring at the shoes and arguing silently with herself when Hannah took things into her own hands and pushed the hobblebushes aside.

In a little hollow under an outcropping of stone, a woman lay curled into a ball. Her skin was darker and richer in color than the earth she had slept on; under a homespun jacket her belly was round and taut: yet another child getting ready to fight its way into the world. The vague curiosity that had come to Elizabeth at the sight of the blue buckles was replaced immediately with dread as the woman pulled away from them, her face blank with fear.

It was more than eight years since Elizabeth had last encountered an escaped slave, but she knew with complete certainty that this young woman had run away from someone who considered her to be property.

She said, "You needn't fear us. Have you lost your way?"

For a moment she didn't move at all, and then she scrambled up into a sitting position, looking from Hannah to Elizabeth and back again. Under a high forehead her eyes were luminous with fever, and a trippling pulse beat at the hollow of her throat, as frantic as a bird's.

"I am Elizabeth Bonner. This is my stepdaughter Hannah."

Some of the fear left the woman's face. Her mouth worked without sound, as if language were a burden she had left somewhere on the trail behind her; when her voice finally came to her it was unusually deep and hoarse.

"The schoolteacher. Nathaniel Bonner's wife." She stifled a cough against the back of her hand.

"Yes," said Elizabeth. "Do you know my husband?"

"I heard stories, yes, ma'am."

Hannah said, "You're ill."

She nodded and the turban wrapped around her head slipped; the girl's hair had been shaved to the scalp not so long ago. With trembling fingers she set it to rights. "Been sleeping on the wet ground."

"Were you trying to find someone in the village?" It was as close as Elizabeth could come to asking what she really wanted to know, but it was Hannah who answered.

"She was looking for Curiosity," she said, evoking the name of Elizabeth's closest friend, a woman she loved and trusted as well as any of her own family. To hear Curiosity Freeman's name in connection with a runaway slave in Paradise made complete sense—and was utterly alarming. And what was Hannah's role in this? Elizabeth might have asked, but her stepdaughter had already turned her attention to the stranger and spoke to her directly.

"Curiosity wasn't where she was supposed to be, was she? She had a birth to attend to, but you couldn't know that. So you left again."

The rest of the fear drained from the young woman's face, and Elizabeth saw that she was burning with more than one kind of fever. There was fierce purpose and an acute intelligence in those dark eyes.

She reached into the pocket tied by a string around her waist and held out her hand to them. In the center of her work-hardened palm lay a thin round disk of wood, its edges carved in a geometric pattern, and a white stone lodged at its center. The sight of it made Elizabeth's heart leap in her chest.

"Where did you get that?"

She coughed again, and her fingers swept to a close over the bijou, a gesture as elegant as the folding of a wing. "Almanzo Freeman set me on the path. He gave it to me."

"Almanzo? But he lives—"

"In New-York City, yes ma'am. More than two weeks now I been on my way. Last stopped just outside of Johnstown."

The last time Elizabeth had made the journey from New-York City to Johnstown, it had taken a full seven days by boat, stage, and wagon. To walk this far from Johnstown would require another two days at the very least; perhaps more, with the April muck at its worst. She could hardly imagine what this young woman had managed on her own, in strange countryside.

"Daughter." Elizabeth spoke in the Mohawk language of Hannah's mother's people. "What do you know about this?"

"I know enough," answered Hannah calmly, in the same language. "But there's no time to explain right now. She's sick, and we can't take her through the village by day."

It was a question, and it wasn't. In her usual competent fashion Hannah had already decided what must be done, and she simply waited for Elizabeth to come to the same conclusion.

And how was she to put a coherent thought together with the osprey screaming and two women staring at her? One of them young enough never to give her own safety a thought; the other with good reason to fear for her life. A young woman in need of help, sent here by Curiosity's son Almanzo, a free man of color living in the city. There were people in Paradise who would take pleasure in returning this woman to whatever punishment waited. Perhaps they would take her child from her.

Elizabeth was aware of the fragile bundle in her arms, suddenly as heavy as iron. She said, "We will take you home with us, Miss—What is your name?"

The young woman straightened her shoulders and took a hitching breath. "Selah Voyager." And then: "I'm thankful for your kindness, ma'am, but I'll just wait here till dark."

"Nonsense," said Elizabeth, more sternly than she intended. "You are hungry and fevered, and this is not such an isolated spot as you might think, so close to the lake. You are much safer at Lake in the Clouds. As are we."

Before they were even in sight of the cabins, the sound of children's shrieking laughter came to them. Selah Voyager jerked to a sudden stop and turned toward Elizabeth.

Hannah said, "There's nothing to fear. The children dive

into the water in the mornings and the cold makes them howl."

But it wasn't the children's laughter that had brought Selah up short: her gaze was fixed at a point behind them. Elizabeth knew without turning that someone stood there, and that this young woman had ears keen enough to have heard him, although Elizabeth had not.

Nathaniel said, "I went down to ask after you two, and here you are almost home without me. I see you've brought us some company."

The truth was, her husband's voice had such power over her that Elizabeth's anxiety simply gave way, replaced by relief and pleasure. His hand was on her shoulder and she covered it with her own as she turned to him.

"This is Miss Voyager," Elizabeth said. "She is a friend of Curiosity's."

The young woman curtsied, stifling a cough in her fist.

"Glad to make your acquaintance." Nathaniel's tone was easy, but his expression was equal parts concern and interest.

Hannah said, "We came up the west way, Da. She's chilled through and I want to get her inside."

"Better see to it, then." He was looking hard at Hannah, reading what she had not said from the set of her shoulders and her guarded expression. "We'll follow directly."

Selah Voyager drew herself up to her full height. "Mr. Bonner sir, I am grateful for your help."

Nathaniel managed a smile. "Don't know that I've been any help to you, but you're welcome on Hidden Wolf."

Hannah put out her arms, pointing with her chin to Elizabeth's bundle. When she had taken it and walked on with Selah, Nathaniel pulled his wife closer to examine her face.

"Another stillbirth?"

She nodded, leaning into him.

"I feared as much when you were so long. Kitty's out of danger?"

"Curiosity thinks she will survive, but the child was too small. We said we would bury her next to the others, and then on the way home—" Her voice went suddenly hoarse.

Nathaniel took her by the arm. "You're so tired your knees are wobbling. You can tell me what there is to tell sitting down as well as standing."

*   *   *

The high valley was an oddity, a triangle cut into the side of the mountain at sharp angles. At its far end a waterfall dropped into a narrow gorge; at the widest point two L-shaped cabins stood among blue spruce and birch trees. Three generations of Bonners lived in the east cabin, nearest the falls, and in the other, slightly to the west, lived some of Nathaniel Bonner's Mohawk relatives by his first marriage.

Nathaniel and Elizabeth came out of the woods into the cornfield on the outer apron of the glen. The smell of the earth waking to the spring sun was strong in the air; the stubble of last year's corn crunched underfoot. At the edge of the field a single stunted pine tree had fought its way up through a spill of boulders. Nathaniel sat there and pulled Elizabeth down to sit in the vee of his legs, the back of her head resting on his shoulder and his arms around her waist. Her hair smelled of lavender and chalk and ink, of the tallow candles that had burned all night in a birthing room crowded and tense enough to make her sweat. That was one story she did not have to tell: he had heard others like it too often.

The sound of the waterfall and the children's voices echoed against the cliffs, coming to them in fits and starts: Lily and Kateri scolding, and the boys' laughter in response. Elizabeth was content to be quiet and let him talk, so he told her what had passed while she was in the village, about Hawkeye and Runs-from-Bears going out to walk the trap lines and the fox Blue-Jay killed with his sling shot when it came after the hens. Matilda Kaes had stopped by with five yards of linen, in lieu of cash payment for her grandson's tuition at Elizabeth's school, and Daniel and Blue-Jay had brought a world of trouble upon themselves by eating a pan of stolen cornbread soaked with maple syrup from the last tapping. Nathaniel wondered to himself why, if the boys had made up their minds to eat themselves sick, they hadn't let their sisters in on it, an oversight which had sent Lily and Kateri straight to Many-Doves to report the larceny.

Elizabeth laughed a little at that picture.

Nathaniel said, "You make a man work mighty hard for a smile, Boots."

She twisted in his arms so that he could see that she was capable of smiling, or trying to. They had lost many things in the last year that could not be replaced, and Elizabeth's easy smile was not the least of them. Her sorrow was as clear as the gray of her eyes.

In August a putrid sore throat had come down on the village out of nowhere. Richard Todd and Curiosity had known straight off what they were dealing with, but it took some weeks before the rest of them came to understand. Even after Hannah read them an extract from one of her books, there was no way to really take in the nature of the beast she called *malignant quinsy*—not until he saw it in the throat of his youngest son.

Hannah made him look, and to this day he wished he had refused. He would no more be able to forget the membrane growing in the soft tissues of the throat than he could forget the boy it had choked to death. Nathaniel thought of the disease as a living thing, a stranger come among them to steal, quick and cruel and unstoppable.

When it was done, not one family had escaped. At Lake in the Clouds they had buried two of their own: Hannah's grandmother Falling-Day, and cradled against her chest for safekeeping, Robbie Bonner, just two years old. Nathaniel still expected to hear the boy's voice whenever he opened his front door.

She said, "Kitty's little girl never even took a breath, Nathaniel. At least we had Robbie for a short while."

"Too short," he said, sounding angry, because he was and always would be. Angry at himself, for letting the boy slip away. The truth was, Nathaniel could not make Elizabeth put down her grief any more than he could put aside his own.

Down in the village the church bell began to toll. Elizabeth started, and sat up straight.

Nathaniel said, "Of all the things that Lucy Kuick brought to Paradise when she bought the mill from John Glove, that damn bell is by far the most aggravating."

"It was Mr. Gathercole who brought the bell," Elizabeth reminded him, yawning.

"And who sent for Gathercole?"

"Mrs. Kuick, yes. I see your point. But it was time, Nathaniel. It is a full two years since Mr. Witherspoon moved to Boston, and people are glad to have a minister."

"Not me. Not one with a bell, anyway."

That got a smile, at least. She ran a hand over his cheek. "Are you going to complain about this every Sunday for the rest of your life?"

"If that bell is all there is to worry about then I'm a fortu-nate man, Boots. Are you going to tell me about that young woman, or not?"

She inhaled sharply and let it go again, resigned. "She's a runaway, I think."

"I figured that much just by looking at her," Nathaniel said. "What else do you know?"

Elizabeth recited the story in her calmest voice, and only the way she worked the fabric of her skirt between her fingers gave away her concern.

"She has a bijou."

"A bijou?"

She nodded. "An African bijou, like the one Joe had when we found him in the bush."

"Not the same one."

"No, but it is similar in design. She showed it as if she thought we'd recognize it. I believe Almanzo must use it as a password of sorts, to let Curiosity know that the person before her was sent by him."

Nathaniel rubbed a hand over his face, trying to order these ideas in his head. "You're guessing that they've been running escaped slaves up here for a while, but that don't make much sense, Boots. You know as well as I do that a stranger can't keep hid in Paradise, especially not one with black skin. You think Curiosity's putting them up at the old homestead?"

"That's not very likely," she conceded. Her father's home stood empty since his death, but it was far from abandoned. "People come and go there so often, I can hardly imagine it would be a suitable safe haven."

"Something's going on, that's for certain. I just hope Galileo and Curiosity ain't got mixed up with escaped slaves."

"Nathaniel—" she said tersely, but he squeezed her shoul-der hard to stop what was coming.

"You don't need to lecture me about slavery. I don't like it any more than you do, and you know that well enough. But this might mean a lot of trouble coming our way. What do you think Curiosity was going to do with that girl after she met her at the old homestead?"

"I don't know," Elizabeth said shortly. "But Hannah does."

"By Christ, I hope you're wrong," Nathaniel said, pulling

her closer to him, feeling her weariness and agitation at odds with one another. "But we better go find out."

Wrapped in her muslin shroud, Kitty Todd's stillborn daughter was so small that Hannah could hold her in one palm and feel the shape of her skull, the curve of her spine, the legs tucked up against the chest no wider than a man's thumb.

Kitty had rallied enough just before dawn to deliver her, feet first, into Curiosity's strong hands. The child, far too early and small even for that, could not be persuaded to take a single breath: gone before her mother ever held her, or saw the color of her eyes.

Kitty would not be strong enough to come up the mountain for the burial, but others might. If Richard Todd got home in time—if he didn't drink himself into a stupor out of anger and grief—he would bring Ethan to watch while his half sister was laid to rest tucked between the graves of Hannah's grandmothers: Cora Bonner, who had come from Scotland to make a life for herself on the New-York frontier, and Falling-Day, once clan mother of the Wolf longhouse at Trees-Standing-in-Water. No doubt someone would read something from the bible over his daughter's grave, but for now she was Hannah's responsibility.

She laid the child into a basket and covered her with a blanket, singing a Kahnyen'kehàka death song under her breath. One part of her, the part that was endlessly curious about O'seronni science and medicine, asked why she was taking the time to sing to a dead child when a sick woman waited. The other part of her, far more patient, took comfort in sending the little girl on to the next world with that simple melody in her ear.

When she returned to Selah Voyager, she found that the journey had taken a heavy toll, filled her lungs so that they rattled with every breath. She was quiet while Hannah examined her, out of fear or weariness or relief or all three. Or maybe she had no questions, maybe she preferred to know nothing of Paradise, thinking it just another stop on the journey. Headed for a safer place, and that not far off now. Hannah could offer that comfort, tell her how close she was, but she hesitated to share knowledge she was not supposed to have at all.

For her part, Hannah was curious. She wanted to ask about the city, how she had met Manny Freeman, what kind of life she had left behind, if she had walked the whole way, and how much she knew about the place where she was going. But she could wait; she would put aside her questions while she attended to her patient's needs. Patience was the hardest lesson, but she had had good teachers in her grandmothers.

On both sides Hannah was descended from healers. It was what she was born to, the only thing that really interested her. She had had good training from the women around her. One white grandmother, one Indian, and Curiosity Freeman. O'seronni medicine and Kahnyen'kehàka, each with strengths and weaknesses; then Elizabeth came to Paradise and brought Cowper's *The Anatomy of Human Bodies with Figures Drawn After Life* and Thacher's *American New Dispensatory,* books that raised more questions than they answered. Finally she had studied for a few months with Hakim Ibrahim, a ship's surgeon who had showed her another kind of truth in the small oval lens of a microscope and more books, these ones ancient, with sinuous, musical names: Ibn Sina's *Al-Qanun fi'l-Tibb.*

All of her teachers hovered near while Hannah treated Selah, taking note of her breathing and the smell of her sweat, how dull and dry her tongue and the whites of her eyes. She listened for a long time with her ear against the smooth brown back, and did not like what she heard. In spite of the liquid in her lungs—or maybe because of it—she was in need of water above all other things, or the fever would overtake her and pull her out of this world and into the next one.

Selah submitted to Hannah's treatment without question. She murmured thanks for the basin of hot water and soap, accepting dry clothes and a blanket with a small smile. She drank the bowl of broth that was put into her hands and swallowed Hannah's fever tea; it was powerfully bitter, but she made no complaint.

Her eyes moved everywhere over the edge of the tin cup, from the shadows at the far end of the common room to the worktable near the door, crowded with bullet molds, a dismantled rifle, traps in various stages of repair. Under the open window, the ink pot on Elizabeth's desk glinted indigo in the sun. Neat piles of paper were held down with rocks, and within reach of her chair were both a crowded bookcase and a churn. Braids of onion, corn, and squash hung from the rafters along with bundles of herbs and roots: just one part of

Hannah's apothecary, and as important to her family's well-being as the tending of the cornfield.

But it was the furs that seemed to interest Selah Voyager most. Some pelts still hung on the walls in stretchers, but most had been tied into bundles and piled along the wall, away from the hearth. The whole winter's work—beaver, fox, fisher, marten, muskrat—waiting to be loaded into the canoes and taken to Albany. To this young woman who was raised to believe she would never have the right to claim anything as her own—not the clothes on her back nor the child she carried—it must look like a treasure beyond reckoning.

Hannah picked up a fisher pelt and put it in her lap.

"Makes a good pillow," she said. "Let me show you where you can sleep."

Selah stroked the fur like a living thing in need of comfort, her fingers long and thin and dusty black against the rich deep brown pelt. Her mouth worked, but nothing came out.

"Time enough later to talk," Hannah said. "When you're rested."

"Will you send for Mrs. Freeman?"

"She'll be here when you wake up." Hannah prayed that she could keep that promise, for herself as well as Selah Voyager.

Chapter 2

Jemima Southern, a single woman of nineteen years, as ambitious as she was poor, always started her week in the same way: at church, taking stock not of her own soul, but of the sins of her neighbors. After Mr. Gathercole's sermon she lingered, not to share news or meet friends, but to gather bits of news like eggs warm from the nest and to hurry them to the widow Kuick at the mill.

It was late when Jemima was satisfied that the women had no more useful information to offer her. She started home at a trot, crossing the bridge with her back straight and her eyes downcast. If she raised her head, she would see her mistress sitting at her parlor windows.

When Lucy Kuick bought the mill from John Glove, she had proclaimed the house where he raised his family unsuitable for her own. A bigger and grander house had been built away from the noise of waterwheels, perched on the hillside that overlooked her property, as well as the lake, the river, the bridge that spanned it, and the village. From that vantage point nothing would escape her notice, not the names of the men who stood spitting tobacco juice into the bushes outside the trading post, nor the fact that Mr. Gathercole was still deep in conversation with Anna Hauptmann and Jed McGarrity on the church step. They might forget who watched them from the house on the hill, but Jemima could not.

If not for the widow Kuick, Jemima would have ended up

milking cows or serving ale when she lost her mother and brothers to the putrid sore throat. Instead she had a mistress who sat in the front pew at church services and went home to take up embroidery, as a lady was supposed to do. Jemima counted herself fortunate to have come into the service of a wealthy mistress, especially as the widow had two passions that Jemima shared: her unmarried son, and gossip.

Born and raised in Paradise, there was little Jemima did not know or could not find out, and nothing she scrupled to share. She was rewarded well for this skill. Of the three maidservants—she had begun service at the mill on the same day as Dolly Smythe and Becca Kaes—only Jemima had a tiny chamber to herself.

Now she came into the dim, warm kitchen and hung her cape on a peg near the door. She took off her pattens and left them there for Reuben to scrape clean of mud. There were some advantages for a servant in a household with slaves. Some advantages, and many disadvantages, most of them having to do with the woman crouched before the hearth, ladling cider over a ham.

Cookie, small and lean and skeptical in all things, was the only one of the seven slaves who was allowed to stay in the house overnight, sleeping on a pallet next to the kitchen hearth. Her Reuben went up to the mill to sleep and came back at dawn. The other men—her older sons Levi and Zeke among them—had been sent to Johnstown for the winter, hired out as laborers while the mill stood idle over the winter.

Cookie spoke without ever looking in Jemima's direction.

"You took your time."

Jemima came to the hearth to examine the pots of squash and yams drizzled with molasses. In another deep kettle, beans simmered in sauce glistening with pork fat. Cookie might be an irritation, but Jemima could find nothing to criticize in the food she put on the table. Her stomach growled loudly.

"Better get up there now, or you'll go without no matter what your belly have to say about it."

"You tend to your work and I'll attend to my own." Jemima left the kitchen at a comfortable pace devised to make Cookie understand that she had no authority over a free white woman, even one who happened to be a servant.

By the time she reached the parlor door Jemima's calm had

fled. She paused to set her muslin cap right and smooth her skirt and saw—too late—flecks of mud on the hem. It would not go unnoticed, but right now the greater sin would be to make the mistress wait.

Lucy Kuick looked up from her needlework only long enough to examine Jemima as she curtsied, one corner of her mouth turning down. The widow had a soft voice with a crackling edge to it, each word bitten off like a wayward thread. "Took you long enough, missy. What news?"

Jemima kept her eyes fixed on the widow's mourning brooch: gray hair woven into a knot and captured under crystal. She used the brooch with its black-and-white enameled lilies to keep her mind off Isaiah Kuick, who sat behind her in the corner. It was the widow's pleasure to have her son read aloud from the bible while she worked on her tapestry. Jemima felt Isaiah's eyes on her back as insistent as a hand; she focused harder on the brooch as she began to relate her news.

She was a good storyteller, with an understanding of how long she could hold off her audience and how best to keep their interest. She began with the smaller things: Anna Hauptmann was now set to marry the widower McGarrity on the following Sunday afternoon; McGarrity, who had been voted constable when Judge Middleton died, had arrested Peter Dubonnet for taking a buck out of season, a fact that couldn't be disputed as Dubonnet had hung the meat to ripen in sight of God and man; Goody Cunningham had come to church in an old ozanbrig shift more suited to fieldwork than Sunday worship; Jock Hindle had got drunk on schnapps and spent the night sleeping on the tavern floor, where he was still. This was a great deal of news for so small a village, but the widow still had not had enough. Her needle jabbed impatiently.

"And Kitty Todd?"

Jemima took a deep breath and recited the details: a long labor, the names of the women who had attended her, the point at which the doctor's man had been sent to Johnstown to fetch his master home from his business there—

"I suppose they sent the Abomination, that Bump."

Jemima acknowledged that the doctor's laboratory assistant had been sent on the errand. The widow was both horrified and fascinated by Cornelius Bump's physical deformities, but for once she let that topic rest as Jemima continued on with her story: a child normal in form but too small to live, a distraught mother, and the speculations on how her husband would take the news of another stillbirth. There were no confessions or revelations to offer, no drunkenness or heresy; Jemima did a bit of embroidery of her own.

"Kitty won't last much longer, they say." She served this conclusion in a whisper, and saw that she had gone too far: the widow's head came up slowly.

"Are you presuming to know the will of the Lord?"

From his corner, Isaiah sighed his concern for her immortal soul while Jemima assured his mother that she presumed no such thing.

The widow's gaze settled on the view while she considered. Jemima saw the line of her back straighten suddenly, the small thin face with its pointed nose and chin fixing on something in the distance. Like a good hunting dog, Jemima thought, and put that thought out of her head before the widow could have a chance to read it from her expression.

"And what of that stranger?" said the widow, stretching out an arm to point, her finger trembling slightly.

Isaiah stood abruptly and moved to the window, close enough to Jemima for her to smell him: dry and slightly dusty, as if he lived on a shelf next to his mother's china figurines of shepherds and milkmaids. She forced herself to look out the window.

A man stood on the bridge looking up toward Hidden Wolf. Tall and well built, dark red hair tied in a queue, dressed like any hunter: buckskin leggings and overshirt, moccasins. There was a rifle in a sling across his back, a sheathed knife at his side, and a tomahawk tucked into a wide leather belt at his spine. At first glance nothing more than another trapper coming out of the bush. At this time of year sometimes as many as two a day showed up in Paradise, looking for a warm meal. They rarely stayed more than a night and left little more behind than the few coins they spent on beer or Axel's schnapps. Jemima was about to say just that when the man turned.

"My God."

The widow leaned forward. "Do you know that man?"

For once Jemima was less concerned with Lucy Kuick's curiosity than her own. She studied the stranger as closely as the distance would allow, her heart beating so fast that she put a hand there to still it. When he had called his dogs and walked off into the village, she took a sharp breath and let it go.

The widow leaned forward and pinched Jemima's forearm so that she jumped. "I asked you a question."

"Liam Kirby," she said. "I hardly recognized him at first."

"Liam Kirby?" Patches of color had appeared on the widow's fallen cheeks. "I know of no Liam Kirby. A relation to Billy?"

"His younger brother, yes. He left Paradise some years ago. I thought—everybody thought he must be dead."

"You see that he is not." The widow picked up her embroidery again. "Go down to the village and see why he's here."

"An old beau come to claim our Jemima, no doubt," said Isaiah, one eyebrow cocked.

Jemima blinked hard. "If Liam Kirby's come back to Paradise, it must have something to do with the Bonners. With Hannah Bonner."

Now she had the widow's attention, and Isaiah's as well. But how much to say to a lady who had taken an instant dislike to Hannah, or to that lady's only son, who had done just the opposite? Isaiah's interest in Hannah was well known to Jemima, and it prickled.

She searched frantically for something that would satisfy them both without giving away too much, not yet. Not until she had time to think this through herself.

The widow leaned forward to peer more closely at Jemima's face, as if she could read things there no one else could see. "Explain yourself, girl."

Jemima cleared her throat. "The Bonners took Liam in when Billy died."

The widow reared back with her head. "Billy Kirby, who burned down their schoolhouse? Nathaniel Bonner took in Billy Kirby's brother?"

Jemima nodded. If she could count on one thing only, it was the fact that the widow never forgot a story. The history of the Paradise school—most particularly Elizabeth Bonner's role in it—was something that had interested her from the first. The widow could not abide the idea of a school where boys and girls sat in the same room, and she had tried to have it shut down more than once.

"They threw him out, no doubt."

"No," Jemima said. "That wasn't it. When they went off to Scotland so sudden that year—"

The widow's mouth contorted, and Jemima faltered for just a moment. She did not usually make the mistake of mentioning Hawkeye's family in Scotland; nothing irritated her mistress more than the undeniable fact that a backwoods trapper and hunter had connections superior to her own. The surprise of seeing Liam had flustered her, but there was nothing to do but push on and hope she could distract the widow from thoughts of Scottish earldoms.

"And that's when he just disappeared. Left one day without a word to anybody, and he hasn't been back since. I always wondered—" She stopped herself.

Jemima had been going to say, *I always wondered if Liam would come back for Hannah one day.* But to provide that information would provoke both the widow and her son; worse, it would give credence to something she had wanted to dismiss from her mind. So she provided a different theory, one she liked a little better.

"Some think that Liam found the Tory gold and stole it from them, and that's why he ran off."

The widow's displeased expression was replaced instantly with one that was equal parts derision and disbelief. "More absurd stories about the Bonners, as likely as snow in July. So this Liam ran off from them; I'd say that showed some good sense. And now he's back. But why?"

Isaiah retreated to his corner. "I'm sure you'll find out, Mother. In the end."

"I don't intend to wait that long." The widow fingered her mourning brooch thoughtfully, and then her head swooped around toward Jemima.

"They'll bury the child this afternoon, no doubt. Only right that I send you up to pay my respects. Say a Christian prayer over Todd's daughter. If the good doctor will consort with heathens and papists it's the best that he could hope for anyway."

Jemima swallowed hard. She had been promised an afternoon off for the first time in three months, but to remind the widow of that would bring repercussions she did not like to contemplate. With a great sigh, Jemima nodded.

The widow bent again to her needlework, looking greatly satisfied with her plan.

$\star$ $\star$ $\star$

Mid-afternoon, Nathaniel and Hawkeye went down to the village to fetch Curiosity. Hannah had banned everyone from the cabin while Selah Voyager slept, so Nathaniel left without asking her the questions she must know were coming her way. Hawkeye never saw the mysterious young woman, and only knew of her what Nathaniel could relate.

Nathaniel was glad of the chance to talk things through with his father. Age made many people impatient, but at seventy-five years old Hawkeye was as steady as the sky overhead, never in a hurry to judge and hard to rile.

Hawkeye listened without asking questions, but when Nathaniel finished he got to the heart of the matter without apologies.

"I suppose you're right; Curiosity is the place to start if you want to ask questions," he said. "But I'm not sure you do. I'd think twice about that, son."

Nathaniel pulled up short. "Can't avoid trouble if I don't know what direction it's coming from."

Hawkeye inclined his head. "You can borrow trouble, though, if you've got a mind to. The way I see it, as soon as the girl is well enough Curiosity and Galileo will help her on her way, and that'll be the end of it. It ain't any of our business if they feel the need to lend a hand. I wouldn't be surprised if Joshua has a part in it too. Who better to help that girl than her own kind, people who been slaves themselves?"

It was the very question that Elizabeth would have asked him this morning, if he had let her. Joshua Hench was free because the Bonners had taken an interest in his welfare, and if he saw fit to help others in his turn, there was nothing surprising—or wrong—about that. Nathaniel could admit to himself that he hadn't been thinking clearly when Elizabeth first told him about Selah Voyager; later tonight he'd have to admit it to her too.

"Maybe so," he said, finally. "But I got a bad feeling about this." And when his father made no comment, he finished: "I hate to think what trouble Curiosity and Galileo might be calling down on their heads."

They walked on in silence for a while. All around them were signs of the mountain coming back to life; another summer ahead, and with it the threat of disease. He was thinking about this so hard that at first he didn't hear his father, and Hawkeye had to repeat himself.

"Did you ever hear tell how it was that Curiosity and Galileo met?"

Nathaniel nodded. "It was back before Elizabeth's grandfather Clarke bought them free and they came to work for the judge. That's all I know."

"They met on the auction block," said Hawkeye. "Both sold as youngsters to the same farmer just outside Philadelphia."

Nathaniel paused. "Why haven't I heard that story before?"

His father shrugged. "They don't talk much about the old days. Sixty years ago, but Galileo can tell you about that morning they sold him away from his mother like it happened yesterday. I suppose he's willing to take his chances to help that girl, or anybody else who comes to him looking to get away. I would be, and so would you."

"I'm willing to give you that," Nathaniel said. "But then there's Squirrel's role in all this. I won't have her risking her own safety, no matter how good the cause."

Hawkeye stopped. There was an expression on his face that Nathaniel knew very well: a kind of sympathy mixed with disquiet that meant he had hard words to share.

"I ain't so sure she's as involved as you seem to think. And even if she is, why she'll be eighteen this summer, but you're still calling her by her girl-name. You're lucky she hasn't gone off already, son. She's more than old enough to start making her own decisions."

"Not if those decisions put the rest of the family at risk."

"You know better than that," Hawkeye said, frowning. "That's not in her nature."

"I'm not saying she'd do it on purpose." Nathaniel rubbed a hand over his face. "But she's headstrong and she's young."

"She's older than you were when you went off on your own," said Hawkeye. "It scared the hell out of your mother and me, knowing what trouble you could get yourself into. But we let you go, and it's time you start thinking about the day you won't be able to hold her back. She won't disappoint you, son. Don't you disappoint her. Show some faith."

Nathaniel started a little at that, but any argument he might have raised left him at the sight of Jemima Southern coming around a bend a quarter mile down the trail.

They stood their ground and waited, watching her come on. She was flushed with walking, and the color suited her. Not a beautiful girl, but comely and solid. No doubt she would be married by now, if it weren't for her cantankerous disposition. Looking at her, Nathaniel had to admit that if Jemima Southern could make a place for herself alone in the world, the same was true of his own daughter.

"Hail there, Mima," Hawkeye said when she was close enough. "Coming to pay our Hannah a visit, are you?"

She drew up short, and pulled her cloak closer around herself. "The widow sent me to pay her respects at the burial." She looked off into the trees instead of at the people she was talking to, a habit that reminded Nathaniel of her father, a man who had been suspicious to the bone and with a temper as quick as fire.

Hawkeye was looking at her with more sympathy than Nathaniel could ever muster. He said, "Thoughtful of you, but we buried that little girl not an hour ago. Elizabeth read a bible passage over her, in case that's what the widow was worried about."

Jemima's chin tightened by way of a smile. She said, "I'll just head back to the mill then." But she stood there on the path without moving, chewing on her lip and looking off into the trees.

"Something you wanted to say?" Nathaniel asked.

She looked up, her eyes flashing. "Did you hear about Liam Kirby?"

That name took Nathaniel by surprise, but Hawkeye didn't fluster.

"Cain't say that we have. Is there news of the boy?"

Jemima sent him a sidelong glance. "Saw him this morning, right in the village. Thought he might have come up to pay his respects. Old friend that he is and all."

Nathaniel said, "If that's the case, I'm sure he'll be by. We'd be glad to see him. Hannah especially."

The girl flushed, and Nathaniel regretted letting his irritation push him to say something so mean-spirited. It was clear enough that Jemima had never stopped thinking about Liam, she wore that on her sleeve. And of course she'd heard the rumors about the stolen gold. Most probably she had come up here hoping to see some kind of confrontation between Kirby and the Bonners, eager to take that news to Lucy Kuick. The thing was, they didn't need any strangers up at Lake in the Clouds until Selah Voyager had moved on.

Hawkeye was thinking in just the same direction. He said, "Maybe you'll come by another time, then. When Elizabeth and Hannah have caught up on their sleep."

But Jemima wasn't done. She stood there on the trail as if it belonged to her.

"Dr. Todd rode in from Johnstown just as I was setting off." She smiled pleasantly. "You'll want to stay clear of him, he's drunk as a lord."

Whether or not they wanted to stay clear of Richard Todd, they were obliged to seek him out, as it was his home they were headed for. They found him in his study with a bottle of brandy three-quarters gone. He was a big man going a little soft around the jowls, his hair thinning fast and the first threads of silver in his reddish-gold beard. Richard listened as Hawkeye told him what little they had been able to do for his child.

"We put her right between your mother and mine," Nathaniel added. Hoping that it would provide some comfort, to know his daughter rested between two women Todd had loved and respected. The man deserved some sympathy, but it didn't come easy: there was a lot of history between them and most of it was hard.

"How's Kitty?" Hawkeye asked.

"Poorly, but she'll pull through. She always does." Not sounding as if he regretted that fact—he was not that far gone—but weary and angry and sick at heart. Just when Nathaniel was starting to soften toward him, Richard cocked his head and looked him in the eye, as plain bad tempered as ever.

"Remember that day I told Elizabeth you couldn't sire a child? The look on her face. But you proved me wrong, so it looks like the joke's on me."

Hawkeye said, "Strange talk for a day like today, Todd."

He shook his head. "I'm confessing something here, Hawkeye. Doesn't happen too often, so you should listen. Nathaniel's got how many to his name now, four? And three in their graves that he can claim as his own. We're even on that score, at any rate. One contest I didn't plan to win."

Nathaniel jolted at that, but his father put a restraining hand on his shoulder. Hawkeye said, "If you're looking for a fight you won't get it from us. We'll just have a word with Curiosity and then we'll be on our way home. We'll take Ethan up to Lake in the Clouds for a few days, if you can spare him."

Richard grunted. "Suit yourselves." He flashed Nathaniel a sidelong glance. "If you're done with this little condolence visit, you can leave me in peace."

Curiosity was waiting for them in the hall. Standing with her arms wrapped around herself and her head turned to rest her cheek on her shoulder, lost in her thoughts. When she was as tired as she was now she somehow reminded Nathaniel of his own mother, another woman who had worn down to leather, each year scraping a little closer to the bone.

When she looked up, Nathaniel knew that she had heard at least some of the conversation with Richard by the expression on her face.

"I already sent Ethan up the mountain," she said. "It don't do the boy good, listening to his ma wail."

Hawkeye said, "Blue-Jay and Daniel will take care of him. We're hoping you'll come along too, Curiosity. If you can leave Kitty for a while and can spare the time."

She pulled back her head to look at them hard. Nathaniel had known this woman all his life, but sometimes it still took him by surprise, the way she read things off people's faces.

"Trouble?"

Hawkeye raised a shoulder. "Maybe. We ain't sure, quite yet."

She took her cloak down from its peg and settled it around her shoulders. "I hope it can wait a few hours. Look like Mariah Greber about to bring her sixth child into the world."

"Then we'll walk you out to the stable," said Nathaniel.

"I was hoping you would."

When they were clear of the house Curiosity said, "I surely would like to take a switch to Richard. Don't know why it is some men got to plead angry when they hurt."

"That's the brandy working," said Hawkeye.

"'Course it is, and more's the shame on him."

Richard Todd was her employer, but he had also been the first child Curiosity ever delivered; she wasn't intimidated by his money, his place in society, or his bad tempers. Not so long ago Nathaniel wouldn't have believed that Curiosity would ever get along well enough with Richard to look after his household, but then the old judge died and for once Kitty had put her foot down: she would not stay on in Paradise without Curiosity and Galileo. For Kitty's sake and his own peace of mind and home, Richard had made an uneasy truce with Curiosity, but they hovered forever on the brink of warfare.

Nathaniel wondered himself at Richard, a man who was always so busy calculating what he didn't have that he lost sight of what was in front of him: Kitty was a good wife, mostly grown out of her flightiness and eager to do right by him. She had brought him a fine son by her first marriage to Elizabeth's brother Julian, and that son had inherited more than half of the judge's holdings. It seemed like Richard had almost everything he set out to get for himself.

Galileo looked up from saddling Curiosity's horse when they came through the door. He squinted hard in their direction, and then a smile broke over his face.

"Now ain't it good to see you," he said "Cain't recall the last time I seen you together at that door."

Nathaniel always took pleasure in coming into this barn. It was as tidy as Curiosity's kitchen, with a sense of contentment and order that came when a man with an understanding of animals was in charge. A stable as quiet and calm as a Quaker meetinghouse, not a bucket or harness out of place.

Galileo was a little younger than Hawkeye, but time sat hard on him. There was a curve to his back that grew worse every year; now when Curiosity stood beside him they were exactly the same height, although Nathaniel could remember very well when that wasn't the case. For a few minutes they talked business: ice-out and crops, pelts and foals and spring lambs. Galileo's gaze fixed on Nathaniel, and he saw how very bad his eyes had grown over the winter, the deepening milky film closing over dark pupils. Squirrel was worried about him, and just recently she had made it known that she was going to approach Richard Todd about the problem.

"I expect you heard the news about Liam Kirby." Galileo addressed this to the men, but Curiosity's head came up with a snap like bone breaking.

"Liam Kirby?"

"He's in the village," said Nathaniel. "We heard from Jemima Southern, but we haven't laid eyes on him yet."

She advanced a step on her husband. "Why didn't you say nothing to me about this?"

"Because you ain't give me a chance," Galileo answered. "Joshua came by with the news, not a half hour ago."

Curiosity drew up in agitation. "If Mariah weren't set on bringing that child into the world today, I'd go find Liam and ask him a few questions. What can he mean by it, just showing up after so long? Leaving folks to worry."

Galileo sent her a sidelong glance. "The way Joshua sees it, young Liam has found hisself work as a bounty hunter."

They all stilled in surprise, even Hawkeye. Nathaniel thought of Selah Voyager up at Lake in the Clouds and the knot of anxiety that had begun to relax in his gut pulled tight again.

"I don't believe it," Curiosity said shortly. "Liam was always a sweet-natured boy. What would make Joshua think such a thing?"

Galileo shrugged. "Heard Liam talking to Jed McGarrity, wanting to know has he seen any strange Africans hereabouts."

Curiosity closed her eyes and opened them again. "I still don't believe it. That's not the boy I knew."

"But it's been eight years," Nathaniel said. "No telling what eight years can do to a young man, if he's in the wrong company. And maybe it ain't a coincidence that he showed up today, looking for runaways. Squirrel and Elizabeth came across a young woman on their way home this morning. Walked here all the way up the big river."

As he spoke Curiosity's expression went blank and watchful, and Galileo stilled.

"She give you a name?" Galileo asked.

"She goes by the name of Selah, and she's asking for you. She's carrying a bijou."

Nathaniel had expected worry and agitation, but all he could see on Curiosity's face was pure relief.

She said, "Thank the Lord for delivering her to safety."

Galileo grunted. "She ain't safe yet. At least we know now what brought Liam back to Paradise." And to Nathaniel and Hawkeye: "Never meant to get you folks mixed up in this."

Curiosity frowned. "They ain't mixed up in it. Joshua will see the girl on her way tonight, and that'll be all the Hidden Wolf folks ever saw or heard of her."

Hawkeye cleared his throat. "That's just about what I figured you'd say. But you ain't heard all of it. Hannah says Miss Selah's got a fever in her lungs."

Curiosity and Galileo exchanged looks, and then Curiosity

straightened her shoulders and mounted her horse as nimbly as a twenty-year-old.

"It will set folks to talking if I go straight up the mountain, and that's the last thing we need right now. Let's hope young Liam don't follow her trail to Lake in the Clouds. As soon as Mariah has delivered her child and I've checked on Kitty, I'll be by."

Galileo handed her the reins and patted her knee thoughtfully. "You ain't had a full night's sleep in two days, wife."

She smiled down at him, a fierce kind of smile. "I'll get there as soon as I may. In the meantime you all keep an eye on Liam Kirby until I have a chance to talk to the boy and set him straight."

Hannah Bonner's Day Book

APRIL 12, 1802. EVENING.

Warm and clear. First bees among the nimble weed. Black phoebes are come early this year.

Yesterday evening Elizabeth and I were called to Kitty Todd in travail and this morning at 4 of the clock she was delivered of a stillborn daughter. The afterbirth came cleanly. Curiosity's good ointment and a bath of tansy, mugwort, chamomile, and hyssop gave the poor mother some relief.

Last night my aunt Many-Doves dreamed of bears in the strawberry fields.

Miss Selah Voyager has come to stay and brought a fever with her. A quickened pulse and rattling low in both lungs. She coughs but brings forth nothing. Her urine cloudy. Gave her an infusion of willow bark and meadowsweet for fever and an onion-and-camphor poultice to loosen the corruption in her chest. Dressed a wound on her leg with slippery elm. Her child moves cleverly but shows no signs of being ready to come into the world. I believe she will recover, if I can keep her quiet long enough and if the bounty hunters she fears can be kept at bay.

Chapter 3

Lily Bonner's father and grandfather went down to the village without her and so she devised a plan: this afternoon while all the women were wound up in the new troubles and the boys were busy trying to distract cousin Ethan from his sorrow, she would slip away to the lake and reappear in the evening with enough smelt to feed everybody. A supper of smelt fried in cornmeal would please her mother, impress her father, and best of all, irritate her brother.

It did not take long to find a piece of fishing net the right size, but Lily had to climb up on a barrel to get the canvas bucket down from its hook on the barn wall. She was finely built and small for her age—shorter even than her cousin Kateri who was a year younger. But she was quick and she managed on her own.

If it weren't for the fact that Hannah was sitting on the porch with her daybook in her lap, Lily would have slipped away right then.

But her sister had that look that came over her when somebody was sicker than she thought they ought to be, as if it were an insult to her personally. It was a look she had a lot, even when she meant to smile, as she did now.

"Little sister, are you going to tote that bucket all by yourself once it's full?"

Hannah's voice carried like the breeze off the waterfalls, and sent a shiver right up Lily's back. It made her jump to have her mind read so easily. Sometimes it felt as if her forehead were made of window glass and every thought there was as plain as the words on a page.

She dragged the bucket over to the porch, and sat down on the step. "I'm strong as any boy."

"Stronger," said Hannah.

Lily sniffed. "The smelt are running, and everybody but me's too busy to notice."

"Where are the boys?"

"They went with Ethan to the fort."

"Hmmm." Hannah fanned herself with the blotter. "Maybe Grandfather will go with you to the lake when he comes back from the village." Her sister was reading her mind again, but this time Lily did not mind so much.

She shifted so she could see into the daybook resting across her sister's knees. Hannah often drew pictures to go along with her notes, but this page was filled only with her neat handwriting. Lily studied the page for a moment.

"Is that her name, Selah Voyager?"

Hannah nodded. "It's the name she has claimed for herself."

"Never heard that name before, Selah. Is it African?"

"I don't know. You can ask her when she's feeling better."

"Is she going to die?"

"Someday," said Hannah. "But not today, or tomorrow either. Why don't you go over to Many-Doves and see if she's got any soup left over for me? I haven't eaten since this morning."

Lily was already at her aunt's door before she realized how gently her sister had weaned her away from her plans. She might have marched right back to tell her so, but Kateri was calling out to her and Lily could not resist being drawn into the half-circle of women around the hearth. Here was something more tempting than fishing: her mother sitting down and her lap empty, her knitting put aside for the moment. Lily stepped over Kateri to get to her, pausing to examine the face of Many-Doves' youngest son, asleep in the cradleboard on her back. Pines-Rustling was there too, piecing new leggings for Runs-from-Bears while she kept an eye on Kateri, who hadn't yet finished her part of grinding the day's corn.

Pines-Rustling was a cousin to Many-Doves; she had come to visit three years ago, and just recently Lily realized that she never intended to go away. This suited her very well;

Pines-Rustling was generous with her many stories of the
Kahnyen'kehàka at Good Pasture, and she had made Lily a pair
of moccasins with the most beautiful quillwork. She admired
them now as she climbed up into her mother's lap.

"I was wondering about you," said Elizabeth. She spoke
Kahnyen'kehàka, except it came out with a strange rhythm
and turned-around sentences, just the same way that Pines-
Rustling spoke English. Only the children were truly comfortable in both languages, but in this cabin everyone spoke
Mohawk. Many-Doves and Runs-from-Bears had chosen to
raise their family away from the Kahnyen'kehàka longhouses
where they had grown up, but Many-Doves only let as much
of the O'seronni world in as she found necessary.

Lily rubbed her face against her mother's shoulder, wiggling
a little to make herself a more comfortable spot. "Sister sent
me, she's hungry for soup."

Many-Doves smiled without looking up from her sewing.
"The visitor must be out of danger if Walks-Ahead has time to
take note of her own stomach."

Elizabeth tucked a stray curl back into her daughter's plait.
"It is very good of you to look after your sister."

Lily wiggled like a puppy, pleased with this picture of herself as Hannah's caretaker. She had always been a serious child,
self-contained and earnest even in her play, but since Robbie's
death she had turned even more inward. She was often at odds
with the other children, arguing with her twin and her cousins
and then going off to play by herself. Daniel mourned Robbie
too, but still he rose every morning to fling himself out into
the world. Since their youngest had gone from them, Lily was
truly content only here on the mountain, with her family
around her.

Too much like me. Elizabeth set her daughter on her feet and
pushed herself up. "Let us take your sister her soup then."

As soon as they were out of the door, Lily said in English,
"What's a bounty hunter?"

Elizabeth stopped. "Where did you hear that word?"

"Hannah wrote it in her daybook. That Selah Voyager fears
bounty hunters."

Her first impulse was to scold Lily for reading her sister's
daybook, but this was an old battle and one Elizabeth feared
she would lose in the end. Lily intensely disliked sitting in the

classroom, but she would read whatever came her way, regardless of warnings and repercussions.

"A bounty hunter is a man who hunts down criminals or escaped prisoners or slaves and returns them for a cash reward."

The small mouth pursed thoughtfully. "Did a bounty hunter come after Curiosity and Galileo, or Joshua Hench, or Daisy?"

"No," Elizabeth said. "Curiosity and Galileo and Joshua did not run away from their owners. Each of them was bought out of slavery, and Daisy was born in freedom. They have manumission papers, you see, a legal document that declares the person in question is free."

The small oval face went very still for a moment. "Do I have manumission papers too?"

She said this calmly, but Elizabeth saw the spark of real concern and fear in her daughter's eyes. She sat down on the step and pulled Lily down next to her.

"You have no need of manumission papers. No one would question your freedom, Lily. You have nothing to fear from bounty hunters."

"Or from kidnappers," Lily prompted.

"Or from kidnappers," Elizabeth echoed obediently, wishing again that the children weren't always so eager to hear stories of what had happened to them when they were just a few months old.

"Everybody knows I'm free because I'm white," Lily reasoned out loud. And then: "Well, then, why can't we write a paper like that for Selah Voyager?"

Elizabeth pulled up in surprise. "That would be forgery, as if we decided to make our own paper money and claim it came from the government treasury. We don't have the authority to write manumission papers for Selah, or anyone. The law would see that as theft."

"But if one person can't belong to another person, how can that be thievery? You can't steal something nobody owns."

It happened with increasing frequency that Elizabeth was taken aback and delighted by the clarity of eight-year-old logic. Now it took her a moment to collect a reasonable response, but Lily waited patiently.

"The problem is that somebody claims to own Selah Voyager," she said finally. "And the law supports that claim."

"Grandfather says that laws are only as good as the men

who write them," said Lily. And then she leapt off the porch in a manner much more suited to her age, and let out a high hoot of laughter.

"Oh, look, Uncle got some turkeys!"

Runs-from-Bears stood at the edge of the woods with a pair of birds slung over one shoulder and a brace of rabbits over the other. With the flick of a wrist he tossed the rabbits to Hector and Blue, who grabbed up their reward and galloped away to eat under the fir tree that was their favorite spot. The dogs passed Lily as she ran toward Runs-from-Bears, her bare heels flashing white as they kicked up her petticoat to show the muddy hem of her shift.

She launched herself fearlessly, grabbing onto his free forearm. He swung her up and for one breathless moment Lily seemed to hang like a hummingbird in midair; then he caught her neatly and she came to rest on his raised forearm. Elizabeth had seen this trick too many times to count, but it still struck her as incongruous: her tiny daughter perched so nonchalantly on the arm of a Kahnyen'kehàka warrior. A stranger would have first seen his size, the weapons he carried, the face mangled by battle and pox scars and decorated with elaborate bear-claw tattoos; Elizabeth saw a man who had taught her to snare and skin a rabbit, how to walk quietly in the endless forests, how to greet an elder in Mohawk without giving offense, and too many other things to count. Runs-from-Bears had helped her through some of the most difficult times of her life; when she looked at him she saw a friend, and so did her daughter.

Lily was talking so fast and so earnestly that by the time Elizabeth caught up, Runs-from-Bears had heard all the news of the day.

"Will you come and meet Selah Voyager, Uncle?"

"I will," said Runs-from-Bears. "When she is well again."

Elizabeth said, "Run ahead now and bring your sister this soup, she is waiting for you."

Lily swung down as she would have done from the branch of a tree, landing lightly. When she had accepted the covered bowl, Runs-from-Bears reached into his hunting shirt and took out a letter.

"Take this to Walks-Ahead too."

Elizabeth was surprised, but the look Bears gave her said

she should wait until Lily had gone from them before she asked questions. Lily did not see this, or did not take heed.

"A letter! Who wrote her a letter?"

"An old friend," said Runs-from-Bears. "She will be glad to have it, but give her the soup first, or she'll forget to eat."

Elizabeth knew no person less prone to exaggeration than Runs-from-Bears, but she could hardly credit the story he had to tell. On his way home he had come across Liam Kirby. The boy had been waiting for him just where the Bonners' property started on the north side of the lake, and he asked Bears to deliver a letter to Hannah.

When Elizabeth thought of Liam over the years since she had last seen him, it was with a strong sense of regret. He had left Hidden Wolf in the mistaken assumption that they had abandoned him forever; of that much she was sure. What was far more difficult and troubling was the question of why he had stayed away once they had come home again. Now, torn between happiness and bewilderment, relief and confusion, Elizabeth kept repeating questions even after Runs-from-Bears had told everything he knew. Liam was alive, well grown, and a likely young man—he carried an expensive rifle, Bears noted, and he had three good dogs with him.

"You'll recognize one of them," he said.

"Recognize his dog?" Elizabeth cocked her head. "Why would I?"

Runs-from-Bears blinked at her in the way that said she was overlooking the obvious, and that he would not carry on the conversation until she had caught up. But there were other, more pressing questions and so Elizabeth put aside the mystery of Liam's dogs.

"Where has he been for so long? And why have we had no word of him?" This was not the question she wanted to ask, but she could not bring herself to say out loud what they all feared: that Liam had left without a word and never come back because he had taken what did not belong to him. Hannah refused to even consider that he would have done such a thing, but the facts were hard to overlook: when they returned home from Scotland in the fall of 1794, Liam had been gone and along with him their silver and the eight hundred gold guineas that had been all that was left of Hawkeye's inheritance. Liam had been the only one outside the family who knew where the money was hidden.

"But why did he not come here directly?"

"He is not sure of his welcome."

"Not welcome at Lake in the Clouds?" Elizabeth's confusion turned to sudden irritation. Then she remembered the letter Liam had sent along for Hannah, and she half-turned in the direction of the cabin.

"Walks-Ahead brought him back to us," said Runs-from-Bears, following the line of her thinking.

Elizabeth said, "She was a child when he left, and so was he."

Liam had run off from Hidden Wolf at thirteen, not quite a man but no longer a child. The attachment he had had to Hannah had been clear to all of them, and part of the reason his disappearance had been so inexplicable. Elizabeth wanted to tell Bears he was wrong: Hannah cared for Liam as if he were a brother, and nothing more. She opened her mouth to say just that, and stopped. She did not want Runs-from-Bears to blink at her again; she was not ready for that yet. Not until she had spoken to Hannah.

Elizabeth said, "I'll go to her now."

"*Tkayeri,*" said Runs-from-Bears. *It is proper so.*

The two families at Lake in the Clouds were in the habit of taking their evening meal apart. In spite of her true attachment to Many-Doves and her family, Elizabeth always looked forward to this time: the children were subdued by weariness and too preoccupied with hunger to concoct any last bit of mischief, while Nathaniel and Hawkeye tended to be most talkative after a day's work, and in no hurry to get up from the table.

But tonight the normal rhythm had been upset. The appearance of Selah Voyager and Liam Kirby both on the same day had stirred the children's curiosity, and they asked question after question until Hawkeye had to rap on the table with his knuckles.

"You three make as much noise as a nest of blackbirds. I'll remind you there's a sick woman in the next room." He sent each of them a stern look, and in turn Lily, Daniel, and Ethan dropped their gazes.

"Now let me say this once and for all. You've heard every story there is to tell about Liam Kirby time and time again. We won't know any more until your sister has her talk with him. As far as that young woman is concerned, Curiosity will be here soon enough to clear things up, but let me remind you of something. I want you to listen to me now."

He leaned forward, and his voice lowered. "She's a guest here, and her safety is our responsibility. If you go talking to anybody about her, if you even say her name, then you're putting her life in danger. Do you understand me?"

Lily and Ethan nodded, but Daniel's mouth set itself in a hard line, one that said he would obey against his better judgment.

Nathaniel saw this too. "Say it, son. Whatever's on your mind."

Daniel glanced at Hannah, and then away. "It's Liam Kirby who's the danger," he said, his voice wobbling with earnestness. "He ran off from here with—" Hannah made a sound deep in her throat, and Daniel paused. "And now he's back, tracking Selah Voyager onto the mountain. I say—" His voice cracked, and a flush crawled up his neck. "Why don't you just send him away, Da? We don't need him here."

Hannah said, "He deserves the chance to explain, little brother."

"And what if it's all true?" Daniel asked. "What if he wants to take her back to the city and collect a reward?"

"He doesn't know she's here, not for sure," said Lily. "Maybe that's not why he came at all." She was looking to her mother for confirmation, and Elizabeth gave it to her.

"That's why Hannah wants to talk to him," she said. "To find out exactly what he wants, and if he knows about Miss Voyager."

"Of course he knows," muttered Daniel. "Uncle found him not five hundred yards from the trail she walked, and those dogs are good trackers."

"If that is the case, then I will send him away," Hannah said quietly.

"Maybe he won't go," said Ethan.

There was always something of a preternatural calm about Ethan, but today more than usual. He wore his worry for his mother like a caul.

Hannah had seen her mother die in childbirth, and she understood very well how vulnerable Ethan was today. If she was angry, she did not show it, but then Hannah rarely did: it was a trick that Lily admired in her older sister but had not yet learned, quite.

She said, "If I send him, he will leave."

The muscles in the boy's throat moved convulsively, as if he would have preferred to swallow down what he felt compelled to say. "From the mountain, maybe. But you can't send him out of Paradise unless he wants to go."

All three of the children looked toward Nathaniel and Hawkeye in an unspoken request for their opinions. Nathaniel drew in a deep breath and blew it out again. "Daughter, read us that letter one more time."

Hannah left the table and went to the desk to stand in the fading light at the window, her plaits shining smooth and blue black down the straight line of her back. She studied the letter for a moment, and then she read in her clear voice.

" 'Tomorrow I will wait at the burned schoolhouse at first light. I will come no further up the mountain unless I come with you. Please talk to me. Things are not always what they seem. Your true friend, Liam Kirby.' "

Hawkeye grunted. "Could mean anything," he said. "I'm curious, for one."

Nathaniel spoke directly to his son. "I don't believe she's in any danger, going to talk to him. We wouldn't let her go if we thought there was. You know that, Daniel, don't you?"

The boy looked up slowly from his plate, and then he nodded.

A firm knock at the door startled Elizabeth. She rose so quickly from her chair that it would have tipped over if Nathaniel had not caught it.

"It's just Curiosity," said Hannah, looking out the window. "And Galileo and Joshua with her. Thank goodness."

Curiosity was so anxious to see the newcomer that she hardly paused to greet Elizabeth on her way to the sickbed the men had set up in the long workroom that ran along the back of the house. Hannah went with her, and Elizabeth busied herself with clearing away the meal. The men sat down to whatever work they had to hand, all except Joshua, who paced the room while he chewed on the stem of his pipe. Elizabeth liked Joshua, who had a dry wit and a surprising way with words, although he did not often choose to speak. Now she tried to calm him by asking questions about Daisy and the children, which he answered politely but as briefly as he could without being rude. He would not be distracted, nor would he provide distraction; Elizabeth concentrated instead on getting the children to their beds in the sleeping loft.

Finally she stood again in the common room, looking at the book that lay open on her desk. Tomorrow she must teach; there were lessons to prepare. But it would be very hard to concentrate until this business with Selah Voyager had been resolved, and so she took up her knitting instead.

"Hard at work, I see," said Galileo with his shy smile.

Elizabeth held up her half-finished stocking for his examination. Not beautiful, certainly, but she was proud of it nonetheless. Learning to knit had been one of the most difficult tasks of her life, but she had come to take comfort in the steadiness of the work.

In her childhood home young ladies knew nothing, cared to know nothing, of spinning or weaving or knitting. Aunt Merriweather discouraged even fine embroidery in the fear that it would lead to the need for spectacles, which she believed must necessarily have a detrimental effect on the interest of eligible young men. At Oakmere, Mantua silk and India muslin, embroidered lawns and satin brocades were ordered by the bolt and turned over to the seamstresses.

But now Elizabeth lived between two worlds, both different from Oakmere, and from each other: the other women at Lake in the Clouds spent much of their time curing deer and buckskin into leather soft and supple enough to make overblouses, hunting shirts, breechclouts, and leggings; down in the village flax was grown and harvested, spun and woven into linen in a laborious process that seemed to never end. In Many-Doves' world, a girl's reputation was built in part by the quality of her doeskin and the beadwork on her moccasins; in Paradise a young woman who could warp a loom was well regarded. Elizabeth stood empty-handed in both worlds.

Marriage had come suddenly, long after she had made peace with spinsterhood. Her cousins had gone to housekeeping with trunks of linens, silver, and china; Elizabeth had come with a good command of Latin, French, German, and the ancient and modern philosophies, a familiarity with literature from Euripides to Pope, a solid grasp of mathematics, but without a spoon to her name, or a single practical skill. This lack was addressed to some degree by money she could call her own—the interest on her small inheritance from her mother, and that part of her portion of her father's estate that hadn't gone to creditors. Money bought fabric and yarn, buttons and thread and ribbon. But there were no seamstresses in Paradise.

Once a year she went to Johnstown to buy what could not be purchased in the village and in return for teaching their children, the women turned that raw material into clothing and household linens. And still Elizabeth had not been comfortable with this arrangement until she learned to knit, taking her lessons from Anna Hauptmann at the trading post for a full month before she turned out her first awkward pair of socks.

She had sent her aunt Merriweather the second pair of mitts she had finished, not to shock the old lady but as a testimonial: Elizabeth had come to New-York one kind of woman and had become another, one who could produce with her own hands at least some of what her family needed.

"You're mighty far away in your thoughts, Boots."

Nathaniel's voice woke her up out of her daydreams. Galileo was humming under his breath as he whittled, Hawkeye and Nathaniel were cleaning rifles, and even Joshua had settled down to examine a trap that needed repair.

"I was indeed," said Elizabeth. "But here I am again. I wonder why Curiosity and Hannah are so long."

"Things to talk through," said Galileo. "Got to know what we're dealing with here before we send the girl on."

Nathaniel and Elizabeth exchanged glances, but it was Joshua who spoke.

"We never meant for you to get mixed up in this," he said, looking directly at Elizabeth. "Never meant to cause you any trouble."

"You haven't caused us any trouble," said Elizabeth. "And neither has Miss Voyager. We would have done the same for anyone in need."

Curiosity appeared at the door to the workroom, wiping her hands on a piece of toweling. "And a good thing too. The girl has got a chest full of trouble. She ain't about to die, though, Hannah has seen to that."

"How long before she can set out again?" asked Galileo.

Curiosity spread out a hand. "A week, I'd say."

"Unless the child comes," added Hannah. "Maybe she should stay until it does. I don't like to think of her out in the bush."

"She won't be alone," said Joshua. "That's one thing you don't need worry about at all."

Hawkeye said, "We don't need to know where she's going."

"Maybe not," Curiosity said. "But there's things you should know, and now's the time to tell the story. You best start off, husband. It began with you, after all."

Chapter 4

"I suppose you could look at it that way," said Galileo. "As I was the only one to home when the first two voyagers came to Paradise. They had run off from old Squire VanHusen—you'll know the farm."

Hawkeye nodded. "German Flats."

"Big family," added Nathaniel.

"That's right," said Galileo. "How many children did the man have, Joshua?"

"Eighteen children of his own, and just as many slaves."

"You know VanHusen?" Hawkeye turned to Joshua in surprise.

"I was born on that farm," Joshua said. "My mama is buried there."

Joshua told his part of the story in his usual deft manner: his father had been a slave of Sir William Johnson's, while his mother belonged to Squire VanHusen; the two farms stood within a mile of each other on the Mohawk. Either Johnson didn't want to sell Joshua's father to the squire, or VanHusen wouldn't buy him, but the family had always lived apart.

"We saw Daddy most Sundays, until Sir Johnson died."

"I remember this," Elizabeth said. "Your father told us the story of how Mrs. Johnson sold him to a farmer in Pumpkin Hollow."

A muscle fluttered in Joshua's cheek as he nodded. "Didn't see him much after that. It was the next year VanHusen sold me

to the Johnstown blacksmith and there I stayed fifteen years almost to the day when Mr. Hench bought me to set me free.

"The way my brothers told it, Mama got word about me
getting my manumission papers and it was her who encouraged them to run. She sent them up here to find me, thinking
I'd be able to help them on their way to Canada. Said she
could die easy, knowing all three of her boys was free. And she
almost got her wish.

"Elijah is still alive and well, but Coffee always was a little
weak in the lungs, and he caught himself a fever in the bush.
Passed on soon after they got here. So that's how the whole
business started."

Nathaniel said, "Correct me if I'm wrong, but as I remember it, VanHusen has been dead more than five years. When
exactly did all this happen?"

"July of ninety-four." Perched on the edge of her chair,
Curiosity spoke up. "While we was on our way home from
Scotland."

The surprise of this statement made Elizabeth put down her
knitting. "That was eight years ago."

"It was indeed," said Galileo. "Eight years and twenty-one
slaves run away to freedom. Coffee the only one we ever lost."

"Twenty-one," echoed Elizabeth. "But how?"

Hawkeye made a soft rumbling sound deep in his throat.

"Don't hush her, Dan'l," said Galileo. "It's a reasonable question. The truth of it is, that first time we didn't have no plans,
and no idea of where to put Elijah to keep him safe except that
he had to be got out of Paradise. Liam Kirby ain't the first
bounty hunter ever to show up here, you realize. So I took him
into the bush. All these years now I been wondering if you had
any idea, and I see we kept things pretty quiet. So I won't say
no more about the where and how unless you ask me."

"I don't think we're asking, are we?" Nathaniel turned to look
at Elizabeth and then his father. When he came to Hannah he
said, "I have the feeling you know more about this than we do."

"Not very much more," said Hannah quietly. "The place
where Miss Voyager is going, you call it Red Rock."

Curiosity blinked at her in surprise. "Sometime you'll have
to tell me how you came to hear that name, child."

"Sometime," said Hannah, steadfastly refusing to meet her
father's gaze. "But Galileo needs to finish his story."

The old man lifted a shoulder. "Don't know as I can finish a story that ain't over yet, but let me see if I can move it along some.

"After Coffee and Elijah, why I thought we was done with the business of hiding slaves. But our young folk, they had other ideas, Almanzo most especially. Now you got to recall that he was sick with the lung fever that summer. I suppose it was laying in bed for so long that did the job. The idea got a chance to put down roots and by the time he was better, that son of ours was ready to free the world. So when Curiosity got home that last week of August, we all set down and talked it through.

"Now the truth is, I'm as proud as the next man of my children, but I cain't deny that they are all three stubborn as mules—"

"They come by it honest," said Curiosity, but Galileo only smiled.

"—and it didn't much matter what we had to say about the trouble they were making for themselves, or for us old folks. They worked it out. Almanzo went off to New-York City and Polly and her husband to Albany. Took almost a year till they had things organized—summer of ninety-five it was that the next voyager came to us. We've been careful, you understand. Almanzo takes his time and he don't set nobody on the path who cain't make the journey."

Elizabeth said, "I don't doubt that he is careful, Galileo. But a young woman in Miss Voyager's condition . . . ?"

Curiosity smoothed her skirt thoughtfully. "This is a special case," she said. "Didn't have much choice." When she looked up at them, her expression was as drawn and strained as Elizabeth had ever seen. Curiosity was a woman who kept her troubles to herself, but something about Selah Voyager had touched her in a way that made that impossible.

Nathaniel was thinking in a different direction. "How is it you knew she was coming?"

"Three months ago we got word from Almanzo," said Galileo. "Come by way of Albany, with our Polly. Said he was planning to set the next voyager on the road as soon as the worst of the thaw was over, and that's what he did. But things got complicated, as they often will." He paused to draw on his pipe.

"Kitty's travails came upon her on the first night of the full moon, and on that same evening Zeke cut hisself right bad at the mill, so Daisy had to go sew him up. Neither of them could be at the judge's old place, the way we planned. The thing was, Almanzo told Selah to look for a black woman at the old homestead once it got to be full dark. And if she didn't see that woman where she was meant to be, why then she was supposed to go hide herself away from the village and try again the next night. That would be tonight, except Miz Elizabeth and Miz Hannah come across her this morning."

"Thank the Lord you did," said Curiosity. "Otherwise I expect we would have lost her. Hawkeye, spit out whatever it is that's bothering you. I can see it sitting in your jaw plain as a plug of tobacco."

Hawkeye had been listening bent forward with his forearms resting on his knees, but he sat up straight to answer Curiosity. "You're right, something don't make sense to me. I can see how she could get to Albany—the men who sail those ships up from the city have got smuggling in their blood, after all. But I cain't see how she would find her way to Paradise from there. Either that young woman is a natural-born pathfinder, or she had a guide."

"She had a guide," said Curiosity. "Of sorts."

Hannah took some folded material out of the basket beside her chair to hold up for them to see: a quilted shift made of scraps laboriously pieced together. It looked like nothing more than the undergarment of a poor woman who couldn't afford muslin.

"A map," Nathaniel said. "She sewed herself a map."

And then Elizabeth saw it too—a narrow strip of blue came up from the hem to branch into a Y. By squinting she could see it: the Mohawk flowing into the Hudson, and a small patch of brown on the spot that must be Albany. Blue thread had been used to trace the Sacandaga River from the Hudson to Paradise, passing through a muddy brown patch that might have been the marsh at Barktown. All along the rivers was a pattern of straight stitches in groups of two.

"It is not out of proportion?" Elizabeth asked.

"It's like a Kahnyen'kehàka map," said Hannah. "It doesn't show distance in miles, it shows how long it takes to walk. You see, two marks for a half-day's walking. You see how the ferry is marked."

"No white man would recognize that for what it is," said

Hawkeye approvingly. "But I have to say, it don't quite seem enough."

"She got the directions memorized too," Curiosity said. "Almost tree by tree."

Galileo nodded. "Ask her to tell them to you when she's well again. Between the map and a good memory, she got herself here."

Hannah looked at Galileo and then Curiosity. "You say that there's people to look after her where she's going?"

"They'll take good care of her, or I wouldn't let her go," said Curiosity.

Galileo put a hand on his wife's arm. "Getting her there is the problem." He looked directly at Hannah. "We ain't talked about Liam yet."

"Maybe Liam isn't looking for her." She said this lightly, but the tilt of her head when she met Curiosity's gaze gave away her anxiety.

"I'd like to believe that, I truly would," Curiosity said in her kindest tone. "But it don't feel right to me, him showing up today. So I got something else to say, something I maybe would keep to myself if it weren't Liam Kirby out there in shouting distance."

She put her hands down on her lap, palms up, and studied them for a moment. "On the day me and Galileo got our papers, we walked away from the Paxton farm with bloody backs. The overseer called that whipping a 'going-away present,' and he put some muscle into it. The last my mother ever saw of me I was sitting on Elizabeth's granddaddy's wagon seat, dripping blood, laughing and crying all at once. And on that day Galileo and me, we swore to each other that no child, no grandchild, of ours would ever know what it was to live the life we was born to. Ain't that so, husband?"

"It is," said Galileo.

"Now you know that both our girls married free men. Polly's children and Daisy's, all of them born free as the Lord meant them to be. What you cain't know is this: that girl lying sick in the next room, she has already had a child sold away from her. A daughter. But this one she's carrying, this is Almanzo's child. Our seventh grandchild.

"I'm not telling you this to oblige you any further, or to ask you for anything more than you already done. We cain't hardly repay you as it is— Don't interrupt me now, Elizabeth."

"But I must. Why did you not come to us, Curiosity? Perhaps we could have bought her papers—"

Galileo shook his head slowly. "Now you must know we tried to see to that ourselves. Between us we got enough money saved."

Elizabeth felt herself flush with fear for them, and she saw the same on Nathaniel's face.

"Then Almanzo is already implicated, if he offered to buy her freedom and she disappeared after he was turned down," said Nathaniel.

"You would be right," Galileo said. "But it ain't our Almanzo who made the offer. There's somebody—"

Curiosity cut him off sharply. "No need to get particular with names, now. Don' matter anyway, because the man who lays claim to Selah wouldn't sell her, and there ain't a law that says a slave owner has to sell a slave at any price if he's got a mind to keep her. So maybe you'll understand that we didn't have much choice, not with a child on the way."

Elizabeth felt herself flushing with embarrassment. "I would never imply that you had neglected—"

"Hush now," Curiosity interrupted her gently. "No need to start with apologies. Just know this, Elizabeth. If I thought it would have made a difference, we would have come to ask for help. Which is what I suppose I'm going to do right now."

She pushed out a breath and drew in another. "Here's the way it look to me. You took Liam in when he was half-dead and you treated him like a son. The boy out there waiting to hear if he's welcome at your door again, and once he's here, why there ain't no telling what he might ask of you, or how you'll feel about it when he do. But understand this. If anybody—Liam Kirby or President Thomas Jefferson hisself—were to threaten that young woman, we will do what need doing."

There was a long silence from the group around the hearth. The fire hissed to itself; somewhere not too far away the pack of wolves who gave the mountain its name began to howl. Then Hawkeye spoke up for all of them.

"Why now, Curiosity, Galileo," he said quietly. "We been neighbors and friends for forty years or more. Curiosity's been at every birthing and deathbed at Lake in the Clouds since I brought Cora here as a bride. Galileo helped me dig her grave, and Sarah's too. We'll be whatever help we can to you and yours, you must know that in your bones." He said this in the tone he used with hurt things, calm and easy, and it did its work. There was another long moment of silence, and then Curiosity smiled.

"I do, Hawkeye. I do know that."

Galileo got up slowly. "That's that, I suppose. Nothing more to say tonight, so we'll leave you to your rest."

Squirrel tried to slip away again when the visitors had gone, but this time Nathaniel stopped her.

"Is it my imagination, daughter, or are you avoiding me?"

She turned to face him, but her gaze flickered first toward Elizabeth. "Of course I'm not avoiding you. But Miss Voyager—"

He held up a hand to stop her. "Ten minutes more won't hurt. Will it?"

For a moment she hesitated, and then she came back to sit again in front of the hearth.

Elizabeth stood there uncertainly until Hawkeye took her by the elbow and turned her toward the bedroom. "Let these two work it out without your help," he said firmly. "You sleep."

She went, but only reluctantly and after sending Nathaniel a pointed look over her shoulder. "We all need our rest."

"I'll be in directly," he promised, and hoped that he was telling the truth.

Hawkeye picked up his rifle. "I'll just go have myself a little walk. If you don't need me."

"Looks like rain," Nathaniel said not to his father directly, but to the room, and still Hawkeye gave him a grim smile. Nathaniel knew that he sounded like Elizabeth when she was trying to distract one of the children from some undertaking that made her uneasy, but then he had legitimate reason to worry.

The truth was, Hawkeye had always walked the mountain in the evening no matter how bad the weather, but in the last few years he had been going farther and staying out longer. Sometimes he didn't appear again till dawn, and once in a while it occurred to Nathaniel that his father might take it into his head to walk west and just keep going.

When he had gone, Squirrel looked up from the basket of

dried greenery she was sorting. "He doesn't sleep well indoors," she said. "You needn't worry about him."

Nathaniel bit back a smile. His oldest daughter had never been a difficult child, but recently he found himself hard-pressed for the right words, especially when she took it upon herself to teach him something she thought he didn't know. Now she was sending him a sidelong glance, not without an edge of guilt and some impatience to it.

He said, "You're not in any trouble, if that's what you're worried about. I just wanted to set some things straight between us."

The crushed chamomile filled the air with a sharp, almost bitter smell. In a quieter tone Squirrel said, "I don't know anything more about Liam than you do, Da. What is there to talk about?"

Nathaniel smiled. "You ain't slow-witted, Squirrel. Don't play at it, it don't suit you."

Her mouth twitched in annoyance, but she said nothing at all.

"You know it ain't Liam I've got on my mind right now. It was Splitting-Moon who told you about the runaways in the bush, wasn't it?"

A little sound escaped her, the kind of sigh that you might hear from a woman when she puts down something she shouldn't have been carrying in the first place.

"When did you figure it out?"

"Don't take much figuring. Twenty-some house slaves and farmhands, surviving eight winters in the bush and keeping hid. That's not something they could do on their own, at least not to start with. They had to have help, and no white man I know in the bush would go to the trouble, much less keep quiet about it. That's when Splitting-Moon came to mind. It's in her nature to help any hurt creature she comes across. Did she come out and tell you about Red Rock?"

Squirrel hesitated while she put down the basket and rubbed her hands. Her gaze fixed on the window over the desk, as if she could see through it and farther. "When she came in the fall to trade she had a little boy with her. He had a Kahnyen'kehàka face—" She touched her own cheekbone lightly. "But his hair was kinked, and he was as dark as Galileo. He called himself Joshua, but she called him Renhahserotha'."

He makes a new light.

"It was the boy who mentioned Red Rock to you?"

"To Many-Doves," said Squirrel. "But long before we ever saw him, we knew there must be others with her. When Splitting-Moon brought us her medicines to trade, she asked for things in return . . . things you wouldn't think she'd have any need for."

Nathaniel let this news settle for a moment, and Squirrel thought that he was looking for more information.

"That's all I know. Many-Doves wouldn't ever let me ask her any questions in the fear she wouldn't come back again. You know her better than I do, Da."

"Not anymore, I don't. I haven't seen the woman since the summer before the twins were born."

Splitting-Moon had left Good Pasture to go live the life of a hermit deep in the bush a year later. She was rarely seen, but stories of the Mohawk medicine woman who roamed the endless forests were told as far away as Montreal.

Now there were only two things Nathaniel could say of her for certain: she had a talent for hiding herself away, and she spent some of the winter in the caves near the lake some called Little Lost, in a corner of the bush few white men knew about. Over the years when she had come to mind, Nathaniel had wondered about her, and why she had chosen such a lonely life for herself. Now it seemed she hadn't been alone, after all.

He had been quiet a long time, and Squirrel looked uncomfortable. She said, "Maybe I should have told you."

"No," he said. "You did the right thing. Go look after our visitor now, and then get some sleep." He turned on his heel to look into the shadows of the sleeping loft.

"The three of you had better go to sleep too, do you hear? Chores in the morning and then school, and I don't care to hear any complaints about sleepiness."

There was a hushed scampering, and then silence.

Elizabeth was sitting on the edge of the bed with the hairbrush in her lap when Nathaniel closed the chamber door behind himself. Even by candlelight her exhaustion was plain to see in the rounded curve of her back and the way she lifted her arm. But she smiled at him and shook her head so that her hair fell in a dark veil over her shoulders, most of the way to the floor.

"Are they settled?"

"Now they are. But I expect they heard every word."

"Of course they did. Tomorrow we will have to have a conversation with them about all of this. Most especially with Ethan."

"You don't need to worry about Ethan. That boy lives and breathes to please Galileo, and he'd put his hand in fire before he'd do anything to cause him harm."

"I do need to worry about Ethan," Elizabeth said. "But not because he might say something inopportune. Did you talk to Hannah?"

"I did." Nathaniel crouched down before the hearth to bank the fire, pausing there for a moment to feel the pulse of heat on his face and chest. He did not especially want to open up the subject of Splitting-Moon; Elizabeth might just decide that she needed to go to find Many-Doves and hear the whole story for herself right now.

He said, "I'll walk her down to the schoolhouse at first light."

Elizabeth exhaled, impatient and trying not to show it. "Do you think that it's truly necessary? Hannah is not afraid of Liam."

Nathaniel thought about this while he stripped to his breechclout. It was hard to think of Liam Kirby as a man at all, much less one who could be a danger, but it was also true that he wouldn't rest easy until he saw the boy with his own eyes.

He sat down next to Elizabeth to begin brushing her hair. It was something he did every night, and every night he was struck by the white skin at the nape of her neck. How strange it was that a woman of such strong will should seem outwardly fragile. Nathaniel's Mahican grandfather had given her the name Bone-in-Her-Back, and it suited her well.

But his eldest daughter was another matter. Clever and quick, yes; she had a mind as sharp as any Nathaniel had ever come across, one that never seemed to rest. Walks-Ahead was the woman-name her grandmother had given her, and while Nathaniel found it hard to use that name, it did suit her: a young woman always looking forward. She exchanged letters with doctors in England and India, letters she gladly read aloud to them but that nobody else really understood, not even Elizabeth. Her reputation as a healer had already spread well beyond the frontier. But she had always been so gentle, inclined more to trust than doubt. Maybe now she stood before an experience that would temper her into something harder; maybe he wouldn't be able to help her.

To the back of Elizabeth's neck, Nathaniel said, "I'm not sure she shouldn't be afraid of him, but you're right. She needs to go on her own."

Elizabeth's shoulders tightened. "It's not in your nature to judge so quickly."

"But it is in my nature to protect my children. And I've been reminded today more than once about how old she is, you don't have to tell me again." He put down the brush and began to plait her hair, finally tying it with the ribbon she offered him.

"What do you say you and me go spend the night under the falls tomorrow? It's about that time."

She cast a frown over her shoulder. "You are changing the subject, Nathaniel Bonner."

"Nothing slips by you, Boots. Is that a no you're giving me?"

Elizabeth pulled up the covers and wiggled underneath, so that the mattress crackled and whispered in response. "You know perfectly well that I've been looking forward to... sleeping under the falls for weeks. If Hannah isn't so preoccupied with Miss Voyager that she can't keep an eye on the children, then yes, of course."

"For weeks, is it?" He leaned over her to smooth the curls that had already escaped the plait. "It pleases me no end to hear that you're so eager."

She swatted his hand away, but there was nothing she could do to hide her blush. "You are incorrigible."

"And you like me that way."

Elizabeth pursed her mouth at him. He kissed it soundly, but her leery expression softened only a little.

"You are so transparent at times, Nathaniel. Simply ask, and I will stop talking about this Red Rock—for the time being, at least. You needn't work so hard to distract me."

He climbed into bed next to her. "Providing you with a little distraction ain't exactly unpleasant, you realize, even if I have to put some effort into it once in a while. I like a challenge, you know that."

She grinned, but pinched him nonetheless. "My point is that seduction is really not the only way to end a conversation."

"Can you think of a better one?"

There was a long pause. "If you put it that way," she said slowly.

He laughed and leaned over to kiss her again.

"Go to sleep, Boots. You're too tired, and I don't especially want to talk about Red Rock and the rest of it any more tonight."

She gave him a long and very thoughtful look. "Yes, all right. Perhaps you're right, the conversation should wait until tomorrow. That's best." She sat up, blew out the candle, and then curled toward him and put her face next to his. There was enough moonlight to show him her eyes, and the expression in them.

"You're a terrible liar, Boots. Go on and say it or you'll lie awake for hours."

With the tip of her finger she traced the line of his jaw. "I've been thinking about Splitting-Moon."

Chapter 5

Just before dawn Hannah woke to the sound of her grandfather moving through the common room. She rose from the pallet she had made for herself near Selah Voyager, checked her patient's breathing and temperature, and slipped away without waking her.

It fell to the twins to stoke the fire and carry water, but this morning Hawkeye had done both, whether to please Lily and Daniel or himself Hannah could not really say. He was gone again now, and she knew that if she went to look she would find him swimming under the falls.

She sat down in Elizabeth's rocker to put on her moccasins. With her cheek pressed against her knee she could not overlook how worn the leather of her leggings had become. For a moment she considered changing: her good linen gown hung on the wall of the sleeping loft, right next to the doeskin overblouse and leggings with bead- and quillwork that she had worn to the mid-winter ceremony at Good Pasture. She imagined herself in one and then the other, and decided finally that she would meet Liam Kirby in her workday clothes.

A stirring and murmuring of voices from her parents' room brought Hannah up out of her thoughts. She stood and the bear tooth she wore on a chain around her neck slid cold and hard between her breasts; she touched it with one finger, checked the contents of the pouch that hung from her belt, and went out onto the porch where her grandfather stood looking out over the morning, lake water running down over his shoulders and his skin flushed with cold.

He spoke without turning to her. "How is she?"

"Sleeping. Her fever is less, but not by much. I'll be back before she wakes."

"You sure of that?"

"Very sure," Hannah said firmly.

In Mahican her grandfather said, "I'm proud of you, granddaughter. Stand tall."

Hawkeye rarely used the language of his childhood; it was a gift he gave her, something that bound them together because there were so few left who spoke it. She was thinking about this, about the power of a rare language, when she crossed into the woods and heard Lily, running light and sure.

Her sister fell into step beside her.

"I won't go back," she said. "I want to see Liam Kirby for myself."

She was barefoot and her hair was unplaited, but Lily had taken the time to load her pocket with small rocks and her slingshot was tucked into the waistband of her overskirt. She was as good a shot as Blue-Jay, but he had far better control of his temper. Hannah said, "There will be no warfare today, little sister. Except maybe when you get back home again and have to make amends with Elizabeth for running off without permission."

"She won't be mad at me, not if I'm with you," Lily said. "And I won't throw the first stone."

And Hannah must be content with that promise, and with the fact of Lily, who could never pause in her examination of the world around her. In short order she had found the tracks of the old bear they called Two-Claws, out of her winter sleep and walking the mountain, a squirrel's skull, and evidence of a ground-bee hive that had been dug up by skunks. For every step Hannah took Lily took four.

Overhead the maple and beech branches were heavy with buds on the point of opening; underfoot crocuses spread out in patches of pale yellow and purple. Hannah thought of all the reasons she needed to be in the forest: to harvest the first buds of the white pine, flag lily root, and a hundred other useful things that the spring brought forth. Suddenly she had the urge to take her sister and go off into the forests to explore for the rest of the day. As if she had spoken this idea out loud, Lily came to a stop at the point where the woods gave way to the strawberry fields.

In a hollow beneath a fallen birch, the ground was covered with hoofprints in a scattering of tiny heart shapes. A doe had dropped a fawn here not an hour ago, and was almost certainly hiding very close by.

"We don't have time," said Hannah, but her sister was already gone. She did not appear again until Hannah was halfway through the field.

"Twins," she said, with great satisfaction.

"How did you get away without your twin?" Hannah asked. "Did he lose the straw pull, or did you have to trade him something?"

Lily pursed her mouth. Instead of answering she said, "Ain't you worried about Liam Kirby?"

"You are changing the subject."

"And you're not answering my question."

"I am a little anxious." She knew how unconvincing her tone must be. The truth was that she felt too many things at once and couldn't put a name to any of it, but Lily would not be satisfied with silence.

"Daniel says he came back to marry you and you'll go away from us to live in the city."

Hannah laughed out loud. "Daniel's imagination has run away with him. Liam is not here to marry me."

Lily gave her a very indignant look. "Of course he wants to marry you. All the men do, or at least all the ones who don't have wives. Even some of the ones who do. They watch you."

"You are being silly." Hannah increased her pace, and Lily began to trot beside her.

"They do watch you." Lily's tone sharpened as she settled in to prove her point.

"That doesn't mean anybody wants to marry anybody. The owl watches the mouse."

"No," Lily said shortly. "Not like the owl and the mouse, not that kind of watching." She thought for a minute. "Don't you want to get married? Do you want to stay with us forever?"

"If I get married someday it won't be to anybody in the village."

"But why not?"

Because it was clear that Lily would not give up until she had all her questions answered, Hannah stopped where she was. "Who would you have me marry then, Lily? Do you have a husband picked out?"

Lily wrinkled her nose, annoyed. "I can't pick out a husband for you."

"I'm very glad to hear it."

"But if I wanted to get married I think Claes Wilde would do very well."

Hannah's jaw dropped. "Nicholas Wilde?"

Lily nodded. "Claes. He's smarter than the rest of them. And he's nice looking—"

"Yes, he is. Clever and handsome both. But he doesn't interest me, and I don't interest him. And here's the reason." She took her sister's hand to hold against her own: white and copper. Lily studied the sight and when she looked up again there was the beginning of understanding in her expression.

"Because your mother was Kahnyen'kehàka?"

"Yes, because of that."

"But I'm going to marry Blue-Jay someday, and he's Kahnyen'kehàka. And Da married your mother."

Hannah sighed. "I didn't say it wasn't possible, it's just unlikely. There's nobody in Paradise—Claes Wilde included—who would want a Kahnyen'kehàka wife. They might look at me—"

She paused. They did look; she could not deny the fact that Obediah Cameron blushed when she walked by, or that Isaiah Kuick stared at her as he would never dare stare at a white woman. Michael Kaes made excuses to talk to her when she brought tisanes for his mother's headaches; even Mr. Gathercole, married and a minister, examined his own shoes as if he had never seen them before when he spoke to her, as if the sight of her face was more temptation than he could handle. Claes Wilde studied her too, but without ever saying a word. Men looking too long; looking away too fast.

Hannah shook herself. "They look at me, yes. But that's as far as it will ever go."

"I don't think they stay away because your mother was Kahnyen'kehàka. I think they're afraid of Da and Grandfather."

"No doubt you're right," Hannah said shortly, so irritated

with the conversation that she would have agreed to anything to end it.

"Now what about Liam Kirby?"

"Liam is an old friend, nothing more," said Hannah. "And he is just as white as any of the men in the village. Whatever happens, I'm not going away with him, and you can tell Daniel I said that."

"Good," said Lily shortly. "He'll be relieved."

They had come in sight of the small cabin that served as Elizabeth's schoolhouse. She had taken it over for her students when she first came to Paradise, and she used it still: in the mornings she taught children from the village; in the afternoon she gave lessons all over again, this time for Many-Doves' two oldest and Curiosity's grandchildren, along with her own twins.

Later today Lily would come only reluctantly to her schoolwork and wriggle impatiently until she was allowed to go again, but right now she disappeared behind the cabin on some errand she did not explain to her sister.

Hannah hesitated and then went ahead without her, angling down the mountain and cutting through the woods toward the lake. It was the quicker route, and it meant that she would not have to pass under Lucy Kuick's window. Widow Kuick seemed interested in whatever Hannah did, and she did not hesitate to share her opinion on matters as diverse as Hannah's footwear, her complexion, her family, and what the widow saw as Hannah's unnatural interest in medical matters where she had no role and should never be allowed one.

It was cool in the woods, but at the first sight of the lake glinting through the trees Hannah broke into a sweat. A strange tingling flowed from her hands up into her arms and over her back, so that the hair at the nape of her neck rippled softly.

There.

On the spot where his brother Billy had once put a torch to a schoolhouse, Liam Kirby sat among the tumbled hearthstones. A long rifle rested within arm's reach. Down at the lakeshore his dogs were knee-deep in water, their attention on a single merganser winding its way through the reeds.

Liam was watching a heron pace through the marsh. It seemed to Hannah that she could hear the water parting and coming together again with every step the bird took. She might have stood there looking for a long time, but the wind gave her away. One of the dogs turned in her direction and let out a soft bark of warning. Liam stilled the dogs with a word as he rose and turned toward her.

Hannah did not have to look very hard to see that this was Liam: there was the same jawline, rough now with beard stubble, the wide mouth, and a nose that had been broken more than once. He had grown into his full height and there were new scars: one on his chin and another cutting through his left eyebrow so that it twisted up into an arch and added an angle to a face that was already sharp with bone. But most disturbing was the guarded expression in his eyes, a new wariness that made him into more stranger than friend.

"You got my letter," he said, his voice creaking a little.

She said, "Let me see you walk."

He blinked at her in surprise, opened his mouth to speak and closed it again.

"All these years I've been wondering how that break healed," she said. "Let me see you walk."

Liam turned away and walked five steps toward the lake and back, stopping where he had begun.

"You're still limping. Does it bother you in wet weather?"

"It bothers me some," he said, and then, more firmly: "I heard about Falling-Day and your little brother. I'm sorry for your loss."

Hannah wrapped her arms around herself. "Thank you."

Liam ran a hand over his hair. "I'm glad you came."

She said, "I've been worried about you." It was the truth, but she hadn't planned to say it.

He looked away over the lake, squinting into the sun. "I thought of writing, but I never could think how to start. In the end it seemed maybe best to let sleeping dogs be."

And what was there to say to that? Hannah rocked back on her heels and studied the way the breeze stirred the marsh grasses. The silence stretched out between them, the uncomfortable silence between strangers who had once been friends.

She said, "You changed your mind, then."

"It got changed for me, I'd have to say." But then he fell silent again while he nervously touched the weapons that hung from his belt, one after the other. He had that look that men got sometimes when they wanted a woman to make things easier, but didn't want to ask for help. Hannah looked away, and at that moment he began to talk.

"When I left here that summer it was because I thought you weren't coming back anymore."

She nodded. "We figured as much."

The corner of his mouth twitched. "Runs-from-Bears came home from Montreal without you and brought word you were on your way to Scotland."

"And he brought you a letter from me."

He smiled for the first time. "And a letter from you. The first one I ever got."

"It was the first one I ever wrote."

"It was spattered with blood," said Liam. "Bears said it was his from the split scalp they gave him, but I always wondered."

Then he lifted a shoulder as if to shrug off some burden sitting there. "The thing was, nobody had any idea of when we'd see you again, not even Bears. And then the lung fever started. Falling-Day took her family and went north to keep them safe from it, and I went south."

"We never heard a word," Hannah said. "I would have written if I had any idea where you were."

"I went to sea."

Hannah looked at him in surprise. "To sea?"

"Shipped out the first time in the fall of ninety-four. It weren't until more than a year later that I heard you were back at Lake in the Clouds, and by that time—" He paused, and looked her directly in the eye. "It was too late."

"Too late for what?"

He dropped his head and dragged a hand through his hair, frowning at his moccasins.

"The rumor is that I ran away because I took the gold hid on the mountain."

Some of the awkwardness between them had begun to fade, but now it came back again full force. Hannah said, "What gold?"

Liam snorted softly. "Have it your way, then. According to rumor there was gold, and I took it."

"It was Dubonnet who started that rumor," said Hannah. "He once accused me of trying to poison him."

"I see the man ain't got any smarter with time," said Liam. "I don't suppose he could tell the truth to save his own life. But that rumor about the gold—"

Hannah cut him off with a raised hand. "I don't suppose you came all this way to talk about old rumors."

Liam sent her a sidelong glance. "So the gold ain't gone?"

"What gold?"

"Never mind." He picked up his rifle. "What I wanted to say is, I left this place with nothing but the clothes on my back. I ain't ever took anything that didn't belong to me, no matter what it looks like. And I ain't ever told anybody what I know about Hidden Wolf. Not about the silver mine nor about the cave under the falls."

"I never supposed you did."

Liam's brow drew together. "Still. I wanted it clear between us."

Hannah said, "So now you did what you came to do." It came out more abruptly than she meant it to.

He drew in a very deep breath and let it out again. "No, I cain't say my business is done. I expect you heard already that I'm earning my living as a bounty hunter."

"Yes," said Hannah evenly. "A blackbirder. We heard."

He avoided her gaze, leaning down to brush his leggings free of dirt. If he took offense at the term she had used, he hid it well.

"I'm looking for an African woman, about your age. Tracked her right to Hidden Wolf."

"Is that so."

"I expect she's somewhere on the mountain, but I didn't want to go any farther without permission. I know how Hawkeye feels about trespassers."

He was asking her more than one question. Hannah's fingers twitched slightly and she clasped them tighter against her sides. "You'd have to get permission from him or my father," she said. "But I expect Elizabeth will have something to say about it too. You know how she feels about slavery."

An eagle had begun circling the lake and Hannah watched it closely, afraid to look too long at Liam and let him see what she was feeling, anger and disappointment and worry too. She would keep that to herself for Selah Voyager's sake.

"This is a special case," Liam said.

He waited for the question that would let him explain away what he was doing, but Hannah was thinking of Curiosity, the expression on her face last night when she told them about putting Selah Voyager on the trail north. *A special case.* She had used exactly those words, thinking of the woman who had put her life in danger to bring a child into a free world.

With complete calm she said, "And how is this one special, Liam? More money on her head than usual?"

He let out a rough laugh. "I knew I couldn't show up here without you standing in judgment on me."

In her agitation, Hannah took a step away from him. "Maybe you've changed, but I haven't. You didn't think I'd approve of the way you earn your money, did you?"

His jaw set hard. "As I remember, your mother's people took slaves now and then."

"The Kahnyen'kehàka kidnapped children to adopt and took prisoners in battle and who they didn't kill they kept as slaves, yes. And what does that have to do with this woman you're after?" Her voice had gone rough with agitation, and she swallowed hard.

"I thought maybe you'd be fair-minded," he said tightly. "And find out the facts before you condemned me. A man's got to make a living. I ain't ashamed."

Hannah drew up to her full height and looked Liam directly in the face. What she saw there was anger and exasperation, but the longer she looked the more those things gave way to the guilt she had hoped to see. Guilt without penitence, but it was a start.

She said, "I'm ashamed for you."

Liam flinched, but his voice was steady and low and completely cold. He said, "The woman I'm after put a knife in a man's throat on the Newburgh dock. When I take her back she'll be tried for murder and hung."

"If she's guilty," Hannah said.

"She's guilty."

"Well, then, I suppose her owner won't be pleased," she said, hearing the bitterness in her voice. "Losing his investment to the gallows."

"I don't think he'll mind much," said Liam. "It was him she put the knife into. This one." He took a hunting knife from a sheath on his belt. The carved ivory handle was grimy with dirt and dried blood. Hannah studied it for a moment and then she looked Liam directly in the eye.

"I hope she's halfway to Montreal by now."

There was a glittering in his eyes, anger as sharp as the knife in his hand. Liam said, "I'll wager she's not much closer to Montreal than I am. If that's where she's headed."

Hannah began to turn away. "I'll give your message to my grandfather and father."

"Tell them that it won't serve anybody if they stand in the way of the law."

In her surprise, Hannah laughed. "I'd like to see you look Hawkeye in the eye and tell him what he owes the law. You've been away longer than I thought, if you believe that will get you anywhere."

Liam turned his head away from her and said, "I have been gone enough years to put this place behind me. I can't remember why I stayed as long as I did."

He meant to hurt her, but Hannah swallowed it down and kept her voice steady. She said, "It was your home. Everybody needs one."

She watched the column of muscles in his throat flex as he swallowed, and then he managed a smile. "Oh, I got a place. Went to housekeeping last fall. I'd like to finish my business and get back to my family."

The words hung there between them, almost visible in the air.

"I can understand that," Hannah said very softly. "I'd rather be home myself right now."

Liam said, "Then I'll say my farewells. In case we don't meet again. Will you shake hands with me, Squirrel?"

It was the name that struck so hard, hearing her Kahnyen'kehàka girl-name out of his mouth. Hannah sucked in a breath and held it, felt her fists like stone at her side. When she took his hand he started at the cold; she felt the shock move up his arm. He was looking down at her, but she turned away without meeting his gaze and never looked back, not even when he called after her.

"Tell them I'll wait at the trading post!"

When she had disappeared into the trees, Liam sat down and bent forward to cross his arms over his head. He squeezed his eyes shut and forced his breathing to slow. Every word she had said echoed in his head as loud as a gunshot.

Hannah. Oh, Christ.

One of the dogs pushed against his leg and nuzzled into the

crook of his arm. Liam slung an arm around her neck and put his face against the fur that smelled of lake water and mud.

"So tell me, Treenie, do you think that could have gone any worse?"

She nuzzled him again and made sympathetic noises.

Liam sat up again and looked around himself. There was something on the stones, white and square: a letter. Hannah had left a letter for him.

It was a good while before he could make himself move and then Liam sat for a longer time looking at the hand-writing.

> Liam Kirby
> At Lake in the Clouds
> Paradise
> On the west branch of the Sacandaga
> New-York State

The handwriting of a young girl, slightly rounded and un-even. A letter from the Hannah that used to be, the one that was gone now, replaced by a woman he had never imagined. She looked so much like her mother, and it occurred to Liam that the dead did come back to life and walk the earth, in the form of the children they had left behind. On the few occa-sions he ever saw himself in a looking glass he could see his fa-ther's face just beneath his own, and when Hannah looked at herself there was Sarah. Men had fought over Sarah.

Clouds passed overhead and sent shadows across the paper. Liam was cold and then warm again. It was Elizabeth who had taught him to read, back when she first opened her school; at this moment Liam wished she had never bothered.

He broke the wax seal and unfolded the paper, ran his palms over the creases to smooth it on his knee.

> Dear Liam,
>   This ship has come to rest in a wide water called a firth with England on one side and Scotland on the other. Scotland is where my grandmother Cora was born, and perhaps my grandfather's people, but it is a very strange and lonely kind of place. We were brought here against our wishes, and will stay only until we can find another ship to bring us home.

In my grandmother's cornfield the bean plants will be winding up the young stalks toward the sun. I think of this time a year ago when we came upon bears in the strawberry fields under a fat moon, do you recall? And they chased us away, and we ran until we fell and then we laughed. Elizabeth bids me give you her best greetings and to say she hopes you are keeping up with your schoolwork. My father says he knows you will be strong, and patient. Curiosity asks you to visit with Galileo when you might. She fears he must be melancholy. She says, too, she hopes you never get it in your head to go to sea.

We never meant to be so long away, but I will bring many stories with me, and you will tell me your stories too.

Your true friend Hannah Bonner, also called Squirrel by the Kahnyen'kehàka of the Wolf longhouse, her mother's people 11th day of June, 1794

A sound came from deep in his chest, something wound so tight that if he let it go completely it might fill the world. Liam ran his hand over the paper again and again. If he had waited another month, even a week, maybe this letter would have reached him. All these years it had been waiting here for him.

He tried to remember back to the days before he walked away from the mountain, but it was so long ago that the boy he saw in his mind's eye was a stranger to him. Impatient and angry, lonely and wanting to move, to go, to be anywhere else but the empty cabin at Lake in the Clouds.

Liam folded the letter and put it in his pack, slipped his rifle sling over his shoulder, and set out for the village.

Chapter 6

Just when Jemima Southern had given up all hope of finding an excuse to go to the village in order to get a better look at Liam Kirby, Isaiah Kuick realized that he was out of tobacco. Normally it would have fallen to Reuben to run this errand, but the boy had been sent down to the mill to scrub down the overseer's lodgings, and so Isaiah did something out of the ordinary: he came into the kitchen.

Jemima was more than willing to put down her mending and take the coins, not from his hand but from the table where he put them. Without his mother in the room, Isaiah seemed unwilling to even look at her. Whether this meant she was a temptation to him or that he truly disliked her Jemima did not know, but for once she had something more interesting than Isaiah Kuick to consider. While he and Cookie discussed when Ambrose Dye might be back from Johnstown with the slaves who had been gone for the winter, Jemima contemplated which path to the trading post would give her the best chance of running into Liam Kirby. Otherwise he might leave Paradise before she ever had a chance to talk to him.

Once out of the house, she picked up her skirts and trotted, but she crossed paths with no one but old Mrs. Hindle, bent almost double under a load of deadwood and arguing loudly with herself. Jemima made a wide circle around her without slowing down.

The trading post was the logical place to find a traveler, but today there was just shiftless Charlie LeBlanc and Obediah Cameron, half-asleep in front of a game of skittles. Anna stood behind the counter sorting through a box of buttons, but seemed glad enough to see Jemima come through the door.

"Tobacco, is it? Fond of his pipe, is Isaiah Kuick. Now why is it he don't come down here himself? Shy, is he?"

She was looking at Jemima out of the corner of her eye. Information about the widow's son was a rare commodity, and one that Jemima would spend wisely. She considered how she might tell Anna what she wanted to know in return for news of Liam, but it was a tricky business; she could easily give away more than she got.

Jemima had just decided to keep silent when the door opened behind her and Anna let out her high shrill laugh.

"Liam Kirby!" She put down the button box with a rattle and came out from behind the counter.

Her screeching would have annoyed Jemima to the point of leaving, but then nobody could ask an impertinent question like Anna so she stepped back to watch and listen, fitting herself into the corner between dusty crates of Turlington's Balsam of Life while Anna walked right up to Liam to put both hands on his shoulders.

"Look at you. Ain't you a sight."

Liam was big, but then so was Anna; she barely had to look up to shout into his face.

"Grown into a man, and not hard on the eyes neither. Your hair's come in right dark, ain't it? And those fine blue eyes you got from your ma, Lord rest her. She was a handsome woman in her youth, and you take after her. Took you long enough to stop in and see old friends. Suppose you heard about me and Jed getting married, two old fools that we are. Next Saturday. You stay long enough and we'll fix you up too. You come home to claim a bride?"

He flushed his irritation for the world to see, from the neck of his shirt to his hairline, an answer just as clear as words on a page and one that made Jemima's stomach lurch into her throat.

"Cain't say that I have." He removed himself from Anna's grip gingerly. "A man ain't allowed more than one, according to the law. I'm here on business."

"Now there's some news. Liam Kirby married. I expect

there's more to tell, it's been near ten years." Anna pointed to a
stool. "Sit yourself down over there by the fire—Charlie,
you'll grow roots in front of that skittles board if you don't
take care. Make some room now, Liam's come to call and he's
got stories to tell. You remember Charlie, Liam, but what you
don't know is he finally found hisself a wife. Married Molly
Kaes but the bloom is off the rose, plain enough. He spends
more time in front of my fire than he does his own."

"Now Anna—" Charlie began, but she cut him off.

"That there's Obediah Cameron, you'll remember him
when he had hair. And here comes Miss Wilde—I'll be with
you in a minute, Eulalia—she's a new face to you, but then
we've got lots of them in Paradise these days. Keeps house for
her brother. I expect you saw the Wilde orchards on your way
in. Have you ever seen so many apple trees? Jemima Southern
there—did you recognize her? All grown-up and thinking she
can hide herself in plain sight. In service at the widow Kuick's
since she lost her folks to the quinsy. Bought the mill from
John Glove, did the widow. You look like you swallowed your
tongue, Jemima. Got nothing to say to Liam Kirby? If I recall
correctly you were sweet on him at one time."

Hot words rushed up and Jemima would have let them fly
right in Anna's face if it weren't for the way Obediah's ears
perked up. The Camerons liked gossip only slightly less than a
tankard of ale, and Jemima must make sure that he got no
ideas about her and Liam that might make their way back to
the widow.

"Liam," she said as coolly as she was able. "Good to see you."

"Ain't it though?" Anna beamed at him. "It's too bad you
got yourself a family, Liam. If our high-and-mighty Jemima
here didn't claim you first, my Henrietta is just about right for
picking. She's in service in Johnstown, a clever girl if there
ever was one and pretty too. If I do say so myself who
shouldn't."

"Now I done enough talking, it's time you sat down here
and told us what there is to hear. Obediah, go fetch my father,
will you, he'll want to hear this too."

"Why don't I just step into the tavern to see Axel—" Liam
suggested hopefully, but Anna flapped her hand at him.

"Oh no, I ain't about to let you go that easy. Let Pa come
to you. He's right spry for his age, though his bones do creak."

Liam sat reluctantly. He looked to Jemima as unhappy a man as she had ever seen, almost as unhappy as she felt inside herself. He had a wife, and the only joy to find in that was the idea of telling Hannah Bonner that the one white man who might have married her was taken.

While Anna and Charlie LeBlanc argued over Liam's head about exactly when it was that Judge Middleton died and how long ago the Kuicks had come to Paradise, Jemima began to work out for herself how she would deliver the news. So intent was she on this that she didn't realize that he was trying to talk to her until he raised his voice.

"Say there, Mima," Liam said. "Is it true Ambrose Dye is still running the mill for the Kuicks?"

"It is." She would have left it at that, but Anna could not.

"Ambrose Dye?" Anna echoed. "What do you want with a man like that?"

"You lost enough at cards to the man back when he first showed up here." Charlie laughed. "I'm surprised you're looking for him."

"As if the widow would let one of her people hang around the tavern playing cards," Anna snorted. "And to tell the truth, he don't seem to want our company anyhow. Bone dry and as solemn as they come. He's gone to Johnstown just now, to fetch home the men the widow hires out over the winter. No doubt he'll start up the millrace just as soon as he gets back. Gets more out of that mill than Glove ever did."

"He's a good miller," Charlie agreed. "But he's strange, is Ambrose Dye. Quiet as a dumb man's grave." He leaned toward Liam and lowered his voice. "Folks say he's part Indian."

Anna snorted. "If he was part Indian he wouldn't be working for the widow. Red skin makes her twitch, you know that."

"He is part Indian," Liam said. "One of his grandmothers was Abenaki. He's called Knife-in-His-Fist up on the Canada border."

Anna let her mouth fall open so wide that Jemima could count her back teeth. "Why, the woman does anything in her power to make Hannah Bonner's life a misery. Ain't that so, Jemima?"

Jemima frowned at Anna, but she spoke to Liam. "Dye's been gone since last Thursday. And if he was here he wouldn't take kindly to you calling him a redskin. Neither will the widow."

Liam shrugged. "I know what I know. You ask him yourself if you don't believe me."

In her irritation Jemima could not keep her mouth shut as she knew she ought. "I doubt Dye'd be any help to you with the slave you're after, if that's what you're thinking."

Liam's head swiveled toward her in a slow arc. "What do you know about the runaway I'm looking for?"

"Nothing," said Jemima. "But I know Ambrose Dye."

And she turned her face away, hoping Liam wouldn't read more into that statement than she meant him to. For once she was glad of Charlie's need to put himself in the middle of every conversation, because he took up cheerfully where she left off.

"Dye's a strange one," he continued. "Seems right mild when you meet him, but from what folks say—why, if he were to come across a runaway no doubt he'd hang him high and leave him for the crows, just to make a lesson of it for the other Africans."

From the other side of the room there was a genteel fit of coughing from Eulalia Wilde, and Anna marched off to see to her needs, leaving Jemima standing there between Charlie and Liam.

It wasn't often that Jemima found herself at a loss for words, but for once she couldn't just come out and ask what she wanted to ask directly: *Where did you go, and do you have that gold?* Just as she was unable to look Liam in the face and tell him that she had hoped he might come back someday and see her for a woman instead of a little girl. Take her out of Paradise and make her mistress of her own place.

Isaiah Kuick would be the better catch, but her chances of getting him seemed slimmer every day. There were other men, but Jemima would hang herself before she married poor. And here was Liam Kirby with an expensive rifle, looking as though he had made something of himself in the world. She had often imagined him coming home to Paradise, but it had never occurred to her that he might be married. Instead she had spent a good amount of time working out just how she could turn his attention from Hannah Bonner to herself.

She said, "You went off without a word, Liam. Thought maybe a panther got you."

He smiled then. "Were you worried about me, Mima?"

"Hannah Bonner, more like. Won't she be disappointed to hear about your family down there in the city."

The little bit of friendliness that had begun to open up in him disappeared just as suddenly as it had come. He looked at her coolly.

"She didn't take the news too hard. Didn't seem to care at all, to tell the truth."

Jemima swallowed down her disappointment. Hannah knew then; she had heard it from Liam himself. They had met someplace, maybe on the mountain earlier today. Maybe last night.

"I doubt that," she said tartly. And then Jemima turned her frustration in Charlie's direction.

"What are you staring at?"

He shrugged one bony shoulder and inclined his head. "Nothing but you getting yourself in a temper, Mima."

"Maybe you can sit around all day on your brains, Charlie LeBlanc, but I got work to do."

Liam said, "Before you go, let me ask you a question."

She willed her expression as still as stone. "For somebody who asks questions so free you got precious little to say about yourself."

"Now that's true," said Charlie. "Tell us where you been for so long, boy."

Liam's gaze flickered away from Jemima. "Went to sea for a few years before I settled in the city."

"Well now, there's a story to be told." Charlie grinned and wiggled himself into a more comfortable spot on his stool. "Take a seat, Jemima."

She answered him on her way to the door. "I've outgrown fairy tales."

"Tell me first when you think that overseer will be back," said Liam. "Got some business with him while I'm here."

Jemima shrugged. "I expect you'll have to wait until the end of the week if you're set on talking to Mr. Dye."

Charlie smiled broadly enough to show all five teeth he called his own. "Why, then you'll be here for Anna's wedding party."

"Not if I can help it," said Liam.

It was the last thing Jemima heard from him as she closed the door behind herself.

There was a singular and simple truth about teaching that made itself felt on Monday afternoon in Elizabeth's classroom: even the best and most conscientious of students were simply incapable of concentrating in a thunderstorm, at first snowfall, or on the day that true spring weather made itself felt—as it had today. And this year was worse than most, because in addition to a cloudless sky and a warm breeze, the Dubonnets had decided that the time was right to turn their yearling hogs out of the winter pens to forage in the woods, and those pigs had chosen Elizabeth's schoolhouse for their afternoon nap.

Over the years Elizabeth had coped with many challenges, but two pigs under the schoolhouse porch on the first day of spring must be interpreted as nothing less than a direct order from the heavens to dismiss her students early. The children were clearly of the same opinion; even Daniel, who could normally be counted on to persevere, had his head cocked toward the door and a distracted look on his face.

But in front of Elizabeth stood her youngest readers: Lucy Hench and Many-Doves' oldest, Kateri. With one notable exception—Elizabeth cast a sidelong glance in Lily's direction—the girls in her afternoon class were well behaved and biddable, but Lucy and Kateri were especially eager to please and serious about their schoolwork. They had been practicing for this recitation for a week, and now Kateri could barely be heard above the grunting of pigs settling themselves in the damp shadows under the porch.

She raised her voice, but the pigs seemed to take this as an invitation to provide a chorus, which they did with increasing enthusiasm and a rustling that made the floorboards tremble:

> HAIL, beauteous stranger of the grove!
> Thou messenger of Spring! [grunt]
> Now Heaven repairs thy rural seat,
> And woods thy welcome ring. [grunt, squeal]
> What time the daisy decks the green,
> Thy certain voice we hear:

Every child in the room was struggling hard to keep from smiling as the pigs' snorting grew louder. Kateri raised her voice until it wobbled:

> Hast thou a star to guide thy path,
> Or mark the rolling year?
> Delightful visitant! with thee
> I hail the time of flowers—

"They're stuck!" Daniel stood suddenly, and then realizing what he had done, he ducked his head. "Pardon me, but I swear at least one of those pigs is stuck fast. Cain't you hear it?"

"Can we go see, Ma?" Lily was already at the door with the others crowding in behind her: Blue-Jay, Solange, Lucy and Emmanuel, even Kateri, her recitation forgotten.

Elizabeth was mustering the good grace necessary to capitulate when a high-pitched scream came from the other side of the door just as frantic squealing began just underfoot. The floorboards heaved, and Lucy jumped up on a desk in one neat hop.

"A panther," shouted Kateri over the screeching.

"The poor hogs," wailed Solange.

Lucy was sobbing through her fingers, her eyes as round as sovereigns. With a sense of foreboding Elizabeth realized that Lucy's gaze was fixed not on the door, but the window. She turned just in time to see Daniel ready to climb through. She caught him by his shirttail and dragged him back, all flailing arms and legs.

"Just what do you think you are doing?"

"Going for help." Daniel's clear green eyes flashed defiance.

"You know there's nothing to be done for those pigs," Elizabeth said. "I will not let you put yourself between a panther and his kill. We will wait."

The squealing stopped just as suddenly as it had begun, to be replaced by the sound of Lucy's soft sobbing.

"You see?" Elizabeth said.

"Wait until that cat eats his way through more than a hundred pounds of pig?" Daniel's jaw set itself hard, and for a moment he looked so much like Nathaniel in a contrary mood that Elizabeth was distracted.

"Somebody will come looking for us," said Lily.

Blue-Jay said, "That could take hours."

Elizabeth thought of sitting here with the children listening to the panther tearing into flesh, and then she imagined what might happen if they tried to leave. The smell of fresh blood was thick in the room now.

Once she had watched a panther drop out of a tree onto a man's back. It seemed a very long time ago and it had lasted only minutes, but she remembered it all with perfect clarity.

"We will sing," she said. "It has been some while since we had a singing party."

Emmanuel said, "Miz Elizabeth, somebody might come by who don't have a rifle. And you know that cat won't like anybody coming too close."

Solange drew in a wobbly breath. "Please let Daniel go, Miz Elizabeth."

Elizabeth looked at her son, so tall for his eight years that she did not need to stoop very much to kiss his face, something she wanted to do very much right now. He looked back at her without flinching, steady in his purpose.

"I'll be careful."

He would try, Elizabeth knew that much. Daniel was clever and quick, but like his twin he had inherited a reckless streak from the Middletons that showed itself at inopportune moments. Blue-Jay had stepped between her children and disaster more than once.

She said, "You may go, but not alone."

"I'm staying with my sisters," said Emmanuel.

"Then Blue-Jay will come with you."

Satisfaction slid across Daniel's face, and resignation across Blue-Jay's. At the window Daniel paused to smile at her over his shoulder before he launched himself through.

Blue-Jay said, "I'll do my best," and then he was gone too.

By the time Elizabeth had walked the five steps to watch, the boys had already disappeared into the forest behind the schoolhouse, headed downmountain.

Downmountain, toward the village.

"Maybe he's going to tell Peter about his hogs," suggested Emmanuel, answering the question nobody had asked out loud: *Why hadn't the boys gone to fetch one of the men from Lake in the Clouds?*

"Our pa is a good shot," said Lucy, wiping her cheeks with her fingers. "Maybe that's where they're headed."

Lily was studying the floorboards with exaggerated interest. Elizabeth lifted her daughter's chin with one crooked finger.

"What is it? What is he up to?"

She shrugged away. "He's been looking for an excuse to go down to the village all day. That panther just did him a favor."

"And why is your brother so eager to go to the village?"

All three of the Hench children went very still. Kateri might have spoken up, if it weren't for Lily's hand on her shoulder.

Elizabeth said, "Does this have anything to do with Liam Kirby?"

"You mean the blackbirder?" Emmanuel was the worst dissembler Elizabeth had ever encountered; she could almost read the whole story from that one word and his expression.

"Is that what you call Liam?"

"That is what Emmanuel calls him," said Kateri. "We call him Tsyòkawe," giving Liam the Kahnyen'kehàka name *Red Crow*. No doubt it would stick, whether or not it was deserved.

"Liam Kirby is a young man of flesh and blood like any other," Elizabeth said, trying to sound dispassionate and failing, even to her own ears. "No doubt you'll see that for yourself soon enough."

"But Lily's already seen him, ain't that so, Lily?"

Elizabeth saw from her daughter's face that it was indeed so. She had disobeyed and gone after Hannah this morning. Now she understood Daniel's rush to get to the village: what one twin dared, so must the other.

She said, "You followed your sister?"

Lily pursed her mouth. "Somebody had to look after her. But I didn't interfere, you can ask Hannah."

"I will do just that. And then your father and I will discuss this with you. In the meantime I believe you have sums to work."

It was a testament to Lily's guilty conscience that she complied without further argument. The others followed suit, forgetting or choosing to overlook Elizabeth's offer of a singing party. And she was glad to be left to her worries.

This morning on her way to teach school, she had passed

Hannah at the strawberry fields and stopped only long enough to learn that Liam was indeed tracking Selah. Hannah had taken great pains to look unconcerned and unmoved, and she had failed completely.

Lily was bent over her arithmetic, but she was watching out of the corner of her eye, no doubt waiting to be asked about her adventure of the morning; she knew exactly how worried her mother must be about Hannah. Elizabeth swallowed down both her irritation and her curiosity. She could not ask her daughter for an accounting of her escapade without seeming to condone her behavior.

Sometime soon Nathaniel would be going to the village to look for Liam. Hannah had said as much, and Elizabeth could imagine the whole scene: Nathaniel stepping into the dim light of Axel's tavern; Liam waiting there for him. No doubt Daniel would be close by. And tempers would flare. Not that Nathaniel would raise a hand to Liam. It wasn't his way to strike out in anger.

And still. Elizabeth tried to see them all together: Nathaniel and Liam, Daniel and Blue-Jay. Tried to imagine how her husband would confront the boy they had taken in and treated as one of their own, but who had left them without a word and now was back, carrying threats before him.

Lily was watching her openly now. She said, "You're going down to the village, aren't you?"

Elizabeth nodded. Then she picked up the first book that came to hand and tried to read, trying to ignore the sound of the panther ripping muscle from bone.

Hannah had retrieved the last of the onions stored from the fall and was bent over the chopping board when Curiosity came in.

"This is one of them cures that is harder on the doctor than the patient," said the older woman. She peered into the kettle of simmering onions and reared back, waving a hand before her face.

"I wonder what the good Lord meant, making so many of the best medicines downright ugly to deal with." And then she took a hard look at Hannah, reaching up to pluck an onion skin from her hair and to wipe her cheek.

"'You have fed them with the bread of tears; you have

made them drink tears by the bowlful,'" she quoted. "But I suppose it's high time I took my turn with these poultices. You let me cut up the rest of this batch."

"I'm almost finished."

"None of that foolishness," said Curiosity, pushing her aside. "You'll run yourself ragged looking after our Selah. She sounding any better?"

Hannah nodded. "Some better. She's asleep right now."

"The best thing for her. No doubt this poultice done her good, but then there ain't nothing like onion and camphor to shift a lung full of muck. Set down there and rest a minute, before you fall over."

Hannah did as she was told, but the fact was that while she had been working all day at a punishing pace, she was still twitchy with energy. Since her morning's errand she had pushed herself hard, moving from hearth to water bucket to sickbed and back again, bathing Selah's head and wrists with vinegar water and changing her poultice, bent over the washboard, the mortar and pestle, the chopping board. She had paused only when Many-Doves brought her food, and ate it standing on the porch before she went back to work; and still she could not reach the state she hoped for, where weariness drove everything about Liam and the things he had said out of her mind.

And now here was Curiosity, who would want to hear exactly those things she had been trying to forget. She had told the story once to her father; she would have to tell Curiosity and all the others who would want to hear it for themselves, recounted word for word, until they were able to conceive of the man Liam Kirby had become.

She said, "Elizabeth should be home by now. Was she still in the schoolhouse when you passed by?"

Curiosity regarded her with eyes narrowed, but she answered the question. "She was there, all right. Dubonnet's hogs made themselves right comfortable under the porch until a panther got after them."

Hannah stirred the cooking onions and waited for the rest of the story, but Curiosity wouldn't be hurried.

"Hand me that other knife, will you? Don't like the feel of this one in my hand. So they was stuck for a good while, until the boys climbed out a window and come to fetch Joshua and his rifle. I went along to see if there was anything left to be butchered. Peter will take it hard, losing both of them hogs."

"And Elizabeth?" Hannah asked, dipping a rag into the bowl of vinegar and water she had prepared for Selah and touching it to her own forehead.

"She went on down to the village to see where your brother got himself to. I expect she hope to find Liam too. And your little sister will be busy for a while, trying to talk Joshua into giving her that panther's head. Unless Hawkeye decide to come home, we got plenty of time for you to tell me about what happened this morning."

Hannah covered her face with the wet cloth and breathed in pungent vinegar, tasting it on her tongue and in the back of her throat and all the way down to the knot in her stomach. When she looked up again, Curiosity was still chopping onions, with tears streaming down her face.

She said, "Selah has been asking for you."

Curiosity let out a rough laugh. "You telling me you ain't ready to talk about Liam?"

Hannah drew in a deep breath to steady herself. "I don't think I ever will be."

"It's true, then? He's after our Selah."

Hannah nodded.

Curiosity's jaw worked hard. "Never thought that boy would turn out such a disappointment, but then I expect neither did you."

"No," said Hannah. "I didn't."

There was a long silence interrupted only by the steady contact of knife to wood. Finally Curiosity said, "Do you think there's any chance of talking sense to him?"

Hannah felt tears push up hot into her throat. She swallowed them back down again so that she could talk.

"I truly don't know. My father has gone down to try. I suppose we'll know more when he gets back." She paused, and so did Curiosity.

"What is it?"

"Liam says the woman he's after is wanted for murder. Her owner caught up with her at Newburgh, and she put a knife in his throat."

Curiosity's gaze fixed on the knife in her own hand, the sheen of the blade and its curve. She put it down and brought the cutting board to the hearth, where she let the mass of onions slide into the simmering pot. Then she sat down in Elizabeth's rocking chair and leaned back to look at Hannah. The lines that bracketed her mouth seemed to have dug deeper into the muscle in the past few days.

She said, "We got to move her along as soon as we can."

Hannah spread her hands on her knees. "It will be four or five days at least."

Curiosity stood so suddenly that the rocker jumped in place; she stretched out a hand to still it. Her expression was troubled, but she managed a grim smile. "Let me go see what I can do to speed things along," she said. And just as suddenly, she turned back toward Hannah.

"I near forgot. Richard say to tell you, he's going to try that Dr. Beddoes's cure on Gabriel Oak tomorrow morning, and he'd be glad of your help, if you care to come along. Don't know as it will do the poor man any good, but you could do with a few hours away from this cabin."

"Yes, I could," Hannah said, feeling suddenly more awake than she had all day.

"I thought you might want to have a talk with Richard while you're at it," said Curiosity.

It was unnerving, how she saw through even Hannah's simplest plans, but it was also comforting. It was rarely necessary to pretend for Curiosity, who understood something Hannah had never been able to explain to her father: over the past few years, she had developed a working relationship with Richard Todd, a man who had once been the Bonners' worst enemy.

Chapter 7

Shortly before dusk, Joshua started down the mountain leading his packhorses, their panniers filled to the brim with the remains of Dubonnet's hogs and the panther pelt. His three children trailed along behind, casting longing looks back toward Lily and Kateri. The girls stood in the path, each holding on to a panther ear so that the head swung gently between them. Lily had plans for the panther's skull, but that was something Elizabeth would have to deal with later. Right now she was worried about Daniel and Blue-Jay, who had not yet come back from the village.

Elizabeth sent the girls on their way home, changed out of her everyday walking boots into the moccasins she kept under her desk, and hitched up her skirt to knee length by pulling the hem through a leather belt. Then she started down the path the boys had taken. It was far steeper than the main trail, but it would get her to the village a quarter hour ahead of Joshua, who would most certainly draw a crowd eager to hear the story of Dubonnet's pigs and the panther.

This slope of Hidden Wolf was so densely wooded that the only way to walk it was in the Kahnyen'kehàka fashion, with toes pointed inward. Elizabeth drew into herself just as all around her the forest was drawing in for the night. She had come to these woods too late in life to ever really learn the trick of moving through them silently; as she passed by, birdsong faded and rose again. For the first time this year she heard the warbling of finches, but there was no time to sit and wait for a glimpse of them.

The creatures who foraged by day were settling into burrows and nests, and where the canopy of trees allowed the sky to show itself, blue was deepening to gold and copper and bloody red. With every footstep the smell of moldering leaves rose up, high and sharp.

At the spot the children called the Dirt Slide, Elizabeth lost her balance and would have fallen if a white pine sapling had not been within reach. Subdued, she slowed her pace. To break a bone and be stranded here until someone found her would complicate things. So she came to the village muddy, with a stinging welt across her cheek, sticky with pine resin. In sight of the trading post Elizabeth stopped to catch her breath, careful not to lean against the wall of the church, newly whitewashed by Mr. Gathercole himself.

The sound of cow bells came to her on the wind, and somewhere closer by a young child's wailing punctuated by the steady bite of axe into wood.

From this corner she could see almost all of Paradise. No matter how often Elizabeth came to the village, she was always reminded of the winter morning she had first seen it, in part because it had changed so little since that day while she had changed so much. What a surprise it had been to her, this awkward little place, log cabins and tree stumps and fields always threatened by the forests that surrounded them. In the years she had called Hidden Wolf her home she had come to believe that Paradise could never evolve into the place she had first imagined; there would be no lawns or parks or cottages or high streets; it could not be England, nor even Boston or Albany. The forest was constant and endless and patient above all things; it only tolerated the village, perched here as if on a cliff that must someday give way.

If she had not known that it was a Monday, the washing hung to dry outside every cabin would have told her so. Chickens scratched among woodpiles and in garden plots that would stay unturned for another three or four weeks, until the last danger of frost had passed. Each spring it seemed unlikely that this narrow valley along the west branch of the Sacandaga would feed and clothe them all: people, horses, oxen, cows, hogs (minus two, Elizabeth reminded herself), goats and chickens, cats and dogs, and one bull kept in a fenced pasture on the edge of the forest, at the eastern edge of the village.

As if the animal population had read her thoughts, a tremendous braying erupted from around the corner of the church and a tomcat tore past Elizabeth in a ginger blur. The dog pack followed closely, but at the last moment the tom managed to leap to the top of the woodpile stacked against the tavern wall, and from there to the roof, where he stood with every hair raised and his back in a perfect buckle. The dogs leapt into the air again and again, as if they might sprout wings by pure force of will. Elizabeth recognized the two loudest, who belonged to Horace Greber; the others were unknown to her.

Except that one of them had left the pack and turned toward her. A red dog.

Treenie. She said the name out loud, summoning the red dog out of her past and into the muddy turmoil in front of the tavern.

The door cracked open and Elizabeth caught her breath. For who else could it be, but Robbie MacLachlan. He would come out of the door and call his dog; she was sure of it, just as she knew with complete certainty that Robbie was dead almost eight years now, and buried in a graveyard thousands of miles away. And even so the sound of his voice was very real to her, strangely high for such a big man, singing softly:

I wish ye the shelterin' o' the king o' kings
I wish ye the shelterin' o' Jesus Christ
To ye the shelterin' spirit o' healin',
To keep ye fra' evil deed and quarrel,
Fra' evil dog and red dog.

The door opened all the way and a young Robbie stood there, tall and broad in the shoulder, straight of back. A full head of hair glinted not white, but mahogany in the last of the sunlight. The man spoke a word and the dogs gave up their baying and retreated, reluctantly.

Then he took a step in her direction, Treenie at his heels, her great flag of a tail wagging. Elizabeth went down on one knee and Treenie came to her, put her head on Elizabeth's shoulder, and made a contented wheezing sound. She smelled of lake water as she had the first time they had met, deep in the endless forests. Now there was white threaded through her coat and her muzzle.

She had last seen the red dog on the Christmas day she had been so big with the twins that she could barely move, when Robbie had left Hidden Wolf for the long journey north to Montreal with Treenie beside him. Where she had been shot by a redcoat, according to the men who had been there that day: Robbie, Hawkeye, and Nathaniel, who appeared now in the door of the tavern, behind this man who was a stranger and no stranger at all.

"Treenie," she said softly. "How can this be?"

"She came home that summer," said Liam. "Just walked out of the forest one morning, when I thought I'd never see any of you again. So I took her with me. I hope you can forgive me that much."

Axel's tavern was nothing more than a shed built onto the side of the trading post with a few tables and a high-backed settle in front of the hearth. It was very cool and dim, and gooseflesh rose up on Elizabeth's arms when she stepped inside. Axel had made himself scarce, and she was glad of it. Now that the initial shock of this reunion was over, she could smell the tension in the air as plain as spilled ale.

Liam stood on the other side of the room, watching Nathaniel closely. She imagined that the guarded expression on his face must be very much like her own, and that made her very sad. Liam had been one of her first students, a cheerful boy in spite of the fact that he lived with a brother who had beat him badly at the least provocation. He was bright in all things that did not have to do with the written word, hardworking, and devoted to Hannah. Elizabeth wanted to find some trace of that boy in the man who stood before her, but Selah Voyager and her child stood between them, and her safety could not be compromised for any reason.

Elizabeth said, "I did not mean to interrupt your discussion. I am looking for Daniel and Blue-Jay."

Nathaniel pointed with his chin toward the door that opened into the trading post. "They're under orders to set still until I come get them."

Elizabeth knew very well that she should go, take the boys home and leave this to Nathaniel, but she could not, not yet.

The red dog snuffled at her hand and she said, "Have you seen her, Nathaniel? Treenie? Robbie was so sure she was dead, and so were you."

"She had a bullet wound in her shoulder," said Liam. "Mostly healed by the time she got back here. I found some salve that Many-Doves left behind when they left and I used that. Seemed to help her some."

Nathaniel had never learned to use words to hide behind, but Elizabeth had been raised as a gentlewoman in an English home where uncomfortable silences must always be filled with conversation. "And she's been with you all this time?"

His face relaxed a little. "My captain took a liking to her. She's been all the way to China and back again."

Elizabeth's head came up sharply. "You went to sea?"

He looked a little surprised, and perhaps disappointed. "Didn't Hannah tell you?"

"There wasn't time this morning to say very much," said Elizabeth.

"But enough," Liam said, and he turned his head to look at her. "You know why I'm here."

Elizabeth studied his face for a moment. She said, "I know why you claim to be here. Have you seen Curiosity?"

Liam's mouth set itself into a firm line. He looked as if he had something to say, but then he just shook his head.

Nathaniel said, "Maybe you want to head home, Boots. We're just about done here."

"Are we?" Liam's head came up sharply. "I'd say we just got started."

"Let me set you straight then." Nathaniel's voice dropped dangerously low. "You want my permission to hunt for a runaway slave on our property, and I gave you a plain answer. We don't allow any hunting on the mountain, and I ain't about to make an exception in this case."

"The law sees this different than you do," said Liam. "If I have to I can go to Johnstown and get a court order."

"You do that," said Nathaniel. "And then I want to be there when you show it to my father."

Liam paled very slightly, but his jaw set itself even harder. "I'm not thirteen anymore, you cain't scare me with that kind of talk."

Very slowly Nathaniel said, "You'll know when I mean to scare you, Kirby."

In the strained silence that followed, Elizabeth forced herself to speak. She said, "Won't you let this go out of friendship, Liam?"

He shook his head. "I cain't. This has to do with murder." And he looked so pointedly at Nathaniel that Elizabeth had to wonder what had passed between them before she came into the discussion.

Nathaniel said, "As far as I can see, it has to do with trespassing and nothing else. So let me say it plain for the last time. If I find you on the mountain—"

"You'll throw me off."

Elizabeth drew in a breath, but Nathaniel didn't flinch.

"I'll put you off. Make no mistake."

His posture had changed, and Elizabeth saw that something new was in the room between these two men, something far more serious than anything that had gone before. There was a fury between these two that she wouldn't have imagined, something that went deeper than missing gold or betrayed confidences.

She said, "What is this about?"

But Liam seemed not to hear her, he was so focused on Nathaniel. He said, "I know what you did to my brother."

Elizabeth felt Nathaniel tense, just as she felt the skin rise all along her spine, as if Billy Kirby himself had walked through the door.

Billy Kirby. She did not often think of him these days, but once he had been around every corner. Billy had been younger than Liam was now when he locked the new schoolhouse with Hannah asleep inside and set a torch to it. Billy Kirby, as blundering and single-minded and short-tempered as a bull. The last words he had ever spoken to Elizabeth directly were the thing she remembered most clearly about him. *We'll find that mine,* he had told her in a soft, easy tone. *And then we'll find you dead in your beds.*

"Billy fell off the north face when he was running from the search party," Elizabeth said hoarsely.

Liam looked hard at Nathaniel. "Is that what happened?"

Nathaniel let out a harsh breath. "So that's what's behind all this. Not the slave. Your brother."

Liam straightened, and the blank expression left his face. He said, "You're wrong. I'm after a murderer, that's all. When I get her I'll take her back to stand trial, the way my brother would have gone to trial if—" He paused and swallowed so that the muscles in his throat convulsed. "I'll set out for Johnstown first thing in the morning and be back by nightfall with that court order. You better know that if she's gone, I'll track her into the bush. If you make me."

"Liam," Elizabeth said quietly. "Should you find this unfortunate woman, do you really think that a runaway slave has any chance of a fair trial?"

Liam picked up his rifle. "At least she'll get one, which is more than my brother got on that mountain. But that's something you'll have to ask your husband about. One more thing," he said, turning to Nathaniel. "You ain't asked, but I want to say that I didn't take anything when I left here that don't belong to me. I ain't a thief."

Nathaniel said, "It's not what you took that concerns me. It's what you told."

Liam's head reared back as if he had been struck, and patches of red appeared on his face and neck. He said, "No matter what you think of me, I wouldn't break a confidence. Especially not one that would put—" He paused. "Put your children in danger."

"I'll hold you to that," said Nathaniel. "Do we understand each other?"

Liam looked down at the floorboards between his feet while he thought. This was Nathaniel Bonner who stood across the room, a hand curled easy around the barrel of his long rifle. A man he had looked up to, once upon a time. To underestimate him would be the last stupid mistake he ever made.

"We're starting to," said Liam. "I suppose that'll have to do for now."

The boys were quiet on the way home, offering nothing in the way of explanations or excuses for their poor behavior, unsettled less by the punishment that was coming their way than Elizabeth's deep silence. They had all felt the sharp side of her tongue on occasion; it wasn't pleasant, but anybody who knew the woman would prefer a furious lecture to the kind of anger that settled deep in the bone and had to be carved out, word by word. Walking behind his wife, Nathaniel studied the line of her back for an idea of what was to come. He could almost feel his son doing the same thing.

Daniel threw a look in Nathaniel's direction, his brow drawn together hard. He was generally a patient boy, but he didn't tolerate his mother's unhappiness any better than Nathaniel did; he expected his father to fix whatever was wrong, and to do it immediately. There were things beyond fixing, but that was something Daniel had yet to learn.

Nathaniel thought of the conversation ahead of him, and a wave of both weariness and anger rose up hard and bitter in his throat. Old wounds once opened were hard to close again.

"Curiosity's here," Elizabeth said as they came up the last stretch toward Lake in the Clouds. "Run ahead and make your apologies for inconveniencing everyone so," she told Daniel. "Blue-Jay, your mother will be looking for you."

When she turned to Nathaniel, her expression was gravely still. "We will discuss Liam later, when the children are in bed."

Anger crawled up his back, but he shrugged it away. "We're going to spend the night under the falls, you and me."

"Under the circumstances—"

"Boots. Curiosity's here to spend the night and my father will keep watch. There's no good reason to change our plans."

He watched as she considered arguments and discarded them, the tilt of her chin increasing with her irritation.

"I need a quarter hour," she said finally.

"I'll go ahead," Nathaniel said, letting her go. "Don't make me wait too long, Boots."

By the time Elizabeth left the cabin it was full dark. Hawkeye followed her with his rifle to hand, and she made no protest. The panther at the schoolhouse was a clear reminder that she could not overlook, no matter how much she would have liked the time alone to think. The simple fact was that she could not manage a musket, the basket she carried over her arm, and the pierced tin lamp all at once, and she needed Hawkeye.

They crossed from the glen into the trees in an easy silence. The light of the lamp picked out touches of color on the forest floor, the first of the season's anemones peeking up from among drifts of pine needles and damp leaves. They pressed up the mountain through stands of birch and sugar maple that gave way gradually to beech and hemlock, Hawkeye matching his pace to Elizabeth's as if she were the elder of the two. At the point where they came to the backbone of the mountain, Elizabeth paused to catch her breath and he paused with her, but he seemed content to wait for her without talking, and no wonder: he had come home to have the twins hurl themselves at him with stories of the day's adventures, and he had heard Hannah's and Elizabeth's in turn. With all of that echoing in his head, he must be as glad of the silence as she was.

The sky opened up for them at the top of the ridge. Overhead a three-quarter moon was almost lost in cloud, and Hawkeye stood for a moment with his head thrown back to study the heavens. His white hair, tied at the nape by Lily with a piece of blue ribbon, reached halfway down his back.

He said, "Rain tomorrow. Do you smell it?"

Elizabeth did not, but neither could she doubt Hawkeye's almost infallible feel for the weather, nor ignore the simple joy he took in the sky overhead and the night itself. The breeze moved on her cheek and Elizabeth turned toward it. There was comfort in its touch.

When they started out again, Elizabeth realized that she felt more at peace than she had all day. She had been holding on to her agitation, afraid that her father-in-law would try to talk her out of it, afraid to let go and unsure why she should fear such a thing. And she found that Hawkeye had tricked her with his silence, and let the mountain and the night sky do his work for him, bringing her the calm she had resisted.

When they came out of the wood, Nathaniel was waiting for them. He took the basket from Elizabeth and they stood on the table of rock with the river thrumming deep in the ground, rushing underfoot to the spot a hundred yards below them where it exploded into the air and tumbled over boulders as tall as a man to the lake below. Down in the glen the cabins were lost in darkness, marked only by the faint spark of a candle at one window. The smell of wood smoke came to them, finding passage out of the caves through cracks to tell her that Nathaniel had laid a fire.

Hawkeye put a hand on Nathaniel's shoulder. The lamp picked out high brows and cheekbones and for a moment they looked more like brothers than father and son.

"You heard?"

Hawkeye nodded. He said, "We'll take care of things to-morrow while Kirby's in Johnstown. You two go ahead now, put all this behind you for tonight." He turned to look directly at Elizabeth. "Can you do that, daughter?"

Elizabeth tried to smile and failed. She said, "I can try."

And hoped that she spoke the truth.

She had made the scramble down to the caves too many times to count, but still she was glad that Nathaniel went be-fore her to hold out an arm at the worst spots. He walked with the lantern held high so she could watch her footing, but she found it hard to look away from the way the light cascaded down over his hand and the broad turn of his wrist. No matter her mood or the number of years she had spent with him, the sight of Nathaniel's hands still pleased her in a way she could hardly explain to herself.

He stopped suddenly and she careened into him with a soft whooshing sound, caught up from falling by his arm locked around her waist. The lantern light lit half his face to show her his curiosity and earnestness, as if he expected her to protest his touch.

"That's better," he said, dipping his head forward to kiss her, a quick stamp of the mouth. Before it could turn into anything more, Elizabeth leaned back to look at him more di-rectly. "What's better?"

"I thought you might take some wooing, and here you are throwing yourself at me."

Elizabeth snorted softly and pulled as far away as she could on the tiny plateau tucked into the cliff. Then she handed him the basket, turned, and climbed up through the cleft in the rock face into the caves.

The waterfall that formed the far wall sent such a wave of icy air through the cave that Elizabeth automatically pulled her cloak more closely around herself. By the light of the tallow candle set on the floor she ducked through the narrow passage to the next cavern and the warmth of the fire Nathaniel had laid for her.

Once they had used this place to hide all their furs and valuables and even themselves, back in the days when some in the village had been set on forcing the Bonners off Judge Middleton's mountain. In the last few years Paradise had been too much occupied with other kinds of troubles to worry very much about their neighbors, but the caves under the falls were still a safe haven, a secure spot known to no one outside the family. Except Liam Kirby, whom they had once counted as one of their own.

I wouldn't break a confidence that puts your children in danger.

A shudder ran up Elizabeth's spine.

Nathaniel was leaning with one shoulder against the mouth of the cave, watching her.

She said, "Do you think if we hide Miss Voyager here Liam will keep his word?"

Moving closer to the fire, Nathaniel crouched down to warm his hands. His expression was very calm and utterly serious, and Elizabeth wished suddenly that she could take back the question she had asked and put aside this conversation. But it was far too late for that.

"The boy wants two things and he cain't have them both," said Nathaniel slowly. "I suppose it depends on which one he wants worse."

"I suppose you are talking about Hannah," said Elizabeth. "But Liam is no longer a boy, he is a married man."

Nathaniel looked up at her, one eye squinted shut. "That don't stop him wanting what he wants, Boots. You know that. Married or not, he feels like he has a claim on her."

Elizabeth bristled. "Your daughter is not a belonging, Nathaniel. You should not speak of her that way." And she turned to the task of setting out the supper she had brought for him, unwrapping cornbread, cold venison, apple cobbler made with the last of the fruit stored from the summer, and a piece of Anna Hauptmann's strong yellow cheese.

"I don't look at her that way, and you know it. But it ain't me we're talking about."

"Liam is not like that."

"Not like what?"

She turned toward him furiously. "Like those trappers who take Indian women for convenience and then abandon them to go home to their wives. Putting them and the children they bear aside like—worn-out moccasins." Her whole face contorted, as if she had bitten into something sour.

Nathaniel took the bread she thrust at him. "Never said Liam was like that."

"But you implied it," Elizabeth said firmly, passing him the venison. "Whatever else Liam has become, he would not have the temerity to make such a request of Hannah. And if he did—" She paused, her mouth pressed hard together. "If he did, then she has been raised to know her own worth. Our Hannah would never give herself so cheaply. You know that to be true."

Nathaniel nodded. "I do. But there's more than one truth here, and you cain't deny it. Liam still wants her. I think it took him by surprise, to tell you the truth, but there it is."

"And just how do you know this?"

"It's in the way he looks at her," Nathaniel said, meeting her eye. "The way a man looks at a woman he cain't get out of his head. The way I look at you, Boots."

Elizabeth pushed out a sigh. "So Lily wasn't the only one who followed her sister down the mountain this morning. I should have known."

Nathaniel saw her struggling, trying to resolve the half of her that was angry at him for following his daughter with the half that was glad he had done so. He said, "I look after my own, and you wouldn't want it any other way."

She gave him a tired smile. "Yes." And then, "Now what?"

Nathaniel finished the last of the venison while he thought, and Elizabeth was content to let the silence stretch out between them. She knew that when he spoke again he would get to the heart of the matter, put words to those things she suspected but that needed to be said anyway.

"He wants her, and it's the wanting that's getting in the way of the reason he came home in the first place," Nathaniel said finally. "Which ain't a runaway slave—she's the excuse."

She sat down across from him. "For what is she an excuse?"

"Revenge," said Nathaniel. "I don't expect he calls it that, though. It'll look more like justice from his point of view."

"You learned a lot about Liam in that short time you spoke to him."

"I see what I see."

The fire whispered between them while she studied his face and he studied her in turn. He could see the question there, in the set of her jaw. What he wanted to do was to draw her down into the nest of pelts he had spread out on the floor for her and hold her there until she could not even remember her own name, much less Liam Kirby's. But he had been with Elizabeth long enough to know that she would fight any attempt to be distracted until she said what she needed to say.

"He thinks you threw Billy off the mountain."

Nathaniel chewed slowly and swallowed. "Seems that way. What do you think, Boots?"

She spread her hands over her skirt and pushed out a long breath. "I know that you did."

And what was there to say to that? Her composure robbed him of whatever explanation he might have offered, and so he said nothing at all.

She cleared her throat. "I have always known, I think. Although perhaps at first I denied the idea when it presented itself. I cannot say exactly how I knew, except that—" She paused. "When you brought his body home, there was something in your manner. Not guilt," she added quickly. "Perhaps it was relief."

The kind of relief he felt right now, to have this out after so many years. Nathaniel nodded. "That's pretty much how I felt."

She nodded. "Did you ever think of telling me what had happened?"

"Didn't see any reason to burden you with it."

Elizabeth gave him that look she reserved for a particularly poor excuse, part amusement and part disappointment. "You know me better, Nathaniel Bonner."

He knew her well, yes. He knew the way she set her mind on a problem and took it apart with logic; he knew that she would not let go until she was satisfied logic could take her no farther. His sensible Elizabeth, who could quote the bible and Greek philosophers and men who had lived their whole lives writing about worlds they knew only from other men like themselves. Elizabeth had once been like them, and she was still like them in some ways. There were things she did not understand, would never understand.

Billy Kirby's face, bruised and bloody, and the sun rising in colors of fire behind him. The wilderness all around, and somewhere deep in the endless forests Hawkeye living a solitary life, because of Billy Kirby. Broken bones and new graves. The stink of wet ash, and burned flesh. The inconsolable weeping of women. Everything in the balance because of this man who stood before him on a rocky ledge, a man who would lock a child into a schoolhouse and put a torch to it. Behind him the chasm, and a cocksure smile on his face that lasted until that last moment—too late—that he understood, finally, what he had brought upon himself.

"Well, then," Elizabeth said, bringing Nathaniel out of his memories. "There is really only one question left. Liam might have suspected what happened between you and Billy, but he could not have known, unless somebody told him. Someone was nearby that morning, clearly. But who could that have been, and why did that person never accuse you?"

Nathaniel brushed the bread crumbs from his lap. "Because whoever told Liam what happened on the mountain wanted him to run off."

"So he could get the gold." Her head tilted in surprise, all the tension leaving her for a moment while she considered the logic of it.

"Looks that way. Don't suppose anybody would be in a hurry to admit such a thing. Now that we've solved that puzzle—" He closed a hand over her ankle, cupped the swell of her calf in the palm of his hand. But she was so wound up in this new mystery that she took no note at all.

"Who could it have been? That much Liam could tell us, if he cared to." She pulled away gently and got to her feet to walk the length of the small cave, her arms folded around herself. The light of the fire sent her shadow up the wall and it jittered with every step she took, her head bowed down with her chin to her chest.

She stopped. "Do you think Richard might have had something to do with it?"

Nathaniel got up, but when he put his arms around her there was a stiffness in her, an unwillingness to let go of this riddle.

"Boots," he said against her hair. "I ain't about to share you with the Kirby brothers tonight, nor with Richard Todd. Not tonight or any other night, for that matter."

She put back her head to look at him. He traced the fine lines at the corner of her mouth with his thumb, cradled her head in his hand and leaned down to kiss her, pulling her up to meet him with his arm around her waist, testing her weight and the shape of her. When he let her mouth go her heartbeat had quickened under his palm, but the distance was still there in her expression.

It was a challenge he had faced many times, but one he had never tired of, could not imagine tiring of: winning Elizabeth. Making her forget everything but him and herself; forcing her to put away the rest of the world.

"Do you remember—"

"No," he said, his mouth at her ear, feeling her shiver at his touch. Moving his mouth down her neck until she shuddered and sighed.

"No more questions, not tonight. No children, no schoolhouse, no Paradise. This is our time, Boots. Let's not waste it."

And so Elizabeth let herself be drawn down, putting everything aside to focus on her husband's face, his beloved face so severe and intense as he worked her buttons and ties, his fingers clever and strong and knowing as he undressed her. She wondered if the candlelight was as kind to her as it was to him, giving back to her the man she had come to know in this very cave, the touch of him, his smells and the look in his face when he was with her, that look that was hers alone.

They came here every spring to remind themselves of that time, to remember where they had started. She had come to him against all good reason and logic, back in those days when she thought of herself as a revolutionary because she wanted to teach school. And how surprised she had been at what Nathaniel had to teach her. About herself, about the very nature of desire and the limits of reason.

He loosened her hair and was spreading it out over the furs, every pull of his fingers sending small shock waves through her.

"What are you thinking about?" He kissed the spot under her ear and blew on it, and she shuddered.

"You. And me. Us."

"That's better." He had a wicked smile he saved for times like this; she tasted it on his skin. He was dressed still and she was not. She might have pointed this out to him but his mouth was warm and busy and distracting. She tried to turn toward him but he caught her, held her pinned at the shoulders and kissed the hollow at the base of her throat.

"Much better."

"Nathaniel?" She needed the sound of his voice, telling her

those things she had never heard from another human being, never wanted to hear from anyone else. He could spin a web with his voice, tangle her in his words and the images he drew with them. Tell her what he was doing, and why, and make her talk in turn.

He pulled away and frowned at her, in concentration and fierce determination and something else, some possessiveness so bone-deep that it claimed the very beat of her heart. He frightened her a little like this and he excited her too, but when she started to tell him that he stopped her with his finger on her mouth, shook his head so that his hair moved around his shoulders.

"Listen," he whispered against her mouth. "Listen."

Chapter 8

From the edge of the woods where Hannah had stopped to scrape the mud from her moccasins, she watched Gabriel Oak and Cornelius Bump make their way toward the outbuilding that served as Dr. Todd's laboratory. Behind Gabriel was his own small cabin, made available to him in partial payment for his services as village clerk and Dr. Todd's secretary. Gabriel was tall and straight, but very frail; even from a distance his poor health was evident in the way he held himself, as if he were about to fall any moment and sure of a broken bone when he did. Everything about him was drawn in shades of gray and black: the fringe of steely hair that showed under the broad rim of the low-crowned hat; the ancient black coat that flapped around him with each brittle step; the ashen cast of the skin stretched tight over high cheekbones.

His companion was Gabriel's age, but half his size: Bump was a small hill of a man, bent almost double. His upper and lower halves seemed to have sprouted as afterthoughts from the hump that was his upper spine. He wore a long jerkin of pale yellow over a homespun shirt of deep indigo; his brown breeches were patched with squares of buckskin dyed turkey red. The fringe of hair that sprouted straight as wire from under his knit cap was the color of clabber sprinkled with pepper. His head, overlarge for his size, jutted up from between the twisted framework of his shoulders. His whole body undulated

with the force of propelling himself forward; he reminded
Hannah of a rainbow trout flexing its way upstream.

She was about to call out to the two men when Gabriel
Oak stopped suddenly and, bending forward, began to cough
into the kerchief he pulled from his sleeve. A consumptive
cough had a sound all its own, as if his lungs were fighting to
free themselves forcibly from their cage of ribs. In the past
year Curiosity and Hannah had tried every remedy known to
them, but Gabriel's cough had defeated them, as they had
known from the beginning that it must. There was no cure for
consumption but the grave.

And still Richard Todd had taken on the case, to everyone's
surprise. Generally he seemed content to leave the care of the
villagers to Curiosity and Hannah while he worked in his laboratory, but he had made an exception in the case of the old
Quaker gentleman. Hannah had the idea that a friendship had
taken root between Richard and Gabriel; whether the doctor
admitted it to himself or not, it was clear to everyone else that
he depended on Gabriel Oak for more than the maintenance
of his household accounts and correspondence. And he had
known Gabriel since he was a boy.

Presented with all these facts, Curiosity only sniffed. She
had her own theories about the relationship between Richard
Todd and Gabriel Oak, but was not willing to share them, just
yet, although sometimes Hannah had the sense that the older
woman would be glad to get whatever it was out in the open.

Gabriel Oak had spent years wandering the frontier and the
endless forests, appearing in Paradise sometimes as a tinker,
sometimes a preacher, most often as a traveling clerk, accepting payment from those who could not put their own words
on paper; often he performed all three services in a single visit.
No matter what work he did during any visit, he spent much
of his time drawing. Sometimes Bump had been with him,
and sometimes not. He had disappeared for longer periods
during the Revolution and made only occasional visits after
that until he and Bump showed up in Paradise in the fall of
1800 and declared that they had come to stay.

When the fit had passed, Gabriel folded his handkerchief—
blood bright—and put it back into his sleeve. Hannah waited
until they had closed the laboratory door behind them, and
then she followed.

*   *   *

The most obvious thing about the laboratory was the pure
stink of it. In between visits Hannah tended to forget how
very bad it was, but even in the cool of a spring morning it
made her eyes water: the sulphur reek of rotten eggs, distilled
urine undercut by ripening manure, and other smells harder to
identify. Stink was never hard to find, especially not after a
long winter in crowded cabins. But the laboratory smells—
sour, sharp, bitter in turn—left a metallic taste high in the back
of the throat so strong that the mouth watered and the urge to
spit was almost irresistible.

A good airing would have helped, but the doctor would not
allow Bump to do more than keep the floor swept and his
equipment clean. Hannah suspected that Dr. Todd was using the
stench to keep idle visitors—and Curiosity Freeman—away.
And still Hannah tried to interest Curiosity in the experiments.
She recited the useful chemicals that were to be won from urine
or dung: hydrogen sulfide, ammonia, nitrates, hydrochloric
acids; but the older woman remained unconvinced.

"Stench is stench." She would wave a hand before her face,
just remembering. "The only thing me and the good doctor
agree on is the fact that I don't belong in that laboratory of his."

Hannah's own discomfort with the odors lasted only until
the current project had caught her interest. There was another
kind of magic here and it had its own language; it was something she intended to learn. If the doctor's sour moods and impatient manner were the price she had to pay to spend time in
this place, that was something she was willing to do.

The laboratory was carefully thought out. Everything had a
purpose and no space was wasted: racks hung from the rafters
crowded with drying herbs wrapped in cheesecloth, and wall
shelves were lined with neat rows of pans and vessels in copper, iron, earthenware, bronze, and glass, all shining in the
light of a dozen candles in sconces backed with a mirror of
polished brass so that the laboratory was bright with reflected
light no matter the time of day or weather. One table was full
of the tools needed for the experiments: mortars and pestles in
a variety of sizes, fermentation vats, tongs and spoons and
scales, covered muffles and sample plates. The other table was
lined with glass jars and pottery crocks carefully labeled: vit-
riol, nitrous acid, acid of sea salt, lime, lye, sulphur, mercury,

bismuth, antimony, zinc, arsenic, cobalt. Baskets under the tables were filled with raw materials: ore, dried dung, and charcoal enough to keep the furnaces fed for the day.

There were three furnaces: the smallest conical in shape, a large melting furnace, and the real wonder and heart of the laboratory, the reverberating furnace, built to the doctor's specifications by a mason who came all the way from Johnstown with a wagonload of specially fired bricks. He had needed two teams to draw the sleigh, and a week to complete his work. Joshua Hench had needed another week in the smithy to make the doors and stacks and fittings.

It was a neat square brick structure that served both as a kiln and a boiler, with holes for the placement of alembics and the other vessels, all but one covered now. Behind a small metal door with sliding vents was the special compartment that reached the high temperatures needed for sintering, with its own stack to guide the combustion gasses outside. To one side a round glass receiver sat like a small world on its own specially built table, and on the other side a woolen rug hung over a roller in a filled water butt. Richard Todd was not moved by stink, but neither was he so foolish as to tempt fire.

When Hannah came in he was hunched over the big leather-bound logbook where he recorded all of his experiments. To her greeting he only shrugged a shoulder.

"You're late."

The very first lesson Hannah learned in his laboratory was that it made no difference how she responded; to talk at all was to invite a lecture.

Instead she greeted Gabriel Oak who had taken his usual place on the patient's chair. She handed her cloak to Bump and took from him her leather work apron.

"Friend Hannah." Gabriel tried to rise, but at Bump's glowering stare he sat again and contented himself with a smile. At close range his complexion had the consistency of wax, all the stranger given the startling blue of his eyes and the intelligence there. "Did you leave your family in good health?"

Gabriel Oak could not be coaxed to talk about himself, but he seemed genuinely interested in the well-being of the villagers. Before Hannah left, he and Bump would have asked for news of the twins and listened with great attentiveness to any story Hannah could think to tell.

"I did, thank you."

"If you're done distracting the patient," said Dr. Todd, pushing himself out of his chair, "we've got work to do here."

Gabriel Oak's morning ended in an exhausted sleep on the cot in the far corner, but not before he took both of Hannah's hands in his own and thanked her in a whisper.

"If you are breathing easier that is thanks enough," she said, pressing a damp cloth to his forehead. "Now you should sleep."

But he was stubborn, this old man, and he squeezed her hands as tight as he was able. "Will you greet your father and Friend Elizabeth and the others on the mountain for me? And give the little ones this, it is nothing very much."

He pressed a piece of folded paper into her hand.

"I will, of course."

He closed his eyes then. While he was drifting off Hannah studied his face, took note of the sound of his breathing. Then she got up slowly and worked the muscles of her shoulders.

It was her usual practice to discuss the experiment with the doctor; he noted down her observations when they differed from his own, and often he would challenge her to volunteer a conclusion. These were the discussions that Hannah looked forward to, but today she had a patient of her own waiting at home. Curiosity would not return to her own work until she could pass Miss Voyager into her care.

Bump had begun his work of cleaning up the laboratory, and Richard Todd was at his standing desk, recording the morning's work. Both of them were concentrating and took no note of the way her stomach growled.

Hannah took her cloak from the wall and hung the leather apron in its place.

Richard looked up from his notes and frowned. "You aren't going already."

He had not put it to her as a question, but Hannah was determined not to be intimidated. "I must."

He studied her for a moment, his jaw thrust forward. "Kitty asks that you join us for dinner. Her spirits are low, and I think a visit from you might do her some good."

Hannah busied herself with her cloak so that he could not see her expression. This was an invitation she could not easily refuse; Kitty was not really her patient, but she was Elizabeth's sister-in-law, and that made her family, of a sort.

"Unless you've got more pressing business."

He had put on his spectacles for writing and now he lowered his head to look at her from over the curved lenses. *As if I were a specimen in a sample dish,* Hannah thought. Richard Todd liked to think himself difficult to read, but Hannah knew the look he got when he was on the trail of something that interested him.

"They are expecting me at home," she said.

"Another hour won't make a difference." He picked up his quill again and dipped it in the ink pot. "Unless there's something else on your mind."

Hannah said, "If you want to ask me about Liam Kirby, it would be better to do that directly."

Bump barked out a short laugh, but Richard wasn't so easily startled.

"Liam Kirby doesn't interest me," he said, his eyes running over the page before him. "But I do have another matter to discuss with you. After dinner."

Hannah considered. If the doctor had an errand for her, or a patient he wanted her to see, he would have said so straight-out. This was something else. She might be able to put aside his attempts to arouse her family loyalty or make her feel guilty, but curiosity was another matter.

"An hour." She bit back the urge to ask any other questions; he had already returned to his logbook, and would have ignored her anyway.

Richard Todd's fine home—the only building built of brick in all Paradise—stood on a little rise just west of the village. The house was like a dowager queen who had lost her way in the woods and settled down, ill at ease, among lesser, ruder beings.

Hannah found Kitty in the parlor, tucked into the settee with Ethan on a straight chair beside her. He was reading to her from his morning's school lessons in his clear, high voice, but rather than falling asleep as she often did, Kitty was listening with her mouth pressed hard together in vexation.

"'These Reflections made me very sensible of the Goodness of Providence to me, and very thankful for my present Condition, with all its Hardships and Misfortunes: And this Part also I cannot but recommend to the Reflection of those, who are apt in their Misery to say, Is any Affliction like mine! Let them consider, How much worse the Cases of some People are, and their Case might have been, if Providence had thought fit.'"

"What a very rational man was Mr. Robinson Crusoe," said Kitty with a narrow smile. "And how shrewd of your aunt Bonner to give you that particular lesson to read just now."

Ethan's open expression clouded as he looked between the book and his mother. He was a compassionate child, and quick to sense unhappiness whether it was spoken plainly or not.

"But—"

"There is no time for a discussion right now. Greet your cousin and then go wash for dinner, Ethan."

He came to Hannah with his brow still creased in confusion and greeted her formally, as his mother had directed. Hannah smiled at him and touched his cheek.

"You must go up to Lake in the Clouds later," she said. "Lily could use your help with that panther's head."

He was such a sober little boy, but the mention of Lily made him smile. At the door he turned to his mother. "It was my choice. I chose *Robinson Crusoe*."

Before Kitty could respond, he had closed the door quietly.

"I meant to imply nothing critical about Elizabeth's teaching," Kitty said, almost fiercely. Because of course she had meant to do just that, and her son had corrected her in his own gentle way.

Hannah came to claim the chair next to Kitty, where she could observe her more closely.

Curiosity was worried, and with good cause. There was a translucent quality to Kitty's skin, as if this stillbirth had used up some vital part of her. She was still bleeding heavily, in spite of all the liver and leeks she had been fed since the birth, and even more worrisome was the low fever that came and went without warning or pattern.

Hannah would have liked to talk to Kitty about her symptoms, to ask about pain and even to examine her, but she knew that her questions would be turned aside with that combination of surprise and offense that was so particularly Kitty's. Richard Todd might value Hannah's assistance in the laboratory, and Curiosity could treat her as a healer in her own right, but to Kitty she would forever be Nathaniel Bonner's half-Mohawk daughter. Not that she was directly cruel; that was not in her. But she was often thoughtless and self-absorbed, and many times the results were the same.

Now she was waiting for Hannah to tell her what she wanted to hear: that Ethan had misunderstood her; that she had done no harm. The things she did want of Hannah were things that could often not be given.

Instead Hannah said, "Is your head aching today?"

Kitty's expression softened with disappointment and guilt as she lay back against the bolsters. "You are heartless. Yes, I will admit it. I should not have said such a thing, but I am tired of being told how a lady bears her loss."

Hannah stood to straighten the rug that had slipped from Kitty's legs. "Richard said you were asking for me."

Her whole expression shifted, as if Hannah had presented her with some unexpected gift. "Did he speak to you, then? You will come with me?"

"Come with you?" Hannah drew back in surprise and alarm as she realized what a neat trap had been set. Richard had sent her here to be drawn into one of Kitty's schemes and she had walked right into it without any suspicion, or defense.

Kitty took no note of Hannah's disquiet. "Yes, to New-York City. It has been years since I've been, and Cousin Amanda has been begging for a visit—"

"You don't mean to travel so far in your condition?"

Kitty shook her head impatiently. "It is for my health that I must go. I have the opportunity to put myself in the care of Dr. William Ehrlich." She said this name with great ceremony, as she might have spoken of President Jefferson or King George.

"I don't know this Dr. Ehrlich," said Hannah. "Is he a friend of Richard's?"

Kitty pointed with her chin toward a letter that lay open on the table next to her. "There is his latest letter. Read it for yourself."

Hannah picked up the paper, but she left it unread in her lap. "Is it worth going so far to consult with this man?"

Kitty turned her face away, and at first Hannah thought she would not answer. Her fingers plucked nervously at the rug in her lap. Finally she said, "Richard has been corresponding with him about my ... condition. He has a genius for diagnosis, apparently, especially in cases such as mine."

Hannah spread the letter over her knee to gain some time to think. "This was written in Philadelphia."

"Yes, but he will be in New-York City for a month and he has agreed to take on my case." She lifted her chin. "Richard thinks he may be able to cure me."

"Cure you? Of what?"

Kitty flushed, as if Hannah had insulted her in some way. "Other women suffer losses and then bear healthy children. My mother lost two before I was born and Elizabeth lost one before Robbie. Why should it not be possible for me to do the same?"

The answer was in Kitty's own face: hectic color had risen on her cheeks and her eyes were bright with new fever. Before Hannah could even think of how to say what she felt must be said, Kitty had reached forward to take her hands.

"You must come with me. Richard won't let me travel alone in my poor health and no one else will come with me, not even Curiosity. Did Richard not speak to you of this?"

"No," said Hannah slowly. "He must have been saving it for a surprise."

While Curiosity was on Hidden Wolf looking after Selah Voyager, her daughter Daisy Hench was in charge of the Todd household. Hannah would have liked to go into the kitchen, where Daisy would be busy putting the last of the meal together. The room would be crowded with Daisy's children, with Ethan in their midst. Certainly Daisy could use another set of willing hands, and there would be the chance to talk a little while they worked. Curiosity's oldest daughter was one of the quietest and most settled souls Hannah knew. No doubt Daisy had heard about this travel scheme and could provide her with details that Kitty must be withholding.

But before she could think of an excuse to slip away, Richard arrived from the laboratory and then there was nothing to do but go in to table, where young Margit Hindle served the meal: ham, turnips and potatoes mashed with butter and pepper, pickled cabbage, cornbread, stewed apples. Margit was new to service and did not hesitate to study Hannah through her lashes, as fine and white as down, as was the hair tucked into her cap. Kitty was too busy with her travel plans to notice that Margit needed correction, and Hannah would not credit rude behavior by drawing attention to it.

The food was good and Hannah was hungry, but she found it hard to concentrate on her plate, so strong was the urge to be away home. Richard sometimes looked at her from over the edge of his wine glass, but Hannah could read nothing from his expression, which made her strangely angrier than she already was about his maneuvering.

"Galileo can take us as far as Johnstown," Kitty announced, and at that the last of Hannah's intention not to be drawn into the conversation slipped away.

"Kitty," she said firmly. "You will have to find somebody other than Galileo to take you to Johnstown. You must realize how poor his eyesight has become over the winter."

Kitty had been arranging her food in neat piles over the pattern of roses on her plate as she talked, but she stopped to blink at Hannah. "What do you mean, take *me* to Johnstown? You said you would come along."

"No, Kitty, I did not," said Hannah firmly.

"But you must." Kitty spoke to Hannah, but she had turned to Richard. "Make her understand, Richard."

"I understand very well why you want me to come with you," said Hannah, struggling with her temper. "And I hope that Dr. Ehrlich is everything you expect him to be. But I cannot travel so far, not now."

There was a moment of strained silence, and then a look of relief chased across Kitty's face. "Oh," she said. "You are thinking of Anna and Jed's wedding. But we don't intend to leave until next week. You can go to the wedding party—but I hope it is not Liam Kirby you are expecting to meet there. I hear that he is married, is that not so, Margit?"

Margit bobbed her head. "That's what he told Anna. It put Jemima Southern in such a foul temper to hear it that—"

"Never mind," Hannah interrupted. "I have no interest in Liam Kirby or Jemima Southern."

They were all looking at her: Kitty in surprise and confusion, Margit with an eagerness that said this conversation would soon be known all over the village, and even Richard was smiling into his wine glass. It was not often that Hannah felt herself go pale with anger, and it took all her self-control to temper her voice.

She said, "And I was not thinking of Anna's wedding party. I have work of my own to consider. I am very sorry for your predicament, but I cannot go with you to the city."

Kitty stood suddenly. "Oh, please," she said, leaning forward. "You are my last hope."

Richard cleared his throat softly. "Sit down, Kitty, there's no need to be so melodramatic. Eat something, you are trembling for hunger. I'll continue this conversation with Hannah in my study. I think it is possible for us to come to an understanding."

"I think not," said Hannah tightly. "And I must get home."

"Your patient can surely wait another ten minutes," said Richard, with one eyebrow raised.

All Hannah's anger left as suddenly as it had come. A challenge, then. Was he guessing, or did he know something about Selah Voyager? It was a chance Hannah could not take. She nodded. "Ten minutes."

"Sometimes I forget you have a temper," said Richard, when he had closed the study door behind them. "But then you've got your grandmother's knack of keeping it to yourself most of the time."

Hannah closed her eyes and opened them again. "You didn't bring me in here to talk about my grandmother."

"No, I didn't." He sat down behind his desk and began massaging the knotty scar tissue on his palm, which seemed to bother him quite often. For a moment Hannah had the urge to ask questions no one had ever dared ask him directly. She knew very well how he had come by his scars, but what would he say? *I was once angry enough at your father to try to kill him, and this is what I got for my troubles.*

But he had evoked the memory of her grandmother, and Hannah could almost hear that familiar voice at her ear, reminding her that Richard Todd was nothing more than a man, and that he could only hold power over her if she gave it to him.

She said, "I have no intention of going to the city. If it's so important maybe you should take Kitty yourself."

He inclined his head. "I don't want to interrupt Gabriel's treatment."

"Not even for your wife's health?"

He sat back in his chair, folded his hands over his middle. "Ehrlich can't do anything for Kitty, you know that as well as I do. If it will comfort her to see the man then she should see him, but I do not expect anything to come of it."

"Then why—"

He waved a hand in dismissal. "It's not Kitty I want to send to the city, it's you."

He took a newspaper from a drawer and pushed it across the desk toward her. It was a well-thumbed copy of *The Medical Repository*, one Hannah had never seen though it was his habit to pass newspapers along to her when he had finished with them.

"You may have heard that the New-York Dispensary opened a new institute in January. They're calling it the Institution for the Inoculation of the Kine-Pox. The last smallpox epidemic put the fear of God in them, and they're hoping to stay the next one."

Hannah looked at the report, but she did not pick it up. "Elizabeth's cousin Will wrote to us about the new institute, yes."

"Good. Dr. Simon is on the medical board, and he will see to your training himself. You will learn how to cultivate the raw material and to carry out the vaccinations. The institution's primary purpose is to provide free vaccination for the poor in the Almshouse, which is where you will work. When you come home again you can show me what you've learned. With any luck this should be the end of the pox in Paradise."

Hannah blinked, and her vision blurred. When she looked up she saw from his expression that she had not misunderstood him. There were a hundred questions going through her head, but only one came out when she opened her mouth. "Does he know I'm Mohawk?"

"Yes."

"He's willing to have a half-breed girl work in his institute." Hannah paused, letting that idea hang there in the air where they could both look at it hard. "Will I be required to scrub floors?"

"No," said Richard, impatiently. "Dr. Simon will extend

every professional courtesy. I wouldn't worry about how your patients react to you, Hannah. The Almshouse inhabitants are thankful for any help they can get. They are mostly Irish and free blacks, anyway."

To offer the truth in the most offensive manner available was to rob it of some of its power and most of its appeal, but Hannah knew that it would do no good to point this out to Richard.

"And why would you do this for me? Because of your friendship with my mother?"

"No," said Richard Todd, but Hannah saw that she had struck a nerve, just as she had intended to do; she had never raised the topic of her mother with him before. No doubt he hoped that she knew nothing of that history.

"Then why?"

"Because I don't care to go and you're the only person competent enough to send in my place. And you've got a natural talent for medicine. I haven't said so to you before. Maybe I should have."

"I see." But she didn't, quite. Hannah could not picture such a place where a red-skinned woman would be allowed to work with white doctors. She would be an oddity of the first order, as interesting to them as a child born without legs or an illness they could not diagnose.

Richard was watching her. He said, "I never thought of you as a coward. You would walk away from such an opportunity because you are afraid?"

He meant to anger her, and of course he had, but Hannah would not show him that.

"There are no guarantees," he went on. "Except that it will be hard and you will wish sometimes that you had stayed at home."

The silence between them stretched out. Finally Hannah said, "Tell me why this doctor would agree to such a thing."

"Valentine Simon is active in the Manumission Society and he's interested in the education of the colored races, but he doesn't suffer fools. You'll have to prove to him that you're worth his trouble. And—" Richard paused. "He's a close friend of Will Spencer's. I expect he read my letter and went straight to Spencer to ask him about you. It took some time, but it's all been settled."

Will Spencer. If anyone could pave a way for her into New-York's medical community, it must be Elizabeth's cousin Will. Another transplanted Englishman, but no loyalist: Will had fled rather than be tried for sedition, as had other members of Corresponding Societies with leanings toward republicanism. He had left England, but he remained Viscount Durbeyfield, the eldest son of the Chief Justice of the King's Bench, and most Americans were still enchanted by a title and influenced by the income that went with it. The Spencers were widely known and highly respected in the city, for good cause.

This opportunity before her was real. A flush of exhilaration made Hannah's fingers jerk, and she wound her arms around herself and rocked forward to think. She said, "You arranged all this without asking me first."

He lifted a shoulder. "I'm asking you now. You don't want to do it?"

But she did. Of course she did. She would spend enough time at the institute to learn whatever there was to know about vaccination. Smallpox had killed and maimed too many Kahnyen'kehàka to count, and the idea that there might be a way to stop it was more temptation than any other incentive he might have offered. When she had vaccinated the whites in Paradise, she could go on to the Kahnyen'kehàka at Good Pasture and then to the rest of the Six Nations.

If she turned him down she would be denying not only herself, but all of her mother's people, and Richard knew it. In return he was asking her to take on Kitty, to relieve him of that burden for a little while at least, until she could be delivered to the care of this Dr. Ehrlich.

He had manipulated her like a child, boxed her in as surely as if he had hammered the lid down with a hundred nails. It stung, and it would continue to sting, but there was nothing she could do but pay that price. In her irritation Hannah said, "And if I won't go?"

Richard smiled again, an unsettling sight. "Then we will hope that the smallpox stays away from Paradise this summer."

It didn't surprise her, the fact that Richard Todd would risk the village, if it suited his purposes. He could be ruthless; his mangled hand was proof enough of that. The Kahnyen'kehàka who raised him called him *Cat-Eater*, a tribute to the fact that even as a boy he would go to any lengths to survive. And there it was, the little bit of power she had over him, the connection they shared. He did not like to be reminded that in spite of his white skin and red hair, he had once been Kahnyen'kehàka; that some part of him would always be Kahnyen'kehàka.

In the language of her mother's people she said to him, "Maybe when I have learned what this Dr. Simon has to teach, I will travel west and find your brother Throws-Far and his children. So that all your family is safe from the smallpox."

A flash of recognition then, in the way his face lost all expression. And he surprised her still, answering her in the same language. "If that is the journey you want to make, Walks-Ahead, then you must first go to the city."

After a long time Hannah said, "I will speak to my father."

"You leave next Monday," said Richard, in English. "After the wedding party." And he smiled, something he did very rarely.

"About Galileo—"

Richard waved a hand. "Of course he can't make the trip. I'll arrange for Joshua Hench to take you as far as Johnstown."

APRIL 15. EVENING.

Chill at dawn with some frost. A flock of horned larks in the cornfield at first light. The chipmunks have come up from their winter nests. Clear skies until evening.

Eulalia Wilde stopped me today in the village to ask if I would look at her ankle, having turned it in a fox hole. She is worried that she won't be able to dance at Anna Hauptmann's wedding party. I promised to bring her an ointment but could not give much hope of dancing anytime soon.

Spent this morning assisting Dr. Todd in his laboratory. He has adapted Dr. Beddoes's treatment for phthisis pulmonalis to Gabriel Oak's case:

Pass vapor of water over charcoal heated to ignition in an iron tube. Carburetted hydrogen gas will pass into the receiver. Agitate over lime water. Dilute with atmospheric air, in the proportion three quarters of air to one quarter carbureted gas.

The gas has the ripe odor of a crowded cow barn, but Friend Oak took it without complaint, by means of a small tube passing through a cork in the mouth of the receiver. Two treatments in ninety minutes brought about giddiness, headache, weakness, and a quickened pulse. After the second treatment his lungs put out a great deal of bloody foul matter.

Upon parting he gave me another of his drawings for my brother and sister, of some sparrows at a woodpile, as true as life and sweetly observed. I fear he must soon pass over, in spite of the doctor's best efforts.

Selah Voyager's fever broke in the night while Curiosity sat up with her. Her skin is now cool to the touch and she is hungry. We continue the willow bark and meadowsweet tea and have started venison broth to fortify her.

This morning Liam Kirby rode for Johnstown at first light as he threatened.

Dr. Todd has asked me to go to New-York City with his wife, where I am to learn the Jennings method of vaccination at the new Kine-Pox Institution. My father bids me reconsider. Elizabeth did not encourage or discourage me, but she left a note on my bed, one of her quotations and I record it here because it rests uneasy in my mind:

Adam was lonely, so he was given Lilith; he wished to lie with her, but she refused. We were created by the same God, she said, turning away from him; why should I lie beneath you? When Adam tried to force her to his will, Lilith cried out the name of the creator, whereupon she rose into the air, and flew away to the Red Sea.

Chapter 9

"What perfectly awful weather," said the widow Kuick. She looked out her window into the chilly wet with a grim smile. "Perhaps we will have snow before the day is over. That would be very appropriate. Yes, most gratifying indeed."

Isaiah was half-asleep over the bible on his lap, but he raised his head. "Appropriate?"

The widow sniffed and sat up straighter as she quoted, raising her voice to fill the room, " 'So persecute them with thy tempest, and make them afraid with thy storm.' "

"Ah," said Isaiah. "The wedding."

Jemima stilled for a moment in her scrubbing of the hearthstones to hear the widow's answer.

"Yes, the wedding. Such foolishness. One husband is enough for any woman, as I told Mrs. Hauptmann myself, and Constable McGarrity too. If he must marry again there are enough young women without husbands to pick from."

Isaiah lifted an elegant hand to hide his yawn. "Does that mean you won't be going?"

"To catch my death in this wet cold?" The widow peered down at her needlework with a frown. "Certainly not. And neither should you, my boy, if you know what is good for you. Jemima!"

"Yes, mum?"

"Tell Becca to put away the black bombazine she laid out for me. You'll go down to the village to make my apologies."

"Yes, mum. What shall I say exactly?"

The widow raised her head to glare at her. "The truth, girl. The truth. While you're there you collect the money Constable McGarrity owes me for Reuben's fiddle playing."

Becca and Dolly were waiting for her in the kitchen, as anxious as hens. Becca's cheeks were flushed with color, while Dolly looked as if she were going to be sick. Jemima walked past them without saying a word and began to put on her pattens.

"Well?" Becca demanded. "Has she given permission? Can we go to the party?"

"I haven't asked her yet," said Jemima, reaching for her cloak.

"Don't count on it," said Cookie from the worktable where she was washing the morning's crockery. "The widow ain't in a generous mood these days."

Jemima desperately wanted to contradict Cookie, but she could not: the widow's mood was as bad as it had ever been. It was always thus in the week before the overseer brought the slaves home after a winter's work in the city, when the widow's mind turned to the season's profits. If the money he brought to her met or exceeded her expectations there would be extra servings of mutton for a week, and the widow would be at her most approachable. If there was less money than she felt was her due, life would be unbearable for a very long time. In either case, she would still send Reuben to play the fiddle at the wedding party. There was hard coin to be collected for his services, after all.

"I told Eulalia I'd be there," said Dolly softly, turning to Becca.

Jemima's temper, so long held tight to her breast, flared. "Eulalia, is it? You could care less about Eulalia Wilde. It's her brother Nicholas you're interested in, hoping that he'll ask you to dance. Everybody knows it, Dolly Smythe. Him too. No doubt he's laughing about it right now."

The tears that sprang into Dolly's crossed eyes gave Jemima little satisfaction. She jerked open the door, but Becca put a foot out to stop her.

She said, "You're the meanest thing God ever put breath into."

"Maybe so," said Jemima. "But you're the dullest and she's the ugliest."

From behind them Cookie called, "Come on back here, let me tell you what folks saying about you, Miss High-and-Mighty!"

"Yes," hissed Becca. "We all know who you want to dance with, don't we?"

Jemima walked away so quickly that she almost lost her footing. When she was out of sight she stopped, and pressed the heels of her palms to her eyes until they ached.

She would go to the wedding party. She must go. Richard Todd had given Anna and Jed permission to use the judge's old homestead, and Reuben was going to play the fiddle. Everyone in the village would be there. For the last week Jemima had thought of nothing else; she knew exactly how it would be, down to the things she would say to each individual, and the way people would look at her. Over the winter she had spent all her free time taking apart the one good dress her mother had owned, sea green with a pattern of yellow and red flowers, and sewing it together again into something more like the dresses she had seen Elizabeth Bonner's cousin Amanda wearing when she came to visit two years ago. It was low enough in the bosom to give the widow apoplexy, if she were to see it.

Jemima would dance with Isaiah Kuick, and with Liam Kirby too, married or not. And Hannah Bonner would watch.

Except that Liam had come back from Johnstown and disappeared into the endless forests, tracking his runaway.

The skies poured down, and Jemima wrapped her cloak tighter around herself.

Jed McGarrity woke on the morning of his wedding to Anna Hauptmann with a sore jaw. A man might grin through a toothache—he had been doing just that for weeks—but there was no hiding a cheek that looked as if it had been stuffed to bursting with chestnuts. An hour after he ducked his head in the trading-post door, Jed found himself trapped.

To his right side was his bride, looking as ferocious as he had ever seen her; to his left was her father, with a bottle of his homemade schnapps at the ready; and in front of him was Hannah Bonner with an instrument in her hand that gave Jed a bad feeling deep in his gut. It was long and thin and it had jaws with teeth, as sharp as a wolverine's.

"That one of them instruments from the medicine case that Hakim fellow give you?" he asked, hoping to distract her for at least a minute.

She gave him a tight smile. "It is. Open up."

He took one last hopeful glance at the door, but there was little chance of rescue. Anna had closed the trading post in honor of their wedding day.

"The quicker we start the quicker it will be over," said Hannah. It always took him by surprise, how gentle Hannah could turn so hard and no-nonsense when she was doctoring.

"Come on, Jed," said Anna. "I ain't never seen you turn coward and today sure ain't the day to start. You'll be running off, leaving me standing by my lonesome in front of Mr. Gathercole, and wouldn't that be a sight."

He opened his mouth to tell her that he would never do such a thing, and Hannah reached right in, as if the two women had planned the whole thing out beforehand. Which of course he wouldn't put past them. Though it did bother him to be so easily got around.

In two yanks she had it. Anna leaned forward to take a closer look.

"More like an old moldy piece of honeycomb than a tooth," she said. "Didn't I tell you not to leave it so long?"

Jed winked at her sheepishly and spat into the bowl she held out for him. "Should have listened, Annie. Won't make that mistake again."

She snorted out a laugh, but she was smiling.

"Take a swallow of my schnapps," said Axel, thrusting the bottle toward Jed. "It won't stop it hurting none, but you won't care so much either."

"Don't start pouring yet," said Hannah. "There's still some work to be done here."

Jed spat again. "Feels fine to me," he said. "Feels good, as a matter of fact. Like the devil finally left off hammering on the inside of my jaw."

"It won't feel good for long if I don't open the gum," she said. "All that poison has to come out."

Jed didn't like the sound of that, but when he started to explain his position she just slipped three fingers in right up to the knuckles. Her head was turned away, as if she was listening to somebody talking in the next room. Then something hard scraped against a tooth and pressed into the swollen tissue. A roar came up from his belly and it was all he could do to keep from biting down.

"There," she said, wiping the little blade she had been holding between her fingers on the sacking Anna had draped around his shoulders and neck. "Spit it all out. It should drain for a while. You need to rinse your mouth every half hour."

"Schnapps?" Axel looked up at her hopefully.

"Warm salt water," said Hannah. "Save the schnapps for the wedding party. I'll come back later today and pack the hole to stop the bleeding."

There was a knocking at the door, but Anna ignored it. "We stand up in front of Mr. Gathercole at five," she said, a little anxiously. "Can you do it before then?"

Hannah hesitated. She had hoped to stay away from the village this afternoon, but all three of them were looking at her with such open and friendly expressions that all the excuses she had rehearsed suddenly faded away.

"Yes," she said. "I wouldn't miss it."

The knocking at the door started again, louder now and impatient. Anna's face screwed itself up in exasperation and she thrust the bowl into Jed's hands.

"You'd think I could close this place for one day," she said loud enough to be heard on the other side of the door as she marched toward it. "Hung a sign out too, plain as a pimple on your nose."

She swung up the bar and threw the door open.

Five men stood on the porch dripping rain. The bigger four were all black men, heads and shoulders tented with oiled deerskins held in place by woven carry bands slung around huge packs. The shortest of the four stood six feet tall, and even he was twice as broad as the white man who had knocked on the door. Long and thin, there was little to see of Ambrose Dye from the depths of his boiled-wool cloak.

"Mr. Dye," said Anna, booming out her surprise. "Don't think the widow expected you back till tomorrow, but here you are on my doorstep sure as rain. Ezekiel, Levi, Shadrach, Malachi, good to see you boys back safe. Zeke, looks to me like you've grown another five inches this winter. I expect Cookie won't be taking that wooden spoon of hers to your britches no more."

The youngest of the men smiled and ducked his head. "Ma will whoop me when she feel the need," he said. "No matter how big I get."

"Now, Zeke," said Anna. "I'm especially glad to see you. Your brother Reuben's set to play his fiddle at our wedding party tonight. I'm hoping you'll come along too. We'd like to have two fiddles, wouldn't we, Jed?"

Jed allowed that if he couldn't play fiddle himself, he would like to have Zeke and Reuben making the music. "If the widow can spare you," he added, with a glance toward her overseer. "For the usual fee, of course."

Anna stepped back to open the door wider. "Won't you step in and dry yourselves in front of my new stove?"

"Hauled it in from Albany just after the first snow," called Axel. "Come and set, give us the news from Johnstown."

But now Ambrose Dye had caught sight of Hannah; she could tell by the way he straightened and then looked away. "We ain't that wet," he said. "Just stopped by for some tobacco on my way up to the mill."

Anna followed his gaze to the table where Hannah was packing up her tools, and her friendly expression went just as suddenly as it had come.

"Suit yourself," she said, and shut the door in his face with a bang. "No more manners than a goat," she muttered, reaching over the counter for the tobacco scoop. "Letting those boys stand out there in the rain because he don't—" She stopped, glanced at Hannah uneasily. "And here's me thinking I'd invite him to the party. I've got a mind to have a word with the widow Kuick about that overseer of hers."

"Never mind, Annie," said Jed. "Give the man his tobacco and he'll be on his way."

But she was waiting for Hannah to say something about Ambrose Dye, who would rather stand in the rain than step into the same room with her. He would chase her away if he could, out of the trading post and the village and off the face of the earth, no doubt. Anger made her throat go so tight that her own voice sounded strange in her ears. She said, "I haven't heard Reuben and Zeke play together for a year or more, Anna. I'm looking forward to it."

If they had asked her straight-out to come, she could have listed a hundred reasons to spend this evening at Lake in the

Clouds, but suddenly none of them mattered. Hannah would be going to the wedding party. Not because Anna and Jed wanted her there, but because Ambrose Dye would want her to stay away.

Elizabeth went down to school in spite of the fact that she had canceled classes in honor of Anna Hauptmann's wedding. There was other work to be done, lessons to be planned and two books that needed mending, and in any case, she liked having the schoolhouse to herself now and then.

When the children were absent, Elizabeth could see the cabin for what it used to be: her father's first homestead, built when he was still a leaseholder. Four years later he had brought her mother here as a bride, and here they had stayed until a bigger house was built on the lake. In the quiet of a rainy spring morning Elizabeth could almost imagine her mother sitting in front of the hearth with her needlework in her lap. Mattie Clarke had been disowned by the Quaker meeting where she grew up when she married outside the faith, but she had never put aside her plain ways. It was her habit and comfort to sit in silence, something Elizabeth had learned from her.

"Hope I ain't interrupting." Curiosity came in, pulling Elizabeth out of her daydreams. She set down her basket by the door.

"Not at all," said Elizabeth. "Are you on your way home?"

Curiosity pushed back her hood and ran her hands over her face. "I am. Lily say to tell you to hurry, she cain't find her blue hair ribbon. Those children are surely looking forward to this party. Smiles to brighten up the worst day wherever you look."

Elizabeth studied Curiosity's face. "Have you had a bad day? Is Selah—?"

"Oh no." Curiosity sat down across from Elizabeth on one of the student benches. "Doing right well, as a matter of fact. Can we set a minute and talk, you and me? Seem like we just cain't find the time these days."

"What is it?" Elizabeth asked. "What's wrong?"

Curiosity wrapped her arms around her knees and rocked forward. "The girl has got to move on. No help for it, with Liam nosing around the mountain. But I hate to do it. Don't like the idea of her out there in the bush, so far from family. And I keep asking myself about Manny, if he'll ever see this child of his."

"Of course he will," said Elizabeth firmly. "Of course. And so will you. Later in the summer she will go on to Montreal and he will join them there."

"It won't be easy for him to leave his work behind."

For a moment Elizabeth thought of Manny at the African Free School, and then she realized what Curiosity was trying to say.

"The voyagers."

Curiosity nodded. "I expect he feeling mighty torn right now."

"But you must be——" Elizabeth stopped herself.

"Relieved. I surely am, I cain't deny it. We never do talk about it, but many the night me and Leo have laid awake thinking about him getting caught. He'd hang before we could get there to say a prayer for him. So I'm relieved, yes. And I'm feeling guilty too. All those souls needing a hand on the way." She shook her head and pushed out a great sigh. "I expect you know that I'm here to ask you for something. Except it ain't easy."

"Anything," Elizabeth said. "You know that."

"Wait till you hear it," said Curiosity. "Afore you go jumping in with that yes." She paused. "Hawkeye all ready to set out north for Little Lost?"

Elizabeth nodded. "He is."

"If I had my way I'd go with them"—she held up a hand to keep Elizabeth from interrupting—"but I cain't. I move too slow, and anyway, it would be as good as waving a flag if I was to disappear like that. It'll be work enough keeping clear of Liam once he picks up the scent."

"It will not," Elizabeth said firmly. "There are very few men who could track Hawkeye in the bush, and Liam is not one of them, as you know well enough."

Curiosity said, "What I know is, her time is close. Too close, maybe."

They were silent for a moment together.

"She really is in good hands," Elizabeth said, but with less conviction. She had great faith in her father-in-law, but she could hardly imagine him delivering a baby. "If Richard hadn't arranged for Hannah to go with Kitty..." She said this more to herself than Curiosity, and did not finish what they both knew.

Curiosity rocked forward again, her expression so tense that Elizabeth imagined she could see the pulse in her throat, just as she could feel her own heartbeat quicken. She knew now what Curiosity had come to ask, but she must wait to hear the words.

"But you could go, Elizabeth, if you had a mind to."

Elizabeth drew in a breath and let it out again. "It's been almost ten years since I last went into the bush. Those were desperate times."

Curiosity's wide-set eyes, so clear and dark, met Elizabeth's evenly. "Desperate times," she said softly. "They got a way of coming round again when you ain't looking."

Elizabeth got up to go to the window. So many trees, as far as a man could walk in a month or more, trees without end. Curiosity was asking her to go into the endless forests with Selah Voyager, to see her safely to the people who would take her in, people like herself, other runaways who had found safety together deep in the bush. On his own Hawkeye could get to the meeting place at Little Lost in two days walking as hard as he could, but with Selah the journey would take four days or five. More, if the child decided to come early.

She wanted to say no. There were so many reasons to stay on the mountain, with her own children. But then Curiosity had once left her family behind to go with Elizabeth on a much longer and more dangerous journey. Curiosity had helped her bring Robbie into the world, and she had been there, too, when he left it. She had taken him out of her arms at the end, and tended to him as if he was her own. It was Curiosity who had brought them through those dark days.

Desperate times got a way of coming round again when you ain't looking.

"Yes," Elizabeth said. "Of course I will go with her."

Curiosity closed her eyes briefly and opened them again, but before she could speak, Elizabeth had started to talk again.

"I imagine you've already figured out what I should do about the school?"

Curiosity smiled. "As a matter of fact, why yes. Seem to me that the urge to go down to the city with Kitty and Hannah going to come over you right sudden. They planning to set out at first light on Monday—won't nobody know if you went north or south, not until they back home again."

"That is a very delicate operation you're proposing." Elizabeth thought for a long moment. "But it might well work. It is believable, at any rate, that Kitty might persuade me at the last minute. What about Richard?"

"You leave Richard to me," said Curiosity.

"Gladly. The twins will be unhappy about this, of course." She looked out the window, as if she hoped to catch sight of them. "There's something I need from you."

"You know you don't have to ask me to look after those children," said Curiosity.

Elizabeth smiled. "I do know that. With you and Many-Doves and Hawkeye they will do very well."

She looked out the window again and remembered Daniel climbing through it, set on rescuing them all. How sure he was of himself, how completely dedicated to the task he had set himself. Her sweet son, at ease in the world in a way she had never been, might never be. He had that from his father, and from his grandfather.

"It isn't so much the twins I'm worried about as Nathaniel. He would take any risk upon himself, you know that. But he won't like the idea of me taking this on. You'll have to help me convince him."

Curiosity had a warming smile, and she used it now. "Why, Elizabeth, I'm surprised at you. Married all this time and you cain't think how to get what you want. That ain't no mystery at all."

Elizabeth sat back. "Is that so? And what exactly is it that I want?"

"You know the man cain't deny you a thing," said Curiosity. "All you got to do is ask him, and he'll follow you to the ends of the earth."

It was easier than she imagined, so easy that Elizabeth wondered if Curiosity hadn't presented her plan to Nathaniel first. Together they would take Selah Voyager to Red Rock; Hawkeye would stay behind to keep an eye on Lake in the Clouds. Selah Voyager was so obviously relieved when they told her that Elizabeth wondered at herself; she should have known that the girl would be frightened, and would want a woman with her.

The plan sat well with everyone but the twins. Daniel had gone off to voice his discontent to Many-Doves; Lily had not yet given up the fight.

"It ain't fair," she repeated, sitting straight-backed in her outrage. Elizabeth tried to focus on the hair she was plaiting, as temperamental and untamable as the child herself.

"Perhaps not," she conceded. "But it is necessary. You know we would not leave you behind otherwise."

Lily would certainly have had more arguments to offer, but she was trying to listen to the men talking in the next room. *Little Lost,* they heard clearly, and *the Prophet.* Runs-from-Bears asked about weapons and Lily sat up straighter. Elizabeth was torn between wanting to listen and feeling the need to distract a daughter with an overly active imagination.

She said, "When I go to Johnstown in September, you will come with me, if you like."

Lily said, "I would rather go to Albany."

"When you are offered a gift it is right that you say 'thank you' before you find fault with it, Lily."

"Thank you, and I'd rather go to Albany."

Elizabeth secured the plait with the hair ribbon that had been found after much searching, wound around a bundle of twigs.

"I will consider taking you to Albany—"

Lily tensed expectantly.

"—if you will make me a promise."

The narrow shoulders sagged. "I know what you want. It's always the same thing, Ma. You want me to be helpful and cheerful and not to argue."

"Of course," said Elizabeth. "But there is something else as well." She went to the shelf on the wall and took down a small book of blank pages she had sewn together. Then she sat down next to her daughter on the edge of the bed and put it in her lap.

"I should like it if you wrote a little every day about what happens while we are gone," she said. And seeing Lily's wary expression she said, "Just a few sentences. So that when we come home we can see what you've been up to."

Lily cast her a thoughtful expression out of the corner of her eye. "That's a job for Daniel, Ma."

"Ah," said Elizabeth. "But then we'd have only your brother's side of the story."

This made an impression. Lily stroked the paper with one finger where Elizabeth had inscribed her name on the cover: Mathilde Caroline Bonner.

She had been named for Elizabeth's mother. *She has Caroline's chin,* her father had announced, when he first saw Lily. *I fear she will carry on in the same vein.*

Her father had feared the women he loved: his sister, his wife, his daughter; he had feared their sense of themselves and their independence. In the past few years, watching her own daughter at odds with the world, Elizabeth had finally begun to understand the nature of such fear.

Lily was studying the paper in front of her with a kind of gentle curiosity that was absent when she picked up her slate at school.

She said, "May I use your pen?"

Elizabeth bit back a smile. Trust Lily to negotiate better terms for herself at every turn.

"You are not satisfied with a quill?"

"There's no flow to a quill, Ma. Makes me feel like I'm scratching in the dirt, like a hen." Lily's expression was so furious and intense that Elizabeth was reminded of her as a toddler, howling at the moon when her schemes proved too ambitious, for even at that age her mind had been so nimble that the rest of her had trouble keeping up.

Nathaniel had brought Elizabeth her pen as a gift when Robbie was born. It was a huge extravagance, but it was also something she had wanted for a long time and Nathaniel hadn't forgotten. A pen was a wondrous contrivance that held more ink than a quill, never needed to be sharpened, and sat easily in the hand. Hers was made of mahogany inset with carved ivory. The shaft tapered down to a delicate nib of copper and silver, and required careful handling. The children were no more allowed to take up their mother's pen than their father's rifle.

The distinction, Elizabeth admitted to herself, was that the men had begun teaching both twins how to handle weapons a year ago. Daniel showed all the signs of becoming as good a marksman as his father and grandfather before him, but Lily was too short still to handle a long rifle.

Elizabeth reached over and pulled her daughter into her lap. For a moment Lily resisted, and then she collapsed against Elizabeth's breast.

"I don't want you to go," she mumbled.

"I know, I know that." And stopped herself from making promises she could not keep.

"If you have to go then Hannah should stay," Lily said more clearly.

Elizabeth rocked her daughter and stroked her head, and said nothing. Lily knew very well that Hannah must go to the city. She had listened to all the discussions, and then consoled herself by writing a list of things she wanted her sister to bring home with her. No doubt Lily would have happily gone without sweets and hair ribbons and her own skinning knife if it meant keeping Hannah at home while Elizabeth was away, but there was more at stake.

Elizabeth must go with Selah Voyager, and Hannah must go to New-York City if the children were to be vaccinated against the smallpox. Not even to comfort the daughter would Elizabeth consider letting that opportunity pass.

After a few minutes, Lily pulled away and rubbed her eyes hard.

"All right," she said. "I'll write something every day. But when you come home, then will you let me practice with your pen?"

"Every evening, if you like," said Elizabeth.

Lily put her hands on her mother's face and looked at her solemnly. "You'll be gone in the morning, won't you?"

"Yes," said Elizabeth, drawing in a sharp breath and letting it out again. "We'll be gone in the morning."

Chapter 10

By the third day of roaming Hidden Wolf with a warrant tucked into his shirt, Liam Kirby had to admit to himself that the two things he wanted most were not going to happen: the dogs could find no trace of the runaway, and the Bonner men weren't going to be provoked into a confrontation.

Sitting in an elm at the edge of old Judge Middleton's homestead in the drizzling rain, Liam looked down at his dogs, sound asleep around the trunk of the tree. They were good trackers every one, but by the time he got back from Johnstown the trail was cold and the rain had done its work. Or maybe, the thought came to him reluctantly, maybe the woman who had put a knife in Hubert Vaark's throat wasn't on the mountain anymore. She might be dead, or maybe Nathaniel had moved her north while Liam was busy talking the magistrate into giving him a warrant. Or maybe she was still sitting in the caves under the falls, just waiting for him to tire of the chase.

From his perch in the elm, Liam had a clear view of the path that came up around the hill and the house itself, every window in the lower floor filled with light. The faint sound of fiddles tuning up came to him, undercut by the trill of a pennywhistle.

People had been trickling up from the village for an hour, most of them on foot. Some he recognized: Peter Dubonnet and his sister, the Camerons, Charlie LeBlanc; others were strangers to him. There was no sign of the Bonners, not yet.

He had been walking their mountain for three days, and never seen any of them.

What he had found on Hidden Wolf was something he had never missed, or thought to look for: his own boyhood. Deep in the bush on the north side of the mountain the last ten years were wiped away like a frost in the June sun. Every familiar tree and beaver pond dragged him back a little further to a place he didn't want to go. Streams where he had fished, the spot where he had set his first trap, the stump of the first pine he had felled. The Big Muddy, where Billy had taught him how to carve the castoreum gland out of the sopping beaver carcass, laughing at him when he gagged on the stench. Another spot, better hidden, where he had showed him the fine points of poaching other men's lines.

No saint, his brother Billy, but in all the years on the seas Liam hadn't thought much about that side of him. Instead he had remembered Billy's hands, as hard as boards, his fists even harder. He remembered the scar on his neck, the blue of his eyes, the way he would howl with laughter when he was on his way to being drunk. He remembered Billy at work. Whatever else he had been, Billy Kirby had never shirked a task. He was willing to put his hand to any work that paid, in coin or goods. When Billy died he left Liam alone in the world, without even a single blood relative.

Now, looking down at his own dogs, Liam thought of the morning Billy had brought home his first tracker, a young dog won in a game of cards from a voyageur passing through in the spring. Liam had wanted to call her Ginger for the color of her eyes, but Billy said who the hell did he think he was, Adam in the garden? Animals didn't need names; they worked or they showed up on the table.

Below him Treenie gave a soft bark of welcome, and Liam was startled out of his daydream. A man was coming toward him, lurching toward him, his back buckled like a cat's. Bump.

The little man stopped. He craned his head and his whole body turned with it as he peered up into the tree, his face as round and white as a new cheese.

"Curiosity sent me," he said. "You best come on in and join the party, says she. Says you can't avoid her forever."

Liam was glad to be sitting in the dark, where Bump couldn't see his face. He should have known Curiosity would have taken note of him sitting out here; nothing got past the old woman.

"Kind of her to offer," he called down. "But I've got business to attend to."

Bump was scratching Bounder behind the ear, talking to the dog in a low, soft voice. Bounder was the biggest of the dogs, more than half the little man's height, but he rolled right over and showed his speckled belly.

"Did you hear me?" Liam called down, louder. "I ain't coming in, you can tell her."

The old man paid him no mind, scratching ears and sweet-talking until the dogs wiggled around him like puppies. Liam let out a bark of his own, all irritation, and swung down to the ground.

"I said—"

"I heard you. My back's bent, but my ears work just fine."

Bump cocked his head at him, looking hard. Liam had the uneasy sense that the little man could see right through him. He hitched a breath, pulled himself in tight.

"Then you'll tell her I ain't coming."

"Curiosity?"

"That's who sent you, ain't it?" And suddenly Liam thought of Hannah. Maybe the Bonners had gone into the house while he was half-asleep and thinking of Billy.

Bump was wiping his hands on a kerchief knotted around his wrist. "You'll have to tell her yourself," said he. "I'm on my way to see to Gabriel. Can't leave him alone for long." But he stood there anyway, studying Liam.

"What? What is it?"

"You do take after your ma," he said. "I can see her clear as day in your face."

Hannah was gone just as suddenly as she had come, and Curiosity too, to be replaced by the shadowy figure of his own mother, dead of a fever when he was no more than four. "You knew my ma?"

"Met her once or twice," said Bump. "Right here in Paradise, shortly after the war, that was. There was a sweetness to young Moira, and she passed it on to you. Don't see none of your pa in you, though. But I expect that's to your credit."

An insult and a compliment, wound up so tight together that there was no way to respond that wouldn't sound foolish from one direction or another. But it was too late anyway: Bump had already turned away, hitching his way back toward the cabin he shared with Gabriel Oak.

"There ain't nothing sweet about me," Liam called after him. "And I ain't afraid of Curiosity Freeman either."

All around him the dogs whimpered in sympathy, but Bump never even slowed down.

The party had all the markings of trouble; Nathaniel saw that as soon as he came in the door of the old homestead.

The hall was crowded with trappers, just out of the bush with the winter's haul, on their way to Johnstown and Albany. They were eager for liquor and female companionship both, but they would find too much of the first and not enough of the second. A trapper coming into the village after months alone in the bush would argue about anything, wager a pelt on the speed of a drop of rain moving over window glass, pull a knife without second thought.

And there was Isaiah Kuick standing in the open doorway of the judge's old study with a tankard in his hand, half an ear turned toward Andy Peach's long complaint about the poor quality of other men's peltry. It wasn't often he saw Kuick in the village, and he had never before seen him in his cups.

From inside the study Nathaniel could hear men's voices raised in laughter and argument both; the air around the door was thick with tobacco smoke and spilled ale. He stepped in to raise a hand in greeting, answered the usual questions and asked the same, turned down a game of cards and the half-empty bottle of schnapps on its rounds. No doubt there would be trouble before the night was through. The question was, who would throw the first punch.

By the look of her, it could well be Jemima Southern, who stood stoney-faced next to the food tables, watching the dancers as if she wanted nothing more than to knock each of them to the ground. She was the only single woman not in the dance, but it wouldn't be for lack of a partner. There were men all around, men so lonely for company or eager to let loose that any of them would have gladly stood up with Jemima and her sour face for a dance or two. The fact that she stood there alone meant something, but Nathaniel couldn't think what, except that even a wedding party wasn't enough to shift the girl's mood.

The dancers moved up the room at a pace fast enough to make the glass in the window sashes rattle while Reuben and Zeke made the fiddle bows fly, coming to the end of "The Fisher's Hornpipe." They stood on upended crates at the far end of the room, two brothers talking with the instruments in their hands. They were the finest fiddlers for fifty miles or more, but it wasn't often that folks got a chance to hear them. The widow charged a full dollar to lend them out to play for an evening, and she sent her overseer along to make sure that they finished promptly at midnight. After that she charged fifty cents an hour. To discourage excess, she said, but nobody was fooled: Lucy Kuick took to coin like a fox to a rabbit.

Dye was sitting in a corner watching the room and the fiddlers both, his expression sullen as a January sky. Right next to him was Liam Kirby, talking into the man's ear. Every once in a while Dye would say a word, and Kirby would nod or shake his head, but his eyes were fixed on Hannah, who was dancing with Claes Wilde.

There had been lively conversation around the table at Lake in the Clouds, the twins speculating at great length on whether or not Liam would be at the party. Hannah had endured the conversation without comment, but Nathaniel wasn't surprised to see the boy here; Liam could no more stay away from Hannah than he could cut off his own right hand. Anybody could see the way he watched her move, the way a man watched a woman he considered his own, even if he hadn't said the words out loud yet, even to himself.

He wondered how long Liam would stay in Paradise once Hannah had left for the city. Wondered if he would forget about the runaway, forget about the wife he had left waiting for him, about his own brother and the mountain and the revenge he had been dreaming about now for so many years, forget about everything to follow Hannah. Nathaniel had to hope that pride would keep the boy from making such a mistake.

"Nathaniel," said Axel, coming up just behind him. "You're looking thirsty."

He accepted the pewter mug from the older man and sniffed.

"Punch too. You've been busy."

"Ja, that's so." Axel laughed. "But a daughter don't get married every day. She's been alone a long time, my Anna. Too long. Don' she look pretty?"

Anna was circling around Jed in the last figure of the dance, and she did look pretty. She was a big woman, but she moved with great agility and smiled so openly up into her bridegroom's face that Nathaniel felt the pull himself, remembering Elizabeth's expression at their own wedding party.

Reuben called out the next dance, "Love in a Village," and Anna put back her head and laughed.

He clapped Axel on the shoulder. "Jed's a lucky man. Now where have the rest of my people got to? Should have been here an hour ago."

"Oh, they're here. The little ones in the kitchen with Curiosity last I saw 'em and your Hannah—you must have seen her, standing up with Claes Wilde? That put a twist in a few handkerchiefs, I'll tell you." He cast a nervous look in Liam's direction. "I expect you'll hear about that from Hannah. And Elizabeth—she's just around the corner there, keeping Kitty company."

Chairs had been lined up along one long wall for those who weren't dancing. Kitty sat like a queen with her feet propped up, wrapped in a shawl with a rug over her knees in spite of the heat from the hearth and so many people crowded into the room. Richard sat to her left, his attention focused on the bottom of his tankard; Elizabeth was on her right, deep in conversation with Dolly Smythe, her head bent at an angle.

All Kitty's attention was on the dancers. Nathaniel had seen Kitty dance in every condition: fevered, swollen with child, barely out of mourning; dancing was to Kitty what the schoolhouse was to Elizabeth, and to see her sitting so quietly while the music played said more about her health than any doctor's explanation. It made him sad for her in a way the lost child had not. For the first time he was glad that Hannah would be going with Kitty to New-York City.

Elizabeth caught sight of him, and raised a hand in greeting. She rose, smoothing the skirt of her good silk gown, and started to make her way across the room.

"The sun rises in her face when she catches sight of you," said Axel. "Jed ain't the only lucky man in the room tonight, Nathaniel Bonner."

"Aye," said Nathaniel. "I cain't argue with you there."

*   *   *

He wanted the chance to talk to Elizabeth in private, but the twins had heard of his arrival and came out of the kitchen to find him, dragging along Ethan for good measure. They had a story to tell, and they would not leave something so important to Elizabeth, who was likely to leave out all the best bits of the drama: how Liam had come in looking dark as a storm, that he had asked Hannah to come outside to talk to him in private, and the sharp words that had fallen between them in this very hall with half the village listening.

"He called her bullheaded, and she told him to go bird hunting if he didn't care for the party," finished Lily.

"And then she went to dance with Claes Wilde though she'd turned him down already." Ethan added this thoughtfully, as if he wasn't sure exactly what it meant.

Daniel said, "Liam's still there, Da. I don't think he's given her up yet."

Nathaniel caught Elizabeth's gaze over the heads of the children.

"Your sister is very capable of dealing with Liam Kirby," said Elizabeth.

Daniel's expression was doubtful, and Elizabeth leaned forward to speak to him directly. "We are here to make sure she is safe. Are you all finished pulling taffy, then? Or have the other children taken over?"

It was a fine tactic, and they hurried away without further thought for their sister or Liam.

"That explains Jemima Southern," said Nathaniel. "I never saw such a sour face. Is it Kirby or Wilde she's begrudging Hannah?"

"Both of them, I think," said Elizabeth. She put a hand on Nathaniel's forearm and went up on tiptoe to whisper in his ear, her breath stirring his hair. "Is everything in order?"

He nodded. "She's ready. Are you nervous?"

"A little. I've been thinking about the last time I left this house in the dead of night . . ."

He slipped an arm around her waist. "That took a good end, didn't it? You went away a single woman and you came back a wife. And with child, too."

She tensed a little, in irritation and pleasure both, at his teasing and began to turn away, but he pulled her back, put his mouth against her temple.

"Maybe we should go upstairs and have a look at your old room," he whispered. "Never did get to call on you there, back then. Or maybe just out to the barn?"

She sputtered with laughter. "Shoo," she said, slapping at his shoulder. "If you're so full of mischief you can just as well work it off on the dance floor. That's 'Barrel of Sugar' they're starting up."

Nathaniel had never cared much for O'seronni dancing, the formal turns and stiff little hops, skipping like children and winding around in set patterns. Touching hands and bowing, and woe to the man who misstepped. This kind of dancing was nothing like the driven measure of Kahnyen'kehàka dance, the thunder of hundreds of feet drumming the earth under a watching sky. But then there were advantages to taking Elizabeth out on the dance floor: the way her eyes flashed with pleasure, and the color that rose in her cheeks. He could no more deny her the dance than he could raise a hand to her in anger.

They moved down the line, passing Becca Kaes, her hair loosened from its pins and tumbling down around her shoulders, Missy Parker laced so tight into her stays that she breathed like an overworked bellows, Obediah Cameron as confused as ever, looking to his brother Ben for instruction but getting it instead from Kitty, who called out from her chair: *Left, Obediah, left.*

At the end of the line Elizabeth smiled and put her hands in his. They circled around Becca and Ben, close enough to the fiddlers now to see how sweat had soaked Zeke's shirt, how Reuben fiddled half bent over, the instrument cradled like a child. The overseer had tilted his chair back against the wall, watching the crowd through slitted eyes.

Then Liam pushed himself off the wall and started across the room fast; Nathaniel caught the flash of Hannah's skirt as she disappeared around the corner into the hall.

The fiddles stopped with a flourish and the voices came up clear and sharp to fill the silence: *wait now.* And Hannah's, as sharp as he had ever heard it: *nothing more to say.* The whole room was turned toward those voices, knowing smiles and troubled ones. Jemima Southern's mouth clamped down like a vise, her arms wrapped around herself. Then the slam of a door, and silence.

"Perhaps—" began Elizabeth, but he squeezed her hand, harder than he meant to.

"She can take care of herself, Boots. You're always telling me so."

"But he followed her into the kitchen." And then, when his expression did not change, she tugged harder at his hand. "It's not Hannah I'm worried for, it's Liam. Curiosity is in the kitchen, or have you forgotten?"

The air in the kitchen was warm and heavy sweet with cooking sugar, bright with the hearth fire reflected in the pans that hung from the rafters. A mob of children—most of them Elizabeth's students—stood motionless, arms bared to the elbow and shiny with butter, hands filled with warm taffy. Daniel came over to stand between his parents with Lily close behind, but every other pair of eyes was fixed on the adults who stood in the middle of the room: Liam, Hannah, and Curiosity.

Elizabeth believed that she had seen Curiosity in every shade of joy and anger over the years, and saw now that she was mistaken. The older woman was angry, yes, that was plain from the way she stood with fists on hips, her shoulders thrust forward. But there was a bitterness in the curve of her mouth and the set of her head, and it said more than any words how badly Liam Kirby had disappointed her.

Liam stood in front of her with his arms at his sides, all the fight taken out of him. He seemed to have forgotten Hannah and everybody else, fixed in place by Curiosity's force of will; she might pull out a gun to shoot him, and he wouldn't be able to move.

Without looking in their direction Curiosity said, "Children, take that taffy out in the hall and keep pulling. And Nathaniel, shut the door behind them if you plan on staying. Don' need all of Paradise listening to what I got to say."

"I'm not going," said Daniel.

"Me either," said Lily.

"That's right," said Curiosity. "This your business too."

"Curiosity—" Liam began, but she cut him off.

"You be quiet, now. All week you been staying clear of me, but you in my kitchen now and I'ma say my piece."

The rest of the children left reluctantly, casting longing

glances back at the scene in the middle of the room. Ethan paused to say a word to Daniel, and then he left quietly and closed the door behind himself.

Curiosity was looking Liam up and down, her jaw working hard.

"You and me, we spent a lot of time right here in this kitchen when you was a boy, as I know you recall," she started in a slow, clear voice. "When your brother didn't think to feed you, that door there was always open, like it was when you needed a place to sleep or when you was hurt. Ain't that so?"

Liam's wary gaze moved to Hannah, and then back again to Curiosity. He nodded. "That's so."

"Now as I recollect, you was a good boy, Liam Kirby. Billy did his best to turn you, but you had something inside you that knew better. Or so I thought."

Liam flushed to the very tips of his ears. "My brother ain't no business of yours." And he flinched as Curiosity stepped closer to him, and as if he expected to get his ears boxed.

"Billy got everything to do with you and me and these folks too. The time has come for plain talk. You know deep in your heart that he was a worthless excuse for a man. The things he done—" She looked at Hannah, and her face contorted with anger. "The man lived and breathed to cause hurt to folks who never did him no harm. And you yourself was one of them, boy. Maybe you don't like to think about it, but none of us have forgot the things he done to you."

"But—"

"Never mind your buts, you listen. Will you stand there and tell me you don't remember the night he burned down the schoolhouse? We almost lost Hannah, and we buried Julian, but when I dream about that night what I see is what your brother done to you. I have seen some sorry things in my time, but I ain't ever saw a child hurt so bad by his own kin. Billy beat you till your bones broke, and when he did that he crossed the line. He was lost for good."

She paused to draw a deep breath.

"Maybe you like to think you forgot that night or put it behind you, but I know you ain't. Just ain't possible to let go of something like that. So let me remind you, boy, and this is something you dursn't forget: these good people saved your life that night, and they took you into their home. They don't owe you nothing, and neither do I, but I got something for you all the same. Now you listen.

"The day your brother died the good Lord was looking out for you. He took Billy out of your life so you would have a chance to grow into a decent man. But you took that opportunity the Lord gave you, and you pissed on it."

Elizabeth saw Hannah startle. Both the twins shifted backward to lean harder against Elizabeth, but neither of them turned their faces away.

Curiosity's voice had gone hoarse. "Don't know what you been doing since you left Paradise. Don't doubt you swallowed down your share of sorrow. I see that in your face. But there just ain't no excuse for the way you earn your living. When you was a boy you sat in this kitchen and ate the food I put in front of you and now you out there in the world hunting down human beings and putting them in chains. Because you don't like the color of they skin, black just like mine. Your brother would be proud of you, Liam Kirby, but when I look at you all I see is pure waste, and it disgust me."

Curiosity's voice had dropped to a harsh whisper, but her words hung in the air just the same. Liam swallowed hard, all the muscles in his throat convulsing. "You finished?"

"I ain't, not yet. Just one more thing I got to say. I hear told that you got you a wife. Is that true?"

He swallowed again. "Yes."

"Then you best leave our Hannah alone. She has told you clear as bells that she don't want nothing to do with you. You go on home to that wife of yours and leave us alone to mourn the boy we used to know. Don't see nothing left of him in you."

The expression on Liam's face reminded Elizabeth of old Mistress Glove, who had lived through a scalping. *Don't miss my hair none*, she had said, running bent and swollen fingers over her scarred scalp. *There's worse things to lose in this life than a little flesh and blood*. Curiosity had taken something from Liam that was gone for good, something beyond flesh and blood. Everything she had said was true and right, but they all were swaying with the shock of it, just like Liam.

"I'll be on my way and I won't bother you again," he said, his voice cracking softly. "But I need to talk to Hannah, just for ten minutes. If she'd be so kind."

"She's standing right here," said Curiosity. She turned to

Hannah and her expression softened. "Are you willing to talk to Liam, child? You don't have to if you don't want to."

Hannah's gaze shifted to Elizabeth and hesitated. There was a question written clearly on her face, but it was Nathaniel who answered.

He said, "You must follow your heart, Walks-Ahead." He said it in Kahnyen'kehàka, and he used her woman-name for the first time. To make her hear, to make the answer as clear as the question she had not put into words.

Hannah's shoulders sagged just for a moment and then straightened. She nodded.

"Outside," she said. "I will talk to you outside."

They walked away from the house into the trees, walked until they could be sure that no one had followed them. Through open windows the sound of fiddle music still came to them, rising and falling with the breeze.

Hannah pulled her cloak tighter around herself and shivered in the damp cold. The rain had stopped and the sky was mostly clear, enough moon and starlight to make out their shadows. She could taste ice on the wind. "A frost coming," she said. "Maybe snow."

The first words she had said since they left the kitchen. All the terrible things she had imagined saying to him, and now she could think of nothing more to talk about than the weather. But then there was no need anymore; it had all been said. Curiosity had used the truth like a knife, cut into him as neat and quick as any surgeon. How deep she had cut, what good it would do, that Hannah didn't know. Some folks seemed to hold on tightest to the thing that hurt them worst; she had seen that before, and she knew she would see it again.

She could feel him searching for his own words, weighing them carefully. He would not speak until he was sure of himself; she remembered that about him, and Hannah realized something she hadn't been able to see before through her anger. This man was a stranger to her in so many ways, but other things, important things, had not changed. Curiosity could find nothing of the boy Liam had been in the man he had become, but he was there, some part of him. That gave her courage, and she raised her face to look at him, making out the line of his jaw and forehead in the faint light of the moon.

Without turning his head, he said, "There's two things I need to say. First off, there's men down in the city who are thinking hard about arresting Manny Freeman. They got this idea that he's been helping runaways move north and they're just looking for an excuse to hang him. Won't need much of one either."

Hannah drew in a sharp breath, but he didn't stop.

"I meant to tell Galileo, but then I don't know if he'd believe me. You're on your way to the city; I thought maybe you could have a talk with Manny. Tell him to step careful. Tell him, it wasn't just luck that took Vaark to the Newburgh dock. Will you do that?"

"Yes." Hannah put a hand to her forehead and rubbed hard, trying to get hold of her thoughts. Manny Freeman was in danger; Liam Kirby had just saved his life. Ten minutes ago he had stood in front of Curiosity and took the worst she had to offer without defending himself or making excuses. He might have stopped her with this news; he could have used it like coin. Such valuable information about her son's well-being was the one thing that might have gained Curiosity's forgiveness, made her look beyond her anger and disappointment to see that there was some hope for this man.

Worse still, Liam had tied her own hands. She could not go to Curiosity and Galileo and tell them about this good thing he had done for them. Not until she could also tell them that Manny had been warned, and was safe. Liam had laid this responsibility on her shoulders, and she had no choice but to accept it. She would reap what he had sowed.

Unless it was too late already. Unless Liam had left the telling of this until it was too late to do Manny any good. Hannah pushed that thought away; as bad as Liam had shown himself to be, she couldn't believe that of him.

He was watching her face, his own expression unreadable. "The second thing is, that man Vaark that got a knife in his throat on the docks, does that name mean anything to you?"

"No," whispered Hannah. "Should it?"

He shrugged. "He was Ambrose Dye's brother-in-law. That means the runaway I'm after is the property of Vaark's widow, who happens to be Dye's sister. I gave him that news not an hour ago, and it sure got his attention."

"I can imagine it did. What else did you tell him?"

Liam was silent for a long time. "Nothing," he said finally. "Nothing but the truth, that my dogs lost her scent some days ago. But I expect he'll want to come with me now when I go into the bush, or he'll set off on his own. He was a blackbirder himself, some years back, and a good one. Now you take that information and do as you please with it. I've had my say, and now I'll be gone."

"Wait." Hannah reached out to touch him and then pulled her hand back. He was turned away from her; she could see the muscle fluttering in his cheek like a trapped bird.

She said, "You came to Paradise to warn them about Manny."

"No," he said sharply.

"Yes. Yes, you did. Why not admit it?"

He shot her a flash of irritation as hot as a lightning strike. "Have it your way."

"And you came to see me."

Liam rounded on her, shaking with fury. "I'm a blackbirder," he said. "I track down runaways for profit and I drag them back to the city. I'm good at it. Six in the last year. They cry and beg and I don't listen. I take them back to beatings and worse, and I collect my money and walk away before the whipping starts. That's why I'm here, on the trail of the woman you've got hid on the mountain. That's the only reason I'm here."

Something sparked in Hannah, an anger she had been holding on to so tightly that she didn't know its strength until she let it go. "You're lying. You wrote me a letter, you came to find me. You're standing here with me now, Liam Kirby, when you could have told my father about Manny, or Elizabeth, or Hawkeye. You're standing here with me because you came to say something. So say it. Did you want to tell me about the girl you married? Is that it? What's her name, Liam, you've never once said her name."

He leaned over her and grasped her arms, his grip hard and desperate.

"Goddamn you for a witch. Yes, I came to see you." His harsh voice, the warmth of his breath against her mouth; Hannah wanted to close her eyes, but she could not look away from his face.

"I came to tell you I should have stayed on the mountain, that I should have waited."

"But you didn't." Her voice sounded flat to her own ears. "You didn't wait. And now it's too late."

He shuddered and pulled her closer, opened his mouth to speak and then closed it. He had no denial to offer her, no explanation, no excuse. And there on his face was the proof that Curiosity hadn't cut deep enough, hadn't been able to reach the thing inside him that he couldn't say, was afraid to say out loud because to do that would be to make it real. Hannah could feel it there, rising up just below his skin, could feel the shape of what stood between them: the girl he had married. Sophie or Jane, Mary or Julia, with blue eyes or green, hair as red as his own, or blond or the color of the earth. Any color but black. She was waiting for him now, waiting for the sound of his step on the porch, waiting in front of the hearth where she cooked his meals, where she nursed his child, sewed his shirts, the girl who was raised to those chores and who cared for no other life or work of her own. A girl content to wait; a white girl.

"It's too late." She was shaking now, too, with something unnamed, unnameable. Shaking with the need to strike out at him, even as her mouth went soft and open to his.

It was a mistake, she knew that very clearly and yet she kissed Liam, because she could see no other thing in the world but the loss of him and the hurting, all the years he had been away and she had missed him, because she had always missed him and always would. He was lost to her but she would kiss him once and it would have to be enough; she could kiss him and take joy in the fact that he was kissing her back, his strong hands on her face, his fingers tangling in her hair, his thumbs on her cheekbones while she tasted his mouth, so sweet and warm. For this one moment she could hold on to him, tender and without reservation.

When they finally pulled apart they were both breathing hard, too hard to speak any of the words that didn't need saying anyway. Hannah's throat was thick with fear and dread: that he would try to keep her here; that he would let her go. And so she turned and walked away, leaving him this time, leaving him for good.

Chapter 11

By ten o'clock Jemima Southern had seen every single one of her plans for Anna Hauptmann's wedding party go wrong. She hadn't danced with Isaiah Kuick or Liam Kirby or even Claes Wilde. Of the three men, Wilde was the only one to ask, but not until he had danced with every one of the married ladies and almost all of the unmarried girls. He came to ask after he had stood up with Dolly and Becca, and after Hannah Bonner had turned him down.

Jemima cut him off without an excuse or a smile, just as she had turned down the Camerons one after the other and Mr. Gathercole with his silly little bows and the trappers who stank of the bush, and even Jed McGarrity, rude as it was to refuse the bridegroom himself. Eventually they stopped asking, walked past her as if she weren't there at all. With every dance her back grew stiffer and she felt the knot in her stomach pull a little tighter. She wouldn't let it show, not here, not in front of all of Paradise. But she watched.

She watched Isaiah Kuick, who showed no interest in the dance at all, or in anything but drink. He sometimes came to the door to scan the room, looking hard at the fiddlers and then going back to join the men in the judge's old study. She watched Hannah Bonner, in one of those gowns they had brought back from Scotland, out of fashion and still too fine for a country dance. The green didn't suit the dark of her skin, but then she didn't seem to care, just as she pretended she didn't take note of the men whose eyes followed her wherever she went.

Hannah Bonner danced with Jed McGarrity and Mr. Gathercole, but turned down most all the single men, sending them away with a smile so she could sit and talk to Dolly Smythe and Eulalia Wilde, until Eulalia's brother Claes came to claim Dolly for a second dance. From the way she smiled up at him with those crossed eyes, it was clear that Dolly Smythe considered two dances as good as a marriage proposal. Stupid Dolly, who would never learn the most basic and important of lessons: the worst thing a woman could do was to show a man that he had power over her.

The hardest insult was Liam Kirby, who never even looked at her though she stood near him for ten minutes or more while he talked to Ambrose Dye. When Jemima had listened long enough to figure out that they were talking about the runaway, she turned her attention back to the dance. Hannah had just stood up with Jock Hindle while his wife sat fanning a face as red as cherries.

"You be gentle with him, Hannah," called out Mistress Hindle. "He ain't so young anymore."

Laughter swelled up and away, and in the silence Ambrose Dye's voice could be heard through the room.

"Red bitch." With no rancor at all, as if he were just calling Hannah Bonner by her true name. "Got no business among white folk."

It was almost funny, the way they all froze to hear the truth spoke aloud. Elizabeth Bonner stood and took a step forward but Hannah put an end to it all by herself, calling out clear and loud.

"Reuben, Zeke, have you forgot what those fiddles are for?"

And just as sudden as the silence had fallen it was gone, lost in the fiddle music and the talk, louder now, as if they had taken a vote and decided it was best to just ignore Ambrose Dye, outsider that he was and would always be.

All of them were content to pretend, all but Liam, who looked as if he had swallowed lye. He stood like that for all of "Molly Brooks," fists at his sides, and then when the dance was done he followed Hannah into the hall.

A laugh caught in Jemima's throat to see him make such a

fool of himself but she swallowed it down, as bitter as winterbloom. And still she could no more keep herself from following him than she could have stripped naked in the middle
of the crowded room.

The argument had already started by the time she got there.
Hannah and Liam, toe to toe, his head bent down toward hers.
Talking low, but clear enough. And Hannah shaking her head,
refusing to meet his eye. The doorway to the kitchen was
crowded with children, mouths gaping and eyes as round as
pennies. Men spilled out of the study to watch, grinning and
elbowing each other. Jemima had the hot urge to slap each
and every one of them. Then it was over and Hannah walked
right up to Claes Wilde where he stood with his sister and
claimed the dance she had turned down earlier, as if that were
her right. Liam went back to his spot near the overseer, with a
face as stiff as bark.

The children disappeared into the kitchen, the men into
the study. Jemima stood and watched the dance, took note of
people coming and going. Nathaniel Bonner came in and
Peter Dubonnet went out. And Isaiah Kuick standing at the
door, staring at her plain as day. All night she had been waiting
for him to take note and there he was, looking at her like she
was a pony with a broken leg, a creature with no good use in
this world.

A great weariness came over Jemima, all of her anger washing out of her, draining away like life's blood. She went into the
hall and opened the front door. Stood there for a moment feeling the chill of an April night, saw the sky crowded with stars
like unblinking eyes. She saw a cloak hanging on a nail and
took it, not caring very much who it belonged to, and then she
stepped off the porch and walked away toward the barn.

She found an empty stall with a scattering of old hay. With
the cloak of boiled wool wrapped around her Jemima fell into
an uneasy sleep; dreamed of her dead mother and woke to the
sound of whispering. For a moment Jemima was confused
enough to imagine herself in the bed she had shared with her
brothers, and then the faint smells of milk and leather and animals long gone reminded her where she was, and why.

But she hadn't dreamed the voices.

"All winter," said Isaiah Kuick. "All the long winter."

"Too long." The overseer's voice, but Jemima had never

heard it like this, low and soft. "I thought you'd never give me the sign."

She tried to calm the beating of her heart, to still the breath that stirred the hay beneath her cheek. Listening with all her concentration to the sound of mouths touching wetly. She was a child again in the dark, unable to sleep through the noise from the next bed. Every night, as sure as the coming sunrise there would be the rustling of bedclothes and sharp words from her father as he pulled and prodded and climbed on top of her mother. His hoarse grunts and her whimpering, like a small animal in a trap; the creaking of the ropes that held the tick mattress, the whole bedstead rocking, on and on and on.

She could not remember her parents ever kissing; she herself had never kissed another human being, but still Jemima knew very well what she was hearing. She blinked hard, willed her eyes to focus. Turned her head just enough to look into the stall across the way, where under an unshuttered window filled with moonlight she could just make out two shapes, twisting and turning as clothing fell away to the floor. And then the line of a naked back bent forward, the sound of flesh on flesh, a sharp gasp.

"Oh Christ, oh Christ."

"Shhhhh." A whisper, soft and softer. "Shhh."

Jemima Southern trusted nothing more than her own eyes, and what she saw was men mating like dogs. What she heard was the talk of lovers who knew each other well, tender words of encouragement, *sweet Lord yes*, and *more*, and *oh please*. Isaiah Kuick on hands and knees and Dye bent over him, using his backside like other men used a woman's front. She could make out the white of Kuick's leg, his arm, his head hung low, mouth open and gasping, in pain or pleasure or both. Dye's free hand busy between Kuick's legs, stroking in rhythm with the pumping of his hips. And then he arched his back and put his face up to the starlight and Jemima saw the most unbelievable and strange thing of all: the man she knew as the overseer—distrustful, cold, mean unto death—that man was gone. The face Jemima saw in the starlight was alive in a way so overwhelming and personal that she must close her eyes, blinded for a moment by a stunned and wordless joy that was not meant for her to see. When she looked again, the two men were still joined together, gently rocking.

This was no strange dream, but a gift. Unexpected treasure, as solid as gold.

Now they're done, she thought. *Now they'll go.* She needed time to sort out the thoughts that raced through her head: her father's voice as he read from the bible, fragments of verses she had not understood but had memorized because he required it of her: *thou shalt not lie with mankind, as with womankind: it is abomination . . . leaving the natural use of the woman, burned in their lust one toward another; men with men working that which is unseemly.* And the widow's voice: *heathens* and *papists* and *eternal damnation* and *Mr. Gathercole, I do hope you'll read from Leviticus today, we are all in need of a consuming fire.*

The widow. Jemima imagined the widow in her chair by the window, always watching, ever keen to uncover transgressions against God and herself. Jemima felt the stab of her embroidery needle, heard that thin voice, so sure of her place in the world, so sure of her son. The way she looked at him, the plans she had for him. *Pride cometh before the fall.* Jemima mouthed the words silently and imagined the widow's face if she were to walk into this barn and see the overseer using her precious Isaiah like a whore. Lucy Kuick's only son was a sodomite.

The men were talking face-to-face, kissing now and then. Their voices were lower and Jemima couldn't make out much of what they said to each other, but the tone was clear enough, gentle and loving and almost more of a shock than what had come before. Then Dye slid down Isaiah's belly and Jemima watched, not so much disgusted or outraged as she knew she should be, but simply amazed and more than a little curious to see a man put his head between another man's legs to suckle like a baby at a full teat. The pleasure it gave both of them was obvious and a mystery too, and she studied it carefully while another part of her mind raced backward through the months she had schemed to get Isaiah into her bed.

She understood now that her open door meant nothing to him, would never mean anything to him. But that didn't matter, not anymore. Once she had hoped to lie underneath him as many times as it took for him to get a child on her, but tonight he had given her something better. Now he could deny her nothing at all.

*   *   *

Then they were standing again, brushing the hay from each other's clothes, hands lingering here and there. Talking days, and times, and opportunities.

Thursday, said Dye, and Kuick laughed.

As if either of us could wait that long.

It was the first time Jemima had ever heard him really laugh, without any trace of mockery.

When they were gone she lay for a while, making plans. Twenty minutes, perhaps half an hour she had watched them, and in that short time her whole life had changed. So deep was she in this knowledge that the sound of footsteps took her by surprise and she froze, thinking they were coming back to start again. If she had stood up too soon and they had found her here, what then? Dye would simply kill her; she knew that without doubt.

But it was Liam Kirby, and he was alone. She knew him by his size and the gleam of his hair in the light of the stars. He stood without moving for a long minute, his hands at his sides.

He was waiting for Hannah, and that made perfect sense: Jemima must watch Liam take Hannah as the overseer had taken Isaiah Kuick; she must listen to the things he would say to her, love talk, sweet words. This was the price she would have to pay for the advantage she had been given, and it was bitter.

After a long time Jemima began to realize that Hannah was not coming. He was here alone, and hiding. Hannah had refused him, and he had sought out this place to lick his wounds. For a moment Jemima was stunned by the depths of her good fortune, and then she whispered his name.

He started, turned sharply. "What are you doing in here?"

"Waiting for you." Her fingers moved to slip her sleeves off her shoulders, letting her breasts spill out as she moved toward him.

He stepped back, but his eyes were fixed on the white flesh, the dark of her nipples. "No," he said. "No."

She reached out and touched him, ran a finger down the front of his breeches as she had seen Isaiah Kuick do not half an hour ago. He jerked, clasped her hand to stop it, held it still. Sucked in breath between teeth clenched hard.

"But think, Liam." His gaze was fixed on her breasts, and he still held her hand against him. She could feel his flesh stirring, his breath on her skin. "Nobody will ever know."

She freed herself, turned her back to him as she raised her skirts high. "You don't have to look at my face," she said, feeling the chill air on her bare flesh. "You don't have to look at me at all. You can pretend I'm...somebody else."

He was silent as she went down on all fours with her skirts rucked up around her waist, her knees spread to expose her sex, her forehead bedded on her crossed arms. Then she heard him groan and he was behind her, loosening his breeches. When he knelt between her legs she felt him shaking, felt the heat of his damp flesh, the soft and hard of him. But he hesitated and she held her breath, understanding somehow that at this moment the wrong word would ruin everything.

He said, "I cain't marry you if you get with child."

"Why, that's all right," said Jemima, rocking her hips backward, brushing against him and feeling him jerk. "That don't matter none, Liam. I'm going to marry Isaiah Kuick, anyway."

He cursed and came to her, leaning forward to grasp a breast in one hand while he supported himself with the other, shoving and prodding to part reluctant flesh, pushing hard and harder still while Jemima bit her forearm to keep from crying out. With a curse he let go of her breast to grasp her buttocks, angling her hips up and spreading her flesh with his fingers to ease his way. Now when he thrust, once and then again, she could not hold back her scream; one last thrust and with that he tore her flesh and seated himself deep inside her.

"Damn you," he groaned. "Damn you to hell."

In spite of the pain she smiled to herself. Wiggled and clenched at him with every muscle until he groaned again and gave in to it. She welcomed the invasion and the burn and the pull and push, his strong hands, his roughness, his teeth pressing into the tender flesh of her neck as he worked his hips, thrusting as if he wanted to climb inside of her. Jemima clenched her teeth against the roaring pain and rocked her hips to meet him, heard him grunt in surprise and pleasure and then the trembling overtook him and he emptied himself inside her in hard little jerks.

He was gasping and muttering to himself, *damn you damn you damn you*. But he was still hard, his flesh trembling wet.

Jemima wiggled and flipped over on her back. She lifted her hips and wound her legs around his waist to pull him back inside her. She would keep him on top of her all night, use her hands and her mouth if she had to, put what she had learned from the sodomites to good use. Make him forget Hannah Bonner and the nameless wife, milk him like a cow, make him spill his seed until he was dry.

After tonight he would never forget her, would never dare ignore her again. When Liam Kirby walked past her he would remember this, remember the way they had been joined in sweat and blood and seed and sin.

One way or another she would marry the widow's only son, but it would be easier if she was with child. She tried to count the days in her head but the heavy heat of Liam rutting inside her got in the way; he pushed her legs apart roughly and then, still not satisfied, he put a hand under her right knee and lifted it, pressed it to her shoulder so that she was splayed open to him. With the next thrust he touched a spot so deep inside her she must cry out again, in pain and surprise and approval. He covered her, pressed her into the hay with his weight, threatened to split her in half, and she gloried in it; put her hands on his buttocks and pressed him home.

If he didn't get a bastard on her this time, she would seek him out again, and how could he refuse? Then Isaiah would claim what Liam had put inside her as his own, or he would pay the consequences.

By the time Jemima made her way home the moon had set and a frost had come down, so that she needed to take the handrail on the bridge or risk falling. She was limping a little, her thighs raw and bruised and sticky, and deep inside a burning itch. Her shoulders and breasts and belly stung where he had marked her with his teeth and the scrape of his beard: she had driven him hard, and he had paid in kind. Every muscle hurt, but for once in her life Jemima Southern was satisfied. She had come to the wedding party to get the best of one of them, Liam Kirby or Isaiah Kuick, and now she had them both. Them, and Hannah Bonner too.

Jemima was thinking about how to sneak into the house so that no one would hear her when she remembered that it didn't matter. She could do as she pleased; she would be the mistress soon enough.

It wasn't until she had dropped her clothes and crawled naked and stinking of barn and man into her bed that two things occurred to her. The first, the most surprising thing, was that she liked the act of fornication. She liked everything about it, but most of all she liked the power it gave her, the way it turned a man twice her size into a child. She liked the act, but she would have to do without it because she could make Isaiah Kuick marry her, but he would never come to her bed. The kind of power she had over him had nothing to do with what was between her legs.

The second thought was not so much of a surprise but it rankled. She had rutted all night with a man who had never called her by name. He had used every opening she offered him and turned his face away when she tried to kiss him. When he emptied himself into her, once, twice, three times, there was nothing in his face of joy or even release, nothing beyond a wordless fury and loathing, for himself, for her.

Pretend I'm someone else, she had told him, but he couldn't forget who she was. Who she wasn't.

For a moment Jemima lay very still, and then she rolled over onto her side, pulled her knees up to her chin to hold all she needed of Liam Kirby deep inside her, and went to sleep.

PART II

Voyagers

THE ENDLESS FORESTS

Chapter 12

In all the rushed preparation for the journey into the endless forests, Elizabeth had never let herself think too hard about what it would mean to walk away from her children and not know when she would see them again. In the course of comforting Lily and Daniel she had managed somehow to convince herself that this journey would require no more than a fortnight. A fortnight, she had explained more than once, would go by very quickly; such a short separation was neither sufficient nor rational grounds for despair.

For the first half-day the exhilaration carried her along. They walked in single file, following Nathaniel on a Kahnyen'kehàka path that he seemed to know very well, in spite of the fact that for very long periods of time Elizabeth could not make it out at all. And yet she was surprised at how easily it all came back to her, the rhythm of this kind of walking, unrestricted by skirts and the fuss of her everyday clothing. For the first time in a very long time she wore a Kahnyen'kehàka overdress and leggings. She had put her hair in simple plaits, and in spite of the pack she carried she felt completely unencumbered.

Mid-April was a good time in this part of the endless forests, most of the spring mud gone and the true heat of summer still a month or more in the future. It was true that the weather was unpredictable. Patches of snow sometimes many inches deep were easy to find, but night frosts were a small price to pay for freedom from the true scourge of the forests. Elizabeth preferred walking cold to the blackfly that came in clouds to invade ears and nose, cuffs and collars, and leave hundreds of painful welts behind. There was nothing to do about the blackfly beyond bear grease and pennyroyal ointment, cures almost as bad as the wrong they were meant to counter.

But the cold could be conquered. Each of them wore winter moccasins lined with fur and laced all the way up the lower leg. Across their packs they had strapped capes lined with marten and oiled buckskins.

Elizabeth had left her school and her students behind, but the habit of teaching she could not put down. She wanted to point things out to Selah, things that she could not know but must learn if she was to spend a season in the bush. The hardwood canopy had just begun to fill in with touches of the palest green; in a few weeks the trees would be in full leaf, and the forest would be lost in cool shadow. Much of what they could see now would be hidden.

Firebirds lined the branches of a white ash like a row of candle flames; overhead a logcock drummed for a meal in the trunk of a dead oak. Moles and mice were busy in drifts of decomposing leaves, but they saw little other wildlife, in part because the three of them—or two of the three of them, Elizabeth corrected herself—were not silent enough; in part because many of them were just rousing themselves out of the stupor of winter.

This bit of forest she knew quite well; it was close enough to home to be within the range of Hannah's constant search for medicinal plants, and Elizabeth liked to go with her whenever she could spare the time. On those outings she had learned most of what she knew of the forest—she could name the trees and most of the plants and their uses—but it was also a rare opportunity to talk to her stepdaughter without interruption. Elizabeth had come to depend on Hannah not only for her help with the children and the house, but also for her conversation, much in the same way she looked to Curiosity and Many-Doves.

They had parted this morning in great haste, even before first light. Hannah had been on her way down the mountain to start the long journey to the city, nervous and ill at ease. There had been no opportunity to talk to her alone about what had happened when she left the kitchen with Liam beyond the simple facts that needed to be shared.

And still it was very clear that something had happened between them, something had been said or done that had marked Hannah. Elizabeth had the idea that if she should come face-to-face with Liam Kirby today she would see that same thing in his face. Exactly what it meant, Elizabeth could only guess, and none of the rational explanations provided any comfort at all.

By mid-morning they were out of territory she recognized, passing into a half-mile-long stretch of sugar maple, moccasins sinking deep into moldering leaves covered with winged seed keys that crunched underfoot. With every breeze more seed keys twirled down from the maples to bury themselves in the forest floor. Where an old tree had fallen and rotted, seedlings spread out in round islands, the tallest in the middle and the shortest around the edges, like an odd peaked cap.

Elizabeth took real joy in the spring forest, but she must keep all of it to herself, because it was dangerous to talk on the trail. Voices carried far in the woods and it could be that Liam Kirby or Ambrose Dye had already started out after them. Hannah's news about the link between Dye and Selah had come as a shock, but there was nothing to be done about it except press on. At the last minute Nathaniel had slung an extra horn of powder around his neck and taken the sack of bullets that Hawkeye pressed on him.

He had every weapon he owned on his person, his rifle slung across his back, a knife at his side, his tomahawk tucked under his belt to lie flat against his back. To these he added a knowledge of the bush that neither Liam Kirby nor Ambrose Dye nor any other blackbirder could match. The journey would be long and bring its own dangers, but Selah Voyager was by far safer walking behind Nathaniel Bonner than she had been in Paradise.

And if the story Liam Kirby had told Hannah was true, Selah Voyager would defend herself and her child, if that should be necessary. Not that Elizabeth could ask. A man who killed to defend himself and his family might be eager to tell the tale, but women were different. A woman who killed in self-defense or anger did not share her story lightly. This Elizabeth knew from experience.

*   *   *

They paused at midday to eat, and because Selah Voyager's condition required it. Not that she had asked, or even seemed to need to rest. The younger woman walked hard, spoke seldom, and never complained. Elizabeth imagined that she was as eager to get to the relative safety of Red Rock as they were eager to see her settled, most preferably before she brought her child into the world.

Now she squatted easily with the great thrust of her belly serving as resting place for a piece of cornbread while she finished her portion of dried venison. She ate quickly and neatly, concentrating on that task and no other.

Then the surface of her belly contorted and the bread leapt away like a live thing, as if her child had known exactly what it was, and had rejected such a meal. It was a comical sight, and they all laughed out loud. At that moment Elizabeth remembered with complete clarity what it felt like to be so full with child toward the end of her pregnancies, how the twins and then Robbie had governed her every movement, every waking and sleeping moment, every thought.

And she was taken by a sudden sense of loss so complete that it left her dazed. A slick panic filled her and she knew with certainty that if she turned around now and went home, ran as fast as she could, they would be gone, lost to her while she was somewhere else, tending to another woman's needs.

Nathaniel reached over and put a hand on her knee. He had read her face and understood what he saw there. It was not the first time she was overcome by this panic for her children, nor would it be the last. But she did not have to explain herself to him and he would never shame her by saying out loud what she knew in her rational mind: Robbie was gone, yes, but Lily and Daniel were a full eight years of age, healthy and strong, in the care of people they trusted completely.

He would not say those things to her because he understood that the fear came from someplace deep inside her where logic and reason had no power. The twins had been taken from them as infants, for a short while but long enough to teach Elizabeth how fear could etch itself into the bone. Robbie's death had reinforced that lesson.

Selah Voyager cleared her throat. "Thank you kindly for the food," she said in her low, slightly hoarse voice.

Elizabeth blinked hard to put the thought of her children away from her. "You're very welcome, Miss Voyager."

The young woman had a smile that transformed her unremarkable but pleasing features, lending her for that moment a radiance that must be called beautiful. She said, "Please, won't you call me Selah?" And then, more softly: "It ain't my slave name, understand. Selah the name my mother give to me on my first birthday."

There were so many things Elizabeth did not know about this young woman and would have liked to know, but she had never thought to ask about what she called herself. She understood without being told that all the runaways sent north by Almanzo Freeman took the name Voyager, at least to start with. Slaves, their owners believed, had no need for or right to a family name; one of a freed slave's first acts was to name herself.

The young woman before them had led a life Elizabeth could hardly imagine, a life she did and did not want to know about. If she inquired, Selah would answer her questions, perhaps out of gratitude, but more likely simply because she had not yet been free long enough to know that she could turn aside a white woman's questions. Elizabeth could not, would not take such advantage, no matter how curious she might be; she would wait, and accept what information Selah Voyager offered.

And she had offered. She had given them the image of a slave who had taken the rebellious step of naming her own child. Most probably her owner had never known of that small act; had it come to his attention he might have laughed at such a futile gesture, or punished her for impudence. Her mother had given her the name Selah; her master or masters had called her something else, Phyllis or Cookie or Beulah.

But all of that was behind her now. She was on her way to a place where she could use the name her mother had given her, where she could name her own child as she pleased. Elizabeth's fears seemed suddenly very shallow and self-indulgent, and she flushed with gratitude for her own good fortune.

"You thinking about your children," Selah said gently. "I expect you must be worrying about them."

"Oh yes," said Elizabeth with a small smile. "I am worried for them. I'm afraid it's the first law of motherhood."

Selah put a light hand on her belly, and nodded.

*   *   *

The first night on the trail Nathaniel led them to a protected spot under an outcropping of rock as tall as himself. It was overhung by balsam branches and it was dry and sweet-smelling, with a cushion of fallen needles underfoot. The trees wouldn't protect them if it should rain or even snow in the night, but they had oiled buckskins to tent over themselves if it came to that, and for the moment the sky looked clear.

Nathaniel went off to see to fresh meat while the women started a fire and settled themselves. They would sleep as soon as they had eaten, so they could be up and on the move before sunrise. Elizabeth was tired enough to sleep on an empty stomach; she couldn't remember the last time she had walked so far, or so long.

She sat down across from Selah, who was feeding the fire with bits of deadwood. "Did Curiosity or Joshua explain our plans to you?"

She nodded. "Three days to the lake you call Little Lost, and we wait there in the caves until the Mohawk woman come for me. Splitting-Moon. Have I got that right?"

Elizabeth took a slab of cornbread and broke it into even pieces. "Yes. We may have to wait three or four days for Splitting-Moon. There is no way to know exactly when she will come."

They had this information from Joshua, whose job it had been to take the runaways to the meeting place. Sometimes Joshua's brother Elijah came with Splitting-Moon, and they would spend a day together talking. Joshua had never asked either of them about the exact location of Red Rock, or even how far it was; what he did not know he could not tell.

Nathaniel and Hawkeye had listened without comment while Joshua related all of this. Later, in the privacy of their bed Nathaniel told Elizabeth what he suspected: that Red Rock was no place at all. It would be far safer for a colony of runaways hiding from the law and blackbirders to keep moving. A permanent settlement was too much of a risk; some trapper would come across it and eventually word would drift back, down the waterways to the city.

Elizabeth related all of this to Selah, who listened without interrupting, her arms wrapped around her belly. Her expression gave nothing away, neither curiosity nor fear.

She said, "There's a blackbirder in the city, name of Cobb.

Saw him a few times myself with a whole gang of men around him, slapping him on the back 'cause he brought in a runaway called Big George everybody had been chasing after for a year." She looked Elizabeth directly in the eye. "Folks say he routed out a whole lot of blacks living free in the forests down south. Brought back the leader's head carrying it over his shoulder on a spike rammed clean through the ears. Put it on display outside the courthouse, to show the other slaves that they'd best not think of running. He look like any other person on the street, but the devil's in the man who can find it in himself to do something like that."

"I have heard of such things," said Elizabeth.

Selah raised her shoulder. "There's worse that goes on, things to turn your hair the color of salt. But what I meant to say is, for all his evil, that Cobb ain't much different than any blackbirder. They got no understanding at all. The truth is, dying's easy when living means going back where you run from in chains."

"You are not going back, in chains or out of them. Cobb has no power here in the endless forests."

"Don't speak of the devil no more," Selah said, holding up a palm. "He might just appear."

"Superstition," Elizabeth said firmly, even as unease sent a shiver slick as grease up her spine.

Selah rocked forward slightly, and when she raised her head her expression had cleared itself. "Tell me about the cold season."

"The winters are hard," Elizabeth said, more than willing to change the subject. "But I expect that by the fall you'll be in Canada with Manny."

Selah touched her belly, moved her hands out over its roundness with fingers spread. "In Canada, or in my grave."

Elizabeth said nothing. It was true that the healthiest and strongest person might die without warning; her own mother had woken one day with a fever and died before sunset. Her cousin Will Spencer had lost a brother to a bee sting that caused his throat to swell shut. And of all people, a woman heavy with child knew very well that she might not survive the ordeal before her. If she did, and the child with her, she would have to keep it safe from too many threats to count: ague, putrid sore throat, dropsy, smallpox, lung fever, yellow fever. Quinsy. Blackbirders.

Selah Voyager was watching Elizabeth, and she had the sudden and uneasy feeling that the younger woman had read her mind.

She said, "You know I killed a man."

"Yes," Elizabeth said, trying not to show her surprise. "I heard as much. So have I."

Selah acknowledged this with a nod, and then she drew a deep breath.

"It was on the dock at Newburgh, two days out of the city. I was looking for a sloop called the *Jefferson*. Manny told me, just walk normal like any servant looking to deliver a message. Anybody stop you, say you're looking for Captain Small. And that's what I was doing when I come around a corner and there was old Vaark."

She paused, her eyes fixed on some point far away. Elizabeth had been wrong; Selah Voyager needed to tell this story, whether or not she was ready to hear it.

"Mr. Vaark was your master?"

Selah nodded. "Bought me from the farm where I was raised up, the summer I turned twelve. Mama still there, I suppose." Selah dropped her gaze from Elizabeth's face to the fire.

"He was a good enough master, was old Vaark. Like to talk the bible, but he wan't quick to raise a fist like some bible talkers. There was three of us house slaves and Josiah out in the stable, and we always had enough to eat and good clothes. Every six months a Sunday free, long as we come back before sunset.

"When I was fifteen the master got me with child, but it come into the world dead. Like that little one you buried the day I come to the mountain."

"She was born too early," Elizabeth said.

Selah nodded. "It happen that way sometime. But the next year my little girl come along, big and strong. She was the prettiest thing. I called her Violet."

There was a fist in Elizabeth's throat, the kind of anger that made it hard to swallow, but she must ask the question and so she forced herself to speak, striving to keep her tone even. "What happened to your little girl?"

Selah's eyes closed and opened again. "The missus, she made old Vaark take my Violet away just as soon as she was weaned. Said she cry too much and keep me from my work. I asked would they sell me too, sell us together, but the master just got to looking sorrowful. He say, ain't you happy here? Don't we treat you good? Like it was an insult to him, me wanting to be with my baby.

"Then she was gone. They never would tell me where to, no matter how I thought to ask. Took me down just as low as a woman can go.

"So the master, he finally come upon the idea of sending me to the African Free School two evenings a week. He got it in his head that it might raise up my spirits if I was to learn to read. The missus didn't like the idea of me spending time with free blacks. Said it would put ideas into my head. But she didn't like me crying all the time neither so she say, go on then, as long as you get your work done.

"And it did stop me crying, but not for the reason they was thinking. You see, there's so many blacks coming and going in the Free School, I thought for sure I'd find somebody who could tell me about Violet, who had bought her and where she was in the city."

There was the flicker of anger across her face, banished as quickly as it had come.

"And did you find out?"

"Oh, I found out sure enough, but not the way I thought. The answer was right under my nose the whole time, but I couldn't make sense of it till I learned to read. Don't think it ever occurred to old Vaark that a slave who can read the bible can read anything else that come her way. One day when I was sweeping out the little room where he keep all his paperwork I come across a piece of paper with my baby's name on it."

She closed her eyes and recited from memory:

To the honorable Mr. Richard Furman,
Superintendent & Commissioner of the Almshouse
in this City of New-York. Gentlemen I hereby
inform you that my Negro wench Ruth was
brought to bed the fifth day of July 1799 with a
female child called Connie. I do therefore hereby
give you notice that I do abandon all my right &
title and all responsibility for the care of said female
child in accordance with the Gradual Manumission
Act signed into law by the Legislature and do hereby

pass the child into the care of this City. This
Certificate of Abandonment made & provided by my
own hand the 6th day of June 1801. Albert Vaark,
Merchant, Pearl Street

"Except I couldn't read so good yet when I found it. Or
maybe I just didn't want to believe the words on the paper. So
I stole it, just put it in my apron and that night when I went to
the school I asked the first person I come across would he
please read it to me, just to be sure. That's how I met Manny.

"He read it to me twice, and every time it was like a fire in
me, burning and burning until there wasn't nothing left of my
heart but a cinder."

"But why?" Elizabeth asked. She could not make sense of
what she had heard. "Why would they do such a thing?"

Selah's mouth contorted, as if the things she had to say were
sour on the tongue.

"The Gradual Manumission Act say, once Violet get to be
twenty-five years of age she could walk away, free. Vaark
didn't like the idea of bringing up a child and feeding her
twenty-five years and then letting her go with no profit to
show. The law say, he don't have to keep her if he don't want
the trouble."

"So when they told you that they sold her—"

"That was all a lie. I knowed it anyway. I knowed down in
my bones once I stopped crying long enough to think it
through. Wasn't no tears left inside me, you see, just enough
hate to burn down the world. All that fire inside me made a
bright light to see by. Who going to buy a black baby who
cain't do no work? They sent her to the poorhouse."

Selah rocked back and forth slowly. "So that morning the
mistress sent me down to fetch buttermilk, I just kept walking.
Walked all the way up to Chambers Street where the poorhouse stand, and I walked right in and I ask, can I see my
child.

"But they turned me away. Woman there said, a slave
woman ain't got no business nosing around the poorhouse,
and did my master know where I was? Nine hundred people
they got in those three stories, and was I thinking of looking at
every one of them?

"I was just as desperate as a woman can be about that time,

but Manny helped me through it. He come looking for me, you see. Come right to the kitchen door looking for me and I went out to talk to him. That's when he told me about the Lost Children. He say it just like that, 'Lost Children,' like other folks might say 'Trinity Church' or 'Pearl Street.' So we sat down out back and he tolt me about all the little black babies put out since the Manumission Act come into law. Some in the poorhouse, but others just put out to make they own way. Black children like wild dogs, living off the street. But my Violet, she was in the poorhouse. It didn't seem so bad no more when Manny said it like that. He come along and give me hope again."

Elizabeth said, "I had been wondering how you met."

Selah nodded. "It was my Violet brought us together. I never asked him, but the next day he started looking for her. I couldn't just wander around the city, you understand, but Manny was born free and a free nigger can go where he want, so long as he stay out of trouble and don't call attention to hisself. Manny could get into the poorhouse now and then, look around for a while, ask some questions.

"There wasn't nothing I could do but wait. Couldn't even let on that I knowed what the master done.

"All that summer Manny kept looking for Violet. We was seeing each other every day by that time. He'd come by Pearl Street or he'd wait for me in the market on the days I wasn't going to school in the evening. And every time he'd have something to tell me. He say, I talked to Dr. Post yesterday when he was coming out of the dispensary. No word yet. He always say it like that, no word *yet*.

"Now by that time Manny had already got it in his head to set me on the path north. But it just didn't set right, the idea of running off not knowing was my Violet alive or dead. Didn't much care to go without Manny, neither. We was as good as man and wife by that time, you understand. But then I come up pregnant, and I didn't have no choice."

She put her hands on her belly, looked down at it as if it could talk to her.

"Truth is, I don't know who got this child on me. I like to think it was Manny. We was together enough last summer that it could well be. But the master, he never would leave me alone. He was one of them menfolk cain't rest till his itch good and scratched. Didn't matter was I big with child or in my courses or how early in the evening the missus locked us in the cellar. There wasn't no lock in this world that would stop old Vaark when the urge came on him."

Elizabeth had to swallow hard to control the nausea that rose in her throat, but Selah didn't seem to notice. The momentum of the story was carrying her forward, and Elizabeth had the uneasy feeling that the worst was yet to come.

"Manny say, it don't make no difference one way or the other, he going to claim this child as his own. So he set me on the path. But then old Vaark, he come after me."

A look came over her, not of regret or remorse or even sorrow, but a kind of resignation.

"Just at first light it was when I come around that corner and saw him. And what I thought was, the only way I was going back to the city was by jumping in that river and letting it take me down. I was ready to do it too, but Vaark, he got between me and the water and he caught me by the arm and wouldn't let go.

"Now you got to understand, he wasn't mad. Never did see him mad. He just get that sorrowful face and say, what a disappointment I was to him, and what was I thinking, running off from a master who treat me so good. Didn't he send me to school, and see to it that I learned to read? And didn't I always have a full belly?"

The corner of Selah's mouth jerked hard. "That's when I put the knife in his throat. Seemed like the only way to keep the man from talking. I know how strange that sound, but it went through my head just like that. He keeled right over and fell into the river, didn't even make much noise. But the river wouldn't take him. Kept him right there. I just stood and watched the way he kept bumping up against the dock, like he was knocking at a door.

"Couldn't have been more than a minute or two afore I came to myself and knew I had two choices: I could jump into the river, too, and put an end to it, or I could try to save myself and the child. So I hid away in the first boat I come across and waited, for somebody to come sail away or for a mob to find me and string me up on the nearest tree.

"But the Lord saw fit to lift the yoke. The captain come along not much later, him and three sailors. All of them so drunk they couldn't hardly walk straight. He look me right in the eye and he say, fare to Albany's ten dollars. You got ten dollars, girl? Which I did, Manny gave it to me and I had it sewn into my skirt. Just as soon as I handed it over he sent one of them sailors to buy a keg of ale and after that they didn't pay me no mind at all. I just sat quiet and watched the river, thinking about the look on old Vaark's face when I put the knife in him.

"Sometime when the night real quiet, I can almost hear the missus saying how I'ma burn in everlasting hellfire for what I done. What I ain't tolt you yet is, she don't have children of her own. The master got children on every slave who come into the house, but not a single one on his own wife, married in front of a preacher and all. Sometimes when I get to thinking about it, I wonder if deep down the missus ain't glad that I put that knife to use."

Elizabeth nodded. "I imagine that you may be right about that."

Selah rubbed both hands over her belly thoughtfully. "I'd do it all over again, that's the pure truth. Hellfire couldn't hurt me no worse than I hurt that morning he took my Violet away. Now." She shook her head. "I bothered you long enough with my troubles, Miz Elizabeth, but it just didn't seem right, all this worry you took upon yourself on my account, and you not knowing. Seem to me that it was only right to tell you what I done. If you don't mind, I'll ask you to pass what I said along to your husband. Don't know as I could tell it again anytime soon."

"Of course," Elizabeth said. "Of course, if you want me to."

"I do. Now I'ma get a drink from that little stream we passed." And she got to her feet, rising up gracefully in spite of her bulk, and went off without another word.

Chapter 13

"It is exactly as I remember it." Elizabeth sat down abruptly on the outcropping of boulders where they had stopped on the shore of Little Lost. "Nothing has changed at all."

"Nothing much changes in the bush," agreed Nathaniel. He hunkered down beside her, but turned to speak to Selah.

"Why don't you put down that pack and sit for a while? No more than a quarter hour to Robbie's place from here, so there's no hurry."

"Well, that's good," said Selah. "It would be a shame to walk on from this place without taking time to look. Just about every day now I think to myself it couldn't get much prettier, but it does. Cain't hardly believe it's real."

"Oh, it's real," said Nathaniel. "Elizabeth learned to swim right in this lake, she can tell you. That was later in the season, of course. Now the water's cold enough to freeze a man's—"

"Nathaniel," Elizabeth said. Selah had covered her mouth with one hand, and looked away politely.

"What is it, Boots?" He grinned broadly.

"Do you think perhaps you should go ahead to make sure that the caves are—"

"Still there? Don't believe there's much chance that they up and walked away. Do you?"

"—not occupied," finished Elizabeth, poking him gently in the arm. "I don't like the idea of sharing my bed with a bear or a polecat, and I for one would like to get settled as soon as possible."

It was their fourth day in the bush. Elizabeth's energy had begun to flag, and while she did not like to admit it, she would be more than content to stay in one place until Splitting-Moon came to find them. Looking over Little Lost it occurred to her that there was more to her weariness than sore muscles: she was looking forward to spending time here with Nathaniel, free of children and daily routines. And in spite of the seriousness of the situation, there was good reason to think that the worst was behind them: Nathaniel had not been able to find any evidence that they were being tracked by Liam Kirby or Ambrose Dye, food was plentiful, and now that they had had some time with Selah, she seemed to be comfortable with them.

Then Nathaniel put a loaded musket next to Elizabeth, and her good thoughts tumbled in on themselves.

"Is that necessary?"

His expression told her that it was. He said, "I'll be back in a half hour. Don't go anywhere."

"I take it you are going to remind me of every false step I ever took in the bush," she countered. But her grumbling was lost on him; he had already started on the path that wound its way up the mountainside.

Selah had found a sunny spot on a boulder where she could dangle her feet, and stripped off her moccasins to take advantage of the water. Elizabeth joined her, sucking in her breath at the cold.

"I had been thinking of a swim," she confessed. "But I see that Nathaniel is right. Very irritating of him to be right so often."

Selah smiled, her gaze moving over the lake. It was no more than a half-mile long, irregular in shape and shallow enough along the shore to count darting minnows. On the other side of the lake the high bank was lined with balsam and red spruce, and the forest seemed as dark and impenetrable as a dungeon.

"Do you suppose there's a lake where I'm going?"

"The endless forests are full of lakes," said Elizabeth. "And swamps and marshes, too, not nearly as pleasant. And bogs, which are even worse. This I know from personal experience. You will never have to search very far for water, that I can promise you."

For a long moment they were silent while the persistent

lilting song of a preacher bird echoed through the woods, countered by the ovenbird's loud staccato.

"Tell me about this man used to live here," said Selah. "Must have been awful lonely."

Elizabeth considered. "His name was Robbie MacLachlan. He came here from Scotland as a young man, after a terrible war. When Nathaniel and I were first married, we spent time here with him and he taught me a great deal about surviving in the forests. He did like the solitude, but I think he was often lonely."

Selah's sober expression said that Elizabeth had failed to give her the story she wanted.

"He was our good friend, the very best of friends. We named our second son for him." Her voice wobbled and cracked, and for a moment she could do nothing more than study the shape of their feet in the water, milk white and a deep rich brown against the sandy bottom where a scattering of pebbles made the shape of a question mark. The sun disappeared behind cloud and the warmth went out of the day, and then came again, just as unexpectedly.

She drew in a shaky breath and let it out again. "Robbie loved to read," she said. "But his eyesight was poor. So we would come down to the lake in the early evening and I would read aloud to him right here on this rock. He would have some kind of work in his hands, carving or mending rope. After I had finished reading he would sing. He had a beautiful voice, and when he sang the birds went quiet in the trees to listen.

"He died far away across the sea," she finished. "Where he started."

Selah reached out, shyly, and touched Elizabeth's hand. She said, "Don't think he's gone from here, not all of him. I never knew the man, but I can feel him all around. Cain't you?"

"Yes," Elizabeth whispered. "I think you're right."

Because Nathaniel needed a good deal more time than he thought he would, he half-expected that Elizabeth would have started up the mountainside to look for him, no matter what instructions he had given her to stay put. Instead he found the two women sitting where he had left them, deep in conversation as dusk settled over the lake.

He knew every expression Elizabeth had to offer, and he could see straight off that she had been thinking about Robbie.

It was something she never could hide, partly because sorrow had a way of overtaking her when she wasn't looking for it. Now she gave him a grim smile, the one that meant that she didn't want to hear any questions, or give any answers. That would come later, when she was ready and not before.

"Ran into some tracks," he said. "I followed them a ways."

"Splitting-Moon?" Elizabeth asked.

He nodded. "I think so. We best move now, before it's dark."

They put aside further discussion in favor of a quick pace, Nathaniel following for once while Elizabeth led the way. He had taken enough time to satisfy himself about the tracks, but he was on guard now, all his senses turned outward, listening hard.

Just as the last of the light was fading they came to Robbie's home camp, which was nothing more than a small natural clearing, surrounded by stands of birch and maple. When Robbie was alive he had kept the underbrush cut back, but now as far as Elizabeth could see there was the usual tangle of bush and vine and fallen timber. The cook pit was still there, lined with rocks too big to cart away, but the trivet and spit were gone. The stripped logs of the lean-to shone a weathered silver in the dusk. For forty years or more it had stood there leaning into the side of the mountain, empty now save for spiderwebs and the dried-out carcass of a fox that had somehow managed to find a way in, but not out again.

The lean-to had never been anything but a way to protect and hide the natural opening into the caves. Once that opening had been fitted with a wooden door, but that was long gone, sacrificed to some trapper's cook fire.

It must have been Splitting-Moon who had drawn the emblem of the Wolf clan above the opening into the caves in red, to claim this place and protect it too. It was a sign to anyone who knew how to move through the bush that this place had been claimed, and that they would come again.

The first thing Nathaniel had done was to find the supplies Joshua had told him about, hidden in one of the last caves under scraped and oiled buckskin. Everything they needed was here: two filled lanterns, a keg of oil, a handful of tallow candles, a flintbox, an empty water barrel, a pot and a fry pan, a pile of old bearskins that would serve as sleeping pallets and blankets both, a bucket and a shovel, some ammunition and powder, a fishing line and net, a couple pounds of no-cake as well as a good supply of corn stored in a double barrel with a tight lid that was meant to keep raccoons and mice out.

Nathaniel brought the bearskins and the lanterns out to the lean-to, where he lit them both and handed one to Selah.

Her face had gone very still, out of fear or simple cautiousness. He smiled at her, and she managed a small smile in return.

The women picked up the bearskins and followed him through the chain of caves, each slightly bigger than the one before until Nathaniel could stand without striking his head. When Robbie was alive he had used this place like a house, dedicating each of the chambers to a different purpose, but now they were all empty. No doubt his tools and traps were being put to good use by the people of Red Rock. It would have pleased Robbie to know that.

Behind him Elizabeth drew in a surprised breath.

"Oh," she said. "Oh, look." It was the one thing of Robbie's that no one had valued enough to carry away: a small oil painting of a horse in a cracked frame, almost unrecognizable now for moss and mold and flaking paint. "I always meant to ask him how he came by this."

"That's a story I can tell," Nathaniel said, running a hand down her arm. "Later."

Selah's face moved in and out of the light of the swinging lantern. "What is that bad smell?"

"Minerals," said Elizabeth. "From the hot springs. Come, we'll show you."

They passed through two more natural chambers. The first one was as black as pitch, but there was some faint light in the second cave. Elizabeth pointed out a spalt in the sloped ceiling, as wide as a hand and three feet long. Right now nothing could be seen through it, but Elizabeth had spent many nights watching the stars from a pallet Robbie had made for her.

"It's light here in the morning," she said. "And we can cook here if for some reason we don't want to use the pit outside. You see, Nathaniel has already brought us a turkey. Very enterprising of you, husband."

Selah had been looking increasingly anxious, but now she put down her pack with a great sigh of relief. "Can I sleep here?"

Nathaniel grinned at her. "You might not like it if it starts to rain."

"Don't mind the rain," said Selah. "It's being so closed up that I don't much care for."

It only took a few minutes to show her the last of the caverns, two of them too small for any real purpose, and then the largest of all, where the air was dense and sour on the tongue, and the heat was enough to make a man at rest sweat hard. A pool of water spread out in front of them, as dark and heavy as oil.

"It is deep enough to swim," offered Elizabeth.

A look of revulsion passed over Selah's face, and she shuddered. "I'd rather jump in that cold lake."

Elizabeth said, "Well then, I'll leave you the lake and you can leave me the hot springs."

The hair on Elizabeth's brow had gone damp and curly, and Nathaniel had the sudden urge to reach out and touch it. She gave him a look that said she knew exactly what he was thinking, a little nervous and pleased, something playful there that promised good things for the night to come.

He said, "Let's see to that bird, and then it's time to get to bed." He grinned at Elizabeth. "Don't want to use up more of this lantern oil than we have to."

After they had eaten, Nathaniel put down his pallet in one of the smaller caves near the lean-to and set to cleaning and reloading his rifle. He had shed his hunting shirt and leggings, content to work in nothing but a breechclout even in the cool of the caves.

Elizabeth found him there after she was sure that Selah was settled and comfortable.

"Everything all right?"

She nodded, her eyes fixed on the way the lantern light played against the bare skin of his chest, the muscles in his shoulders and thighs. When they had first been married, Elizabeth had often been shocked to come upon him near naked just like this; then she had slowly come to accept the fact that she could not talk him into clothing. He was simply most comfortable in a breechclout. It had taken almost a year for her to admit to herself that she liked him like this. It was something she had never said out loud.

Much of her girlhood training had been left behind in

England, but there were simply no words she knew how to say that would convey the simple truth: she took a great deal of joy in the sight of her husband's near nakedness.

She finally cleared her throat. "I gather that porcupine nest in the corner is abandoned?"

He raised a brow at her. "It is. You've got prickles enough for me, Boots."

She snorted softly. "Then perhaps we should put the nest out, Nathaniel. There's hardly room enough for me here as it is."

He was pouring gunpowder from the horn into the pan almost without looking. "We've managed in smaller spaces, as I recall, but we don't need to worry about that tonight."

"And why is that?"

"Because you won't be sleeping here."

"Really, Nathaniel," she said primly. "I must sleep sometime, and so must you."

He put back his head and laughed. "What a wanton I've got to wife."

She sat down abruptly. "If I'm a wanton it's all your doing, Nathaniel Bonner. And if I jumped to the wrong conclusion, there's good cause for that too. Many a night you've kept me from my sleep."

He leaned closer and tugged at her plait. "So I have, I cain't deny it. But what I meant about tonight was, you'll be sleeping back there with Selah."

Elizabeth knew the look in his eyes very well, and it had nothing to do with her sleeping anywhere but right next to him.

"And why would I do that?"

"In case that bear you were worried about comes around, wanting to share your bed. He'll have to go through me first."

She regarded him silently for a moment. He was thinking of Liam Kirby; she knew that without being told. Perhaps the tracks he had found earlier were not Splitting-Moon's at all; perhaps he was more worried than he had admitted. Before she could ask, he reached over and ran a thumb across her lower lip. "Now understand, Boots. I'm going to keep you here for a while first, until you're good and wore out."

She flushed because he meant her to, because she could no more resist his touch than she could stop breathing. But there was no need to rush things, and so she pulled her hairbrush out of her pack—the one luxury she had not left behind at Lake in the Clouds—and held it out to him.

"I take it you're willing to brush my hair before you... banish me."

His fingers moved over hers as he took the brush. "Oh, at the very least. Come on over here, Boots."

This was the best time of all, the thing she looked forward to all day long. Every evening when the children were in bed and the work was done she would sit down in the vee of his legs on their bed and Nathaniel would brush her hair and plait it for her. Sometimes they talked, but more often it was a quiet time.

Elizabeth concentrated on the pull of the brush through her hair, the way it made all the nerves in her scalp come alive. One by one her muscles relaxed as the brush did its work. Now and then Nathaniel stopped to untangle a knot with his fingers, and with each gentle tug a shiver moved down her spine to pool warm, low in her belly. When he moved the mass of her hair to one side and nipped at the exposed skin of her shoulder she arched against him.

The truth was, no matter how hard her day or dark her mood, these fifteen minutes when Nathaniel tended to her were enough to make everything good again. By the time he finished, putting down the brush to rub her scalp, cupping her head and then her shoulders in his hands to knead gently, she was boneless and pliable, liquid enough to spill.

Sometimes Elizabeth wondered if all over the world other women were sitting in front of their husbands like this, if it was something that everyone did and nobody talked about, like other acts between husband and wife.

"I wonder if Mr. Gathercole would call this sinful," Elizabeth said out loud.

She felt his teeth at her shoulder, nipping hard enough to make her yelp. "What was that for, may I ask?"

"I don't like you bringing up another man's name just now, Boots." Warm breath at her ear, his voice low and rough, the touch of his tongue—she let out a soft moan and he smiled against her neck. "Anyway, a preacher's got no business in this cave with us. I imagine he'd take one look and throw a fit, anyway."

"Do you?" As hard as it was, Elizabeth pulled away and got

to her feet. "He has a wife; they have a daughter. This . . . business can't be totally foreign to him."

"What business would that be?" Nathaniel reached out for her, but she stepped away.

"Oh no," said Elizabeth. "We're not going to get caught up in that conversation. Not yet. I'm going to bathe first." She picked up the lantern and glanced at him over her shoulder.

"I'm sure Mr. Gathercole would approve."

He lunged for her, his fingers brushing against her hip as she shrieked a high laugh and darted away. The sound of her laughter trailed behind her like a veil.

"You'll wake Selah," Nathaniel called.

"Don't worry none about me," came Selah's quiet voice. "I'm fast asleep."

That was enough to quiet Elizabeth. She ran the rest of the way to the last cavern in silence, hanging the lantern on a hook on the wall in one movement while she loosed her leggings with the other, kicking her way out of them and pulling her overdress up over her head, determined to be chin deep in the water before Nathaniel could catch her. Her heart was beating so loud in her ears that she didn't hear him coming and didn't know he was there until his hands were on her.

He pulled the overdress off and jerked her back against him in a single movement. "Why, Boots," he whispered. "You weren't thinking of getting in that water without me, were you?"

She tried to turn to him, but he tightened his grip. Gathered her hair with one hand and put it over his own shoulder, so that all along her naked back she could feel him, the smoothness of his chest, the breechclout caught up against his middle, how ready he was. He slid one hand down her belly, hard against soft, lower and lower still until she went lax against him, the back of her head resting in the hollow of his shoulder.

"That's better." His mouth on her temple, hot and cool all at once. She whimpered as his fingers worked their way between her legs, the roughened skin of his fingertips seeking and finding until her knees began to buckle.

"Have mercy," she whispered.

He took her down to the hard floor, spread her open beneath him.

"Is it mercy you want?" Heavy flesh hovering, touching

her lightly and withdrawing again. A severity had come over his face, as if she might decide suddenly and without warning to deny him. All the hundreds of times she had taken him into her body and he still held himself back at this last crucial moment before they came together, demanding that she commit herself anew, pledge herself and her body again and again.

She pulled his head down to hers and kissed him open-mouthed, raised her hips in welcome. "I want you, I want this." Her flesh parted to accept him, unfamiliar for that moment until he had centered himself inside her and was transformed, no longer Nathaniel but as much a part of her as her own heart.

He smiled against her mouth. Held her tight against him with one hand on the small of her back, and rolled them into the water as he surged into her.

She gasped in shock and surprise at the heat of him deep inside her, the heat of the water everywhere else like stroking fingers, like a thousand nimble and curious tongues probing breasts and thighs, folds of tender flesh stretched taut and straining.

He was moving against her, inside her, all around her, muttering harshly, making her gasp. He pulled her into the deeper water where he could stand and she could not. She wrapped her legs around his waist and he bent her back across a forearm, lowering his head to suckle one breast and then the other while her hair floated all around them.

Mine. He whispered it against her wet skin. *Mine.*

When the long shuddering started to move through her, wave upon wave, he pulled her up against him, breast to breast. She heard herself making inhuman sounds and his voice at her ear, *aye* and *aye* and *aye, that's it, aye, come to me, come.* The shuddering began to slow and he slipped a hand between them, used his fingers to make it spin out and out, to take the last bit of her sanity and self-control.

When he carried her back to the ledge he was still hard inside her, as hard as he had ever been.

"But you aren't done." Her own voice far away and dazed, her body still keening.

"Neither are you, Boots." His laugh was as rough and unrelenting as his kiss was soft. "You're nowhere near done at all."

Chapter 14

By their sixth day in the caves, Elizabeth's good spirits began to give way to disquiet and restlessness. Nathaniel watched it happen, but for once he had no comfort to offer; there was reason to worry, and it would do no good to pretend otherwise.

Every day he went out hunting; every day he stayed out a little longer and went a little farther, looking not so much for game, which was plentiful, but for some sign of Splitting-Moon. He brought back a steady stream of turkey, grouse, rabbit, and duck—nothing so large that the meat would go to waste, or have to be smoked. He brought no news at all.

He kept his growing worries to himself, and watched Elizabeth do the same. Sometimes at night he could almost hear her mind working, but so far they had not talked about what they were both thinking. If there was no way to get Selah Voyager to Red Rock, what then?

There were three possibilities that came to mind, and none of them appealed much. He could go out and do some serious tracking until he found the runaways, leaving the women here to fend for themselves. That could take up to a week or more, if it turned out that Red Rock wasn't any one place in particular and the group was on the move. Elizabeth had been on her own in the bush before, but never by choice.

Or they could go home, just take Selah back to Hidden Wolf and keep her and her child hid on the mountain. That would be the easiest solution, but now that Liam Kirby had brought Ambrose Dye into the search, it was also the most dangerous.

Then there was Canada. They could take Selah all the way to Montreal, where she'd be safe from blackbirders and Manny could join her. There was a woman in Montreal who would take Selah in without question, but Nathaniel knew pretty much without asking how Elizabeth would react to this idea of adding another four weeks to a journey she hadn't wanted to make in the first place, and that with a pregnant woman or, more likely, a newborn.

Elizabeth would flat out refuse to go to Canada, but whether she admitted it to herself or not, any kind of movement would suit her better than the waiting.

In some ways Elizabeth's growing restlessness was more trouble than anything else. She liked to think of herself as a creature of habit, but the truth was, she just didn't take well to the routine that went along with a life in the bush. The playfulness that had taken her through the first few days was still there at night, but in the day she was jittery, and in an unsettled mood Elizabeth was likely to get herself and everybody else into trouble.

For her part, Selah seemed as calm as ever, but she tended to keep to herself and spent long hours sleeping in the caves under a pile of bearskins. Sometimes she would get a distracted look, and sit quietly with her hands on her belly. For a few minutes all her attention turned inward, as if she were having a conversation with the child on whether or not it was ready to come into the world. Elizabeth went very still when this happened, relaxing only when Selah let out a deep sigh and picked up whatever work she had put aside.

Selah provided Elizabeth with distraction, for which Nathaniel was thankful. Every day she managed to find something she needed to know that Elizabeth could teach her. Yesterday they had spent most of the morning putting together makeshift compasses, something Robbie had taught Elizabeth when she first came to spend time with him here. The day before they had gone looking for the first fiddleheads, or wild onion, or anything else that would add some flavor to the regular diet of meat and cornbread.

"Fishing," announced Elizabeth. She had come up behind

him where he sat by the cook fire, barefoot and with her hair slightly damp and flying free. She bent forward from the waist so that it fell to the ground and grasped it all in her hands as if it were a tangle of wayward rope. Peeking out from between the strands, she looked at Nathaniel and said, "I would like it if you came with us and showed Selah how to use a fishing spear."

"That could be arranged." Nathaniel watched the hair slide into her hands on one side, pass through the busily working fingers, and emerge as a fat plait.

"No meat today," Elizabeth said firmly.

He made a hiccuping sound of agreement. "Trout, if we can get some."

She righted herself to finish her work, her gaze still fixed on him. "You are very accommodating these days, Nathaniel Bonner."

"And you are looking for a fight, Boots. Maybe you should just haul off and punch me in the nose, get it over with. If that would improve your mood."

She sat down on the old log that had served as a bench for as long as Nathaniel could remember, polished down by years of use until it gleamed like a great bone. A smile jerked at the corner of her mouth.

"Am I looking for a fight?" She put back her head to look straight into the sky. "Yes, I suppose I am. I thank you for the kind offer, but I don't need to punch you in the nose. It will be enough to improve my mood if we get a few fish for our supper."

"If that's all it takes we can go fishing every day, Boots."

She was silent for a long minute while she watched two crows arguing in the branches of a fir. Nathaniel saw the question in her face before she had put it into words.

"Do you suppose Splitting-Moon might have met with an accident?"

He met her gaze. "Maybe. Maybe not. Could be ten different things holding her up. She could be here in an hour, for all I know."

"Then you are not worried?" She narrowed her eyes at him.

"I didn't say that."

She pushed out a very large sigh and stood. "The child will

not wait much longer. Here is my suggestion. If there is no sign of Splitting-Moon in three more days, then we must have a council and decide what to do next."

For the rest of the day Nathaniel couldn't quite shake the idea that Elizabeth had already made up her mind about what to do next, but wasn't yet ready to let him in on her plans.

They set out not for Little Lost, but for the river Robbie had always called No-Name that wound its way along the small valley on the other side of the mountain.

The weather had taken a real turn toward spring. Elizabeth counted this among the day's blessings, along with the trout lily that had sprung up overnight to carpet the forest floor and the sight of a blue heron rising up out of the river, all dangling legs and brilliant white in the sun.

As they made their way down to the river, Elizabeth thought of how good it would be to just get into a canoe and paddle away. They would climb in, all three of them, and run with the winding river, through the mountains without stopping, to join the next river and then the next, until they found themselves on Lake George. Elizabeth had the sudden and almost undeniable urge to see the lakes and the open sky overhead, and she went eagerly to the spot where Robbie had kept his canoe.

It was gone, of course. There was no sign of it at all, nothing but an abandoned nest and a scattering of eggshell. Elizabeth must be content with fishing.

Selah said, "Any chance we might come across a bear?"

It was a question she asked often, and Elizabeth couldn't figure out if she was afraid or curious.

"We might," said Nathaniel. "Elizabeth had her first encounter with a bear right here." He pointed to a tree while he grinned at her. "She climbed that pine to get a better look."

"I climbed that pine to get away." Elizabeth could not help but laugh at his playfulness, and the memory of that morning. "I had scabs on my hands and knees for a week."

Selah said, "Don't think I could get up a tree with this belly."

"You won't need to," said Nathaniel. "A black bear wants to get away from you worse than you want to see it go. Just stay clear, and never get between any bear and her cubs. And don't climb a tree. A bear in a serious mood will just follow you right up."

"I saw a man got in the way of a bear, when I was a girl," said Selah. "Out on Long-Island. Tore his face right off and took out his throat. His own kin couldn't recognize him."

"I'm not saying it never happens," Nathaniel said, more seriously now that he saw how concerned she really was. "But there's no reason to fear the worst, not if you keep your head and do what needs doing."

He had been sharpening the blade at the end of the fishing spear with his whetstone, but he looked down the river and stopped.

"What is it?" Elizabeth craned her neck to look upriver. She could see nothing, but there was the sound of something big in the underbrush.

Nathaniel had put down the fishing spear. "Moose."

"Moose?" Selah's tone was part curiosity and part anxiety.

He pointed. "A moose with a new calf is a bigger worry than any black bear. She'll be testy."

A quarter mile away at a marshy bend in the river, the moose had come out of the trees with a calf just behind her, wobbling and butting against her udder. This seemed to concern her as little as the afterbirth that still hung around her hocks like bloody and bedraggled skirts; she was intent on the river, and she stepped into it almost daintily, moving toward a clump of bulrushes. First she drank for a long minute, and then she pulled up a great mouthful of greenery. That was when she caught sight of them.

"Good Lord," whispered Selah, with real awe in her voice. "Look at those legs, they must be six feet long."

Nathaniel swung his rifle into his hands, but Elizabeth knew by the lack of tension in his arms that it was more precaution than real concern.

The moose looked at them for a long minute. Then she dropped her head and her nostrils flared as she made a loud, fluttering noise. It was warning enough for Elizabeth.

"Nathaniel, wouldn't it be best if we left this part of the river—"

He shook his head without taking his eyes away from the moose. "No need to worry unless she flattens her ears."

The moose considered them for another long minute, took

a last mouthful of rushes, and ambled back into the trees with her calf scrambling along behind.

"Wasn't that a sight," breathed Selah. "Don't think anybody back on Pearl Street ever saw such a thing."

In the excitement she had backed away a few steps, so that her bare heels protruded over the lip of the riverbank. She was rocking back and forth, her arms wrapped around herself.

Elizabeth said, "Be careful that you don't lose your balance—"

A loud hissing erupted from the bank below Selah's feet, a high and sizzling sound like hot fat in a wet fry pan.

Nathaniel was ten feet off, but his head came up like a shot. He dropped his rifle and bolted toward Selah, reaching over his shoulder for his tomahawk with one hand, and for his knife with the other.

"Jump to the side!" he shouted.

Selah looked up with a dazed and puzzled expression, as if he had ordered her to gallop like a horse. The hissing had frightened her, but she did not see what Elizabeth saw plainly behind her: a snapping turtle the size of a tree stump lunging up the bank toward Selah's bare ankles, its thick neck extended and the jaw gaping open.

"Jump *now!*" Nathaniel bellowed and she did, hopping high and right, but not quite far enough: the turtle's jaws clicked shut on the hem of her overdress with a sound like a door slamming and she went tumbling to the ground, grunting in surprise.

Selah was trying to scramble away, her belly digging a furrow in the ground. On her hands and knees she and the turtle were almost the same height, and it looked for a moment as if the snapper had mistaken Selah for one of her own errant children and was intent on dragging her back to the river where she belonged. Elizabeth grabbed Selah's right arm and pulled, but the turtle didn't seem interested in giving up its mouthful of doeskin, not even for the ankle right beneath its nose.

Then Nathaniel's tomahawk came down hard, severing the leathery folds of the neck at the point where it joined the shell. The hissing stopped just as suddenly as it had started.

Selah propped herself up on one elbow, shaking her head to clear it. Her overdress was muddied and streaked with grass, and there was a swipe of dirt on her forehead. She had broken out in a sweat and for one moment Elizabeth thought she would faint.

She sat down beside Selah and took out her handkerchief to wipe the dirt away.

"That was a bit more excitement than we needed this morning," she said. "Are you all right?"

"Never seen a turtle so big," Selah whispered. "Seem like all the creatures in the bush three times bigger than they need to be. It put the fear of God in me, I cain't deny that."

Nathaniel crouched down to wipe the blade of his tomahawk clean on the grass. "Once a snapper gets started it can't change the direction of a lunge," he said in a perfectly calm tone. He leaned over to look at the bloody head clamped to Selah's overdress like a curious piece of outsized jewelry. Elizabeth shuddered to see that the sulphur yellow slitted eyes were still open, and the expression was as ferocious as ever.

"Jumping to one side is usually enough," Nathaniel continued, pressing his fingers into the jaw hinges until the mouth gaped far enough open to disengage it. "I expect she's got a nest in that bank and that's why she came after you."

He held out the head, still dribbling blood. "Do you want this? The turtle is the symbol of great strength. The Kahnyen'kehàka people believe that the turtle carries the whole weight of the world on its back. It's good luck if you dry it and wear it in a pouch around your neck."

That Nathaniel would suggest this did not surprise Elizabeth—she knew enough of Mahican and Mohawk beliefs to understand his purpose—but she was surprised that Selah consented. She put a hand to her throat as if to imagine the pouch there, and touched the wooden talisman that Manny had given her when she ran, hanging by a rawhide string.

"Turtle stew for dinner then," Elizabeth said, trying to strike a lighter tone. She prodded the ridged shell. It was covered with algae, and looked like nothing more than a great rock.

A thoughtful, almost distressed look came over Selah's face. She closed her eyes, and for a moment Elizabeth thought that she was going to be sick after all. Then she spread her hands out over her belly, and her eyes opened with a click.

Elizabeth saw two things: in Selah's face, a dawning relief quickly replaced by grim determination; and a patch of wet spreading out over her lap. A familiar smell rose up, the smell of flood plains and life brewing.

"We may have to wait on that turtle stew," said Nathaniel, one brow raised. "You best get her up to the caves, Boots. Soon as I've got some of this meat I'll follow you."

By sunset the contractions were strong and regular, and Selah had paced a trail around the clearing. When Elizabeth brought her water she stopped to drink, but she turned away corn-bread and meat with a shake of the head.

"I'll just bring it up," she said, stopping to rub her stomach. "But later on I'll have a bowl of that turtle stew, wait and see."

Elizabeth had helped with some twenty births since she came to Paradise, and she had seen how every woman came to the experience differently. Some seemed to lose track of the world around them and flounder in confusion; some lost courage early on; others turned irritable and rancorous; some seemed to find an almost mystic state of calm. Selah was simply focused, minute by minute, on what her body might be asking of her, as if childbirth were a puzzle to be solved.

When the last of the light was gone and a fine drizzle had begun to fall, she reluctantly agreed to move inside, where she walked up and down the length of the stone corridor, stopping sometimes to lean against the wall.

Nathaniel started a small fire in the cave where Selah slept, set out the candles that would be needed later, and filled the water barrel. Curiosity had given Elizabeth a package of things she might need in case Selah went into labor, and now she opened it for the first time.

Each item was wrapped carefully in muslin: a pair of scis-sors, a small ball of string, needle and thread, a scalpel that Elizabeth recognized as belonging to Hannah, a bundle of soft muslin cloths, swaddling clothes, and three small stone bottles, each tightly corked and with a tag attached. The handwriting was Hannah's, and the sight of it touched Elizabeth. She would very much like to have Hannah here right now.

At the very bottom was a note in Curiosity's hand:

> If you come to read this I expect Selah is in travail. There never was a woman who set such a store on doing things just right as you, Elizabeth, so I thought

I better say a few words and remind you of what
you know already. First off, remember that she's got
to do the work herself. For the most part the best
thing you can do for her is to just stand back and
speak calm words. Tell her to holler when the need
come over her. You have seen yourself that most
times a third child will come sliding into this world
like the heart of a boiled onion from its shell. But
the most important thing is, don't let her rush
herself. Most trouble come because somebody gets
impatient.

Elizabeth read the note twice, and then she folded it neatly
and put it back where she had found it.

*A third child will come sliding into this world like the heart of a
boiled onion from its shell.* Most times. Elizabeth thought back to
the morning that Daisy Hench had brought her Solange into
the world, and the calm good spirits that had prevailed in that
birthing room. Mariah Greber's third daughter Hope was
much the same, and Willy LeBlanc's arrival had taken Molly
by surprise as she hung wash, so that there was barely time to
call for help. And Robbie, Elizabeth's own third child.

She had labored all through a warm night in June. The
twins had been born in the middle of a storm, with only
Hannah to attend Elizabeth; by comparison Robbie's birth had
felt almost dreamlike. The birthing room had been very quiet
for the most part, not the quiet of dread or despair but ab-
solute calm and something that could only be called joy.
Nathaniel had been nearby, and all the women she loved and
trusted most in the world: Curiosity and Hannah and Many-
Doves. Elizabeth could close her eyes and see it whenever she
pleased: Curiosity holding Robbie up for them to see in the
first light of dawn.

She braced her shoulders, took a deep breath, and went to
get herself ready.

Nathaniel came to talk to her while she changed.

"She's been through so much," he said. "She's not likely to
panic now."

"I think you're right." Elizabeth wound her plait around
her head and secured it with a kerchief.

He was silent for a while, but Elizabeth could feel his unease.

"Did you want to say something?"

He grunted softly to himself. "I suppose I do. The thing is, Boots, I don't mean to tell you your business—"

She turned to him, and raised an eyebrow. "But?"

"But you might want to talk to her, during."

Elizabeth heard the irritation in her own voice. "I wasn't planning on taking a vow of silence for the duration, you know."

He cleared his throat. "That's not what I mean, and you know it. It's just that you tend to go quiet when you're anxious, and I got the idea that you don't even know you're doing it. When you were in labor with Robbie, Curiosity talked to you the whole time. I seem to remember she made you laugh more than once. And things went easier for it, as far as I could tell."

Elizabeth did not answer at first. She was changing into her second, cleaner overdress, and wondering whether she should cut her nails. Hannah would quote Hakim Ibrahim to her if she were here: *the devil lives beneath the nails.*

"I see your point," she said finally. "But Curiosity is much more at ease in a birthing room than I could ever be. I'll do my best to make her comfortable."

He cleared his throat. "To tell the truth, it was more you I was thinking about, Boots." Nathaniel reached out and cupped her face in his hand.

Elizabeth stepped forward to put her arms around his waist. With her forehead against his shoulder she took a deep breath and then another, and slowly the tension that had cramped the muscles of her shoulders and back began to leave her. She trembled, and it seemed to her that he was trembling a little too, in sympathy for what she must go and do alone. To stand like this in Nathaniel's arms was more comfort than any talk, and when she pulled away she could smile at him with honest good humor.

"Elizabeth?" Selah's voice came down the corridor. "Elizabeth?"

"Things seem to be moving along," said Nathaniel. "You call me if you need a hand, I'll be just outside."

*   *   *

Elizabeth remembered the most difficult part of her own labors as the time just before the urge to push came over her. In those endless minutes her stoicism had evaporated, and she had not been able to keep herself from howling in agony. Selah had come to this point in her travails, but she would not let herself scream even after Elizabeth read Curiosity's advice out loud.

She was squatting with her back against the wall. Elizabeth crouched with her, holding on to her hands. In the pause after a particularly long contraction, when Selah's strength seemed to be ebbing, she asked, "Have you thought what you want to name this child?"

Selah's gaze had been turned inward, but now she came back to the world long enough to focus on Elizabeth. She managed a small smile. "That depend," she said. Her voice was hoarse, and Elizabeth reached over to get a dipper of water. Her own shadow jerked and danced on the wall in the light of the fire and the candles.

Selah swallowed and wiped her mouth with the back of her hand.

"What does it depend on?"

The long tendons in Selah's neck stood out when she rested her head back against the wall. "On whether this child look like my Violet or not."

Elizabeth closed her eyes. She had meant to distract Selah, and instead had reminded her of Hubert Vaark. Before she could decide whether an apology would make it worse or better, another contraction had started.

When it was over Selah said, "Sometimes you got to wonder what people are thinking when they name children. There's an alderman down in the city used to come by Pearl Street, his name was Mr. Mangle Minthorne. Now why would his mama call him Mangle? He look normal enough. I always wondered if maybe it was a hard birth and she held it against him."

Elizabeth had to smile. "There's a family in Paradise, Horace and Mariah Greber. They have five girls called Faith, Charity, Hope, Prudence, and Constance. Then the sixth child came along not long ago, their first boy."

The muscles in Selah's stomach had begun to contract again, like a small mountain intent on moving itself. Elizabeth held Selah's hands until it was over, and then she wiped her brow.

"More water?"

Selah shook her head, and she managed a smile. "Five girls and finally a son come along. What a happy day. What did they name the boy?"

Elizabeth smiled, as she did whenever she thought of the morning Horace Greber had announced his new son's name at Sunday services. For once he lost his dour expression and smiled so broadly that his whole face had folded into great pleated wrinkles.

"Mariah wanted to name him Paul after her father, but Horace had another idea, and he got his way. They named the boy Hardwork."

Selah's head snapped up, and she let out a croaking laugh. "What?"

Elizabeth nodded. "Horace said he never would have believed it would be so difficult to produce a boy, and he didn't want his son to forget it."

Selah giggled hoarsely until the next contraction started and then for the first time she let out a great groan. When it was over she said, "There is a lawyer in the city called Mr. Plunket Plunderheit," and she put back her head and giggled again. The next contraction drew out and out, and ended in a long shuddering.

"Are you ready to push?"

Selah grunted in response. She was panting as if she had run a mile, and had another mile before her.

"Don't rush," Elizabeth recited. "I'm not supposed to let you rush."

"Not rush?" Selah looked at her as if she had said, *let's not have this baby after all.*

"So you don't tear." Elizabeth said this more firmly. "You don't want to tear."

"What I want," Selah said, fixing her with a furious expression as she bore down with all her might, "is to get this child *out.*"

Elizabeth had seen women push for hours to expel a child, but Selah seemed to have other ideas. There was no time to be anxious or to anticipate complications, because in three great, groaning pushes the baby's head was free, and in one more it rotated slickly and slid into Elizabeth's waiting hands.

He was a big child, well rounded, and he wiggled and flexed like a fish, arms and legs jerking as if he meant to swim away through the air. Then he opened his eyes and looked straight at her, and his lips spread in something that Elizabeth could only think of as a smile. He blinked, his expression all surprise and curiosity.

You remind me of your grandmother. Elizabeth almost said it out loud, but then she stopped herself.

"A son," Elizabeth said. "You have a healthy son."

Selah let out a shuddering sigh and held out her arms. When Elizabeth handed the boy to her, Selah's hands fluttered closed over him like dark wings. Under the waxy white coating that had eased his way through the birth canal his skin was almost exactly the same shade as hers, the deep rich color of good loam with nothing of red or yellow in it at all.

"Thank you," Selah said clearly. "Thank you."

Elizabeth did not want to be thanked, not until the afterbirth was safely delivered. With hands that were shaking slightly she checked and found that Selah's great rushing had brought with it only two small tears that wouldn't need to be sewn.

When the thick cord that still joined mother and son had stopped pulsing Elizabeth tied it carefully in two spots and picked up the scissors. She paused and took a deep breath, almost hearing Curiosity's voice at her ear.

Better too much than too little.

She had said it out loud, and Selah made a sound deep in her throat, of agreement or worry Elizabeth couldn't be sure. The scissors made a crisp sound as they severed the cord, and at that the boy let out his first cry. It grew quickly into a great squalling that continued until Selah directed him to the breast.

Delivery of the afterbirth was what concerned her most, but it came in one last push, whole and intact.

"Don't throw it away," Selah whispered. "I want to bury it myself."

Nathaniel was waiting out in the open when Elizabeth finally came to find him. His hair was damp with rain but he was smiling when she walked directly into his open arms. A shuddering passed through her in great waves, relief and joy and exhaustion.

"A boy," she said finally, her mouth against his chest. "She's going to name him Galileo. She says—" Elizabeth's voice cracked, and her throat swelled shut with tears.

"What, Boots?"

"She says the boy looks nothing at all like his sister Violet. And I didn't know if I should be happy for her, or sad."

Nathaniel held her until she was done weeping, and then they went in together to formally greet Almanzo Freeman's firstborn son.

Chapter 15

On the brightest and sweetest of spring evenings Nathaniel came back from Little Lost with a brace of trout and a stranger. One moment Elizabeth had been scouring out the pot with sand and rehearsing to herself the plan she would present to Nathaniel, and the next she looked up to see a solution she had not considered standing before her.

"This is Elijah," Nathaniel introduced him, although the resemblance to his brother was plain enough to see. Elijah was as well built and muscular as Joshua, with the same jaw and nose and set of the shoulders, but there were raised tattoos on his cheekbones and a long silver ear-bob dangled from his left lobe, almost exactly like the one Nathaniel wore. Across the chest of his fringed hunting shirt he had strung a simple wampum belt, and he carried a rifle slung across his back with easy familiarity. His skin was black, but everything about his demeanor and the way he moved spoke of the Kahnyen'kehàka.

Selah had been nursing her son in a patch of sunlight, but she tucked him into the muslin sling she wore across her chest and got up to meet Elijah, touching his hand with her own and examining his face closely.

"Elijah," Elizabeth said, "you must be thirsty, would you like some water?"

"Thank you." His voice was hoarse with disuse. Elizabeth had the sense that he was reaching for English words, as if it had been so long since he used his mother tongue that he had misplaced it.

"I'll show him," Selah said. When she had taken Elijah off toward the fresh water that came out of the rock face just behind the lean-to, Elizabeth put her hands on her hips.

"Well?"

Nathaniel said, "He's alone."

"I can see that. Why is he alone? Where is Splitting-Moon?" She heard the impatience in her voice, and stopped herself. "Did he say anything at all?"

"Not much. I expect he'll explain as soon as he's caught his breath."

Nathaniel sat down next to the cook fire and began to clean the fish with quick, economical movements of his knife. He was worried, she could see that, but his patience had the upper hand right now. Elizabeth crouched down by the fire and poked at it with a stick so fiercely that the sparks leapt up.

"Better the fire than me," Nathaniel said behind her and she bit back sharp words, knowing very well that he would just smile at her and make her laugh, steal her mood from her that easily.

When Elijah came back to sit with them she could not ask him the hundred questions she wanted to ask; in spite of all the stories they had heard of him, he was a stranger and hungry, and the formalities must be observed. Food offered and accepted, and then news of Paradise.

Nathaniel explained why they had come in Joshua's place, and Elijah listened, asking a question now and then of Nathaniel or Selah.

When the worst of the story had been told, from Liam Kirby to Ambrose Dye, Nathaniel said, "There's been no trace of either of them or anybody else for a mile around. I don't know what that means, exactly, but it looks like you'll be safe taking Selah back to Red Rock for the time being, at least."

Elijah looked at them in turn, his dark eyes unreadable. He said, "Dye been in the bush before, looking for us. I doubt he'd come any closer should he try again."

"That's good to know," Nathaniel said. And they sat silently, waiting for Elijah to tell them whatever it was that had brought him here alone. Kestrels called nearby and the baby murmured in his sleep against Selah's breast. She ran a hand over the curve of his back and then she let out a great sigh, giving up the waiting to ask a question she couldn't hold back anymore.

"How many of you are there at Red Rock now? Manny couldn't tell me for sure."

Elijah blinked at her and Elizabeth saw something frightening there, a sorrow on the verge of brimming over, sorrow enough to fill the world. She stood up suddenly, because some part of her knew already what he was going to say. More disaster: a stray bullet, a forgotten trap, snake bite, rock fall. There was no end to it.

"Splitting-Moon?" She heard her own voice wobble and break. "What is it? An accident?"

He shook his head. "About two weeks ago she met up with a trapper on his way out to the great river," he said. "Traded him a good beaver pelt for a whetstone, but she brought back a fever with her." His gaze moved past Elizabeth to Selah.

"Little-John and Digger died, one right after the other. The children went next, all three of them and then Andrew and Parthenia. She was the oldest of us."

He paused, and Elizabeth thought of the little boy Hannah had described, Splitting-Moon's son. Elijah's son. He had lost his only child just days ago, and he sat here telling them the story as if it had happened to somebody else. Because, she knew very well, it wasn't real to him yet, because he wouldn't let the loss close enough to claim it as his own, not yet.

He sat straight-backed, and looked at each of them in turn. "All but two of us come down with it, but it didn't hit everybody the same. Just before I left Splitting-Moon said the fever had burned itself out. But I ain't sure, maybe she was just trying to get me to go, quiet like. So I don't rightly know how to tell you how many we are. Maybe nobody at all."

"Splitting-Moon?" Elizabeth asked again.

There was a convulsive twitching at the corner of Elijah's mouth. "She took sick," he said. "Her fever went so high it was hard to touch her for a while. But she's out of danger. She couldn't rest easy knowing there was a voyager here waiting. And there's a message I need to pass on to Joshua, if you'd be so good."

"What word?" Nathaniel asked softly.

"Not to send anybody new our way. As soon as everybody can walk we're leaving, heading north," said Elijah. "We can't stay in the bush so we'll head for Canada, whoever's left."

Elizabeth sat down again before her trembling legs could give her away. There was something else, something worse that he wasn't saying. She could see the same thoughts moving across Nathaniel's face, but Selah's expression was more of confusion, and distress. She said, "Why would you want to leave Red Rock?"

"Don't want to," said Elijah steadily. "But we don't have much choice." He dropped his gaze to the fire. "The fever left Quincy and Splitting-Moon both pure blind."

"Lord save us," whispered Selah, rocking her son closer to herself.

Elizabeth felt Nathaniel's arm come up around her, and she was thankful for that prop. Splitting-Moon had lost her son and her sight. *Be merciful to me, O Lord, for I am in distress; my eyes grow weak with sorrow, my soul and my body with grief.*

She had last seen Splitting-Moon when she still lived in the longhouse at Good Pasture, in training to be Ononkwa—medicine woman—after her grandmother. Elizabeth could summon Splitting-Moon's face when she closed her eyes: a serious young woman with a sadness about her. She seemed happy only when she went into the forests to seek the plants and roots and barks she needed for her medicines. Now that had been taken from her, that and so much else. Without her sight she could not leave the bush to trade for the things they must have. Without her son she was still the woman she had been, and she was someone else entirely.

Splitting-Moon was the foundation of Red Rock; she had taught this man and the others how to hunt and move in the forests, how to survive the winter and the rains and the treacheries of the bush. She had led them, but now she would need to be led.

A merciful God. Elizabeth let out a coarse sound and turned her face to Nathaniel's shoulder, pressed herself against him and then straightened, to find Selah watching her.

"She is your friend," Selah said.

She needs your help.

No one said the words, but they were there just the same, almost visible in the air. Nathaniel was watching her, as if the decision were hers alone; as if she could say words that would fix this terrible wrong.

Elijah said, "She wouldn't want you to put yourselves in danger." He turned to Selah. "I'm here to fetch you back to Red Rock and then we'll go north. There's ways into Canada through the bush, you understand." He paused, and when none of them said the obvious thing—*how will you follow trails through the bush you don't know and Splitting-Moon can't see?*—he continued.

"We can live free in Canada, won't have to hide no more." His voice grew stronger, as if he were reciting something he had learned by heart but did not quite believe. "I'm going to take Splitting-Moon to Good Pasture. Some of us will go on to Montréal, but you can do as you please."

Selah was listening to him, but she was watching Elizabeth. There was understanding there, and compassion. Selah knew what Elizabeth was going to say, and so did Nathaniel. He took her hand and squeezed it.

Elizabeth said, "We will take you as far as Good Pasture." And to Elijah's look of confusion: "All of you. All of Red Rock."

Nathaniel walked the mountain one last time at dusk, to make sure that no one had trailed Elijah to Little Lost, and to prepare himself for the coming argument with Elizabeth.

There were few options before them, and all of them were bad. No matter how many times Nathaniel went over the situation, he always came out to the same conclusion: he could see no way to do this but to start by taking Elizabeth back to Paradise. While he did that, Elijah could bring his people to Little Lost, and then Nathaniel would meet them to start the long walk north to Canada and the Kahnyen'kehàka at Good Pasture. It would take three weeks at least to get them that far, maybe twice that, depending on how much the fever had taken out of them. It could be up to two months before he got back home again, assuming they could keep clear of the law and the army and blackbirders.

Elizabeth was waiting for him outside the caves, alone. From inside the caves came the soft sound of Selah singing to her son, as she had begun to do more often in the last few days.

My Lord calls me,
He calls me by the thunder;
The trumpet sounds within-a my soul,
I ain't got long to stay here.
Green trees are bending,
Poor sinner stands atrembling;

The trumpet sounds within my soul,
I ain't got long to stay here.
My Lord calls me,
He calls me by the lightning,
The trumpet sounds within-a my soul,
I ain't got long to stay here.

By the light of the banked embers of the cook fire Elizabeth sat with her arms wrapped around herself, her head leaning to one shoulder as she hummed along with Selah. She moved over to make room for him on the log and then they sat together for a long time without talking. But there was nothing calm about this silence; he could feel her tension growing, almost hear it happening, like the steady winding of a clock.

He put his arm around her, but it took a minute or more for her to give in to it and relax against him. With Elizabeth it was usually best to say the worst straight-out and so Nathaniel pulled her closer and put his mouth against her hair. "I'll take you back tomorrow, Boots. You don't want to be away from home for another six weeks."

She stiffened against him, and then pulled away. The faint light from the dying fire drew her face in simple lines and showed him the one expression he had not foreseen: pure disbelief. She hadn't even anticipated that she might need to go home without him. Nathaniel braced himself for a longer argument than he had expected.

"Six weeks? Nathaniel, that is ridiculous."

He drew up short. "I think I can reckon how long it will take, Boots. Fifteen sickly folks won't be able to trot through the bush, you know."

Her mouth curled down at the corner. "If we were to walk that far, yes, of course."

"Were you planning on sprouting wings and flying?" He was working hard to keep his tone easy, but a great wariness had come over him. Elizabeth had a plan; he could see that on her face, and Elizabeth with a plan was a formidable force, a storm on the horizon.

She tilted her chin at him. "There's no need to be sarcastic, Nathaniel. It's very simple, really. On the big lake it will take two days to get to the Québec border."

"The big lake. Elizabeth, even if we could get enough canoes for fifteen people, the law would pick us up on the first
day, you know that yourself—"

She gave him a look of utter disgust, and held up her hand to
stop him. "Well, of course we should be arrested, if we were
traveling in canoes. Give me more credit than that, please."

Nathaniel saw the furrow between her eyebrows, and
knew that she had taken real offense. And maybe with good
cause, he admitted to himself. Obviously she had worked out a
complicated plan, and she deserved to be heard out. The
problem was that with Elizabeth's plans she usually managed to
put herself right in the middle of some kind of danger.

"Go ahead, Boots. I'm listening."

Some of the irritation left her face. "With an open mind?"

"Aye." He sighed. "Go on."

"It's very simple, really. If we assume that there are indeed
blackbirders looking for escaped slaves, then we must present
them to the world as something else."

"And that would be?"

"Quakers," said Elizabeth, and then more quickly: "A
group of Quaker missionaries on their way north to Canada.
With you and I as the leaders."

Nathaniel had a faint idea where this was going. "And how
do you plan to turn a dozen blacks who've been living hard in
the bush into Quakers? The clothes alone—"

"Do you remember the letter I had from Captain Mudge
six months or so ago?"

"Grievous Mudge?"

Elizabeth nodded impatiently. "Do you know another? His
sister has been widowed and is come to live with him. The sister who was a missionary in Africa for twenty years. Surely
you must remember, you laughed so hard when I read the letter to you—"

"The sister who sends barrels of clothing to Africa,"
Nathaniel finished. "She put Mudge in a temper because she
sent away one of his shirts—"

"All of his shirts, except the one on his back," Elizabeth
corrected. "Mrs. Emory has left her mission, but she is determined to clothe all of Africa by post. But I am getting ahead of
myself, let me start from the beginning."

Nathaniel leaned back on his elbows. "By all means."

"From what Elijah has told us, the rest of his people must be a few miles east of here, isn't that right?"

She waited for his nod.

"So it is maybe twenty miles from there to Mariah and the *Washington*. Given their condition, it will take two or three days to take them that far. Two days to sail up to Lacolle. From there another two days' walk to Good Pasture."

"You want Grievous Mudge to sail the *Washington* to Lacolle," Nathaniel said, more to himself than to her. "After his sister dresses us all up as Quakers."

"Yes," Elizabeth said impatiently. "I think that much must be clear by now."

"Bear with me a minute here, Boots. I can see Mrs. Emory's part in this, but tell me why it is that Grievous Mudge would want to risk his schooner and a gaol sentence to run a whole shipload of escaped slaves up to Québec."

She sat back and looked at him in surprise. "I thought that would be obvious, Nathaniel. He is bored. Why else does he write letters and complain? He will welcome the opportunity to be out on the water again, and the challenge."

Nathaniel shook his head, and tried very hard to bite back a smile.

"I hope you are not laughing at me, Nathaniel Bonner," Elizabeth said severely.

"It would never occur to me to laugh at you, Boots. You amaze me, is all."

She pursed her lips, only slightly appeased. "But?"

"But let me ask you this. You know the navy is all over the water. I doubt we can get past Grand Isle or Lamotte without being boarded at least once, maybe twice. You don't think a dozen black Quakers would make them a little suspicious?"

"It will not," she said, a little tenser now. "What could be more reasonable than former slaves converting to the Quakerism that brought them their freedom?"

"And what are you going to do about the manumission papers the law will want to see?"

Elizabeth's jaw tightened. "Very simple," she said. "I will write them myself." And she swallowed so hard that he could see the muscles in her throat flexing.

Nathaniel put his arm around her and drew her back to him.

"You're talking about counterfeiting the papers. Manumission papers and travel papers both, for all of them."

"I believe *counterfeiting* is the term, yes. Or perhaps *forgery* would be more appropriate, although I must admit I am not sure of the distinction between the two. And of course fraud and grand theft. We will be breaking any number of laws of the state of New-York and the United States and most probably Canada as well. But I have come to a conclusion. The mere fact that a law exists does not provide a moral reason for obeying that law. And I can see none in this case."

"You've thought this through."

"Yes, of course. I've been thinking about it for a good while, ever since your youngest daughter reminded me that laws are only as good as the men who write them."

He kept silent for a minute, trying not to laugh out loud, in delight and defeat, both.

She said, "Go on, then, Nathaniel. Just say what you have to say. Tell me why it won't work and why you think I have to go home without you."

"Oh, it'll work," he said, pulling her onto his lap. She struggled a little, and he held her tighter. "I think it'll work just fine if Mudge is willing to go along with it. And I expect you're right about him. Smuggling's in his blood."

She relaxed a little against him. "But?"

"No buts," he said, running a palm up her back. "It's just sometimes you still surprise me. If there's a man to be broke out of gaol, it's you I'd come looking for, but I never thought of you as a forger. Next thing you'll be suggesting we rob a bank or two on the way home."

"Have your fun at my expense." She tried to pull away, but he wouldn't let her go.

"Or maybe some fur smuggling." He smiled against her neck. "Just to keep you on your toes."

"Will you be serious for one moment?"

"I'm dead serious, Boots. I think it'll work. In fact, now that I think about it, I don't see another way to do it."

She relaxed suddenly and completely. "You're not just saying that?"

He shook his head. "Ah, Boots. The war would have been a year or more shorter if they had had you as a general. If you had been born a man, that is. Which I'm glad you weren't, all things considered."

He wanted something different from her now, but her thoughts were far away from him, moving out through the forests. Her mood was shifting from determination to contemplation and from there to sorrow.

"You're thinking about Splitting-Moon," he said.

She nodded. "This is the least we can do for her. And for Selah, and for the rest of them. They've been through enough. Two weeks more away from home is a small sacrifice in comparison."

Nathaniel looked at the darkening sky and thought of the dangers of the journey ahead of them, of Splitting-Moon sitting unaware under the blaze of stars, of Daniel and Lily safe on Hidden Wolf. They were surrounded by familiar things and by family and friends, as safe as children could be in the world. The other two had grown beyond his reach and his protection: Hannah somewhere in the city making her own way; Luke, farther still, across the wider water. For them he could do less, or nothing at all.

But they would do this thing for Selah and Manny and their child, for Splitting-Moon and Elijah and their son, for Galileo and Curiosity and all the others.

"We'll start tomorrow," he said.

She made a humming noise deep in her throat, acknowledgment and acceptance and worry all at once.

"Let's go to the hot springs now." Her voice soft and hesitant at his ear, all her defiance and daring gone. He had married an English spinster who would commit larceny in the name of a cause she found to be just, but in the light of day she still could not talk about the things they did together when he took her to their bed. Hardheaded and tenderhearted, she was no mystery to him but always a puzzle, his rebel of a wife who blushed like a schoolgirl when he told her plain what pleasure she was to him.

In the new dark with all of the color draining out of the world he could not see this particular blush, but he knew it was there. He traced it with the tip of a finger, up from her collarbone over the soft skin of her neck and the crest of her cheek, claiming it and her for himself. Elizabeth in all her furious wanting, his alone.

Chapter 16

The Great Lake had many names and faces, but in simple fact it was nothing more than a very large body of fresh water, an inland sea bordered on one side by the endless forests of the New-York frontier and on the other by the Green Hills of Vermont. The water that some called Champlain and others only the Great Lake narrowed on its lower end into a ribbon that twisted and twined its way south. These were the facts; this is what Elizabeth told her students year after year.

But of course it was not really the truth, not the whole truth of the lake; standing on the bluff above the protected cove known as West Haven, Elizabeth must acknowledge that to herself. As far as she could see the world was water, a deep and turbulent jade near the shore and jet at its heart, where the storm was already hard at work. A bony finger of lightning touched the horizon and then crackled in satisfaction. Another storm, the third in two days. As if the spirit of the lake had been sitting at Captain Mudge's table when they made their plans and set itself against such foolishness.

Elizabeth wrapped her borrowed cloak tighter around herself and rocked back on her heels with the rising wind, lifting her face to the spray of lake water, mixed now with the warmer rain. She could not stand here much longer, or she would draw attention that they had worked so hard to avoid. Behind her was not only Captain Mudge's home, but the village of Mariah, smaller than Paradise and made up mostly of fishermen and sailors and their families. But the nearest neighbors were far too close for comfort, and Elizabeth had no doubt that they were all very curious about what was going on in Captain Mudge's house. And here she stood at the lookout, a Quaker missionary lady without the sense to come in from the rain.

In the house they would be sitting with the captain at the round table in his little parlor, Nathaniel and Elijah and Splitting-Moon marking three points on the compass with Captain Mudge the fourth, true north. Splitting-Moon would sit with her hands resting lightly on the table in front of her, her head cocked to one side as if she were studying the painting of a shipyard that hung over the hearth, listening intently while they went over maps and charts inch by inch and waited out the weather. Splitting-Moon spoke only a little English and Captain Mudge no Kahnyen'kehàka and so the conversation would move in stops and starts while Nathaniel or Elijah translated. Sailors and soldiers and Kahnyen'kehàka medicine women could be patient, or at least they knew how to hide their worries, a talent that Elizabeth had never possessed in abundance.

And so she stood in the storm, looking down at the captain's schooner *Washington* where it lay at anchor in the cove along with a handful of smaller fishing vessels that rocked in the wind, testing their ropes like dogs eager to be off to the chase. Tomorrow they would board the *Washington* and start north for Canada, a strange thought, the very strangest, for Elizabeth had once vowed never to set foot in Canada again.

She turned back to the house and caught a flash of movement from the corner of her eye. For a moment she paused, trying to make out a familiar dark shape in the deepening shadows of dusk and storm. Nothing. He would show himself when he was ready, and not before.

The path to the house led through a neatly laid out orchard, apple and pear trees all shivering in the wet. She kept her gaze fixed on the ground, unsure of herself in borrowed shoes that pinched at the heel, and wondering if giving up her moccasins as Mrs. Emory insisted hadn't been one precaution too many. Jode took her by surprise, appearing out of a tangle of raspberry canes without a sound.

"Ah." Elizabeth caught a fist against her chest in surprise and relief both. "Jode, we were worried about you."

Captain Mudge's sister had managed to find some kind of

clothing for all of them over the course of their first day in
Mariah, but Jode stood before her now as she had first seen him
in the bush, in nothing but breechclout and leggings, with
summer moccasins on his feet. And she was taken again, as she
always was, by his elegant and vibrant beauty, lithe and power-
ful, with skin not black or brown or any shade that could be
named, because it seemed to shift with the light, sometimes
more copper and then ochre or cinnamon. In the misting rain
the skin of his scalp glistened some color that could not be
named at all, shaved smooth in the fashion of a Kahnyen'kehàka
warrior with a single roach of hair slicked down with bear
grease at the crown. His Kahnyen'kehàka name was Leaping
Elk, and it fit him well.

The muzzle of an old rifle stuck up over his shoulder, and
his chest was crisscrossed with wampum and carry-straps hung
with powder horn and bullet pouches. In the faltering light
the carved handle of his knife gleamed the yellow of old bone
in its beaded sheath. The neighbors might raise a disapproving
eyebrow over Elizabeth standing in the rain, but the sight of
Jode hung about with weapons would evoke a very different
reaction.

He was looking at her with vague distaste, and Elizabeth
realized she had been startled into speaking English. She repeated herself in Mohawk, and then hesitated. "Won't you
come into the house and eat something?"

"I don't need to be fed by you," he said. "I can hunt for
myself and the others."

"Of course you can," Elizabeth said shortly; it would do no
good to try to placate him with gentle words, and even less to
let herself be drawn into an argument. "Do you not worry
that you might be seen?"

He looked at her down the bridge of his nose, an expression
as gracefully disdainful as her aunt Merriweather had ever produced. The truth was that if Jode did not choose to be seen no
one would see him. He had come into the bush as a little boy
with his mother, and he remembered almost nothing of the life
they had led before on a farm outside Albany. At eighteen, he
was the youngest of those who had survived the fever, and he
was by far the angriest of all the escaped slaves, caught up in his
grief for his mother. The boy wanted nothing more than to
care for the family he had left, but they must leave the endless

forests and everything he held familiar. The one thing he could hold tight in his fist was his own anger, anger enough to burn down the world.

They had been traveling together for four days, and every day Nathaniel seemed surprised that Jode had not yet disappeared back into the bush to make his own way.

"Will you at least come and speak to Splitting-Moon, so she doesn't worry about you?"

The impassive expression wavered for just a moment, the dark eyes flicking toward the house and then back to Elizabeth. Nathaniel was wrong to worry about Jode disappearing; where Splitting-Moon went, there would he go.

"Tonight, I will come," he said. And slipped away into the dark.

Elizabeth had not yet decided what to make of the captain's widowed sister. At first appearance Mrs. Emory looked like any other woman of late middle age, a solidly built woman with an open expression and a busy way about her. Her hands were as small as a child's and always full of some kind of needlework. Her son and his wife had taken over the mission she had run with her husband, and her whole joy in life seemed to be sending barrels to them filled with clothing, religious pamphlets, and dried fruit. Even after so many years in the heat and sun of the Guinea coast, she still seemed to think that a good pair of breeches or a skirt could magically transform a man or a woman into the most perfect of beings: a civilized Christian sure of not only a heavenly reward, but happiness on earth.

What Mrs. Emory lacked in reason and understanding, she made up in gentle goodwill, and Elizabeth was thankful that she had opened the door to so many unexpected visitors of three different races without any hesitation. Elizabeth's concerns about this scheme of hers simply disappeared when she discovered that Mrs. Emory had no patience with slavery, and neither did she seem to care very much about the legalities of the task they had been asked to take on. She would leave the laws of man to her brother, but the challenge of food, clothing, and medical attention for so many she saw as a personal assignment sent her way by her departed husband.

But there was a price to pay, because Mrs. Emory was also

given to a furious curiosity that she could not contain. She met Elizabeth at the door to take her wet cloak, ticking like a mantel clock in her dismay.

"I thought I'd have to come out after you, Mrs. Bonner, did I not? In this cold rain, too, and without your tea. And what were you doing so long in the rain? Mr. Quincy has been asking for you, wanting you to read the bible. And of course Mrs. Bonner will read to you, said I to him said I, as soon as she's come in from the weather but now he's gone off to sleep, fevered still, poor man, although Miss Uffa is much improved, is the Almighty not merciful? So many years in the bush without the comfort of his Word, but deliverance came to them as surely—"

"How is Stephan?" Elizabeth interrupted softly, and Mrs. Emory was content to be led off in a different direction. She nodded her head vigorously so that her jowls wobbled.

"Oh, he's doing ever so well, ate two bowls of our Katie's good broth and did he enjoy it? The others too, all of them fed until they could take no more and resting as well they should, poor lambs. Oh, and Mr. Bonner has been asking for you, Mrs. Bonner, and doesn't he seem distracted? With good reason, of course, so much to take on, the best of shepherds but too many sheep, is that not the case? But we must remember, the Lord our God is a merciful God. Mr. Bonner's in the parlor with the captain and the others, will you go through and I'll send in Katie with your tea. Oh, but look, look at your shoes—"

"I'll dry them in front of the hearth," Elizabeth said over her shoulder, and then stopped at the sight of Katie in the hall with a tray in her hands. An African woman as tall as Nathaniel, she was hard to overlook. She had come from Africa because she wouldn't be separated from Mrs. Emory and brought her three boys with her. Elizabeth had rarely heard her speak, but she liked the woman for her calm and quiet competence.

"Go on through then, Mrs. Bonner, Katie will set your place while your shoes dry out."

Selah was sitting in the corner with her son at the breast, half-asleep herself. Elizabeth took the baby from her so that she could rest more easily. Katie went about her work, unaware or unmoved by the fact that the escaped slaves could not take their eyes off her, a woman who had left Africa to come here of her own free will.

Nathaniel put a hand on Elizabeth's knee under the table.

"Tomorrow, Boots," he said. "We'll go down to the ship just before first light."

Elijah turned his attention back to the table. "If the storm passes."

"It will pass," said Splitting-Moon, her face turned toward Elizabeth. "It is already passing." Her cheeks were deeply marked by barely healed grooves she had torn in her skin on the day her son had died, but her voice was as strong and steady, with a hard edge like the bloody crust of a wound that would never heal.

"And Quincy, will he be ready to travel?"

There was a short silence around the table. Captain Mudge leaned forward, pulling on the great bundle of tobacco-stained bristle that served as a mustache. "Quincy will stay here with us," he said. "My sister will nurse him until he is well enough to follow."

"He is dying," said Splitting-Moon calmly, as if the captain hadn't spoken at all, and there was nothing to contradict. "We will say goodbye to him before we go. Bone-in-Her-Back?"

Elizabeth sat up abruptly and the baby made a dissatisfied sound against her shoulder, the small mouth with its suck-blister making a perfect O. "Yes?"

"There was someone at the window behind you just now, I heard steps."

The captain grunted. "That'll be the milch cow wanting to get into the barn—"

"No cow," interrupted Splitting-Moon. "A man."

All three men stood quietly and reached for their weapons.

"Move away," Nathaniel said softly. "Into the corner with Selah—" And he stopped at the sound of a crow's caw. One corner of his mouth turned down in surprise and then up again, in relief.

"Three-Crows," said Captain Mudge, sitting back down again.

"Three-Crows?" Elizabeth echoed, as Nathaniel left the room. "The Mahican?"

Three-Crows was an old friend of Hawkeye's, someone they saw at Lake in the Clouds now and then. "Captain Mudge, how do you know him?"

"Everyone on the Great Lake knows that old rogue," said Captain Mudge. "There never was such a man for talk. Sary thinks she's going to convert him with venison stew and small beer, so he stops by here whenever he's in the area. Happy enough to listen to her preaching while he looks for the bottom of my tankard, is Three-Crows. No doubt he'll be off south tomorrow." He sounded quite pleased with the arrangement, most probably because it gave his sister another focus for her ministry besides himself.

"Maybe he would be willing to take a message to Lake in the Clouds," Elizabeth said. "To reassure the children."

Splitting-Moon's face turned into the candlelight with a stricken expression.

"Your good fortune is still with you, Bone-in-Her-Back," she said, in French this time, the language they had used together before Elizabeth had known much Kahnyen'kehàka. A language that drew them together and separated them from the others. "You have been given a way to comfort your children."

Bonne chance.

Three-Crows was a tough old Mahican of an age with Elizabeth's father-in-law, a small man with straggling gray plaits, his neck and arms like so many lengths of woven leather. He was dressed in a combination of clothes, some of which Elizabeth recognized as Mrs. Emory's handiwork, and some he had been wearing for years, including a pair of buckskin leggings so old and thinned with age that they hung like flaps of his own skin from his hips. On his chest was a tangle of wampum beads and medicine bags and teeth strung on rawhide; for weapons he carried nothing more than a knife and a war club with a head carved to the likeness of a snarling bear. His hands shook a little, most probably with old age and drink both. A slave to the bottle, Mrs. Emory had whispered to Elizabeth when she came in to greet the newest visitor, her mouth set in a purposeful line.

Mrs. Emory stood off to one side with her hands crossed over her bible while Three-Crows worked his way through her stew, willing to let the men have him for a time to discuss their business. Elizabeth was content to listen, too, while Nathaniel laid out their plans. He trusted Three-Crow's judgment—when he was sober—and valued his knowledge of the great lake.

Three-Crows used a crust of bread to wipe the last of the stew from the plate.

"Blackbirders about," he said. "More than usual. You sure they ain't on to your scent?" He spoke English with an accent like Hawkeye's, all softened consonants and oddly off beat, and his voice had a deep rasp to it, as if it were about to fail him.

"Could be," Nathaniel said. "Where'd you see them?"

"All over. The last one on the tail of the lake, two days ago."

Selah cleared her throat. "You know any of them by name, sir?"

Three-Crows reached for his tankard. "I know them all. The one on Lake George, he used to be up north a lot, the Kahnyen'kehàka called him Knife-in-His-Fist. You must know of him." He directed this last to Splitting-Moon in her language. His gaze lingered on her face, studying the blank and sightless eyes without embarrassment or apology.

"Knife-in-His-Fist had an Abenaki grandmother," said Splitting-Moon. "He turned his face away from her people."

Elizabeth said, "He is a man about my height, with a deep scar here"—she drew a line that extended from the corner of her mouth almost to her right ear—"and missing an eye-tooth?" Three-Crows nodded.

"Dye," said Nathaniel. "We've been expecting him to show up, sooner or later."

"Perhaps you have, but I had hoped we might avoid this complication," said Elizabeth, and started when Mudge thumped the table with his fist.

"This man Dye, he got a ship?"

Three-Crows shook his head. "A couple dogs, is all. And a temper."

Mudge thumped the table again so that the pewter plate jumped. "Dam—Close up your ears now, Sary, because I'm going to use them words that get you so wound up." He cleared his throat, his jaw sawing hard. "Then the hell with Dye, say I. Damnation, say I. Unless the man can fly he's no threat to us. I carried Mrs. Bonner all the way to Sorel in the spring mud, ain't that so? Mrs. Bonner and them babies, with the redcoats on our tails. The *Washington* will get you and yours to Lacolle safe and sound, be there a hundred damned blackbirders on the lake."

Elizabeth smiled at him, that smile that she used when somebody needed calming; Nathaniel had seen it work on harder cases than Grievous Mudge, and it worked now.

She said, "Of course you will, Captain. That is why we came to you."

Late in the night Nathaniel found Elizabeth back in the parlor, sitting at the table with its clutter of maps and papers. By the light of a single candle she was cutting a new quill from a turkey feather, the tip of her tongue caught between her teeth in concentration. She was very pale, from sleeplessness and worry, and it hurt him to see it.

"Come in, Nathaniel," she said without looking up. The penknife whispered as she scraped to sharpen the point. "You make me nervous watching there in the dark."

He came to stand beside her, reaching out a hand to grasp her shoulder and feeling the tightness there. "You've got a cramp in your neck."

"Hmmm. I was about to come to bed but I needed—"

"To go over those papers again."

The manumission and traveling papers were neatly laid out on the table, each written out on a different kind of paper, each with a different ink. She had labored over them every night for hours, but the truth was she would never be satisfied. If he asked her she would point out all the imperfections: a poorly chosen word, or an inconsistency in the handwriting she had tried to effect. Elizabeth would never be satisfied with these documents she had fabricated; once she had made up her mind to break the law she would not rest until she had met the challenge.

"I had to rewrite the ones that mention Quincy. And of course that means that I had to sign my father's signature again. I think this time it is more true. Can you imagine how angry he would be to know the part he's playing in this? The dead have no idea how useful they can be on occasion." She looked down at her handiwork and one corner of her mouth went up, in reluctant amusement. "You'll have to sign it again too, Nathaniel." She pointed to the bottom of the sheet.

Nathaniel picked it up and read to himself.

To All people to whom these presents may come,
Know ye that I, Nathaniel Bonner of Hamilton County
in the State of New-York, through and by the power &
authority vested in me by the Yearly Meeting of the
Society of Friends in New-York, do remove to Canada
twelve manumitted and freed Negroes or persons of
colour, to wit: Elijah Middleton, about thirty-five years
old and of dark complexion, Moses Middleton, about
thirty years old and with a yellow complexion, slightly
built & his wife, Conny Middleton, a woman of
medium color with light eyes, about twenty-five years
& Jode Middleton, about eighteen years and mulatto
of complexion, her son. All four of these Negroes
belonged to Judge Middleton & by him were
transferred to the said Society of Friends and thereafter
manumitted and freed. Further I remove...

"Boots, if you had a year you couldn't do a better job."
When he had signed the spot she indicated, he put the quill
down and set his hands on her shoulders to work the tight
muscles. Elizabeth let out a little whimper and arched up to
meet him. After a long minute she said, "I wrote a letter to the
children as well." Her voice had gone suddenly soft and he
didn't need to look at her face to know that she was near losing control over the tears she had been holding back for days.

Nathaniel leaned down to fold his arms around her. In her
ear he said, "They'll like that, having a letter. I expect they'll
argue over who gets to sleep with it under the bed tick."

"Of course," said Elizabeth, smiling a little and rubbing her
cheek against his arm. "I am counting on it. A good argument
will keep them from worrying too much about us."

The clock on the mantel struck two, and Elizabeth looked
up in real surprise. "So late. Did Jode come?"

"He was here for a good hour."

"Ah." Elizabeth let out a great sigh. "And is he coming
with us to Canada?"

"Splitting-Moon thinks he will," Nathaniel said. "But we
won't know for sure until we board the *Washington*—and that
in about three hours, let me remind you."

"You're worried about him."

"Oh aye," Nathaniel said easily. "About him losing his temper at the wrong time, about Dye, about the garrison at Lacolle. There's plenty to worry about, Boots. We don't need to go looking for anything new."

She reached out to take his hand, pressing hard. "We'll manage it together, you and I. We've managed worse."

"Aye, so we have." He ducked his head and blew out the candle, leaving the clutter of maps and plans and papers behind in the dark. They were left with the sounds of the sleeping house and the wind in the trees, the sharp smells of tallow candle, wood smoke, mutton stew. Fear.

Elizabeth let herself be pulled out of the chair and into her husband's arms. It was good to stand with him like this, ready to be led off like a child to her bed, wanting nothing but sleep and forgetfulness for the few hours that were left before they must leave this place and head north. She was far more frightened than she cared to admit, for herself, for him, for the people who slept in the rooms above them, for their children. She let herself relax against Nathaniel to feel the simple fact of him, his calm determination, more comforting than words would ever be.

"I could carry you," he said, his mouth pressed against her hair.

Elizabeth smiled in the dark, because it was true; because he would carry her and did carry her, even when she walked beside him.

Chapter 17

They went down to the ship without lantern or torch to show the way, strung together along the footpath like buttons on a string. Captain Mudge led with Elijah close behind. Splitting-Moon followed her husband by means of a rawhide thong looped around his waist on one end and her wrist on the other, just as Kahnyen'kehàka warriors had once led kidnapped women and children away from their homes.

Why this image came to Elizabeth she did not know, but it made her shudder. She was second to the last in the line, with Nathaniel bringing up the rear. Her husband at her back had always been enough to steady her resolve, but now she saw before her a dozen people, every one of them here only because she had thought to suggest it. They might have made their way north through the endless forests with Nathaniel to lead them, but she would not have him gone so long: it was her impatience that had brought them here. Elizabeth shivered in spite of the broadcloth cloak and heavy skirts, her pulse drumming wildly in her throat.

A movement off to the left and she drew up short.

"No cause for alarm," said Nathaniel softly. "Just Katie's sons standing guard. Any blackbirders hanging around here will have to get through them first."

"I wish Jode would come." Elizabeth spoke to him over her shoulder and got no answer, because of course there was nothing to say; the boy would come or he would stay behind.

The smell of the lake grew strong and stronger and then the wild roses and juniper that lined the path gave way to hard-packed dirt embedded with thousands of mussel shells. Shacks of sail menders and rope makers kept watch in the shadows like sagging old soldiers; someone had nailed a piece of paper to a door and it flapped weakly in the breeze. Barrels and buckets and hogsheads, the ruins of a canoe and a cold fire pit, all the smells that added up to docks: rusting metal and rotting fish and tar and a hundred other things Elizabeth could not name.

A lantern flickered into life at the foot of the gangplank to show Captain Mudge standing there in its light. Elijah started straight up, but Splitting-Moon hesitated and turned toward the warmth of the lantern, her face a strange copper moon hovering for that moment between land and water. Elizabeth stepped onto the wharf, slick with dew and fish oil, and almost lost her footing.

In the shadows beneath the captain's tricorne Elizabeth could not make out his face but she felt the fine tension that rolled off him, a hum like bees in the distance. He boarded after Nathaniel, quick for all his girth, and called out to the sailors—good and silent and well-paid men, he had promised—and just that easily the sails were raised to catch the wind.

There would be no more turning back. Elizabeth hesitated at the rail, caught by the sight of the brightening sky in the east. The sun would come soon and when it set again they would be more than halfway to Canada. If the winds were kind; if the revenue agents and blackbirders and border guards happened to be looking the other way.

Nathaniel pressed her elbow. Elizabeth followed the others to the aft cabin house, and there was Jode, standing tall and defiant until he caught sight of Splitting-Moon. He looked away, and straightened his shoulders, shrugging off the boy in him that wanted to go to her and put his head on her breast.

She had forgotten the noise a ship could make, wood and rope and sails and wind all groaning in tandem, a clutter of sound that itched until it bored its way beneath the skin and became as unremarkable as the rush of one's own breathing. They were crowded, all of them, into the aft cabin house that served as captain's quarters and chart room, barely large enough for four. Selah and Splitting-Moon took the berth and Stephan, the weakest of the men, the only chair; some sat on the chart table and the rest of them sat on the floor, shoulder to shoulder. They sat in silence and listened to the wind that moved the *Washington* like a skitter bug across the surface of a pond.

Elizabeth thought she might never be able to sleep again and so it took her by surprise, one moment to be sitting across from Uffa, studying the solemn thin face, and the next to wake to a cabin filled with bars of sunlight from the shuttered windows that opened onto the deck.

"I dreamt of Julian," she said aloud, to hear her own voice and to mark the dream.

"You always dream about your brother when you're on the water." Nathaniel eased his arm out from under her head and flexed it to loosen cramped muscles.

Pico handed her a dipper from the water barrel that sat near the door. She drank most of it and rubbed the rest into her eyes to open them to the day.

"Where is Jode? Did I dream him too?"

One corner of Nathaniel's mouth turned down. "He's up on deck with Isaiah."

"Is that a good idea?"

He shrugged. "As long as we don't all crowd up there at once."

"Two by two, like Noah." Uffa had a hoarse, almost toneless voice, but its strangeness was tempered by her smile. She held out her open ditty bag toward Elizabeth. "Hungry?"

In each canvas bag Mrs. Emory had packed a great bounty and variety of food: venison jerky, cornbread filled with nuts, flatbread spread with pork lard, blood sausage, onions in crackly skins, dried apples and pears, a pungent cheese that crumbled on the tongue. Elizabeth took some dried apple and a piece of cornbread and, when the older woman's brow creased in concern, a bit of the sausage as well.

The men ate in silence but the women whispered among themselves in English and Kahnyen'kehàka and Dutch. Splitting-Moon, Selah, Conny, Flora, Uffa, Dorcas—Elizabeth studied each of their faces and remembered them as she had first seen them, weeping soundlessly over a new grave scratched out of the forest floor. There was a watchfulness about these women, but neither their sorrow nor the long walk to the lake had been enough to break them. Dressed in the clothes Mrs. Emory had provided, hastily dyed in shades of muddy gray, the women put Elizabeth in mind of winter sparrows crowded together for warmth, and willing to take comfort and hope where they found it.

The men worried her more. Stephan because of his fragile health, Charlie because of his prolonged silence—Elizabeth doubted that she had heard more than five words from him together—Pico and Markus for the depth of their mourning, and Jode and Elijah for the pure power of their anger. Quaker gray could not dull that, or even hide it.

"Would you care for some of African Katie's bread?"

Elizabeth was startled out of her thoughts. Dorcas had eyes the color of brandy, a soft sweet voice, and a mass of scar tissue on her cheek where there had once been a brand mark. An *R*, Dorcas had explained, making the shape in the air with a sweep of one finger. Runaway. And she had opened the deerskin pouch she wore around her neck to show Elizabeth the part of herself she had refused to keep but could not discard, a dry and wizened dark curl of flesh.

"So I never forget," she had explained.

"There's no need to whisper," Elizabeth told her now. "You could sing at the top of your voices and no one would hear you out here on the water."

But the women smiled at her suggestion in surprise and unease, as if she had told them that they could fly.

The door opened and Jode appeared there, looking awkward and out of place in leather jerkin, homespun shirt, and breeches. Behind him was Elijah, who carried what looked like a great chunk of polished bone in two cupped hands.

"Now what have you got there?" asked Dorcas, standing up to get a better look.

Elijah stepped over people to reach Splitting-Moon. "A tooth. At least that's what the old sailor claims. Said Splitting-Moon could tell us about it."

It did indeed look like a tooth with its three long pronged roots, but it was the size of a large man's fist. Elijah put it in his wife's cupped hands, and she ran her fingers lightly over the surface, weighing the shape and then holding it up to sniff.

Elizabeth said, "Which old sailor?"

"Little man with a red cap. Calls himself Tim Card."

"Tim Card!" Elizabeth put a hand on Nathaniel's arm. "Do you remember I told you about Mr. Card? The last time I sailed with Captain Mudge he was on board. Oh, the stories he told... About pirates, and privateers, and Button Bay."

Selah said, "I suppose a giant tooth has got some story behind it." She had taken the tooth from Splitting-Moon and was turning it in her hands. "Look here, grooves. Like he was gnawing on something."

"The old man claims it's an angel tooth," said Jode, who hadn't moved from his spot by the door. "Says that all along the waterways you can dig and find the bones of angels that fell in the battle for the heavens."

"Never thought I'd see no angel bones," said Stephan, his voice still a little raw from the fever he had left behind.

"That old sailor told us he seen leg bones almost twenty feet long where he found that tooth." Jode said this in his usual diffident tone, but the excitement was clear on his face. "Don't believe in angels, though."

Pico reached up from his spot to swat at Jode with one of Mrs. Emory's religious pamphlets. "How do you know that tooth didn't come from an angel?"

The boy snorted, and looked away over his shoulder.

Conny said, "Well, I believe it. Mrs. Emory read to me from the bible not two days ago about big angels coming down to earth."

"That wasn't nothing to do with angels." Uffa frowned down at the tooth in Stephan's hands. "It was giants. Ain't that so?" She turned to Elizabeth.

"From Genesis," she agreed.

"Go on and quote." Nathaniel poked her lightly, not even trying to hide his grin. "You know you can't leave it."

Elizabeth poked him back, but she raised her voice so that they could all hear.

"'In those days were the giants on the earth, and also afterwards, when the sons of God had come in to the daughters of men, and they had borne children to them; these were the heroes, who of old were men of renown.'"

"I swear, there must be a hundred books in that head of yours." Selah smiled at her from across the cabin. "Can't see how you remember all them words."

"Now how do you get from giants in the earth to fallen angels, that's what I want to know," sniffed Flora. "And maybe it ain't real anyway. Could be carved, out of ivory or some wood. Nathaniel ain't said a word, and neither have you, Splitting-Moon. Is it real?"

Nathaniel said, "It's real. I've seen the bones, and so has Splitting-Moon."

They all went very still, but their faces were bright with differing degrees of disquiet and interest. Jode just looked irritated. To Splitting-Moon he said, "You never told us stories of giants."

She turned her face in his direction. In the bright morning light the scars on her face stood out in crimson ridges, as if she had painted herself for battle. Her head tilted to one side slightly and she smiled a little, the smile a mother reserved for an impatient child.

"There are hundreds of stories," she said. "It will be many years before you have heard them all, and longer still before you understand them." She said this softly, but Jode dropped his head as if she had shouted.

"Can we have the story, then?" Dorcas leaned forward. "It would help pass the time."

Splitting-Moon let the silence draw out and then she cleared her throat and raised her voice so that it filled the little cabin.

"In the longhouse my fathers tell the story of the giants who lived among us long ago. They speak of Weetucks, who stood as tall as the top of the tallest trees, and his brother, Maughkompos, who stood still taller. Maughkompos could stand in the middle of the great river and catch up a sturgeon as big as a man in one hand. Weetucks could knock Sister Bear out of the tree where she hid from him. No animal could run fast enough to be safe from the race of giants. No teeth were long enough to hurt them, no claws sharp enough.

"They were such good hunters that little by little the giants killed many of the animals in the forest and drove away the others. The deer and bear and elk and buffalo and the beaver, all of them left and went to the far north, where no giants walked the earth. And our hunters came home empty-handed, and the people grew hungry and cold, for there was no meat or even a single beaver pelt to be had.

"The Master of Life saw what trouble the giants had caused among his people, and he was angered. So he called forth lightning and smote them all, and wiped their race from the earth. Their bones he left behind, to remind my people of the giants, and how they brought about their own end."

"Greed," announced Dorcas, switching from Kahnyen'-kehàka to English. "It was greed that done it."

Charlie stood suddenly, his whole body shaking. A man of middle years, short of stature but strongly built, he put Elizabeth in mind of the stunted oak that stood just outside her schoolhouse, not only for his build but because he seemed to have been struck to the core by the loss of his wife and daughter. Elizabeth often heard him weeping in his sleep; he moved through the day like a dream walker.

"Pride cometh," he called out in a harsh voice, raising his fists to his face. "Pride cometh and then the fall. The angels fell and the giants and we fell too. God used that fever to smite our prideful selves. We grew proud and he punished us, sure enough. He took the children." He turned his head to look at each of them, pointing with a trembling finger. "He took your Joshua and your Mariah and Billy and my girl, my sweet girl, my Meg." He swung around suddenly toward Selah. "He took our children and he'll take your boy too."

He collapsed as abruptly as he had stood, and drew his knees up to his face, bending forward as if he could disappear inside himself by pure force of will.

All the women seemed to turn toward Selah at once, but she held up a palm to stop them, shaking her head very slightly. Then she got up from the berth where she had been sitting with her son in her lap and picked her way across the room to Charlie. A whistle sounded on the deck and the captain's voice rose in command, and then Selah crouched down next to Charlie and put a hand on his head. She stayed there like that without saying a word and they all waited with her until a shudder ran through the bowed shoulders and Charlie lifted his head.

The two of them looked at each other for a long time, the young woman and the older man with tears running unchecked down slack and stubbled cheeks. Selah never smiled but there was an openness to her expression, a seeking that seemed to reach him. He blinked at her and blinked again, his mouth working without making any sound at all.

Selah said, "Will you hold my son for me? I'd sure like to

go stretch my legs a while, but I'm afraid to take him up on deck, in case I slip. Will you hold him? His name is Galileo, named for his granddaddy."

Charlie swallowed so hard that the muscles in his throat clenched convulsively. He said, "Galileo was the one who showed me the way to Red Rock, when I was first a voyager."

"This is his grandson," Selah said in her calmest voice. "Will you look after him for a little while for me? I would appreciate it."

A trembling went through him. After a long moment when no one moved or spoke or even breathed, his shoulders came up and his back straightened by degrees, and then, finally, his fists relaxed.

Selah put the sleeping child there in the cradle Charlie made of his arms. The baby flexed in his sleep, eyes fluttering and his mouth working noisily until he settled again.

"Thank you," said Selah. She got up gracefully and turned away to Elizabeth and Nathaniel. "Will you come up on deck with me? I'd like to walk a little."

The day passed slowly, divided between walks on the deck and the cabin, food and sleep and talk, and one short period in which the weapons—brought to the ship in the dead of night and hidden behind a false bulkhead—were taken out to be checked and cleaned. Quakers did not bear arms, and it was as Quakers they would pass safely into Canada; as uneasy as it made them all, the rifles and muskets and hunting knives were put back in their hiding place.

With every ship that passed without note or hail Elizabeth's smile became a little less forced. Most were just merchant vessels, schooners and bateaux and great clumsy rafts that hugged the shore, but one navy cutter overtook them without a second look. Nathaniel saw how ready Elizabeth was to be cheered, how pleased she was by the good spirits in the crowded cabin, where the voyagers had fallen into the kind of storytelling that makes time pass, each of them trying to best the one that went before with the most outrageous or oddest tale.

They spoke of childhood pranks and tricks played, of spiders outwitted by flies and cats made to look foolish by mice, of people who grew wings and witch women whose love potions found unlikely targets. Pico told the story of a bullfrog in a pair of breeches that made Elizabeth laugh until she cried. They did not speak of death or the graves so recently dug, of escaping to the north or the lives they had run from; neither did they speak of the future, of the lives they might lead in Canada.

With each story the fear that had given them the energy to come this far was driven back a little. All of the voyagers began to show more interest in the world outside the cabin, even Charlie, who had been roused from his grief by a giant's tooth. Most of them ventured on deck for a few minutes to see the countryside on either side of the lake, the blue haze of the mountains rolling away to the west, the startling green of forests that crowded down to the lakeshore. Jode went on deck more and more often, drawn by fresh air and sharp wind and the sight of the sailors at work. As the day wore on the other men grew restless and went up in revolving groups of twos and threes. Nathaniel watched them from the window that opened onto the deck and caught pieces of their conversations.

They wondered about everything, the working of the sails and the windlass and the wheel; they asked each other questions that couldn't be answered about the things they saw on shore: how long a rotting hulk had been settling into a stretch of shoreline and how it had come to ground itself, how many kinds of ducks could be found on this water, if a strong man could swim from one shore to the other, how long it took to build the big rafts that moved timber to the mills. Sometimes Captain Mudge came to give them a few words about their progress, and Tim Card found them a willing audience when he could spare the time from his duties.

The old sailor was never at a loss for a story to tell; simply by scanning the lake something would come to him. As he listened at the cabin window, it seemed to Nathaniel that most of Card's tales seemed to be woven together, bits of Indian stories, of myth and bible stories and wars. It made a strange picture, little Tim Card with his bristled chin and tufts of white hair sticking out of the holes in his cap, surrounded by black men twice his size who bowed their heads politely, listening with real interest to stories of fur smugglers, Tory duplicity, and fallen angels.

Elizabeth came to stand beside Nathaniel, leaning against

the window casement with her arms crossed low and her chin on her chest. She listened with a half-smile as Tim pointed out landmarks and refought, moment by moment, the Battle of Champlain and the burning of the American fleet. His voice drifted to them in snatches: *General Arnold* and *snuck out from under their noses* and *gave them a run the likes of which.*

In her Quaker gray Elizabeth seemed not quite herself, contained somehow and made smaller, but when she turned her head to smile at him the fire and fight of her were still bright on her face. She held out a hand and he took it, to trace the calluses and ink stains and to press her palm against his mouth and touch her skin with his tongue so that she jumped and pulled her hand away, sending him a look that was meant to be a reprimand but didn't quite manage to hide the spark he had ignited.

She pursed her lips and pointed with her chin to the men who stood with Tim Card at the rail. "With every mile they are more returned to themselves."

Nathaniel put a hand on her shoulder. "I was just thinking the same thing about you, Boots."

"Were you?" She lifted her face, heart-shaped and pale and sincere, to him to show him her surprise. The gray of her eyes seemed almost silver in the sunshine, and he noticed for the first time a thread of white in her hair. At that moment he could see the resolute old woman she would become someday, steely in her bones.

He said, "What do you think you would be doing now if you had never left England?"

She inclined her head. "Looking after my cousin's children, visiting my brother in debtor's gaol, and writing extracts from library books, no doubt. What do you think?"

"Sometimes I wonder if you might have got it in your head to write books, like your Mrs. Wollstonecraft."

She put a hand to her mouth and laughed. "This is a new approach, Nathaniel. Most usually when you are taken with a fit of remorse and worry for my well-being you simply tell me I should have been safer had I stayed in England. Now you have me giving up fame and fortune as a lady writer to come to the wilderness. Very inventive."

Nathaniel put an arm around her shoulders to pull her to him. "You would have been safer, that's true."

She pressed her face to his chest and laughed so that her shoulders shook and he felt the warmth of her damp breath through his linen.

"If you keep laughing at me we'll have to have a little talk. One of those discussions you like so much." He said this against her ear, and felt her laugh shift to a different kind of shudder. "When we're alone."

She pulled away and touched her face with the handkerchief she pulled from her sleeve. "Don't be silly," she said finally. "We won't be alone for another two days at least, Nathaniel Bonner. You'll just have to save your . . . lecture until then." And she ducked away before he could pin her there against the wall to prove her wrong, laughing at him over her shoulder.

A great shouting on deck and she froze just like that, the smile wiped from her face. The door was flung open and Elijah appeared there with Jode and Pico close behind.

"We're heaving-to." Elijah said it tonelessly, his voice almost lost in the noise coming from the deck: orders shouted, the groaning of the ship, and sailors moving double-time.

"What is it?" asked Splitting-Moon. "Why are we slowing?"

Nathaniel leaned out the window to repeat the question to one of the sailors as he trotted by. He didn't like the answer he got but he passed it on anyway.

"Customs signaled. They're coming on board."

Elizabeth said, "But we are still hours from the border." She was fighting to keep her tone even, but it didn't matter—every face in the cabin was still with fear.

"It's sooner than we expected, that's true. But it won't do any good to panic."

That got him what he needed: she flashed him a hard look and her fear gave way to indignation. Before she could protest he leaned down to look her directly in the eye.

"You've stood up to the governor of Lower Canada, to common criminals and Jack Lingo and to peers of the realm, Boots. I think you can manage a few customs agents." He turned to the others as he reached to take his hat from its nail on the wall. Broad brimmed and low in the crown, for now he must be the Quaker he professed himself to be.

"Cover your heads and put on your sober faces. We're going up on deck to take the air, all of us."

Jode made a move toward the false bulkhead, but Elijah stepped in front of him, put a hand on his shoulder and said nothing at all. The boy jerked free, but he could not stare Elijah down. When he dropped his gaze the older man said, "Stay close to Splitting-Moon."

Elizabeth had dealt with customs officers before, and on this very ship. At that time, with Nathaniel and his father being held in Canada as spies, she had been too distracted wondering how she was going to break them out of gaol before they went to the gallows to take any note of such things.

Now she must pay attention, and she did not like what she saw. They had passed from the southern part of the lake—the Broad, as the captain called it—to this region of islands and shoals to weave their way along the New-York shoreline. To the east a handful of schooners and cutters lay at anchor in a small harbor of an island, among them a ship flying the colors of the American navy and another of the customs patrol, but more disturbing still: a bateau headed their way. She counted six oarsmen, a number of customs officials and marines. Trailing after the bateau were two canoes, but it was the marines that had caught Elizabeth's attention.

"Marines assigned to customs officials? Is that normal?"

Nathaniel shrugged. "Those canoes worry me more."

"They look like Kahnyen'kehàka to me," said Elizabeth. "Don't you know them?"

"Stone-Bird in the far canoe," said Nathaniel. "Probably been downlake, trading."

Elizabeth caught the tone of his voice, tight and uneasy, and looked again to see what she had missed. "Surely that must be good news, if they are headed for Good Pasture? We need not travel alone."

And she stopped, because at that moment she realized what she was seeing—who she was seeing—in the second canoe. The nearer canoe. Two men, and one of them was Liam Kirby.

Nathaniel caught her elbow as she swayed. "Steady on," he whispered. "Steady."

"But—"

He squeezed her arm hard enough to leave a bruise. "Don't let on."

Don't let on. Panic crawled up her spine like milling wasps. She shook her head sharply to clear it and when she looked up again Liam Kirby was still there, paddling toward them in this gilded hour before sunset with the light on his hair, such a deep and startling red that there could be no mistake. A few more moments would bring him to the *Washington*.

Elizabeth's mind raced but she could think of nothing but Liam standing in the damp shadows in Axel Metzler's tavern and the anger etched deep into the bones of his face when he spoke of his brother. If he had wanted a way to revenge himself upon Nathaniel he would find one here, on this deck.

Nathaniel pulled her closer and spoke so low that she could barely make him out. "I don't think he's seen us yet. The angle's wrong. Come."

She followed him wordlessly until they stood near the far rail with the voyagers. It was a singular talent Nathaniel had, this ability to move through the world in the worst of circumstances as if he were simply walking across his own porch on a bright day. A talent that Elizabeth would have paid a high price to possess, especially right at this moment. She forced herself to take three deep breaths.

No escape. Nowhere to run. No weapons but their wits. She choked down a hysterical sound, more laugh than scream.

"Ahoy!" Captain Mudge called out to the approaching bateau. He stood at the rail with his hands crossed at his back and his beard fluttering in the breeze like a tattered flag, the very picture of an old sea captain at home on these waters. He seemed not at all worried by the customs officers or the canoes or anything else, but then he could not recognize Liam; he did not realize the trouble within reach.

"What are we going to do?"

"Hold steady."

A swelling anger swept away her fear. Anger at Liam Kirby, at Nathaniel, at herself most of all. She could not help but look over the faces that had grown so familiar to her already, these people who had withstood so much; she had brought them to this. They should have listened to Jode, who stood at the rail with Selah to one side and Splitting-Moon at the other. The simple strength of their combined concern for him kept the boy there as securely as a child on a tether.

The bateau reached the *Washington* with a bump and the

customs officer came up the rope ladder, small and sharp with bright, darting dark eyes that fixed on the captain. With a great cry he clasped one of Mudge's hands in both his own and shook it fiercely.

"Jed Allen," said Nathaniel.

"Another Allen?"

He shrugged, a muscle in his cheek fluttering softly. "You can't spit on this lake without hitting one of the Allen kin."

Elizabeth tried to clear her thoughts. Was this good news, or bad? She said, "Will he recognize you?"

"I doubt it. Haven't seen him in twenty years or more."

The captain and his cousin were exchanging news, but Elizabeth could not concentrate on anything but that spot where Liam Kirby would first show his face. He would come on board and point them out for imposters and criminals; he would take not only Selah and her child, but all of them. Every one. In her stomach fear roiled like the sea itself, hot and brackish.

Jed Allen turned and leaned over the rail to shout down at the bateau. "Mr. Thistlewaite! I need you here!"

"The clerk," Nathaniel whispered at her ear. He had stepped back so that he could speak to her and watch what was happening at the same time. "If Kirby does come on board, there's a chance he won't give us away, with you here. Just a chance he won't want to see you go to gaol."

"Selah." She hissed the name. "Where can she hide?" Even as she said the words she knew the answer: nowhere. The deck was open to examination; to reach the false bulkhead where the weapons were hid, Selah would have to cross the length of the ship. It would be like waving a flag.

"Here's the clerk, now. Keep a calm face and don't turn around."

The clerk was an elderly man, but he came on board as nimbly as a boy and landed with a soft thump. He carried a great register book in a sling across his chest and a lead pencil stuck in the corner of his mouth like a pipe, but most important was the fact that Mr. Thistlewaite was dressed much as they were, in simple gray, and his hair was cut in a straight line across his forehead. A Quaker, then. Surely there was some good sign to be read in that fact.

"Mr. Thistlewaite!" Jed Allen shouted. "Are you ready?"

The old man fumbled the great register open across a barrel, took the pencil from his mouth, and nodded.

"I am ready, yes indeed."

"Make record of the cargo!" Mr. Allen's voice was all thunder and bark now that he had taken up his business, but his cousin the captain seemed not in the least intimidated. He ran his fingers through his beard and glanced down over the rail at the men who had still not come on board. *He's looking at Liam,* Elizabeth thought. *But he doesn't know that.*

"A dozen keg of nails, three dozen barrels of potash," recited Captain Mudge. "But there's no need to write that down, man, it's none of it bound for Canada and I won't be paying tax on what stays in New-York State. It's passengers we're transporting, as you can see. Quaker missionaries."

Both men turned to look at them, Mr. Thistlewaite squinting through his spectacles and Mr. Allen craning his head forward in a motion like a chicken swallowing.

"Quakers, by God." Mr. Allen seemed to take them in for the first time. "Where did you dig up Quaker missionaries, Grievous? And black ones, on top of that?"

"Bound to preach to the Mohawk," said the captain, ignoring the question that had been asked. "They've got their work cut out for 'em."

"The Mohawk, is that so. Mr. Thistlewaite, did you hear that?"

"I did, yes indeed."

"And what do you think of such a thing?"

The older man blinked in surprise. "Why, not much at all, no indeed. God's work, so it is." The bateau bumped against the *Washington* again and Mr. Thistlewaite glanced down toward the water. When he raised his head again he met Elizabeth's gaze and held it for just a moment too long.

Mr. Allen swung back to the captain. "You've seen their papers, have you, Grievous?"

"I have," said the captain very solemnly. "They look to be in order."

"That's good enough for me. Is it good enough for you, Mr. Thistlewaite, or do you want to make a record in your book?"

Elizabeth pressed her handkerchief to her mouth while she watched the old man struggle with the question. Behind the lenses of his spectacles his eyes seemed overlarge, more than human, owllike, seeing things left in the shadows and dark places. A servant of two masters, his own conscience and the job he had been entrusted to carry out. Elizabeth saw all that on his face but there was more as he looked over the faces of the voyagers. Pity, and resignation.

"No, sir, no indeed," he said finally. "But there's the matter of Mr. Cobb and his associate waiting, sir. He'll want to have a look, so he will."

Mr. Cobb. Elizabeth must have made some sound in her throat because Nathaniel had taken her arm again and his grip was hard.

There's a blackbirder in the city, name of Cobb . . . Don't speak of the devil no more, he might just appear.

"Damn the blackbirders!" barked Mr. Allen. "They've boarded every ship to come through here for the last week and found not a single runaway for the trouble. This is Captain Grievous Mudge, Mr. Thistlewaite. If Grievous Mudge has seen the papers and is satisfied then so must Mr. Cobb be satisfied."

"Indeed, sir," said Mr. Thistlewaite. "But he's coming on board all the same and Mr. Kirby with him."

A sudden calm came over Elizabeth, as if she were a vessel filled to the brim with fear and could simply take no more. Then she realized Nathaniel was turning away, toward hushed voices and the rattle of metal. She turned too, and there was Splitting-Moon with Selah's child in her arms.

Selah herself stood at the rail, holding a twenty-pound keg of nails wrapped in a tangle of rope, some of it looped around her arms and neck. There was nothing of fright in her expression, nothing but resolution. She was four strides away; she was already gone. She met Elizabeth's gaze and mouthed a single word.

Curiosity.

With her arms wrapped around the keg Selah rolled over the rail as silently and gracefully as a bird launching itself from a cliff and disappeared into the great lake, just as the blackbirders stepped on board the *Washington*.

Elizabeth swooned. When she came to herself again moments later she was still on her feet, suspended between Nathaniel and Jode, two strong men shuddering with a rage they dared not vent. All around her the faces of the voyagers were blank with a stunned fear. And Selah was not among them; Selah was gone.

Elizabeth heard a whimpering coming from her own throat. Nathaniel's arm tightened across her back. Senseless noise coming from his mouth in a low whisper, the same sounds over and over until they began to make sense. Meant not just for her but for Jode too, a low chant in Kahnyen'kehàka.

"She sacrificed herself for the boy. Think of the boy, now. Think of the boy."

Curiosity's grandson. Behind them he was fussing, a small hiccuping cry. Elizabeth freed herself with a jerk and turned. Splitting-Moon was rocking the baby against her chest, humming to him. His mother's death song.

Elizabeth took the child without a word and his weight, the solid fact of him, brought her back to herself and anchored her among the living. She paced her breathing to this child she had helped into the world; a child she would have to deliver now to his grandmother.

She forced herself to raise her head and consider the men who were here to stop her.

The unremarkable Mr. Cobb stood almost directly in front of her, his head bent over the papers she had forged so carefully. There was nothing of the mad dog about him; he looked to her more like a traveler long on the road, ill-tempered and over-wrought. Liam held himself apart, standing as far away from them as he could, his arms crossed on his chest and his expression unreadable. Selah had chosen her own kind of flight from these two, but the others could not; her son could not.

She sought out Liam's gaze, and held it. Watched his expression shift from righteous knowing to uncertainty, from uncertainty to anger, from anger to discomfort. He looked away once when Mr. Thistlewaite spoke to him and then back again, hesitantly, like a child drawn to the fire he has been warned about.

The boy in her arms whimpered and Elizabeth gave him her little finger to suckle, but she did not give up Liam's gaze. If he had it in his heart to betray them, he would do it looking at her; he would do it knowing what he wrought.

Cobb was asking questions. Nathaniel answered in the

calmest and most reasonable of tones; as if the world were a sane and reasonable place. He recited, word for word, the answers they had practiced together while Elizabeth held Liam's gaze. While Cobb called out the names and matched them to the faces who claimed them, she held Liam's gaze.

There was another long silence while Cobb studied the papers with the air of a schoolboy confounded by a calculation. A crease appeared between his brows.

"There are twelve blacks listed here, but I see only eleven. One of the wenches is missing."

"Dead in childbirth," said Nathaniel. Speaking one part of the truth. Elizabeth shuddered to hear it.

Cobb's gaze rested for a moment on the child in Elizabeth's arms. He grunted. "And what about that red nigger back there? I don't see any mention of her here."

A muscle fluttered in Nathaniel's cheek, the worst of signs, but the man before him could not know that. He said, "She is Mohawk. She has never been a slave."

Cobb's thin mouth turned down and seemed to disappear into his face. "That's what's wrong with the whole damn country. A red nigger Quaker." He shook his head in disgust and then a sly look came over him. He glanced toward Liam over his shoulder.

"A Mohawk woman here, Kirby," he shouted. "Maybe you want to have a taste, seeing how you're still looking for the one that run off from you." Cobb snorted a laugh, the tip of his tongue thrust out between his teeth.

Elizabeth felt Nathaniel jerk in surprise and then struggle to calm himself, even as she watched Liam first flush to the roots of his hair and then go pale with the fury of a patient man. She caught his eye and he went very still and in that moment she knew that they were saved. Somewhere a Mohawk woman— not Hannah, surely he could not be talking about Hannah— was unaware that she had saved a handful of people standing on this ship. Cobb had saved them by summoning her image to stand here. The Mohawk woman who was not Hannah, unnamed, unknown, had finished the job that Selah had begun.

With one last look at Elizabeth, Liam turned away and said a few words to the captain, and then he left the *Washington,* disappearing down the ladder rope.

In her relief, Elizabeth clutched the boy to her so fiercely that he wailed. Cobb pivoted toward the sound, still laughing. He pulled a piece of paper from his jerkin and held it up. A poster, much folded and water stained.

"It's this woman I'm after." He circled with it held high, raised his voice toward the crew. "Any sign of this runaway wench?"

His circle brought him back around to Elizabeth and Nathaniel, and he stepped closer with his poster, held it up to their faces. "You haven't seen this black? None of your Quaker friends got her hid in a cellar somewhere?"

It was a crude piece of work, poorly printed on rough paper. *Five hundred dollars reward for the capture of the runaway slave and murderess called Ruth.* A rough drawing of a young woman with a bloody knife in an upraised fist. Wild-eyed, treacherous, unknowable.

Just this morning Selah had laughed with the rest of them at Pico's stories. When most mothers would have run in fear at Charlie's outburst, she had smiled kindly and asked him to hold her son. Selah, at the bottom of the lake with a keg of nails cradled in her arms.

Cobb stood watching her, his expression eager and curious and twitching with want. His stink lay about him like a shadow, full and ripe, so that the knotted fist deep in Elizabeth's belly suddenly punched upward without warning. She bent forward with the force of it, her body curled over the child as she spewed bile across the deck, spattering Cobb from foot to waist. He let out a cry of disgust and jumped back, swatting at himself.

Someone took the child, and Nathaniel held her shoulders while she retched. When Elizabeth finally raised her head, Cobb was gone.

Late that night, as the *Washington* sat anchored in Canadian waters, the longboat took the voyagers to the spot where Stone-Bird had promised Captain Mudge he would wait for them. Splitting-Moon sat in the bow between two oarsmen in a circle of light from a lantern that swayed overhead on a pole. With every stroke of the oars the light played out to gild the rippling water.

Standing on the deck of the *Washington,* Elizabeth watched as the boat slowed and then stopped. One by one, the voyagers slipped into the lake to wade to shore in darkness. Jode had already reclaimed his buckskins and leggings and weapons; in the night he might have been any Kahnyen'kehàka hunter. The women trailed behind with skirts kittled up, their arms wrapped around each other. Elizabeth could not see them once they were away from the boat, but she could hear them weeping for relief and sorrow.

Beside them, Captain Mudge said, "They'll be safe now. Stone-Bird will see them to Good Pasture, you can be sure of that."

Nathaniel answered him, empty talk of weather and trails and distances to be covered; Elizabeth turned her face away. Let the captain believe her to be overcome with grief and anxiety, if only to hide those feelings she found so distasteful in herself: she was faint with relief to see the last of the voyagers. Let Stone-Bird deal with them, with Stephan's fever and Charlie's weeping and the women's bent backs. They were no longer her concern; she would put them out of her mind and heart and conscience, and turn all her attention to the boy.

The longboat had already begun to make its way back to the ship, the rhythm of the oars cutting water as steady as a heartbeat. Within the hour the captain would give the order and the *Washington* would turn about and sail south, toward home. Where her own children waited; where Selah's son would find a home with his father's people.

Nathaniel's breath on her hair, warm and slightly sweet. She raised her eyes to him, saw the way the lantern light etched the lines on his face and made his expression more severe. The downward turn of his mouth, the resolute set of his jaw when he looked at the sleeping child in her arms.

"Take us home." She was surprised to hear herself say the words aloud, but Nathaniel was not. He laid a hand against her cheek, and nodded.

NEW-YORK CITY

APRIL 19, 1802

Midday. Fort Hunter.

Left Paradise at first light. Threatening rain clouds to the west for most of the day, but the roads remained dry. Flies a plague to horses and people alike. Hooded mergansers on the rail of the ferry when we crossed the Mohawk, a good sign. The river very high but the crossing uneventful.

Kitty claims not to be in pain but she willingly took willow bark at midday and again in the late afternoon without her usual complaints.

In Johnstown we saw a young boy selling newspapers, large of head and with a normal trunk but his limbs only half their expected length. He stared at me quite openly. I expect he had never seen a Kahnyen'kehàka woman dressed as I am for this journey, as I had never seen one of his kind.

I will be glad when it is behind us.

Chapter 18

Kitty Witherspoon Middleton Todd was, as Hannah had known she would be, a difficult patient and a worse traveler. Frail and fractious, she was capable of manufacturing indignities and pains to complement the real ones that were part of any long journey. And she was exactly the distraction that Hannah needed. During the day, at least, Kitty allowed her no time to think of Liam Kirby and the things they had said to each other; there was little opportunity to worry about her father and Elizabeth on their way into the bush with Selah, Manny Freeman, or what waited for her at the Kine-Pox Institution.

Kitty was one kind of distraction, but there was Ethan as well. Hannah had anticipated that Kitty's son might need as much of her attention as his mother. He was a good and biddable child, but any nine-year-old boy would have to be kept amused and out of danger during river crossings and in the city crowds. By the end of the first day, Hannah realized that she had underestimated Ethan, who turned out to be the very best kind of partner in the undertaking before them.

In his own quiet way, Ethan achieved more with his mother than even Curiosity. He could settle Kitty's nerves with a few words and he had strategies to distract her from the schemes she seemed to hatch hour by hour, without affronting or insulting her. By the time they reached Johnstown, he had proven his worth many times over.

He and Hannah came to an unspoken agreement: Ethan would cope with his mother's nonmedical needs. After all, the worst Kitty could be accused of was the self-centeredness of the chronically ill; there was nothing of real cruelty in her, and at least once every day she expressed such delight with the journey that it was impossible to stay irritated with her for very long.

It fell to Hannah to deal with ferry masters, coach drivers, and innkeepers, because once Joshua left them at Johnstown and turned the team back toward Paradise, their progress depended on successful negotiations with strangers.

After the second night Hannah decided that innkeepers were by far the biggest challenge. They seemed to believe that it was their right to cheat a red-skinned woman, no matter how well she was dressed or how educated her speech, and every one of them was amazed and affronted that Hannah should take exception to such treatment.

Albany, Hannah reasoned, would be easier. They would not have to inquire for accommodations, as Richard had given plain instructions: they were to spend their one night in the city at the Black Swan. The inn was very near the docks, and had a reputation for cleanliness and reasonable rates.

All Hannah's hopes for a simple transaction fled as soon as she came in the door. The innkeeper took one look at her and turned his back, informing her over his shoulder that while he did have rooms to let, the cost had recently tripled. He spoke loudly, and in a purposely broken English that suggested she would understand nothing else.

She waited until he turned to face her. "Squaw no speak English?"

"But of course I speak English. Better than you do, sir, by the evidence. Mr. Homberger, is it?"

It had been foolish to embarrass him, Hannah saw that by the way the blood rose to his face. She considered leaving to find another inn, but it was growing dark outside and Kitty was exhausted.

He still would not meet her eye. "If you speak English then you must have understood me. Our rooms are beyond your means, miss."

"That must be a very recent change," Hannah said. "As you have not yet posted the new rates there on the wall."

There was a long pause, and then Mr. Homberger's curiosity won out and he examined her from head to foot, peering at her over his spectacles. "I see I must speak plainly."

"Yes," said Hannah. "That would be best."

He said, "We are not accustomed to receiving travelers of your persuasion."

"And what persuasion is that, Mr. Homberger?"

"Those who do not require clean sheets, or any sheets at all," he said coldly. "I believe you would be most comfortable in our stables. For those accommodations I will charge the posted rate."

Hannah was overcome by the almost irresistible urge to let out a screaming war whoop, just to see how the innkeeper might react. Instead she said, "I suggest that you read these letters of introduction."

"That can make no difference at all," he announced, even as a tic began to jerk at the corner of his eye. He cast a nervous glance at the papers in Hannah's hand.

"This one," she said, ignoring him completely, "is from Dr. Richard Todd. I trust you are familiar with his name, as he owns the property on which your inn sits. It may be true that people of my persuasion don't always understand the complexities of land ownership, but by my reasoning that makes him your landlord. It is Dr. Todd's lady and son who are waiting outside in that carriage you see there."

The color had drained from Mr. Homberger's face, but Hannah went on.

"This second letter was written by Mr. William Spencer, also known as Viscount Durbeyfield. The viscount is cousin to my stepmother. We are on our way to visit him in New-York City, at his invitation. And this one, this is my favorite, I think. It is from General Schuyler. Under other circumstances we would have taken up lodging with the general and his lady while in Albany, but they are away. I trust you recognize his name, sir?"

It gave her no satisfaction or pleasure to see Mr. Homberger's distress, and Hannah didn't care to listen as he explained how she had managed to so completely misunderstand his intentions. Within ten minutes they had been settled in the best rooms the inn had to offer, but the operation had been far more draining than the whole day's journey.

And there was still Kitty to deal with. She complained of the wait in a drafty carriage, the view from her window, the size of her bed, the aches in her back, side, and head, and the biscuit she was served with her tea. Even Ethan was not equal to all of that, and it took their combined efforts to see her settled.

When Hannah finally did climb between the clean sheets Mr. Homberger had so begrudged her, she dreamed. She dreamed of Lake in the Clouds in the middle of winter, of snowdrifts and the kind of cold that turned bones brittle. She dreamed of Liam Kirby at the woodpile, his axe rising and falling in a steady rhythm. He was naked to the waist in the bitter cold, the muscles in his back clenching hard as he worked. And with every bite of the axe into the wood, blood swelled up, turning snow from white to red.

In the morning Hannah woke to the knowledge that the worst of the journey was over. Richard had arranged for their passage on the schooner *Good-News* in advance; she had a confirming letter from the captain in her possession, and there would be nothing for her to negotiate about the fare or the cabins or her right to be on board.

They would sail this morning, and if all went according to plan, they would be met at the city docks by Will and Amanda Spencer tomorrow afternoon. Amanda and her household servants would take over Kitty's care and Ethan would be claimed by his cousin Peter, the Spencers' seven-year-old son. Hannah would be free to seek out first Manny Freeman, and then Dr. Simon at the Kine-Pox Institution.

Hannah was sitting with her daybook and her travel journal before her when Ethan knocked at the door. He was dressed as neatly as his mother would have him, in a dark blue coat and fawn-colored pantaloons, but there was a smudge of breakfast jam on his chin and his neck linen was rumpled, some small signs of boyish behavior that Hannah was glad to see, no matter how they might irritate Kitty. Hannah offered him some of her own breakfast.

He sat down across from her and took a bun. "What are you writing?"

Hannah put down her quill and corked the inkhorn she wore on a thin chain around her neck. "A little of everything. My daybook about your mother's condition, and a travel journal, as I promised Elizabeth. And how is your mother this morning?"

He swallowed visibly. "She would like to stop here for a day or two. She thinks we should find a doctor to bleed her before we travel on."

Hannah picked up her teacup to hide her irritation. Kitty was seriously ill, there was no doubt of that, but to bleed someone in her condition was the worst kind of O'seronni medicine; even Richard had agreed to that much. And still Kitty had decided she wanted to be bled, and worse, she had sent her son to announce this decision, hoping to avoid Hannah's displeasure completely.

Ethan understood the silence. "Don't worry, Hannah. I showed her this." And he took a piece of newsprint from inside his coat, unfolded it, and put it on the table. It had been carefully clipped from the *New-York General Advertiser.*

> Mrs. Leonora VanHorn is pleased to announce
> that she is recently returned from France and
> Brussels with a great deal of the very finest lace,
> now for sale in her establishment on the Broad
> Way at Wall Street. Of special interest is the large
> selection of exquisite lace, including Duchesse
> Appliqué, Point de Rose Appliqué, Point de Lille,
> Mechelen, Valenciennes, and Alençon.

"Very nicely managed," said Hannah. "You did not point out to her that this is dated two months ago, I take it."

Ethan was studying his roll very closely. "It made her so happy to hear about the lace," he said. "I didn't see any need to ruin her mood."

"Let me say this once again, Ethan." Hannah leaned across the table and whispered. "This would be a very long and difficult journey without you."

He produced a wide smile, and Hannah noted as she often did how much Ethan looked like his father. He had Julian Middleton's unruly dark hair, the same square chin and high cheekbones, and straight brows over dark, slightly slanted eyes. There was a great deal of Julian in the boy's face, but Ethan had none of his father's character at all. Julian had been self-indulgent, irresponsible, and destructive, but Ethan was none

of those things. Nor did he have very much from his mother.
In some ways he was very like Richard, who had married
Kitty when Ethan was still an infant in arms. Like his stepfather, Ethan had a great curiosity about the world, a keen understanding, and a sober nature.

But where Richard was self-absorbed and easily irritated,
Ethan was compassionate to a fault and tended to melancholy.
In Paradise this was countered by Daniel and Blue-Jay, who
worked very hard to keep Ethan occupied with the business of
boys. For the past four days, though, he had been his mother's
closest companion, and it showed. Hannah wondered if their
division of labor had been a good idea, after all.

He said, "Maybe I shouldn't have shown it to her. She truly
believes she would profit from a bleeding."

"Your mother is nervous," Hannah said. "And with some
reason. But once we arrive in the city and are settled at
Amanda's, she will be glad that we pressed on."

Ethan seemed to have hardly heard her. He had turned all
his attention to the view outside the window: sailboats and
barges and lighters on the great river, the wharves crowded
with hogsheads, barrels, and bales arriving from downriver or
being loaded for the journey south; gentlemen in fashionably
long tails and high beaver hats, merchants wrapped in canvas
aprons, sailors and servants and slaves, all of them in a hurry to
get somewhere. It must be exciting to a nine-year-old boy, because Hannah could not deny that it stirred her own blood.

Without looking away from the river, he said, "Maybe we
will stay in New-York and not go home at all. Aunt Spencer
would like that very much, I think."

Hannah closed her daybook. "Did your mother suggest
that she would?"

He nodded, all of his composure suddenly gone. What she
had before her now was a young boy of nine years, torn between wanting to please a mother he loved and afraid that it
would mean losing everything familiar. Hannah felt a new
flush of irritation with Kitty, who almost certainly had been
hatching plans without any thought of the distress she was
causing her son. Whether she was in earnest was debatable, but
right now that was not the most important question.

"Would you like that, Ethan?"

"I want to go home," he said. "I'm glad to go visiting in the

city, but then I want to go back to Paradise. I think—I think
Curiosity and Galileo would miss me."

"Along with everyone else," said Hannah firmly. "Of
course we will be going home. Now come and finish this jam,
will you? It would be a shame to have it go to waste."

As soon as they stepped from the lighter onto the *Good-News,*
Kitty retired immediately to her cabin for a nap and insisted,
to everyone's surprise, that Ethan and Hannah stay on deck
and enjoy the air. The combination of this sudden and unexpected freedom from her charge and the fact that they were
now putting Albany behind them did a great deal for Hannah's
spirits. And she found that she was very glad to be on board a
ship again.

The *Good-News* was no different from any of the other
schooners that ran up and down the Hudson from Albany to
Manhattan and back again. There were at least a dozen of
them in service, from spring until the freeze made the journey
impossible, and they were all very much alike. Simple quarters
for paying passengers, and belowdecks the stink of sweat and
tar and worse.

But to stand at a ship's rail in a good breeze was something
Hannah had missed. Other sea journeys came back to her with
complete clarity, so that she relived in just a few moments herself when she was not much older than Ethan, the summer she
had left most girlish things behind. For those months she had
lived day to day, caught between fear and exhilaration beyond
measure.

Within ten minutes the wind had cleared Hannah's head of
Mr. Homberger and his sheets, of the press and pall of the city,
and even of Kitty's thoughtlessness. Ethan seemed to benefit
just as much as she did. He stood next to her, his hands clasped
firmly around the rail, and when the schooner's sails were up
and filling with the wind he raised his face to hers.

He had made the journey from these docks to the city
twice before, and on this very schooner. For an hour he
pointed things out to her as if she had never been on the Great
River before, but Hannah listened without interrupting while
he talked about Stony Point, Castleton, Roah Hook, and the
stories of the Coeyman's Creek ghost every child could recite.
When he tired of standing at the rail he insisted that he must

introduce Hannah to everyone he knew, from the sailors to
Captain Nedele, a lean old man with skin like crumpled and
singed paper, no hair on his head but great tangled tufts over
his eyes and sprouting from his ears, and a bulbous purple nose
squashed hard to one side, like a small, mistreated turnip.

The captain looked at Hannah with eyes squeezed almost
shut, and then he took his pipe from his mouth and pointed it
at her.

"Miss Bonner, you say. Nathaniel Bonner's girl, ain't you?"

When Hannah agreed that she was, he opened an almost
toothless mouth and laughed. "Why, now ain't that something.
I fought beside your grandfathers and your great-grandfathers,
too, in the war against the French. Better men you'll never
find. You tell Hawkeye that Jos Nedele is still on the water and
that he sends his regards. You won't remember this, but I saw
you once, must be more than fifteen years ago, down in
Johnstown. You was sitting up on Hawkeye's arm like a little
bird. How is he?"

"Very well," said Hannah. "A little restless, these days."

"That's old age," said the captain, chewing thoughtfully on
his pipe stem. "It takes some men that way. The years pile on
and little by little an itch starts deep in the bone. Got to keep
moving, or die trying." He sucked noisily on his pipe and blew
a cloud of smoke out over the rail. Hannah started in surprise
at the smell: not the sweet smoke of white men's tobacco, but
the bitter-sharp oyen'kwa'onwe of her mother's people. It was
a smell so distinct that it summoned men long in their graves:
Sky-Wound-Round and Chingachgook, Stands-Tall and all
the rest, men as real to her as the captain himself.

"I'll tell you what, missy. You set down to table with me
this evening. I've got stories you'll want to hear, about them
days when the three of us fought together, me and Hawkeye
and Stands-Tall. This young fellow here, he might like to hear
about what happened at William Henry, when we got overrun
by the Frenchies and the Huron."

Ethan accepted the invitation with all the good manners he
had at his disposal, but when they had left the captain and
walked on, Hannah saw the confusion in his face.

"Hannah," he said. "I've heard those old stories a hundred
times, and you must have heard them a thousand. Doesn't he
know that?"

"I suppose he does," she said. "But that's not the point. My mother's people say that the most precious thing an elder can offer you is a story. No matter how many times you hear it, there will always be something new to learn. If you know how to listen, that is."

Ethan said, "But the stories I really want to hear nobody will tell me. My mother won't talk about the night my father died, and my stepfather won't tell me about the years he spent with the Kahnyen'kehàka at Good Pasture, and Curiosity, why Curiosity has a million stories and she'll tell ten a day if I ask her, but she won't tell me what I want to know either."

He was studying Hannah's face closely, as if she might be the person to give him what he needed, the stories he must have in order to make sense of his family and world. He was not old enough to understand that it was not her place to give him what he was asking for. That was Kitty's right, and responsibility.

Hannah said, "Sometimes the most important stories are the ones we have to wait for the longest."

Ethan nodded reluctantly, and Hannah saw the day coming when his questions would not be so easily evaded.

Hannah had last passed through New-York City with her family on the long journey home from Scotland. She had been eager to start up the river that would take them most of the way to Lake in the Clouds, so eager that she had found it difficult to concentrate on anything else.

Her clearest memories were of the departure itself. A lighter had rowed them to the middle of the river where the schooner *Nut Island* was anchored, and they had boarded her at midday. For the rest of the afternoon Hannah had stood at the rail with Hawkeye, looking back at the Manhattan shoreline, remarkable primarily for the fact that it was so quiet. There was nothing to see at the wharves but a few storehouses and a tavern called the Pig and Whistle, fishing dories and farmers' carts, and beyond that farmland and forested hills. Now and then they had caught a glimpse of a country house through the trees, but soon there was no sign of a city at all.

It was hard to believe that in the years between that journey and this one so much could change. Once they had passed Harlem Cove, timber gave way quickly to acre upon acre of fields where farmers were busy with spring plowing, then fine houses with lawns running down to the water, and suddenly a forest of masts, spires, and great warehouses three and four stories high.

The sailors began to work the sails, maneuvering the *Good-News* to her place among dozens of ships, small and large, that were nosed up to the piers like men crowded around a table. The wharves crawled with men of every shade of color from bone to obsidian, humping great boxes and puncheons and bales, loading and unloading wagons, rolling hogsheads, and every one of them seemed to be shouting, sometimes at nothing at all. Men more formally dressed waved quills and carried ledgers as tall as a two-year-old, bellowing orders and threats. Cages of chickens, ducks, and geese were piled as high as a man, horses stamped and snorted, and pigs and dogs alike roamed the wharves, adding to the stink and the noise. Most strange of all were the hundreds of workers who were dumping barrow after barrow of refuse and stone into a long stretch of water cordoned off by wooden poles driven into the river bottom.

Hannah watched until she was forced to accept what her eyes and her rational mind told her: the men of the city had taken it upon themselves to seize the sea, to turn water into land, and they were succeeding.

Standing at the rail with Ethan on one side and Kitty on the other, Hannah could find no words at all for what she was feeling, not so much fright or revulsion or even confusion, but the simple knowledge that she did not belong here, could never belong in a place like this.

"Isn't it glorious," Kitty announced, clasping her hands together hard, as if to contain the urge to throw out her arms in an embrace of all Manhattan. "Have you ever seen a city so alive, Hannah? Have you ever seen anything so exciting?"

Yes, Hannah wanted to say. *I have seen a mad dog snapping at its own tail.* But she kept this thought trapped with a tight smile.

Ethan put a hand on her arm, as if he had heard what she could not bring herself to say: *This is no place for me.*

"Look," he said calmly. "Aunt and Uncle Spencer."

"Oh, how good of her," said Kitty, her face radiant with satisfaction. "Amanda is come to meet us. I can hardly wait—"

She stopped in mid-sentence, and both Ethan and Hannah turned to her to see that she had gone very pale.

"Mother?"

Kitty looked at Ethan as if he had asked her a puzzling question, and then her eyes rolled back in her head and she fainted into Hannah's arms.

"Your mother was just overcome by excitement. Tomorrow morning she'll be impatient to go out shopping, Ethan, wait and see."

"But she was bleeding," whispered the boy.

They were standing in the hall outside Kitty's room in the Spencers' fine home on Whitehall Street. Dr. Wallace, Amanda's personal physician, and the famous Dr. Ehrlich had been summoned even before the Spencers' carriage had left the wharves, and both men were waiting when they arrived at the house. Kitty, conscious but disoriented, had disappeared into her room with them in close attendance, along with Amanda's housekeeper, a black woman called Mrs. Douglas.

"She was bleeding," Hannah agreed, because she could not deny what they had all seen: Kitty's skirts spattered with blood. "She was bleeding, as all women bleed, once a month."

No doubt Kitty would faint all over again to hear Hannah offer this particular explanation to a young boy. Worse, it was not the entire truth. Healthy women of childbearing age bled, but not like this.

Ethan's desperate expression softened a bit. "All women?"

"Yes," said Hannah firmly. "All women who are old enough to bear children, for a few days every month. When we are home again you must ask your stepfather, and he'll explain it to you. But it is a private matter, one not discussed in company."

Lily and Daniel both would have argued with Hannah about this. They would want to know why such an interesting fact as monthly bleeding should not be discussed with anyone who could provide an explanation. But Ethan knew his mother, and he understood without being told that to raise this topic with her would bring consequences neither of them wanted to contemplate.

Downstairs in the foyer a door opened, and Hannah heard

Will Spencer speaking to one of the maids. Then Peter's voice rose up to them, breathless and eager.

"He's looking for you," Hannah said. "You might as well go along, I'll call you when you can see her. I promise."

Ethan hesitated one more moment, and then ran along the wide hall and disappeared down the stairs, leaving Hannah to collapse onto a chair.

Her head was throbbing and she was trembling, from hunger but also simple exhaustion. Hannah made herself breathe deeply, once and then again, and when she opened her eyes she noticed the painting on the opposite wall for the first time. A pheasant draped across a table as if waiting to be plucked and cleaned; a carved crystal decanter filled with wine the color of blood; a bowl of apples, pears, peaches. A single orange.

Hannah closed her eyes again and saw before her a wide, flat basket filled with figs, apricots, dates, smooth-shelled nuts. Hakim Ibrahim holding out an orange to her, the first orange she had ever seen. It had looked to her like a small sun caught in the web of his fingers, his skin the color of earth mixed with ash. In her own hand the orange was heavy, dense, smooth to the touch. The Hakim took another and showed her how to open it, thrusting his thumbs into the skin so that the juice showered the room with its scent, light, sweet, and still faintly sharp.

That morning they had been talking about another woman who lost a child, a Scotswoman, long dead now. A melody came to Hannah unbidden. A song the Scotswoman had sung standing at the rail in a sweet, low voice.

> Be wary o' the cold damp
> Be wary o' the mists
> Be wary o' the nicht air
> Be wary o' the roads and the bridges and the burns
> Be wary o' men and women and bairns
> Be wary o' what ye can see
> And what ye canna

The Hakim had eyes as dark as her own and a high brow creased in concentration under a neatly folded red turban. He was not like O'seronni doctors she had known; he never hurried, and when he had thought through a problem he presented his reasoning along with his conclusions.

What had he said about the Scotswoman? *She is not yet healed from her loss, either in mind or body.*

"You are very far away in your thoughts, Hannah."

It was Will Spencer's familiar and friendly voice, but she started anyway, jumping up from her chair, catching a hand against her heart as if to calm it.

"Oh dear," said Amanda. "We didn't mean to frighten you."

The idea that Amanda Spencer might frighten anybody at all made Hannah smile.

"I think you must have been dreaming," said Will.

"Yes," said Hannah. "I was. I was dreaming about Hakim Ibrahim. He used sandalwood oil in a case like Kitty's, to quiet the womb. I had forgotten that until just now."

Amanda's sweet smile faltered a little, and Hannah reminded herself where she was. Amanda Merriweather Spencer, Lady Durbeyfield, had probably never before heard the word *womb* spoken in mixed company, but she was too well trained a hostess and far too kind to let her dismay show openly.

Hannah said, "Forgive me, I was thinking out loud."

"There is nothing to forgive," said Will Spencer. "We would all be thankful to have the Hakim here for Kitty, isn't that so, Amanda? We owe him a great debt. Sandalwood oil, you say? I believe it would be possible to locate sandalwood oil here in the city. I will send out some inquiries."

Amanda put a small hand on her husband's arm. "There is time for that tomorrow," she said firmly. "Right now I am going to show Hannah her room, so that she can collect herself. We dine at four, so you have an hour."

Will nodded, a little reluctantly. "Very well, then. Until then."

Hannah was sorry to see him go. As a girl she had come to like and admire Will Spencer for his honesty and his interest in her life. In her experience there were few Englishmen who were able or willing to really talk to a young girl; there were fewer who would bother with a half-breed. Will always reminded her of Elizabeth when she first came to Paradise, as open to the world around her as anyone who had been raised

among the Kahnyen'kehàka. It was so rare a thing among the
O'seronni that at first it had been hard to trust, in both of
them.

Sometimes it seemed to Hannah that Will Spencer and her
stepmother Elizabeth might be the same person in two selves,
twins born to different mothers. It was something she had discussed at length with her grandmother Falling-Day and her
aunt Many-Doves, but never with either Elizabeth or Will.
They were too English to understand that such things were
possible.

"Here we are," said Amanda, opening the door to a room
two doors down from Kitty's. "Ethan is right next to you, you
see, in case he calls for you in the night."

The room was large and airy and beautifully furnished, exactly what Hannah had expected of the Spencers. While
Amanda spoke of baths and tea and anything else that Hannah
might need or want, she saw that her trunk had been brought
up and her things put away.

"I hope you will be comfortable here. We are so glad to
have you with us," Amanda finished.

The words of a lady raised to run a mansion or a manor,
but there was nothing artificial about the way they were said.
Hannah knew that it was her turn to say something equally
well bred, to compliment her hostess and thank her for her
hospitality, but before she could think exactly what might be
expected, Amanda surprised her by leaning forward to take
her hands.

She said, "I know this is very strange for you, Hannah. The
city must be overwhelming, and I imagine you are thinking of
home with great longing. But we are glad to have you here,
for as long a visit as you can manage. Please let us do what we
may to make your stay a happy one."

Hannah opened her mouth to say something, anything, of
gratitude. Amanda squeezed her hands again. "Never mind,"
she said. "There is nothing that needs to be said. We are family, are we not? You are my own cousin Elizabeth's beloved
stepdaughter and as long as you care to stay with us you must
think of this place as your own home."

For a long while after Amanda was gone, Hannah sat on the
edge of the fine bed, tracing the heavily embroidered motif of
flowers and bright birds with one finger. She was comfortable

here, she should have said that to Amanda, along with the rest of the truth: *I am so comfortable and feel so protected that the idea of leaving this house is overwhelming.*

Just outside the door the city was waiting for her. There were people she must see and talk to and learn from, and things for her to teach in turn. Dr. Simon and his institute, Manny Freeman's world of runaways and blackbirders, and Liam Kirby's family.

The thought of Liam came to Hannah as quickly and suddenly as a brain fever and with it the understanding that she could not pretend to herself that she was not curious. She could not imagine his home, knew nothing about how he lived, had never heard his wife's name, and she must know all of those things, somehow. When she left this city she would take those answers with her. So she could put Liam Kirby behind her forever.

Dear Dr. Todd,

We are safe arrived. The Spencers met us at the dock and brought us away in a carriage. Mrs. Todd was put straight to bed after a faint spell. She is in great good spirits but her pulse is as ever irregular at times and her courses continue unabated. Although she will not own it—she is afraid to be confined to her bed when she has so many plans for this time in the city— I believe her head aches almost constantly. Dr. Ehrlich was waiting for us at the house on Whitehall Street and spent a long time with her. Dr. Wallace was also in attendance. Of Dr. Ehrlich I can say very little except to repeat one of my stepmother's favorite quotations: "A little learning is a dangerous thing." You will have to hear the doctor's conclusions (if indeed he has any) from him directly as he will not share them with me.

Ethan traveled well and is in excellent health and spirits now that he has Peter as a playmate.

Tomorrow I go to the Kine-Pox Institution for the first time.

The Spencers send their very best regards as do I, your student

Hannah Bonner, also called
Walks-Ahead of the Kahnyen'kehàka

Chapter 19

On her first night in the Spencers' home, Hannah practiced a small rebellion by opening her windows to the night air.

The maid who closed them to start with was called Suzannah. She had arrived at the door to collect clothing that needed laundering, and stayed to let Hannah know that she was the housekeeper's granddaughter, seventeen years of age, and that in the fall she was going to marry a cordwainer by the name of Harry Dabbs.

Hannah had listened politely while Suzannah went about her job of making the room ready for the night, rehanging the gown Hannah had worn to supper, turning down the bed, plumping pillows, positioning the chamber pot, and finally closing all the windows against the night air.

As soon as she was gone, Hannah had opened all the windows again, and while she did that it occurred to her that in all her eagerness to talk, Suzannah had never asked any questions of Hannah at all. Partly, Hannah was sure, because she already knew a lot; the servants were usually better informed than anyone else in the house. But almost certainly she had not asked Hannah anything because it was part of her training; a servant who asked personal questions—even if she happened to be the housekeeper's granddaughter—would find herself scrubbing pots and out of the reach of guests. Standing at the windows to breathe in the night air that Suzannah had so feared, Hannah asked herself a question instead.

Who, in this great and crowded city, could she really talk to?

She had opened the heavy draperies for good measure, leaving only the lace undercurtains moving uneasily in the breeze. Then she went to bed and lay awake with that one question on her mind.

The answer, of course, was that there was nobody for her to talk to except the five people in this house who were bound to her by familial ties, responsibility, and common history. Once she walked through the doors into the city, she would be truly alone.

Hannah woke at sunrise to the disconcerting sound of her name being called. She sat up in the broad bed and pressed her fingers to her eyes, willing her head to clear, listening hard until she could make sense of it.

"Hannibal!" This was followed by a high giggle. "Watch out now, Hannibal!" A young boy's voice, but not Ethan or Peter.

The house was perfectly quiet all around her. Whoever Hannibal might be, somebody was looking for him outside. For a moment Hannah wondered if good manners required her to ignore what was going on in the street under her window, but then curiosity got the better of her.

She did not bother with the steps that were meant to help her negotiate the long drop to the floor; instead she slid over the side until her bare feet met not cool planks or a knobby rag rug, but a slightly itchy wool carpet.

Across the street was a small enclosed park called Bowling Green, where they had walked last night after supper while Kitty rested. Hannah had been preoccupied with worry, about Kitty but also about her doctors, who had smiled at her questions with fatherly condescension and never answered at all. She had agreed to the walk because she thought it might clear her head and help her to organize her thoughts, never realizing that to stroll in Bowling Green at dusk was to be on social display.

Every path had been crowded with fashionable people, some of whom the Spencers had only greeted and others who had been introduced to Hannah, Delafields and Gracies and Varicks without end. The ladies had tried not to stare at the sight of a young Indian woman in lace and silk, but many of the gentlemen,

especially those who were old enough to leave social niceties behind them, were less apologetic about their curiosity.

One stooped old man with a great black cigar plugged into
the corner of his mouth and wispy hair that floated around his
head like fern fronds had been introduced to her as Mr.
Henry. He had puffed hard on his cigar while he studied her
with narrowed eyes, and his mouth stretched wide in a delighted smile.

"So the Mohawk medicine woman is arrived, eh? Dr.
Simon told me all about you, girlie. What, no drums and
masks?" And he had laughed uproariously at his own wit. Will
and Amanda had both been offended for her and apologetic,
but Hannah told them the truth: she preferred Mr. Henry's
coarse honesty and open interest to hooded glances and whispered comments.

At this hour of the morning Bowling Green was all but deserted within its circle of poplar trees just coming into leaf, but
the streets were not. The city scavengers were hard at work,
collecting rubbish that had been thrown into the street sometime between last night's walk and now. Three big men with
kerchiefs tied across their faces shoveled great piles of offal,
drifts of paper, a broken chair, a dead cat, and every other
manner of trash into a cart. The cart, the horses, and the men
were surrounded by a halo of flies, so thick and busy that
Hannah could hear the buzz.

When the scavengers moved on, a whole crowd of young
boys stayed behind to empty buckets of water and then sweep
the flagstone walkways that separated the fine homes sur-
rounding the park from the cobbled street. The houses were
all of stone and brick, three and four stories tall, and Hannah
knew that in each of them a legion of servants or slaves were
hard at work attending to those hundreds of tasks that must be
done while employers still slept.

"Hannibal!" The giggling came again, louder now. A boy
about the age of Hannah's own brother Daniel ran up the side-
walk flicking a wet brush before him like a rattle. She could
not see the boy he was after, but she heard muffled laughter
and the great splash of a bucket being upturned, it seemed by
the squealing over someone's head.

The door almost under Hannah's window opened suddenly
and with it all laughter was cut off.

"What trouble you two will get up next, I cain't hardly imagine." The impatient tone was softened by reluctant amusement. Hannah could not see the housekeeper where she must be standing in the door, but she recognized Mrs. Douglas's voice.

"Come on now, before you catch your death. What you thinking, getting that woolly head of yours wet in an April chill? Hannibal, you best get on in, too, before Mary decide to use that brush to skin your backside. Come on now, Marcus. Put that bucket away proper, and I'll be waiting at the kitchen door with a towel. I seen a thousand children in my time, but there never was such boys for foolishness."

The door closed on her grumbling. Hannah listened, but she could not hear Mrs. Douglas moving through the house. She imagined that the old black woman must be trembling with laughter as she made her way through the halls to the kitchens.

She would come through the swinging doors with her hands on her hips and the women busy with the day's baking and cooking would pause, floury hands held in midair while they listened to the story of two boys in a water fight out on the public street where God and man could watch. And then Marcus would come to the door and they would laugh while Mrs. Douglas rubbed his head dry with a piece of toweling, talking the whole time about the kind of hardship that waited around the corner for black boys who forgot their manners, duties, and good sense.

The kitchen would smell of yeast, of meat turning on the spit and cornbread in the oven, of vinegar and cinnamon and ginger. The door would open and close as the other servants came and went with well water, fish fresh from the river, onions from the root cellar, eggs slipped from the nest by quick brown fingers. They would stay to talk for a minute, to swallow down cornbread spread with the drippings from yesterday's joint of beef, to chop parsley for the soup pot.

Most of the servants in this house were black, but none of them were slaves or even indentured; they could move about the city as they pleased once their work was done. No doubt some of them went to the Free School, and knew Manny Freeman.

Hannah looked down again at the empty walkways winding through Bowling Green, studied the houses where wealthy men still slept behind drawn draperies and closed windows. With sudden purpose, she went to the dressing room and searched out her simplest gown.

She picked out Marcus right away by his damp hair and the gleam in his eye. He was seated at a long trestle table between Peter and Ethan, where all three boys were applying themselves to breakfast with enthusiasm. Hannah was almost sorry when Ethan caught sight of her, jumping up with his spoon in his fist, grinning so joyfully that all of Hannah's doubts about this journey disappeared. Whatever else might come of their time in the city, Ethan had put his worries behind him for a while at least, and that was worth a great deal.

"Miss Hannah." Mrs. Douglas greeted her with a polite but puzzled smile. "We can bring your breakfast up to your room if you too hungry to wait. No need to come belowstairs, you realize. Didn't anybody show you the bell pull in your room?"

All around the crowded kitchen dark eyes were fixed on her, but there was neither friendship nor animosity in any of them. They simply didn't know what to make of her, an Indian woman who had been welcomed into the house as a guest, a colored woman they must treat as though she were white.

Hannah said, "I would like to sit down and eat with the boys, if that isn't too much trouble."

Mrs. Douglas hesitated just long enough for Hannah to realize that the older woman was concerned. No doubt she had seen and heard many things out of the ordinary in the Spencer household, but Hannah knew that this was very possibly the first time that a guest had asked to eat in the kitchen with servants and children.

Hannah said, "I am far more comfortable here than in the dining room. It reminds me of home. Please let me stay."

They made a place for her at the trestle table, and the housekeeper filled a plate with hot biscuits, ham drizzled with honey, and a great mountain of cornmeal mush topped by a puddle of melted butter. Hannah assured Mrs. Douglas that it was more than she needed or had hoped for, and gradually the kitchen settled back into its normal rhythms.

"Today we are going to Wall Street to see Dr. King's orang-utans," Ethan announced. "And then to Mr. Bowen's wax-works. There's a likeness of President Jefferson." He went on outlining a day's outing that would have exhausted anyone but a child who had been cooped up on a sailing boat for two days.

"I expect we'll have to pour you into your beds tonight," said Hannah, and all three boys nodded their heads in cheerful agreement.

"Will you be going along too, Marcus?"

The boy swallowed. "Yes'm. I go wherever Peter goes." He held up his head proudly. "I'm in training to be a manservant."

"A manservant do more listening than talking," called Mrs. Douglas. "That's a lesson you ain't learned yet."

"My father is taking us," said Peter. "He's not going down to his offices at all today. You're coming too, aren't you, Hannah?"

"I can't this morning," she said, cutting into her ham. "I promised Curiosity and Galileo that I would see Manny right away. I have a package for him." And a message, she thought, and caught Ethan's eye. He ducked his head to study the tines of his fork.

Ethan was the only other person who knew that part of the reason she had to see Manny was to pass on news of Selah. He also understood very well what a delicate business it was, and he had promised faithfully to never speak of it to anyone. What he didn't know, of course, was that Liam Kirby had given her another message for Manny, and by far the more worrisome one.

Tell him to step careful, and to stay out of Micah Cobb's way. Tell him, it wasn't just luck that sent Vaark to the Newburgh dock.

The clock in the hall chimed seven, and Hannah wondered when she would be able to slip away. Certainly not before she had checked on Kitty, and Will and Amanda had come down to breakfast.

Marcus had stopped eating to watch her, his brow furled. He said, "Miss Hannah, how do you know Manny Freeman?"

"We grew up together," said Hannah. "He is almost ten years older than me, but I spent a lot of time with his family. Do you know Manny from the Free School?"

"Everybody know Manny," said Marcus. "Ain't that so, Grandma?"

Mrs. Douglas came to the table with a great copper bowl of egg whites tucked in the crook of her arm. "That's true enough," she said, whipping the whites with a fork.

"Maybe you can tell me how to find the Free School," Hannah said. "I'd like to see him today, if I could."

"You don't need to go all the way to the—" Marcus started, and then stopped at the cold look his grandmother gave him.

Mrs. Douglas said, "We see Manny from time to time."

Peter had been very quiet until now. He was naturally timid, the kind of boy who was so happy to be in the company of older boys he admired that he didn't trust himself to speak. But he obviously felt he needed to break that rule, because he stood abruptly as if he had been ordered to give a formal recitation in front of a stern teacher.

"But we see Mr. Freeman almost every day," he said in his high, soft voice, his narrow brow furled in confusion. "He comes to visit with my father. Sometimes he comes with Dr. MacLean and sometimes Mrs. Kerr and sometimes alone. They stay in Father's study for a very long time and they talk about society business. Sometimes Father lets me stay, if I am quiet." His voice dropped, and he leaned across the table toward Hannah. "Sometimes Mr. Freeman brings me a carved animal for my collection. He is very good at carving."

Mrs. Douglas was looking decidedly uncomfortable, her mouth pursed into a tiny, tight O. She said, "You boys run off now and leave me to my work." And to Hannah: "Miz Hannah, if you would be so kind and wait for just a minute?"

When the boys had disappeared into the garden, Mrs. Douglas handed her bowl to another woman and sat down heavily across from Hannah. For a moment her energy seemed to desert her, leaving her face to old age and worry. There was a streak of flour on her brow, and Hannah had the urge to wipe it away.

Mrs. Douglas had a kind smile. She said, "Peter is a sweet child, always so eager to help that he maybe said more than he should."

Hannah realized with considerable surprise and disquiet that the housekeeper was admitting that Peter had been reporting secrets not meant for her to hear, and asking her to forget all of it.

She said, "You don't know me, but I hope you'll believe me when I say that I wouldn't repeat anything that might

cause Manny Freeman or the Spencers or..." She paused, and
considered the intelligent, wary look in Mrs. Douglas's eyes.

"Or any voyager harm."

A flickering across the old woman's eyes, recognition and
fear and relief too. Then she leaned across the table and put a
hand on Hannah's forearm, squeezed hard.

"I got to be getting breakfast on the table," she said. "But I
hope you'll come back and talk to me again sometime soon."

"I will," Hannah said, immensely relieved and pleased that
she had managed to build some kind of understanding between them. "I will come back. But if I could ask you first for
directions to the Free School—"

Mrs. Douglas nodded. "I'll ask Cicero to show you the way
in an hour's time or so. Will that do?"

Hannah assured her that it would serve very well, and then
she found her way to the next breakfast table, where Will
Spencer was sitting alone and reading his newspaper.

Will insisted that she sit down to keep him company in spite of
the fact that she had already had her breakfast. With what he
meant to be a stern expression, Will informed her that
Amanda was with Kitty and had left instructions not to be disturbed.

Hannah said, "I appreciate your concern for me, but I am
supposed to write to Richard today to report on her condition
and treatment. It's my responsibility, even if her doctors dislike
that idea."

Will narrowed his eyes at the mention of the doctors.
"Tomorrow is time enough for you to take all that on your
shoulders. I insist on having my way on this for today at the
very least. And you have other engagements as well. This afternoon I will take you to the dispensary and introduce you to
Dr. Simon. After that you may be better able to write to Dr.
Todd."

"What about Dr. King's monkeys?" Hannah smiled. "The
boys will be very disappointed to miss them."

"The boys will miss nothing at all," said Will. "And you
will not be left on your own to go out into the city. Now tell
me, how did you leave your stepmother and father?"

This brought Hannah up short, for the one thing she had
failed to discuss with Elizabeth was how much information

about the current trouble at home should be passed on to Will
Spencer. It was hard to imagine Elizabeth keeping anything
from Will, but then to involve him in the smuggling of slaves
was something that Hannah did not like to take upon herself.
Neither could she lie to him directly.

If Will was disturbed by her long silence, he showed no sign
of it. Finally Hannah said, "Liam Kirby came back to Paradise
a few weeks ago, looking for an escaped slave. He hasn't found
her, as far as I know."

Will blinked at her, his face impassive. "I remember Liam
from Paradise," he said finally. "You were once very good
friends. He lives here in the city now, you must know."

"Yes." Hannah stood abruptly. "I really should look in on
Kitty, she will think I've forgot her altogether."

"Come now," Will said with a smile. "I won't ask questions
about Liam Kirby if you prefer not to talk. But you can't run
off until I've given you all this post that your old friend the
Hakim left for you."

"The Hakim? Hakim Ibrahim was here?"

"Last week. He was sorry to hear that he would miss you,
and he sends his very best wishes."

Hannah slumped back in her chair and searched in vain for
something to say that wouldn't sound childish and discouraged, but Will had already turned his attention to the pile of
newspapers and packages beside him. After some sorting he
brought a great armful to Hannah.

"I know you must be disappointed, but I think this will
help a bit."

She began to sift through the unexpected bounty, dividing
it into piles. A large batch of extracts from letters and medical
journals that the Hakim had copied out for her, bound with
string; a very heavy package she could not identify by shape;
another of books; a small box securely nailed shut; and seven
letters. Five were addressed to her father or to Elizabeth, but
two were for her.

"I will leave you to your post," said Will, and withdrew before Hannah could make herself look up from the letters in
her lap to thank him.

The thicker letter was from the Hakim, and would most
probably require that she open the box and packages as she
read. She put that one aside to save for later. The other letter

was from her cousin Jennet at Carryckcastle in Scotland. Hannah had not seen any of her Scots relatives in seven years, but her correspondence with Jennet had kept the connection very much alive. She had the room to herself, and so she opened it carefully and unfolded the pages.

> *Dear Cousin Hannah,*
>
> *It's four months or more since we've had word from Lake in the Clouds. No doubt a fat letter will come the morrow with news enough to satisfy what my mother calls my unladylike curiosity, but as the Isis leaves the Solway Firth this afternoon bound for New-York, I cannot wait any longer to put down on paper what news there is to tell, good and bad.*
>
> *My father writes his own letter to your father, and still bids me report that we are all thriving, and in good health. As an obedient daughter I must do as he asks, and now to that I add my own words: it's no so true as I would like it to be. Father is overtired of late and in some pain, though he would rather cut out his tongue than admit such a thing. He has got the habit of resting in his greenhouse when he thinks nobody will take note and has no strength even to care for his beloved tulips. My mother his guidwife says that the Earl of Carryck can take his rest where and when he pleases, and what better place than among the flowers and plants that give him such pleasure?*
>
> *The simple truth is that he is as stubborn and wily as ever he was, as stubborn as all the earls of Carryck afore him. No doubt my brother Alasdair for all his sweet devilment will grow to be just like him, for it's a trait bred in the bone and there's wee use denying it. How else to explain a man of eighty-one years who claims he needs no doctor to help him to his grave? And still he could not turn away Hakim Ibrahim when he arrived with the Isis just ten days ago. We were gey pleased to see him, for all my father's protests. The Hakim's tonics and teas and oils seemed to bring some relief, enough at least to make my mother sing again in the mornings. The earl even spoke of riding out with Luke to see the tenants.*
>
> *Then just yesterday the Hakim asked to see my mother alone in the surgery and when he left she was white-faced and more snappish than I've seen her in a good long while. She announced to me that the earl would outlive us all, no matter what the doctors had to say about it. But in truth she's*

frightened, as are we all. Even Alasdair seems to ken what lies ahead, and for all his tumbling about and noise he comes of an evening to lay his head on Father's lap and let himself be petted, like a wolf cub almost tamed.

The truth of it is, the earl has been putting his affairs in order for six months or more. How many times have I heard him tell my mother that with such good men to depend on she need not bother herself with the affairs of the earldom. There's Ewan Huntar wha has been our factor these three years since he returned hame from his studies in Edinburgh. Never will I understand why a man needs Latin to see to the running of the castle and the tenants and shipping, but the earl is weel pleased with Ewan and says he has the sense for money and the head for law. Luke can turn his hand to inkpot and ledger too but he's pleased to leave it all to Ewan. He and Nezer Lun bear the responsibility of keeping Carryck strong and the men ready to defend kith and kin from Campbells or even Englishmen, should it come to that.

In that much Luke has changed no a single mote. He's still most content rushing about on horseback. He and Nezer spend all their days thinking up one drill after another to keep the men sharp and ready, and when they tire of parading up and down and turning the heads of the lasses from the village, then they gallop off to the hunt and are gone for days at a time.

It's seven years since your father and mine made the agreement that brought your half brother here to Scotland. Betimes it seems as if the others forget that Luke was born far away in Canada and never set foot on Carryck lands until he was as old as you and I are now—but I remember, and so does Luke. My lady mother claims that he's a Scott of Carryck through and through, but she kens him no so well as I. When we go riding it seems that Canada is all he cares to talk about, how vast it is and how green with trees and about his Granny Iona the runaway nun, and the great river named after a saint crowded with blocks of ice as big as houses in the spring so that men leap from one to the next and lay wagers on who'll land first in the drink.

Perhaps it has to do with his mother's going hame to Montreal last year. He seldom speaks of missing her, but I see it in his face and every day a bit stronger, the wanting to be away. For a while I thought that Ewan's sister Katie might tie

him down to Carryck with a bairn. Your brother is as fond as
any man of the lasses, but he's no completely daft and all her
twitching and giggling have brought her naught but a sorry
reputation. Luke is no more interested in gypit Katie Huntar
than am I in her brother Ewan, and should my father lay
praise upon his keen and balding head from dawn till dusk.

Were it no for my father's poor health I should go down the
Firth myself and board the Isis for New-York, if only to prove
I'm still the Jennet who showed you the fairy tree and faced
down the Pirate (I meant to say straight off that the Hakim
brought news of Stoker: he has a new ship called Revenge and
he plies his wicked trade in the Sugar Islands), and not such a
melancholy creature as I must seem from this letter of mine. For
all our sorrows we find a good deal to laugh about, as we did
yesterday when wee Alasdair put his head in an empty honey
bucket in order to lick the bottom and couldn't get out again. We
laughed until we wept, all of us, and Alasdair too, rolling around
on the ground and kicking his legs so that I had to sit on him
before Luke could get a hold of the bucket and cut the hoops.

You make no promises about coming to Scotland, so I
suppose it's up to me to do the traveling, Hannah Bonner.
You'll be thinking that we've kept your brother far too long
and it's high time that he visit home again, and so my newest
plan is this: if we canna keep Luke here, I'll bring him to you
in the endless forests, and what great adventures we'll have.

This letter will reach you in the spring, and so I'll close
with good wishes for a healthy summer, one that brings neither
sickness nor new sorrows to you or your family.

> Your fond cousin and true friend,
> Jennet Scott of Carryckcastle
> The fourteenth day of February in the Year of Our
> Lord 1802

For a long time Hannah sat with Jennet's letter open before
her on the table, so deeply lost in her thoughts that when the
clock struck eight she started and could not remember where
she was. She would not have been surprised to look out the
window and see rolling hills covered with heather, but instead
there was just the view of the next house, and a maid washing
windows.

Hannah wondered about the earl, and whether he could still be alive and what illness might have taken him. She knew that the Hakim would have written to her about that in his letter, but she wasn't ready yet to give up Jennet. In any case the next mail packet was likely to bring news of the earl and maybe bring her Jennet and Luke too.

Hannah could almost see them standing at the rail of the *Isis*. In her memory they were still as she had last known them, Jennet at ten, a tiny thing with a wide and smiling mouth and a long shock of blond hair that curled around her face; Luke with his mother's fair coloring, tall and very lean, with their father's breadth of shoulder and Granny Cora's high brow and wide-set eyes. He had been a man grown even then, and he had teased her as an older brother is supposed to do.

A letter from Luke lay on the table, addressed to their father. He wrote two or three times a year, dutifully reporting on his life in Scotland, what he was learning of running an estate and farms, how he was progressing in the handling of weapons and the art of war. And still Hannah's real sense of this half brother she had never really known came from Jennet's letters and not his own. He was twenty-six to her almost eighteen years, and they had spent a total of a month in each other's company, just before he left to claim a place for himself at Carryck. For that first year in Scotland he had been the heir to the earldom, and then Carryck's lady surprised everyone—herself not least—by producing one last and unexpected child, a son.

Their father had sent a letter to ask if Luke wanted to come home to Canada where he had been born and raised by his grandmother Iona, or to Lake in the Clouds where he would always be welcome. But Luke had answered with nothing of regret or blame for what had been lost to him. He would stay in Scotland for as long as he could be of service to Carryck.

"He'll be back," Hawkeye had said, when Elizabeth read the letter out loud in front of the hearth on a winter's evening. "He's not so much a Scott as he is a Bonner, and his roots are here."

Hannah read over Jennet's letter again: *You'll be thinking that we've kept your brother far too long and it's high time that he visit home again, and so my newest plan is this: if we canna keep Luke here, I'll bring him to you in the endless forests, and what great adventures we'll have.*

Jennet's schemes were numerous and detailed, but this one, Hannah sensed with both excitement and vague uneasiness, was likely to come true.

"Miss Hannah?" An elderly black man stood at the door with his hat in his great hands. He had a quick, kind smile and he reminded her immediately of Galileo.

"Yes?"

"I'm Cicero. You were wanting to go over to the Free School to see Manny?"

"Yes." Hannah stood, her eyes moving one final time over Jennet's letter. "Is it close enough to walk?"

He tilted his head in surprise. "Why, yes, miss. It ain't so very far. Take maybe twenty minutes, a half hour, was you to want to look around and see a bit of the city."

"Yes, I'd like to walk a bit," said Hannah. "I will just put these things away and then I'll be right with you."

They started up the Broad Way on the east side of the street, walking on flagstone. Between the houses on the other side of the street there was a flash of mild blue now and then from the river, the same pale shade as the spring sky overhead.

Cicero pointed out the mayor's residence and the homes of a number of aldermen and lawyers, and Hannah supposed that these must be families that the Spencers knew well. She wondered at the carefully trimmed bushes and flowers as regimented as an army battalion, nowhere a blade of grass out of place.

The traffic was tremendous, worse than Albany and beyond anything Hannah could have imagined. Coaches and carriages of every shape and size, delivery carts, men on horseback. A pearly pink hog was nosing around in the gutter and moved only when a carter used his whip on the broad back. There were no ladies out at this hour of the morning but there were too many gentlemen in fine coats and tall hats to count, all of them in a hurry to be somewhere. They walked alone or in pairs, and none of them took any notice of Hannah and Cicero, which suited her very well.

There were also servants and workers, a man Hannah thought must be a baker for he was wrapped in an apron and dusted with flour from head to foot. A black man went by carrying a great sack over his shoulder and he and Cicero greeted each other softly.

The vendors were the most pleasant surprise because all of them, women and men alike, sang to advertise their wares as they moved along. A young girl with a box suspended from a string around her neck sang in a high, clear voice: "Come get the first strawberries! Early strawberries! Sweet sweet strawberries!"

It was truly astounding, the variety of things that were sold on the street. Gingerbread, cider, shoe buckles, neatly tied bundles of kindling, pots and fry pans, brooms, great bundles of lilac and smaller ones of violets, newspapers. A cart went by, the driver so encrusted with grime that Hannah could not be sure of his skin color and he sang too. "Charcoal! I've got your charcoal here!" Just after him came two chimney sweeps hung all around with the tools of their trade, scrapers and buckets and long-handled brushes. They sang together in an easy harmony:

Sweep O-O-O-O
From the bottom to the top
Without ladder or a rope
Sweep O-O-O-O

A crowd of boys shouldered through the crowd, raggedly dressed and gaunt faced. Cicero put a hand on the stout cane he carried in a loop on his belt and kept a close watch; Hannah had the sense that he would not hesitate to strike, if he felt the need.

A very young woman in clogs and a mobcap that came down over her ears was offering buttermilk in a simple singsong. She carried a bucket in one hand and a tin cup in the other, and she called out to Hannah. "Buttermilk, miss! Sure and there's naught better to lighten the complexion!"

Cicero let out a great grunt of disapproval, but Hannah merely walked on, determined not to be sidetracked by the attention she would not be able to avoid. The girl's Irish English had reminded her of Jennet's news of the pirate Stoker again, which made her smile.

As they made their way along the Broad Way they passed shop after shop, many of them larger than cabins that housed a family of six in Paradise.

"That there is Mr. Caritat's circulating bookshop," said

Cicero solemnly, pointing with the top of his head. "Mr. Caritat is often a guest at the Spencers' table." In front of the shop window, two gentlemen stood head to head arguing over the open page of a volume they held between them. One of them had just cut some pages open and he jabbed with the small bookknife to punctuate his sentence. The other gentleman was Dr. Ehrlich, but he did not see her or did not care to.

She would ask Will Spencer to take her to Mr. Caritat's bookstore some other time, and maybe if there was the opportunity to the stationers as well for some fine paper to take to Elizabeth as a gift.

They passed a printer and then a music shop. The door opened as they went by, letting out a warble of fiddle music and then cutting it off again just as another crowd of boys went howling through the street, one of them with a huge ham hock clutched to his chest like a baby. Close behind came a butcher in a bloody apron, grim faced and determined. There were jewelers, silver- and goldsmiths, hatters. Over one door painted bright blue hung a beautifully drawn sign: Steven Green, Master Linen Draper, originally of Norwich. Hannah did not know exactly what it was a linen draper did, but she did not want to ask Cicero just now, as she had the sense that he would stop walking to answer her question and do so in great detail.

"Oh look," she said, stopping after all. "Mrs. Leonora VanHorn, Milliner."

"Do you know Mrs. VanHorn?" Cicero asked her, smiling politely.

"No," said Hannah. "But I know Mrs. Todd will want to make her acquaintance. I understand she carries lace from Brussels."

In the next block the smell of roasting coffee and tobacco smoke came drifting from the windows of a coffeehouse. The doors stood open and they could see into the long room crowded with men, all talking loudly. Just next to that was the City Hotel, as large as the warehouses on the pier. The front door was flanked by small trees in tubs. Hannah stopped to look at them, wondering how someone had come upon such a strange idea that a tree might be happy with so little room for its roots to spread.

Here Cicero turned onto a side street and the noise of the

Broad Way receded. There were more shops, a saddlery and a coachmaker, offices, and smaller, more modest houses. There were vendors here too, with brooms and eggs and fish fresh from the river, their voices mingling as they sang out. A group of children played in the lane with a three-legged dog who looked at Hannah with somber pleading in its eyes. Pigs were busy in the gutters, and in fact the whole street smelled much worse than the wider Broad Way, strewn as it was with trash and offal and manure. She could hardly imagine what it must be like in the high heat of late summer.

Two more turns and they had come upon a long red-brick building with neat white shutters.

"This here is the African Free School," said Cicero. "Most likely you'll find Manny in the porter's lodge, just back there. I'll just stop in and visit with Mr. Solomon until you ready to go. Manny will find me for you."

He bowed from the waist, handed her the parcel he had been carrying for her, and left.

Hannah followed a narrow path that led behind the school building, passing classrooms as she went. In each of them students were reciting, and the sound of multiplication tables mixed with the conjugating of verbs and poetry recited in a harmonized singsong.

The path took her to a wide-open area behind the school, no doubt where the younger children played in their recess. She found the porter's lodge just as it had been described to her, a small building with two window sashes on either side of an open door and a slate roof. Stepping into the dim hallway from the bright April morning, Hannah could first smell more than she could see: beeswax and mineral oil, leather and wood shavings. Her vision adjusted and she made out the bright rag rug on the floor and at eye level a piece of needlework simply framed: *In My Father's House There Are Many Mansions*. Two doors faced each other, with a neat hand-printed card tacked on each: one read MECHANIC and the other PORTER.

Hannah was trying to decide where to knock when she heard a step and someone blocked the light from the door behind her.

A familiar voice said, "Can I help you, miss?" even as Hannah turned.

Manny's smile was so true that all Hannah's worries about coming simply fell away. "Hannah Bonner!" He took both her hands to shake at once. "Why, look at you. Just look at you. Ain't it a pleasure to come upon a face from home. It's been two years at least. Now come on in here, come on. What are you doing in the city?"

He opened the porter's door and ushered her in, talking the whole time with such animation that Hannah hardly answered one question before he had asked another one. In short order he had given her the best chair in the room, offered to fetch her tea or water, and seated himself across from her.

Manny had not changed so very much, it seemed to Hannah, but there was a new watchfulness about him; he seemed sometimes to be looking inside things rather than at them. He was more like his mother in temperament than either of his sisters was, but he looked most like his father. They had the same high brow and straight posture, and even the same way of sitting. Both of them were of slightly more than average height and strongly built.

A natural lull came into the conversation and Manny dropped his head to study the floor with a thoughtful expression.

He's wondering about Selah, Hannah realized. *Wondering if there's any news. He's not even sure she made it to Paradise, or if she's alive.*

She cleared her throat. "Curiosity sent this parcel for you, some of her soap and ginger cakes and a jar of preserves. And I have a message. More than one message." She paused, and looked out the windows over the yard to the school. The only person in sight was an old woman standing outside the next house, peeling potatoes over a barrel, her head bound with a kerchief the color of egg yolks.

Manny's voice wavered. "You can talk here."

Hannah smiled. "Selah is safe."

His whole posture changed, relief running through him to bend him forward from the waist. Manny put his forehead on his knees and his shoulders heaved once, and stilled.

Hannah said, "When I left, my father was just about to set out with her for Red Rock."

He raised his head. "The child?"

"Hadn't come yet when I left, although I would think it

must have by now. Selah was fevered when she first came to us, but strong and well when I left. She and the child both."

"I thought she was dead," Manny whispered, more to himself than to her. "After Newburgh I thought—" He shook his head.

"Selah asked me to tell you not to worry for her. I don't suppose you can stop worrying, but I think the worst is over now that she's on her way to Red Rock."

Manny let out a great and ragged sigh, but his relieved expression had already given way to new concerns.

"Liam Kirby?"

Hannah jerked in surprise. "You know about Liam Kirby coming after her?"

He looked away, out the window to the old woman hunched over the barrel. "We keep an eye on all the black-birders working out of the city. Mostly we know where they are and who they're after."

Hannah said, "Who is 'we'? The Manumission Society?"

Manny's head jerked around to her. "Christ, no. The Manumission Society couldn't get caught up in moving slaves. It would bring this whole school down if it ever came out that one of the trustees was involved."

"But—" Hannah thought of Peter's earnest expression at breakfast. How had he put it? *They stay in Father's study for a very long time and they talk about society business.*

"Manny, is Will Spencer in the Manumission Society?"

His gaze was level, and his expression very still. "No. Never has been."

Hannah sat back, and waited.

After a good while Manny said, "I ain't sure it's the best idea to talk any more about this. I'm thankful that you took the time to come and give me the news, Hannah. Couldn't be written down in a letter, you understand."

Hannah nodded, but her thoughts were still with Peter and the story he had told in the kitchen. What Manny would not say aloud was too clear to ignore: Will Spencer was helping the runaways.

It wasn't our Manny tried to buy the girl free, Galileo had said, and Curiosity's expression, the way she had cut him off: *No need to get particular with names, now.*

It made perfect and undeniable sense that Will would be

part of a secret society that worked to move slaves north into freedom. William Spencer, Viscount Durbeyfield, once of England, presented one face to the world: a man of the best family, excellent connections, perfect bearing and manners. There were many men like him, men who led exemplary lives and spent untold hours smoking opium or drinking brandy in darkened libraries. Will Spencer's secret vices were rebellion, revolution, reform.

The dangers were tremendous. A situation much like this one had forced them to flee England and leave everything familiar behind. Hannah thought fleetingly of Amanda and Peter, of all that he was risking.

Manny was watching her, but Hannah knew that she could not get any more information from him, or from anybody but Will himself.

"Did you say you had more than one message? From my folks?"

"No," said Hannah. "From Liam Kirby. He said—" She paused, and tried to collect her thoughts. "He said there were two things to say to you. First, to stay out of Michael Cobb's way."

"Micah Cobb," Manny corrected her.

"Micah Cobb. To stay out of his way because he's been watching you and he's looking for a reason to arrest you." *To see you hang,* Hannah thought, but he would know that without her saying the obvious.

If this was news to Manny, it didn't seem to upset him very much. "And the second message?"

"This one I remember word for word. He said, 'Tell him it wasn't just luck that sent Vaark to the Newburgh dock.'"

The muscles in Manny's jaw rolled and clenched. He stood and went to the window, leaning with one hand high on the wall. "Anything else?"

"Not in a direct message to you, no. But he mentioned the widow Kuick's overseer. The way Liam was talking, I got the impression you must have had some business with him. Do you know Ambrose Dye?"

Manny nodded. "I know who he is, yes."

Hannah realized that what she was seeing now was Manny so angry that he was having a hard time containing himself. And there was nothing she could do to help him, because when he looked at her he saw Nathaniel Bonner's daughter. Manny would not put her in danger, in part because it just went against his nature, and in part because he would have to answer to her father if anything should happen to her.

Hannah stood. "I probably should go back now. I haven't even seen Kitty yet today and this afternoon I have to go to the dispensary..." She was running on, but she couldn't stop herself. "Dr. Todd has arranged for me to learn how to give smallpox vaccinations."

Somehow she had managed to say something to break Manny's distraction, because his head came up sharp.

"Will you be working at the poorhouse?"

"I don't know," Hannah said, spreading her hands out in front of her. "I don't know anything except that I am to be trained by Dr. Simon."

Manny said, "Then you'll be working in the poorhouse. That's where folks come to get vaccinated, the ones who can't afford to pay a doctor." There was new energy in his voice. He started to say something, and then cut himself off.

"Will I see you again?" Hannah asked.

"I'll come by the kitchen to say hello to Mrs. Douglas early tomorrow morning, if you don't mind."

"I don't mind at all," Hannah said, more intrigued than anxious. "I'll look forward to it."

APRIL 25, 1802

Walked through the city in the company of Mr. Cicero, Cousin Will Spencer's butler. He took me to see the African Free School where I visited with Almanzo Freeman, who was glad of the news of home I brought to him.

On the way back to Whitehall Street Cicero gave me a lesson in the types and uses of vehicles here in the city. Each has its own name and it seems to be a matter of great importance not to mistake a barouche for a cabriolet or a gig for a phaeton. Beyond the pony carts and ox carts and coal carts, which are easy enough to distinguish even for me, there are also coaches and chariots, curricles and gigs, whiskies and chaises, some with two wheels and some with four, some with high sides and some without, some with coverings of leather that can be folded back when the weather is fine and others with glass in window frames. The largest are pulled by four or even six horses, and the smallest have room for only one passenger who must also hold the reins of a single pony. Some of the finest coaches are painted in bright colors with gilt edging while others are very battered. Today I saw a hackney carriage (which may be rented for a little money, driver, horse, and all) pulled by a gelding whose tail and mane had been dyed purple, and plaited with dried flowers.

A neighbor, the eldest son of the head of the city council, called soon after we were arrived at home to see if I should like to take a ride in what he called his high-flyer. Cousin Amanda brought me this invitation with a concerned look, and bid me politely refuse. Her exact words were "Let him break his own neck if he must, the silly boy."

When he drove away I saw what she meant, from my window. The wheels of the high-flyer are as tall as a child of twelve and there are steps to climb to the seat. For all that it does look like good fun, I have followed Amanda's advice and will keep my neck and head in good working order, given all there is for me to learn at the Kine-Pox Institution and hospital.

When she is nervous, Kitty babbles at great length; I write silly things of no real importance, to save myself the trouble of putting down in ink the things that I have learned about Cousin Will Spencer that will keep me awake this night.

Chapter 20

By the time they left by carriage for the New-York Dispensary, Hannah had almost talked herself out of raising the topic of runaway slaves and blackbirders to Will Spencer, mostly because she was very aware that her father and her stepmother would have very different opinions on the matter. Elizabeth liked to think of herself as ruled by reason, but she often let her heart lead her; Elizabeth would want her to do anything in her power to help Manny, and that meant approaching Will.

But she knew very well what her father would want and expect of her: she must fulfill her promises. To Richard Todd, that she would see his wife and stepson safely home; to her family, that she would not do anything to put herself in real danger. She had warned Manny, and he would pass along that warning to Will Spencer and whoever else was involved; that should put an end to her involvement.

Except, Hannah thought, as Will pointed out buildings and parks and theaters, she knew that she could not put aside or forget or explain away the way Manny had reacted to that last message. His expression had stayed with her all morning through all the planning for outings and visits and shopping, the complex negotiations with Kitty about how much rest she required every day. The boys had been absent from the table because they had gone with Peter's tutor to see the orangutans and waxworks, and taken along a picnic packed by Mrs. Douglas.

It wasn't just luck that sent Vaark to the Newburgh dock.

From what Hannah understood of the whole business, Selah had not run on a whim, but had left the city well prepared with maps and memorized instructions and help along the way. Manny had provided all of that, Manny and the mysterious society Peter had mentioned so artlessly. But something had gone wrong, and Mr. Vaark—Selah's owner—a word that could not be ignored for all its implications—had known to look for her on the docks at Newburgh, where he had died. Where Selah had killed him.

If it wasn't luck that had sent Vaark to Newburgh, what had? Or who? Was there a spy at work?

"You are very far away in your thoughts," said Will. "Are you thinking about the Hakim again?"

"No," Hannah said, smiling. And then, looking away out the carriage window: "I visited Manny Freeman this morning at the Free School, and I was thinking about him."

Will was quiet for a long moment. "We will have to talk about that later this afternoon," he said finally. "Here we are at the dispensary."

It was an unimposing building, a house that had been converted into offices where doctors could treat the sick rather than visiting them in their homes. From Will, Hannah knew that there were thirteen physicians and surgeons who contributed their time to the dispensary, as well as a full-time apothecary. The Kine-Pox Institution itself was in the Almshouse, but they were to meet Dr. Simon here first.

"There's no need to feel anxious," Will said. "Dr. Simon is an excellent doctor and one of the finest men in the city."

Hannah said nothing, but she thought of the men who had spent so much time with Kitty yesterday and refused her questions. Then she reminded herself that she was here on a very simple matter. She had studied all the available materials on the *variolae vaccinae*—including the pamphlet that had come in this morning's post from Hakim Ibrahim—and all that remained was to practice what she had read about in theory, under the supervision of an experienced doctor who could answer her questions.

She was not coming to this New-York Dispensary alone. All of her teachers were at her back; she would not shame them, or herself.

*   *   *

A young black man who introduced himself as Archer showed them into a meeting room, before Hannah could get any sense at all of the dispensary beyond the smells common to any place where the sick were treated.

Eight men sat around a round table, all very distinguished in appearance, most with elaborate beards and mustaches. The youngest was perhaps thirty, and the oldest—wearing a very outdated powdered wig—was more than sixty. Dr. Ehrlich and Dr. Wallace were both present, and Hannah was vaguely pleased to see them. She would ask again about their examination of Kitty, and they would not be able to avoid or ignore her in this company.

The room was thick with pipe and cigar smoke and for a very strange moment Hannah thought of the council fire at Good Pasture. When there was a problem to be solved the sachem called together men experienced and wise enough to contribute to the conversation as they smoked oyen'kwa'onwe in a pipe that passed around the room. But at any Kahnyen'kehàka council fire the clan mothers would be there too, to make sure that the men did not forget their responsibilities, or lose their heads. As men were wont to do, Curiosity would say.

I am Walks-Ahead, she reminded herself. *I am the daughter of Sings-from-Books of the Kahnyen'kehàka people. I am the grand-daughter of Falling-Day, who was a great healer, great-granddaughter of Made-of-Bones, who was clan mother of the Wolf for forty years. I am the great-great-granddaughter of Hawk-Woman, who killed an O'seronni chief with her own hands and fed his heart to her sons. I am the stepdaughter of Bone-in-Her-Back.*

What had Elizabeth said, that morning that she left? *Hold your head up and meet their eyes. Don't smile until they see you for who you are, and understand that you won't be put off or dismissed.*

"Gentlemen," Hannah said to the room, and they all rose to their feet as if she were the schoolmistress and had called them to order.

Some of them looked skeptical and others curious. The youngest of the men sat down almost immediately to scribble something on a piece of paper while two others came forward to greet her.

The elder of them was so round that all of him wobbled as he walked. A cascade of chins hid his neck, and above his beard his complexion was so high in color that Hannah thought he might burst if she touched him. If he were to fall over with an apoplexy she would not be in the least surprised.

"The Reverend John Roberts," said Will. "President of the board of directors of the dispensary."

"I look to the details of funding and support so that these good men can go about their business without distraction," explained the reverend, and he waddled back to his chair while Will introduced Dr. Simon.

Hannah's first thought was that Richard Todd and Will had not told her what she really needed to know about Dr. Simon. Of middle age and dressed in Quaker gray, he had the kind and intelligent expression that had been described to her, but there was nothing soft about him at all, and without knowing exactly why, she was reminded of her uncle Bitter-Words, who had been Keeper of the Faith at Barktown, before the last of the Kahnyen'kehàka had left Trees-Standing-in-Water.

Will went on with the introductions: Mr. Furman, superintendent of the Almshouse; Dr. Hosack; Dr. Benyus, who bowed deeply from the waist; Dr. Pascalis, who had some paralysis on the left side of his face that dragged down the corner of his eye and mouth both. The last of the men, the one who had taken his place to write, turned out not to be a doctor at all, but a journalist.

"Mr. Henry Lamm, of the *New-York Intelligencer*. I hadn't been expecting you today, Mr. Lamm." Will Spencer was always polite, but there was an unusually sharp edge to his tone.

Mr. Lamm inclined his head and sat down again to write. "Dr. Wallace invited me," he said, without looking up from his notes.

"Let's get started, shall we?" This from Mr. Roberts, who sat far back from the table to accommodate his girth.

Hannah cast a questioning look at Will, but he looked as puzzled as she felt.

"Gentlemen?" Will sent the question out into the room, but it was Dr. Simon who responded, clearing his throat first.

"My colleagues are very interested in Miss Bonner's background and training," he said. "If she has no objection, they would like to ask her a few questions."

"There was no mention of this—" Will began, but Hannah held up a hand to stop him.

"I have no objection."

Will hesitated. "As you wish."

He thought she was being foolish or foolhardy or simply stupid to agree to such an inquisition, but Hannah was far more angry than she was anxious. These men had come to see her as the boys went to see the orangutans, to satisfy their curiosity. Most of them meant no harm and would ask her simple questions about fevers and broken bones, but not all of them.

By his expression she could see that Dr. Ehrlich was here to expose and embarrass her, and the journalist was here to see what news could be made of it.

But Hannah was overcome with a sudden and complete calm. For three years she had endured Richard Todd's impatience, the endless questions designed to distract from the obvious, his poor tempers. She had treated sore throats and set broken bones and dosed fevers; she had helped many and saved a few and watched others die, her little brother and her grandmother among them. All of it she had recorded in her daybook, every step she had taken on this journey.

Let Dr. Ehrlich—let all of them—do their worst.

Chapter 21

Hannah woke the next morning to find Ethan standing next to her bed in his nightdress. He was turned toward her open window, his head tilted to one side as he listened to a creaky deep voice raised in a singsong.

Here's white sand, choice sand,
Here's your lily white s-a-n-d
Here's your Rock-a-way Beach s—a—n—d.

"Do you hear it?" Ethan asked her.

"Yes," Hannah said, rubbing her eyes. "I hear it. It's only a street vendor, Ethan. You know, like the man who brings the milk or the woman who sold you boys some gingerbread yesterday on your way to the theater."

He turned his face to her, blinking slowly. She reached out to touch his cheek, and he stepped back a little, shaking his head. Then he raised his chin and echoed the song that they could still hear, faintly, as the vendor moved down Bowling Green.

"'White sand, choice sand, lily white sand.' He's singing about Lily. Is Lily in the white sand? Is she lost in the white sand?"

Gooseflesh rose on Hannah's arms, but she forced herself to move slowly so that she would not startle him out of his walking sleep. Very carefully she folded back the covers.

"Come, Ethan, sleep here a while. Come lay your head. Lily is at Lake in the Clouds safe and sound in her bed. She is asleep, and so should you be. Sleep."

He let out a great sigh, of relief or weariness or sadness that he had not made her understand, but after a moment he climbed up on the bed and closed his eyes. Hannah lay awake next to him, shivering in spite of the warm bedclothes and thinking of her sister. Lily white sand. Lily white. Lily.

After a good while she realized that no amount of O'seronni sensible reasoning would allow her to ignore what a dream-walker had come to tell her. She got up, lit a candle, and wrote a letter.

> Dear Lily and Daniel (for in that order were you born):
> Yesterday your cousins Ethan and Peter and their friend Marcus went to see a large monkey called an orangutan who is kept in a cage. There is a picture of an orangutan in one of your mother's books on the jungles of Borneo. A man called Dr. King charges money for the privilege of seeing this animal (who is called Samson, for his great strength). The boys report that Samson is in the habit of pelting Dr. King with bits of rotten food, and that he has three times escaped from his cage. This reminds me of the story of Mrs. Sanderson, which you have heard many times. If you were here perhaps we could find a way to help Samson escape and he could come and live on Hidden Wolf. There is a longer letter for Curiosity that will have come today with more news of the city. If you are very good I'm sure she will share it with you. In the meantime I will ask you to sit down right now, today, without delay, and write to me. Your cousin Ethan dreamed of you last night and I would like to know that you are well.
>
> Your loving sister Hannah Bonner, also called Walks-Ahead by the Kahnyen'kehàka, her mother's people

Will was the only one up and about to see her off to the Almshouse for her first day of work with Dr. Simon. She left the posting of the letter to him, and resisted the urge to tell him why it was important. He had many fine qualities, but Hannah wasn't sure that Will's open-mindedness would extend to dream-walking. She must trust him to see that the letter found its way home, and quickly.

Just before seven, Cicero delivered Hannah to the Almshouse, a rambling, shabby building that sat across from the beautifully kept city hall park like a boil on the nose of an otherwise elegant lady.

Cicero started the long climb down from the driver's box, but in her eagerness Hannah opened her own door and jumped lightly to the ground.

"That's not the way we do it, miss," said the older man, dropping his chin to look at her through overgrown eyebrows, divided by a deep and disapproving furrow.

"I'll try harder, Cicero, really I will, but—" Hannah sidestepped two old women who shuffled down the street with arms twined together like branches. "I don't want to be late."

His nose twitched in distaste as he looked at the Almshouse. "I'll be back at four sharp, right here. Don't you make me come in that place to find you, miss."

"Four exactly," Hannah echoed, and waited until Cicero had climbed back on the box and clucked to the team. He seemed to have assigned himself the role of her protector in the city, and Hannah was both touched and irritated by his concern for her, but she was also very glad when the carriage had disappeared into the traffic on the Broad Way and she was free to study the Almshouse.

It was three stories high and far bigger than the fine homes on Bowling Green, but it had been hard used in its short life and it seemed almost to sag in the middle. There were faces at many of the small windows, children and old people mostly. One face was so old and its expression so vacant that Hannah couldn't be sure if it belonged to a man or a woman. Sometimes the very old gave up on this world to concentrate on the next, and it was that kind of waiting that Hannah saw in the face that was watching her now. Wanting nothing, expecting nothing.

A building this big, filled with people too poor or old or sick to feed themselves, with no families to claim or care for them; such a thing was almost beyond comprehension. She wondered if it had to do with the city itself, so many people crowded together. Whatever the cause, the city was full of people who were so desperate for help that they might be

willing to overlook the color of her skin. That was what she
would find out today, for better or worse.

When she walked up the steps and opened the front door
she was greeted by the smells of porridge and boiled onions,
too many bodies too close together, chamber pots waiting to
be emptied, flesh gone foul, sour stomachs spilling over. A little boy came hurtling past her and bumped into her bag so that
she had to steady herself with one hand against the door frame,
or begin by falling on her face.

"Watch yourself, little bugger!" screeched a voice nearby.
Hannah wasn't sure if this was meant for her or the boy, but
she decided it was better not to find out.

The entryway was filled with people, most of them elderly,
all of whom studied her openly.

"Look, Josie." An old man wrapped in a striped blanket
turned to his neighbor. "An Indian princess come to the poorhouse. Maybe she'll want to share your bed, eh?" And he let
out a huffing laugh that quickly turned into a cough.

There was a raised desk at the far end of the room, and next
to it a row of children standing patiently with bundles clasped
to their chests. The oldest of them, a boy, held a crying baby
that seemed to be covered from scalp to toe with a scaly rash.
The porter was making notes on a pile of papers with a ragged
quill, and he didn't look up until Hannah stood directly before
his desk.

He was maybe thirty, with a shock of greasy hair that fell
forward over his brow. His fingers were ink stained and so was
his chin with its few dark hairs, which he was stroking in a distracted way. When he looked up at her he smiled with only
one side of his mouth, drawing attention to the cleft in his lip,
poorly hidden by a feathery mustache.

"May I help you?" He had to raise his voice to be heard
over the crying baby.

Hannah introduced herself and asked for Dr. Simon.

The porter's stained fingers stopped wandering through his
chin hairs while he looked at Hannah more closely, taking in
the plain gray wool work gown and apron in an old-fashioned
cut, the cloak of boiled wool and her medical bag.

"The new assistant?"

"Yes. For a short time, anyway."

The oldest of the children raised his voice to ask a question in a language Hannah didn't recognize. He had eyes the same shade of gray as Elizabeth.

"Irish orphans," said the porter. "Both parents died on the passage over. They want to know if you have a war club in your bag." He translated this question as if it were perfectly reasonable, but not especially interesting.

"You speak Irish, Mr.—"

"Chamberlain. I do. My mother is Irish."

"You can tell them that I carry no weapons. Tell them that I'm a doctor."

One corner of his mouth jerked, but he did as she asked and got in return another, much longer question from the boy.

"You're the first Indian they've ever laid eyes on, miss, and the first woman doctor. You can see by the look on his face that it will take more than my word."

The boy was looking at her expectantly, and so Hannah opened the bag to show them that it contained nothing more than her medical instruments, her notebooks, two full-length aprons, and the food that Mrs. Douglas had packed for her when she refused breakfast. The smallest of the children put his head so far inside that his hair fell forward and Hannah could see the lice crawling on the back of a dirty neck. When he looked up again his eyes were perfectly round.

"Arán."

Hannah gave the porter a questioning glance.

"It's the bread he's looking at."

"They're hungry?"

He nodded. "They always are. As soon as I get the paperwork finished they'll go off to the bathhouse and then the kitchens. And then Dr. Simon will want to see them in the Kine-Pox office."

Hannah took out the bread wrapped in a piece of linen and handed it to the oldest boy. "Tell him to divide it evenly. Now where do I find Dr. Simon?"

The children had fallen over the bread and paid no more attention to Hannah.

"Somewhere in the sick wards, most likely." He reached under the table and a shrill bell rang twice, once short and once long.

"Mrs. Sloo will show you the way."

A small woman had appeared at Hannah's elbow, as quick

and silent as a shadow in spite of the fact that she was easily as wide as she was tall. Under a startling white mobcap perfect iron gray curls were lined up in a row across her forehead. Dark brown eyes huddled close around a tiny fist of a nose, and below that was a full-lipped mouth perfectly shaped, but no wider than a spoon. Both sides of that astonishing mouth were turned up in a smile that showed a line of perfectly white and even teeth, as small as a child's, in gums the color of ripe cherries. It was a face of contradictions, but with a quick, intelligent, and clearly impatient expression.

"The new assistant, I take it." Mrs. Sloo looked Hannah up and down. "I'm the housekeeper, twenty years now, old place and new. Mr. Sloo's the keeper of the bridewell, not the gaol, mind, but the bridewell. Expect you passed by there on your way uptown."

Then she was off, walking at a rolling pace that defied her size, her skirts snapping around her.

"You'll want to know your way around," she said, putting back her head to throw her voice up toward the ceiling. "This is a big place, easy to get lost. Mr. Furman's office there, the superintendent. A devil for detail is Mr. Furman. Mr. Cox, purveyor. You'll want to stay out of Mr. Cox's way of a morning till he's had his coffee. He's a right bear without his coffee, is Mr. Cox. This hallway takes you out to the kitchens and bake house. Breakfast at six, dinner at noon, supper at six is how we working folk do it. I expect you're used to breakfast at eleven and dinner at four, but you'll adjust or go hungry, like everybody else. That way to the washhouse and beyond that's the workhouse, that's where you'll find all the able-bodied men from seven till six. The able-bodied work here or they don't eat. Cobblers, hoopers, what have you. Two carpenters do naught but make coffins. Most of them we use ourselves and the rest Mr. Cox sells or barters. A fierce man in a barter is Mr. Cox.

"Out that way you'll find the cow barn and the gardens. We raise most of our own vegetables or we did anyway when we weren't so crowded. We've got them sleeping and eating in shifts these days.

"It's Mr. Cox's business to scare up whatever it is we can't grow or raise. Keeps him busy. That there's the records office, where Mr. Eddy does his work. The indenturing and so forth, where orphans come from and where they go, the vessel book, papers enough to bury a standing man. Last year he found masters for forty-three of our young ones. Joiners and butchers and what have you, the girls in service."

She pivoted around suddenly to look up at Hannah. "You'll have seen two of our girls, went into service at the Spencers' on Whitehall. Amanda Blake and Bertha Dawson. Good strong girls, know their place and their work too. Bertha was born in the old place, on a Tuesday. Girls born in the poorhouse of a Tuesday—the ones that live long enough—are all called Bertha. What day of the week were you born?"

Hannah was so taken aback by this question that she stopped. "I don't know."

Mrs. Sloo sniffed and continued her strange toddling walk. They had come to a set of double doors and she opened these inward to a large room where thirty or more women were at work. "Mostly spinners and weavers in this room. Used to have the oakum pickers in here too, but the creosote stink got to be too much. Can't have the girls sicking up into the flax."

She shut the doors just as suddenly as she had opened them, before Hannah could get any feel for the place or even make eye contact with the children who were bent over flax combs.

"That there's where the seamstresses work, the tailors next to them. We don't hold with men and women working in the same room, not here. This stairway goes up to the dormitories. Men on the third floor, women and children on the second. Eight hundred and seventeen all told, with the two new ones born in the night still living. And these doors will take you into the sick wards."

She stopped just short of the double doors and knotted her red chapped hands together as if to keep herself from touching them.

"This is as far as I go." Her tone had shifted from the businesslike to something else, and Hannah saw that the tiny mouth had set itself hard. "You'll have to find your own way from here."

"I think I can manage," Hannah said.

Mrs. Sloo leaned forward, her round face tilted up to Hannah's as if to examine the color of her eyes. "If you know what's good for you you'll turn around and go home."

Hannah stepped back in her surprise.

"You think I can't read a newspaper? I know all about you. Not even twenty years on you, and there you stand. I'll tell you this. Latin won't do you any good beyond those doors. You're no use in the lying-in ward as nobody will want a red woman to midwife, and the sick wards are no place for a decent female, nor not even for a Mohawk princess who fancies herself a doctor. No good can come of it, that much I promise you."

"Newspaper?" Hannah echoed.

Mrs. Sloo sniffed loudly, turned on her heel, and trundled her way back down the hall.

On the other side of the double doors the short hallway looked much the same, with pale green walls and an uneven floor of wide oak planking. Doors lined both walls, and on each of them was a carefully polished brass plaque: Visiting Physicians, Suspended Animation Rescue, Apothecary. A line of people, men and women both, were waiting quietly outside this last door, all of them dressed in linsey-woolsey, most of the men in heavy clogs. One of them held a bloody rag to one eye while the other, bright blue, stared at Hannah in open disapproval. The apothecary door stood open, and Hannah had a glimpse of shelves lined with bottles and jars. A man stood with his back to her bent over a mortar, a small woman waiting to one side with her hands folded in front of her. The apothecary's hair stood out in a halo of frizzed curls around his head, backlit by the sun.

"Not now, Mr. Furman!" he thundered without turning around, and Hannah went on.

Another set of double doors opened into a very different kind of room, one as wide as the building itself and lined with beds, each of them occupied by a man, all of whom were looking directly at her. She saw yellowed skin and sunken eyes and swollen joints, a face overwhelmed by carbuncles, a belly swollen as large as a woman on the verge of childbirth. Each of these men was sick unto death; Hannah could see it in their faces.

She said, "I'm looking for Dr. Simon and the Kine-Pox Institution."

This got her nothing but more stares, and so she stepped farther into the room. "Dr. Simon is expecting me."

A door swung open at the far end of the ward. The man

who appeared there was tall and angular, with quick dark eyes underscored by shadows, a strong nose and chin, and hair that had been cut so short that it showed every curve of his skull. "Miss Bonner?"

"Yes." Hannah let out a great sigh of relief.

"Dr. Simon's office is this way."

As soon as the door was shut behind her Hannah said, "Are there no women on the wards at all?"

He cast her an unapologetically curious glance. "Mrs. Sloo tried to scare you off, eh? Never mind, she does it to everybody. There's women enough coming into the men's ward, day in and day out. Visitors and the cleaning women, and Mrs. Graham comes with the charity ladies once a week at least, with broth and bible pamphlets."

His way of talking was both dismissive and a little forward, but Hannah had expected as much. He was testing her, of course, to see what she was made of. Hannah wondered if there would be anyone in this whole place who might welcome her without giving voice to their misgivings.

"I expect they've never seen an Indian here."

"Oh, they've seen Indians, but not dressed like you are."

Before Hannah could decide whether to be insulted or curious about this comment, he continued.

"Most of them didn't talk to you because they can't. A good sixty percent of the inmates have only Irish or German. Just two Americans on the ward right now, and you won't get much out of either of them."

"And why not?"

He stopped to look at her. "Blue Harry—the man with the swollen abdomen—is stone-deaf, and Old Thomas doesn't talk to anybody except Mrs. Sloo, or so they say. I've never heard it, myself. That's the lying-in ward, there. Six beds, all of them full. We could do with twenty and still keep them filled. Here's Dr. Simon's office."

He opened the door with a flourish. "He'll be right in, Miss Bonner." There was a moment's hesitation while he studied the door frame. "Have you read the newspaper this morning?"

The question took her by surprise. "You are the second person to mention the newspaper to me. I haven't read it. Should I?"

He shrugged again, shoulders moving abruptly under his coat. "I would, if I were you."

Irritation slid down Hannah's back and straightened it. "You are very mysterious, Mr.——"

"Dr. Savard. I'm Dr. Simon's assistant."

"Dr. Savard. What newspaper are you talking about?"

"It's there on the desk," he said. "The *New-York Intelligencer.* You can't miss the article, it's called 'Red Prodigy.'"

Chapter 22

New-York Intelligencer
April 20, 1802

We have both seen and heard of such examples of extraordinary acumen in the Aborigines of this country as caused us to deplore the unhappy fate of the Indian tribes. It seems to us that no civilized nation of Europe has yet produced any individual—much less one of the gentle sex—of the same astonishing powers as were exhibited yesterday at the New-York Dispensary by a young lady of the Mohawk. We were present when the esteemed physicians of that institution met with the young lady, who presented herself as a student, wishing to learn the methods of Dr. Jenner's vaccinations against Smallpox, that she might carry this skill with her to the frontier.

Even the late Mrs. Wollstonecraft, whose little volume on the Rights of Women shocked and perturbed so many, would have been surprised to see her philosophy bear fruit so soon, and in one so young, for the lady in question is a mere eighteen years of age. She is tall for her sex, and her proportions are equal to that of those exquisite models of art which the genius of antiquity has left as a standard for modern taste. It is true that her complexion is of a dark copper shade, but her eyes are entirely destitute of the ferocity which is a general characteristic of the Indian tribes, and of the Mohawk in particular. They are quick and penetrating and at the same time have the placid regard which always fascinates and attracts attention. This young lady shows all the advantages of being raised in a civilized home. Her speech and dress most especially (she wore a simple but elegant, if somewhat outdated, lawn gown with a sash, bodice scarf, and shawl embroidered in green) display a taste uncommon to savages. But her mental talents surpassed even the considerable charms of her person.

The physicians gathered to interview the young Mohawk in the modest meeting room of the Dispensary. They began by asking her to recount her training in medicine. She complied in an unadorned, most refined language, and in doing so recounted a history that rivals Herr von Goethe's astonishing tale of Wilhelm Meister's Apprenticeship. In her short life her teachers have included such diverse personages as her own grandmother and great-grandmother, both healers and clan mothers of the near defunct Mohawk nation, Dr. Richard Todd of Albany and Paradise, whom she has served in an informal apprenticeship for the last three years, and Hakim Ibrahim Dehlavi ibn Abdul Rahman Balkhi, a Musselman physician of great repute who visited with this city's physicians just ten days ago.

Dr. Valentine Simon, the gentleman responsible for so much of the good work among the poor of this city and the founder of the Kine-Pox Institution, asked her a number of questions. On the treatment of burns, cramp colic, fevers, and a number of other common complaints the young Mohawk lady answered to the general satisfaction of the physicians. A larger discussion ensued on the topic of the treatment of malignant quinsy, which she had occasion to see and treat in her own village last summer, and of consumption, which Dr. Todd of Paradise has been treating with revolutionary methods from abroad. The physicians asked detailed questions, which she answered as concisely as she had answered all others.

A dispute broke out among the physicians on the subject of the Bilious or Yellow Fever, sometimes called the American Plague, which has struck so cruelly at our cities in the last ten years. While the physicians argued the ques-

tions of origin, contagion, and treatment, the young lady
listened politely without interruption. Dr. Ehrlich, visiting
from Philadelphia, then asked her opinion on the subject,
to which the young Mohawk replied that she knows the
disease only by its reputation and conflicting reports, and
found herself therefore unable to express any opinion at
all. Dr. Ehrlich pressed her on the issue of Dr. Benjamin
Rush's regimen of large doses of cathartic, specifically mercury and jalap, followed by copious bleeding.

At this the young lady hesitated, and then replied that she
was predisposed to the opinion of a Dr. Powell of Boston,
who claims that ingestion of mercury is far more damaging
than the disease it is meant to cure. She added in assured
tones that she was disinclined to excessive bloodletting, especially in the case of such a debilitating disease. In response to such strong opinions Dr. Ehrlich suggested that
her unorthodox and incomplete education in medicine had
overlooked the teachings of the immortal Hippocrates,
who advocated for extreme diseases, extreme methods of
cure. The young Mohawk woman replied to Dr. Ehrlich
with more of Hippocrates but now in Latin: Primum est
non nocere. First do no harm.

It is our opinion that nature rarely combines such prodi-
gious talent, self-awareness, and magnetism in an individual, and we are aware of no other case in which such rare
gifts have been bestowed upon an Indian or even a lady of
such great personal charms. We join the physicians of the
New-York Dispensary in welcoming this phenomenon to
our city, and wish her the best of luck in her work.

Chapter 23

The strangest part, Hannah thought to herself when she had read the article twice, was that the journalist—Henry Lamm, she reminded herself—that Mr. Lamm had meant to praise her. Others would read what he had written and call it complimentary, and in fact she could not point to any factual errors or exaggeration. She had surprised him with the simple fact that she could speak an articulate sentence, and that was the problem exactly: people expected things from her that she could not provide, and she had no choice but to surprise them. In the end there was no way to respond to such a sly combination of praise and censure; Hannah understood somehow that to reject what Mr. Lamm would surely think kindness and generosity would make an enemy of him. The well-to-do most often reacted badly when their charity was closely examined.

"At least he does not mention my name," she muttered, and heard at that moment a soft movement behind her. Dr. Simon had come into the room and she had not noticed.

He said, "Mr. Lamm believes that he has extended a courtesy by not naming you."

Hannah put the paper back down on the desk and managed a smile. "It would have been more courteous not to print this at all. I don't like being a curiosity."

Dr. Simon inclined his head. His neck linen was spattered with blood that hadn't yet dried.

"I can appreciate the difficulty. I must take some responsibility for the fact that he was allowed into the room yesterday. Is there some way that I may make amends?"

"Yes," Hannah said firmly. "You can put me to work and keep me busy, Dr. Simon."

"That much I can promise you, Miss Bonner." Dr. Simon gestured toward the door. "Shall we begin?"

At four o'clock Hannah came down the steps to the sight of Cicero on the driver's box and Will Spencer holding the landau door for her.

"I wasn't expecting to see you." She accepted his hand up into the carriage. "I'm glad you came, but it's good that you didn't bring Kitty." She looked down at herself; her gown could not look in worse repair if she had spent the day fighting her way through the bush. Will did not seem concerned at all, but he did look closely at her as he settled himself.

"She would be taken aback, that's true."

"She would be horrified," corrected Hannah, with some satisfaction. "I'm afraid this is what comes of vaccinating Irish orphans. Tomorrow I will know better what to expect."

"Tomorrow," said Will, "your eye will be very charming shades of black and blue."

With two fingers Hannah touched the swollen flesh very lightly. "Just a three-year-old in a panic. She didn't mean to do it."

"I hate to think what she might accomplish if she put her mind to it," said Will. "You had a good day otherwise?"

Hannah drew in a deep breath. "I haven't really had time to think. But yes, it was a good day. I learned the basics of the vaccination method and then I assisted the doctors. There are a number of patients who should be in the New-York Hospital, but as they are very close to death Dr. Simon has kept them in his wards. Oh and Will, Dr. Simon is going to lend me his translation of *Seats and Causes of Disease*. I have some extracts that Hakim Ibrahim sent me, but not the whole—"

She paused, realizing that she had been running on without considering how Will might react to such details, but there was nothing but simple curiosity in his expression.

"I also learned a few words of Irish. 'No biting' being the most helpful. And now I've talked enough. How did Kitty fare today?"

"Well enough, I think, although she was very pale when

she came back from her excursion. Dr. Ehrlich called on her—I think he was disappointed not to find you in."

"No doubt," Hannah said dryly. "I suppose he bled her again."

"I couldn't say. You will find her napping, I think. And you had another disappointed visitor this morning. Manny Freeman."

"Manny Freeman," Hannah echoed. "I had forgot all about his coming by. I wanted to talk to him about—" She stopped, and Will blinked at her in a way that reminded her suddenly and quite unexpectedly of Runs-from-Bears. And what a strange thing that was, because Hannah could not think of two men who resembled each other less in physical appearance.

Will said, "If you can wait another half hour for your dinner, I think we should have a talk. Shall I ask Cicero to take us for a short drive?"

Hannah nodded. "Yes," she said. "I think that would be a good idea."

Later Hannah had no memory of the first part of the drive, because all of her attention was focused on Will Spencer's face as she told the story of what had happened in Paradise since the Sunday morning she and Elizabeth had found Selah Voyager under a hobblebush.

When she had finished, recounting as much of her conversation with Liam Kirby as she could recall and felt comfortable sharing, Will said nothing at all for a long time. Instead he stared out the window, turning his hat in his hands.

Hannah didn't mind waiting, and she didn't mind the silence; she had grown up in a household where quiet contemplation was highly prized, and she trusted Will Spencer. But now that she had laid out the whole story, piece by piece, she felt the weight of it again.

"This is a very dangerous business," Will said finally. "I should send you straight home to Paradise."

Hannah sat up straight. "I'm very tired of this silliness, Will, I must say."

He raised a brow at her. "Silliness?"

"Mrs. Sloo tells me I belong neither in a birthing room nor in the Almshouse sick wards; Dr. Ehrlich tells me I don't belong in medicine—something Mr. Lamm found it necessary to print in his newspaper, as I'm sure you're aware by now—"

Will inclined his head:

"—and you tell me I don't belong in the city at all. I expected more of you, of all people."

It was not often that Will Spencer showed strong emotion, but Hannah saw that she had managed to push him that far.

"You do not understand, Hannah." He was angry and offended both, but so was she.

"I do. I understand that Manny is in danger of his life, and that you've been helping with the...the voyagers. Can't you just say as much and stop being so mysterious? I'm not a child who can't be trusted to keep silent."

Will's jaw worked once or twice as he turned his attention out the window again. He said, "You are more like Elizabeth every time I see you."

"I will take that as a compliment."

"I meant it as one." He pushed out a deep breath. "We call ourselves the Libertas Society, and in the last eight years we have helped one hundred thirteen slaves to freedom. Sometimes we have provided money anonymously or arranged to buy someone's freedom through a third party, but more have run away with our assistance. Some of those north, through Curiosity and Galileo, some to England. We also are involved in stopping the kidnapping of free blacks and the unlawful transport of blacks to the Southern states, where they can be sold into permanent slavery. There are seven of us, including Almanzo. I cannot tell you who the others are, because we are each of us sworn to keep those names secret. What else do you want to know?"

"Does Amanda know?"

"Yes," said Will. "In theory she has known from the beginning, although she is never informed of the details. For her own protection. After the trouble in England I promised her I would never keep...my activities...from her again. And of course I've made provisions, if something should go wrong—" He stopped himself.

"But Elizabeth doesn't know."

"No. I saw no reason to implicate her, and in fact Curiosity and Galileo insisted that your family be kept out of it."

His expression was very calm now, even relieved. Hannah realized that she and Will Spencer had something in common: neither of them had the freedom to talk openly about the work that was most important to them.

In a gentler tone she said, "And what happened at the Newburgh dock? Who could have betrayed you, and Selah?"

"I don't know," said Will. "But I will find out. The answer is somewhere in that building." And he gestured with his chin out the window.

They had left the city proper and were now on an unpaved street. There was the stink of tanneries and slaughterhouses, livestock and pig slurry. Not far ahead of them came the bawling of cattle and the landau slowed down suddenly, Cicero chirping calm words to the team. The air filled with dust from the milling animals.

"The Bull's Head," said Will as they inched their way past a tavern flanked on both sides by cattle pens. "The drovers bring the cattle here from the countryside, and the auctions are held there, in the tavern."

"What does this have to do with the voyagers?" asked Hannah.

"Micah Cobb and the Swamp Boys meet here, every Friday and Wednesday night. A sort of association of black-birders, you'd have to call them. That's how they divide the work up among themselves."

"This Cobb is behind what happened on the Newburgh dock?"

"Yes. The only question is where he's getting his information."

Will leaned forward toward Hannah. "I've answered your questions, and now I'm going to ask you for something. This is a dangerous business, and it's coming to a head. You did us a great service by passing on Liam Kirby's message, but I'm asking you to step back now and let us take care of it. Will you agree?"

Hannah hesitated. "I am worried about Manny."

Will's expression hardened, just enough for Hannah to see the conviction there, and the strength of purpose. He opened his mouth to speak but she stopped him with a raised hand.

"Did I ever tell you that my grandmother Falling-Day gave you a Mohawk name?"

"Did she." She had managed to surprise him.

"She called you 'The Dreamer.' It's a great compliment among my mother's people to be called a dreamer. She said that you live most of your life in unseen worlds and come into this one only when you have some purpose to serve. I think you have a great purpose to serve with your Libertas Society."

Will's jaw worked thoughtfully, and when he looked away Hannah thought he was trying to hide a grin. She had amused him, but he did not wish to insult her. Finally he said, "In that case, you will give me your word that you will leave Micah Cobb and the blackbirders to us."

"If that is the only way I can be of help to you, yes."

Will sat back and ran a hand over his face. "Thank you. I give you my word that we will do everything in our power to make sure that no harm comes to Manny. He will be leaving here very soon."

"Curiosity and Galileo will be relieved when he is away, and safe." She did not say the rest of it, that relief would come at a high price; their only son would never be able to come home again unless he left his wife and child behind.

"So will we all. Now I think it is time to go home and see that you get your dinner." And he called up to Cicero, who began to turn the team immediately.

Now as they passed the Bull's Head there was a woman standing in the doorway of the tavern, tall and slender and bow-backed with weariness. Dark hair wound around her head, copper-skinned; a half-breed. She caught Hannah's eye and her expression changed as did her posture, her back straightening so quickly that Hannah was reminded of her grandfather's hunting dogs when they got the scent of a wolf. Alike and not alike; cousin and enemy. A rippling shock raced up Hannah's spine and down her arms to tingle in her fingers, as if the strange woman in the doorway of the tavern had pointed a gun at her.

The carriage came to a sudden halt again, jerking Hannah's attention to the opposite side of the carriage where a procession had appeared. Two young boys pounding on drums were followed by a long, skeleton-thin man in a butcher's apron. In one hand he carried a large and well-polished cleaver, and with the other he led a cow on a rope. He stopped at Will's window and smiled broadly, showing two deep dimples and eyeteeth that had been filed to points.

"Good day, sir, good day. The finest bit of beef you'll see this spring, sir. Bought her at auction just this morning. Will you have some of her?"

While Will negotiated with the butcher about what cuts of meat he would take and at what price, Hannah turned back to the tavern, but the woman was gone. When the butcher had gone on his way, Hannah touched Will's sleeve and pointed with her chin.

"There was a person standing there, an Indian woman. Did you see her?"

He cleared his throat. "Yes. Her name is Virginia Bly. The innkeeper's wife."

"She's the first Indian woman I've seen since I came to the city," Hannah said. "She gave me the strangest look—"

"Have you not heard her name before?"

"I have not. Should she be familiar to me?"

Will studied the door frame thoughtfully. "I thought Liam Kirby might have mentioned her. He is married to Bly's oldest daughter, Jenny. You didn't know?"

Hannah forced herself to look at Will, although she knew he would see more in her face than she wanted to show. "That he is married, yes. I knew that. But Mrs. Bly could not know me. Why would she look at me like that?"

Will hesitated. "How much did Liam tell you?"

"Enough," said Hannah. "As much as I care to know."

They were silent for a very long time. When Hannah raised her head, Will had turned away politely to study the activity on the streets as if he had never been in the city before. He was as ever the English gentleman who would not pry in private matters.

Hannah swallowed down her irritation and her curiosity. Just yesterday she had decided that she wanted to know something of Liam's life here in the city, and she should be satisfied to have had that opportunity with so little trouble.

Be careful what you ask for; it was one of Elizabeth's favorite sayings, and Hannah felt its full force as the landau took them back to the city in silence.

APRIL 24, 1802. EVENING.

My first full day at the Almshouse. As a part of my introduction to the practice of smallpox vaccination Dr. Simon vaccinated me. He made small incisions in both my upper arms with a sharp lancet, hardly deep enough to draw blood. Into these incisions he rubbed virus material taken this morning from an orphan who was vaccinated eight days before. Dr. Savard then showed me how records are kept and materials are stored.

I observed for the rest of the morning and in the afternoon I assisted in the women's ward. The patients here are all too poor to pay the four-dollar fee to be admitted to the City Hospital. Many are newly arrived by ship and have no money, friends, or language, and of those, I am told, more than a few end up buried in the paupers' graveyard.

Dr. Savard is to introduce me to most of my duties here. To me his manner is curt but not directly insulting. To the patients he is less abrupt but distant. Mr. Magee, who seems to be both caretaker and orderly, asked me if I had ever taken a scalp. He asked this question in Dr. Savard's hearing. Dr. Savard looked very pointedly at Mr. Magee's bald head, arched an eyebrow, and laughed aloud. He has a wit as quick as Will Spencer's but little of kindness or patience to temper it; he indulges his sense of humor at the expense of others. And still he performed a service, in that Mr. Magee has asked me no more silly questions.

Dr. Simon says that everyone will soon be accustomed to me and will go about their business normally. I hope he is right. I can learn a great deal from the doctors here, if they will let me work.

April 26. Evening.

The air in the city is heavy with soot; I have heard birds but seen no living creatures beyond men, dogs, pigs, sparrows, rats, and horses this day. I feel a thunderstorm coming.

Examined seven patients vaccinated before I arrived here. None have yet reached day eight. Four new vaccinations, two observed and two performed with Dr. Simon's guidance. He seems well pleased with the preservation technique suggested by the Hakim in his last letter and will adopt it in the clinic.

My own vaccination day two. Sites on both arms dry, no symptoms.

Examined five orphans and dosed them all for worms; assisted in two normal deliveries, mothers and infants all in good health, and a stillbirth. The mother, a girl of fourteen years, turned away and would not look at her child. Removed dead tissue from Mrs. Hallahan's suppurating breast. She is in great pain and opium provides little relief.

One thing I had not expected to need here was a knowledge of foreign languages. The little bit of French I learned from lessons with Elizabeth was all but used up by the arrival of a number of Acadians, and I floundered until Dr. Savard came to my rescue. Every day we see patients who are newly arrived from the docks and have no English. Twice I have been called upon to speak Scots and find that I am grown clumsy with it from long disuse. My grandmother Cora would be disappointed and my cousin Jennet outraged.

When Irish is needed, I must call on Mr. Chamberlain from the porter's desk. Mr. Holbein from the carpentry shop does for German, Mrs. Gronewold for Dutch, Mr. Luedtke for Danish and Swedish, Dr. O'Connell for Spanish and Italian as he learned these languages when he was a ship's surgeon. Dr. Savard speaks the French language fluently. According to Mr. Magee, who has stopped asking me questions and instead plies me with gossip whenever I am near, no matter how little interest I show, Dr. Savard lived much of his early life in France and then in French Canada. Mr. Magee also informs me that the doctor wears his hair shorn very short because he detests lice. A very strange preoccupation for a doctor who works with the poor of this city.

There are on occasion African servants and slaves who come to us for care but thus far all of them have had some English. I have seen no Indians at all, which does not surprise me in this overcrowded city.

Of all the white immigrants the German are the most openly disliked and are often treated very badly. It is a revelation to me to see that O'seronni hatred can also be turned toward their own in this way.

I have begun a list of the most crucial terms in all these languages, which I keep in my apron pocket. Thus far I have recorded "please" and "thank you," "where is the pain?," "hold still," and "I can help you."

APRIL 28. EVENING.

Today I found the room they call the nursery, where the orphaned infants are kept. What misery.

APRIL 29. LATE AFTERNOON.

Overcast for most of the day; some showers. Two buntings on my windowsill this evening, chased away by a robin, the robin then dislodged by a crow who stares at me with a sharp black eye and reminds me of Dr. Savard. Another curiosity about the doctor: he seems to have memorized much of Dr. Morgagni's writings, which he quotes at great length in Latin or English as his mood dictates. I am glad now of the hours Elizabeth made me spend with Latin grammar, as I am mostly able to follow his mutterings. When Dr. Savard examines a patient he asks the question out loud: Ubi est morbus? Where is the disease? as he begins his questioning.

Examined sixteen patients vaccinated in the last month; three of whom had reached day eight. Two of these showed the expected white vesicle raised at the edges and depressed at the center, with a turgid margin. Dr. Scofield, who continues to speak to me in a loud voice as if I were deaf, supervised while I used the lancet to extract the virus from these two patients. The third patient, a twenty-seven-year-old farm worker called Marie LeTourneau, was revaccinated with the fresh material. It may be that she has already had the pox or been exposed to it, thus the lack of reaction to the first vaccination attempt.

My own vaccination, day five. Sites on both arms lightly inflamed and tumid to the touch. Slight headache in the morning hours. No fever or swollen glands nor any other symptoms. No sign of eruption or vesicles.

This morning at eleven a man called Matthew Johns was brought into the ward. The patient was about forty years of age, resident in the Almshouse four weeks, with no prior history of serious illness beyond the broken arm that had cost him his job as a dockworker (a simple fracture of the ulna set by Dr. Simon and largely healed). A short man, thickly built and strong. Symptoms of shortness of breath, erratic pulse, profuse sweating, and ashen complexion. While he was answering questions put to him by Dr. Savard, he suddenly threw up both arms over his head with such force that his fists hit the wall and made it shudder. At the same time he let out a great bellowing cry like an ox struck by a dull axe. His face flushed a deep and angry red and his eyes bulged as if pushed from inside his head. Mr. Johns was instantly dead, with no pulse at the throat or wrists.

Dr. Scofield made a record of death due to violent apoplexy. As the patient had no family or next of kin and was a ward of the city, Dr. Simon has released his remains to the hospital for autopsy, which has been scheduled for eight this evening. He has invited me to observe.

In the late afternoon Mr. Eddy, who keeps the record books, came into the Kine-Pox office and argued with Dr. Savard for a quarter *hour about the cost of the ivory vaccinators we must have for our work. Dr. Savard refused to answer his questions with any seriousness of tone, which put Mr. Eddy in a very poor mood. The louder Mr. Eddy spoke in his irritation the softer spoke Dr. Savard. Just before he left Mr. Eddy took note of me and announced that he objected most strenuously to my presence. According to Mr. Eddy, an unmarried young lady—and this word came to him with great difficulty—has no place in the Almshouse wards.*

Dr. Savard then offered to marry me on the spot, which caused Mr. Eddy to leave in a state of great agitation. When I remarked to Dr. Savard that he seems to enjoy baiting Mr. Eddy he said he was in all seriousness; he would rather marry than have to vaccinate another Irish orphan, a task which falls now entirely to me.

APRIL 30.

A letter from Curiosity with no news of my father and stepmother but the curious report that Jemima Southern and Isaiah Kuick are man and wife. She says that the widow is as displeased as Jemima is satisfied with her new prize. The village will speak of nothing else. For the first time I am glad not to be home. Included in her letter was one from my brother Daniel asking questions but giving no answers, and a drawing done by my sister of Blue sleeping with his head on his paws. It is a little awkward in execution, but still I am amazed and a little unsettled at how well she has rendered his likeness. She has sprained her ankle, but seems otherwise in good health and remarkable spirits. I still do not understand the message the dream-walker brought to me.

Manny came to visit while I was in the kitchen with Mrs. Douglas just before dinner. He brought more news of a neighbor's plan to remove herself and her slaves to the South. This is causing great concern and uneasiness among the servants.

He refuses to say when he will leave this city. I believe he is waiting for news of the voyager, and is reluctant to leave for fear of missing a letter.

Today Mrs. Douglas spoke to me of Kitty's bleeding, which has increased rather than decreased since our arrival as evidenced by the state of her linen. I asked if Dr. Ehrlich had been informed of this, to which Mrs. Douglas only pressed her lips together and refused to say anything at all.

We agreed that Kitty is to be fed a broth of beef and leeks twice daily to fortify her blood. Ethan will sit by her side and make sure she takes it all.

The boy's spirits are so much improved since we are here that I cannot regret this journey.

Chapter 24

The first week at the Almshouse went by so quickly that Hannah might have lost track of the days if it were not for Kitty, who spent the dinner hour reminding her that she was sacrificing a great many pleasures in the pursuit of her medical training.

"You have turned down three invitations in three days and oh, yesterday's musical evening at the theater, did I mention that we sat behind Mr. Astor and his lady? It is said that he is a fine musician."

"Not the story of his forty flutes again, Kitty, please." Will held up a hand in mock horror.

"I think it is a very revealing story. To come from Germany with nothing but flutes to sell and look at him now."

"Mr. Astor's fortune has far more to do with furs than flutes," Hannah said firmly, and stopped herself there. She would not be drawn into another argument about Astor's fur trade practices, something Kitty knew little about but was willing to defend nonetheless.

"Mr. Astor aside," Kitty said. "You are avoiding my point."

Hannah considered her own fatigue, the fact that she had three pages of notes to record in her daybook, and finally Kitty's expression, which was as stubborn as it had ever been. It was obvious that further resistance would be unproductive.

"I'm listening."

"It is simple. You spend all day with Dr. Simon, and now

he is asking for your assistance in the evenings as well. It is too much."

"Yesterday was an unusual circumstance."

"Was it. Well, I hope he is not going to ask again. I'm sure you would have liked the musicale much better than whatever task he set you."

For a moment Hannah had the very dangerous urge to tell Kitty exactly what she had been doing, and how much more instructive it had been than any musicale. But Elizabeth had trained her well, and Hannah could not insult Will and Amanda Spencer with a description of an autopsy at their supper table. And beyond simple good manners, she had promised Dr. Simon. Dissections were very unpopular with the public, primarily because some doctors had got into the habit of robbing graves for their students to study. She must keep her silence, no matter what she had seen and learned; no matter the dreams that woke her in the night.

She said, "I have no plans to go back to the dispensary this evening."

"That is good news." Kitty studied Hannah with pursed lips. "And you must promise me that you will be home by noon tomorrow or you won't be ready for the guests at four."

Hannah looked up from her plate and caught two smiles— Will's amused one and Amanda's, far more concerned and sympathetic.

Will said, "It is just a small party, Kitty. An old friend on his way back to England and some friends, nothing more."

Kitty made a strangled noise that meant she was not going to let Will Spencer understate the excellence of his guest list.

The idea of a recitation of the life history and family connections of each person who would come through the door tomorrow evening made Hannah a little desperate. The only hope was to distract Kitty by changing the topic.

She said, "Ethan mentioned to me that you fainted this afternoon."

The thin, pale face went quite still for a moment. Then Kitty turned to Amanda, as one sister might turn to another looking for an ally when a mother began to ask difficult questions.

Amanda cleared her throat gently. "Perhaps the second outing was a little too much after all."

Kitty pressed her lips together. "It was nothing, just a little dizziness."

But of course it was more. Dr. Ehrlich's treatments seemed to be doing very little good at all, and Hannah had the uneasy feeling that if she were to examine Kitty she would find her much worse off than she had been even a week ago. She suspected that some of Kitty's irritable mood had to do with the fact that she was in pain, but she would not be questioned by Hannah; she had put all her hope in the doctor, who bled her when she requested and otherwise left her to her whims. Because, Hannah knew quite well, he had no other treatment to offer.

A vision of Mr. Johns came to her, his chest laid neatly open, ribs cut and spread, muscles folded back to reveal the heart. She had spent enough time studying anatomy books to know that what she was seeing was not normal; for some reason, this particular heart was twice the size it should have been, and embedded in a nest of blood vessels that were as brittle as dry bark. A ragged tear in the muscle wall was plain to see, the tissue worn as thin as intestine.

Inside of Kitty there was something wrong too, something that would remain a mystery even if—even when—it killed her. This thought made Hannah regret her impatience, but Will had already decided to intercede in the disagreement.

Will said, "May I propose a compromise? If Kitty spends somewhat less time satisfying social obligations"—he held up a single finger to keep her from interrupting—"and Hannah spends somewhat more, you may both be better satisfied. Hannah?"

She gave him a dry smile. "I am happy to compromise. Kitty, I will come home at midday tomorrow and give the party my full attention if you will promise to rest the half day beforehand, and the whole day after."

Kitty hesitated. "Will you let me choose your dress for the party?"

Hannah thought of the three gowns she had brought with her, any of which would suit. There was little havoc even Kitty could manage with such limited resources. She nodded.

After a week Hannah's daily routine was well established; she arrived at the Almshouse at seven, worked with Dr. Scofield or Dr. Savard for most of the morning in the Kine-Pox Institution office and then in the wards. If she was asked, she assisted in the apothecary until it was time to accompany Dr. Simon to the New-York Hospital to see how his other patients were progressing. Every day Mrs. Douglas gave her bread, cheese, and cold meat tied up in a napkin, and every day Hannah forgot about it until Cicero came to get her so that she could join the Spencers for dinner at four.

The doctor kept her so busy that there was little time to spend with Ethan, and even less to worry, not even about Manny. There was no time for homesickness either, although she sometimes wondered whether her father and Elizabeth had returned yet from Red Rock and if there might soon be a letter with news from home. Certainly her days were too busy to spend any thought on Liam Kirby, his whereabouts, his wife, or his mother-in-law.

No matter how firmly she put these things from her in the daylight hours, in the night she often woke from dreams that faded away almost immediately, leaving behind vague images of Virginia Bly standing at the doorway of the Bull's Head.

"Will it be much longer, miss?"

Hannah realized that the young man standing in the doorway of the pharmacy had been waiting while she daydreamed over the mortar and pestle. She focused her attention on the task at hand. By the time she had sent him on his way with ointment for his mother's shingles, it was almost noon and time to go. The people who were still waiting outside the pharmacy door she must leave to Mr. Jonas, the Almshouse apothecary, who would dose children for worms and dispense headache tisanes for the rest of the day with short temper but great efficiency.

Dr. Savard came in just when Hannah was beginning to worry that Mr. Jonas had forgotten her.

"Are you here to take over?"

"Most certainly not. Mrs. Sloo sent me to find you." He scratched in a distracted way at the bristle on his chin. "She's asking you to come by and lend a hand with a new inmate. Damn me if that ropemaker with the broken foot hasn't given me lice."

Dr. Savard's easy profanity had increased every day that Hannah had known him. Whether this was a sign of his approval and a compliment, or an indication that he didn't take her seriously, she had not yet decided.

"Mrs. Sloo asked for my help?" She hung the leather apothecary apron on its hook and smoothed her skirt. "I am surprised. I haven't seen her since my first day here."

"She's seen you, of that you can be sure. There's an Indian come begging at the door, doesn't understand English."

He was examining the creature he had drawn from his beard with one corner of his mouth turned down in resigned disgust.

"Mrs. Douglas checks my head every evening and goes through it with a fine steel comb. Perhaps that would help."

The doctor squinted at her, his brows drawn together. "But of course, what a good idea. I'll have my housekeeper tell the butler to send my manservant out to buy a steel comb."

An early lesson Hannah had learned was never to argue with Dr. Savard when he turned to sarcasm. She picked up her bag.

"I'll stop to see Mrs. Sloo on my way out."

He drew up to his full and considerable height. "On your way out? Feeling the need for a stroll along the promenade? Or perhaps you've an important meeting with the mayor?" He crossed his arms and lowered his chin. Like a bull pawing at the ground, Hannah thought, a bad-tempered bull looking for somebody to charge. Any other time she might have risen to the challenge as her arguments with Dr. Savard tended to be instructive, but today there was no time.

"Dinner with some friends of my cousin's," said Hannah. "I promised to attend."

"Let me guess, the mayor and the head of the city council."

"No," Hannah said. "But I believe the mayor's nephew will be there."

"Ah, dining with Senator Clinton, is it? Fine company for a doctor's assistant from the backwoods."

Hannah had been goaded by men with far sharper tongues than Dr. Savard; someday, she promised herself, she would tell him so. "I'll be back tomorrow morning at seven."

"That's all right then," he said, returning to the finger-combing of his beard stubble. "I wouldn't want to keep such riches all to myself."

*   *   *

"I can't decide if she's deaf and dumb or if she never learned a civilized tongue." Mrs. Sloo jerked her head over her shoulder toward a shape huddled in a corner of the waiting room. "But the child is dead a day at least. Maybe you can get it away from her. Tell her we'll give it a decent Christian burial and that we'll feed her before she goes back to wherever she came from."

Mrs. Sloo folded her hands in front of herself and gave Hannah her sternest look. "She can't stay here, tell her that. There might be a bed in the bridewell for her tonight if they aren't too crowded. And you'll want to be quick about it; Mr. Spencer's carriage is waiting for you out on the street."

She might have been fifteen or thirty or a hundred. A young-old-ageless woman not quite alive and nowhere near dead; she looked at Hannah with eyes dark as blood and hard as bone, and the arms around the silent bundle in her arms tightened.

"Food." The word whispered in English, like a secret between friends, a password.

"The only word she knows, or admits to." Mrs. Sloo's toe tapped impatiently.

Hannah ignored her to focus on the woman. She was wrapped in a torn blanket coat, and her head wobbled slightly, as if her neck could not quite bear the burden. Hannah thought of the body that had once been Mr. Johns on the dissection table, his muscular throat laid open to the knife, the stark white of tendon, the dark blue of stilled blood, the red muscle, yellow fat, the *color* of him.

"Let me see the child." Hannah whispered too, chilled by the disapproval that radiated from Mrs. Sloo.

The woman looked at her blankly, but the flexing in her arms meant something.

Hannah touched her own chest and named herself formally, in her own language. *I am Walks-Ahead, daughter of Sings-from-Books of the Kahnyen'kehàka. We are the People of the Longhouse, Keepers of the Eastern Door, the Mohawk of the Six Nations of the Hodenosaunee People.*

The woman blinked at Hannah as if she twittered rather than spoke. She tried again in her grandfather's language, naming him and his father and grandfathers of the Mahican.

Nothing.

"Maybe she's from one of them tribes to the south," said Mrs. Sloo behind her, as if she might have said *a different breed of dog.* "Try one of those."

In her amazement Hannah turned to look up at the little woman, mounds of flesh topped by a perfectly round head, the row of curls, the tiny mouth pursed in distaste.

"What tribes do you mean?"

The older woman flapped her little hands in front of herself. "What do I know? Gibberish is gibberish. Never mind, I'll get Moroney to help. Should have done that to start with."

Agnes Moroney, with hands like warped washboards, a woman with the strength and the understanding of a man; Hannah had seen her toss a drunken and contentious tanner into the street with a flick of her wrists.

"No," Hannah said, turning her back. "Leave her to me. This is a medical matter."

A huffing came from behind her, the sound of offense taken and stored carefully away, and still Hannah waited until Mrs. Sloo was gone. There would be a day of reckoning, oh yes, but she could not worry about that now.

"Food," said the woman with the dead baby, still whispering.

"Yes," Hannah said. "Come with me, I will give you food. Away from here, in a safe place."

The dark eyes blinked again. After a long moment punctuated only by the wailing of a hungry child on the other side of the wall, the woman nodded.

She would give them no name, not even after she had eaten her fill at the kitchen table. Mrs. Douglas was busy with preparations for the dinner party, and so Hannah served her, cornbread spread with beef fat, venison pie, spring onions, pickled cabbage, currant tart. Whatever she put on the table, the woman took to herself quickly and neatly, stopping now and then to suck her fingers clean and wipe them on her blanket coat.

Peter observed this ritual with rounded eyes but kept his silence, in part because Ethan seemed to find nothing unusual about the visitor's table manners and in part because Mrs. Douglas sent him a series of very pointed looks to remind him how any guest in the Spencer house must be treated. Hannah knew that if she gave him any encouragement he would ask questions, and so she said nothing at all and simply watched the visitor.

For her part the woman took no note of the boys or the cooks or the coming and going of tradesmen or of anything but the food before her and Hannah, who sat across from her at the table. She ate with one hand because she still held her child against her chest under the blanket.

When she was finished she rose slowly and pushed the plate a little away from herself. There were some crumbs at the corner of her mouth, and a trembling there that touched Hannah more than anything she could have said.

"There is a bed for you here, and fresh clothes. If you want them."

The woman gave her no answer, but when Hannah left the room, she followed.

At three, when the stranger was soundly asleep with her child in her arms, Hannah realized two things: she had broken the promises she made yesterday evening to Kitty, and she had an hour to get ready for the dinner party. She was standing in the hall outside her bedroom thinking through these things and wondering where to start trying to make amends when Amanda appeared. She was wearing an evening gown that shimmered deep indigo and her expression was distracted, but she stopped in front of Hannah and looked at the closed door.

"How is she?"

Hannah lifted a shoulder and spread out a hand in a question of her own. "She's asleep, finally."

"She hasn't—"

"No, not yet."

Amanda closed her eyes briefly and then opened them again.

"I'll send Suzannah in to sit with her. You must come now, Kitty is waiting for you in her room."

For once Hannah was unable to hide her exasperation. "I suppose I must listen to yet another lecture about the importance of millinery."

Amanda straightened suddenly, and new color came into her face along with a flicker of something severe in her eyes. For the first time Hannah saw a little of her mother in her, Aunt Merriweather's sharp eye and sharper temper.

"Hannah Bonner," Amanda said. "That is most unkind of you. It is true that Kitty can be very trying at times, and I understand that her silliness—I suppose that is the only word—about shopping and parties is irritating to you. But you know her too well to think so poorly of her, Hannah. Who understands better than Kitty what that woman is suffering? Do you think she would put a visit to the shops above that? Kitty spent an hour this afternoon cutting cloth and sewing a shroud for that child."

Hannah had drawn back in surprise and alarm. "I didn't mean—"

"You did mean." Amanda's chin trembled, and her usual soft expression came over her features. "You have been working very hard and this must affect you very deeply—" She looked at the closed door again, lost in her own thoughts.

"It was very kind of Kitty to make a shroud."

Amanda nodded. "It helps her to keep busy, I think. She spends so much time thinking about the little girl she lost, you know. Now will you do something kind for her?"

"Yes," Hannah said. "Of course."

Amanda had a sweet smile, and it brought Hannah great relief. "Go to her then, she's waiting, and let her dress you. It will give her a great deal of joy. I will follow as soon as I've spoken to Mrs. Douglas about our visitor."

"Miss Whitmore has made some adjustments in the shoulders and the bodice based on your own clothing," said Kitty, one knuckle pressed against her chin as she studied the gown that had been spread across her bed. "I think this will serve very well. Hannah, you must put it on right away so that she can make sure of the fit."

Hannah looked from Kitty to Amanda and to the seamstress, who was busy rummaging through her workbox, her mouth bristling with pins.

"I can't wear my own green silk?" She tried to say this as gently as possible, but Kitty's chin came up as if she had been challenged to a duel.

"You promised that you would let me choose your gown."

"I did, but—"

"And I chose this one. This is too fine a party for you to wear Miss Somerville's cast-off green silk. The color never

suited your complexion anyway." She looked down at the
heap of pale silk in shades of ivory and cream and pale yellow
with as much affection and satisfaction as she looked at her
son. "It will give me great pleasure to see you in this."

"Very well," Hannah said grimly. "I will wear the gown."

"And Catherine will do your hair," Kitty continued in
what was meant to be her sternest tone, undercut by the suspicion of a smile at one corner of her mouth.

Hannah touched her plait where it lay on her shoulder and
thought of sweet Amanda, her voice shaking with anger.

"I am yours to outfit as you see fit."

Kitty smiled triumphantly and clapped her hands together.
"I will make a masterpiece of you."

"As long as I do not have to see myself in the looking
glass," Hannah said dryly. "You may do as you wish."

But there was no way to avoid her own image; it presented itself in the great ormolu mirror in the hall, in another that
hung over the mantelpiece, in the mirrors behind every candle
sconce. Even if Hannah could have avoided catching a glance
of the mischief Kitty and Catherine had wrought in the mirrors, the same message was to be seen in the faces of the
guests. The men would not hide their admiration; the ladies
could not conceal surprise behind careful smiles. A memory
came to Hannah, Elizabeth's clear, elegant hand and the lines
she had written.

*Lilith cried out the name of the creator, whereupon she rose into
the air, and flew away to the Red Sea.*

The idea of wings to fly away on was very appealing, but instead Hannah was cocooned head to toe in Kitty's finery. The
high-waisted silk taffeta gown was cut very low indeed, something that did not bother Hannah in principle—she had grown
up working the cornfields next to women who worked bare-
breasted under the August sun. Except of course Kahnyen'-
kehàka men didn't take any special note, while these gentlemen
were working very hard not to study exactly that part of the female anatomy which had been put out for inspection.

The green silk was far more modest, and it seemed to
Hannah that it would have made things easier on these guests
Kitty so wanted to please. It also had long sleeves, which
would have saved the worry that the short sleeves of Kitty's

gown might not cover the vaccination sites on Hannah's upper arms. But there was no help for any of it; she had made a promise and she would keep her word. She wore the gown; she let Catherine intertwine her hair with folded silk gauze and a string of pearls, all of which was wound very artfully around the crown of her head and reminded her, strangely enough, of the antler headpiece worn by a sachem.

She had no wings to fly away with, only the long ends of the silk gauze that trailed down her back to end in deep silk fringe that swayed when she walked, and the silk net shawl heavily embroidered with flowers which she must carry draped over one arm, at Kitty's insistence.

"How beautiful you are," Amanda had said, taking her hands and smiling. "If only there were time to have your portrait taken—I must see about that."

"Oh please," Hannah said, shocked once more when she thought she could be shocked no more. "Don't go to the bother."

"It is no bother," said Amanda. "Your stepmother and father would be so proud to see you; we must make a record."

Hannah bit the inside of her cheek and held her tongue. Her father would be more alarmed than pleased to see her thus; she knew that much, but would not argue the point.

In the good parlor everything shone with the gentle light of the spring afternoon, the white marble of the fireplace and the ivory figurines that sat on the mantelpiece, crimson velvet draperies and silver buttons, crystal chandeliers and the emeralds wound around Miss Sarah Lispenard's throat. Elizabeth had told her the story of Aladdin's cave of wonders when she was a child, and Hannah had the strange feeling that she had somehow stumbled into such a cave and, more troublesome, that she would have trouble finding her way out.

Kitty drew her away into a corner at the first opportunity.

"You mustn't look so serious. You will frighten people off."

"I am bound to say something very wrong," Hannah said. "Let me apologize now for embarrassing you."

"Nonsense," said Kitty. "What you need is a little . . . trick to sustain you. And I have the perfect one. Pretend that you are Elizabeth. Say what she would say, and you will do splendidly."

The oddest thing was that Kitty was right. Hannah pretended that she was Elizabeth as Will introduced her to Senator Clinton, to Mrs. Kerr, a widow known primarily for her good works among the city's poor, and to Mrs. Kerr's niece, Sarah Lispenard, who rustled prettily in white silk and taffeta and tried not to stare at Hannah, but without success. Mr. Howe, on the other hand, did not try to hide his interest. Tall and unusually thin, Mr. Howe walked with the support of a cane although he could be no more than thirty. There was a glassiness to his gaze that made Hannah think that if she were close enough, she might be able to catch the sickly sweet scent of laudanum that clung to men who lived with wounds that never quite healed.

She decided he must be a retired soldier, but found instead that Mr. Howe was another English immigrant—his elder brother had been to Cambridge with Will Spencer—one who had given up the practice of law to become a journalist and editor. Hannah was beginning to wonder just how many newspapers one city needed. But Mr. Howe never mentioned Mr. Lamm's article, for which she was grateful.

The introductions moved along quite well while Hannah pretended to be Elizabeth, but every once in a while she found herself wondering whether Will's friends might be members of the Libertas Society. She was considering Mrs. Kerr when Amanda claimed Will and Kitty appeared to draw her aside again.

"You must meet Mr. Davis." Kitty nodded toward a group of men standing at the other end of the room, among them Miss Lispenard. "A great adventurer, he's just come all the way from the Missouri. And can you guess who that is talking to him?"

Hannah said, "That is Miss Lispenard, who very much admires my bravery and takes great pleasure in painting fans."

"No," Kitty said shortly, using her fan to tap Hannah's wrist smartly. "Not Miss Lispenard."

"Then you must mean the tall man with bowlegs she is flirting with."

Kitty drew in a sharp breath. "Hannah Bonner, behave yourself. That is Captain Lewis."

Hannah cast a glance over her shoulder. "Whatever fame he claims for himself, it looks as though he spent a lot of time looking for it on horseback."

This time Kitty's shocked gasp gave way to a strangled giggle, but she dug her fingers into Hannah's forearm and lowered her voice another notch. "Captain Lewis is personal secretary to President Jefferson. He is only in town for a few days. Is he not handsome? It is a great honor to have him here, a compliment to Will and Amanda."

"Because he is handsome, or because he is President Jefferson's secretary? In either case, he seems more interested in Mr. Davis than he does in the party."

Kitty clucked her tongue softly in disapproval, but her cheeks were flushed the same deep rose color as her gown, and her eyes flashed her enjoyment. Suddenly Hannah was very sorry that she had been so difficult about the party, if it was going to bring Kitty such pleasure.

She said, "Come, let's ask Will to introduce us to this excellent Captain Davis."

"Mr. Davis and Captain Lewis," Kitty hissed, delighted. "And you will not lack the opportunity to speak to him. Amanda has asked him to see you into dinner."

"Miss Lispenard will be disappointed."

Kitty tried to look understanding, but she could not quite hide a satisfied smile.

Chapter 25

The president's personal secretary was everything Kitty hoped he would be, Hannah saw that from her triumphant expression when Captain Lewis bent low over her hand. His hair was very like Daniel's, dark and wavy and reluctant to be tamed. When he turned to Hannah she was surprised to find that his hand was callused and hard, a working man's hand. A soldier's hand, she corrected herself, taking closer note of his uniform and bearing.

"The young lady I read about in the newspaper." His deep voice was softly Southern, but his gaze was intense and direct.

Hannah managed a polite nod. "I am afraid so."

"If I might say, you don't look like a student of medicine, Miss Bonner."

"I suppose that's true," Hannah said, flushing with irritation. "But then I would expect the president's secretary to be a bald old man with chin whiskers and very bad teeth."

"Hannah," Kitty squeaked, but apparently Captain Lewis was unwilling to be affronted. He laughed out loud.

"Mrs. Todd, don't stop her. It's refreshing to find a young lady who speaks her mind, and in such vivid images. But our hosts are waiting, and Mrs. Spencer has asked me to escort you to dinner. May I?"

Captain Lewis looked certain of his answer but Kitty looked alarmed, and with good reason. She knew very well that Hannah was capable of refusing the offered arm. Something she might have done, if it were not for Will who was waiting at the door and watching her.

He tilted his head and raised one brow, as if to ask if she needed his help. As if Hannah Bonner, also known as Walks-Ahead of the Kahnyen'kehàka Wolf longhouse, might need to be rescued from Captain Meriwether Lewis.

Hannah allowed herself to be escorted to the dining room where she found that Amanda had arranged for her to be seated between Senator Clinton and Captain Lewis. To her relief the captain turned his attention to Miss Lispenard and the half of the table that was involved in a discussion of trade on the Mississippi. It suited Hannah very well to be free of the captain's attention, but it clearly disappointed Kitty, who kept peeking around a great pyramid of doves baked in pastry shells to give Hannah very pointed looks.

Senator Clinton was less interested in trading troubles on the frontier than he was in Hannah's education and Elizabeth's school, and he asked a great many questions.

"It must be very tiring for Mrs. Bonner to teach two sessions each day," he concluded as he took more goose from the platter offered him. "In my experience most ladies benefit from a nap in the afternoon."

"There are few ladies with more energy or enthusiasm than my cousin, Senator." Amanda offered this tentatively; it was as close as she would come to correcting a guest.

Hannah said, "As the children will not consent to be together in the same room she has no other choice."

"Perhaps not," said the senator. "If the village would hire a second teacher. There are some very likely young men finishing their studies at the African Free School; I'm sure that any of them would be thankful for the post. That person could then take on the education of the Negro and Indian children and your stepmother could continue with the others."

Hannah knew very well what Elizabeth might say to such a suggestion, but she could hardly imagine the senator's expression if she were to tell him.

"I have corresponded with Mrs. Bonner," said Mr. Howe from across the table. "An extraordinary lady."

There was a moment's surprised silence, which Amanda broke in her gentle way.

"I sent my cousin Mr. Howe's pamphlet on political equality in the city," she said. "I believe your correspondence followed from that?"

Mr. Howe said, "It did indeed. Mrs. Bonner has an incisive mind and a most unusual way of looking at things. I have been thinking of asking her to write an article for the newspaper. Under a pen name, of course, as George Eliot did."

The senator's glass came to a sudden halt on its way to his mouth. Hannah watched him struggle with surprise and disapproval, and then swallow both with a good amount of French wine.

Mrs. Kerr leaned forward and tapped sharply on the table with one finger, her watery blue gaze fixed and severe.

"Mr. Howe, have you not spent enough time in the bridewell pursuing the rights of Irish freemen? When will you be satisfied?"

"When more than twenty-three percent of the men living and working in this city have the right to vote for those who govern it." He gave her a very broad smile. "Irish or not."

The old lady pressed her mouth together so firmly that the small chin rumpled like a peach pit, but there was something of reluctant admiration in her expression.

"Miss Bonner, have you heard the story of how Mr. Howe took up the cause of two Irish ferrymen who had the misfortune to come before an unscrupulous judge?"

"That is a serious charge," said the senator, dropping his chin to his chest.

Mrs. Kerr flicked his admonishment from her fingers like water. "It is indeed, and I can state it with some certainty, as I have the misfortune to be the judge's aunt. He is my poor sister Sophie's only child. As you well know, De Witt."

"Mrs. Kerr," said Amanda. "You have left out the best part of the story."

The old lady drew up. "Then you must tell it, child, if you think you are up to the job."

"Is this really necessary?" asked Mr. Howe.

Amanda smiled at him. "It is a very good story, Mr. Howe, and you have no cause to be embarrassed."

"It is simply told," said Senator Clinton. "An alderman of this city who shall remain nameless"—he paused to look at Mrs. Kerr with one brow raised—"was in a hurry to get from

Brooklyn to the city and he ordered the ferrymen to shove off twenty minutes before their scheduled time. Two recent immigrants, I forget the names—"

"Malone and O'Shay," supplied Mr. Howe.

"Malone and O'Shay, yes. Mr. Malone and Mr. O'Shay took exception to the way the alderman abused them—"

Mrs. Kerr thumped the table with the flat of her hand. "You have gutted the tale like a two-day-old fish, De Witt. The Senate is having an unfortunate effect, as I warned you it would." She turned to Hannah.

"This alderman—one of the Livingstons, I'm not afraid to say, though De Witt has scruples, given that he married into the family—he called the ferrymen lazy rascals and threatened to throw them in the bridewell because they would not do as he ordered, and they stood up to him, as the Irish often will. A brash people, the Irish. I wonder if they will ever learn that discretion is sometimes the greater part of valor. They gave the man as good as they got. 'We're good as any buggers!' That's what they said, you mustn't blush to hear it told truthfully, Mrs. Spencer. And when they reached Manhattan that rogue Livingston called a constable and had them marched to the bridewell, thrashing them with his cane the whole way."

She slashed the air with her finger to demonstrate, and fixed Hannah with a terrible stare. "Ask me how I know this, Miss Bonner, and I'll tell you. I was on that ferry, and I saw the whole thing." She sat back. "And never have I been more shocked. I've seen some things in my day—war wears a woman down that way, you know. But never have I seen anything like those two young men standing up to Jonathan Livingston in their rough clothes and clogs. It did my heart good.

"And the next day when they were brought before the judge—my nephew, I am ashamed to admit, a Federalist of the worst stripe and I blame my poor silly sister for marrying as she did—he heard evidence only from the alderman, asked for no other witnesses, and he did not even allow those men counsel. Asked for no witnesses! And with his own aunt in the courtroom, who saw the whole thing with my own eyes. And said so clearly." She drew in a terrible breath.

"But he would not let a woman speak in his courtroom. Now men may speak of armies that take it into their heads to rule cities, but in these new times the real threat sits upon the bench in a courtroom. Men who will not scruple to use the solemn responsibility vested in them to see their own causes advanced, and lawyers who hover about like crows in a battle-field, waiting to pick over what remains of justice. I have no fear of muskets—I have fired upon the enemy myself on more than one occasion—but a courtroom, that's another matter."

"But where does Mr. Howe come into this story?" asked Hannah, who was torn between amusement, concern, and confusion.

"He was in the courtroom when the judge sentenced those two young men to six months' hard labor, to teach them not to insult men in office."

"And how is it you ended up in the bridewell with the ferrymen, Mr. Howe?"

"He did not," said Amanda. "By the time the assembly sent Michael to the bridewell, the Irishmen had escaped." Her mouth twitched, and she sent Mrs. Kerr a sidelong glance.

The senator cleared his throat. "They say the guards were bribed, although it was never proved."

Hannah tried again. "But wait. I am still unclear on why the assembly—"

"I wrote an editorial." Mr. Howe answered the question that Hannah had been trying to ask. "The judge and the assembly took exception to my choice of words."

"Such as 'tyranny' and 'partiality,'" said Amanda. "And he wrote that the ferrymen had been punished only to suit the pride, ambition, and insolence of men in office. I remember the wording exactly."

Mrs. Kerr let out a fierce laugh. "And right he was too, but of course they couldn't have the truth put out plain for all to see. So they sentenced Mr. Howe who sits there before us to a month in the bridewell—"

"And two thousand supporters carried him there on an armchair," finished the senator. "Then three thousand met him and carried him home in a phaeton when his sentence was finished. You should run for office, Michael, with such support from the masses."

"Ah, but the masses can't vote in the city elections," said Mr. Howe. "And beyond that, I get far more enjoyment writing about the men who do run. When will you come back to the city government, Senator?"

There was a ripple of laughter around the table.

"You must have other things to occupy your pen," said the senator, signaling to have his wine glass filled again. "There is always some scandal going on in the city."

"Yes," said Hannah. "There's Madame du Rocher and her slaves."

Hannah had spoken up at exactly the moment that the rest of the table had also fallen still, and her words seemed to echo. She glanced down the table at Will, who looked both curious and resigned at this turn in the conversation.

Captain Lewis's attention had shifted too, but there was nothing of the tease in him now. The discussion of the Mississippi at the other end of the table faltered and came to a stop.

"Slavery is not a crime in New-York State, as I understand it." This question was directed to Hannah, but it was the senator who answered it.

"A very complex topic, and an unsuitable one in this company." He sent a pointed look in Miss Lispenard's direction.

"De Witt," Mrs. Kerr said in a tone that bordered on the sharp. "There are no children here. Two young ladies, yes, but both of marriageable age and both educated—highly educated in one case, and over my brother's odious objections in the other. But educated nonetheless and capable of forming opinions." She turned toward Amanda. "Mrs. Spencer, this French lady is your neighbor?"

She nodded. "She has leased the small house across the green, this past year. I have rarely seen her in all that time. She has been in great . . . personal difficulties."

"Yes, I read the papers," said Mrs. Kerr dryly. "And have you any cause to believe she is abusing her slaves?"

Amanda looked toward her husband. To Hannah's amazement and disquiet, he shook his head.

"Then why raise the subject?" Captain Lewis turned first to Amanda, then to Will and finally to Hannah. "Unless you would like to argue about abolition. It is a topic that has been taken up by many great men over the past twenty-five years, and you see where they have got with it, Miss Bonner. It is not to be."

Hannah felt herself flush, not so much in embarrassment as anger. She looked around the table and saw so many different expressions. Kitty was horrified at the turn in the conversation, Will was involved but not terribly concerned, Amanda vaguely worried, Miss Lispenard curious, Mrs. Kerr eager, Mr. Davis distracted, Senator Clinton anxious and impatient, and Captain Lewis distinctly irritated. The easiest thing would be to hold her tongue, but then that was what the captain wanted and Hannah did not like the idea of giving in to him.

"Sir," she said to him in her calmest tone. "Abolition may not be a popular subject in the South, but the fact that the legislature of this state passed a Gradual Manumission Act into law would seem to indicate that it is, indeed, to be, as you put it. At least here. And before you leap to Madame du Rocher's defense, you should know that by all appearances she intends to leave this state with her slaves to evade the act, which is of course in itself a violation of the law. Finally, since we were speaking of the newspapers, it seems to me that such widespread illegal activities—and I understand that slave owners often take this step to evade the law—warrants the attention of the journalists of this city. In my opinion, of course."

Mrs. Kerr sat back in her chair with a sigh, as if she had just finished a very satisfying meal. Her smile—and a number of other smiles around the table—could not be overlooked, and the captain colored. He cleared his throat.

"You have a great many opinions for a young...person."

"The benefits of education," said Hannah. "As Mrs. Kerr pointed out."

"And the pitfall," said Kitty. "But I'm afraid it's all to lay at my sister-in-law's doorstep. She is an avid reader of Mrs. Wollstonecraft's writings."

Senator Clinton said, "I would have assumed so, given what I have heard here tonight. Let me just say this much and perhaps we can find a more suitable topic of conversation. If indeed Madame du Rocher plans to break the law, of course such action cannot be tolerated. Ah." He broke into a relieved smile at the sight of Mrs. Douglas in the doorway. "The sweets. I see you asked the cook for a meringue, Mrs. Spencer. Very good of you to remember."

Mr. Davis said very eagerly, "I certainly did miss sugar while I was in the West. Honey and molasses are sweet enough for some, but I'll take sugar in my coffee if it's to be had."

Just as suddenly as the awkwardness had come over the

table it was gone. Hannah wondered at it, until she caught
Mrs. Kerr's conspiratorial wink.

The Indian woman and her child disappeared from the house
so quietly that no one could say when they had gone.

"Suzannah came down to the kitchen at half past eight,"
Mrs. Douglas explained for the third time. "And when she
went back a quarter hour later, the woman was gone." She had
sent two of the men out to look for her, without success.
"Like she just went up in the sky," Mrs. Douglas finished. "Just
flew away."

Hannah lay awake for a long time thinking of the woman,
and then she dreamed. In her dream she flew over a bloodred
sea, the woman's child strapped to her chest. In the way of
dreamers she suddenly found herself over Lake in the Clouds
and without hesitation or fear she dove from the sky into water
so deep and dark and so warm that it must revive even the dead.
The water pulled her down and down, until she found herself
inside the earth itself in a cave filled with strange flickering light.
Around a fire that burned up from the rock itself were faces she
knew: her grandmothers Falling-Day and Cora Bonner, her
great-grandfather Chingachgook, Robbie MacLachlan, and little Robbie sleeping in his lap with his curls damp around his
face. Her own mother with an infant in her arms. *Your twin,* she
said, holding out the child. *Come take him.*

She said, *I already have this child to look after,* only to find that
the child was gone. Instead of arms she had wings, great power-
ful wings with feathers in white and gold and silver. Hannah
could not take the child her mother held out or even pick up the
one she had lost on her way to safety. Should she ever find it.

The low moaning of the wind moving through the trees woke
her, rising and rising again to shriek like a woman in childbirth. Hannah lay disoriented for a moment, looking at the sky
and not quite making sense of what she saw there, dawn or the
flicker of lightning. A strange, warm lightning the color of the
sunrise.

She was out of bed and at the window in three great leaps,
almost falling in the tangle of her nightdress around her legs,
steadying herself by grabbing onto the brocade draperies.

No storm, not even a house afire, but a scene on the street

below her window so strange that it took a moment for Hannah to make sense of it. A team of matched bays and a fine closed carriage, its roof loaded with luggage. And behind that another team, this time six draft horses hitched to a great wagon.

Both the carriage and the wagon were empty, but around them the Broad Way had become a great rippling river of men and women with torches held high. A light mist was falling from a cover of clouds so low that the torchlight reflected back in an odd glow, gold and rose and silver, enough to pick out faces with great clarity. Every one of them was black.

The river of people swayed as one, and from it came the moaning that had woken her.

The door of the house opened and a lady stepped out to stand on the stair. She was dressed for travel in a long cloak. Under an elaborate hat dressed in feathers her face was very pale but when she spoke her voice, high and clear, echoed across the square.

"You have no business here. Leave at once."

Servants came out of the door behind her, each of them with their arms full of smaller pieces of luggage and boxes.

"Hannah?" Ethan's voice at her door, and then he came scuttling across the room in his bare feet. He tucked himself against her side, and she put an arm around him.

"Is your mother awake?"

It was not cold, but he was shivering so that his teeth clicked when he spoke. "No. Is Madame du Rocher going away?"

"I think that is her intent, yes."

The crowd had begun to twist and flex like a great snake waking from sleep, cutting off the servants so that they could neither get to the carriage nor return to the house. Hannah counted five of them and then suddenly they were just gone, absorbed into the crowd of other dark faces. The moaning had shifted into a lilting chant, boiling up from the depths.

Liberté! Liberté! Liberté! Liberté!

Madame du Rocher raised her voice again. "I have summoned the night watch! Go now immediately or I will see that the skin is flayed from your backs!"

The chant began to echo down the street, and all around Bowling Green men were appearing in the doorways in nightdress. An old woman ran toward Madame du Rocher shaking her fist, screaming, *"Maudit! Maudit!"*

"Look," said Ethan, tugging hard on Hannah's arm. "Look!"

A pile of refuse had been set on fire and in its light a man had climbed up onto the fence that surrounded the green, with one arm slung around the trunk of a poplar to steady himself. In the glow of the fire, Manny Freeman raised his other fist into the air and one of the windows at the front of the house exploded. A horse screamed and both teams began to pull in the traces.

Madame du Rocher retreated into the house and the sound of glass breaking filled the street.

Liberté! Liberté! Liberté! Liberté!

"A riot," Ethan whispered. He pulled away and ran from the room, but Hannah could not make herself move. The crowd had pinned her in place just as surely as they had forced Madame du Rocher back into the house.

Men and women both were running forward, hurling rocks and rubble and handfuls of dirt.

Liberté LIBERTÉ liberté LIBERTÉ!

An elderly black man appeared in the doorway waving his arms over his head, but his shouting was lost in the chant. Two young men ran up the steps and lifted him bodily, dragging him away to disappear into their number. Someone had loosed the teams and the horses surged off through the crowd, the empty wagon rocking wildly on its wheels.

From the north side of Bowling Green came the sound of musket shot.

"Come away from the window," said Will behind her. "The constables are come, and the blackbirders will be with them. You don't want to see what will happen."

At dawn, unable to sleep, Hannah found her daybook, much neglected in the past days, and scribbled the few lines she could not banish from her head.

May 1. Dawn. This night I watched a battle outside my window, and it was a revelation to me. What a strange place is this city, blind and deaf to a war fought day by day on its very streets.

In the morning Will was waiting for her in the carriage, intent on using the quarter-hour journey to the Almshouse to speak to her in privacy. The lines that bracketed his mouth were very deep, and his hair, normally perfectly combed, stood up in spikes at the back of his head.

"Did you sleep at all?"

He raised a hand as if to push aside the question. In his usual calm manner he said, "Manny must leave the city today, under cover."

When Hannah closed her eyes she saw him clearly, outlined in flame, his head thrown back while he shouted with the others, his fist closed around a stone. "Was he recognized?"

Will lifted a shoulder. "Madame du Rocher's slaves took the opportunity of the riot to disappear. Only one has been recaptured."

Hannah sat up straighter. "Did Manny have something to do with that? Did you?"

"No," Will said. "We have never operated in such a fashion. It is far too dangerous. But Bly has accused Manny nevertheless and it will be in the afternoon papers. If Manny is found they will try him and most likely find him guilty, given the evidence."

"But they can have no evidence, if he was not involved in the escape."

Will pressed his hands together. "When Bly is finished with the slave he captured last night, she will give evidence to anything. She will swear that Manny organized the whole riot and encouraged them to run, or anything else that Bly wants her to say."

Dread washed through Hannah, moved up from her belly in a flush that crawled out to her hands and made them tingle. For a long moment she could not speak at all.

"He may have left already," Will said. "Or he may be in hiding and looking to the safety of the du Rocher slaves. He understands what Bly and the blackbirders are up to, of that you can be sure. Hannah, if there is anyone who can find his way out of the city, it is Manny."

These were good, sensible words but they could not banish the images that rose unbidden before Hannah. Curiosity and Galileo, Selah Voyager round with child. How would she ever carry such news to them?

Will was not finished. He said, "I wanted you to be aware of the situation, in case the constables decide to question you." He leaned forward to cover her hand with his own. "I will do everything in my power to make sure he gets home safely."

Hannah looked Will in the eye, and found no comfort in what she saw there. "But you don't know where he is. Is the blackbirder called Cobb after him, the one...the voyager feared so?"

"I understand how worried you are for your friends," Will said. "But now you must leave it to the Libertas Society. Can you do that?"

She said, "You did not answer my question about Cobb."

There was a brittleness in the way Will looked at her, worry and irritation and simple powerlessness scraping the bone. He looked away and then back again.

"Cobb went north," he said finally. "There's a reward he's after."

"So he is no threat to Manny." It was a question he would refuse to answer but Hannah must say the words anyway.

Will said, "We are here. You must try to put all of this out of your mind for now."

But she could not put any of it aside, not the idea of Manny in hiding somewhere nor of Cobb headed north. So preoccupied was she with these facts, she had walked half the length of the sick ward hallway before she realized that there were already people waiting outside the closed apothecary door, and that she had last seen faces like these by torchlight. A young woman with a high forehead, her skin the color of tea, her mouth filled with broken and bloodied teeth. A tall man with shaved head holding his wrist at an unnatural angle. A younger man with a scarred face, his eyes darting uneasily around himself as he cradled his ribs with both arms. When she stopped before them he met her gaze defiantly and went very quiet, as if he were waiting for her to decide between calling the constables and treating their wounds.

She said the first thing that came to her. "You're here to be vaccinated, no doubt. Come this way, it will be just a minute until I get the office ready."

Later it would occur to Hannah that she had been very fortunate to avoid the doctors while she treated the three rioters in the institution office. She set the broken wrist, thankful that the skin was not broken; she cleaned out the woman's mouth and removed the remains of two broken teeth, and packed her jaw with gauze to stop the bleeding.

The man with the scarred face watched her work but his expression never changed. When she began to examine him, he turned his head aside and looked at the wall.

"You have some broken ribs on the right side. I will bind them, but you will have to take care."

He grunted in reply, but he raised his arms in the air while she wound the bandage. His torso was covered with scars, ivory and delicate pink against black skin. A long scar an inch wide curved across the tight plane of his abdomen. It looked as though someone had tried to gut him with a dull knife and come very close to succeeding, but far worse than that was the scarring left by lashings. His back had been flayed to the muscle in places, and more than once.

That he had survived such beatings told her what kind of man he must be, one who would survive because his anger would not let him die. His back pronounced him a slave more clearly than anything he might have told her.

"How did you know to come to me? Did Manny send you?"

He studied her for a moment, his expression unreadable. Then he nodded.

"Is he safe?"

He blinked at her, and it occurred to Hannah that he might not understand. The French words came to her almost without bidding. *"Manny, est-il en sûreté?"*

It was the woman who answered, her words coming muffled through her swollen mouth, in the accent of the islands. "We are none of us safe, miss. Not even you, not now."

Chapter 26

Early Monday morning as Cicero handed Hannah up into the carriage for the ride to the Almshouse, he pressed a note into her hand. The paper was thin and the ink was poor, but it was written in a strong, careful hand, one that Hannah did not recognize.

> *A man needs medical help. If you will attend to him, be outside the Almshouse kitchen door at three this afternoon. We will see that you are back by four. Mr. Spencer has no part in this, and neither should he, for his own welfare.*

Hannah worked all day with the note folded in her bodice, measuring its shape and weight with every breath she took. A man who needed help. A note from a stranger about a stranger, passed to her by Cicero, who never even met her eye when he put it in her hand. A man who needed help, who dared not come to the Almshouse or the dispensary or the hospital, all places where someone without money could get treatment.

It might be Manny. It might not.

It was the worst kind of folly, and yet Hannah found herself planning. She could be away from the sick wards for an hour, if the work in the vaccination office was finished. Dr. Simon would assume she was in the nursery; Dr. Scofield would assume she had gone to the hospital with Dr. Simon; Dr. Savard might come looking for her, but it was unlikely: Dr. Simon would be amputating a leg this afternoon, a procedure that called for many assistants.

A man needs medical help.

It could be fever or a broken bone or a knife wound. Hannah checked the lancets and scalpels she had been given by Hakim Ibrahim, instruments she had used with the supervision of Dr. Todd or Curiosity or Dr. Simon. She checked the vials and bottles strapped to the side of the bag. Her supply of willow bark for fever tea was low, and she refilled it from the crock in the apothecary.

At two, when she had finished with the last of the day's vaccination work and she was about to close the office, Dr. Simon came in. Hannah could hide her distress, but not her surprise.

"I was just on my way to change some dressings," she said. "I thought you would be at the hospital by now?" Making a question of it, the way Amanda did when she was offering direction to her husband.

"I was about to leave when a visitor arrived," said Dr. Simon, with his usual quiet smile. And with that an idea came to Hannah, outlandish and very appealing all at once: she could put the note in his hand, and let herself be guided by his counsel. Dr. Simon's antislavery sentiments were public knowledge; he would not do anything to harm people in need.

"Yes?"

"And then I remembered your vaccination."

Hannah glanced down at herself, confused now. "I don't understand what an unexpected visitor has to do with my vaccination. Am I overlooking something?"

"Is this not the eighth day since you were given the virus?"

"Yes." She flushed a little to admit such absentmindedness, but Dr. Simon did not seem to be worried by this lapse on her part.

"I have a special favor to ask of you, then. Today I received a letter from President Jefferson."

Hannah forced herself to smile and listen.

"He is very interested in this work of ours, you see, and he has asked for a supply of our virus, as fresh as possible. His secretary is here and he will take it with him to Washington. He leaves this evening."

"Captain Lewis." Hannah had forgotten about the president's personal secretary entirely in the aftermath of the riot.

Dr. Simon nodded. "Yes, he mentioned to me that you have been introduced. That is a fortunate coincidence."

Hannah made a sound in her throat, but the doctor took it for agreement.

"The president has given the captain the assignment of learning everything he can about vaccination. He has had samples of virus from many doctors, but he would like ours as well, to see if our method of preparing it for transport might be superior to the others he has been shown."

Hannah had turned away so that the doctor could not see her face, busied herself with straightening papers on the desk. "I have no objection," she said. "It doesn't matter to me where the virus goes once you've taken it."

There was a moment's silence and Hannah could not help it; she must turn to see his face. Dr. Simon was rarely at a loss for words, but he seemed now to be searching.

"Is there something else, sir?"

"If Captain Lewis had come earlier in the day I would not have to ask you this, but I see you've already finished with the other eighth-day vaccinations."

"I have. But I've said I don't mind if the virus taken from me goes to Washington with Captain Lewis. Is there some other problem I'm overlooking?"

"Captain Lewis would like to see the preservation method from its start. I am concerned for your modesty."

Hannah could not hide her smile. "I see. Maybe it will help you to know that when I met the captain I was wearing a very fashionable evening gown I borrowed from Mrs. Todd," she said. "Today he will see far less of me than he did that evening. If we can do this quickly, I have no objection."

Hannah put on a sleeveless kirtle while the doctor and his guest waited in the hall. She could hear them talking as she set out the lancet and the rest of the materials the doctor would need. *Generosity,* she heard the captain say, and the doctor in response: *She has surpassed my highest expectations.*

She didn't know whether to be irritated or complimented and so Hannah satisfied herself with saying exactly what was required of her when they came in, and nothing more.

Dr. Simon, never unduly worried by long silences and concerned with providing all the information that the president might want, seemed not to notice at all. But Captain Lewis was ill at ease. Hannah was far more comfortable observing him than he was her.

His height surprised her, and she had forgotten the way his hair fell forward over a high brow. He had a straight nose and wide-set eyes that were bloodshot. Though he would not look at her directly she could see that he was suffering the effects of too much wine and not enough sleep.

Dr. Simon was far too polite to take note. He began to lecture in the tone he used with his students, quick and competent and full of sober enthusiasm. He held up the lancet.

"The vesicle is perfect, exactly as you see it in the diagrams. When I open it—" He made a decisive movement with the lancet, and Hannah registered the sting. "A very gentle touch is all that is required. You see the fluid, which many describe as pearly. This fluid contains the virus itself. Would you hand me one of the vaccinators, please? You see, those bits of ivory. It is a delicate business to catch all of the fluid on the end of the vaccinator, but you see it is flat at one end, and a hollow has been carved into it. Here we have it, kine-pox virus. Miss Bonner is now immune to smallpox."

Captain Lewis asked good questions of the doctor, and listened carefully to the answers. Hannah might as well have been a statue sitting before him for all his attention, and it irritated her that he did not include her in the conversation.

"How long will the virus need to dry on the vaccinator?" asked the captain.

Dr. Simon said, "We have recently discovered that it is best not to let the virus dry on the ivory. Or I should say, Miss Bonner suggested it to me when she first arrived. Perhaps you should explain this, Miss Bonner."

Hannah kept her expression still. "It was not my invention. Another physician wrote to me about his methods. The virus seems to remain active longer if the entire vaccinator is put in a small glass vial of purified water and sealed with wax."

"A tremendous improvement," said Dr. Simon, who had moved to Hannah's other arm and was bent forward to extract the virus from the second vesicle. "And so much easier to pour the contents of the vial into an incision than to rub it raw with the vaccinator itself."

There was a knock at the door, and Dr. Simon looked up. "That will be Dr. Savard, we must go. Miss Bonner, may I ask you to finish with the captain? He would like to see our vaccination records, and I'm sure he has some questions."

Hannah could not deny Dr. Simon such a simple request, but very much wanted to be rid of both of them. When he closed the door behind himself she first glanced at the clock that stood on the desk.

Captain Lewis said, "Perhaps this is too much of an imposition?"

Hannah cast him a sidelong glance. She took a plug of wax from a dish on the worktable and sealed the vaccinator vial, and then held it up for his inspection. "Here you are. Fresh vaccination material for the president. It is important that there be no air at all left in the vial, please note. The record books are on that table behind you. If you have no questions I have some work to attend to."

"I do have one question," said the captain. "Will you be vaccinating your own people when you go home?"

Hannah pulled up short. "Yes. That is why I am here."

"And you will keep records?"

"Of course."

He looked thoughtful for a long moment. "It would be of some assistance to me—to the president—if you would agree to send us copies of your records."

All of Hannah's irritation left her suddenly, to be replaced by surprise. "Why would the president be interested in the vaccination records of a small village on the edge of the wilderness?"

"The president is interested in a great many things," said Captain Lewis.

Some men were most easily taken to task with silence, and Captain Lewis was one of them. He might be able to put other women in their place with a mention of the president, but she would wait until he had answered her question truthfully.

After a long moment he said, "I need to learn about the actual practice because I may find myself in a place where I have to carry out large-scale vaccinations."

"Ah," said Hannah. "You are planning on traveling to the Missouri."

Captain Lewis stilled suddenly. He opened his mouth and then shut it again.

Hannah said, "It is a very reasonable deduction, Captain. At dinner you asked Mr. Davis so many questions about provisions for his journey and the conditions on the way, and now you stand here asking about vaccinating a great number of people. Whatever other work you undertake for the president, I hope you are not a spy. I fear you wouldn't last very long at all. Your expression gives away far too much."

He let out a great rush of air and rubbed the flat of his hand along his jawline, as if a tooth had begun to ache. "I have been indiscreet."

Hannah turned away to tidy things on the desk. Behind her he cleared his throat roughly.

"I must ask you not to speak of this to anyone. Not to Dr. Simon or to Mr. Spencer."

She glanced at him over her shoulder. "Then you do travel west, I see."

He winced slightly. "That is the president's hope, but Congress has not yet been approached about this expedition. It is all very...sensitive."

"France and Spain would not approve," said Hannah, almost to herself. And then: "You need not look so surprised, Captain Lewis. I can read a newspaper as well as any man. And even understand what I read."

"I have offended you. I apologize. But if I could have your word that this discussion will go no further—"

"You have my word," Hannah cut him off. "You may plan your journey without fear of interference from me."

"By your expression I can see that you do not approve."

Hannah was not quick to anger, but Captain Lewis seemed to know what to say to irritate her most. "And would it surprise you if I did not approve?"

He did not try to hide his surprise. "On what grounds?"

Hannah crossed her arms and rocked forward with her chin lowered, working very hard to stop herself from speaking the things that she most wanted to say. She must choose her words carefully, not so much because she was worried about offending the president's secretary—she feared that could not be avoided—but because she wanted him to understand her.

"For many years my grandfathers predicted that sooner or

later the whites would need more land and begin to move
west." She paused, and saw by the captain's expression that she
was not far from the mark.

"And if that were so?"

"You see the color of my skin, Captain Lewis. I know very
well what will happen to the Indians once the west is open.
You will speak of treaties and land purchases but in the end
you will take what you want. By force."

There was a long silence, and Hannah saw that she had
struck a nerve. He was very angry, but to his credit—she must
grant that much—he did not offer false explanations or excuses. She was both relieved and disappointed in him, and she
turned back to her work.

"If there is nothing else, Captain?"

He said, "Will you send me copies of your records?"

"Will you promise to vaccinate Indians as well as whites as
you go west?"

He blinked at her. "For as long as I have active vaccination
material, yes."

"Very well, I will send copies of my records."

The captain picked up his hat and hesitated at the door.
"You are a most unusual young lady, Miss Bonner."

"Yes," said Hannah. "I am. And a very busy one too."

When she got to the kitchen doors just before three Hannah
found a boy waiting for her, no more than eight years old,
barefoot and bareheaded, with a quick smile and nothing to
say at all. Hannah had to trot to keep up with him as he dashed
up one alleyway and down another, five minutes or more in
which they never touched foot on a main street. They came
finally to the back entrance of an old brick building in the
Dutch style, with a gabled roof and windows shuttered even in
the spring sunshine. The alleyway and the steps were covered
with a fine dusting of flour, and the smell of baking bread was
in the air.

Hannah followed the boy again, this time down five steps
into a cellar. The first room was overheated and poorly lit by a
single betty lamp hung from the ceiling. The corners were
crowded with bags of grain, and in the middle of it all stood
Manny.

Relief and anger surged so strongly in Hannah that she put

down her bag to take both his hands in hers. They were cool to the touch and his pulse was steady and strong; she could see no sign of illness in his face.

"Manny Freeman," she said. "If you are not hurt it will be my duty and great pleasure to injure you myself. Why are you still in this city?"

He managed a smile, but the expression in his eyes remained untouched. "There's nothing wrong with me that some sleep won't cure."

"You haven't answered my question."

"There's no time for that," he said. "Come."

The next room was slightly larger, darker, and crowded with people. Some lay on pallets on the floor, and others sat. In the far corner was a slop bucket and a water barrel. Every one of the people in the room—all of them black—looked at Hannah with expressions that ranged from barely contained anger and agitation to exhaustion. She nodded to the woman whose broken teeth she had extracted, but saw no sign of the two men.

"Over there," said Manny, pointing her toward a tick mattress that had been spread across some crates. The man who had been given the privilege of a bed elevated off the floor seemed to be sleeping. Hannah recognized him from Bowling Green, where she had seen him now and then driving Madame du Rocher's carriage. He was of middle years, strongly built and wide through the shoulders.

Next to him an elderly woman Hannah didn't know sat wrapped in shawls. In one hand she had a dipper while with the other she held down a corner of his mouth to let the water dribble in. The neckline of his shirt was wet, and Hannah wondered if he was swallowing anything at all.

Manny said, "He's been like that since Friday night."

Hannah went to the older woman and hunched down next to her. "What's his name?"

"Thibault." She had a whispery voice, as if it had once been broken and never quite recovered.

"And yours?"

"Folks call me Belle." She put down the dipper and used a piece of rag to wipe the man's chin.

"Have you been with him the whole time?"

She shook her head. "On and off since they fetched him

here late Friday. There ain't much I could do for him, but I don't like to be the last word."

With both hands the old lady lifted Thibault's head to turn it. There was a depression in his skull just behind the ear, as long as Hannah's hand and three fingers wide.

"A club?"

"Hickory," said a voice behind her, heavy with the accent of the French islands. "A hickory club as long as a man's arm."

Hannah put her ear to Thibault's chest to listen to his heart, not that it would make any difference. Inside this man's skull the brain was swollen and bleeding, pressing on bone until it exhausted itself. Beneath her ear she heard the evidence, a heart once strong whose beat was faltering, thready and irregular.

When she sat back on her heels Belle turned her face toward the darkest corner of the room where a young man stood, stone-faced and unblinking.

"Fetch that light down here, Dandre, will you please."

"Let me." Manny came forward to do as she asked.

"Hold it close, now. Let it shine on his face."

It was a striking face, not so much for the strong features or the well-formed mouth but for the look of peacefulness. The old lady lifted one eyelid with a splayed thumb and there was the evidence that could not be denied: in the flickering of the lamplight the pupil stayed as dark and round as a tarnished copper penny.

"Gone?" The old woman had turned her face and Hannah realized now why they had fetched her from the hospital. Not because they didn't trust Belle, but because the old woman did not trust her own eyes, which were covered with a pale film.

"Gone," said Hannah. "No reaction to the light."

Belle eased the man's head back down as gently as an egg. "Eyes gone, the spirit gone too. The rest of him just don't realize it yet. He was a good man, Thibault, but he as mulish in the other world as he was in this one."

Hannah caught Manny's gaze and nodded her agreement.

He drew in a shuddering breath. When he let it out again he said, "How long?"

"A day at the most, if you stop giving him water. Perhaps no more than an hour."

The young man Belle had called Dandre came out of his

corner. In the dim light Hannah recognized him as another one of Madame du Rocher's missing slaves, one she had met in the kitchen, deep in conversation with Mrs. Douglas. A good-looking young man with hair shaved close to the skull and large eyes the color of molasses cut with honey. Now his face was swollen and his lower lip mangled, but it was his expression that shocked, the burning fury of him. He took the dipper out of Belle's hand and threw it against the wall with all his strength, and then he stood hunched forward, his whole body shaking with sobs.

Hannah felt Manny's hand on her shoulder. She followed him back to the first room.

"I'm sorry," she said finally. And when he could not find anything to say, Hannah put a hand on his sleeve.

"What will happen to them?"

He blinked at her as if he were waking out of a deep sleep. "They'll be gone tonight."

"And you with them?"

He nodded.

"Will you be taking them north?"

His head came up and he looked at her hard, his eyes bright and dry. "You know better than to ask questions like that."

Hannah stepped back from him, surprise and hurt pushing aside those things she had wanted to say to him, the things she knew that Curiosity would say if she were here.

He said, "I need another favor from you." From his jerkin he took a piece of folded paper. It appeared to be from a newspaper, but in the dusty dim light of the basement Hannah could not make out much about it.

"There's a child I'm looking for. She may be in the poor-house someplace, or they may have placed her out. Or maybe she's dead. One way or the other I want to know. This is all the information I have." He took Hannah's hand and closed her fingers over the paper, squeezed tight.

"I'm not sure that I can—"

He cut her off with a shake of his head. "If you can get a look at the record books you might be able to find some mention of her. You know where they keep the records?"

Hannah thought of Mrs. Sloo waddling her way past Mr. Eddy's office. *An exacting man, our Mr. Eddy, tolerates no sloppiness.*

Keeps track of the comings and goings. The orphans mostly. A power-
ful lot of work, and paper enough to bury a man standing.

And Mr. Eddy himself, the pale oval face and colorless eyes,
the way he looked at her when she passed him in the halls.
What would he do if he found her in his office among his papers? But Manny was waiting for her to say something, and
Hannah could not deny him this, not out of hand.

"And if I find some record of the child?"

The question surprised him, she saw that in the way his
shoulders stiffened. "I don't think you will, to tell the truth. I
been looking for her a long time now. The only way to make
sure is to get into that office and I never have been able to get
that far. I'm hoping you'll have better luck."

"Manny," Hannah said, lowering her voice. "Who is this
child? Is she . . . yours?"

"She's Selah's," Manny said. "That makes her mine too. If
you can get to the records I'd be thankful. If you can't do it
without putting yourself in danger, then let it be."

"And if I do find her after all?"

"Then bring her to my ma and pa. Now you best get
along, it's almost four. If you see my folks before I do—"

Hannah made a protesting sound, but he ignored her.

"You tell them what you saw here today, and that I'm on
my way home, as soon as these folks are safe."

"Is there such a thing as safe for them? For you?"

Even as the words escaped her Hannah regretted them, but
to her surprise it earned her a smile, one that took her back
unexpectedly to her childhood and the boy Manny had been.
It was Manny who first showed her how to bait her fishing
hook and taught her how to whistle like a poor-will; in return
he had called on her when he needed help to play a trick on
his sisters. It was a gentle smile, without worry or anger.

"There is indeed," he said softly. "In one kind of Paradise
or the other. You best get going now, Jean is waiting to show
you the way."

MAY 12, 1802. EVENING.

Heavy rain for most of the day. This morning there were four eggs in the sparrow's nest on my windowsill.

Three letters by the afternoon post. One from Curiosity, with news of home but no word of the voyager. The second letter was from Captain Lewis, with greetings from the president and a list of questions to be answered regarding vaccination on the frontier. To this he added a personal note and wishes for my good health and an uneventful journey home. The last letter was from my brother Luke, with news of the earl's death. He lived a long and honorable life and he will be remembered for his bravery and wisdom. Young Alasdair is now the new earl of Carryck. Luke writes also that Jennet is to be married to the factor Ewan Huntar, as her father wished. I expect I will hear more of this from her in tones very different from my brother's.

Madame du Rocher has left this city in the dead of night. Only one of her slaves had been returned to her. The rest are gone away for good and good, says Mrs. Douglas. May she be right.

MAY 14, 1802. EVENING.

Today Mrs. Graham, who had been away visiting a married daughter in Boston, came and spent all day in the wards. She divided her time between reading the bible to people who speak no English and generally getting in the way. My only conversation with her was very brief, as I did not wish to be interviewed on the state of my everlasting soul. She is supposed to be a very good and generous lady but the tribute she demands for her charity is very high indeed.

Dr. Simon took pity on me finally and asked me to assist him at the hospital. There we saw the interesting case of a young woman with a blockage of the urethra, which we were able to clear. Whether it will come again or not is a question that can't be answered, unless it were possible to look inside her living body.

MAY 15. EVENING.

Beautiful warm weather and a high wind to wash away the stink of the city. Today an Irish orphan boy of about five years bit Dr. Savard hard enough to draw blood. His face went very pale but he made no sound of protest or pain, and neither did he let the boy go until he had finished treating a burn on his ankle. Later when I asked if he wished me to tend to the bite wound he gave me such a fierce look that I was taken aback.

Six new vaccinations this morning.

At three in the afternoon Blue Harry slipped into a final sleep and died quietly. Mr. Magee is very sad at the loss of an old friend.

Spent an hour in the nursery in the morning and another in the afternoon. Dr. Simon knows where I go when he cannot find me. He makes no comment at all.

MAY 16. EVENING.

Today a letter from Curiosity. No news of my father and Elizabeth, but Friend Gabriel Oak is at peace and laid to rest. Dr. Todd conducted the autopsy and Curiosity was present. She reports the lungs much ulcerated and wasted away, as expected.

In Paradise the flax and barley and rye have been set in the fields along the river. At Lake in the Clouds the women will be planting corn.

Today I treated a young woman who had been badly beaten, ribs cracked and a gash on her face that I closed with six stitches. It will leave a scar in the shape of a sickle that curves away from her mouth. She is the fourth woman who has come to us in such a state since my time here. When I asked if she had no other way to earn her bread than to sell her body she said she is well paid for her bruises and expects nothing else.

What a hard place is this city for women especially. Dr. Savard claims that most of the women who make a living this way—and there are legions of them—will not see thirty years. Disease and violent injury kill most, but a good number freeze to death every winter for want of a simple fire.

MAY 20. EVENING.

Clear and warm with a cool breeze. By all accounts, Almanzo Freeman is no longer in New-York City. May his journey be an easy one.

Examined five vaccination subjects and extracted virus from one. Assisted Dr. Simon and Dr. Scofeld with the amputation of a gangrenous leg below the knee. Patient is a boy who either speaks no English or does not wish to speak. He has been recorded in Mr. Eddy's record book as John Smith 24.

Mr. Matthias Greenaway, who is the Master of Scavangers and a member of the city council, underwent surgery to remove cataracts this afternoon in his own home on Park Avenue. Dr. Simon invited me to observe. Mr. Greenaway was given enough opium to render him insensible and then he was tied securely to a table with straps across his forehead, shoulders, waist, hips, knees, and feet. Dr. Ellingham performed the surgery with assistance from three others. Corneal incision near the limbus was made by puncture with a sharp curved needle, enlarged to both sides with a blunt curved needle and then with a curved scissors. A flat instrument of about a finger's width was then put into the eye by an assisting doctor, and while it held the cornea away from the lens, Dr. Ellingham used a sharp needle to open the capsule. Next the instrument was passed between the iris and lens to free adhesions. Finally Dr. Ellingham exerted gentle pressure to dislodge the cataract. The operation was then carried out on the other eye. The whole undertaking was handled with great speed.

My grandmother Falling-Day was distrustful of O'seronni doctors who were so eager to cut into the body with their knives, but even she must see the miracle of this. To bring light where darkness has fallen, what greater service can a healer provide?

Every day I feel my grandmother near me and sometimes I feel her disappointment to see me put aside her gentle medicines for harsh O'seronni ones. Sometimes I ask her if I cannot have them both, but there is never any answer.

I will speak to Dr. Todd and see whether or not it might be advisable to suggest such an operation to Galileo Freeman.

Today marks one full month since we came to the city. By my records I have performed more than thirty vaccinations and retrieved viral material from almost as many. I have seen a great many surgeries, five autopsies, and assisted in sixteen births. In the time I have been assisting in the Almshouse I have seen forty-seven deaths, more than half of those infants or children less than two years.

Many of the fruit trees along the Broad Way are in blossom.
Today I saw a woodpecker in Bowling Green. I was taken by such a
strong homesickness that it was some time before I could speak.

Another letter from Captain Lewis, repeating much of what was
said before as if he forgot that he had already written. A letter from
Curiosity. No news of my father or stepmother or of the voyager.

June 1. Late Afternoon.

Examined ten vaccination subjects and retrieved virus material from
three. Six new vaccinations, four children and two young men. Dr.
Simon says that I am now proficient in all stages of the Jenner
method. He has written to Dr. Todd to tell him that my education in
this matter is complete enough to send me back to Paradise.

In one week we depart this city for home. On that day I will vaccinate Ethan so that by the time we reach Paradise I will be able to
retrieve fresh virus from him in Dr. Todd's presence. I will also take
vaccination material with me should Ethan's attempt fail.

Dr. Simon has asked me to continue to assist in the wards and
vaccination office until we depart the city. I would not know what to
do with myself if I had no work, and so I accepted. According to my
records I have seen patients with abscess, aneurism, arrhythmia, as-
cites, childbed fever, cholera morbus, contusion, cataract, cancer, dys-
pepsia, dysentery, dislocations, epilepsy, fevers, fractures, gonorrhea,
hoemoptoe, hernia, ophthalmia, palsy, pthisis pulmonalis, scarlatina,
and wounds.

A new patient was brought into the wards by the constables who
found him in the street, robbed and insensible. Aged about fifty years,
from the condition of his hands a mason or bricklayer by profession.
Dr. Simon's diagnosis is of the terminal stage of the disease called
morbi venerei but referred to by the doctors here as syphilis and by the
patients as the French disease or French pox. The patient's symptoms
include a large protrusion on the left shoulder which is an advanced
aneurism of the aorta, highly irregular heartbeat, blindness, loss of
reason, and extreme ulceration of the nose and legs. I have seen this
disease in many guises since working in the Almshouse and yet Dr.
Simon is reluctant to speak to me about it. He prefers to think me innocent not only in deed but also in my knowledge of what passes between men and women.

Dr. Savard was less concerned with my unmarried status and proved willing to discuss the case, though I fear that his talkativeness had a great deal to do with the bottle of brandy he keeps in the bottom drawer of a cabinet in the kine-pox office. He copied a passage for me from Morgagni regarding death due to aneurism.

Today Kitty lost consciousness for close to an hour. Upon waking she asked to be bled again. She speaks of staying on here for the rest of the summer so she might continue in Dr. Ehrlich's care.

I must still write my weekly report to Dr. Todd, and this time I will speak more bluntly about his wife's poor condition. He will receive my letter with hers, and what a contrast that will be. Kitty speaks and writes only of amusements and shopping, though it seems to me that there is a growing desperation about her.

Chapter 27

At ten to three o'clock on the last Saturday she would spend in the Almshouse, Hannah sat at the desk in the Kine-Pox Institution office with a piece of paper before her and a newly sharpened quill in her hand. She read the words she had written once again.

> *My assistance is required here for another few hours at least. One of the doctors will see me safely back to Whitehall Street when my work is done.*

All week Hannah had been consumed by this moment and it came to these few dozen words. She was taken by the sudden and almost irresistible urge to tear up the note and write another one.

> *Dear Will and Amanda—*
> *If I am not with you by ten this evening, you will most probably find me in gaol for breaking into Mr. Eddy's records office in an attempt to find information about a lost child. I undertake this offense against the Almshouse of my own free will, and if I should end up before the magistrates I will have all the comfort of knowing that while I have brought notoriety to you and myself I was fulfilling a promise to a friend.*

Instead she put down her quill, folded the note she had written, and wrote out the directions on its face. If all went well she might one day be able to tell Will about all of this, why she had deceived him and to what end.

From the pocket of her work apron she took another piece of paper, this one soft with handling. She had read it so many times since Manny gave it to her that she hardly needed to look at it and yet she did, because it was the only place she could turn for assurance that what she was about to do was good and right.

She wished for her grandmother Falling-Day, or for Many-Doves. From her grandmother she had heard every day what she owed to herself and to her clan, what it meant to be Kahnyen'kehàka, what it would take for her to survive in this white world. Every day since her grandmother died Hannah had heard Many-Doves repeat those same words to her own children. *Make your own way in your world and in theirs; leave the poison called alcohol to the white men who brought it here; do not get involved in their wars; give them no opportunity to make you their prisoner.*

If she could talk to one of them in the language they shared maybe she could make sense of all of this, understand how it had become necessary to go against the things they had taught her. But all the guidance she had now was this paper.

When Manny gave it to her, she had expected nothing more than a description of the child he was looking for, Selah's daughter. To her surprise and great unease she found something very different: a carefully copied letter addressed to the director of the Almshouse, Mr. Furman—a man she had seen only once, and who, as far as she could tell, spent as little time as possible in the building.

> *I hereby inform you that my Negro wench Ruth was brought to bed the fifth day of July 1799 with a female child called Connie. I do therefore hereby give you notice that I do abandon all my right & title and all responsibility for the care of said female child in accordance with the Gradual Manumission Act signed into law by the Legislature and do hereby pass the child into the care of this City. This Certificate of Abandonment made & provided by my own hand the 6th day of June 1801. Albert Vaark, Merchant, Pearl Street*

The names Ruth and Connie had been crossed through and over them were written Selah and Violet, in Manny's hand.

Hannah read the words a dozen times and a dozen more trying to make sense of it, and then she realized that the other side of the paper was not blank. He had copied the letter on the back of an advertisement.

It was a notice like a hundred others she had seen nailed to doors and posts throughout this city and at every tavern and inn between here and Johnstown. Each was very much like the last: a name, a description, the circumstances by which a slave had slipped away, the promise of a small reward, of hell-fire and eternal damnation and whippings.

But this notice was different: there was a drawing of the runaway, a woman with a witchy, feral look about her—*Selah,* Hannah reminded herself. *This is meant to be Selah Voyager.* And there was the reward, the unheard-of reward of five hundred dollars for the capture of the escaped slave woman Ruth who had murdered her rightful owner on the Newburgh dock. To be paid by the inconsolable widow, announced the poster. To render this city safe.

Hannah ran her finger over the words on the page. A woman with dark skin was not entitled to take revenge on the man who stole her child. A woman with white skin was entitled to revenge the death of a husband, but she must call it something else, find some excuse to call for blood.

All up and down the Hudson people would be studying this drawing. Women would shudder righteously and denounce the savagery of Africans; men would speak of the law and of justice and all of them would be thinking of the money, a fortune, enough to buy a small farm and keep a family for years. Shelter and food and peace. Men would be headed north in the hope of winning such a prize. None of them would ever see the letter Vaark had written to the Almshouse, or know the name of the child who had been taken from her mother because she was not profitable enough to keep.

Hannah felt the anger rising in her, filling her as water filled an empty jar. She put Manny's note back in her pocket and left the office, closing the door behind her.

At the porter's desk she found the first thing she must have: a group of boys tossing pebbles against the wall and wagering on the way they would fall. She pulled one of them aside and showed him a ha'penny. The bargain was struck that easily: he would deliver her note to Whitehall Street, and if he returned within a half hour, the porter would have another ha'penny for him.

When he was gone, bare heels flashing as he ran, Hannah went to the one place in the Almshouse that required all her concentration and strength of will.

The nursery was a room without windows and crowded with cots, and in each cot were two or three or even four babies, the youngest newborn and the oldest no more than two. Yesterday she had counted fifty-three of them, most undernourished, many sick, all of them left to the care of the city, abandoned or orphaned or lost.

Today somewhere between five and ten of those fifty-three would be gone, one or two old and strong enough to be sent to the children's ward. The rest would be buried in a common grave in the paupers' field; the empty cots would be filled again before the day was out. Thousands of babies had passed through here, and Selah's little girl had most probably been one of them.

She opened the door to the stench of unwashed swaddling cloths and tallow candles that did little to lighten the dimness. The two matrons who worked in the nursery overnight nodded to her, both of them far too glad of another pair of capable hands to take any issue with the color of her skin. This was one place where Mrs. Graham never came to read her bible; none of the society ladies who visited the wards trailing servants and silk shawls spent time here.

In the middle of the room an old man sat on a low stool. Hannah knew him only as Jakob; she had never had a conversation with him because, as far as she knew, he had learned no English in the twenty years he had been in the Almshouse. He spent all his time in the nursery, day and night, and it was more his place than anyone else's.

While Hannah paused at the door, Jakob began to sing to the three babies in his lap. A new quiet came over the room at the familiar sound, the same old lullaby he always sang, for the way it quieted the infants or maybe just because he knew no other. His gaze shifted constantly while he sang, sliding past Hannah without interest or concern and reminding her, as he always did, of an old sheepdog with eyes for nothing in the world but his charges. The babies in his lap would be the sickest, and he would hold them until they needed to be held no more.

Hannah closed her eyes and thought of her grandmother Falling-Day, who had known how to comfort a hurting child. She heard the familiar voice at her ear: *What cannot live must die.*

She went to the nearest cot and picked up a newborn, yellow of skin and eye, all tendon and bone and slack muscle, too listless to suckle the little finger she put in its mouth. Its skull was misshapen, with a tracing of blue veins as insubstantial as cobwebs. Each of the infants had a piece of paper pinned to its swaddling clothes. This one said: *Unnamed female, number 174. Born 25 May, mother dead in childbed. Brought to the Almshouse on the same day by a neighbor who would not give her name. In sorrow shall ye bring forth children.*

Hannah concentrated, but she could detect nothing of the child's spirit. What she held in her arms was an almost empty cocoon, without animating force. After a moment she crossed the room and held out the child to Jakob, who paused long enough in his song to look, the creased mouth surrounded by a gray bristle puckering as he studied unnamed female number 174.

When Jakob had made room enough on his lap for one more, Hannah went back to the cots.

She stayed in the nursery feeding and washing and rocking one infant after another until the church clocks scattered throughout the city began to strike seven and she knew that the doctors would all be gone. There was no more time to waste.

She said this to the child in her arms, a little boy with skin the color of coffee, but she said it in her own language. The bright eyes blinked and then he opened his mouth to coo at her with great seriousness. He was one of the strong ones, sturdy enough in body and spirit to survive this place. He would live to move to the children's ward and from there to one of the workrooms, where he would be trained to groom horses or burn charcoal or make buttons. Maybe someone like Amanda Spencer would claim him in a few years to train him as a house servant, if he was lucky. If he left this nursery before the next round of lung fever or croup made short work of them all.

"You're here late tonight."

Hannah drew in a sharp breath and reminded herself to smile. The woman who stood next to her had a thin face made lopsided by the fact that she had lost all her teeth on one side. She was the youngest of the nursery matrons, the one who had not yet been overwhelmed and hardened by sorrow. Once in a while Hannah had heard her laugh.

"I lost track of the time." It was the truth, but not the entire truth.

"A young lady must have better things to be doing." The matron held out her arms for the boy. "Best get along home now."

I do have something else to do, Hannah thought of saying. *And wouldn't you be surprised to hear what it is.*

Stealing the key to the records office was the easiest part. It hung in the caretaker's little cubbyhole, in a row with a dozen other keys, each carefully labeled in Mrs. Sloo's even, blockish hand: kine-pox office, apothecary, storeroom, records office. It seemed such a small thing to take one key and replace it for a short while with another. Mr. Magee himself would take no note; he was already in bed. For a moment Hannah listened to him snoring on the other side of the wall. His ability to sleep through every kind of commotion was legend in the Almshouse.

Sometimes a doctor would come to look in on an interesting case in the evening, but even this threat had been removed—to Hannah's relief and uneasiness both—by the fact that an autopsy was scheduled to begin at the hospital at exactly seven. A woman bloated and heavy with child, found dead on the docks with nothing to identify her. Dr. Simon would wonder why Hannah had missed such an opportunity, but she wouldn't be here to explain.

The door to the records office presented itself; a door like any other. On one end of the hallway, doors led to the main building, and on the other to the infirmary. Hannah waited for a moment, listening for footsteps. Then she turned the key in the lock.

Overfilled as it was from cellars to attic, the Almshouse was never a quiet place. Hannah stood very still for a long time in the middle of Mr. Eddy's office and listened. The familiar wails and conversation and squabbling worked to calm her galloping heart while she looked around herself. The room was criss-crossed with evening sunlight from a single window, and each shaft of light was heavy with dust. She pressed both hands against her face until the urge to sneeze had passed.

Paper enough to bury a man standing, Mrs. Sloo had said. Looking around herself, Hannah saw what she had meant. It was a neat room with a large desk and a chair as the only fur-niture, but deep shelves reached around the entire room, in-terrupted only by door and window. The shelves stretched from floor to ceiling, with a ladder that ran on a track to reach the highest ones. Every shelf was filled with half-boxes and every half-box with record books facing spine out. To Hannah's great relief, all of them were labeled.

She climbed the ladder to the top in the far corner of the room and began to work her way down, starting at every new sound in the hallway. It was far busier than she had ever imag-ined, and she realized now how lucky she had been to even get this far without being noticed. It took considerable effort to focus on the records before her, which turned out to be very dull: correspondence with the city council and mayor, minutes of meetings of the trustees, records of monies spent on food and raw wool and timber, gifts received, accounts with merchants all over the city.

Most of the boxes had not been disturbed in a very long while and Hannah was sometimes forced to use her handker-chief to wipe dust from the cards. It took a half hour to work her way down one wall, and still she had failed to find a single reference to orphans or abandoned children or slaves of any age. She began to move more quickly, listening with only half an ear as people passed by. Hannah's worst moment was hear-ing Mrs. Sloo's voice, but it turned out that she had no interest in the records office; she had collared one of the weavers and brought him into the relative silence of the hallway to quiz him about a loaf of bread that had gone missing from the kitchen. The traffic did not stop until the charwoman came by with a sloshing bucket and began scrubbing the floor.

She sang as she worked in a language Hannah didn't recog-nize, the melody underscored by the rhythmic movement of the brush over the floorboards. By the time she was finished the light was almost gone and Hannah had found the apprenticeship records: names and trades and the terms on which a ward of the Almshouse was sent to live and work for a carpenter or a ropemaker or seamstress. Hundreds of names filled these books in a small, cramped hand, but none of the children listed here were less than ten years old.

In the last of the light, Hannah climbed down from the ladder and stood considering the stub of candle that sat in a dish on the desk when a familiar voice shouted just outside the door.

"Christ on the bloody cross!"

There was the sound of glass shattering and, following it, the thud of a body hitting the floor.

Hannah stepped off the ladder and into the shadows with one fist pressed against her chest. Three things occurred to her all at once: Dr. Savard was back early from the autopsy, he had made a mess of some kind and fallen perhaps because he was drunk, and she would be trapped here until it was all cleared away. From the smell of distilled alcohol that was filling the air it seemed that he must have dropped a specimen jar; by the sound it had been a very large one.

"Mr. Magee!" he bellowed. "Mr. Magee, I need you!"

There was no chance at all that his voice would carry so far as Mr. Magee's bed, something the doctor knew himself. A shiver ran up Hannah's back at the tone in his voice: even in the most extreme moments she had never seen Dr. Savard lose his composure. Just as that thought came to Hannah he stopped shouting and said in a much lower voice, "Goddammit, if I bleed to death it'll be on your sorry head, man."

Dr. Savard was bleeding; he had cut himself. He needed help, but how badly? She stepped back again and brushed against the shelves, dislodging a cloud of dust.

It wasn't a very loud sneeze, she told herself. And then she sneezed again.

Outside the door there was sudden silence.

"Who's there?" barked the doctor.

As he rattled the doorknob Hannah entertained the thought of climbing through the window. She sneezed again.

"Miss Bonner?" His tone was dry and completely neutral.

Hannah cleared her throat. "Yes?"

"What a fortunate coincidence. I need your assistance, if you'd be so kind as to come out here."

*   *   *

"It will take ten stitches or more to close it," Hannah said sometime later. She was bent over Dr. Savard's hand, working by the light of hastily lit candles. "It could have been much worse. You're lucky."

"Oh, very fortunate indeed," he replied. There was a swipe of blood on his cheek and dribbles of it all down his shirtfront, as well as a line of sweat on his brow, but his expression was as mocking and detached as ever. "Be so kind as to pass me the bottle in that bottom drawer, I will need some distraction from your needlework."

Without looking up from his hand, Hannah said, "When the last of the splinters are out."

"Of course," said Dr. Savard. "I wouldn't dream of inconveniencing you."

Hannah dropped another glass shard onto the examination table. "My stepmother says that white men use sarcasm to hide something they would like to say but may not."

He grunted. "As you well know, I am not inclined to withhold my opinion on anything. Speaking of hiding things, what exactly were you doing in the records office?" After a while he said, "You resort to silence, and I resort to sarcasm. To each the weapon of his own choosing, Miss Bonner."

Hannah brought two candles closer to improve her view of the injury. The doctor had interrupted his fall on the wet floor with his hand, which landed on a piece of the broken jar. The cut ran in an angle across his palm from the base of his little finger to the juncture of the thumb and wrist. It was deepest in the pad of muscle below the thumb, and in fact if the angle were only slightly different he might have done himself more serious injury by cutting into the artery.

With the tips of her fingers she pressed along the edge of the cut to be sure that there were no more glass shards. Dr. Savard looked away and said nothing at all.

"No more splinters," she announced.

"Then if I might remind you—"

Hannah avoided his gaze as she opened the drawer and retrieved the bottle he had asked for, the candlelight sparking hints of red in the deep brown of the brandy. It was half full, and it made a little clinking sound when she put it down before him.

"I should think you've already had enough." She wondered at herself, that she should make such a comment to him when she knew how it would be received.

But he was more curious than offended. "And how do you know how much brandy I've had to drink, Miss Bonner?"

Hannah was preparing the suture needle, but she looked up to meet his gaze. "The more formal your speech, the more you've been drinking. When you are completely sober your language would make any lady faint."

He blinked in surprise. "You've made a study of my habits, I see."

Hannah said, "I'm ready to start. If you are going to drink, then you had best go ahead with it now."

"You would prefer I take laudanum?" he asked, reaching for the bottle with his uninjured right hand. "Or should I take nothing at all and sneer at the pain, as your Mohawk warriors are trained to do?"

She glanced up at him and saw the challenge in the dark eyes. He was embarrassed and ill at ease and in pain, but Hannah was not inclined to humor him by entering into the argument he wanted. She said, "You must please yourself, Dr. Savard. As you always do."

He snorted softly, the corner of his mouth twitching.

Hannah began to stitch. From the corner of her eye she saw how his right hand tightened on the unopened bottle.

"You needn't take such small stitches," he said finally. "I don't mind the scar."

"It will heal faster this way," Hannah replied calmly. "Unless that was an order?"

He exhaled loudly, as if she were a stubborn student and he a poorly used teacher.

Hannah worked as quickly as she could, and after a minute she was so focused on the work that she forgot the man attached to the hand. The flinching of his fingers at every movement of the needle meant only that there was no nerve damage; the sounds he made now and then were irrelevant.

When she had placed the last stitch she stopped to consider her work. Even Dr. Todd might be satisfied with her, for once. She went to her own bag and came back with a corked bottle.

Dr. Savard cleared his throat. "And what do you intend to do with that?"

She met his gaze. "I intend to wash your wound out with it. What did you think?"

His gaze skittered away and then back again, and to Hannah's great surprise, he flushed a mottled red. "You're always pulling some root or leaf or some strange Musselman cure out of that bag of yours."

For once she let herself smile. "I'm sorry to disappoint you but it's nothing so exotic or effective as Dragon's Blood. If I had any, I would use it."

He straightened. "I'm a man of science, Miss Bonner. I studied in Edinburgh, which is widely regarded as the best school of medicine in the world. Your magical remedies are of no interest to me. Now what is in that bottle?"

She didn't try to hide her smile as she took out the cork and held it under his nose. "Nothing very shocking, just a distillation of winterbloom and slippery elm to keep the wound from getting inflamed."

Dr. Savard frowned at her, his nose twitching. "That will sting like the very devil. I'm not sure it's worth it."

Hannah considered the neat line of stitches in his palm, and she thought of the Hakim. How would he convince a reluctant patient, one who happened to call himself a doctor? Appeal to his better nature, he would say. On the other hand Curiosity would laugh aloud at such childishness and shame him into it; neither approach seemed the right one for Dr. Savard.

She said, "Well then, let's experiment."

His combative expression gave way to distrust. "With my hand?"

"Listen, please. You say that you are a man of science. Let me wash half the wound, from here to here." She traced a line from the middle of his palm to the base of his palm, and his fingers twitched.

"If both halves of the wound heal at the same pace and in the same way, I will concede that you are right and there was no need to bother. And of course as a man of science, you will concede the opposite, if it turns out that it does help in the healing process."

He scowled at her. "You are very clever, Miss Bonner. There is no way for me to refuse your suggestion without appearing small-minded and stubborn."

She drew her brows together and said nothing.

"Very clever indeed," he fumed. "I will enter into this little experiment of yours. On one very small condition."

Hannah saw, too late, that she had underestimated him and put herself in a corner. She could walk away, of course, but then she looked at his palm again. She had seen wounds like this go bad very quickly.

"You want to know why I was in the records office."

"Of course."

"I will meet your condition, if you will promise me not to tell anyone else about this. Anyone at all. No matter what you think of the merits of my . . . undertaking. Or of my reasoning."

Dr. Savard did not often grin, and it made Hannah uncomfortable to see him do it now. "You've piqued my interest," he said. "Very well, go ahead with your experiment. I agree to your terms."

Hannah kept her own expression neutral as she took his hand and tipped the bottle over his lower palm. He jerked hard at the first touch of the liquid and let out a hiss between his teeth.

After a long moment he said, "Now that you've had your fun—"

Hannah took Manny's note from her work-apron pocket and handed it to him. While he read, she put away the bottle in her workbag and tidied the examination table, trying not to look at his expression as he turned the paper over and read the other side.

When he raised his head she said, "I'm trying to find some record of what happened to the child. As a favor to her father."

"Who is—"

"A friend of mine."

There was nothing to read from his face, neither surprise nor censure nor approval. His eyes were very dark and Hannah found she could not hold his gaze.

Dr. Savard was silent while she wrapped his injured hand in a piece of linen and tied the bandage neatly. When she looked up he was staring at her with a look that bordered on anger.

"Does this have anything to do with the way you disappear for an hour now and then in the late afternoon, in the direction of the kitchens?"

Hannah blinked at him. "I must go now. They will be waiting for me on Whitehall Street."

He said, "I'll see you home," and held up his newly bandaged hand to stop her protest. "I have no intention of letting you walk the length of Manhattan unaccompanied, Miss Bonner. Save yourself the argument."

"If you would simply have the desk clerk call a hackney carriage for me—"

"Doesn't it strike you as odd that I was carrying a specimen jar here at this hour of the evening?"

Hannah pulled up in surprise. "I hadn't thought about it. I suppose it is odd."

"A mob broke into the autopsy room at the hospital this evening to claim the cadaver."

"But I thought the body had been found on the docks?"

Dr. Savard lifted a shoulder. "It seems that the men who delivered her to the dissection room stretched the truth a bit to get their pay."

"Grave robbers."

"These gentlemen prefer the term 'resurrectionists.' The lady's husband took issue, of course, and the mob got ugly, to say the least. They decided that while they were there they would destroy everything they could get their hands on."

"Was anyone hurt?"

He lifted a shoulder. "Some bumps and bruises. William Ehrlich got himself a black eye, but the worst of it is we'll have to take autopsies somewhere else for a good while. I hoped to save at least one laboratory specimen, but you see I was not very successful."

"So you rescued the—" She paused, thinking of the mess on the hallway floor, glass and blood and chunks of something unidentifiable. "What was it?"

"A cirrhotic liver," said Dr. Savard. One corner of his mouth turned up. "It was the closest thing to me, in more ways than one." He cleared his throat and looked at his palm critically. "So you must understand that given the mood on the streets, I cannot let you leave here unaccompanied."

After a long moment Hannah said, "It will be just a moment while I change out of my apron."

As it turned out the only carriages they saw were already engaged. After a few minutes in which the doctor paced up and down the Broad Way waving his arms unproductively, he fetched a whale-oil lantern from the Almshouse and they began the walk to Whitehall Street by unspoken agreement.

Hannah carried her own bag, as Dr. Savard had one hand that he could not use and needed the other for the lantern on its short pole. It creaked agreeably with each step, sending an oval of light swinging back and forth between them. The shapes of the buildings and trees were easily made out against the night sky. Coffeehouses and shops were silent, but the tavern doorways were lit by darkly smoking torches or lamps. Now and then they passed a private watchman who patrolled the street with a lantern of his own. There was no sign of ruffians, but Hannah did not point that out, mostly because she didn't want to add to the noise.

Coaches and cabs pulled by iron-shod horses moved briskly along cobbled streets; laughter and voices raised in argument drifted from everywhere and nowhere; dogs barked; shop signs creaked with every gust of wind.

"I don't know how people stand the constant racket of the city." She said this out loud, to her own surprise and to the doctor's.

"Really?" He raised his head to listen. And then: "I don't suppose the world is silent at night even on your mountain, is it?"

"No," said Hannah. "There is sound enough. But not this constant buzzing."

He made a noncommittal sound. "You would become accustomed to it with time."

"No," said Hannah. "I would not." To change the subject she said, "You must be in some considerable pain."

Dr. Savard made a sound deep in his throat.

"Was that a denial?"

He sent her an irritated look. "Of course I am in pain. But it will pass. Most things do."

"Willow-bark tea would be some relief."

"Watch your step here."

They skirted a pile of refuse that had been cast out into the road, the light catching the eyes of a rat that had settled itself in a nest of rags.

As they passed the darkened doorway of a milliner's shop two figures moved deeper into the shadows, followed by a hoarse giggling.

"Oooh, look, Susie. Dr. Savard come out this evening for a stroll. How very good to see you, Doctor."

"Miss Susan, Miss Mariah. Good evening to you both." He raised his voice without slowing. To Hannah he said, "Ladies of the night, as Dr. Simon refers to them so shyly. Prostitutes, in other words." His tone was matter-of-fact and unapologetic.

Hannah looked over her shoulder, but could make out nothing of the women.

"Dr. Savard's out walking with a lady, Mariah. He's got no time for us." There was a hiccup of laughter.

"I recognize that voice," said Hannah, slowing. "I treated her just yesterday for—" She paused.

"Blennorhagic discharge?"

"Yes."

"Many of them have it, it's why they come to us."

"But they are contagious."

"Yes."

"And . . ."

"Professionally active, yes. The phrase you're looking for, Miss Bonner, is *caveat emptor.*"

"No," Hannah said, irritated finally by his tone. "I wasn't thinking about the buyer at all. I was thinking how painful it must be for her."

He shrugged so that the lantern swayed. "Hunger is a harsh mistress."

Hannah said, "You are very cold on this subject, Doctor."

In the light of the lantern his expression was sober. "I prefer the term *detached.* It is a necessity when practicing medicine among the poor. I'm afraid that's a lesson you haven't learned yet."

"It is one I hope I never learn."

"You are very young."

"And you are stating the obvious. What does my youth have to do with it?"

He looked away into the dark, as if he might find the right answer there. "I was like you, once. I found that optimism is a liability in the practice of medicine, especially here."

Hannah said, "How kind of you to share your superior knowledge and understanding of the world." And she started off again at a much brisker pace, to the sound of his soft laughter and a new sound, a distant shouting undercut by the high piercing of a constable's whistle.

She stopped and turned back toward Dr. Savard, who had also turned in the direction of the noise. More whistles now, and the shouting more distinct.

"Is Dr. Simon safe?" Hannah was embarrassed to realize that she should have asked this question earlier.

"I expect he's safe enough by now. We had best press on."

A few minutes later he said, "So I take it you had no luck in your search in the records office?"

Beneath the brim of his hat Hannah could make out nothing of his expression. "No, I did not."

She lifted her face to the night breeze, glad of its cool touch.

"You are planning to leave the city very soon, as I understand it."

Hannah said, "We will leave before the end of the week, yes. Mrs. Todd is no better and her husband wants her to come home."

"Mrs. Todd is Dr. Ehrlich's patient, I believe. He has mentioned her now and then."

It was not really a question, but Hannah made a sound of agreement. She could not think of anything to say about Dr. Savard's colleague from Philadelphia that might not give offense, but to her surprise she did not need to.

"The man whines and buzzes like a mosquito," said Dr. Savard in a conversational tone. "If only he were half as intelligent."

She hiccuped a laugh, pressing a hand to her mouth. The doctor looked at her impatiently. "He is a disaster as a physician and you know it."

After a moment Hannah said, "Mrs. Todd is much worse now than she was."

"How very diplomatic of you. You could call him a pretentious charlatan and have done with it."

"I might," Hannah said. "If I weren't so worried about Kitty."

"Give me her history, then," said Dr. Savard. "We might as well talk of that as anything else."

Hannah slowed. "Do you mean it? I have been wanting to discuss her case with someone, but Dr. Simon seemed reluctant."

"Then you should have asked," he said brusquely. "Get on with it, you've got fifteen minutes."

He let her talk, asking questions now and then for clarifica-
tion. Hannah told him what she knew and what she only suspected. The simple process of reciting Kitty's history was
enough to strip away the last of her optimism.

"I fear she will not live out the summer," she ended.

They had come to the beginning of the park at Bowling
Green. The gardeners had been at work; the smell of cut grass
was heavy in the air. The park was quiet but all around it the
houses pulsed with light and movement like a halo. Down the
street a line of carriages waited in front of the Delafields',
where a party was under way. Amanda and Will would be
there, and Kitty with them, if she was strong enough today.

"Miss Bonner."

"Yes?" Hannah was startled out of her thoughts.

"Let me ask you this. You have seen how much work there
is to do among the poor of this city. You are already an excellent medical practitioner. Will you not consider staying on to
see to the needs of those who really need you?"

Hannah stepped back from him, awash in surprise and irritation and a strange satisfaction. He was looking at her with
such intensity that she had to turn her head.

"You have nothing to say?"

She pressed a hand to her throat, felt the thundering of her
pulse. "I'm thankful for your good opinion."

He waved this away with his bandaged hand. "No, no. I am
not looking for thanks. I am offering you an opportunity to do
what you were born to do. The poor of this city need you.
Will you stay for them?"

The thought of living and working in this city felt so
wrong to Hannah, so far from the way her world was meant
to be, that she could hardly think of how to answer him politely, or even give any real credit to the compliment he had
paid by suggesting such a thing.

You might as well ask me to fly, she thought of saying. Instead
she said, "My people need me too, Dr. Savard. If I stay here I
will be turning my back on them."

He shook his head impatiently, as if she were a dull student
who refused to take his meaning. "Are you speaking of the
people of Paradise, or of your people? Of the Mohawk?"

"Some of my people are in Paradise, and some are not.
Does it matter where they are, or what they call themselves?"

"Yes." He looked away over the park, the muscles in his jaw knotting. "It does matter. A village of a hundred people hardly needs two doctors. There is more important work to be done. On the other hand, if you are speaking of going to live among the Mohawk—"

"Dr. Savard," Hannah interrupted. "Your idea of what is important and mine are worlds apart."

Just as suddenly as the intensity had come into his expression it fell away, replaced by the man she had worked with for the past weeks: detached and cool and unknowable. A teacher, and a good one; never a friend.

He inclined his head. "Of course. I beg your pardon, Miss Bonner."

The silence that fell between them was heavier now, fraught with things that Hannah could hardly name. She said, "The house is at the other end of the park. Thank you for seeing me this far."

"I'm dismissed, then." His old half-smile was back, and she was relieved to see it.

"If you insist," Hannah answered in the same tone. "You will remember the willow-bark tea for the pain?"

"How could I forget it?" He held up his injured hand in a salute. "Good evening, then, Miss Bonner."

She had walked on a few steps before she stopped and turned back. "You never gave me your opinion on Mrs. Todd's case."

"You never asked for it."

"That has never stopped you before, Doctor."

She could see only part of his face, but she knew that he was smiling by his tone. "Ah, but she's your patient, isn't she?"

Hannah hesitated. "I'm asking for a consultation, then."

He turned his face up to the trees as if they had some wisdom to share. Of the stars he asked the question she should have anticipated. *"Ubi est morbus?"*

"The uterus," said Hannah. "The source of her disease is some weakness or unhealed rupture of the uterus following the delivery of a dead child. But how to heal it?"

He was looking at her with his usual irritation and urgency. "Miss Bonner, I ask you again: *ubi est morbus?*"

"The source of her disease is not in her uterus?" Hannah asked, astounded and unsettled and provoked. "But where, then?"

"The source of her disease may not be in her uterus *alone,*" said Dr. Savard. "You have been blinded by the obvious. What Mrs. Todd requires is something or someone to worry about besides herself, Miss Bonner. Distract her mind and you will have a chance of healing her body."

"You believe the hemorrhaging to be hysterical in origin?"

He shook his head sharply. "Your patient is not some lady with vapors complaining of chills and aches. The physical damage is real enough—"

"But the healing process begins elsewhere," finished Hannah for him.

He smiled at her, and touched his hat with his bandaged hand. "You begin to think like an anatomist, Miss Bonner." It was the highest compliment he had to pay, and with it he turned and left her.

Chapter 28

Mrs. Burroway was the senior matron in charge of the nursery, dry as old bread and hard to rattle. Presented with Hannah's proposal, she refused to be surprised or even to question her motivations. She simply went to the desk in the corner and wrote out a few sentences. Hannah signed the paper and fished a few coins from her apron pocket.

"I'll send young Michael along shortly," said Mrs. Burroway. "You can trust him not to drop her."

With that lukewarm reassurance Hannah was free to walk away from the Almshouse, empty-handed as she was. Cicero had collected all her own things as well as the trunk of books, medical supplies, and vaccination materials Dr. Simon had assembled for Richard Todd. And she had already taken leave from the doctors and patients and from Mr. Magee, who enclosed one of her hands in both of his own and wished her well in awkward, overly formal language that he must have learned by listening to the doctors.

"We'll miss you," he had said finally. "Even Mrs. Sloo will miss you, mark my words. She likes a good fight, does Mrs. Sloo, and you gave her what she likes."

"She wouldn't like it if I were to stay on," Hannah said.

He lifted one bony shoulder in disagreement. "I wouldn't be so sure. She's a woman determined to be vexed, is Mrs. Sloo."

And so Hannah left the Almshouse smiling. She was looking

forward to the walk back to Whitehall Street, her only chance
to be alone today. Once she stepped through the door there
would be all the furor of packing, the household as full of motion and unease as an anthill before a storm. The boys would be
occupied with their most recent and involved plot to smuggle
Peter and Marcus onto the sloop bound up the Hudson. Their
hope was to join Daniel so that the four of them could establish
a boys' paradise on the mountain. Amanda and Will kept thinking of one more thing to send to Elizabeth or the twins,
Curiosity or Nathaniel, so that the pile of luggage waiting in the
hall had already grown to tremendous proportions.

And there was Kitty, distraught at the idea of leaving and
full of last-minute demands.

*She needs something or someone to worry about besides herself.
Distract her mind and you will have a chance of healing her body.*

Hannah was turning this over once again when she turned
the corner onto the Broad Way to find the streets crowded
with people as far as she could see, and none of them going
anywhere.

She asked a passing shopgirl what was happening and got
only a look of surprise and shock in response, as if a statue or a
painting had suddenly spoken. It seemed that many people in
the city had never seen an Indian at all, and most of those had
the idea that the color of Hannah's skin meant human language was beyond her. It happened so often when Hannah
was out in the city that she had almost stopped being insulted.

One of the Almshouse boys caught Hannah's eye, slinking
through the crowd in a way that could mean nothing good at
all. She stopped him for an explanation and got instead that
look that boys reserved for very slow grown-ups. He told her
what everyone else seemed to know already: the Tammany
Hall parade was about to start. And then he was gone into the
crowds.

Whatever Tammany Hall might be, it seemed that the parade was popular with the people of New-York. The whole
city seemed to be here: washerwomen and merchants, tinkers
hung about with ladles and pots and strings of forks looped
around their necks, housemaids, ladies in elaborate hats and
walking cloaks, chimney sweeps. People were crowded into
doorways; they hung out of windows and peered down from
roofs. Those who spilled into the street itself jostled and

poked, jittered and fidgeted in their excitement, so that each step forward was more difficult, and then it was simply impossible to go anywhere at all. Dogs howled and a pair of oxen raised their noses to bellow at the sky; the drover swore and slapped and pulled at his animals, desperate to move them out of the way of the coming parade. Children darted up the street and back again, screaming out progress reports.

Most of the street vendors had been caught up in the stream of people like timber caught in an ice jam: a knife grinder leaned against his cart, sound asleep with his head tilted back against the grind-wheel while the roasted-peanut vendor was surrounded by an eager and impatient public.

Hannah was tall for a woman, but no matter how she lifted up on tiptoe and craned her neck, she could see no way to escape.

At her elbow an old lady with a single clutch of small black teeth and a white crusting of sugar on a pendulous lower lip squinted up at her. She said, "Forget it, dearie, you're stuck here until the parade is gone. Might as well enjoy the show, eh?" She peered up at Hannah, her eyes squinted almost shut. The grime in the creases around her eyes was so dark that it looked at first glance as if she had been tattooed.

"Miss Bonner!" A tall man raised his hand in greeting as he made his way toward her from the row of private carriages parked to watch the parade. "Mrs. Kerr asks if you'd like to watch the parade with her."

Hannah raised a hand to block the sun. There was Mrs. Kerr waving a handkerchief so fiercely that the ostrich feathers on her hat—dyed orange and green to match her striped gown—swayed like branches in a strong breeze.

What Hannah wanted to do was to get home, but if she must watch the parade she might as well see it clearly. She let herself be guided to Mrs. Kerr, who fussed until she was settled among velvet cushions sprouting silk tassels three fingers thick.

"Isn't this just fine," said the old lady. "I was hoping to see you again before you leave for home. And see, here come the revelers."

A procession appeared from around a corner, bursting in a roar of color and sound upon them.

Children came first, all of them boys, trotting in wild,

sweeping curves, bells and rattles on rawhide strings tied around their waists, bells swinging from hips and knees, bells sewn to sleeves. Some of them carried drums on leather belts, and they pounded out a heavy rhythm.

An old man with flowing white hair and beard trotted alongside them on a donkey that had been decked out in streamers of every color. He had a bucktail tied to his beaver hat and stripes of paint across each cheekbone, and he threatened the children who rushed up to him with great swipes of a rusty tomahawk, sending them screaming and laughing in every direction. A young boy bolted forward to grab at the saddlebag that hung low over the belly of the animal, but the old man captured him and dragged him over the donkey's neck to whack noisily at his rump with the flat of the tomahawk.

"The elder Mr. Mason," said Mrs. Kerr, raising her voice to be heard over the crowd. "His son is one of the sachems, and he dearly loves a parade."

"The braves!" the crowd screamed. "The Tammany braves!"

Then the chanting began, and the skin rose on Hannah's neck.

"The heart and soul of Tammany," explained Mrs. Kerr. "Respectable businessmen, all of them."

A hundred men came trotting down the Broad Way, all of them white and each painted to look like an Indian. They wore caps with tails of horsehair at the crown above faces smeared with paint.

"De Witt would like to scalp each and every one of them with their own tomahawks." Mrs. Kerr was laughing. "The silly sods."

"Senator Clinton doesn't approve of this...demonstration?"

Mrs. Kerr waved a gloved hand. "He has no use for Tammany. These are all Aaron Burr's men, you see."

Hannah didn't see at all; she recognized the names of some of the most prominent New-York politicians, but had never taken the time to learn much about their factions or battles.

The men from Tammany Hall were dressed in buckskin leggings and hunting shirts, some of them with elaborate capes decorated with quillwork and beading. Others wore their own clothes with only the gaudy face paint and a bucktail pinned to a hat. Even the men who had kept their beards and long mustaches had painted themselves, so that they reminded Hannah more of the minstrels she had seen at Scottish fairs than of the Indian warriors they meant to be.

But the worst of it, the thing that left Hannah breathless, was the masks.

They wore masks made of braided cornhusks and masks that had been carved from living willow in a ceremony that required three days to appease the spirit of the tree. Many were carefully painted and decorated with long swatches of horsehair and bits of metal nailed around the eyeholes. These masks were as familiar to her as the faces of her own family: none of them had been made by white hands, and every single one of them had a sacred purpose.

"Laughing Beggar," Hannah whispered to herself as a man ran by.

"What was that?" Mrs. Kerr cupped a hand around her ear.

"That mask," Hannah repeated as she pointed. "It is called 'Laughing Beggar.' My uncle wore a mask just like that one at the last Maple Festival."

To drive away evil spirits, she would have added, but there was no hope of being heard now as the men had begun to chant, and the crowd echoed them. Nonsense syllables strung together like the babbling of babies, accompanied by the beating of drums and feet against the road.

When the braves had passed, a smaller group of men appeared, walking sedately.

"There's Burr," said Mrs. Kerr. "The vice president, you know, but always scheming for more. You see how he simpers and smirks and makes love to every man who casts a vote. Itching for a crown to wear, even if he has to forge it himself."

The last party in the procession was led by a large man with such a massive head and huge round belly that he looked in danger of pitching forward. Behind him walked a woman almost as tall as he. Hannah recognized Virginia Bly from the Bull's Head even at a distance. The three younger women who walked behind them Hannah had never seen before, but from their coloring she guessed that these were the Bly daughters. All four of the women were dressed in the finest doeskin overdresses; even from a distance Hannah could make out the heavy bead- and quillwork.

The procession had come to a stop. Mr. Bly climbed up onto a large wooden stand in the middle of the street to hold out his arms. His cheeks were painted with random swipes of red and yellow and black; his dress was half O'seronni and half some strange O'seronni idea of what a Kahnyen'kehàka warrior might wear. But the headpiece was no hastily put together combination of feathers and rawhide.

A long train of eagle feathers cascaded down from a skull-cap made of splints covered with fine beaded doeskin. It was the headpiece of a great warrior, of a sachem who had won many battles for his people. In some longhouse to the north, in a village on the Mohawk or Sacandaga or in the valleys where the Seneca and Onandaga lived, women had sat together for long hours over that headpiece. Women like Virginia Bly; women like Hannah's mother and grandmothers. The urge to rush forward and grab it from his head was almost more than she could resist.

Bly raised his voice, deep and loud enough to resonate over the crowd.

"My friends! Let us bow our heads and remember the Great Grand Sachem of the Thirteen United Fires. May he remain in the protection of the Maker of Life, the Great Spirit who has raised him to his exalted position. May the wisdom of the sachems who went before him guide him to transcendent splendor of his greatness."

As he droned on the crowd began to disperse, first single people slipping away and then larger groups. When Mrs. Kerr reached forward to rap with her cane on the box, Hannah jumped in surprise; she had been so taken up by the spectacle in front of her that she had all but forgotten where she sat.

"George, drive on as soon as you are able. Take us along the shore for a little, away from the crowds. Miss Bonner needs some fresh air and the chance to regain her composure."

"I want to walk back to Whitehall Street," Hannah said.

"Do you? Through this crowd?" Mrs. Kerr looked out over the street. "Or would you prefer to ride a while with me and hear about Virginia Bly and her daughters? You needn't look so surprised. Your expression gives away a great deal, my dear."

The urge to protest was so strong that Hannah tasted it like salt on her tongue. "Why would I want to hear about Virginia Bly and her daughters?"

Mrs. Kerr fluttered her fingers at this question. "Do not play the innocent with me, Miss Bonner. If you don't care to hear the story I have to tell, I will see you straight back to Whitehall Street." And then, after a moment in which Hannah weighed and rejected every possible response: "I thought so."

It was five minutes or more before the noise of the crowd was behind them. Mrs. Kerr seemed satisfied to sit and watch the oyster boats along the shore. Hannah could not bring herself to ask questions, simply because she could not think where to start.

Finally Mrs. Kerr seemed to remember that she was not alone. Her gaze shifted to Hannah.

"I go to watch that parade because it amuses me to see men make such fools of themselves, but of course you would be offended." Another long silence followed.

"Mrs. Kerr—"

"Virginia Bly had five daughters," the old lady began, as if Hannah had not spoken. "The three youngest you saw today. There are many rumors about those three, the favorite being that at night their mother keeps them locked in a room with the windows nailed shut. That rumor happens to be true. Her two elder daughters ran away, you see, and she is determined to keep these ones at home.

"The man who is probably still speaking back there on the Broad Way is her husband, the innkeeper at the Bull's Head, where Will Spencer took you the afternoon you heard from him about Libertas. Did you think he would not tell us about that trip? We depend on one another for honesty, Miss Bonner. Of course he told us.

"Now you must realize that Libertas watches Harry Bly closely. For example, I can tell you that yesterday he took Micah Cobb's place in a meeting of the blackbirders. Mr. Cobb has gone north in search of..." She paused to consider her words. "A mutual friend of yours and mine. Of course you must be worried for that friend, but as of this moment I have no news to report. What I can tell you—and what you want to know—is the story of Virginia Bly's eldest daughter, Jenny. Who is Liam Kirby's wife."

Hannah flushed with confusion and embarrassment. "Since you speak so openly to me, Mrs. Kerr, I hope you will pardon my own bluntness. I'm not especially interested in discussing Liam Kirby or his wife with you, or with anyone."

The older lady sat back among the cushions with an abrupt laugh. "Someday I must meet your stepmother and congratulate her on your education. Such quickness of thought and speech in a woman of your young age is to be commended. I will admit that I have started this conversation badly—"

"You need not have started it at all," Hannah interrupted, unable to govern her temper. "This is a personal matter, and to be very honest, I am surprised and disappointed that Will Spencer would have shared any of my history with you."

"Now you are jumping to conclusions, Miss Bonner," Mrs. Kerr said more sharply. "Will Spencer did not divulge any confidence to me. What I know of your situation I know from Liam Kirby himself."

Hannah felt the blood draining from her face. She opened her mouth but no sound would come out.

"Shall I go on?"

"I'm not sure."

"Well, then. I will begin. You may stop me at any point, although I doubt you will.

"You are wondering how I know Liam. It seems an unlikely acquaintance, that is what you are thinking. And of course you are correct, but only because you don't know that my late husband had a small fleet of merchant ships, and he loved nothing better than to go off to sea now and then to see to business himself. A boy at heart, you see. A man who has no children—for whatever reason—will ever be a boy.

"Mr. Kerr dreamed of going to sea, but his father would not let him join the navy. So he made up for it in his later years by traveling on his own ships. That is how they met, Mr. Kerr and Liam Kirby, on a voyage to the Spice Islands. When you saw him in Paradise I will assume he told you about his years at sea."

Hannah said, "You knew Liam was coming to Paradise?"

Mrs. Kerr shook her head so that her feathers danced. "Miss Bonner, if you make me jump about in this story we will both end up more confused than we started. Now, as I was saying, Mr. Kerr and Liam first met on board the *Nutmeg*. The red dog caught Mr. Kerr's eye first—he was devoted to dogs, you see. At one point we had six of them, each bigger than the last. Dogs can be comforting creatures but I do draw the line at sharing my bed with six of them... I digress.

"When the ship returned to New-York, Mr. Kerr brought Liam and his dog home to Park Street, as was his habit with young strays. My husband was an unconventional man, Miss Bonner, or he would never have taken me as wife. What interested him he must have near him, and so young Liam spent much of his time with us when he was not at sea. I grew very fond of him."

"And he told you about Lake in the Clouds?"

"In time he spoke of the home he had left behind," said Mrs. Kerr. "But not in great detail. For the most part he talked about his brother, your father, and how you had disappeared into the Scottish countryside."

Hannah could barely breathe, much less speak, but Mrs. Kerr did not seem to want any commentary.

"We need not go into his accusations. The point is that he spoke of you often, and he believed you lost to him forever. Then he came back from a long absence—a journey to China, if you can imagine such a thing—and he caught sight of Jenny Bly.

"That was the end of his career on the seas. He took up work here in the city, carpentry for the most part, and twice a week he called at the Blys', or he attempted to call on them. Virginia Bly would not take his interest in her daughter seriously, you understand. A young man with no connections and no prospects would not do for her daughters. But Jenny gave Liam enough encouragement to keep his hopes up, most probably simply because it plagued her mother, who had finally managed to find suitable husbands for the girls. Jenny was meant for Mr. Hufnagle—a German coffee merchant new to the city, widowed, and twice her age. A white man with resources, you understand, was her goal. One willing to marry a red-skinned young woman with a generous dowry.

"Every day Mr. Kerr would hear about Liam's progress, or I should say, his lack of progress, with Jenny Bly—Liam was renting a room above our stables, you see. By that time Mr. Kerr had fallen quite ill, and he took great comfort in Liam's visits. He was excessively attached to the boy. As was I, I must admit.

"Although I have no children—or perhaps because I have

no children—it seems to me quite obvious that Virginia Bly was to blame for what happened next. Strong-minded young women can no more be driven than a flock of cats. They will strike out in the end, and that is what happened. She announced to the girls that they would be married in short order, and at that, they ran off. Liam was beside himself with worry."

Mrs. Kerr paused to look Hannah directly in the eye. "There is nothing very unusual about this story thus far, you must be thinking. A young woman dissatisfied with her parents' choice of a husband defies their authority. But imagine this: your father is so outraged that you would dare to flaunt his wishes that he puts a price on your head. That is what Bly did. He put a price on the heads of his two eldest daughters and he set Micah Cobb loose to bring them home, as if they were nothing more than stray dogs. And Mr. Cobb did bring them home, within two days. He is very good at what he does."

"Mrs. Kerr." Hannah heard some desperation in her own voice, but she could hardly bear to listen to the rest of the story. "If you could—"

"Get to the point of it? I am almost there now, Miss Bonner. The merchants Virginia Bly had bribed into agreeing to marry her daughters disappeared with the scandal, of course. So she married the eldest, Jane, to Micah Cobb—a man who had dragged her home tied hand and foot like a calf. Jenny was promised to Micah's brother Jonah—a disgusting specimen if ever there was one—but she managed to slip away again, and when she came back the next day, she was Liam Kirby's wife."

"Wait," said Hannah, rubbing the ache that had begun to gather at her temple. "Jenny Bly married Liam to thwart her parents?"

"Liam does not see it that way, but yes, that is my conclusion."

"So she is estranged from her family because she married against their wishes," Hannah said. "Is that the point?"

"No," said Mrs. Kerr, her fist tightening on the head of her cane. "It is not. You are an impatient young woman at times, Miss Bonner."

Hannah bit back a sharp response. "I apologize. Please go on."

"Three months after the young women were married, they disappeared again."

"They ran away," Hannah said. "That could not have been a surprise."

"I did not say that Jane and Jenny ran away, I said that they disappeared."

Hannah pulled up short, sure at first that she had misunderstood.

The older woman contemplated her gloves for a long moment. "Liam believes that she did run away. Most of the city seems to be of the same opinion. In any case, none of the blackbirders have had any success in finding either Jenny or Jane."

A flush of irritation made Hannah's fingers jump so that she had to wind her hands together to quiet them. "You think they are dead? Murdered?"

"I think that is a possibility," said Mrs. Kerr. "What I know as a certainty is that if those two young women came to harm, it was not at Liam's hands. Liam will not rest until he finds his wife."

"That is a poor excuse to live his life as a bounty hunter," Hannah said.

"It is no excuse at all," Mrs. Kerr agreed.

A small and frightening thought came to Hannah, the image of a young woman bent over a plate of food with a dead child tied to her chest. "Mrs. Kerr," said Hannah slowly. "Can you describe Jenny to me?"

For the first time since the conversation began Mrs. Kerr's expression softened. "You saw her younger sisters, and she looks a great deal like them, dark of hair and skin. She has unusual eyes, though. Too green to be called hazel, but shot with brown."

"How tall? As tall as me? As her mother?"

The older lady looked off into the distance with her eyes narrowed, as if she were trying to call Jenny Kirby out of her memories and into flesh. "She is taller than you, I think. Not quite so tall as her mother, but then I have never seen another woman of Virginia Bly's height. Why do you ask?"

"There was a young woman who came to the Almshouse," Hannah began slowly. "But she was very small of stature."

"Ah." Mrs. Kerr shook her head. "I see. You can rest

assured that it could not have been either of the Bly daughters, then."

Frustration boiled up suddenly in Hannah; she could not hold it back. "Mrs. Kerr, I have no idea what I am to do with this story you've told me."

The older lady smiled. "Put it away, then," she said. "Until you have figured that out."

Hannah asked to be brought no farther than the north end of the Bowling Green so that she would have at least a few moments to regain her composure, but once she had taken her leave from Mrs. Kerr she found herself flushing with a new anger, as ungovernable as the sun itself. Words filled her mouth that she dared not say, not to anyone, not even to herself. What kind of place was this that bred people like Virginia Bly and Micah Cobb, that could take the Liam she had known and turn him into such a man?

Mr. Livingston's butler cast her a curious glance as he went by; one of the Delaney kitchen maids called out wishes for a good journey as she shook out her apron. Each time Hannah had to force herself to answer politely.

"Good afternoon, Miss Bonner," called Mr. VanderVelde as he went into the green with his dogs.

As if I belonged here. She swallowed down her anger over and over again, but it always forced its way back into her throat, a new and cancerous growth winding itself around tendon and muscle and throbbing, like drums, like an old wound. Like a new one.

Mrs. Douglas was waiting for her in the front hall, more anxious than Hannah had ever seen her.

"There's somebody from the poorhouse waiting for you in the kitchen." A wail came from the kitchen, and the dignified Mrs. Douglas jumped a little.

Hannah remembered suddenly why she had needed to be home promptly. "He brought the baby?"

Mrs. Douglas nodded. "Said he was paid to deliver it to you and he didn't care to wait. He wanted to leave that child as if it were a letter or a parcel or a basket of apples, can you imagine? I told him, I said he best wait for you, Miss Hannah. I figured there was some mistake. Are you fevered?"

Mrs. Douglas folded her hands in front of her. *Because she wants to put a hand on my forehead and does not dare,* Hannah thought. *Because of the color of her skin; because of the color of mine.* As Curiosity would have done without hesitation, or Elizabeth, or Many-Doves. And with that thought the anger left Hannah; she came back to herself and remembered what she owed these people for their kindness and generosity. Nothing that happened out in the streets could change that: her anger had no place in this house.

"It's no mistake, and I'm not fevered," she said. "But I can't explain right now, Mrs. Douglas. I am so sorry you were concerned, I didn't mean to be so late. But right now I must go see Kitty and take the baby to her."

A look came over Mrs. Douglas, dawning understanding and something like admiration. She pursed her lips and then broke into a smile.

"Of course you do," she said. "I see that you do."

Hannah found Kitty sprawled across her bed, still in her nightclothes and her face swollen with weeping. As soon as Hannah closed the door behind herself Kitty sat up, hugging a pillow to her chest with one hand while she buried her face in her handkerchief. In the overbright late-afternoon sunlight her complexion had a bluish tinge that Hannah did not like at all.

"I don't know how I'll go on without Dr. Ehrlich, Hannah. I really don't. Just when I was starting to feel myself. Richard has no compassion." Kitty's misery was real, but Hannah was too nervous herself to do much more than make sympathetic noises.

She said, "Mrs. Douglas asks if you've finished the broth that she sent up to you."

Kitty fluttered her fingers toward the table where the tray sat, untouched. "I have no appetite, and let me just say right now that I won't be bullied into eating." She raised her face from the handkerchief to flash a furious and defiant look in Hannah's direction. Then her expression shifted instantly into surprise.

"What do you have there?"

Hannah came to sit on the edge of the bed. "What I have here is a dilemma, Kitty, and I need your advice." She folded back the blanket to reveal the face of a newborn, wrinkled and calm and wise as a woman who had lived a hundred years. A fringe of dark red hair peeked out from beneath a dingy muslin cap, the same red as two delicately drawn eyebrows. Her eyes were the muddy color that would eventually turn brown.

Hannah raised a finger to smooth the child's brow. "Her mother came from the south of England, like Elizabeth. She was called Margaret White. Her husband died of a fever on the passage over and she had no way to make a living and so she ended up at the poorhouse."

"White," echoed Kitty. She was staring down at the child as if she had never seen such a creature in her life.

Hannah said, "Mrs. White died in childbed. I knew her a little; she meant to make her way as a seamstress to support herself and her daughter."

"A little girl?" Kitty's voice came steady, although she would not meet Hannah's gaze.

"Yes."

"She's healthy?"

Hannah lifted a shoulder. "She is very small, but her heart is strong and she has no trouble breathing. And she suckles well."

A flush crept up Kitty's neck as she reached out a hand to touch the small hand that had escaped the swaddling clothes.

"Does she have a name?"

"A child isn't given a name at the Almshouse until it reaches six months." *Unless it reaches six months,* Hannah corrected herself silently. "But if she stays there they will call her Ann, as she was born on a Thursday."

"She doesn't look like an Ann at all," said Kitty.

The baby's eyes were moving restlessly, lighting first on Hannah's face and then on Kitty's. Then she opened her mouth into a perfect round no bigger than a pea and let out a high, hooting cry.

"She's hungry," Kitty said.

"She was fed with goat's milk just an hour ago. I asked Mrs. Douglas to send for more."

Kitty's mouth pursed in disapproval. "Goat's milk will upset her stomach. Mrs. Douglas could find a wet nurse, I'm sure."

The baby squeezed her eyes shut and began to cry in earnest, as if to agree.

"It would be best to call her after her mother. Margaret White is a pretty name." Kitty glanced nervously at Hannah.

"If Elizabeth agrees, of course. You intended to bring her to Elizabeth and Nathaniel to be raised at Lake in the Clouds?"

Hannah pressed a fist against her mouth to hide her smile. She could not help thinking of her stepmother and the endless discussions they had had about truths and half-truths, lies and white lies, the strange distinctions that O'seronni made to comfort themselves. It was a lesson she had learned, finally, and it was one she was often called on to use with Kitty.

She said, "There are so many infants in the nursery, I thought if I could help just one ... do you think I did the right thing? I'm not sure how Elizabeth will feel about taking on another child. Especially one that needs suckling."

"You know Elizabeth better than that, Hannah. She wouldn't let a child go uncared for if it was in her power to help. Of course you did the right thing."

Kitty put out her arms for the child. They were crisscrossed with the evidence of Dr. Ehrlich's lancet, bird tracks against skin as pale as new butter. "May I hold her?"

Just as soon as she was in Kitty's arms, the baby's wailing subsided to a hiccuping whimper.

"She's so hungry," Kitty whispered. "If I had any milk—" She glanced up at Hannah apologetically.

Hannah kept her gaze averted as she went to the door, where she paused. "Maybe you do have milk, Kitty. It has not been all that long. I'll go talk to Mrs. Douglas. Do you need anything else?"

Kitty had already begun to unwrap the crying baby to examine her, and she had trouble focusing on Hannah long enough to answer her question. "Yes, we'll need swaddling clothes and some decent linen. This cap won't do at all. Please ask Amanda to come, I'm sure she will have something appropriate. And I'll need Suzannah's help. It's time that I dressed."

Hannah sent a silent thank-you to Dr. Savard as she went down the stairs, her pulse still thundering in her ears. Will looked up when she entered his study, and came immediately to his feet.

"Good God," he said. "I've never seen you look so anxious. What's this about a baby? Mrs. Douglas was almost beside herself. Is something wrong with Kitty?"

"There's nothing wrong," Hannah said, holding up both

her hands to stop him. "In fact, as of this minute I have new hope for Kitty."

Will sat down again, a thoughtful look replacing the worried one. "Your expression reminds me of Aunt Merriweather on the day Lydia's engagement was announced. You must have managed some great coup. Are you going to tell me about it?"

This made Hannah smile even more broadly. She looked up toward the closed doors on the next floor, listening for the sound of a child's cry and hearing nothing at all.

She said, "I was so worried about what is wrong with Kitty's physical body that I forgot about her spirit. My mother's people understand that a wounded spirit can hinder the body's healing, but I lost sight of that when I spent all my time with vaccinations and microscopes and dissections."

Will was looking at her thoughtfully. "And how is it that you remembered so suddenly?"

"Someone reminded me," Hannah said. "A teacher. A friend."

Chapter 29

"I know such a long visit has been trying at times, but I hope you will miss the city at least a little."

Hannah glanced at Will Spencer where he stood at the rail of the *Good-News,* his hands clasped behind his back and his gaze fixed on the horizon. In a few minutes the longshoremen would finish bringing the last of the trunks on board. Kitty and Amanda had already gone belowdecks with the wet nurse to see to the arrangement of the sleeping quarters and to settle the child, dressed now in yards of the finest muslin and lace. There was no sign of the boys, either, who had decided to explore the ship in their last minutes together. *Looking for the right spot for two stowaways,* thought Hannah, but she kept this thought to herself as she studied the city everyone hoped that she would miss.

From this vantage point it was as loud and frantic as it had seemed on the day they arrived; familiarity did nothing at all to tame it. Hannah could not pretend that she regretted leaving, not even for someone as generous and good-hearted as Will Spencer.

She said, "I will miss you and everyone on Whitehall Street."

He laughed openly. "You are very diplomatic."

"Dr. Savard said the same thing to me the other day when he asked me my opinion of Dr. Ehrlich." Hannah looked away over the water. "He meant that I was holding back my true opinion."

"And were you?"

She considered. "Yes. But there is no need to do that with you, so I will tell you what I will miss, and what I won't." She paused.

"I will not miss Dr. Ehrlich and his love of the lancet, but I will miss the discussions you and I had over early breakfast every day. I won't miss the way people on the street stare at me or the things they mutter, but I will miss the way Amanda came to me every evening to ask about my day. I will miss Mrs. Douglas, but not Mrs. Sloo. I will miss working at the Almshouse and the hospital, as I learned so much there and could learn so much more. I won't miss the Almshouse nursery but I will dream about it. I won't miss the stink of the streets but I will miss walking by the water. I will miss Dr. Simon's library and the daily newspapers but I won't miss him especially in spite of his generosity, as he never was very comfortable with me. I will miss the way Mrs. Douglas hung bags of lavender among my clothes and made sure I had extra handkerchiefs when I left for the Almshouse. And I will miss the roasted peanuts I bought sometimes from the little man on the corner, because they were very good, and he is blind and he never asked me silly questions. Will that do?"

Will held up both hands in surrender, laughing good-naturedly. "Let me ask a different question. Did you accomplish everything you set out to accomplish?"

"I wrote that very question in my daybook yesterday," Hannah said. "In some things I accomplished more than I had hoped."

Once Hannah had thought Will too much of a gentleman to pry, but over the past weeks she had learned that he could use silence to carve a conversation to his own ends. Since the day he had shown her the Bull's Head, Liam's name had never been raised between them, but it hung there now, almost visible.

She said, "Mrs. Kerr came looking for me yesterday."

Will rocked back and forth on his heels while he studied the deck beneath his feet. When he looked at her again his expression was very sober.

"I thought she would. Did she tell you what you wanted to know about Liam?"

Hannah squinted into the sun. "She told me everything. And nothing at all."

There was a burst of voices on the dock, a sailor and a longshoreman nose to nose over a trunk. Hannah watched until the two men had been pulled apart and sent in different directions.

Hannah said, "Do you believe that Jenny Kirby and her sister ran away?"

Will pressed two fingers to the bridge of his nose, a gesture Hannah had come to recognize as a sign of extreme discomfort on his part. He said, "I truly do not know."

"Then I have only one more question," Hannah said. "I might have asked Mrs. Kerr, if I had been able to gather my thoughts. Is Liam truly a blackbirder, or is that all some elaborate game he plays while he looks for his wife?"

Will pushed out a breath. "The answer to that question is not as simple as you would expect."

"Simplify it then, for me."

"Very well," said Will. "Yes, Liam is looking for his wife. Yes, he is a bounty hunter. And yes, it was the former that brought him to the latter."

"Mr. Spencer, sir!" A breathless voice hailed them from the dock, and they both turned toward it. It was Oliver, one of the Douglas grandsons employed on Whitehall Street. "Mr. Spencer, sir! Granny Douglas sent me to try to catch you up. Post come for Miss Bonner, just a few minutes ago."

Will raised a hand to wave the boy over. "Let's have it then, Oliver."

The boy darted up the gangplank, dodging out of the way of a sailor with a barrel on one shoulder while a birdcage swung from his free hand, full of finches fluttering nervously. Breathless, the boy handed the post to Hannah directly. She thanked him while she shuffled through the letters.

"Three at once." Will could not hide his curiosity, but he would not ask the obvious question.

"One from my stepmother." Hannah held it up so that he could see the familiar hand. "They are finally home again, then." She saw on Will's face the same relief that she felt. Over the last two weeks she had been less and less able to pretend she was not worried about the long silence from her parents. At night all the things that might have delayed them in the bush marched through her mind like foot soldiers who would not be dismissed, even by sleep.

She broke the seal and opened the folded sheet right there, because Will must have whatever news there was before they sailed.

"'Dearest Daughter,'" she read aloud. "'Your father and I are returned home, both of us in the best of health, as indeed we found all the family to be, although your sister Lily is still not quite recovered from a badly sprained ankle.'"

"Thank God," said Will.

Hannah continued: "'We have brought with us Curiosity and Galileo's grandson, a sturdy, vigorous child. His mother has left this world for the next, a report which must sadden you greatly. Indeed, we are all in mourning for her. Many-Doves has taken the boy to nurse alongside Sawatis.'"

"Ah, Christ." Will turned his face away.

Hannah drew in a sharp breath and let it go again. Tears rose up in her throat, anger and frustration. Selah was dead, in childbirth or of a fever; or maybe—this thought came to Hannah and she could not put it away—maybe at the hands of the blackbirders who had frightened her so. *Liam Kirby*.

Will's voice startled her out of her thoughts. "Does she say how it came to pass?"

Hannah scanned the rest of the letter. "No, nothing at all. Will, this will break Manny."

He put a hand on her shoulder. "He is stronger than that, Hannah. And there is his son, you must remember. Go on and finish so that I can tell Amanda all the news."

Hannah forced herself to focus on Elizabeth's neat handwriting.

"'Curiosity and Galileo are eager for some word of their son, as you can imagine. We hope it is in your power to provide them with that comfort. Curiosity's grief is tempered by her work in the village and in particular because she has been much occupied by caring for Reuben at the mill. The boy was badly burned in an accident and is not expected to live, though he continues on day by day in great distress. We are all eager to have you here as soon as it is possible for you to leave. Whatever news you bring us, good or bad, we will manage best together. Your loving stepmother Elizabeth Bonner.'"

"Thank God we are away," Hannah whispered when she

had finished. "Or I would have to set out on foot." Tears ran freely over her face, and she blinked them away.

"Poor Curiosity," she whispered. And then: "Can you get word to Manny? Can you ask him to come home to Paradise?"

Will's expression was so willfully empty that Hannah was reminded of Dr. Simon when a patient asked him a question that he did not want to answer, simply because it cost too much to say the words out loud.

"Will," Hannah said more loudly than she intended. "Is he dead?"

"No!" He shook his head. "Manny is not dead."

"You know where he is?"

"I have a good idea where he is," came the reluctant answer.

"Then can you get word to him? Tell him his parents need him."

"I can try," said Will Spencer. "I will do my best."

It wasn't until many hours later when all the goodbyes were behind them and the *Good-News* had begun her journey up the Hudson that Hannah remembered the other letters.

Sitting on her narrow berth with them in her lap she could work up only vague interest in either letter. The one from Jennet was heavier, three or four sheets at least and the first word Hannah had had from her since her father's death. No doubt it would not be an easy letter to read.

The second letter was more of a surprise and a mystery too: it bore her name in Dr. Savard's handwriting.

"Go up on deck with your post," Kitty suggested from her berth, hiding a yawn behind her hand. The baby slept contented at her side, the small mouth working thoughtfully.

"Are you sure?"

"Yes, of course I am. Take advantage of the last of the sun. Esther and I can manage very well. And perhaps you could send Ethan down to me. He has bothered the captain long enough."

Hannah went gladly, not only for the sun but to be away from the irritation of the wet nurse's silent but constant observation, something that was hard to ignore in the tight confines of the cabin.

Kitty had hoped that she would be able to produce enough
of her own milk to feed the child, something that might have
been possible if she had persisted, but by the second day she
had been so worried for the baby's welfare that she interviewed the wet nurses Mrs. Douglas had found. The girl they
hired was newly arrived from Germany; she spoke only a little
English and seemed reluctant to share information about herself, but she had plentiful milk and unlike three of the other
candidates Mrs. Douglas had found, she was willing to make
the journey to Paradise and to stay until she was no longer
needed—so long as she was properly paid.

Hannah was able to bear Esther's scrutiny only because it
was mute; she asked no questions at all.

When she had extracted Ethan from another of the captain's stories—this one about a ghost ship that sailed the
Hudson by the full moon—and sent him down to his mother,
Hannah found a coil of rope that would serve as a place to sit
with her post. From this improvised throne she could watch as
the river narrowed and the mountains shrugged shoulders up
out of the darkening countryside. The evening breeze wound
around her, lifting the hair that strayed from her plaits to touch
damp skin as tenderly as a mother.

She reread Elizabeth's letter first, looking for some clue about
Selah. There was nothing at all, as if she feared that the information might fall into the wrong hands. Or maybe, Hannah told
herself, she could not bring herself to put the words on paper,
to give them that kind of power and permanence.

Hannah considered Jennet's letter for a long moment,
measured the light remaining in the sky, and put it aside for tomorrow.

The seal on Dr. Savard's letter opened with a crack.
Hannah unfolded two sheets of heavy paper and read.

Dear Miss Bonner,

*First, my apologies that I was not present at the Almshouse to
wish you a good journey home and the best of fortunes in your
continuing medical education. May this short letter serve that
purpose.*

*Second, news of professional interest: today I vaccinated the
two hundredth child against smallpox, a record of which Dr.*

Simon is deservedly proud. The child, a girl of seven years and recently arrived from Scotland, showed her teeth but did not use them.

Third, your experiment on my person. I find that I cannot reject your hypothesis; the lower half of the wound is all but healed while the upper half still suppurates. This morning I treated the entire area with your concoction. It stung mightily, and reminded me of you.

By way of payment for your valuable consultation and treatment, and as a token of my regard and respect, I enclose a copy of a document which will be of interest if not comfort to you and your friends.

With best regards
Your colleague
Paul deGuise Savard dit Saint-d'Uzet

The second sheet had been copied out in his hand, with a notation at the top that read "Deaths 1801, July–September, Page 12." Each line contained a name along with age, family status, place of origin, cause and date of death, as well as place of interment. Half of the entries listed unnamed infants who had died within their first month in the Almshouse; most of them were under four, and all of them had died of the croup. They were Irish, German, American, African; some of them had been born in the Almshouse. Some had been orphaned but most were recorded as abandoned, surrendered to the state, or indigent.

She was the last entry on the page, as if Dr. Savard had run out of ink or time or perhaps simply because he had made his point. Connie Vaark, mulatto, two years of age, abandoned to the care of the city three months previously, had choked to death on the thirtieth day of September in the company of a dozen other choking children and was buried with the others, nameless, motherless, in a common grave in the African Burial Ground on Chrystie Street.

Of course Hannah had known that Manny's search might end like this. To anyone who had spent time in the Almshouse nursery these facts could be no surprise at all. Dead children were as common as crows, nothing more than facts to be recorded neatly on the page, black on white.

Whatever news you bring us, good or bad, we will manage best to-gether. Elizabeth had written those words, and Hannah trusted her stepmother. But how could such a thing possibly be true; how could she take this news to Curiosity and Galileo, to Manny, who had still to learn that his wife was dead. It would fall to her to explain, to help them see it for themselves how a child could be left to die in such a place as the Almshouse.

Manny had asked this favor of her, but it was too much.

The sun dragged bloody clouds down to the other side of the world over the edge of the Palisades. Standing at the rail, Hannah watched until her eyes teared.

The wind toyed with Dr. Savard's letter, tugged at it, folded it and spread it out again. When Hannah opened her fingers the two sheets sailed out over the dark water like wings, white on black.

PARADISE

Chapter 30

When her parents had been gone for a week, Lily Bonner began to wake just before dawn in the hope and fear that they had come back in the night. While she could not wait to have her mother and father home again, Lily dreaded having to admit that she had failed to keep a promise: in seven days she had not written a single word in the little book her mother had left her.

She started every day by taking it out and counting the pages. Inside the cover of fine doeskin, there were twelve pieces of paper that had been sewn down the middle to make twenty-four pages, bright white and bigger than her own hand. And she still could not make herself pick up a quill. For the first week she had considered just writing the most obvious things: *Went to the Big Muddy today with Bears. Ground corn for a long time. Many-Doves is making a new pair of moccasins for Kateri and she let me do some of the beadwork. Helped Bump plant cabbage. Helped Many-Doves and Pines-Rustling plant beans and squash seeds around the corn plants.*

But to waste good sunshine and expensive paper to tell her mother things that she knew without being told, that just didn't sit right. Lily wanted to write things that would surprise her mother, things she couldn't figure out for herself, things to make her frown or laugh or ask questions that nobody could answer. She wanted the little book to be like the newspapers that Aunt and Uncle Spencer sent from the city. When a newspaper came, no matter how out of date it was, Lily's mother would call them together in the evening and read aloud, and her face would go pink with eagerness. Lily liked newspaper evenings even when she didn't really understand what she heard, because they made her mother so happy.

She knew that the only way she was going to have any real news was if she spent time in the village, where grown-ups seemed willing to talk about just about anything in the hearing of a little girl who didn't seem to be paying attention.

With her mother gone, there was no school but there were still chores, more than ever now that the ground was warm enough to break and planting had begun. And the grown-ups had worked out a plan: the three older children would spend the first part of the day at Lake in the Clouds. When their chores were done and they had had their dinners, they could go down to the village if they wanted to, as long as they were within Curiosity's calling range; they could explore on the mountain, as long as they stayed off the north face; or they could stay at home, in which case they were likely to be drawn into whatever extra work Hawkeye or Many-Doves or Runs-from-Bears could find for them.

Lily figured out by the second day that Daniel had made some kind of promise—most probably to their father—to keep an eye on her. It was the only way to explain why he invited her to come along when he and Blue-Jay went off to catch frogs or shoot arrows or make some changes to their fort. Sometimes Lily agreed, mostly out of curiosity, but also out of concern. If it made her brother happy to think he was protecting her, she would let him. Lily thought that he might be lonely, but unable to admit it.

Mostly Lily spent her time in the village. She always stopped by the trading post before going on to the Todds' house, because it seemed to her that pretty much everybody except the widow Kuick found their way to Anna or Curiosity, every day. They came to buy or sell or trade, tobacco and eggs and linsey-woolsey and seeds and venison, to ask advice or help with sick animals or cheese that wouldn't set or warping a loom; everybody left some news behind. Mostly it wasn't very surprising news, but every once in a while there was something that might interest her mother, and Lily kept track of those things in her head.

She could spend a half hour or so in the trading post, listening

to the men who sat at the back playing cards or draughts or skittles. They were so busy talking that they didn't pay any mind at
all to who was nearby, but Lily could only stay so long before
somebody would take note and ask her nicely what she needed
and was she sorry she hadn't gone along to the city with her aunt
Todd or to Albany with her mother?

It irked her that people really believed her mother would
go to Albany and leave her behind, and it irked her even
worse that she couldn't tell them the truth, that she hadn't.
People were supposed to think that her mother and father
were in Albany, and to give them any other ideas would be the
worst kind of betrayal. Lily thought of Selah's calm expression
and the baby she was carrying and the urge to answer questions and even to be around people who would ask them left
her cold. Then she would go off to Curiosity and Galileo.

The kitchen at the Todds' house was as much home to her
as the hearth at Lake in the Clouds. She could stay as long as
she wanted and ask questions if the urge came on her, or just
listen. If the weather turned bad while she was there,
Curiosity fed her and put her to bed, and nobody at Lake in
the Clouds would worry about where she had got to. Except
that she didn't like to leave Daniel to sleep alone in the loft,
and so she usually did go home.

But of course there was no sitting idle in Curiosity's
kitchen; she would set Lily to carding wool or spinning or stirring the wash or polishing pewter, but she didn't mind that,
because the conversations in Curiosity's kitchen were well
worth it. It amazed her, the things grown-ups would say in
front of a child who could keep her tongue and look bored. As
if she were deaf, or too little to understand what it meant
when a woman missed her monthly, or that Peter Dubonnet
had got the sudden urge to go hunting when Baldy O'Brien,
the hated tax collector, came in from Johnstown.

So two full weeks after the wedding party Lily didn't know
what to think when Curiosity met her at the kitchen door and
wouldn't let her come in. Lily didn't get more than a glance of
the room, but she saw Dolly Smythe sitting at the table with
her face in her hands and her shoulders shaking as if she had a
fever.

"There's work in the garden," Curiosity had said, in the

voice that meant she wasn't going to tolerate any discussion. "Make yourself useful, child." And she closed the door.

Curiosity often sent Lily to help in the garden. Generally it suited her fine, because she liked being outside and Bump was almost always there to talk to. Bump was one of her favorite people; he called her "Miss Lily" and told her stories of his travels during the wars and the western frontier and the Indians he had lived with for a time, of a great warrior called Sky-Panther he had once seen, and of the early days in Paradise, when her grandmother and grandfather Middleton had lived up in the schoolhouse and her Granny Bonner had been alive.

Now Lily hesitated, not exactly trying to hear through the kitchen door but wondering why Dolly Smythe was here. The widow wasn't the kind of mistress to let her servants wander around the village to visit friends in the middle of a workday. It was possible that the widow had decided she didn't want Dolly in the house anymore, although that was hard to imagine; Dolly was a hard worker and clever, and her manners never caused anybody to click their tongues, not even the old wives who watched the unmarried girls like cats watched their kittens, ready to use their teeth to make a point if they saw the need. Lily's mother thought a lot of Dolly Smythe, and that was recommendation enough.

There was no sign of Bump in the garden either, which was another mystery as he had hoed three new rows and left the basket with the twisted seed papers on the step of the shed. Lily stood in the middle of the kitchen garden smelling the good smell of warm sun on fresh-turned earth when she thought of Dr. Todd's laboratory. Maybe that's where Bump was, helping the doctor. With a glance over her shoulder at the closed kitchen door, Lily went around the shed to look in that direction.

There was no smoke coming out of the chimneys, but she had just about made up her mind to go have a look anyway when Lucy Hench came up behind her.

"You looking for Bump?"

Lucy was two years younger than Lily, but she was tall for her age. She was what Curiosity called a simple soul, which meant that she wasn't especially bright but she was kind and well-meaning, and in general Lily liked her a lot, although she could not play with her for more than an hour without getting bored enough to scream.

"Your granny sent me out here to help him in the garden. Is he in the laboratory?"

"Nope," said Lucy. "Nobody's in there right now. The doctor went up to see the window."

"The widow," Lily said automatically, but she knew that Lucy would go on calling Mrs. Kuick "the window," as if she were made of glass.

Lucy said, "Don't know where Bump has got to. Do you want to play dolls with me?" She held up a rag doll wrapped in a handkerchief.

"I've got this planting to do," said Lily. "What's wrong with the widow, do you know?"

Lucy shrugged one shoulder. "Don't know, exactly. When Dolly came down to fetch Dr. Todd, she said the window had taken a fit and was throwing things, and could he come quick before she killed somebody."

"The widow was throwing things?"

Lucy nodded, rocking her baby against her chest. "Sure you don't want to play dolls? This one of mine, she's got the canker throat and she's about to die. You could doctor her."

"I can't," said Lily, working hard to sound as if she would have really liked to. "Do you want to help me in the garden?"

Lucy made a disappointed face and set off to find her sister Solange, who had a doll with eyes and a mouth.

The widow had taken a fit. This was certainly news worthy of being written down, but Lily wasn't sure what it meant. Last year old Mr. MacGregor had taken a fit right in the middle of the trading post and died with a purple face, but he hadn't been throwing things at the time. One of the Camerons had thrown a rock through a window, but he had been drunk. She couldn't imagine the widow Kuick drinking anything stronger than weak cider.

And there was nobody who could explain it to her. Curiosity was in the kitchen with a weeping Dolly Smythe and there was still no sign of Bump at all. Lily turned around once more to look for him and saw that Gabriel Oak was sitting in the sunshine in front of his cabin. He raised a hand in greeting.

Lily looked around herself at the deserted garden and the

closed kitchen door, and then she set off to pay Gabriel Oak a visit.

Even in the full heat of the sun he was wrapped in a cloak with a shawl around his shoulders. Lily knew from Hannah that he was very sick, but now she saw it for herself in the way his skin was stretched so tight over his bones. She wondered if she should have stayed in the garden and not bothered him, but he gave her a smile that reminded her of Daniel when he wasn't trying to be fractious, sweet and lonely too, somehow.

"Friend Lily," he said. "Will you sit with me a little while?"

Gabriel Oak was the only Quaker Lily knew, and she wondered if they were all so polite and quiet and easy to talk to. There were two stools, and she climbed up on one.

"I was looking for Bump," she said. "I'm supposed to help him in the garden. But everything is confused today."

He blinked at her slowly. "Cornelius went with Dr. Todd. An emergency, I expect."

"I thought maybe he had." Lily looked down toward the village, but there was nothing to see there at all except a few dogs sleeping in the road. Lily squinted a little and saw that two of them had bloody muzzles, and there was a tangled mess of orange fur spread out in front of them.

"Look," said Lily. "They finally got Missus Gathercole's cat. They've been chasing it just about forever."

Gabriel Oak looked very hard in that direction. Finally he said, "Thou hast very good eyes, Friend Lily. From thy grandfather, no doubt."

Lily said, "Daniel does too, he can see even farther than me. He says he's going to be a sharpshooter in the next war. If he has his own rifle by then."

"Is there to be another war?" Gabriel Oak looked interested, but not very concerned.

"The newspapers say so," Lily said, more doubtfully now. "My grandfather says it's none of our concern."

"Thy grandfather sees clearly in more ways than just one."

They were silent for a moment together and then Lily let out a great sigh. "Curiosity won't let me in the kitchen," she said. "I wish I knew what was going on. Did you see Dolly Smythe come?"

"I did."

Gabriel Oak picked up his sketchbook while Lily told him the little that she knew from Lucy and what she suspected. He let her talk without interrupting her, but every once in a while he would look up and nod, and Lily never got the sense that he was pretending to listen, as grown-ups often did. Before she knew it she had told him about the blank pages in the book and her plans for it.

"If I knew what was wrong at the mill I could write that down for my mother."

"Friend Lily," he said in his soft, deep voice. "There are things other than words to put on paper, and more than one way to tell a story." And he held up his sketch.

He had drawn Bump at work in the garden while Lucy watched him from the fence. Bump's mouth was open and Lily could almost hear him singing and Lucy humming along with him because, as Curiosity liked to say with a smile, her sweetest granddaughter couldn't carry a tune in a bucket. Without really knowing why, Lily said, "He likes that song best of all, the one about the soldier coming home."

Gabriel Oak was smiling at her, as if she hadn't said anything strange at all.

"How do you do that?" she asked. "How do you make them so alive I can hear him singing?"

"I can't tell thee the how of it," he said, taking the sketch back. He touched it gently with his pencil, stroking a curve into the line of Bump's poor back.

"I don't understand," Lily said. "How can you not know how you do what you do?"

His brow pulled itself together. "I've wondered that myself for many years," he said. "The closest I can come to explaining it is that some are given a particular gift. A few can weave words into a story, others can carve wood into shapes that seem more real than real. Some can make music, as do young Reuben and his brother. I can draw pictures." He looked at her and beneath the fringe of his hair his gray eyes were kind and maybe a little hopeful. "Hast thou done any drawing, Friend Lily?"

Lily thought of her slate at school, its rough surface and the dust of the chalk ground deep into her fingers, as dry and unpleasant as digging for onions. Her copybook was not much better, rough paper that she wrote on with quill and the ink her mother made, or even worse, a quill filled with bullet lead. Line after line of poetry scratched out stroke by stroke.

"No," she said. "Do you think I could learn how?"

He said, "Some of it can be learned, if thou art willing to study the science of it. Whether or not the gift is in thee, that will show itself. When I was a younger man I gave drawing lessons to the ladies of Baltimore."

Lily blinked in surprise. Generally Bump told stories and Gabriel Oak listened, but it seemed that he was in a story-telling mood today. She wondered what he meant by it, if he might be willing to give her lessons. That seemed unlikely, but it was exciting, anyway.

She said, "Did any of your students have a gift?"

He closed his eyes for a minute as if he could look back over time. "Some did, yes. But the gifted ones weren't always those who were willing to work the hardest."

"I'm a hard worker," she said, meeting his eye directly.

Gabriel Oak smiled at her and Lily watched, absorbed, as he took a long wooden box from the folds of his cloak. The top slid back to reveal more black-lead pencils than Lily had ever seen at once, short and long, thick and thin. There was a porte-crayon with a piece of graphite held tight by a small clamp; Lily's mother had one of those too, but she didn't have a lead pencil.

Lead pencils were made one at a time and had to be ordered from Boston or Albany or even France, where the best ones were made at high cost. The only people Lily had ever seen using a pencil were the surveyor who came from Johnstown when the widow Kuick got into an argument with Dr. Todd and Lily's own father about the boundaries of their properties, and Gabriel Oak.

He was examining one of the smaller pencils, turning the square shape in his long fingers. Then he took a file from the box and began to work the end to a point. The wood dust smelled sweet; Lily watched it sift down to his lap.

When he handed it to her she turned it in her own fingers, feeling the smooth wood, so polished by use that she couldn't make out the seams where the top was joined to the sides. She said, "I've never used a pencil before."

"We'll start from the beginning, then," said Gabriel Oak. "That's generally best."

*   *   *

Richard Todd and Bump came in by way of the kitchen, where they found Cookie crouched before the hearth. She had a cut on her forehead that had left a great bloody patch on her kerchief, and she glared up at the doctor as if he were responsible.

"Oh, thank God," said Becca Kaes, standing up from the table. She was shaking so hard that she had to wind her hands in her apron to steady them.

"Becca." The doctor nodded, one corner of his mouth turned down in curiosity or irritation, or both. "What is the problem?"

A shrill shouting started up at the other end of the house and was cut off by the slam of a door.

Becca shook her head and pressed the back of her hand to her mouth as if to keep herself from screaming. She drew in a ragged breath and let it out again.

"The master is engaged to marry Jemima Southern." Her voice was hoarse, and she looked quickly behind her as if she feared someone might have heard. "The widow is displeased."

The other side of the doctor's mouth turned down. "That's why you sent for me? There's no medicine I can give her that will make the match more to her liking. It's Mr. Gathercole you need to tend to this kind of distress."

Becca came forward and grasped his forearm, her chapped fingers digging into his coat hard enough to make him step back from her. "She's very displeased, Dr. Todd. She broke every piece of glass in the good parlor and she's got Isaiah and Jemima in a corner and she's talking..." Her voice dropped to a whisper. "She's unbalanced."

Cookie's small, thin face turned toward them. She said, "The widow ain't unbalanced. She just mean as a mad dog with its tail in a trap, is all. It's a bitter pill she got to swallow, but she'll do it in the end. This time she will, yes, indeed." And she smiled with such satisfied malevolence that the rest of them looked away in discomfort.

"Bump," said Dr. Todd. "There's nothing for us here."

"Please, sir," said Becca, looking very close to tears now. "Please, just... have a word with her."

*   *   *

Jemima Southern stood in the corner of the good parlor and surveyed the destruction the widow Kuick had wrought. It gave her a sour satisfaction to see the Turkey carpet covered with tangled needlework, scattered books, and shards of glass. Every painted dog and porcelain shepherd, every smirking kilted Highlander and blushing powdered lady had been sacrificed to the widow's rampage.

Good, thought Jemima. *Less to dust.*

Not that she would be dusting anymore; those days were gone now, for good.

Beside Jemima, Isaiah Kuick stood with a blank expression, as if he were watching an actress on a stage and not his own mother, convulsed with rage. When the last china vase shattered against the wall he said nothing, and when his mother howled at him, *Idiot you idiot you godforsaken whoremaster you'll burn in hell for this* he had blinked and said nothing.

Because he would indeed burn in hell. They had come to an understanding, she and Isaiah: she would help him on his way to hell, and he would make her his wife.

In the two weeks after the night in the barn, Jemima had watched him and taken note of his comings and goings. Twice she had followed him to Dye's quarters by moonlight, and stayed outside long enough to know what they were about. And then just this morning she had found Isaiah Kuick alone in the parlor.

She had laid it all out before him, as simply as she could: her courses were late; she was with child. Before he could tell her that it was none of his concern, she had wiped the mystified smile from his face by speaking the sentence she'd rehearsed again and again for a week, slowly and surely and meeting his gaze without flinching.

"This child was conceived the night of the wedding party in the barn at the judge's old place, and if it wasn't you that got it on me, then there's something your mother might like to hear about the overseer and her son."

He had looked at her with sudden understanding and none of the shame or fear that Jemima had anticipated, which put her off a little, but she pressed on, regardless.

"You do the right thing and marry me, and I won't expect you to share my bed. I won't care where you spend your nights."

She had been prepared for arguments and she had thought through her options. If he balked, she would swear a rape on him and sue for support of her child, or she would get up in church and announce to Mr. Gathercole and his congregation that they had two sodomites among them, and provide details. He could choose one of those, or he could marry her and continue to meet Ambrose Dye, so long as he took more care and didn't indulge his unnatural urges in barns where anyone might happen to pass.

The bargain was struck that simply, as she had hoped it would be. The widow's son was a sodomite, but he wasn't stupid. When Jemima thought over the way the conversation had gone she was filled with a deep sense of satisfaction, to have managed with so little fuss—right until the last, when she had asked him the one question she could not keep to herself.

"Tell me why you stare at Hannah Bonner whenever you come across her," Jemima had said, and for the first time in the conversation she was unable to keep her tone even. "You can't be thinking about bedding her. Or do you?"

Isaiah had finally managed to look surprised. He said, "I have no interest in bedding her, no. I look at her the way I'd look at a painting by Rembrandt or Michelangelo, if there were such a thing in this village. She's simply the most beautiful thing Paradise has to offer."

The sting of that had still not lessened, and never would. But she must concentrate on other things, important things.

The worst was over: the widow's fury would burn itself out, and tomorrow or the day after they would stand up in front of Mr. Gathercole. And the widow would stand there with them, and she would wish them well and welcome Jemima into her home no longer a servant, but a daughter-in-law. No matter what she really felt, the widow Kuick would smile as long as they were in company and say the things that were expected of any lady of good breeding. Jemima was to be the mother of her only grandchild, after all. She would see to it.

The truth was, Jemima had had her courses two days after the night in the barn, but she had a plan. Liam Kirby was still in Paradise, and she knew where to find him: he spent all his time wandering the mountain looking for his runaway. Never mind that everybody had begun to wonder if there had ever been a runaway; maybe—and this was a thought that came to Jemima reluctantly—maybe the whole story about blackbirding had been his way of getting close to Hannah Bonner again. The important thing, Jemima reminded herself, was that Hannah was gone and Liam wasn't. She would go find him on the mountain and get what she needed from him; now that she was engaged to the widow's only son she had some freedom, and she would use it, today.

The widow had fallen into the chair by the window, silent for the moment while she stared for once not out at the village, but at her own hands where they lay in her lap. When she raised her head this time her gaze focused on Jemima, and the expression there—cold and not quite human—sent a shiver down her back after all.

"Whore," she whispered, her voice cracking with the effort.

"Call me what you like," said Jemima. "Your words cannot change what I have growing in my belly, or the act that put it there."

Such hate in a human face; it was an impressive thing to see. She said, "Isaiah, find that Indian witch and tell her to do away with it. There's a tea that will do the job. Get rid of it, before it ruins your life."

She said this to her son as if he already had dominion over Jemima's body.

"I'll drink no tea," Jemima said. "If you try to force me I'll swear an assault on you before the constable."

The widow's color rose another notch and for a moment Jemima wondered if the rage might even kill her, or if that was too much to hope for.

"Isaiah," said his mother. "Send her away from here. Give her what money she needs, and send her away."

"No," said Isaiah, in a patient tone. "I can't do that, Mother."

Jemima knew very well that he was thinking of Dye; his loyalty was not to her at all. He would do this to protect his lover and to keep him, and still it gave Jemima great pleasure to hear him deny his mother. She let her triumph show and the widow's face contorted with disgust and fury.

A knock at the door and the widow sprang up from her

seat with new energy, flew across the room as if she expected
an avenging angel sent to smite the unrepentant sinners.

Dr. Todd came in, not looking concerned at all but cross,
and ill at ease.

The widow was startled to see him, as if he had discovered
her in some shameful act. Jemima had to admire how she
came back to herself, drawing her shawl tighter around her
shoulders and composing her face, nothing there now of rage,
just condescension and good manners.

"Dr. Todd," she said. "We were not expecting you. And as
you can see——" She looked around the room and seemed to
take in the extent of the wreckage with some bewilderment.
"We are not in a position to receive callers today." And she
held up her chin haughtily.

"I'm not here on a social visit," Dr. Todd said. "You've got
your servants shaking in their boots, Missus Kuick. It looks
like Cookie will need some stitches. What is the meaning of all
this?"

Color flooded up from the widow's papery neck. "A family
matter," she said stiffly. "And none of your concern."

Dr. Todd threw Jemima a pointed look. "Jemima, you've
got a cut on your cheek."

Jemima touched herself with one finger, felt the warm
smear of blood. She hadn't even noticed when it happened.

"It's nothing," she said.

"Mr. Kuick?" Dr. Todd asked.

Beside her, Isaiah cleared his throat. "We were discussing
wedding plans. Jemima and I are to be wed."

Jemima could no more keep herself from smiling to hear
those words spoken out loud than the widow could keep from
letting out a single strangled gurgle of surrender. It was done
now; it was said.

Jemima's hand brushed against Isaiah's. He shuddered and
moved away from her, just ever so slightly, a half-step. But Dr.
Todd had seen it, and when he looked at Jemima this time she
saw that he moved beyond curiosity to some dawning understanding.

A flush ran through her, hot and cold at once.

"I wish you joy," said Dr. Todd. "And now I'll see to
Cookie."

"Dr. Todd," Jemima said in her coolest voice.

He paused at the door. "Yes?"

"Please send Becca in, this mess needs to be swept away."

One eyebrow arched in surprise at her tone, but he nodded, and closed the door behind him.

Lily had forgotten all about the widow Kuick's fit by the time she started home. Even when Bump came back to work in the garden and Dolly Smythe came out of the kitchen to talk to him, Lily could not be drawn away from her spot next to Gabriel Oak. The widow's fit didn't seem important anymore, because her head was full of drawings.

Under her arm Lily clasped a sheaf of paper filled with shaded circles and squares and lines, and the most magical thing of all, two linked rings that built the structure of the human face. Just as soon as Gabriel's pencil had finished drawing the line where the circles came together, and on that line the placement of the eyes, something small and bright had flared in Lily's mind: it made such sense, she didn't know how she had missed it before. Lily reached into her pocket and ran her fingers over the two black-lead pencils and the piece of India rubber Gabriel Oak had lent to her.

She had just come in sight of the schoolhouse when she heard a rustling in the bush and her brother jumped out onto the path with a loud war whoop, waving his wooden tomahawk over his head. He had slicked down his hair with mud and painted his face in yellow and blue stripes, but the green of his eyes stood out anyway for all the world to see, the same green as the new leaves on the maple trees.

Lily said, "I heard you coming." Because she had, and because it would irritate him: a warrior struck silently.

"I could have been a bear, for all the attention you were paying," he said reproachfully. "Could have killed you with a single swipe of a paw."

"But you aren't," Lily said. "And you didn't." She walked on, and he followed her.

"Where's Blue-Jay?" she asked.

"Many-Doves needed him. What's that you've got?"

"Paper."

"I can see that much. What's it for?"

She stopped and turned to him. "Gabriel Oak is giving me drawing lessons."

Beneath his war paint, Daniel's expression was thoughtful. "Why would he want to do that?"

That was a question Lily could not answer, so she shrugged.

"Let me see," Daniel said, reaching out, but she side-stepped.

"Your hands are dirty. You can see at home."

When I'm good and ready, and not before. This last she didn't say out loud, but she could see by Daniel's expression that she had hurt his feelings. Before she could think how to fix that, he had turned away.

"I'm going home the short way," he announced.

"I'll come too."

He threw her a furious look. "No."

"You can't stop me, Daniel Bonner."

But he could, almost. She was wearing skirts, and he was in leggings; she had her precious bundle of paper and he had both hands to use. And he was angry, and anger made him move even faster than normal.

Daniel cut up the worst part of the slope, whacking at the underbrush with his tomahawk and never looking back to see how Lily was faring. She was panting hard when they hit the first crest with that deep burn in the lungs that came with pushing so hard uphill. Her free hand was throbbing with scratches too, but there was no time to try to make peace with her brother. Daniel ran off, and she followed.

Lily knew now that he was headed home by way of Eagle Rock, a route that the boys took often, although it had been forbidden to them. It was the fastest way home, and the most dangerous. He was trying to make her turn back.

"I'm not scared," she whispered to herself.

Eagle Rock was a boulder almost as tall as a house, half-buried in the mountainside. From the top of it you could see where the Lake in the Clouds waterfall came out of the mountain; you could see the village and the schoolhouse and at this time of year, when the trees weren't filled in yet, you could follow anybody moving on the south face on the mountain. They came here sometimes with their father or grandfather or Runs-from-Bears, but never from below.

Lily came up the last bit of the slope under the Eagle Rock ledge, and found Daniel waiting for her. He was crouched down low among the bushes and his face had gone very white.

Before she could ask him what was wrong he had pulled her down next to him and put a hand over her mouth.

She was too short of breath to struggle. When the thundering of her blood finally ebbed, Lily understood why Daniel had dropped to the ground. A man and a woman were standing not twenty feet away. If she were to stand up she would be able to see them clearly, and they her.

Strangers on the mountain. A hot flicker of fear erupted deep in Lily's belly and she pressed her face to the rough earth, feeling the scrape of stone.

Daniel put his head next to hers, nose to nose so that her eyes crossed when she tried to look at him. His smell was a comfort and disturbing too, because it reminded Lily of their mother, but his expression was angry, his mouth pressed together hard.

"It's all right," he whispered. "They'll go soon."

"Strangers?"

He shook his head. "Kirby," he whispered. "And Jemima Southern."

Lily's fear gave way to surprise. That Liam Kirby had been roaming the mountain for the last two weeks was no news at all; their grandfather and Runs-from-Bears kept track of him, waiting for Liam to tire of his search for Selah Voyager. But Jemima Southern on the mountain was another matter entirely. Lily remembered the trouble at the mill and wondered if her coming here had anything to do with the widow's fit. Lily listened hard but the wind was high and she could make out only a few words now and then, Liam's voice agitated and impatient: *on my way to the great lake* and *work to do;* then Jemima's laughter in response, like swarming wasps.

I'll swear a rape, Lily heard her say in the argument that followed. And *your wife.* Jemima talked and talked while Liam said less and less, and then there was the sound of a hand striking flesh and a small cry not so much of pain as satisfaction. Voices raised again, angrier now, and the sound of struggling.

"Is he hurting her?" Lily had to ask, but Daniel shook his head.

"Cover your ears," he whispered. And Lily gave him a look that said she would no more cover her ears than she would take them off and hand them over. Daniel's mouth was twisted in disgust, but no matter what questions Lily whispered, he gave her no answers at all.

And it occurred to Lily that Liam Kirby and Jemima Southern were doing what married people did behind closed doors, that mysterious thing that put color in her mother's face and made her father laugh as he never laughed otherwise, the thing they liked so much that they kept it to themselves. Children weren't supposed to ask about it because it was private, but Lily had some ideas about what was happening behind the door when it was closed, ideas she hadn't discussed even with Daniel or Hannah because they were unsettling and strange. There were animals enough around to watch, and animals didn't worry about keeping things to themselves. And neither did Liam and Jemima, it seemed.

Then suddenly Jemima laughed, a short harsh laugh that echoed off the rock, and for a moment Lily had the idea that all of Paradise could hear her, as if she had stood up on Eagle Rock and blown a trumpet to draw their attention. A satisfied laugh but bitter. As if she had managed to wrestle something of value away from Liam only to find it was broken anyway.

Daniel pressed Lily's arm hard enough to raise a bruise in order to keep her quiet, and finally they heard the sound of someone moving off through the bush, upmountain. And more footsteps, coming their way.

They were on the only path that led away from Eagle Rock; that thought struck Lily just as Jemima's shadow fell over them.

"Look here," she said. "Spies. The apples don't fall far from the tree, so it's said."

Daniel leapt to his feet. "We ain't spies. This is our mountain, and you're trespassing."

Lily got up too, but Daniel stepped in front of her to keep himself between his sister and Jemima Southern.

Jemima leaned forward, and Lily saw that her face was splotched with color and her lower lip was bloody, as if she had bit it. Her bodice was untied and her hair had come down, and there was a glitter in her dark eyes that reminded Lily of spiders.

"What you saw here ain't none of your business," she said, looking at each of them in turn. "You'll keep it to yourselves if you know what's good for you."

All the fear in Lily was gone, replaced by a flush of irritation and anger. "First of all, we didn't see anything at all. And second, why should we listen to you?"

Jemima hissed and grabbed her hard by the elbow, pulled her forward so that Lily came face-to-face with the spill of breasts in the open bodice. Jemima smelled of sweat and fear and something else, something strange and sharp.

"Let her go!" Daniel pulled out his tomahawk and thumped Jemima on the shoulder with the flat of it, but she dug her fingers deeper into Lily's arm and turned on him. Jemima was strong, and a wildness had come into her expression that made Lily's stomach cramp.

"First you'll listen to me, you little infidels. If you breathe a word of seeing me up here on this mountain with Liam Kirby I'll make you pay."

"You had best let her go," Daniel said in the kind of calm, pointed voice that sounded just like their father when he was truly angry. He was almost as tall as Jemima, and for a moment Lily had the sense that he was on the edge of doing her real harm.

Jemima didn't seem to see the threat in his face, or maybe she didn't care. She said, "I'll come after that half-breed sister of yours. I mean it. I won't have nothing to lose anymore if you talk, so I might as well settle some scores."

"My father will kill you if you hurt any of us," Lily shouted in her face.

"Then we'll all die together," Jemima said, and let her go so suddenly that Lily stepped backward onto the sheaf of drawing paper. It began to slide away and over the edge of the incline, one page fluttering after the other like birds. Lily snatched after them and suddenly the earth beneath her feet was gone.

She heard Daniel draw in his breath as she hung suspended over the incline and he was reaching for her but it was too late; she was tumbling, over and over and down. *Protect your head;* she could hear her father saying it and she crossed her arms up over her face, knowing with a separate part of her brain that this must hurt, that she should be feeling pain.

A spruce tree stopped her with a thump. Lily lay there for a moment looking at the sun filtering through the branches overhead, moving not at all because it was too much work to breathe.

Then Daniel was leaning over her and she was never so glad of anything as the sight of her brother with his muddy hair and his yellow-and-blue face: two linked circles, forehead to nostrils, eyebrows to chin, and in the intersection his green eyes wide with terror.

She wanted to tell him not to look so scared, but she couldn't get enough breath to use her voice. Lily reached up and touched his cheek, felt the stickiness of the war paint on her fingers, and saw that there was water in his eyes. Her brother on the verge of tears, that was something she didn't see very often.

He said, "You got the breath knocked out of you."

"I lost my paper," Lily heard herself croak.

"I'll get it for you, every single piece, I promise. But you've got to stay here, Lily. Promise me you won't move until I get back with help."

Lily frowned at him. "No. I can walk." She tried to push herself up on her elbows, but a stab of pain ran up from her left ankle and came out of her mouth in a squeak.

"Promise me," Daniel said again, his eyes flickering toward her leg and back again to her face. "Promise me."

"Is it broke? Can you see the bone?"

"No," he said. "No bone. But it looks broke. Promise me you won't try to move."

Lily called after him, "Slow down or you'll fall too!" And then he was gone.

She was still clutching a single sheet of paper in her hand. Lily spread it out as best she could. Not one of her drawings, but a blank sheet, torn and smudged. With her other hand she felt for her pocket and the shape of the pencils. Neither of them had broken in the fall, and she was glad of that. Lily put her head back and stared up through the branches of the tree and the sky and at Eagle Rock, not so very far above her.

Jemima Southern had disappeared with the wind, and so had Liam Kirby.

Not so very far to fall, she whispered to herself, and felt the throb in her ankle keeping time with the beat of her heart.

She might have fallen asleep in the dappled shade under the trees if it weren't for the ache in her bone or the way that the scrapes on her arms and face had started to burn. Lily was just thinking about trying to sit up against the trunk of the spruce when she heard Runs-from-Bears coming up the incline as fast as he could move, with Daniel just behind him.

Lily let out a great and relieved sigh when they were standing over her, but then she saw the look on Bears' face and she remembered that they shouldn't have been here in the first place.

"What made you come up this way in skirts?" It wasn't like Bears to ask such an obvious question; that was one of the things that Lily liked best about him, that he understood things without a lot of talk.

"It was my fault," said Daniel. "Don't be mad at her."

Bears made a sound deep in his throat that meant he was seriously displeased, but he picked Lily up with great care and settled her so that her legs hung over his arm. Lily got a look at her ankle then, swollen and already changing color.

"We just wanted to get home the fast way," she said to Bears, and this time the sound he made was a little softer.

"You must have seen Liam Kirby," he said. "He's been up here all morning. Did he have anything to do with this?"

"No," Lily said, louder than she meant to.

"She just slipped," said Daniel, telling just enough of the truth to keep the secret; it was one of his best tricks, but Lily wondered that he was using it now. It was hard to believe that Jemima's threats had silenced him so easily, and what was even worse was that Lily would have to stay silent too, at least until they had had a chance to talk things through.

But Runs-from-Bears was not fooled; Lily could see that on his face as clear as the bear-claw tattoos that marched across his forehead. For a minute he looked at Daniel hard, and then he made another sound deep in his throat before turning away to start down the incline with Lily in his arms.

Chapter 31

Just when Lily was about to desair of another lost morning sitting in front of Curiosity's hearth with her foot propped up on a pillow, and no more scrap paper to draw on, Blue-Jay and her brother came bursting into the kitchen. Lily was so glad to see them that she almost smiled before she remembered how mad she was. She would leave the smiles to Curiosity, who looked up from her bread dough and laughed at the sight of them, both out of breath.

"You boys look to be in an awful hurry," she said. "And a good thing too. Your sister about to bust at the seams."

Lily pressed her mouth together and made a great show of stroking Curiosity's old tomcat, who had claimed her lap for his morning sleep.

"A messenger's come." Daniel swallowed hard.

Blue-Jay said, "With word from your da."

Lily sat up so suddenly that Magnus rolled off her lap, but before she could reach for her crutch, Curiosity stepped right in front of her and put out a hand.

"Hold on now."

"But a messenger's come." Lily tried to reach around Curiosity, but the old lady just raised her eyebrows so far that they disappeared underneath the blue-and-white-checked kerchief.

"Not so fast, missy. I'll tie you down if I have to. You know I'll do it."

Curiosity was looking from one boy to the other with a grim expression. "Out with it, now. What news?"

Daniel shook his head hard enough to send his hair flying. "Nobody hurt, everybody safe. Selah had a boy, she's calling him Galileo."

"Praise God." Curiosity pressed the flat of her floury hands to her face and closed her eyes for a moment. "Got to go find that husband of mine, give him the good news." She headed right for the door without even taking off her apron, not stopping until she had stepped over the threshold, where she paused and turned back to Lily while she wiped the flour from her face.

"Don't you be getting up from that chair, Mathilde Caroline Bonner." She meant to be firm, but she was smiling so broadly that it didn't work. "I mean it now, you hear me good."

Nobody was quite sure if Lily had cracked a bone in her ankle or just sprained it, but Curiosity had made up her mind not to take any chances one way or the other. Every morning she unwrapped the ankle and had a hard look. Then she'd call Dr. Todd and he'd have a look too, and they'd ask her to turn the foot one way and then the other. Finally they spoke a few words to each other and Curiosity bound up the ankle again from toes to shin, even though the swelling was gone and even the greenish-yellow color that matched Magnus's eyes exactly had faded to almost nothing.

Lily turned on her brother and Blue-Jay. "When are they coming home?"

The boys exchanged a look, and then Daniel shrugged. "He didn't say."

Lily pushed herself up out of the chair as far as she could without disobeying Curiosity. "What do you mean, he didn't say? Who brought the message?"

"Three-Crows," said Daniel, and Lily sat back down with a groan.

Three-Crows was an old Mahican hunter who wandered the Great Lake from Canada to Ticonderoga, picking up news in one place and putting it back down in another. Hidden Wolf was far off his normal route but he came by once or twice a year to see Hawkeye and talk about the old days. There were a few things Lily knew for sure about him.

Three-Crows would eat everything put in front of him and some things that weren't; he wouldn't stay long at Lake in the Clouds because Many-Doves wouldn't let him drink spirits; and he couldn't be hurried into sharing his news. He was as set in his ways as Magnus, who brought a single mouse every morning to put on Curiosity's doorstep and slept in the same spot in front of the hearth every night.

When Three-Crows came to Lake in the Clouds he started by announcing what kind of news he had to offer. Sometimes he'd say just enough to keep you interested—like the news about Selah's baby—and then he would make you wait for the rest.

Right now Lily knew he would be hunkered down on the porch with Hawkeye, listing every Indian they knew in common to see if either of them had news the other did not. If somebody they had known when they were boys had died, then they would tell each other the whole story of that person's life. After that Three-Crows would tell the rest of his news in order of importance, from the least to the most: the quality of the winter furs and what prices they were fetching; who had a new canoe or a new wife or trouble with the law; what the politicians were telling themselves; what wars the whites were fighting, where, and why. They would have the same old debate they always had on how to stay clear of O'seronni quarrels without picking sides.

Even Runs-from-Bears would not sit for long on the porch when Three-Crows came to call, and Bears was always glad to sit with the Kahnyen'kehàka elders when they got to telling stories. Bears stayed out of the way because all the telling would be done in Mahican, and nobody on Hidden Wolf spoke more than a few words of Mahican except Hawkeye, Nathaniel, and Hannah.

Of course Hawkeye wanted to know when his son and daughter-in-law were coming home, but he wouldn't interrupt his visitor or even try to hurry him along. Two old Mahican men with a pipe of tobacco would need most of the day to get to what everybody was wanting to know.

"What I don't understand," Lily said more to herself than the boys, "is how he came across them to start with. Three-Crows won't go into the bush." And she looked up to see that the same thought had already occurred to Daniel and Blue-Jay both.

"That means he saw them on the lake. But what would they be doing on the Great Lake with Selah Voyager?" She put the question out for anyone to answer, but if either of the boys had anything to say it was chased away by the sound of scratching at the door, which swung open only far enough to admit Bump's round head cocked at that odd angle that always took Lily by surprise because it made her think—uneasily—of a chicken's neck newly twisted.

"Time for your lesson, Miss Lily. Gabriel's waiting. Boys, help me with the lady's carriage, will you?"

It was the same joke he made every morning when he came to fetch her with the wheelbarrow, but Lily smiled politely while she thought through this new problem.

If she sent the boys away so she could have her drawing lesson in peace, Daniel would take offense again and maybe he'd make her wait for whatever news Three Crows finally spat out. But if she invited them to come along they would look over her shoulder at what she was drawing, talk to Gabriel and ask him hundreds of questions, and ruin her lesson. She had missed yesterday because Gabriel wasn't feeling strong enough after he finished with Uncle Todd in the laboratory. She didn't want to waste the little time she'd have with him today.

Bump said, "You boys hear about the bear Claes Wilde found cold as the grave right at his front door, come first light?"

The boys swung around to him. "A bear?"

"Yes sir. It's a bear for certain, or the best imitation I ever saw. Must stand six feet tall, and when Claes opened the old fellow up, guess what he found."

He leaned so far forward that Lily thought he might topple right over and hit the floor with his nose.

"A porcupine quill, stuck clear through the heart. A bear near as big as a cabin brought down by a porcupine."

Blue-Jay looked politely at the floor, but Daniel's brow folded itself in a way that meant he couldn't keep his doubt to himself.

"You know a porcupine can't shoot a quill into a bear's heart, Bump. That's impossible."

Bump rolled the shoulder that stuck up so high that it looked like a mountain wanting to take a walk.

"So you'd think. But you can head right down to Claes and see for yourselves if you don't believe me. I expect he'll be busy butchering for a good while."

The boys loved to visit with Gabriel Oak, but neither of them could forgo the possibility of a bear killed by a porcupine. They were out the door before Lily could ask when they would be back, but at least Blue-Jay turned to call to her.

"We'll bring news as soon as we've got it!" And he went loping off after Daniel, solving Lily's problem about her drawing lesson, which was less satisfaction than she had thought it would be.

"Always in a hurry to get gone," she sniffed. "Who cares about an old bear."

Bump closed one eye to look at her. "Is that so. And here was I, hoping to take you down there to see for yourself after your lesson. Now don't scowl at me, Miss Lily, you'll be wrinkled as an old prune before you've got a full decade under your belt. What's sitting on you so heavy this morning?"

"I want to go home," she said. *I want to go home to shake news out of Three-Crows.* But she couldn't say that, not to Bump or even Gabriel Oak, because she had given her word that she wouldn't talk about any of it. People were supposed to think that her mother was in New-York City with Kitty and Hannah and Ethan, and that her father had gone up to Good Pasture to see to Kahnyen'kehàka family business.

Good Pasture was just a day's walk north of the Great Lake. Maybe that's where they were headed, but why?

"Won't be long before you're home again," said Bump. "But think on this while you're waiting. Life moves fast enough without putting spurs to it."

Lily bit her lip to keep the sharp words that wanted to come out on her tongue, because as mad as she was she couldn't be mean to Bump.

He held out his arm to lean on so that she could climb into the wheelbarrow without putting weight on her foot. When she was settled, Magnus stretched himself hard and jumped in for the short trip up to Gabriel's cabin curled across Lily's middle. The wheelbarrow went down the kitchen steps with a bump-bump-bump that made Magnus put his claws into Lily.

She hiccuped out a little screech, but then she was out in the air and the sun and just like that she felt better.

On the horizon the mountains stood out green and blue against a bluer sky. The air was full of birds and the smell of last night's rain, and Magnus was purring against her chest in time with Bump's humming. Then Lily saw Gabriel Oak sitting in front of his cabin waiting for her and she decided that Three-Crows and his news could wait, for a few hours at least.

There was a book sitting on the little worktable in front of her stool, one Lily had never seen before. It was bigger than most, with cracked covers that might have once been brown but were now stained and even blackened in parts, as if it had been rescued from a fire more than once. The spine was gone, and the whole was bound together with twine. The bindings were swollen and straining at the burden of papers layered in between the leaves.

Gabriel said good morning and then went right back to his drawing. Lily knew that it wouldn't do much good to talk when he was caught up in his work and so did Bump, who just went about the task of helping her get out of the wheelbarrow. When he was sure that her foot was propped up on a bolster the way Curiosity had showed him, he laid out her paper and pencils and her little book—her sketchbook, Lily reminded herself—on the table where she could reach it. Then he went off to his chores, humming to himself.

Lily should have begun her own work, but instead she sat studying the book that Gabriel had left for her to see. Under her fingertips the cracked leather boards were smooth in some places and grainy in others. The book felt so full to bursting that Lily would not have been surprised if it had moved in her hands, opened its covers in order to find some ease from the burden it carried. As full as her mother had been with Robbie, just before he came into the world. Lily blinked in surprise that such a thought might come to her about a book.

"Can I look inside?" She hadn't meant to interrupt Gabriel, but the question came out anyway.

He gave her one of his distracted smiles without looking up from his sketch. "That is something for thee to take away and study later, to help thee pass the time in quiet contemplation. For now we'll start with Magnus, I think. Canst thou see the bones of him beneath the fur and fat and muscle, Friend Lily?"

The cat blinked sleepily at her with his slitted yellow-green eyes, one ragged ear cocked forward as if to hear her answer. Lily put the book in her lap aside and picked up her pencil.

If Gabriel Oak was having a very good day, he could work with Lily for two hours before he started coughing. On bad days it would be a half hour or less when he pulled out his handkerchief and pressed it to his mouth, and then Bump would come to help him back into his cabin, where Lily had never been invited and most probably never would be, another one of the nonsense rules that grown-ups made and couldn't be argued out of.

In the week since Lily had been staying at the Todds' so that Curiosity could keep an eye on her—something Lily thought Many-Doves could have done very well, but nobody listened when she said so, not even Many-Doves herself—it seemed to Lily that Gabriel's bad days were getting to outnumber the good ones. Today, though, his voice and hand were unusually steady as he guided Lily through her exercises. Circles and triangles, boxes and cones, shaded from one side or the other, from above or below.

Everything in the world seemed to be built out of a few simple shapes, once you knew how to look. Drawing was mostly learning to see the shapes that built the bones of a thing—a tree or a face or a bucket—and once that much was done, it was all a matter of catching light and shadow to show how it all fit together. Lily spent most of her time drawing on scraps of paper Gabriel gave her, from sunrise to sunset and beyond, if Curiosity would let her work by candlelight, and every drawing just made her want to do another one. To see if she could, again. If she could make things truer and clearer and more alive.

Curiosity didn't disapprove, exactly; she'd watch Lily work and raise her eyebrow, cock her head. "Now look at that," she'd say. And, "You going to wear that lead pencil down to nothing in no time, but that surely is pretty what you got there. Your mama going to be proud to see how hard you working at these drawing lessons."

And still Lily hadn't drawn anything in the little book, although every day she meant to start.

"Daniel wants to know when I'll draw him a picture of Lake

in the Clouds, but he wants it to be in color," Lily said into the silence.

Gabriel cocked his head thoughtfully. "Does he?"

Lily studied the sleeping cat stretched out before them and the way the sun seemed to lift color out of his coat, ginger and orange and mottled brown, the raw red of a healing scar over his haunch, the way the insides of his ears shaded from the dull dun of eggshells to a delicate pink, like the sky just after sunrise.

She said, "Don't you ever make likenesses in color?"

Gabriel raised his head to look into the forest. There was a sadness in his expression Lily had not seen before, and she felt a sudden panic, that she had made him think of something that might hurt. Then he smiled a little and turned to look at her.

"Thy grandmother was a Friend, but thou canst not know much of the life or the teachings."

He had not asked a question, but Lily nodded anyway. "She died in England. When my mother was just a little older than I am now."

Gabriel picked up his pencil again and moved it gently over the paper, as if it would help him find the words he needed. "My father was a Friend of the plainest sort. I can hear him still speaking sternly to my sister Mary when she brought home a silken hair ribbon she found in the street. He believed that to wear such colors was a terrible burden on the soul."

"But why?" Lily asked, thinking of her hair ribbons back at Lake in the Clouds, wound together in a rainbow. She did not wear them often, but she liked having them.

"Because they encourage vanity and worldly excess, as do so many things. We had only one likeness on the wall, an engraving of the Peaceable Kingdom. Does thou know the prophecy of Isaiah, Friend Lily?" Without waiting for her to answer, he quoted in a low singsong: " 'The wolf also shall dwell with the lamb, and the leopard shall lie down with the kid, and the calf and the young lion and the fatted beast together, and a little child shall lead them.' "

He smiled at her. "It is a wondrous vision. When I was small I climbed up on a chair to study that likeness. I could draw it now, I think, line for line. Then one day I picked up a bit of charcoal and began to draw on the hearthstones, and it was as if a great light had been lit inside of me. A Friend prays his whole life to find Inner Light, and I thought I had found it in that piece of charcoal when I was just your age."

Gabriel stretched out his hand, long fingers slightly bent, and looked at it as if he had never seen it before.

"What did you draw?" Lily asked.

"The likeness of my sister Jane as she sat knitting. It was an awkward thing, but still it was very like her. So much that it frightened me a little to see what I had done, so I did what I always did when I was in doubt, I went to my father. He was a printer, and kept his shop in the house."

"Did he recognize your sister?"

Gabriel swallowed so hard that Lily thought he would start coughing, but the moment passed. "Yes, he did. I can see his face still, the shock in it and the disappointment. He had eyes the color of cornflowers, and they were filled with tears to see what I had wrought. On that morning he made it his Concern to lead me away from such worldly indulgence."

Lily sat up straighter. "Your father wouldn't let you draw? But why not?"

"What I saw as a gift, he saw as a trespass on Divine law. He was a good man, Friend Lily, and I wanted to please him but I could not forget what it felt like, to put those simple lines down and to see my sister there in them. When I was sixteen I left my father's house to make my own way in the world. He died the following year."

"That's very sad," Lily said, thinking of her own father and mother and remembering quite suddenly that there might be news, now, about when they would be home again.

"It is sad indeed, but I did not tell thee the story to see thee weep. Thou asked if I never use color, and here you have the answer. I have lived a willful and disobedient and often selfish life, but in this one thing I have stayed true to my father's hopes for me. I draw the world as I see it, but in the shades of gray that are my birthright. So I cannot teach thee how to put color on paper. But there is a secret I have learned over the years, and I will share it with thee."

Lily waited while Gabriel paused, different expressions moving across his face, doubt and weariness and other things she could not name. His thumb ran gently along the pencil.

"The more that is taken away, the more clearly will thou see what is left behind. It is true of Magnus sleeping there in his dis-

guise of fiery fur, and it is true of worldly possessions, and it is
true of the human heart." And then Gabriel let out a small, dry
laugh, something Lily had never heard from him before and it
startled her greatly.

"When thou hast learned to value what is left behind, then
thou wilt be ready to find another teacher, one who can teach
thee about color."

Lily's mouth felt very dry. She said, "Do you think I will
ever come so far?"

"I have no doubt of it, Lily. None at all. Now I think that
thou should have another look at Magnus, thou hast missed the
angle of his ears."

The cat had turned over in his sleep and was splayed on his
back with his belly to the sun and his paws stuck straight up. It
was a silly sight, but Lily could not find it in herself to smile or
even to do as she had been told. She felt as she did after she had
eaten too large a meal, filled up now with words and sleepy, in
need of quiet so that she could make sense of the things Gabriel
had told her. There were so many questions—she wanted to
know where he had gone at sixteen and how he had earned his
living, who had taught him as he taught her now—but they
would have to wait until she had thought it all through.

She said, "You look very tired. Shall we stop for today?"

He reached out a hand and let it rest on her shoulder, something else he had never done before. "There is all eternity to
sleep, Lily. Ah, here is Friend Curiosity."

She was coming up the slope toward the cabin with a basket over her arm, walking like a girl so that her skirts swirled
around her legs and snapped back again. Curiosity in the best
of moods, well pleased with the world. *Her son has a son,* Lily
remembered and it saddened her not to be able to share such
good news with Gabriel.

"Dinnertime," Curiosity called. "Come away now, Lily,
and let the man eat in peace. Bump on the way up from the
barn."

Then she stopped in front of them and opened her mouth
to say something, but no words came out. Her expression had
gone very quiet and empty, but there was a sharpness there,
some surprise that did not sit well. Lily followed the line of
her gaze to Gabriel, who had lifted his face up, his eyes narrowed against the sun under the fringe of gray hair and the

broad brim of his hat. His skin was very white, and his eyes were rimmed with red.

"Gabriel Oak," she said, her voice a little hoarse. "What have you done?"

He blinked at her slowly. "We have had a good morning, Friend Lily and I." He produced a grin that lifted only one side of his mouth and made him look like a boy. Something had passed between them that Lily did not understand and was not meant to understand, except that Gabriel had somehow got the best of Curiosity.

She had the crease between her brows that meant she wasn't about to be charmed, not even by Gabriel Oak.

"I'm ready," Lily said, uneasy and unsure if she were somehow to blame for whatever had so displeased Curiosity. "I'm ready to go now."

"Hold on just a minute," said Curiosity. "How much did you take, Gabriel?"

"Enough, I think." He was still smiling, but not quite so broadly.

Curiosity sucked in one cheek and let it go again, and then she let out a great breath. "Well, then, we'll just set here with you a while longer."

She silenced Lily's question with a quick flick of her fingers. "We got a matter to settle."

Gabriel blinked at her, sleepy and content. "I made a promise, did I not?"

Curiosity didn't answer him. She said, "Lily, have you done any drawing in that book your mama gave you yet?"

Lily shook her head.

"Time to get started then. Open it up, now. I'll stand right here while you work. Don't worry none, I ain't going to look over your shoulder. Take his likeness as best you can."

"You want me to draw Gabriel?" Lily's voice rose up in surprise, wavering a little at the end.

"I do."

"But I'm not—"

"Friend Lily," Gabriel said softly. "I made a promise that I cannot keep without thy help. Wilt thou help me?"

"Yes," Lily whispered.

"Concentrate on this task before thee. It is within thy power."

The more that is taken away, the more clearly wilt thou see what is left behind.

Lily studied Gabriel. His skin shimmered damp in the sunlight so that for a moment it seemed that she could see through it to the skull itself. The great hollows of cheek and temple, the line of his nose, the deep cleft above his lip where sweat shone in the sun like dew in the curve of a leaf.

"Will you take off your hat?"

He did as she asked, and she began to work, linked circles and then caught the shape of his deep-set eyes, turned up a little at the corners where the wrinkles were deepest. The color didn't matter to her pencil but she could not overlook it either, eyes as blue as her own—like flag lilies, like cornflowers—but fever bright, and brighter still, like window glass reflecting a bloodred sunset. His usual kind expression was there too, but lost a little in the heat of his fever. He wasn't watching her or anything at all, his gaze was fixed in the distance while he waited for her to do this thing he had asked of a little girl. Younger now than he was when he drew his sister Jane and found out the truth about himself.

Panic clenched, rose up from her belly like a fist to lodge in her throat. She put down the pencil to flex her fingers and then she felt Curiosity's hand on her shoulder, as sure and calm as her mother's. The fear left her, ran away down her back and disappeared into the ground like a strike of lightning.

The more that is taken away.

Lily let her pencil work. All the rest of the world went away while it moved on the paper, putting down Gabriel's bones, circles within circles and the planes between them. The beginning and the end of him. And then she was finished, a simple drawing, nothing more than lines meeting and parting and meeting again to build a likeness of her friend.

"A little too broad in the chin," said Lily. "And the ears aren't quite right."

"Shhhh." Curiosity leaned down to look, her eyes moving quickly over the paper.

"Now see," she said finally in her softest, sweetest voice. She smelled of linen in the sun, of cinnamon and the color of her own skin. "Now see what you made. Wouldn't your grandmother be proud?"

Curiosity was looking at Gabriel Oak when she said it, and

Lily would remember her expression for a very long time to come, sad and happy at the same time and satisfied, above all things.

In the evening when there was still no word from Three-Crows or Daniel or anyone else, Lily opened Gabriel's book, working the knots in the string with fingers that trembled a little. When she was done the book sat before her with its warped boards and blackened face like a great horny toad ready to leap.

She turned over the front cover, curious first and foremost about what kind of book it might be, and read with considerable effort:

> **An Apology for the True Christian Divinity, as the Same is held forth, and Preached, by the People, called in Scorn, Quakers; Being a full Explanation and Vindication of their Principles and Doctrines**

The first flush of surprise and disappointment lasted only a second, until Lily looked at the inside of the cover she had set aside. The handwriting was old-fashioned and hard to read but the familiar name was there: she put her finger on it and whispered the words to herself aloud as she read, something her mother would not like but it seemed the only right way, to say the words out loud from the page.

> **Josiah Oak bought this Good Book 5th day, 2nd Month in the Year of Our Lord 1748 for his son Gabriel, that he may Endeavor to Walk in Divine Light**

Below the faded ink Gabriel's father had put on the paper, he had made marks of his own: a whole world of faces, men and women and children, some laughing, some serious or concerned or distracted. Beneath each he had written a few words: *Sister Jane, aged 18; Aunt Catherine, with her cat Theobold; Brother Thomas, lost to a fever aged 23; Mother in contemplation; Great-grandmother Clarke; Father.*

Josiah Oak was an old man in the drawing, with sunken cheeks and deep lines around his mouth, pain lines Hannah would call them, but there was nothing bad or cruel in his expression, no matter how Lily studied him, looking for a man who would send a son away because he wanted to draw. He had died so long ago and still Lily could know him a little, from the set of his jaw and the look in his eyes. This was the way Gabriel had seen his own father. The bones of him.

Lily turned the pages carefully, afraid that if she made any sound at all what she had in front of her might disappear. She saw now what Gabriel had meant her to have. Not the book, or what the book had to say—the printed words were long and complicated and did not interest her—but for the world inside it. Gabriel had drawn in the white spaces and sometimes along the edge of the words, trees and cabins and a clump of fireweed, a child with a scarred face, an old lady with a sour look that reminded her of the widow, two Indian boys playing a game with dice, one of them laughing while the other scowled. *Seneca camp*, he had written below them.

Most of the drawings had something noted, sometimes just the name of the place where the drawing had been made and a date. *On the Delaware, spring 1749. Meg Brewster of Philadelphia. Mr. Leonard, Barber, 1750. A tree struck by lightning, Marysville.*

"I've been talking to you for five minutes, girl. Have you gone pure deaf?"

Lily looked up at Curiosity, who stood fists on hips in front of her. "Gabriel gave me this," she said, her hands spread over the pages. "I don't know why."

Curiosity's expression softened.

"Do you know why he would give me this?"

One corner of her mouth twitched a little, not in laughter at all but as if she were trying to decide what to say. "It'll come to you in time, child."

When she had carried Lily into the kitchen and deposited her, she stood back. "Tomorrow you can put some weight on the ankle," she said. "Walk around the garden a little."

Just a few hours ago this good news would have driven everything else out of Lily's head, but the book in her lap was so heavy, and her fingers kept moving back there, tracing the cracks in the leather.

Curiosity didn't seem to notice; she had already turned her back to talk to Daisy, who was washing fiddlehead ferns from the basket in her lap. Lily thought of asking them to light a candle—it was far too dim in the kitchen at dusk to read anything—the urge to open the book was that strong. She had not even come to the first of the papers that were layered between the pages.

"Strangest wedding I ever heard of," Daisy was saying to her mother. "Wasn't nobody there except the preacher and his wife. The widow caught herself a chill, so they say, and stayed in bed. Her only child and she wouldn't stand there and watch him be married. Anna did go on about it."

Lily sat up a little straighter, her hands stilling on the book.

Curiosity said, "I keep thinking of Martha, rest her soul. She would be pleased to see her Jemima settled so well."

Daisy let out a soft grunt of disapproval, started to say something, and then she cast a glance in Lily's direction and stopped herself. "One thing for certain, I never saw a man so blank faced on his wedding day. Kuick looked like he was walking in his sleep."

"It all happened right fast," Curiosity said dryly.

"Dolly will have some news to share. She coming today?"

Curiosity shrugged. "I expect Jemima will make her work till full dark, though she's unlikely to get her full wages."

Lily didn't like to ask questions when they were talking for fear that they would just stop, but now she couldn't hold back.

"Dolly Smythe is leaving the widow?"

Daisy looked up from her basket with the smile that reminded Lily of her own mother.

"She is. The new Missus Kuick don't care to have Dolly scrubbing her floors or working her loom."

"That suit me just fine," said Curiosity. "I'll be glad of the extra pair of hands, I surely will. The only question I got is, I wonder how long it'll take for Becca to give notice, just her and Cookie taking on all the housework alone while Jemima lays abed."

And then the two women exchanged glances and Curiosity closed her mouth up tight. All week Lily had been listening to Curiosity and Daisy worry over the changes at the Kuicks', but they were far too mindful of her sitting in the corner and always stopped short of the things Lily most wanted to know about.

At night sometimes she lay awake thinking of what happened at Eagle Rock, of Jemima's face twisted with anger, the grip of her hand, the way she spat out her words.

Nothing to lose if you talk.

When Curiosity and Daisy started in on Jemima there was never any mention of Liam Kirby, who had disappeared into the bush without a word to anybody that very day.

Maybe because Hannah was gone, or maybe because he wanted to get away from Jemima. Both, Daniel had said when they talked about it one morning when they had a few minutes alone. And to these reasons of Lily's Daniel added his own, the least appealing of all: Liam was still hoping to pick up Miss Voyager's trail, and he had gone north to the Great Lake to take up with other blackbirders, men who hunted like wolves when the need was on them.

It gave her a bad feeling deep in her gut to think about it. In the dark she wished herself at home where she could wake Daniel and they would talk until it all made some kind of sense. Alone it just stuck in her head like a cocklebur and wouldn't be shook loose. Maybe together they could go to Hawkeye and tell him the story. He would listen with that quiet look he got when something hard had to be said. Then he might even smile at the idea that Jemima could cause them any harm, the laughing kind of smile that meant the idea was too odd to take seriously or the grim smile that meant that Jemima might try, but she would regret it mightily if she did.

And then Lily looked up and saw her grandfather standing in the door of Curiosity's kitchen, taller than the door itself, as tall as any mountain. As if he had heard her thinking about him, as if she had called his name loud enough to hear at Lake in the Clouds. The sight of him loosed something tangled inside her so that she felt her bones go loose and tears pushed up without warning. She wiped them away while he was greeting Curiosity and Daisy, because she didn't know why she was crying and she didn't want him to see.

He came to kneel next to her chair. Lily leaned a little forward to get more of the smell that always clung to him, pine trees and Indian tobacco and gunpowder and hard work. Different from her father, who liked to chew mint, but the same too.

"Is there news?"

"There is," he said. "Three-Crows brought you a letter from your mother."

"But—"

"Read the letter first." He smiled when he put it in her lap to show her there was nothing to be afraid of, and then he leaned forward so that the eagle feather tied into the side braid above his ear tickled her face, an old trick that still made her laugh. His face could be hard as iron when he was worried or angry but now he was relieved, she could feel it herself.

"I'm going to pay Gabriel my respects, and then we can talk."

Curiosity lit a candle for her to read by and stepped away to leave her alone, something that must have been hard because Curiosity wanted news as much as Lily did. So she opened the folded pages—the sight of her mother's handwriting was so familiar and so welcome that Lily touched the paper to her cheek—before she began to read out loud, a little shyly because she had never liked recitation, and had always left that to Daniel.

Dearest children,

Our travels have taken us unexpectedly to Mariah on Lake Champlain, where we are guests of an old friend. You will remember Captain Mudge who came to call at the Schuylers' when we visited there last. He made each of you a wooden boat to sail on the river and allowed Lily to trim his beard with his pocket-knife when she declared it much too long. Captain Mudge's sister, Mrs. Emory, who spent many years in Africa, has kindly given us some figures carved of ivory to bring home to you. Our old friend Three-Crows brings you this letter as a favor to your grandfather. We expect that you will treat him as an honored guest and that you will endeavor to listen politely and to curb your impatience.

Tomorrow the captain will take us up the lake on his schooner, the same one on which you sailed when you were infants, called the Washington, *Mrs. Freeman or Runs-from-Bears would tell you the story again, if you were to ask. This journey will take perhaps ten days all told, and then we will set out for home from the Big Carry overland. Your father calculates that you should begin to look for us in thirteen days and that it might be as many as twenty, depending on the weather and other things we cannot anticipate. Your grandfather and Runs-from-Bears will know if and when it is time to be concerned at any delay; in this and in them, you can trust completely.*

We regret very much this change in our plans but it could not be helped. You will be disappointed, but you must not worry, for we are all in good health and spirits and hopeful of a good ending to this undertaking. We expect that you will continue to be helpful and cheerful and obedient to Many-Doves, Mrs. Freeman, Runs-from-Bears, and your grandfather; most of all we trust that each of you will keep the promises you made to us.

Be good and loving to each other, our two halves, two wholes. We think of you with affection and great pride,

Your loving parents,
Elizabeth Middleton Bonner
Nathaniel Bonner

Lily read the letter twice, and then another time, but they were all agreed that it raised more questions than it answered.

"The rest of the story must have come through Three-Crows," Lily said, a little unsettled by the look on Curiosity's face. "Hawkeye will tell us why they're on the lake."

Curiosity made a sound deep in her throat that meant she was far less than pleased with another delay. Then Galileo came into the kitchen and Lily was asked to read the letter aloud again.

They sat wondering about what could have caused such a big change in plans, if it might have been blackbirders that kept them from taking Selah to Red Rock and what was it they planned to do with her once they got to the Canadian border. Daisy went back and forth to serve Uncle Todd his supper while her parents talked in a low whisper, as if he might hear them from the dining room.

Lily never could understand why Uncle Todd would want to eat alone while Aunt Todd and Ethan were away; he could be in the kitchen with people, but this evening at least she was glad of his ways because Curiosity and Galileo would never talk so freely in front of him.

"She was being careful," Galileo said, it seemed more to convince himself than anyone else. "Don't mean bad news, necessarily. It wouldn't be wise to say too much in a letter, might fall into the wrong hands."

"I have got to set down and write that letter Manny been waiting for."

"Let's wait, see what Hawkeye have to say," said Galileo softly. "He's coming now."

Lily was glad when her grandfather picked up a stool and settled it and himself down next to her. Galileo, Curiosity, and Daisy all drew up close, Galileo with his arms folded and propped against his knees so that he bent forward, Curiosity and Daisy with fingers wound tight together, sitting close enough to touch shoulders. Hawkeye was a good storyteller and nobody interrupted him, even at the worst parts when Curiosity drew in a sharp sigh.

When he was finished there was quiet for a long minute, the kind of quiet that sets on a house when somebody is laid out in a coffin to look at one last time. Lily tried to imagine it, twelve people dead in five days, young and old. She had seen her brother dead and Falling-Day too, both of them so still in the wood box that her father had built for them, but she could not make herself see twelve dead people all at once. If you counted everybody in both cabins at Lake in the Clouds from Sawatis to Hawkeye, youngest to oldest, that would be twelve people.

A brain fever that could put twelve people in their graves inside of a week was worse than any sickness Lily had ever heard her sister Hannah talk about. Worse than croup, worse than yellow jack.

Curiosity cleared her throat; her voice came rough and thick. "Lord have mercy on their souls."

"They died free," Daisy said. "There's that much to be thankful for."

"If anybody can get the rest of them to Canada, Nathaniel can." Galileo said this in his own firm voice, the one he used with the horses and oxen and creatures he meant to send in a particular direction.

Lily said, "I don't like it." Because she didn't, not at all. All day she had wanted news, and now she wished she had never heard it.

"Together your daddy and ma can manage just about anything," said Curiosity, reading her. "Don't you doubt it."

Hawkeye leaned forward and lifted Lily as easily as he might lift a sack of cornmeal, settled her on his lap so that she was surrounded by the hickory hardness of his arms beneath the soft leather of the hunting shirt. Another time she might have been insulted to be treated like a babe in arms but now it seemed just right, and she was glad of him and of Curiosity and Galileo and Daisy too, all of them sitting together in a circle.

"I'm going to take her home tonight," he said over Lily's head. "Daniel is feeling mighty alone right now."

Curiosity gave him a vague smile. "All right, then," she said. "But don't you let her put weight on that ankle more than an hour a day until I say otherwise."

Hawkeye generally walked everywhere but this time he had come down to the village on Toby, the ancient piebald gelding as quiet and gentle as an old toothless dog, the horse that pretty much belonged to the children as the men walked faster than Toby did. The Kahnyen'kehàka took pride in walking, but Lily was glad to see the old horse.

Galileo handed Lily up so that she sat astraddle in front of her grandfather with her sore ankle tied to a bolster and the rest of her wrapped in a blanket. Curiosity had put all her things in the side basket, and then she stood back with her arms folded tight.

"It surely was nice to have you, child. I'll be up to see you tomorrow afternoon."

Bump was standing by the garden fence and he raised a hand to her, white as linen in the gathering dark. Lily waved back and called out to him but he stayed silent and later she wondered if she had imagined him there.

Galileo touched her hand and then they were off. Lily was glad that Hawkeye didn't try to talk to her because she was so confused, to be heartsick at leaving when all she had wanted was this, to be going home again to sleep in her own bed.

They headed home around the west end of Half-Moon Lake, Toby's long legs whooshing through the high grass, mud sucking at his hoofs where they skirted the marsh. She leaned back against her grandfather and listened to his heartbeat and the frogs singing in the marsh louder than any children at play and the steady rhythm of Toby's breathing.

It was almost full dark but the lake drew all the starlight to itself, flickering like a copper penny tossed up spinning into the sky at midday. When light left the world they would be blind (*like Splitting-Moon,* she whispered to herself) until the sun came again. Lily closed her eyes and opened them again trying to imagine that loss, living in a world stripped of color and shape and shadow.

If she looked hard enough she could make out the shape of the mountain ahead, as familiar to Lily as her mother's face, the line of her father's back.

"I'm glad," she said. "I'm glad you came to get me."

Hawkeye made a humming sound deep in his throat, but that was all she needed.

PART III

Crosswinds

Chapter 32

June 14, 1802

Married only a few weeks and finally in possession of all the feather beds, china dishes, silver knives, beeswax candles, and copper tubs she had ever imagined, Jemima Southern Kuick came to the conclusion that life would be better still if she only had an orphan for a husband. She was sitting in the parlor across from her mother-in-law when this thought came to her on a rainy June morning. They were alone, as they usually were for a good part of the day.

The hidden costs of becoming a wife had begun to make themselves known, and the most surprising was this: marriage had freed Isaiah Kuick from this parlor and his mother's company, and sentenced Jemima to take his place.

"Privilege has its duties, missy," said the widow, her bristled chin bobbing. "And you'll do what's proper, stand next to my son—"

"My husband," interrupted Jemima in a monotone.

The widow's mouth twitched. "Next to my son when they put that boy in the ground at noon. It's the right thing to do when one of the slaves dies. Mark that, now. The right thing. It falls to you." She jabbed her needle in Jemima's direction. "It falls to us to provide an example to the village."

Jemima turned the pages of the newspaper in her lap. It was a month old but far more interesting than the widow in a lecturing mood.

"And if I don't care to get my feet wet?"

"If you don't go see Reuben buried his mother will pout," said the widow. "And you won't like Cookie in a pout. She'll burn the porridge and lose your left shoe and misplace my basket of wools and that will go on for months. The slaves are sly creatures when it comes to getting their own back, missy. Don't you forget it. You must say a few words of praise about the boy, as my representative."

"Anything to save you the trouble of moving out of that chair."

"I'll have a respectful tone from you!" The widow's thin cheeks flushed a color so deep it was almost blue. Pushed just a little farther, her temper would roar to life and she would reach for something to throw. First the empty teacup and saucer that stood on the side table at her elbow and then a book, as there was nary a china figurine left in the house. When nothing else was available she was not above launching knitting needles like spears. Jemima knew without any doubt at all that if her mother-in-law were strong enough to pick up furniture to hurl it through the room, she would do so.

She turned the page of the newspaper while she watched the widow from the corner of her eye. For a short while she had been amused by the sight of a refined lady hopping from one foot to the other like a two-year-old who wanted a sugar-tit she couldn't have; now she was ready to bolt if the need should arise.

"It's like living with a sharpshooter with an itchy trigger finger," she complained to her husband on one of the rare occasions they spent a few moments alone.

Isaiah had been on his way out to meet Dye in some dark corner and he listened to her with a combination of impatience and amused disregard. He would not take her part against his mother. He wouldn't even be bothered to remember her first name. Isaiah called her "Missus Kuick," as if they were a couple married fifty years and bound by the old customs.

The truth was, Jemima must admit to herself, she had been far too liberal in her negotiations. The bargain she had struck with Isaiah Kuick gave him more freedom than was good for him; he spent more time out of the house than she had imagined, and thus far she hadn't been able to think of any way to take back the upper hand without causing as much damage to her own cause as to his.

And still it afforded her great satisfaction to imagine telling the widow the truth about her son and his absences from her parlor.

Now her mother-in-law was adjusting her shawl around her shoulders with tight little jerks. She pursed her mouth and squinted in Jemima's direction.

"You'll go see the boy buried, and I'll tell you why. This is one opportunity you won't miss to show off that wedding ring you snared for yourself."

Jemima swallowed down her irritation and produced her sweetest smile.

"But why would I do such a thing, Mother Kuick? I have nothing to prove to anyone."

"Oh, don't you now? Not even to Missus Elizabeth Bonner and her heathen of a stepdaughter?"

Lucy Kuick had an awful huffing laugh that showed all the gaps in her back teeth.

"The look on your face, missy, now that is worth a great deal. Caught you off your guard, did I? That's what you get for sitting on your great backside all the day long. Things sneak up on you when you're napping. The whole crowd of them are back, came in late yesterday evening dragging half of the city with them."

"Georgia must have brought you the news." Jemima could have bit her tongue for showing even that much interest.

"She did indeed. That and more. She's worth her wages, I'll say that much. Does her work and more, and not a surly bone in her. Knows her place and doesn't look for more than her due. Should have sent to Johnstown for servants to start with. There are some lessons you could learn from Georgia, missy."

Jemima wondered what the widow would do if she should pick up a book and throw it through one of the glass windows she was so proud of. She would do it too, if not for the fact that there was already too much gossip in the village about what went on in this parlor. But there were other ways to deal with the widow, and so Jemima picked up her own untouched cup and poured out her tea on the widow's good Turkey rug, the one Mr. Kuick had given her as a wedding present.

She could move fast when the need was upon her, and still the first book thumped against the door with surprising force before she had pulled it all the way shut.

"May you rot in hell!" screeched the widow.

Jemima was halfway down the hall before the hailstorm of books stopped.

It wasn't until she had closed her bedroom door behind her and turned the key in the lock that she could breathe again. She stood in the middle of the dim room with one fist pressed to her heart and the other to her mouth, swallowing down panic like hot water.

Nathaniel Bonner had come home from the bush two or three days ago, and now Elizabeth and Hannah were back from the city, far sooner than Jemima had hoped. All of the Bonners together at Lake in the Clouds, young and old sitting around the table. Talking.

Jemima could almost hear the questions. *Tell us again how you came to sprain your ankle, daughter. Tell us again about Liam Kirby, when did he leave here, and what finally drove him away? Tell us again why you were at Eagle Rock that day, Daniel.*

She ran a hand over her belly, still flat and firm in spite of the fact that her courses were late, and her breasts ached. Liam Kirby had run off, but not before he started the child in her, the child who was the cornerstone of everything she was trying to build for herself. The child was her only real protection from the widow. There was an old saying that went through her head a lot these days: the Lord helps those who help themselves.

"I helped myself." Jemima whispered the words out loud. She had planned well. Except, of course, for the fact of the Bonner twins sitting up on the mountain with their folks, talking.

It had got to the point that they trailed her around, waking or sleeping, as she had last seen them at Eagle Rock: Daniel's painted face creased in outrage, turning him from a child to a younger version of his father. His sister howling like a demon as she tumbled down the slope. It made Jemima break into a sweat to think what would have happened had the girl broken her head instead of only spraining her ankle.

But there was hope. It seemed so far that the twins had taken her threats to heart and kept quiet. So far. But maybe not; maybe they had already told the whole tale. That insistent voice at her ear, the voice that would not let her sleep soundly. The bitterest pill was this: Jemima had bested Hannah Bonner and got Liam Kirby for herself, but she must keep that victory to herself or put herself in danger of being discovered.

Something that might happen anyway, if Daniel or Lily should decide to confess what had happened at Eagle Rock.

Children could be forgetful. Children needed a firm hand, and someone to remind them now and then what was expected of them. Her own father had used a switch or a piece of harness for that task, but Jemima was not so worried or desperate that she had forgotten who the children belonged to. If she should put a mark on either of them the Bonner men would come looking for her; there was no doubt of that at all. But there were other ways to put the fear of God into a wayward child, and Jemima had spent a great deal of time contemplating all of them. The problem was that she saw the children so seldom.

They would be at the burial, in that much the widow was right. Jemima would have to change her clothes and go out into the rain after all.

There was a scratching at the door.

"Missus Kuick?"

"What is it, Becca?"

"Mr. Kuick sends word that he's ready to leave for the burial. The slaves are all waiting down at their graveyard." Becca's tone was as neutral as she could make it but the smirk was there, hidden behind the door. Jemima meant to turn her out as soon as another servant could be fetched from Johnstown, but now and then the urge to do it immediately was almost overwhelming. If it hadn't meant disrupting the household and putting the widow in a temper she would do it, just for the satisfaction of getting rid of Becca and her impudent ways.

"Tell him I'll be there directly."

"Yes, Missus Kuick."

On her back Jemima wore a gown that had been her mother's second best, an ugly deep green with red facings, worn thin at the hems and wrists, tight across the shoulders, patched more than once at elbow and hip. The rest of her clothes hung on pegs on the wall: two linsey-woolsey dresses she had not worn since her marriage and would never wear again, and the dark brown bombazine she had inherited from her mother and worn as her Sunday best for the last year.

Jemima had lost no time in ordering new clothes made for herself. The first of them hung on the wall like a butterfly among moths, heavy silk in a pink-and-green paisley pattern. The only silk available at the trading post, but good enough for Matilda Kaes to get started sewing while more was ordered from Johnstown. Jemima fingered the lace insets in the bodice and tassels that hung from the sleeves to swing as she walked.

Any of her old gowns was more appropriate to a burial than this new silk. To wear it would infuriate her mother-in-law and shock the village. Anna McGarrity and the old wives would never come to see a slave boy buried but they would hear about it within the hour, and then they would talk about nothing else for a week.

Jemima took the silk down from its peg and began to plan the rest of her day.

Elizabeth had been home for six days and still she hadn't gone down to the village, mostly because she dreaded the questions that would come her way, and the fact that she would have to lie, something she had never done very well or very successfully. Nathaniel could show himself and did without hesitation; no one would think to question him about how long he had been gone or what business had kept him away. The only question that came his way had to do with his daughter being away, and that he could answer honestly: he would be a happy man when the whole family was together again.

Day after day Elizabeth found excuses to keep to the mountain. She passed her time with the children, listening to Daniel and Blue-Jay tell stories of their adventures, sometimes finishing each other's sentences with perfect timing. She spent hours sitting with her Lily, looking through the little book she had made for her daughter in the hope that it would encourage her to write.

Elizabeth had expected to find Lily's impatient handwriting on the pages and found instead one drawing after another. Some were no more than geometric exercises in shape and shading and perspective, some portraits amazingly like the people they were meant to be. The drawings that touched Elizabeth most were of small, odd objects: a shoe—Curiosity's shoe, easily recognized—lying on one side next to a clump of grass, a broken bottle, a carved pearl button hanging loose on a shirtfront. Each drawing was more accomplished than the last, and each of them had a story to go along with it that Lily was eager to tell.

"My mother could draw," Nathaniel told his youngest daughter. "She spent hours drawing pictures for me, all of the family she left behind in Scotland, the village where she grew up. It's a gift you have from her."

Lily had always been an unsettled child, jumping from one occupation to the next and easily bored. Elizabeth had never seen her so absorbed. She listened with increasing surprise to all the stories about Gabriel Oak, of the things he had taught and the things he had said. Lily had gone so far as to write many of them down on the last page of her little book.

"I wrote them down after we buried him," she explained with great seriousness. "So I don't forget him."

"He was a good friend to you," Nathaniel said. "You could not forget him."

Elizabeth said, "I am sorry to have missed the chance to thank him for all his attentions to you while we were gone."

"You can talk to Bump," said Lily. "He's mighty sad since Friend Gabriel died."

Bump was one person Elizabeth could imagine talking to without worry, but still she did not go down the mountain. When she was not with the children, Elizabeth spent her time with Many-Doves and Pines-Rustling, weeding the cornfield or the herb garden, or at the hearth, her hands full of work that tired her out physically even if it could not wipe her mind clean of Selah Voyager and Liam Kirby.

Curiosity came every afternoon on horseback after she had stopped by the mill to change young Reuben's dressings. She came to assure herself that her grandson was healthy and thriving, and simply to sit, idle for once with the baby in her lap while she listened to the women talk.

This was a Curiosity Elizabeth did not know and had never imagined. The Freemans were no strangers to death: Polly's first husband crushed by a falling tree, Daisy's second son lost to colic, older losses of parents and brothers and sisters that still burned bright. But Selah's death seemed to have caught Curiosity unprepared. She had turned inward, distracted and silent, her head always cocked toward the door as if she were waiting for someone long overdue. Some good stranger who would stand with his hat held politely before him to say that it was all a mistake, that Selah was healthy and well and how ridiculous they had all been to think that a strong woman who had been through so much could just will herself to drown.

Curiosity answered when people spoke to her, she smiled, frowned, made decisions, did her work. But only the children seemed to be able to really reach her, and then only for short periods. For the most part she sat with her grandson in her arms, one hand spread over the curve of his skull. She rocked him when he cried and hummed to him, and when he cooed in the way of a baby first waking to the world, she held long conversations with him about the weather and the crows in the trees and the days when people could fly.

It would have made more sense to leave the boy with Daisy, who was his father's sister, and eager to have him. But Daisy had stopped nursing her youngest years ago and had no milk, and so when dusk came Curiosity left her grandson to Many-Doves' care and went down the mountain to her husband.

"How long does mourning last?" Daniel had asked Elizabeth when three days had passed and Curiosity seemed more distant than ever.

Forever, Elizabeth had thought to say and then stopped herself.

Nathaniel said, "It's like any deep wound, son. It heals as it heals."

"I think she's waiting for word of Manny," Lily volunteered. "I think Manny could make her feel better, if he came home to get his boy and she could see them together."

"Hannah will be back home soon," added Daniel. "Maybe she'll bring some new medicine from the city that will fix Reuben's burns. That would help Curiosity a lot, she wouldn't be so angry anymore."

Nathaniel met Elizabeth's eye over their children's heads, surprised and pleased and a little unsettled by this combination of innocence and wisdom.

Later Elizabeth could not stop thinking about what Daniel had said so matter-of-factly. Curiosity was angry, angrier than she had ever been.

Elizabeth went looking for Runs-from-Bears and found

him repairing the handle of the old washtub out behind the barn, out of hearing of the children.

"Tell me about Reuben," she said. "About his accident at the mill."

Runs-from-Bears put down the hammer and picked up a piece of wire. "Don't know that it was an accident."

Elizabeth wrapped her arms around herself because, in spite of the warm summer afternoon, gooseflesh had risen all along her back. "Tell me."

"There ain't much to tell," said Bears in his even way. "The story goes that the boy was carrying a sack of quicklime on his shoulder when the seam gave way. Covered him pretty much from head to foot. By the time he could jump into the millpond the damage was done. Burned off pretty much all his skin."

A quicklime burn was as bad as fire, but unlike fire it could only be put out by water. Some said a quicklime burn was worse than anything a flame could do. Once when Elizabeth had still lived in her father's old homestead, she had seen a kitten fall into a sack of quicklime out in the barn; Galileo had put an end to the unearthly screaming with a quick blow of the scythe, but not quick enough to keep Elizabeth's gorge from rising.

Now she forced herself to concentrate on the gleam of sunshine on Bears' dark hair, threaded here and there with gray. When she could talk again she said, "What makes you think it might not have been an accident?"

Runs-from-Bears looked over to the porch of his cabin, where his daughter Kateri was grinding corn and singing to her little brother, who swung gently in his cradle board hung from a nail on the wall. It struck Elizabeth again that no matter how little men of different races might resemble each other physically, they were all prone to the same expression when they looked at their children: concern, fierce pride, awkward tenderness.

He said, "There wasn't anyone there but the overseer when it happened. The boy won't talk or can't talk, but the men down at the mill have got their suspicions."

When Elizabeth passed the story on to Nathaniel that night as they made themselves ready for bed, he went very still.

"You knew?"

He nodded. "Aye. My father told me about it. It explains some things."

"Is that all you have to say?" Elizabeth could hardly contain her fury. "It explains some things?"

Then he turned to her, and the stillness in his expression made her pull up short.

"I can go down there right now and put a bullet in Dye's head. It would be a pleasure, if that's what you want. Just say the word, Elizabeth."

"No." She sat down next to him, deflated. "Not that he doesn't deserve it. But . . . no. Why hasn't Curiosity said anything? Why hasn't Galileo? It is against the law to treat even a slave in such a manner. He could be charged and arrested, could he not?"

Nathaniel ran a hand down her arm, laced his fingers through hers and squeezed tight. "First off, there's no proof that Dye had a hand in what happened to the boy. He's a harsh man but I ain't ever heard of him killing anybody—not even a slave—for the fun of it. A boy like that, strong and well trained, he's worth a lot of money to the widow."

"Then you don't believe that Dye was responsible."

"I didn't say that. The thing is, we don't know what happened, or why."

Elizabeth jumped up from the bed, desperate to be moving. "I still don't understand why Curiosity said nothing at all about this. Do you think—could it be that she . . ."

"Spit it out, Boots."

She stopped, took in a great breath and let it out again. "Do you think she might blame us for Selah?"

What she wanted was a quick denial, but Nathaniel didn't give her that. He ran a hand over his beard stubble and finally shook his head. "No," he said finally, leaning down to unlace his moccasins. "I wondered about that myself, but I think it's a sight more complicated."

"Explain," Elizabeth said, more curtly than she meant to.

He shrugged. "Curiosity wouldn't hold what happened against us, you know her too well to doubt that. But both of them, Curiosity and Galileo, they seem to be drawing away. I think they want to keep their distance to protect us, in case there's real trouble coming up on Reuben's account."

This thought jolted Elizabeth just as much as the picture of the boy covered with quicklime. "Do you think that they . . . are they going to . . . take revenge?"

"I don't know that they've got anything planned," Nathaniel interrupted her. "And I'm not going to ask. You shouldn't either."

"Nathaniel, if they take the law into their own hands, the repercussions—" She stopped herself. "I want you to talk to Galileo. You or your father. Someone. Or I will talk to Curiosity."

"It's not Galileo we've got to worry about," said Nathaniel. "Nor Curiosity. If anybody has got it in their heads to go after Dye, it'll be one of Reuben's own."

Elizabeth was not much acquainted with any of the Kuicks' slaves simply because they were not often allowed into the village, but she knew them by sight and by the stories she heard. Ezekiel and Levi were big men, quiet and competent and ready with a smile, and Reuben had been much like his older brothers. Their mother, though, was another matter. Curiosity had spoken of Cookie now and then. *Like a kicked dog biding its time.* Elizabeth recalled that comment exactly.

"This is very bad, Nathaniel."

"Let's just bide our time," he answered her. "Curiosity says the boy cain't hold on much longer, and then there'll be the burial to get through."

The next evening Hannah came home to Lake in the Clouds by the rising of the moon. The dogs gave no warning, so she took them by surprise when she opened the door.

Daniel saw his older sister first and he dropped the rope he was braiding to launch himself at her with a whoop. Lily was still a bit unsteady on her injured ankle but she followed close behind, tipping up the basket in her lap so that buttons rattled across the floor.

The twins made so much noise, asked so many questions, and flung so much news at Hannah's head that Hawkeye had to restore order by picking up his younger grandchildren by their shirts and holding them in the air like wiggling puppies.

"I swear you two have forgot all your manners. She might as well be a raccoon up a tree for the way you're belling. Now let your sister catch her breath." His tone was just irritated enough to get the twins' attention, and they settled down into a sudden and reluctant silence.

As much as Elizabeth wanted to rush forward herself, she held back while Hannah greeted her grandfather and then went to Nathaniel. She spoke to him first in the language of her mother's people, and said all the things that were expected of a good daughter. She looked happy to be home, happy and thankful too, but there was a weariness about her that went beyond the cost of a long journey. Hannah had left the last vestiges of her girlhood behind her in the city.

Elizabeth wondered if Nathaniel could see this change in his daughter. She hoped he could not.

"It is good that you've come home to us," he answered Hannah in the same language. "It is right that we are together again."

Daniel went running to fetch everybody from the other cabin and they crowded together on the porch to hear Hannah's stories by the light of rushes dipped in pitch to keep the mosquitoes at bay. Lily thought it was worth the stink to be able to sit in the open and watch the moonlight dancing on the falls as they talked together.

Many-Doves brought Selah's baby for Hannah to see. He was a big healthy child with rolls of fat under his chin and down his arms and legs, like an overstuffed doll. Hannah sat with him sleeping in her lap while she answered all the questions that came her way, from Kateri who asked her whether they had seen any sea monsters to Grandfather, who asked about the captain of the ship that took them down to the city.

It was one of Lily's favorite things to do, everybody sitting together on the porch on a summer night. She leaned back against her mother's legs; she could reach out a hand and touch her brother or her father, she could climb into her grandfather's lap if she wanted, or into Hannah's.

Blue-Jay asked Hannah to start from the beginning and she did just that, making it funny where she could so that laughter floated off into the dark and Grandfather and Runs-from-Bears made noises deep in their throats. Later when it was time for the story of what had happened on the Great Lake with Selah and the voyagers they wouldn't be able to laugh anymore. That was a story Lily didn't really want to hear again.

By the time Hannah had told about coming to the city and all the family in the house on Whitehall Street, the grown-ups decided it was time to send the children off to bed. Kateri and Blue-Jay went without complaint but Lily begged and wheedled and argued even when Daniel gave in without much of a grumble. It wasn't until she had earned herself an extra afternoon weeding the cornfield that she gave in, marching in a fury to the sleeping loft.

Her brother was waiting for her with arms crossed on the sill of the open window, the breeze fluttering in his hair while he listened to the grown-ups talking on the porch. She started to ask him was he completely out of his mind and did he like the idea of spending the rest of the summer weeding corn? But he hushed her with an impatient look and scooted over to make room.

"Quiet," he whispered in her ear. "She's just getting to the good part."

Voices drifted up from the porch in fits and starts with the breeze, but a child with good ears could make out just about everything.

"You could have reminded me," Lily whispered at him. "Instead of letting me get myself in trouble."

Daniel just wrinkled his forehead and pulled her down beside him to listen.

They stayed that way for a long time while Hannah talked. She told stories of the hospital and the patients and orphan children Lily knew she was not meant to hear, things so sad and awful that Daniel couldn't keep his sighs to himself and Lily had to nudge him to remind him that they weren't supposed to be listening.

Then their father's voice came up to them, clear and sharp from underneath the window where they knelt.

"Daniel. Lily. Bed."

Lily went to bed, but she could not be commanded to sleep; she studied the shadows and wished she were brave enough to go back to the window.

"We had better not," came Daniel's whisper from the other cot, as if she had spoken her thoughts out loud.

Lily turned on her side toward him. She could make out only the line of his shoulder and head in the dark, but she knew he was looking at her.

"He wasn't so very mad," she said. "He calls me Mathilde when he's really mad." But she stayed where she was, and so did her brother.

After a while she said, "I thought I wanted to go see the city, but I've changed my mind."

Daniel made a humming sound in agreement, and then she heard him sit up. "Lily, what are we going to do about Jemima?"

He came over to climb into her cot next to her, as he always did when there was something very important to discuss, or when he was worried; most nights there was something to talk about.

"There's nothing we can do," said Lily. She felt Daniel's resistance in the set of the shoulder that touched hers.

"But she was trespassing. We're supposed to tell."

"Liam Kirby was with her, so he was trespassing too. Do you want them to get all worried about Liam Kirby again now that he's finally gone?"

Her brother's face was a pale oval, as familiar as her own face; she could draw him in the dark, if she had to. She could draw her brother if she were blind.

Daniel shook his head and his hair gave off the smell of pine sap.

"I suppose not. I just don't like the idea of Jemima Southern wandering around the mountain and making threats. It ain't right."

"She sure was scared about us telling," Lily said.

This was a conversation they had had many times already, and each time it ended just here, because they knew that there was something important at stake, something they didn't understand and couldn't ask about. It had to do with what went on between men and women, and that was one subject they didn't talk about very much.

"She acted like we was going to take a treasure away from her," said Daniel, echoing her thoughts.

"The thing is to stay clear of her for the rest of the summer," said Lily. "What we have to do is to keep out of

Jemima's way and maybe she'll just forget about the whole thing."

Later, Lily woke uneasy and confused. There were voices in the great room, whispering in the dark. Her mother murmured, and her father's voice came in response, low and a little rough.

She rolled onto her stomach and raised her head to look over the rail.

A single candle sat on the mantelpiece throwing an oval of soft yellow light out around itself and up the wall. At the very edge of the light, Lily's mother stood pressed against the wall with her father leaning in over her, one hand stemmed high on the wall. His other hand was on her shoulder with fingers spread so that his thumb rested in the hollow of her throat, where a single button had come undone.

Lily rubbed her eyes but they still stood there in perfect symmetry: the line of her father's arm; the angle where his hand met the wall; the curve of his back; all those lines coming together to make a space that only her mother could fill. In the candlelight she turned her heart-shaped face up to him and a strand of hair fell down to curl on her neck. He said something and she laughed, the sound cut off suddenly when he dipped his head to hers.

Lily lay back down and closed her eyes, crossed one arm over her face to trap the picture they had given her, forever in her mind's eye. Too precious even for paper.

It was a rainy morning, cool and sweet smelling. For the first time since they were returned from Canada, Elizabeth woke with a sense of well-being. Because there was a new child at the Todd house that meant some hope for Kitty; because Hannah was home again, changed by her time in the city but not wounded; because for all the sadness of the letters from Scotland she had brought home with her there was good news too: Luke content with his fate; young Jennet settled and married. Because her children were whole and safe and Liam Kirby was gone and would never come back to Hidden Wolf again.

It was true that they had less news of Manny than they would have liked, but what they knew was not desperate.

There was reason to believe he was well and would soon be home; Will had said so, and Will could be trusted. Another blessing to count. The summer stretched out before them with its troubles, but they were home together, and together they would manage.

Elizabeth was stirring the breakfast porridge and planning her day with renewed energy when the dogs began to bark. Toby, grazing near the porch, nickered in welcome and a familiar whinny came back in response: Hera, Curiosity's mare.

"Here's Curiosity come to hear your news," she said to Hannah. "She rides up every day to see young Galileo."

Hannah looked directly startled. "I'm surprised Kitty let her go. There's the new baby, and all the stories to hear, from Kitty and Ethan. And the wet nurse, I haven't told you about her yet—"

"Daughter," said Elizabeth softly, taken aback at Hannah's strange manner. "It is just Curiosity. There is no need for such agitation."

Hannah nodded; started to say something and then shook her head. She wiped her hands on her apron and went out to meet Curiosity.

Elizabeth put another bowl on the table and watched through the open door.

They stood there together, each clasping the other's forearms, two dark slender figures backlit by the sun and outlined in gold. For that moment it was hard to tell them apart, the young woman and the old; sorrow bent both backs, and regret bowed their heads together.

Elizabeth let out her breath, pressed her hands to her mouth so that she would make no sound. When she could trust her voice again she called, "Won't you come in and eat with us?"

Curiosity broke away and came to the door, and Elizabeth started to see her face, drawn down in weariness and grief.

"I cain't stay," she said. "I just come up to fetch Hannah, if she'll come along to lend a hand. Reuben passed on at dawn and I need her help laying him out. And we got a lot to talk about, the two of us."

Elizabeth let them go without her because she could not bear the idea of sharing the task of tending to another dead child, nor did she want any part of the conversation. She stayed behind to see to her own family's needs, but she could not keep her thoughts from following Curiosity and Hannah down the mountain. But while she ladled out porridge and spoke to the children and mended a tear in Hawkeye's hunting shirt and examined Lily's drawing of Nathaniel, Elizabeth grew more and more certain that she had been wrong to stay behind.

"I am a coward," she muttered aloud to herself, and Nathaniel's head came up sharply from the bullet mold before him on the worktable.

She blew out a breath. "I should have gone with them to help," she said. "To be with Curiosity."

Nathaniel studied her for a moment, and then dropped his gaze back to his work. "You don't have to take up every burden, Boots. And you're no coward."

She made a clicking sound in her throat, a sound Nathaniel recognized very well: Elizabeth denying herself the argument she wanted, swallowing down sharp words.

He finished wiping out the bullet mold with the oily rag and got up to put it back on the shelf where it belonged, taking longer than he needed so that when he turned around again she had had time to compose her expression.

"Go on and say whatever it is you have on your mind, Nathaniel," she said to his back. "I can feel you working up to it."

He laughed at that, a gruff laugh; she had him down to rights.

"The boys were friends, but I don't want the youngsters at the burial. Not with things so up in the air."

Her shoulders stiffened slightly, but the movement of the rag never faltered. Nathaniel braced himself for the argument that must come. She would insist that the children be present at the funeral, not so much out of friendship or good manners or propriety; those things concerned her far less than they had when she first came to Paradise.

The reason she would want them at the burial was the reason he wanted them kept away. It was the one friction point between them: Elizabeth lived in fear of raising up children ignorant of the workings of the world, overly protected and inward-turned; Nathaniel lived to protect them, and to teach them, first and foremost, how to protect themselves. In his quieter moments he recognized that he and Elizabeth were well matched in their worries, each tempering the other. So he expected an argument from his wife, and instead got something else, something that worried him more than any sharp words.

"Yes," she said softly. "I fear you are right."

Chapter 33

Jemima pulled her shawl down more tightly over her bonnet and shoulders, stamped her feet in her stiff new leather boots against the creeping damp, and counted again: one coffin of green wood wet with rain, three Indians, seven whites, sixteen blacks—a few free, the rest slaves—and not a single child in the crowd gathered around the muddy hole in the slaves' burial plot. From her place at the foot of the open grave Jemima could see the Bonners at the back of the mourners, but there was no sign of the twins.

"We commend the body of this child to the ground." Mr. Gathercole was using his preaching voice, crackling and high and as pleasing as a swarm of blackfly. "Ashes to ashes, dust to dust."

They stood three abreast, Mr. Gathercole, Jemima, and then Isaiah. Behind them was Ambrose Dye; Jemima could feel him at her back, standing too close. In another time and place she would have spoken a few choice words to cure him of his impertinence, but now she must simply bear it. If she stepped away from him and closer to her husband, it was likely that Isaiah would simply move away in turn, and Jemima would not take that chance, not with Hannah Bonner looking right at her.

Being caught like this between her husband and his lover was strange indeed, both oddly satisfying and uncomfortable in a way she didn't want to think about.

Directly across from them Cookie and her sons stood at the

head of the grave with all the Negroes gathered behind them. Curiosity and Galileo were there, Daisy and Joshua Hench. Even Jock Hindle had allowed his two slaves to come. And all of them were looking hard, eyes as hot as a fever moving fitfully from the preacher to Isaiah to the overseer and back again.

There were rumors all over the village, whispers as unstoppable as the leaves that fluttered down from the trees in September. The blacks suspected Ambrose Dye of murder, although nobody ever put it that plain. Nobody, black or white, would come out and make such an accusation without hard proof.

Jemima knew that Dye had murder in him, but she couldn't believe that he had anything to do with killing the boy. It made no sense. First, because Reuben was worth a great deal of money and Dye was tightfisted, and second, because a white man could be charged with killing a slave if he couldn't prove cause. He would hang if he drew the wrong judge.

Even if it came to that and the judge was content to fine Ambrose Dye for his temper, the widow would not put up with an overseer who went about so carelessly with her valuable property; she would put him out with a reference. He would have to go out to Johnstown or farther to find the kind of work he did, and leave Isaiah behind. As much as Jemima liked that idea, she could not imagine that Dye would risk so much.

Unless there was something she was missing.

From the look on Curiosity's face she thought that the old woman might know what that something was. She had nursed the boy until he died, after all; if anybody knew what had happened that day at the mill, it would be Curiosity. Not that the word of an old black woman would mean anything. When Judge O'Brien came through on his circuit two things were certain: crimes against property would be punished to the full extent of the law, and no black, especially not a free black woman, would be allowed to testify as a witness in his court.

Curiosity could no more speak up than she could shoot Dye on a crowded street. She would keep what she knew to herself, no matter how heavy a burden it might be.

Reuben's mother, on the other hand, looked dried out and hollow as a gourd, worn down, as if something vital had been drained out of her. Cookie was such a strong presence in the house that Jemima forgot how small she really was, no taller than a ten-year-old child but ropy with muscle. Standing between her grown sons she seemed to have shrunk even more. Jemima had the sense that if she should touch her, Cookie would simply topple over with a rustling sound, crack to a million dry pieces that would blow away with the wind.

Grief could do strange things to a woman. Jemima's own younger brothers had outlived their mother by a few hours; at the time she had not realized what a blessing that had been.

While Mr. Gathercole droned on Cookie was creeping forward inch by inch until she stood with the worn toes of her clogs extending out over the edge of the grave. She swayed once and again, and Jemima held her breath, sure that she was about to see a mother fling herself on top of her child's coffin. She had heard of such things, but never seen the like.

Levi put a hand on her shoulder and the moment passed just as the preacher came to the end of his service.

"Who would like to say a word?" Mr. Gathercole turned his head right and then left. "Who would like to speak for this child?"

Everyone except Cookie turned their eyes to Jemima. As the mistress of the slaves the widow Kuick would have said a few words about the unfathomable will of the Almighty, about Abraham's sacrifice, and the call to judgment. Things Jemima should say in her place; things she would say, if she could only open her mouth. Anybody who had spent their Sundays in church or with a bible could do what was required of her now, but to her surprise Isaiah cleared his throat roughly and stepped forward.

"Reuben was a good boy." He spoke clearly, in a deep and rich voice that Jemima had never heard before. It was a sound that seemed to reach Cookie as nothing else had. A look of confusion crossed her face and then she straightened her shoulders and raised her head.

"Of sweet and tractable disposition. He was quick and bright and clever. He was respectful of his elders." Isaiah paused, the muscles in his jaw flexing hard. His eyes were reddened at the rims, as if he had been crying or was about to. And more than that, Jemima could hear no trace of mockery in his voice, see nothing in his posture but real sorrow. She had to struggle to hide her surprise.

"His special talent was music," Isaiah went on. "When he could not play his fiddle, he sang. It was a joy to hear him. I am sorry——" His voice cracked and broke and he cleared his throat.

"He was born to this household, and he would have grown to be a fine man in it. I am sorry that he is gone. I extend my sympathies and the sympathies of my mother and wife to Reuben's mother Cookie, who has served us well and faithfully for many years, and to his brothers, Ezekiel and Levi, who have been with us since they were born. We will miss Reuben as you will miss him."

Cookie blinked and blinked again; opened her mouth and shut it. Ezekiel leaned down to whisper something at her ear and she shook her head sharply.

Isaiah said, "Mr. Dye has a few words to say as well."

Many of the blacks had been rocking back and forth on their heels as they prayed and listened, but now every single one of them went as still as the boy in his coffin. A spark jumped among them, suspicion and anger flaring high and bright. A shiver ran up Jemima's back; so much hatred focused so clearly, so absolutely, on the man standing just behind her.

"Mrs. Kuick," Isaiah said quietly. "Please step aside and let Mr. Dye come forward."

Jemima did as she was bid, edging the preacher aside so that she could keep her view of Cookie, of Isaiah and of Ambrose Dye. There was some mystery here she had not imagined, and the key to understanding it was within her reach.

Dye stood straight and tall, his head erect, and folded his hands at the small of his back. He looked over the blacks the way he always did, his thin lips pressed together in a frown. Jemima rarely had a chance to see him this close. He had scraped himself raw shaving, and a trickle of blood had dried just above his Adam's apple.

"Reuben learned right quick when he wanted to," he said, his voice booming out over the gathering as if he were calling a dance. "Never shirked a task, never talked back. A good worker, with a feel for wood."

He made a move as if he wanted to step away from the grave, but Isaiah stopped him.

Later Jemima would wonder at how a few simple movements that meant nothing taken one by one could add up to something so big. She saw Isaiah's hand raise itself to grasp Dye's

shoulder, saw the fingers grip and tense: a common gesture between men, one that said *wait,* and *don't go yet.*

Jemima watched Isaiah's hand leave his lover's shoulder and
trail down the length of his arm. Dye jerked, and something
passed between them as urgent and fast as lightning. Nothing to
do with the needs of the flesh; nothing of love or lust, but
something deeper and more complicated. As if they had made
a pact of some kind and Dye had to be reminded of his part of
the bargain.

The overseer cleared his throat and said, "He'll be missed at
the mill. By all of us." A long pause, stretching out and out.
Dye straightened his back and dropped his gaze to study the
coffin.

He said, "We regret the senseless accident that sent Reuben
too early to his reward."

A murmur moved through the crowd like a gusting wind.
Gazes shifted from the overseer to Isaiah and back again to the
overseer. Ambrose Dye, who had once dealt with a runaway
by breaking all the bones in his feet without flinching or pausing. *As if he couldn't even hear the screams,* Cookie had said when
she told the story to Dolly. *As if he was stone-deaf.* That man
stood in front of the slaves he thought of as chattel, and declared himself regretful.

And just that simply, Jemima knew that the rumors were
true. Something had happened that day at the mill that had
nothing to do with the story they had been told. Somehow
Dye had let his anger get the best of him.

If she closed her eyes, Jemima could almost see it.

Reuben walking by a window where he shouldn't have
been, or into a storage room where he wasn't expected. Dye
coming to his feet with a roar, Isaiah turning away to hide his
face. Reuben's expression, first startled and confused, then
blank with understanding, and finally wild with fear.

Exactly what happened then, how that last desperate and
furious step came to pass, that didn't matter. What did matter
was the look on Cookie's face. She knew the overseer was responsible for her son's death, but did she know why? Had he
told the story, or had that been burned out of him, as Dye intended?

They were all waiting for Cookie to speak. She might end
all of this with a nod, a word, a shrug of her shoulder; she

might open her mouth and let the truth pour out, hot and sour. She had the power now; she could take everything away that Jemima had worked so hard to get for herself.

Or maybe she would not say out loud what she knew; maybe the anger to be seen in the sea of black faces burned too hot for such a reasoned and hopeless gesture. Jemima thought fleetingly of the riots in the French Indies, blacks rising up and white blood spilled. Heads on spikes, women raped until they begged for death, children flayed raw. She saw the possibility of blood in Cookie's face, the black eyes fixed on Dye without blinking.

Cookie was the only slave allowed to stay in the main house at night. Every evening she sharpened knives, set bread dough to rising, put oats or peas to soak before she went to sleep on her pallet in front of the hearth. The weapons available to her were many: fire, steel, the leaves of certain plants cut up fine and sprinkled like rosemary over a joint of lamb. The question was whether or not she was beyond caring about the bloodbath that would follow.

The others were touching her, but she would not be turned away. She held Dye's gaze and things passed over her face too terrible and terrifying to name.

When she opened her mouth the sound that came out was strangely her own, calm and steady. She said, "It's hard times when folks got no safe place to go but the other side."

Then she held out an arm, elbow locked, and opened her fist. A shower of earth fell over the coffin that held her youngest child, her son. With one last look, first at Isaiah and then at Ambrose Dye, she turned her head to the side and spat on the ground, turned further and walked away.

The crowd parted for her and then fell in behind.

Jemima heard herself breathing fast and hard. Whatever they suspected, whatever they knew, they would not speak the words out loud, not today. She was safe, for the time being.

The rain started to fall in earnest while Hannah, Bump, and the Freemans walked away from the graveyard in the direction of the Todds', so that conversation was impractical. Hannah was not unhappy to have the quarter hour to think. Once she had presented herself to Richard Todd she would be too busy to do anything but answer his questions, and there was a great deal to think about.

She walked behind Curiosity, who had taken her husband's arm in a gesture that would look to most as nothing more than the companionable ways of a couple long married. Hannah thought that it probably had as much to do with the fact that Galileo's eyesight was so poor, but she liked to see them together regardless of the reason. Their easy familiarity and the comfort they took from one another was soothing after the things she had seen this day. She had helped lay out many a person for burial, but seldom had she seen anything as sad as Reuben or his mother, washing the boy's ruined body with gentle hands.

At the burial Hannah had been overwhelmed by a strange but persistent image of Cookie hovering over them in the air, suspended there by the pure force of her anger, skirts fluttering in the wind while she spat a curse down on Ambrose Dye's head.

They all held Dye responsible for Reuben's death, even Curiosity, in spite of the fact that she had no proof, and admitted that openly. In the long hours by his bedside she had heard him speak only a few words, and those came in fever delirium at the end. *Come dance with me, Mama,* and *Hand me that fiddle,* and *God strike me blind if I don't.*

The truth was twofold. First, they would never have enough proof to accuse Dye of anything, and that made him innocent in the eyes of white law. Second, and more important, the widow's slaves, the people who knew him best of all, could not, would not, imagine Dye innocent of anything at all.

The part of Hannah that was Kahnyen'kehàka understood that second truth better than the first one. Cookie and her sons wanted revenge, yes. Of course. But they could not have it without bringing a world of trouble down, a bloodletting that would move far beyond them to other people they cared about.

Curiosity glanced over her shoulder at Hannah and produced a small and very tired smile.

"I'll call a meeting at the trading post tomorrow evening." Richard Todd did not bother to look up from the sheaf of

papers on the desk before him. He was reading through
Hannah's notes from the Kine-Pox Institution office for the
third time with a quill in his hand, making notes to himself
and asking her questions now and then, sometimes questions
he had asked already and she had answered; whether to test
her memory or her ability to keep her temper, Hannah was
not sure.

Richard had worked out a plan to vaccinate the whole village, and he was so well satisfied with it and himself that anything Hannah had to say was of no interest at all.

Hannah knew the people of Paradise, a cautious and distrustful lot on the whole. Many of them would no more line
up to be vaccinated than they would walk up to a bear and
slap it on the nose. Richard knew that too, of course, but he
intended to bully them all into seeing things his way. He told
Hannah about his plans not because he wanted her thoughts or
suggestions, but because he thought out loud.

He would send Bump down to the trading post, the tavern,
the church, and the blacksmithy to start the word moving.
Any man who showed up to listen to what he had to say tomorrow night at the trading post and brought his family along
would get a free tankard of ale for his troubles.

Hannah drank the last of her cold tea and put the cup down
on the tray with the remnants of their dinner. The study was
crowded with boxes brought back from the city, books Dr.
Simon had sent as a gift to his colleague, gifts from Will and
Amanda, all the supplies that Richard had ordered.

A deep basket of nuts, candied fruits, and sweetmeats from
the Far East sat on top of the new edition of Thacher's
Dispensatory; boxes of tea and coffee and tobacco vied for
space with six dozen sealed jars of raw chemicals. A scarf woven of silk and fine wool had been flung over a box of vaccination supplies. Amanda had worked the pattern of twining
ivy in silk thread, but Hannah knew that Richard might well
use it to pull hot plates from the furnace and never even notice
what he had done if it were not put away soon.

The most expensive item he had asked for was a new lens
for the precious microscope that sat on its own table by the
window. Hannah had carried the lens herself for the entire
length of the journey, wrapped in many layers of silk and

muslin inside a canvas bag, like the most fragile and valuable of eggs.

"Now maybe I should send you to Philadelphia to learn Dr. Rush's treatment for yellow jack. As you did such a fine job with Dr. Simon. His letter is full of praise."

"You needn't sound so surprised," Hannah said.

He cleared his throat, which she was meant to understand as an admonition. She went on anyway. "I have no interest in going to Philadelphia, or anyplace else for that matter. Don't you want to talk about Kitty?"

Then he did look up, his head cocked to one side. "Your letters were very detailed. I have all the information I need. Or maybe you want to complain about Dr. Ehrlich to my face."

Hannah shrugged. "No, the less said about him the better. But I would like to talk about her treatment."

He narrowed his eyes and dropped his chin to his chest to peer over the tops of his spectacles. "There is no treatment, you know that. Good food to build up her blood, restricted exercise."

"And something to occupy her mind," Hannah finished for him. "You haven't said a word about the baby."

He grunted, a low and dismissive sound but not an angry one. "She may keep the child if it amuses her."

A flush of anger took Hannah by surprise; she had believed Richard could not shock her, and she was wrong. She said, "She is a little girl, not a puppy."

Richard blinked at her tone, a little surprised, not entirely displeased. "She shall have what she needs," he said, unruffled. "Short of adoption. Do we understand each other?"

"Which 'she' are you talking about?"

He threw up both hands in surrender. "Both of them. Both of them. I've had enough of this topic. What of the vaccination schedule? When will you take care of your own family?"

"This evening," said Hannah. "I brought enough stored virus to vaccinate everyone at Lake in the Clouds, except Runs-from-Bears and Pines-Rustling, of course, as they both have natural immunity. But there's one more issue about Kitty that we must have clear between us."

"Oh really," Richard said, shifting in his seat in high agitation. "And what is that?"

"It would be disastrous for her if she should..." In spite of her best intentions, Hannah found the words she had practiced so faithfully, the sentences she had gone over with Curiosity again and again, had failed her. But it didn't matter, because Richard knew already what she was trying to say. His usual disdainful and impatient expression drained away to be replaced first by regret and finally by a combination of fear and embarrassment and simple vulnerability; things he managed to hide from the world day by day.

He said, "There is no need to fear. I will not endanger my wife's health. I am surprised that you would suspect that I'm capable of such irrational behavior."

Hannah exhaled. She said, "Everyone is capable of everything, at any time. Another lesson from the city, one of the less pleasant ones."

Richard held her glance for a beat too long, and then looked away without troubling to challenge her on anything at all.

Chapter 34

June 15; full moon

"Now you tell me if I've got this wrong," said Anna McGarrity. "But it seems to me that I ain't seen the two of you together in my trading post for more than a year." She leaned over the counter and held out doughnuts to Elizabeth and Nathaniel, one in each sugary hand.

"Why, Anna," Nathaniel said. "I'm surprised you take any note of who comes in here. Newlywed as you are, and all. And you still blush like a bride too."

Anna looked pointedly at Nathaniel's free hand, which was planted firmly on the small of Elizabeth's back. "Some folks never do stop acting like newlyweds, looks like to me. For my part, I thank the good Lord for a man who knows what to do with his hands. Ain't that so, Elizabeth?"

It was true that Elizabeth liked Nathaniel's habit of touching her, just as it was true that Anna's willingness to talk of such things made her uncomfortable. She bit into the doughnut to save herself the trouble of an answer, and in response Nathaniel's fingers curved around her waist.

"You see, Anna, you're not the only one who can still blush," he said, laughing.

Elizabeth swallowed and said, "Two can play at this game, Nathaniel Bonner. Just you wait."

That made both of them laugh. Elizabeth would have walked away, but they had been propelled to the counter by the slow tide of people filling the room, and there was nowhere else to go.

Anna said, "There's no running off now, Elizabeth. Look at this crowd. It ain't often we see so many folks in here at once." She began to stack the doughnuts in neat pyramids. "Except maybe the time Charlie LeBlanc lost his wager on a shooting match and had to set still and let Old Man Cameron shave his head. Now just stay put and keep me company while I'm busy feeding these folks."

Nathaniel caught Elizabeth's eye and winked. In spite of all there was to worry about he was in a good mood, with an easy smile for anyone who came his way. It was having Hannah home again, Elizabeth reasoned, and word of Luke. All four children present or accounted for, all of them healthy and safe.

"Missus Bonner!" called Molly LeBlanc from across the room. "Good to see you again. Be glad to see my Willy getting back to school!"

"I'm sure she will," Nathaniel said under his breath. "Anything to be shut of that scoundrel for a few hours."

When Nathaniel was in such a mood the only course was to ignore him, and so Elizabeth kept her attention focused on the room. It was the first she had seen of many of her students and their families since she dismissed the school, and they greeted her so warmly that she was a little ashamed at her reluctance to come into the village.

Nathaniel was right in one thing: those who seemed happiest to see her were the parents of her most difficult students. Jock Hindle worked his way up to the counter to tell her as much.

"Seems like those boys of mine get into three times as much trouble when school is out. I still don't understand how you get them to mind without a switch or at least a primed rifle over your arm." He reached over to help himself to the doughnuts.

Anna smacked good-naturedly at his hand so that a cloud of sugar and cinnamon rose into the air. "Hold on now, Hindle, let me see your money before you go stuffing yourself."

With a grimace the older man fished a few coins from the deerskin pouch tied to his belt. "Never thought so many folks would take the doctor up on his offer. A man cain't turn around in here without getting a mouthful of his own hair." He scowled down at the coins in his palm, stirred through them with a thick finger, and flipped the one he wanted to Anna with a flick of his thumb.

Nathaniel said, "Oh, I don't know. Cain't imagine many folks passing this up."

"I won't complain about the business," Anna said. "But I got to say, it don't seem quite right, a doctor bribing folks with ale. See Mr. Gathercole over there with my Jed, I swear he's going to bust trying to figure out how to disapprove of the drinking without saying anything that'll get in Richard's way."

"Poor Mr. Gathercole," said Elizabeth, sending Nathaniel a sidelong glance. "Doomed before he even begins." She could not quite avoid his pinch, but she did manage to swallow the squeak that followed. Mr. Hindle had turned away, and Nathaniel took the opportunity at hand.

At her ear he said, "You and me are going to have a Mr. Gathercole talk right here in front of the whole village if you don't stop rubbing up against me, Boots."

"Empty promises," she hissed back at him as she pushed Nathaniel's hands away. To Anna she said, "I am surprised to see the widow here."

Anna squinted in the direction of the hearth, where the widow Kuick had claimed the good rocker for herself. "Left her servants and the blacks at home. No sign of her son either, but she takes Jemima with her everywhere. Like one of them little dogs rich folks keep on their laps all the time."

"I wonder if it was the free tankard of ale or the idea of seeing Richard take off his shirt that got the widow to come down and rub shoulders with the rest of us," Nathaniel said.

Anna laughed at that loud enough to make people turn around. Elizabeth could not hide a smile, but she elbowed her husband in the ribs for good measure.

It was strange to see the widow here. Elizabeth could go for months without seeing her at all except at church services; she doubted that the lady had ever put foot in the trading post before. She sat there now with Mrs. Gathercole to her left on a low stool, like a lady-in-waiting. The minister's wife looked ill at ease and flushed in the crowded room, one of Anna's doughnuts balanced untouched on her knee. Curiosity had mentioned just recently that Mrs. Gathercole expected another child late in the year.

As did Jemima Southern. Jemima Kuick, Elizabeth corrected

herself, looking at the young woman who had once sat in her schoolroom and caused no end of trouble.

She stood alone in the crowd in her fine silk dress, her breasts almost spilling out of the bodice. Where her husband might be was a question no one would dare ask her. Marriage had done nothing to mellow Jemima's temper or sweeten her expression, and Elizabeth was sorry to see it. She would have wished Jemima well for her mother's sake, as Martha Southern had been a good woman, as sweet as her daughter was sour. It seemed that Jemima had found a mother-in-law like herself, unwilling to be pleased, always ready to find fault.

The widow took no note of Jemima's unhappiness nor of Mrs. Gathercole's discomfort. She sat straight backed and disapproving as any queen thrust unexpectedly among her lowest subjects, her gaze flicking from one unwelcome sight to another.

Mariah Greber came up so that Nathaniel had to squeeze aside. She had her infant son in one arm and the youngest of her girls on her free hip. The girl presented herself to the world as a great tangle of hair and a mouth opened in a high-pitched howl.

"Can you stop up this gal's mouth with one of your doughnuts, Anna?" Mariah shoved the child over the counter. "Otherwise I'll have to drown her like a kitten and be done with it. I'll pay you just as soon as I can find Horace; he's over there someplace with Axel and the trappers. All I can say is, thank the good Lord Dr. Todd will stand no more than one measure of ale to a man."

Anna took the girl with a sympathetic cluck and Mariah disappeared in the direction of the trappers who stood with their heads bent together and shoulders hunched while they talked. The men who spent their lives in the bush were a solitary bunch and rarely came into the village, but news of free ale moved fast in the bush and was enough to make any of them walk ten miles.

The group parted and she caught sight of a big man in their center, a man with the expression of a slow child, dull and confused.

"Good God," she said, truly taken aback. "Look, Nathaniel. Dutch Ton, but with a clean face." She craned her head to see if she hadn't imagined the old trapper. "He hasn't been in the village for three or four years at least. I always forget how big he is until I see him again."

"He wouldn't be here now if he hadn't let me scrub him down with lye soap and a long-handled brush," said Anna, holding a cup of cider up to Charity Greber's pouting mouth. "There never was such a stench. Sticks to him like mud to a hog. Why, he had so much rancid bear fat in his hair and beard it took four soapings and half a gallon of turpentine to get rid of it all. I said to him, Ton, it ain't the bear fat that keeps the black-fly away from you, it's the pure stench, so I did, said it plain. But he just smiled. Then I burned his clothes and sold him a new set to wear. I expect he'll wear them till they fall to shreds on his back and then he'll wrap himself in an old bear pelt until he can find his way back here."

"I wonder if he's introduced himself to the widow," Nathaniel said. "I'm sure she'd like to make his acquaintance." Anna put her head back and laughed.

All the windows and doors stood open to the evening breeze, and children ran in and out, darting between legs and under tables. Cornelius Bump had climbed up on a barrel of salt fish to get a view of the room and he waved in Elizabeth's direction, his round head bobbing.

Many-Doves and Runs-from-Bears stood near the door, and with them Joshua and Daisy Hench and Curiosity and Galileo. As if they dared not come in any closer to the widow Kuick. Elizabeth pointed this out to Nathaniel and he raised his head to look just as the twins wiggled their way through the crowd to them.

"Pretty much everybody's here but the Todds and Hannah," said Daniel, hopping from one foot to the other with excitement. "Should I run and fetch them?"

"No need," said Anna, pointing with her chin at the door. "Here they are now."

In spite of all she had heard from Hannah and Curiosity about Kitty's condition, the sight of her was a shock. Elizabeth's sister-in-law had always been slender and pale, but now she seemed as frail as a woman of eighty years. And yet there was an air of contentment about her: her complexion was good, neither too sallow nor too high, and she smiled warmly and spoke to everyone who greeted her with real interest. She waved in Elizabeth's direction and called out.

"You must come by tomorrow and see our Meg!"

"There's a chance," Curiosity had said to Elizabeth. "That baby might be just what she needs to help her pull through. As long as she don't catch pregnant again."

Neither of them had said out loud what they were thinking: how would Richard Todd take to the idea that Kitty could not provide him with the children he wanted? To thwart Richard was to ask for trouble; this Elizabeth knew from personal experience. She studied him, but for the time being nothing unusual was to be seen in his expression.

He stepped up on a crate in the middle of the room and the crowd went suddenly quiet.

They're afraid of him. Elizabeth knew that, but it always amazed her again to see the proof of it. He was an impressive figure, there was no denying it. Richard had always been a big man but middle age and sedentary habits had added layers that made him more substantial still; whiskey had roughened his complexion and shortened his temper. A cantankerous old man in the making, Curiosity said of him, and Elizabeth saw the truth of that in the way he looked over the people of Paradise, as if they were unruly children who had earned a caning.

He raised one hand to silence the whispering at the back of the room.

"Glad to see there's enough common sense left in Paradise to get most of you here. Now I never have been a man for a lot of talk—" His head swung from one side of the room to the other, looking for somebody brave enough to disagree with him. Satisfied, he carried on.

"Let me call on the old folks here to start with. Many of you have lived through smallpox yourselves. Seen it kill whole families. I see faces here been carrying pox scars fifty years. Ain't that so, Goody Cunningham?"

The old lady nodded. "That's true. The pox took both my folks, and then it robbed me of what little beauty I called my own."

Muffled laughter rose up from the back of the room where some of the older boys stood together, and Richard turned a sharp eye in that direction. The sound died away abruptly.

He said, "It's been a long time since we saw smallpox in Paradise. Too long. The young ones don't know enough to be afraid of it and the middle-aged ones have forgot what it was like."

"I remember." Runs-from-Bears spoke up, his deep voice carrying through the room. "I remember watching my four brothers burn up with fever and die."

Richard paused again, and Elizabeth thought how good it was that the widow Kuick was behind him and he could not see her expression, outrage and disgust and plain disbelief.

He said, "Last summer the smallpox was in Johnstown, and this summer it could well be knocking on our door. Except now there's less reason to fear it, if you'll do what needs doing and not make a fuss about it.

"You all know Hannah Bonner. Born and raised right here in Paradise, and she's been in every one of your houses at some time or another, bringing you tea for your fevers or looking after your sick children. The grown-ups here will remember that both her grandmothers were rare healers in their own ways. For the past five years Hannah's been apprenticed to me and I think enough of her to have sent her down to the city to learn how to do these vaccinations against the smallpox.

"Now let me say one more thing before I ask her to explain all this to you. You'll pay attention to what she's got to say and you'll ask civil questions or you'll answer to me. When she's done explaining I'm going to roll up my shirtsleeves and let her vaccinate me right here for you to watch. She can vaccinate four people today, and I'll be looking for volunteers. Those of you who never had the pox all need to be vaccinated, most especially the children."

He looked around the room once again, as full of fire as any preacher. "Let me say this. If you don't let the children be vaccinated out of superstition or for some other fool reason, then it'll be on your own heads. I warned you."

Hannah stepped up on the crate next to Richard's. She was wearing one of the gowns Kitty had bought for her in the city, saffron-colored calico with clusters of red flowers and flowing vines. It was cut modestly over the breast but still it showed her figure to advantage. Standing next to Richard she looked tall and slender and serious with her hands folded in front of her, and Elizabeth felt herself near tears for no good reason at all. At her back she felt Nathaniel shudder, too, with the shock of a daughter turning from child to woman before their eyes.

Then Hannah smiled, such a warm and true smile that everybody in the room relaxed and smiled back, even old Isaac Cameron, who was easily the gruffest man ever put on the earth. Everybody except the widow Kuick and Jemima.

Hannah said, "I'm glad to be back home—"

From the back of the room Lily called out, "Well, it took you long enough!"

There was a murmur of laughter.

Hannah said, "Ethan, will you come up here, please?"

Richard got down from his crate and Ethan hopped up in his place.

"By God, that boy looks like his daddy," said Anna. "As if Julian was standing right there, Lord have mercy on his troubled soul."

Hannah helped Ethan pull his shirt over his head so that he stood before them with the linen clutched to his bare chest. He was browned by the sun, muscled in the way of young boys, sleek and unselfconscious and beautiful.

Hannah turned Ethan in a circle for the room to look at. "If you look closely you'll see that on each arm Ethan has a single blister. He was vaccinated eight days ago, the morning we left the city and started for home. It takes eight days for the blister to get to this stage, when it's ready to be lanced. What I'm going to do is to take the clear liquid from his blisters and rub a little of it into small cuts on the doctor's arms. Ethan, tell the folks here about your health for the last eight days."

The boy looked up at her as if the request mystified him. "Why, I've been fine, you know that, Hannah."

"No fever?" called out Missy Parker.

He shook his head.

Charlie LeBlanc stepped forward. "Now you tell us, boy, did it hurt when she cut you and rubbed that cow juice in?"

Ethan's chin tilted up. "It ain't cow juice, it came from a man called Mr. Jonas down in the city, from his blisters. And it didn't take much, just a little scratch. Nothing to get worked up about."

There was a snort of laughter from among the trappers.

Richard said, "Tom Book, if you got something to say, then say it."

"All right then," said the trapper. He had a dirty bandage over one eye and a crust of blood on his nose, and he blinked in the way of a man who has been looking at the bottom of an ale tankard for far too long.

"Let me see if I got this right," he began in the slow and arduous way of the truly intoxicated. "You're claiming that you put cowpox on that boy, and now he's never going to get sick hisself with smallpox." He snorted again and a bubble of blood appeared at his nostril. "It don't make sense no matter how you look at it. People ain't cows."

"It might not seem to make sense right now," Hannah said, "but I can tell you this. Nobody who's had this cowpox vaccination has ever come down with smallpox, though others around them have. Hundreds have been vaccinated here and in England. It's like this: your blood gets a taste of the pox—any kind of pox—and then it has what it needs to fight the sickness off after that. Folks here who had smallpox a long time ago, none of them have ever had it again, isn't that so?"

Gertrude Dubonnet said, "I nursed my brothers through it back in sixty-nine and caught it myself. Never come down with the pox again after that."

"That's why we only need to vaccinate people who've never had pox," Hannah said. "I was vaccinated as soon as I got to the city because I've never had it."

There was a lot of restless shifting in the room now, men's voices low and uneasy.

"Enough talk," said Richard. "Let's get on with this. Who's going to come up here now and stand next to me? Who's as brave as this boy?"

"I am!" called out the twins in one voice. They pushed their way to the middle of the room, with Blue-Jay and Kateri close behind. The Hench children followed, all four of them. Then the room went completely silent and nobody moved at all.

Richard crossed his arms and looked out over the crowd, his expression darkening. "Horace Greber, why don't I see any of your children up here? You think the pox won't like the look of them? What about you, Charlie? Jock? Jan Kaes, you got young grandchildren who need to be vaccinated."

There was an uneasy shifting and murmuring, and then Greber cleared his throat. "You said three or four vaccinations

today, Dr. Todd. Got more there than you can do already as
it is."

"So you'll have your children right here in eight days' time
to be vaccinated, then. Is that right?"

Greber tilted his head up at him and squinted. "Well,
maybe. If none of the ones she pokes today fall over dead or
grow horns and a tail."

There was a ripple of laughter in the room. Nathaniel
tensed, and Elizabeth squeezed his hand hard to remind him of
their agreement: this was Hannah's business, and they would
leave it to her.

It was Ethan who spoke up first.

"I didn't fall over dead, Mr. Greber. None of your girls will
either. And I'll drop my breeches to prove I haven't grown a
tail if you want to have a look for yourself."

An outraged sound rose above the laughter as the widow
Kuick pushed her way out of the crowd of people at the back
of the room, her heels rapping on the plank floor. In her dusty
black silk and black shawl she looked like an agitated crow.

"Foolish boy to speak to your elders thus! Irresponsible parents to allow it." She sent Kitty Todd a look that might have
caused her to faint, if she had not at that moment been looking
to her husband.

"Now, Widow—" Richard began, and she cut him off with
a chop of her hand.

"You will let me finish, sir! Mr. Greber shows more common sense than you do, Dr. Todd. No thinking person in this
village is going to let that—that—Mohawk woman take a
knife to them or to their children, and I'm surprised at you for
suggesting such a thing. Infecting people with filth taken from
a cow. What kind of godless foolery is this?"

A trapper Elizabeth did not recognize shouted, "I say keep
the white children out of this. Let the colored do what they
want, a little cow shit won't hurt them anyway."

Elizabeth kept her attention on Hannah, who had not
flinched once while the widow talked. Standing above the
crowd on her crate she was serene and unsurprised; she had been
prepared for a scene like this.

It was Richard who shouted for silence, and they gave it to
him reluctantly.

"Mrs. Kuick," he said, barely restraining his anger. "Step

aside if you don't want to be vaccinated and leave the rest of us
to do as we see fit."

"I will not!" She had flushed such a deep color that the tip
of her nose looked almost blue. "I will not stand by and watch
such an abomination happen before my eyes. And I will not do
business with anyone who lets themselves be seduced into this
godlessness!"

She looked around the room, her head jerking from face to
face so that the soft wattles of flesh at her jaw trembled. The silence drew out and out, and little by little her expression quieted and something of satisfaction took its place.

"You begin to see reason," she said, drawing her shawl more
closely around her shoulders. "You see, Doctor. The good people of Paradise know a witch"—she looked over her shoulder at
Hannah and shuddered—"when they see one."

For a moment, Elizabeth thought that Nathaniel would not
be able to hold himself back, and with a curious kind of de-
tachment she wondered if he or Richard would reach the
widow first. Then a voice rose up, strong and sure, from the
crowd.

"I'll be vaccinated. Me and my sister both." Nicholas Wilde
held up a hand, and the color that had begun to fade from the
widow's face sprang back again.

"I'll step up too," Axel Metzler shouted out, and in his agi-
tation his English began to slide toward his native German.
"Bei Gott und Himmel, listen to me, all of youse. If little
Hannah Bonner—who never did nothing but help folks—if
Hannah is a witch, then I'm Tommy Goddamn Jefferson."

Voices rose up from all over the room, some louder than
others.

Jed McGarrity said, "My Jane ain't ever had the pox. I'd like
her to step up too, although she's fourteen already and can decide for herself."

Jane McGarrity was Elizabeth's oldest student and of the
girls the most difficult, but she was proud of her complexion
and protective of her beauty. She was also one of the many
young women with an eye on Nicholas Wilde. "I'll come up if
my pa wants me to," she said, ducking her head and blushing
prettily.

Old Isaac Cameron thumped the floor planks with his cane
until he had everyone's attention. Then he pushed his way to

stand in the middle of the room, between Richard and the widow. "I ain't been a boy for seventy years." He raised his hoarse and cracking voice to a high wobble. "Never had the pox, but all my years I have lived in fear of it. I seen what it does, and I don't care to ever see it again, specially not when I pick up a looking glass. It's an ugly old mug, by God, but it's mine and I like it the way it is." He rubbed a hand over his freckled pate and then he grinned up at Hannah.

"Come on down here and scratch me, missy. I expect I'll take a little cow spunk without fainting." He craned his head to look at the trappers. "Worse than women, all of you."

The widow said, "Mr. Cameron, you forget—"

The old man poked his cane in her direction and she stepped back, her hands pressed to her heart.

"Now don't you go shouting at me, Lucy Kuick, you old harridan. Maybe you got other folks around here so scairt that they don't dare speak their minds but I'm too old to put up with your bitching, mill or no mill. If I want to let Hannah Bonner victualize me then that's exactly what I'll do. If you're set on a throwing fit you'll find a pile of them fancy chamber pots with flowers painted on the inside over there. See how hard you can toss one of those, we'll get a little wager going."

The widow's red-rimmed eyelids fluttered, but she held on to her composure. "Mr. Gathercole, are you going to allow him to speak to me that way?"

"Don't go looking to the preacher for help." Cameron wagged his head. "You got something to say to me then say it, woman."

"Very well, then," said the widow. "You'll burn in hell for this." She had control of her voice, if not her complexion. She was speaking to Cameron, but her gaze was fixed on Hannah.

"Maybe I will," said the old man, and he grinned wide enough to show off three lone teeth the color of aged oak. "Maybe so. But there's lots of reasons to burn, Lucy. We each of us seek out the one that suits us best."

In the end they had to draw lots to see who would be vaccinated first, and so Nicholas Wilde, Jane McGarrity, and Solange Hench stood in a row with the doctor while Hannah and Curiosity set to work. Enough people had marched out of the trading post behind the widow Kuick that there was space enough for everyone who was interested to come up close and watch.

Elizabeth and Nathaniel stayed back at the counter with Anna, who could hardly hide her troubled expression.

"What about you folks?" she asked finally. "Aren't you going to step up too?"

Elizabeth caught Nathaniel's eye, and when he nodded his agreement she slipped the sleeve of her gown off her shoulder and showed Anna her upper arm.

"Hannah brought some of the serum back with her in a glass vial," she said. "As she wasn't sure that it would still be effective she vaccinated all of us with it. If it doesn't take then we will have to be vaccinated again with fresh serum."

"But the Lake in the Clouds children marched right up there like they was ready to get scratched," Anna said. "Does it need doing more than once?"

Nathaniel said, "Once is enough if it takes, but our two've got more loyalty than good sense. If Hannah claimed she could sew on heads as good as new, they'd be first in line at the guillotine just to prove her right."

"So all the Hidden Wolf folks have got scratched then," Anna said thoughtfully. "I guess that explains why they left so quick. Right after the widow."

"Anna, what's got you worried?" said Nathaniel. He leaned toward her across the counter. "That we got vaccinated first or that we got vaccinated at all?"

Elizabeth had always known Anna to be as thoughtful as she was plainspoken; the fact that she could hardly meet Nathaniel's eye was unsettling.

Finally she said, "I suppose then it makes sense that your Mohawk kin will be coming by to get vaccinated too. Not that it matters if they do, you understand. They get the pox like anybody else. Worse, it seems like. My only worry is that the widow Kuick is looking for any excuse to stir up trouble after that slave got away . . ." Her voice trailed off.

"What have you heard?" Nathaniel's tone was calm, but the muscles in his jaw flexed.

"Dye has been talking," she said. "To the men in the tavern, two, three nights a week when he never used to show his face at all. Like he wants to see how much trouble there is to be made." Her voice trailed off apologetically.

"Anna, please just tell us what you know," Elizabeth said quietly.

Anna pushed out a great rush of air and lowered her voice to a whisper that Elizabeth could barely make out. "I don't know much at all, but I heard some things. There's a rumor going around that there's a new child at Lake in the Clouds. A black child, appeared out of nowhere."

Elizabeth drew a deep breath and then another one. She cast a glance in Curiosity's direction, hoping that for the moment at least she would be spared the knowledge that Selah's son was no longer so safe as he had been.

Nathaniel said, "And if there was such a child?"

Anna shrugged. "All Dye wants to talk about is that runaway that nobody could catch. You remember which one I mean? The poster was up here for a while. Liam Kirby said he tracked her to Hidden Wolf but then his dogs lost the trail and he gave up." She hesitated, and looking in Hannah's direction, she lowered her voice even further to a rough whisper.

"Me, I think that Kirby's giving up maybe had more to do with your Hannah leaving for the city. I've got eyes in my head and I know you do too." She paused and looked around once again. "But the fact is, he never did get that slave. Maybe you heard tell that the man she run from was Dye's brother-in-law. She killed him, but she still belongs by law to the wife. Dye's sister."

Nathaniel nodded. "So they say."

Elizabeth wondered at her husband, that he could sound so detached, as if Selah were still among the living. Which she must be still, to the men who were looking for her and her child.

"Well, she run off pregnant," Anna finished slowly.

"And Dye thinks that the runaway left her child behind on Hidden Wolf?"

"No," said Anna, frowning at Nathaniel as if he were a bright child playing at ignorance. "The point is, if there's a child, it don't belong to the runaway. It belongs to Dye's sister."

There was a moment's pause, and in that space the sound of Richard Todd's voice and then Hannah's, not quite an argument but always on the edge of one: the usual sharp back-and-forth that both of them seemed to need, if not enjoy. Nathaniel ran a hand down Elizabeth's arm and threaded his fingers through hers. She was glad of his touch, and leaned into him.

"The whole thing seems pretty unlikely," Nathaniel said.

"That's what I told him," Anna said, more eagerly. "But he's worked up. Looking for any excuse to go poking around the mountain. Which is why I asked about the Indians coming to Hidden Wolf to be vaccinated. You know how Dye is about anybody with red skin. And the widow's even worse."

"What even gave you such an idea that the Mohawk would come to be vaccinated?" Elizabeth asked, trying very hard to keep her voice calm.

Anna's round, plain face came up suddenly, the brow creased in confusion. "Why, because two Indians I don't know are out on the porch now with Many-Doves and Bears. Didn't you see them at the door a few minutes ago?"

Nathaniel had walked off before the last words were out of Anna's mouth, with Elizabeth close behind.

The doctors at the Almshouse had trained Hannah well; she could answer all his questions while she went through the vaccination procedure, and not lose her concentration or her temper. She was glad of that training now, because Richard Todd questioned her every move, and insisted on full answers about each step before he'd let her continue to the next. He was familiar already with the procedure and so Hannah understood that his questions were not for her, but for Nicholas Wilde and the others who watched closely and listened. If they understood, if they accepted, then the rest of the village would come around eventually.

Nicholas Wilde rolled up his sleeves when his turn came and kept his face turned away from Hannah while she worked, but color crept up his neck and his breathing quickened. With one part of her mind Hannah understood that this was something other than fear, but there was no time to consider why Nicholas Wilde's heart beat so fast.

When she had finished with him he thanked Hannah politely without looking her in the eye, and left. Jane McGarrity watched him go with an expression that was many things all at once: longing, disappointment, sullen resignation. Then she jiggled impatiently until Hannah was finished with her.

Solange was the youngest and the last to be vaccinated, and

she had questions to ask too, one after the other while she eyed the lancet with growing concern.

"You chatter like a squirrel, child," Curiosity said in a calm voice to her granddaughter. "There's no call to be so worried. You saw how easy it goes."

"If I can stand it so can you," Ethan offered, and Solange flashed him an insulted look.

"Just close your mouth for a minute and breathe deep," Hannah said, and she made the first small incision. In practiced motions she accepted the last ivory vaccinator from Curiosity and spread the serum over the cuts. She had just picked up the lancet to make the incisions on Solange's other arm when the girl straightened suddenly and she leaned away.

"Who's that?"

"Don't try to distract us now," Curiosity said, more sharply this time. "Let Hannah finish, it won't take but a minute."

"I'm not trying to distract you," Solange wailed just as Ethan said, "Hannah, do you know those Indians?"

Hannah finished with the lancet and the vaccinator before she looked over her shoulder. Her father and stepmother were standing just outside the door, and with them were two men she had never seen before.

"They aren't Mohawk," said Ethan, craning his neck. "At least they don't dress like Bears or Nathaniel."

Just at that moment the taller of the two turned to look in the door.

A stranger, a Seneca by his dress, and possibly the most frightening human being Hannah had ever seen. It was not so much his size—the men of her own family were as tall and strongly built—or his features, which were pleasant enough but unremarkable. It was the expression in his eyes, cold and sharp and alive. *Like a panther hunting,* Hannah thought. His head had been shaved for war, leaving behind a long scalplock at the crown. A single hawk feather dangled from the rawhide tie, coming to rest behind a small ear pierced with three silver studs.

The stranger caught her gaze and he stilled, muscles tensed.

Solange hiccuped her distress, the sting of the lancet forgotten. "Look, Grandma," she whispered. "Don't that look like the meanest man you ever saw?"

"Little girl, you hush," said Curiosity. "Cain't tell nothing about a man from the look of him. I hope you ain't going to be one of those people who cain't see the roses for the thorns, missy."

Grumpily Solange said, "He don't look much like roses to me. Not to Hannah either, the way she's looking at him."

Then the stranger smiled. He smiled at Hannah and at Hannah alone, and just that simply, everything changed.

"See now," Curiosity said softly. "See?"

Eager to find out more about the strangers, Ethan and Solange flew out the door without a word of farewell, leaving Hannah and Curiosity alone for a moment in the trading post. From the open door to the tavern came the sound of Anna's voice as she pressed the last of her doughnuts on the men who had stayed behind to debate the good and bad of being vaccinated. Hannah wiped her lancet three times before she closed it into the instrument case, and she listened to the other conversation, the one that was taking place on the porch.

The men were doing most of the talking: *He-Makes-Them-Ready,* and *hungry,* and *how many years?*

"What are you waiting for?" Curiosity pushed her gently. "Go on now, they'll come looking for you next."

"Who?" Hannah said, "Who are they?"

"Don't know that young man who came to the door to look at you," Curiosity said. "But that other voice I hear you should recognize yourself, girl. I know it's been more than a few years but I hope you know your uncle Otter's voice when you hear it."

For once Lily Bonner was happy to put aside her drawings and run errands. She ran with her brother and Blue-Jay all the way home; she ran to tell Pines-Rustling the good news; she ran to draw water and to stir the coals in the hearth; she ran about in the cabin from workroom to table to hearth and back again. There was soup to warm for the travelers and cold meat and bread to get ready. The boys were hard at work stacking firewood out in the clearing between the two cabins; tonight they would have a real fire, a Kahnyen'kehàka fire. Because Strong-Words—whose boy-name had been Otter—had come home from the west, and brought a friend with him.

Many-Doves had been so happy to see her youngest brother that she had cried out. All the women, even Lily's mother, even

Hannah, had not been able to hold back tears; the men cleared their throats and thumped each other on the back and spoke too loud saying very little at all.

This morning—it seemed so long ago she could hardly believe it was true—Reuben had been buried and she had been so angry to be left behind; now she could hardly stop smiling, because there was a homecoming to celebrate. There would be stories around the fire, more stories even than Hannah and Ethan had brought from the city. Strong-Words had been gone a very long time, and he must tell it all.

Lily had heard many things about this mysterious uncle. Her mother held him in great regard because he had helped her once when she had been in the deepest despair, and alone. Lily knew about the time Grandfather had gone to Canada to fetch Strong-Words home and ended up in gaol for his efforts. She knew Strong-Words' temper had gotten him and everyone else in trouble; she had heard whispered stories she was not supposed to hear about Strong-Words shooting at Uncle Todd. This was something she didn't understand at all; Uncle Todd could be mean and he was always cranky, but there must be something else in the past that no one wanted to tell her, most probably something that happened long ago in the time of the wars.

Once Lily had asked her father when she would be old enough to hear the whole story and he had given her the look that was both thoughtful and a little irritated and told her that twenty years or so would do it. It was not the answer she wanted but she knew that pushing would do no good at all.

Mostly Strong-Words was known, here and at Good Pasture, as a storyteller. And he had brought his brother-in-law, a Seneca called Strikes-the-Sky who had fought with him in the wars waged on the western frontier. Maybe they had taken scalps; maybe they would tell about it, something Lily's father and grandfather would never do; about this she knew better than to ask. Even Daniel and Blue-Jay didn't ask about such things, and when they included them in their games they made sure to be well out of hearing of the men.

The soup was just hot enough when Lily heard her father's familiar owl call. The boys ran with her to meet them while Pines-Rustling waited on the porch with the babies. Their people came out of the woods, Kateri riding on her father's shoulders, all of them smiling.

In the last of the summer-evening light they came into the glen. At the bottom of the lake under the falls Strong-Words stopped, held up his rifle high, and let out a high yipping call that echoed up the cliffs and back again.

In the crook of Pines-Rustling's arm little Galileo mewled and cried.

"It's all right," said Blue-Jay to the baby. "It's just Strong-Words telling the spirit of the mountain that he is home again."

There was as much food as they could cook on short notice and a fire as high as a man, stories and laughter and voices raised in friendly disagreement. Lily was so happy that she could hardly sit still; she wandered from her mother's lap to her father's, from Grandfather to Runs-from-Bears and started all over again.

Strikes-the-Sky sat quietly, eating and talking when someone asked him a question but mostly staying out of family talk. After half an hour of watching him Lily knew a few things, even if she didn't know how to feel about them.

The first thing was simple enough: Strikes-the-Sky was the handsomest man she had ever seen next to her own father. She couldn't say why he was handsome, if it was in his nose or the set of his eyes or his brow or chin, but he was. The strangest part of it was that he had two faces, the serious one that he wore like a mask, and the real one, when he smiled. Both of the faces were beautiful and frightening too: the serious face made a person want to run away, and the real face made the same person run right back. Like a fire burning too hot on a cold night, when a person needed to hover near but could hardly stand the heat.

The second thing was harder, but just as clear to see. Strikes-the-Sky had come to claim her sister Hannah—no, that wasn't right. He had come to claim her sister Walks-Ahead for himself. Lily wasn't sure when he had got that idea—maybe he had come all the way from Seneca country for no other purpose. Or maybe he had just realized himself that Hannah was the reason he was here.

Not that he said anything of the kind; nobody did, but it was true anyway. While he ate or listened or answered questions, Strikes-the-Sky watched Hannah. He watched her like other men watched her, as if he had come across some unexpected treasure that would disappear if he dared to look away. The difference this time was that Hannah was watching him too.

Hannah meant to hide it, but she couldn't do that any more than she could grab the stars out of the sky and hide them in her pocket. It shone on her face as bright as any moon, and everybody saw it. The women first, who exchanged glances and then soft smiles; then Grandfather and Strong-Words, then Runs-from-Bears, who whispered something to Many-Doves and got elbowed for his trouble. Then finally Lily's father, whose face went very still and serious.

"Come help me get water." Daniel pulled at Lily's arm roughly.

"It's your turn," she said to him, unwilling to look away from Strikes-the-Sky, who was unwilling to look away from Hannah. "You do it."

"Come now," Daniel insisted, and Lily gave in finally and went off in the dark with her brother. Blue-Jay was waiting for them.

"What is it?" Lily said, glancing back at the fire over her shoulder.

"You know what it is," Daniel said impatiently. "Look at the way he's staring at Hannah."

"He can look if he wants to," Lily said, a little sullenly. She wasn't sure how she felt about Strikes-the-Sky, and she didn't much like being forced so quickly into taking sides. "What does it matter if he looks?"

Daniel's mouth narrowed down, the way it always did when he wanted something but couldn't think of a way to get it. From that Lily knew that her brother and Blue-Jay had been arguing about Strikes-the-Sky for a while. If Blue-Jay were willing to go along with whatever plan Daniel had in mind, he wouldn't have come to get her in the first place.

"They are looking at each other," said Blue-Jay. "You can't stop that once it's started."

"And everybody's watching them look," added Lily. "That doesn't help either."

"It's like a lightning strike," said Blue-Jay to Daniel, whose expression was growing darker with every word. "My father says it happens that way sometimes between a man and a woman. It happened that way between your mother and father."

Daniel gave Blue-Jay a furious look and stomped off into the dark. He would be gone until he had figured out a better argument, or learned to see things differently.

Lily didn't follow her brother. She stood with Blue-Jay while watching the scene around the fire, an easy quiet between them. They watched the grown-ups moving around and listened to the voices that came to them over the sound of the waterfalls, serious now as Strong-Words and Strikes-the-Sky took turns telling about the wars to the west. *They push,* Lily heard Strong-Words say very clearly. And, *they will never stop pushing.*

Blue-Jay's dark eyes shone eager in the dark as he listened. He was like every boy and man Lily knew: war stories made him spark like flint. Ready to catch fire; willing to burn. Lily did not understand it.

Strikes-the-Sky stood and the firelight threw his shadow up into the heavens. He was straight and strong, and Lily's fingers itched for a pencil to see if she could catch the truth of him, put his spirit down on paper. Then when she was an old woman she would look at that paper to remind her of this night when she knew that it was really going to happen: Hannah would go from them soon, to start her own family.

She said, "Maybe he will want to stay here with us."

Blue-Jay made a sound deep in his throat. "He will want to take Walks-Ahead away," he said quietly. "To the west, to his people."

"She might not want to go," Lily said, more firmly. "She doesn't have to go if she doesn't want to. My father won't like it." And then another thought came to her, one that was even more unsettling. What if she didn't go alone? What if Strong-Words' stories of the west were enough to make Many-Doves and Runs-from-Bears pack up their family and go too?

She touched Blue-Jay's arm lightly, and he looked down at her. Lily opened her mouth and shut it again. Then she said: "It's like standing on the edge of a cliff."

Blue-Jay said nothing at all, because he understood her without a lot of talk; he knew exactly what she was thinking. And because she was right.

Chapter 35

———

June 16

Hannah woke with a start just before dawn, agitated and alert, as if someone had chased her out of her dreams and into the waking world. She pressed a hand to her racing heart and reached for the dream, but it was already gone. Waiting for her to come back to bed, like a lover. She shook her head to clear it of that unwelcome and unsettling image.

Then she remembered that Strong-Words had come home. He was her uncle, but as a child she had always thought of him more as an older brother. Then he had been a boy called Otter, and he had taught her how to dive into the lake under the falls and showed her secret places on the mountain. He had taken her hunting with him when she was hardly old enough to skin a rabbit; it was Strong-Words who taught her many of the Kahnyen'kehàka stories that she now told in her turn to the young ones.

He had come home to tell new stories, of the Seneca and the Shawnee and the Battle at Fallen Timbers, where he had first met Strikes-the-Sky, two years older but war-tested. He had left here as Otter with nothing but his weapons, and come home a husband, a father, a leader of warriors. A stranger to her, in ways she had never imagined when she was a little girl and her family had seemed as steady and constant as the mountain itself.

And he had brought Strikes-the-Sky with him, who looked at her and made her want to look back.

She was used to the way that white men stared at her; her

long weeks in the city had resigned her to the fact that she must learn to live with these stares that no white woman would tolerate. She ignored them, or when she could not, she had learned to say the words that would make most men turn away. Some had the sense to be embarrassed; others hid their discomfort with anger.

Things were the same when she was among her mother's people at Good Pasture: men studied her. The looks they sent her way were more disturbing, because they were strangely pleasing to her.

The young men at Good Pasture wanted her, yes. They wanted her for her body and her face and her voice, as the white men did, but to the Mohawk she was no mystery. They knew her as a healer; they knew her as a good daughter and sister. They knew that she was the granddaughter of Falling-Day, and the great-granddaughter of Made-of-Bones. They might want to touch her, but there was more to it: they looked at her and thought not only of the feel of her but of the line of strong women she came from. Because she was strong too, and that did not frighten the men at Good Pasture.

Last year at the Midwinter Ceremony a young man of the Turtle longhouse, a young man braver than the rest, had asked her to go walking, to dance so that he could watch her, to come in turn and watch him play baggataway; he would have put his blanket around her shoulders when his team won, if she had come close enough to let him. She had liked him for his simple good manners and the way he laughed so easily, and so she had sometimes gone walking with him.

When he had waited long enough Hannah let him draw her into the shadows and touch her face and kiss her shyly; she had moved away before she could learn the taste of him. When she left Good Pasture to come home to Lake in the Clouds, she had not thought much about him. At night when she woke from unfamiliar dreams that made her body twitch in unfamiliar ways, she remembered the shape of his mouth alone.

In the spring his mother had sent a corn cake to Many-Doves and a question: when would they come back to Good Pasture? There were things she wanted to discuss. It was the old way of starting the marriage negotiations, and that pleased Many-Doves. Hannah was surprised and flattered in a way she could not deny, but most of all she was unsettled.

Once Many-Doves saw that Hannah had not expected the gesture and did not welcome it, she sent the offering back with Spotted-Fox, who had stopped on Hidden Wolf on his way to trade furs in Albany. To Hannah's relief, Many-Doves had not told anyone at Lake in the Clouds about any of it, not even Runs-from-Bears or Elizabeth. Hannah did not need to explain, or even to think about it anymore. The truth was, she could hardly remember what Walking-Elk had looked like.

Not even a day ago she had seen Strikes-the-Sky for the first time, and she knew already that she would never forget his face.

She could go to Many-Doves and ask her what to do; that was the way these things were handled. She could ask Elizabeth, who would listen quietly and give her good advice. But the idea of speaking out loud what she was feeling made Hannah so anxious that she had to get out of bed.

On the table she saw the neat pile of her daybook and the vaccination records she had begun last night, and that reminded her that Dr. Todd was expecting her this morning. There was work in the laboratory, the notes from his autopsy of Gabriel Oak for her to read, and he wanted to go over the rest of the notes from the Kine-Pox Institution with her.

She was hungry, but Curiosity would feed her. Hannah dressed quickly, smoothed her plaits, packed a basket with the things she would need, and slipped out of the cabin.

Otter and Strikes-the-Sky had put down their pallets on Many-Doves' porch, and Hannah could not help but notice that they were already gone. They might be swimming under the falls, or in the caves or any one of a hundred places on the mountain. She swallowed her curiosity and trotted most of the way to the village.

The Todds' kitchen was empty but for Bump, who was finishing his porridge. He smiled broadly to see her and raised a hand in greeting. Perched up on a stool he reminded her of a robin; he was wearing a faded red waistcoat and his head bobbed as he ate. "You're early this morning, Miss Hannah."

"Yes, well . . ." Her voice trailed off, and she felt herself smiling awkwardly. It wasn't that she was at a loss for words, but that she had the strongest urge to tell Bump about Strikes-the-Sky. There was something about the old man that made her want to talk, as if he were a chest with a sturdy lock, a safe place to put all the dangerous ideas that wanted to tumble out of her mouth.

He must see her discomfort, but he seemed determined to put her at her ease. Bump hopped down to the floor and pulled out the cap he had tucked under his wide belt.

"I'm off to stoke the furnace in the laboratory. If you want to come along the doctor will follow in a few minutes. Unless you were wanting to give Mrs. Freeman the news from Lake in the Clouds first?"

The house was full of early morning sounds: Curiosity in the dining room talking to the doctor; Dolly singing softly as she swept the hall. Outside the thunk of an axe, and the slow heavy song of a dove. Somewhere upstairs the baby cried and was quieted. While Hannah listened to all of this Bump watched her, his eyes kind and still sharp under the tangle of eyebrows.

"You know about our visitors, then," she said.

"Oh, ayuh. I expect everybody's heard by now. The story grows like a beanstalk in the July sun. Down to the tavern they'll be saying your uncle brought a dozen warriors with him all hung about with scalps and looking for more. Men who are fond of their ale like to dig up a little trouble now and then."

"I fear you are right," Hannah said, suddenly more comfortable in this conversation than she could have ever imagined.

"Look at it this way, Friend Hannah." Bump hitched his way across the room to the door. "It gives them something to worry over besides your smallpox vaccinations."

He went out into the kitchen garden and Hannah followed him. The smell of lavender in bloom hung sweet in air so still and clear that she could count the trees on the highest ridge. Behind her she heard Curiosity come into the kitchen, the clatter of dishes, a few words exchanged with Dolly, short and sharp and not like Curiosity at all.

Hannah thought of Reuben's burial for the first time since she had first set eyes on Strikes-the-Sky. She was embarrassed to have let him put everything else out of her mind.

She let Bump go ahead, and went back into the kitchen and to Curiosity.

"Did you get any sleep at all?" Hannah stood across the table from Curiosity. There were deep circles under her eyes and a weariness there that went beyond grief.

"Not too much," she admitted. "I told that Dutchified nursemaid not to eat pickled cabbage, but did she listen?"

"But Curiosity, she doesn't speak English," Hannah said, something she had pointed out many times, so far without any success at getting her message across.

Curiosity waved a hand in dismissal. "Hmmpf. Seem to me like she understand more than she let on. In any case she went and ate the last of that cabbage and her milk went sour and gave that child a bellyache. Ain't none of us got much sleep. Except the doctor, of course. That man could sleep through the last trumpet." She said this with no malice at all, as if she admired Richard's talent for shutting out the world, and expected nothing else of him.

"How's our Leo this morning?" Curiosity finished, brightening a little with the change in subject. "Or maybe you don't know. Look like you rushed on down the mountain in a hurry if you got here before Richard finished his breakfast."

Hannah reached for a biscuit from the platter and broke it in half. "I didn't have a chance to look in, but he was well last night."

"Never mind," said Curiosity with a yawn. "Now that I don't have to go nurse Reuben I can ride up straightaway this morning. Got to get the baby ready to go anyway. Galileo will be ready to travel by dinnertime."

Hannah swallowed the last of the biscuit and took another. "Go? Go where?"

Curiosity had turned to put more wood on the fire, and she looked over her shoulder with an expression that was more impatience than anything else.

"We got to get young Leo away right quick. Would have done it last week if it weren't for Reuben. We're going to take him to Polly in Albany; she still nursing her youngest and nobody will take no note of another black baby in a city that big."

"This is about Ambrose Dye, then."

Curiosity pulled a kerchief from her sleeve to wipe her face. "It is indeed. I'll kill the man myself before I let him put hands on that child. Lake in the Clouds just ain't safe enough, not now."

"Curiosity—" Hannah started and then stopped herself. Any promises she might offer would sound hollow and trite and she could not even believe them herself.

She said, "I hadn't thought it through."

The older woman grunted softly. "Look like that visitor already drove everything else out of your head."

That prickled, but Hannah tried to keep a calm expression. "That is not fair."

The older woman blinked hard. Then she pushed out a great breath and pulled in another one. "Maybe so. You'll just have to forgive me, Hannah. I ain't quite myself."

She sat down heavily on a stool, and Hannah rounded the table to touch Curiosity's brow with the back of her hand. Her skin was cool and damp; the calico wrapped around her head was wet through with perspiration.

"You've been pushing yourself very hard," Hannah said. "You'll get sick next and then we'll be forced to tie you to your bed."

Curiosity gave her a half-smile. "Sometime it do seem like the whole world come down on a body all at once. But I'll rest easier when the boy is safe away from the widow's overseer."

An image of Ambrose Dye came to Hannah, looking down at Reuben's coffin with an expression empty of all emotion. He had known the boy since birth, watched him grow, seen him with his mother and brothers, heard him laughing, and still his death had seemed to touch him less than the loss of a hunting dog.

We regret the senseless accident that sent Reuben too early to his reward. That hard voice, so harsh and wooden, as if he were reading words from a page put down in a language he didn't understand. Words meant to dampen the fire, but instead he had breathed new life into it. It smoldered all around them.

Hannah said, "Of course you have to take him away. How long will you be gone?"

"A week at the most. It's been a good while since we seen Polly and her children. Richard and Kitty will just have to make do while we gone. Kitty needs some watching, but she doing better than I expected and Richard's got an eye on her..." Her voice trailed off. It was unlike Curiosity, this hesitant tone.

"You only have to ask," Hannah said.

Curiosity blinked, as if she had forgot Hannah standing right in front of her. "It's Cookie I'm worried about, but I don't know that anybody can do anything about it if she get it in her head to go after Dye. My Galileo was the best chance, but she won't even look at him when he talk to her." She shook her head. "I suppose the only thing you can do is keep your eyes open wide and watch. If something should start to happen, why then the best thing would be to send your daddy or your grand-daddy down as a witness; that way Dye can't overreach himself so easy. And stay clear of the overseer yourself, child. You understand why I'm telling you that?"

Hannah nodded. "I do."

"Well, then, I done all that I can." Curiosity pushed herself up and spread her hands over her apron to smooth it.

"Now tell me about the homecoming last night. It sure was good to see young Otter, though I will admit it was a surprise to see him all growed up. He got himself a family?"

Hannah told Strong-Words' story as best she could, from his early travels west to the Seneca woman who had chosen him as her husband and given him four children, the last just before her uncle started off on his trip east.

"I can see how they'd give him a man-name like Strong-Words," Curiosity said. "But I still cain't imagine that boy I used to know as a man with a family to look after. He ain't changed that much from what I hear. This Stirs-the-Wind has got to be a strong woman if she can take on Otter—I mean Strong-Words—and four youngsters too. And three of them boys." She snorted a little laugh. "That's a woman I'd like to meet someday. Now tell me about that friend Strong-Words brung along with him, his brother-in-law I think he said. What's his name?"

"Strikes-the-Sky." Hannah's voice faltered, because she could think of not one thing to say that wouldn't open up the subject she feared above all others.

"And just why did he come along?"

Hannah shrugged. "He hasn't said, and neither has Strong-Words."

"Some things plain enough without talking," said Curiosity. "Look like Strong-Words has took up matchmaking. Brought you home a husband."

Hannah bit back the words that wanted to spill out of her. Instead she said, "If that's what he had in mind he'll be disappointed. And why would you think such a thing anyway?"

She disliked the slightly frantic tone of her own voice, and even more than that she disliked the way Curiosity was looking at her, as if Hannah were a child hiding a piece of gingerbread behind her back and lying about it with crumbs on her face.

"Hold on there," Curiosity said softly. "No cause to get angry. I'm just saying that I saw some things. I saw the way that man was looking at you. And I saw the way you was looking back at him too."

The biscuit crumpled in Hannah's fist, and she busied herself brushing the crumbs away to the floor, where the cat wound around her ankles waiting for just such a windfall. When she could talk again she said, "You're imagining things, Curiosity. There's nothing to see."

Curiosity cocked her head to one side and pursed her mouth; it was an expression that Hannah knew well, one that meant she was holding something back. Finally she came over to Hannah and hugged her very hard.

Hannah was surprised, as she always was, at the strength in Curiosity's thin arms and the comfort they provided. She relaxed a little against the older woman. She had long outgrown Curiosity's lap but it was almost as good to stand here in the kitchen with her and take her ease.

Hannah said, "I'm sorry, I shouldn't have snapped at you."

"Shhhh," Curiosity said, pulling back a little to look her in the eye.

"There really is nothing to tell you about Strikes-the-Sky," Hannah added, more gently.

Curiosity smiled. She said, "A hole ain't nothing either, but you can still break your neck in it."

Hannah let out a thin laugh.

The older woman said, "You give that man a chance, now, you hear me? Don't go turning away before you hear what he got to say."

"Yes, all right. I'll try."

Curiosity shook her head so hard that her turban wobbled a little. "You surely are a piece of work. Don't try, child. Do it. No reason to look so embarrassed either. You don't want to spend your whole life looking after our bumps and scratches, do you? The time come to think about raising up a family of your own. A man can be a comfort sometimes, when he ain't feeling ornery." She grinned a little, her old sharp grin.

"Elizabeth didn't come to that conclusion until she was ten

years older than I am now." Hannah winced to hear her own petulant tone, but Curiosity only laughed.

"Age don't got nothing to do with it, and you know it. If Elizabeth and your daddy had come across each other when she was fifteen they'd have ended up together back then. Now maybe you're trying to tell me that young man ain't the right one, and if that's so why then you don't need to make no excuses. Send him on his way. That what you want?"

Hannah leaned against the door, crossed her arms across her chest, and dropped her chin to fight tears that threatened to spring up so suddenly and uninvited.

"He's a stranger. I've spent a total of six hours in his company in a crowd of people, and last night my little brother pulled me aside to say that he would give me his permission to go west with Strikes-the-Sky if I promise to come home to visit every year. My little brother has me married off already and I haven't even spent an hour alone with the man. I don't understand how something like this can happen from one day to the next."

"Something like what?" Curiosity asked softly.

Hannah shook her head because she dared not speak, and slipped out the door.

When Jemima Kuick answered the knock at the widow's parlor door just after dinner to find Hawkeye standing there, she was struck pure dumb. Two ideas came to her, neither of them good. The first was that the twins had finally told their story, and Hawkeye was here for her; the second, far less frightening, was that he had figured out how Reuben had got burned, and he had come to accuse Dye of murder. She wouldn't mind the idea of Dye hanging, if it weren't for the fact that when the whole truth came out Isaiah might end up right next to him.

Hawkeye said, "Well, Mima, ain't you going to invite me in?" He didn't smile but he didn't look angry either, which meant he wasn't here about the twins and what had happened the afternoon at Eagle Rock when Lily fell.

At the sound of his voice the widow's head snapped up sharply. "Mr. Bonner," she said in her haughtiest tone. "What do you mean, coming here without invitation or summons?"

Jemima didn't have much use for any of the Bonners, but she knew better than to talk to Hawkeye like he was a beggar with an open hand. The widow underestimated him or gave herself too much credit, or both; either way Jemima would stand by and just watch her reap her just reward. If she were to run down to the tavern and take wagers on which one of these two would win in a battle of wills, not even Charlie LeBlanc would be stupid enough to put his money on the widow.

"Mrs. Kuick." Hawkeye ducked his head to keep from hitting it on the door frame as he came in. He was too big for the room, too big for the house itself.

"What do you want, Mr. Bonner?"

"Well, I didn't come to drink tea with you, if that's what you were thinking. We got some business to discuss, you and me."

And then without asking or waiting or even looking at the widow for permission, he sat down on Mr. Kuick's chair. A deep armchair upholstered in brown velvet with embroidered linen on the arms and back; the chair that nobody was allowed to sit on or even touch, not even Isaiah. The chair that the widow dusted herself every day. Hawkeye sat down across from the widow just like that and took no note of her thunderous expression.

"Of all the temerity—" she began in a sputter, but he cut her off with a wave of the hand.

"Save your breath," he said easily. "Don't like being here any more than you like having me, so I'll just say what I got to say right out so we can get this settled and I can be on my way."

The widow let out a strangled sound. "Hurry up about it then, if you must."

"Oh, I must all right. What I want to know is, are you sending your man Dye to trespass on Hidden Wolf or is he doing that all on his own? The reason I ask is simple. I need to know how many names to put on the warrant. Just his, or yours too. I'll have Jed McGarrity write it up all proper so it's ready when the judge comes through on his circuit. Of course if I should catch Dye at it between now and then I'll just shoot me a trespasser and that'll leave you to explain to the judge on your own."

Jemima had never seen the widow blanch, but she did it now. All the color left her face and then rushed back just as suddenly in such a deep flush that she looked as if she had painted herself as gaudy as any stage actress.

"How dare you," the widow whispered. "How dare you threaten me with the law."

Other folks might start to shake when the widow got to whispering, but Hawkeye just leaned forward with his hands on his knees, his brow pulled down low. "Oh, I dare all right. You best not underestimate me. A body makes accusations against me and mine and then carries a weapon onto my property, why then the law's the very least I got in mind."

"Leave here at once," the widow said, pointing with a trembling finger at the door. "Before I call my son and have him put you out."

"I'll leave here when I've had an answer from you," Hawkeye said, leaning back again. "Then I'm headed down to see McGarrity to sign the warrant. Unless we can get this settled here and now."

The widow said, "Your accusations are ridiculous. I have never directed Mr. Dye to break the law, nor do I believe that he would do such a thing. I will have you up on charges, sir. For your assault on my character and morals."

Hawkeye pushed out a deep breath. "Before you go off to complain about my manners, why don't you make sure you know what you're talking about. Call the man in here and ask him. If you think you can trust him to tell the truth."

It was a bold move on Hawkeye's part, and Jemima had to admire him for it. If the widow refused to call Dye in, it would look as though she didn't trust him, or worse, that she did have some part in his trespassing and could not risk his testimony. That would put her in Hawkeye's power in a way that was not to be borne.

But if she did call Dye in, then she had no choice but to support him in whatever lies he told, or look as if she had no control over her employees. If Dye told the truth, that he had been trespassing on the mountain—Jemima knew for a fact that he had; twice she had seen him coming out of the forests well past the Kuicks' property line—then he would have to be dismissed immediately.

The problem there was a simple one: the widow liked Dye; she liked the money he made for her and the way he handled the mill and the slaves. He left her alone, which was what she wanted. All was well with her world if she could sit here like a queen and leave the work to men like Dye, bound to her by what she believed to be loyalty. If only she knew the whole of it. Jemima sucked in her lower lip to keep herself from smiling.

The expression on the widow's face said she understood the trap that Hawkeye had set and would concede him this first small battle. She yanked the bell pull so hard that Jemima would not have been surprised if it had pulled right out of the wall. Instead she heard the faraway tinkling of the bell in the kitchen.

"I will send down to the mill for my overseer," she said coolly. "We will finish this conversation as soon as he is here, but we will finish it in the kitchen." She looked Hawkeye up and down very pointedly, lingering on his moccasins. "This is not a matter for my good parlor."

Hawkeye had a frightening grin, and he used it now. "I don't care where we do the talking," he said, unfolding his long frame from Mr. Kuick's chair. "But we'll get to the bottom of this before I leave here today, that much I promise you."

Jemima fled the widow's parlor just behind Hawkeye, dodging Georgia, who had come to answer the bell. She had no intention of listening to the widow rant until the overseer could be found.

She had just slipped past Hawkeye when the widow yelled down the hall. "You make sure that man goes straight to the kitchen and nowhere else! Do you hear me, Jemima?"

Hawkeye winked at her. "She thinks I'll pocket the good silver while she ain't watching. Maybe you best tie my hands, too, and march me to the kitchen at the end of a musket."

Jemima didn't bother to answer him, but neither did she do as she had been told. While he headed for the kitchen she went in the other direction, along the front hall, through Isaiah's empty study and then the back hall that ended in the door that led down to the root cellar.

At this time of year, before the new crops had started to come in, the cellar was almost empty. Bushels and baskets and folded burlap sacks were her only company when she came to the cellar, which was why Jemima liked it here. She paused to listen for the sound of steps. When she was sure no one had followed her she moved aside the plank that leaned against the wall and ducked into the short passageway that ended in a tangle of bush and blackberry vines.

The widow was afraid of another Indian uprising and she

had wanted a secret escape, a way out of the house should the need ever arise. Except of course it wasn't secret at all: the house had been built by men who lived in the village, after all, and the passageway saw almost as much traffic as the kitchen door. This was the way that Isaiah slipped out at night to meet Dye, and Jemima had long suspected that the maids used it to sneak out when the urge was on them. For her own purposes she used it only during the daylight hours, simply because she didn't like having every step she took tracked by Georgia and reported back to the widow.

The passageway took her out into the far end of the kitchen garden, behind a clump of evergreens. From there Jemima could go where she liked: up the mountain where she was not welcome, down to the village where she was not wanted; to the mill, which was forbidden to her. Or she could stay right where she was and contemplate the situation at hand. Georgia had trotted off toward the mill to fetch Dye. Whether or not Isaiah showed himself when she delivered her message, Jemima had no doubt he was somewhere nearby and would hear about Hawkeye's accusations. The question was, Would he leave Dye to handle this on his own, or would he try to calm the waters with Hawkeye as he had done at the graveside?

Either way Jemima would be in the kitchen to hear what Dye had to say. She hunkered down to wait.

Below her the Sacandaga rushed eastward, separating the mountain from the rest of Paradise. From here she could see most of the village, including the cabin where she had been born and raised up. At that time the land it stood on had belonged to old Judge Middleton; now it belonged to his grandson Ethan and was in Dr. Todd's control. He had rented it to the blacksmith when he married Daisy Freeman, and since then they had added another room and a porch, and the kitchen garden was twice the size it had been.

Daisy was there now, weeding her butter beans while two of her children played nearby, the sun shining bright on their woolly black hair. But for the rush of the water Jemima thought she could hear the girls laughing.

Her father would have never stood still to see free blacks living in the village at all, much less in a cabin built by a white man for his family. Back in those days when they were always hungry but knew right from wrong.

Georgia's voice brought Jemima up out of her daydream, and she curled up tight so that there was no chance of Dye catching sight of her as he strode on past with Georgia running at his heels. Jemima waited for a count of twenty and got up to go back into the house when the clatter of horses' hooves on the bridge made her turn.

Riders coming down from the mountain, and in a hurry; maybe Nathaniel on his way to lend his father some backup with the widow. Maybe with something else on his mind entirely.

She waited until the horses came into view and then stood, so surprised by the riders that she had to look twice to convince herself that she wasn't imagining things.

Curiosity and Galileo Freeman were trotting through the village on horseback, both of them dressed for a long trip. Galileo's rifle was in its sling on his back, for all the good it would do him, half-blind. The saddlebags were filled to bursting, but stranger than that, Curiosity had a bundle tied across her chest with a shawl. A bundle that squirmed and wiggled. A child's fist rose up from the swaddling. A black child.

Daisy had come up on her feet in the middle of her bean patch. She raised a hand toward her parents and waved; nothing of surprise there at all, neither in her expression nor in the way she watched them with her hand at her brow to shade her eyes.

The children called out after them. "Goodbye! Goodbye!" Daisy hushed them and sent a concerned look up toward the millhouse. Jemima could not be seen where she stood, but she stepped back anyway, feeling the scrape of blackberry vines on her bare arms.

The horses never slowed. The Freemans rode through Paradise in broad daylight and nobody lifted a finger to stop them. They disappeared on the Johnstown trail just like that, without a backward glance.

Jemima stood and watched until the dust settled and the Freemans were gone. Then she listed for herself the things that she knew.

First, the rumors that had been drifting through the village since the spring about the runaway and her child were true.

The Bonners were running slaves, and the Freemans with them. That made them thieves, all of them. Thieves and liars and hypocrites.

Hawkeye stood in the kitchen right now with Dye, making threats; calling names, making demands.

Second, they were well organized. Cookie would be part of it; no doubt she stood at the door keeping watch, hiding her satisfaction. Maybe she had given some signal that Dye was out of the way and the Freemans should ride. Jemima had been worried about poison, but Cookie's revenge was less obvious and most probably more of a satisfaction to her. She helped the Bonners steal from the widow and from Dye; stood there smiling while the Freemans took the child away toward safety and Hawkeye tied the widow in knots with the cold, slow flow of his righteous indignation.

Third, they were sure enough of themselves to move by daylight. Most probably they had been doing this so long that they stopped being careful. And now they had given her the last weapon she would need to keep herself safe.

Jemima breathed a deep sigh of relief and thanksgiving. When she could trust her expression, she went into the kitchen to watch Hawkeye deal out what Dye had coming to him.

Chapter 36

———

June 17

Hannah kept herself so busy that there should have been no time to think of Strikes-the-Sky and for that very reason, she explained to herself, she could think of little else. While she worked in the laboratory with Richard Todd, talked to Bump, ground willow bark, examined an infected scratch on Dolly's leg, while she ate or walked or answered questions put to her, another part of her mind was considering Strikes-the-Sky. The way his expression shifted so suddenly from arrogance to curiosity and back again, the sound of his voice and the oddities of his language, the way he held a cup when he drank, the sound of him laughing at one of Lily's stories, the tone he took with the boys: serious and forthright, interested in their games and opinions. The few words he had said to her: *thank you,* and *please,* and *in the west they talk of your skill as a healer.*

The two men had met at the Battle of Fallen Timbers, a fact that made Hawkeye sit up and take note. What he wanted to know was, first and foremost, how they had escaped with their hides intact and, second, how two Hodenosaunee warriors had ended up fighting so far west.

Otter and Strikes-the-Sky looked at each other and then Strikes-the-Sky said, "Back then Little Turtle was holding fast to Ohio for the Shawnee. I went because I thought it was our last chance to keep the whites at bay."

"And since Little Turtle gave up the fight, what do you

think now?" This question came from Runs-from-Bears, who was ignoring the hard looks his wife sent him.

"Now I will go and stand with Tecumseh, who is younger and hasn't forgotten how to fight," Strikes-the-Sky said calmly.

"And will you go fight with Tecumseh as well?" Many-Doves asked her younger brother.

He said, "Of course. I promised my wife that I would make sure her brother-in-law doesn't lose his scalplock."

His playful tone did nothing to soften his sister's grim expression. She said, "Better you should stay home with your wife. How she puts up with you I can't imagine. And you—" She sent a sharp look at Strikes-the-Sky. "You are no better."

"I never claimed to be," Strikes-the-Sky said amicably. "And before you ask I will tell you that your brother's wife only puts up with me because her sister took me as husband and she feels obliged."

They had already heard about his wife, dead now three years. Tall-Woman she had been called, for her height and the habit she had of standing up in the face of trouble. When this was told late on the first night of the visit Hannah had asked a question, her first.

"How did Tall-Woman die?"

Strikes-the-Sky looked at her directly when he spoke. "She was new with child and there was a pain in her belly." He touched the hard plane of his stomach near the navel. "Fever and great pain. Our healers could do nothing for her."

Neither could I have, Hannah might have said but she did not. She might have said: *I have seen inside the body of a woman who died like that. The child quickened outside the womb and caused a rupture.* But she didn't say that either. She would not add to his grief, but she must respect him for it.

Hannah went over the conversation around the fire again and again in spite of her strongest resolution to concentrate on other things. She was losing patience with her wayward thoughts when Charlie LeBlanc sought her out in the laboratory. What he had to say was this: his Molly was in travail and ready to bring her fifth child into the world, and could she please come as Curiosity was away? He didn't have much to pay her but he would be glad of her help.

The first flush of relief—Charlie had brought her a reason to stay away from home and the visitors—was soon replaced by irritation with herself for such cowardice.

Molly was good-natured and cheerful in all things in spite of the fact that she had married dirt poor and had more boy-children and work than any one woman deserved. This labor was no different; she talked and scolded the boys and directed chores and prodded Hannah for gossip in between pains.

While Molly never said so, it was clear to Hannah that it was the hope of a girl that sustained her through travails that went on far longer than any of them expected.

The LeBlancs' first daughter didn't show herself until the sun was up. Her four brothers, ages one to eight, greeted her with no less astonishment than Charlie; they had all come to the conclusion that Molly just wasn't capable of producing anything but males, and didn't know where to start with the tiny red-faced girl who looked at them with wide eyes. Charlie, who was often seen carrying all four boys at once, shied from picking up his daughter until Molly shamed him into it, and then a smile cracked his face in half.

"That's what a man looks like when he falls in love," said Molly with some satisfaction.

Hannah hummed a reply that said nothing at all.

If there had been room in the small cabin she would have taken her rest—long overdue—right there near the new mother; even the boisterous LeBlanc boys would not have been able to keep her awake. But she made herself walk the ten minutes to the Todds' house and went to sleep on the cot in the little room off the kitchen that Curiosity used to treat the sick and isolate surly children.

Hannah paused only long enough to take off her moccasins and send Ethan up to Lake in the Clouds with word that she would be home as soon as she could, but perhaps not until the next day.

She woke disoriented and unsure of where she was or what time it might be, and realized that Dolly stood at the foot of the cot with a tray of food.

"I hear there's good news up at the LeBlancs' today," she said by way of greeting. "Molly sure is happy to have her a girl. They are going to call her Maddy, after Charlie's mama. A big child, I hear?"

"Good-sized, yes." Hannah accepted the bowl of broth that

Dolly offered and drank it all in three long gulps. "What time is it?"

"Close to noon," Dolly said, and then at Hannah's surprised expression: "The world won't fall apart 'cause you slept for a few hours, Hannah Bonner."

Hannah produced a smile, but it was hard work. She intended to call on the four people she had vaccinated last night to check the incisions, and Dr. Todd had given her a list of patients to see: Mary Gathercole had a sore throat and her mother a worsening rash; Jed McGarrity was complaining about another sore tooth; Ben Cameron had chopped off a toe with a careless swing of the axe and the dressing needed changing; and Matilda Kaes was suffering greatly with the rheumatism in her back. Curiosity was gone for a few days at least but Richard Todd had no intention of leaving his laboratory as long as Hannah was home to look after less interesting complaints.

"The only reason I come in here to bother you is your sister has been waiting out in the kitchen for an hour now," Dolly explained. "She's ate through near all the gingerbread and if you don't go see what she's got on her mind she'll bust soon. It's got something to do with that visitor up on the mountain, but she won't tell me no more than that."

"Strikes-the-Sky," Hannah said. "His name is Strikes-the-Sky."

"I heard all about it from Mama, after you finished with the vaccinations."

Hannah said, "The village must be talking."

Dolly took the blanket that had fallen to the floor and hung it out the open window to air. When she looked back at Hannah over her shoulder, her expression was thoughtful.

"Nobody holds nothing against you, Hannah. You know that."

In her surprise Hannah could not think at first what to say, and Dolly took her silence as encouragement. She said, "Once the first batch of vaccinations is done they'll calm down some, you'll see."

Hannah had thought they were talking about Strikes-the-Sky, and now she was glad that she hadn't said as much. She reached for her moccasins to hide her face, and stayed that way until Dolly had left.

*   *   *

"I did not ask Molly LeBlanc to have her baby last night, you know," Hannah said to Lily. They were sitting on the garden bench in the sun, and the day was already so hot that Hannah was tempted to open the first few buttons on her bodice. Lily had taken advantage of her age and tucked up her skirt to free her legs to the breeze. Hannah looked at her ankles and was pleased to see that there was no swelling or distortion to distinguish them.

"I wonder about that," Lily said primly. "I surely do."

"You are acting as if I arranged a birth specifically so I could avoid the visitors."

Lily cast her a sidelong glance. "Strikes-the-Sky was disappointed that you weren't there last night when we were sitting around the fire."

Hannah pressed a hand to her stomach to still the fluttering there.

"I suppose he told you that. Announced it to the world, did he?"

Lily gave her a disgusted look. "I can see things without being told. What I can't see and what I want to know from you is why you're going out of your way to avoid him. I think he's wonderful."

"Lily Bonner," Hannah said, torn between amusement and irritation. "You hardly know the man."

"I do know him," her sister insisted. "I can tell about him from the way he tells stories. And besides that he's handsome. Here."

She pulled a small roll of paper tied with a string from the pocket tied around her waist, slipped off the tie, and smoothed out the drawing on the bench between them.

"It took me three starts but I think I got his likeness pretty well in the end."

"My God," Hannah breathed in surprise.

"You like it?" Lily was pleased, all her petulance gone and a shy smile on her face.

It was a simple drawing, but there was something about it. Lily had captured his confidence and put it on the paper, as real as the line of the jaw or the curve of the ear. And he was handsome; there was no denying that.

"This is beautifully done," Hannah said simply. "What did Elizabeth say about it?"

Lily shook her head. "She hasn't seen it. I did it for you. To show you."

Hannah ran a finger over the paper. "You did not need to prove to me that you can draw, little sister. I see the evidence of that every day."

"Not to show you I can *draw*," Lily sputtered in annoyance. "To *show* you. Him. Strikes-the-Sky."

It was true that Hannah could hardly take her eyes away from the drawing, but she didn't know what else she was supposed to see beyond the face she knew already. "What do you want to show me about him?"

"He's strong and good and he tells excellent stories. And he's not afraid of you like most of the other men. He's perfect for you."

At this Hannah did laugh, to hide her distress. "No one is perfect, as you well know."

Lily shook her head in disappointment, as if Hannah were being purposely dense. "He's perfect for *you*. I'd marry him if I were old enough but that wouldn't be right. He's yours, and Blue-Jay is mine."

"Lily," Hannah began slowly. "I don't know where you got such an idea, but you shouldn't talk about a human being as if he were a book or a handkerchief. When you are grown you will find out whether or not Blue-Jay is the right one for you. In the meantime, Strikes-the-Sky doesn't belong to anyone."

Lily's expression was a strange combination of obstinacy and worry. "You don't see what's plain to everybody else because you are afraid. You're not used to wanting, and it scares you."

The truth of that shook Hannah hard, and for a moment she was silent as she gathered her thoughts.

"Why are you in such a hurry to marry me off?"

"Because you're getting to be an old maid," Lily said with her usual forthrightness. "And you told me yourself no white man would suit you. I can see that there's no one in the village you respect enough to love. So here Strong-Words brings you the perfect husband—"

"I doubt that's what he had in mind," Hannah interrupted.

"—and you won't even talk to him. Worse than that, you run away whenever you can, as if he were a monster."

"Just exactly what would you like me to do?" Hannah asked, her irritation getting the best of her. "Sit in his lap at supper?"

Lily's mouth pursed thoughtfully. "Now you are making fun."

"Oh please." Hannah threw up both hands in surrender and disgust. She stood, and made an effort to smile at her sister. "Enough of this silliness. I have work to do."

"Will you promise to be there tonight at the fire?" Lily asked.

Hannah was halfway to the house when Lily yelled, "If you'll promise that, I won't bother you about him anymore!"

She glanced over her shoulder. "Don't make promises you can't keep, little sister."

"I see you took the picture!" Lily called after her, and her laughter followed Hannah into the house.

By the late afternoon it was so hot that the world seemed to buzz with it, and every breath felt as though it had to be drawn through damp toweling.

The blackfly and the heat were enough to banish any idea Hannah might have had about taking the long way home, and on top of that there was a storm coming. When the path wound its way to the edge of the mountain she saw it in the far distance, flexing soundlessly under thick layers of cloud.

She rehearsed her excuses for closing herself in her room. Her daybook, medicines to be prepared, letters to be written. And none of it sounded in the least bit credible. Her father would give her a questioning look and Elizabeth a concerned one, but they would not order her to join the visitors, nor would they try to make her feel guilty. Lily would do that all on her own.

The thunderstorm broke over Hidden Wolf with a vengeance just as they were finishing supper. Because they could not sit with their visitors by the fire the boys had readied, everyone was obliged to crowd together around one hearth, and so Hannah found herself sitting across from Strikes-the-Sky; close enough to reach out and touch him, if the need should arise. Hannah shook herself when that thought came to her, and fixed her gaze more firmly on the shirt seam she was mending.

They talked for a while about baggataway matches played long ago between the Mohawk and the Seneca, a conversation that had the boys almost hopping with excitement. Daniel wanted to get his stick down from its peg on the wall to show Strong-Words and Strikes-the-Sky the dried batwing he had tied to the handle, but Hawkeye stopped him with one raised brow. Daniel in an excited mood with a baggataway stick in a crowded room was not the best idea.

"I remember your older brother well," Nathaniel told Strikes-the-Sky. "He was a fearsome player. Once I saw him jump clear over a man's bent back to get to the goal."

"Did you hear, Walks-Ahead?" Daniel asked, poking Hannah with an eager finger. "Did you hear that our father played baggataway against Strikes-the-Sky's brother?"

"And me," said Runs-from-Bears. "I played that day too. There must have been close to two hundred on the field."

"Last year we played twice in the village," said Blue-Jay. "But there were only twenty of us. Nicholas Wilde is a good player, and so are the Camerons. Maybe we could play again while you are here."

Hannah sensed her father and grandfather exchanging glances, and knew very well what they were thinking: a game of baggataway might defuse the tensions in the village, or set them burning.

"You will play baggataway at Good Pasture," said Many-Doves to her son. "When the corn is in."

The familiar clamor rose up from all the children at this announcement. Every fall Runs-from-Bears took his older children to Good Pasture to spend two months with their own people, and every year Daniel and Lily campaigned to be included.

Elizabeth said, "There are more cheerful things to talk about, surely. Strong-Words, you have not told us very much about this Handsome-Lake you mentioned. It sounds as though he is a sensible man with good ideas to share."

Otter said, "He has done good, most of the time." But he did not sound entirely convinced; Hannah made a note to herself to ask him more about this later.

"It is because of him that his village has given up all hard drink," added Strikes-the-Sky.

"But not your village?" Many-Doves asked.

"Not completely," said Strong-Words. "But we make progress. He-Makes-Them-Ready says if we will keep the old ways we must give up the things that the whites brought to us, and that includes alcohol."

"Hmmm." Many-Doves made a sound deep in her throat, one that said she did not think much of this. "If Cornplanter can ban hard drink, then He-Makes-Them-Ready should be able to do it too. Unless he doesn't have the backing of the clan mothers."

Strong-Words hesitated. He said, "Some find it hard to go back to the old ways. I see you sewing with steel needles, sister. And the hoes you use to weed the corn, they are steel too, are they not?"

At this Many-Doves only smiled. This was just her little brother trying to start up the old argument, the one that he had never tired of. It always began in the same way: he announced that the Indian nations would have been better off if the whites had never set foot on the continent, Runs-from-Bears disagreed, and for hours they would debate, arguing their positions to the family gathered around.

One by one all the adults would choose sides. Hawkeye and Many-Doves always agreed with Strong-Words in the end; Nathaniel with Runs-from-Bears; Elizabeth would refuse to choose one over the other, in spite of the teasing that came her way.

When they were alive both her grandmothers had sided with Nathaniel. That had always irked Strong-Words, who could not convince his own mother of the truth of his argument. Falling-Day had always ended the discussion when she said, "If I threw away the whole nettle because of its sting, we would not have the medicine it gives us to soothe wounds. We take what is useful and leave the rest."

To the children who were scattered through the room this old argument was very new. Sprawled on the floor, they listened, wide-eyed, with none of the usual fidgeting. As Hannah had once listened, watching the faces of the adults as they spoke and looking for weaknesses in their arguments to store away and think about later.

Now Hannah was old enough to take a position of her own, as long as she was willing to argue it. And of course there were others here who were new to the game: Pines-Rustling and Strikes-the-Sky. She glanced at him before she remembered that she meant not to and found that for once he was not looking at her, but at Strong-Words, and with an expression she could not quite read.

"We think we cannot live without steel, but that is because our imaginations have gone as soft as our memories," Strong-Words said. "Bows and arrows suit a hunter in the endless forests better than guns ever will. We could go back to the old ways if we were not so lazy."

"You scrape a hide clean with flint instead of a fine-honed knife before you go talking about *lazy*," said Runs-from-Bears. "And while you're at it, go fell a couple trees in the old way with fire and then tell me that you're willing to give up working with axe and saw. I wouldn't want to be without a knife in the bush," he said. "Nor would I give up a rifle for a bow and arrow with women and children to defend."

Otter shook his head. "All you've said is that steel is quick. Quicker than the old way, and nobody could deny that. Nobody would deny that a horse is faster than walking, or that it takes less time to buy a bolt of cloth than it does to cure enough skin for a shirt. What I'm saying is that quick ain't necessarily the best way to do things, at least for our kind."

"Look out now," Runs-from-Bears said to his wife. "Not only is this brother of yours going to take my knives away from me, but he wants your calico too."

Many-Doves lifted a shoulder and said nothing, unwilling or simply not ready to join in the conversation.

"I for one will take a razor over a clamshell when it comes to shaving," Nathaniel offered, rubbing a hand over his chin. "And it ain't a matter of quick, it's a matter of keeping my skin."

There was soft laughter in the room, and even Strong-Words joined in. Nobody ever brought up the fact that Hawkeye and the rest of his family would not be here at all if the whites had stayed off the continent.

"You could just give up shaving, Da," Lily suggested.

"Oh no," Elizabeth said. "Not that, please. He will scratch constantly and stare at himself in the mirror and complain of his ruined looks. He is as vain as any Kahnyen'kehàka warrior about his smooth cheeks and chest."

"Listen to her," Nathaniel laughed. "Putting it all down to my vanity when it's stubble burn she's worried about."

Elizabeth blushed, but she carried on resolutely. "That brings up a question," she said, looking at Strikes-the-Sky and then Strong-Words in turn. "Did you pluck your scalps, or use a razor?"

Strikes-the-Sky let out a deep, short laugh. "I use a razor. Strong-Words lets his woman pluck his scalp until his impatience gets the better of him."

Otter held up a hand to stop the laughter. "I'm just as weak as the rest of us," he said. "But we could learn to live in the old way again."

"This would not be an issue if you were not so set on going back to battle," said Many-Doves, with a pointed look at her little brother's scalp.

He ignored her. "Name one thing we couldn't learn to live without," he said. "One thing that came to us from the O'seronni. Each of us. Sister, you start."

Many-Doves put down her sewing for a minute and tilted her head in thought. "You are right, I like my sewing needles," she said. "But then there's the cooking kettles. I have them from our mother. Every time I scrub them out with sand I think of her."

"You could make pots of clay. Our grandmother Made-of-Bones had such pots."

She shrugged. "If we lived among the people, maybe," she said. "If there were fifty of us in the longhouse. But not living as we do now."

For a moment Hannah wondered if Strong-Words would argue that they should all be living in longhouses; it was the one argument that might end in harsh words. Many-Doves and Runs-from-Bears were determined to raise their children in the old Kahnyen'kehàka territories, even if it meant that they must live apart from the rest of their people. Most of the Kahnyen'kehàka—the ones who had survived the plagues and the wars and hard drink—had been driven north to Canada. Even Trees-Standing-in-Water was gone now.

But Many-Doves was determined to stay in this place where her mother had chosen to live and die and Runs-from-Bears would not cross her in this.

Hawkeye cleared his throat. "I'm mostly on your side of this argument, Strong-Words," he said, "but the truth be told, I ain't willing to give up my hunting knife nor my tomahawk. A' course I still have my father's war club and I couldn't do without that neither."

"You'd give up your rifle?" Daniel asked, as if his grandfather had offered to cut off his hand.

Hawkeye shrugged. "If there wasn't such a thing as a rifle or a musket I wouldn't know what I was missing, would I?"

One by one they went around the room. Pines-Rustling admitted that she would be loath to give up the good strong thread that Mrs. Kaes spun for her in trade for leather cured for moccasins, and Blue-Jay admitted that he liked cone sugar better even than maple when he could get it.

Kateri, who was a quiet child and loath to speak her mind with so many to hear, stood up all at once and the room quieted. "If my mother let us take our corn to the mill to grind, then I would not want to give that up. I am thankful for the three sisters—" She cast a glance that was all smoldering discontent at her mother. "But grinding corn all day long when there is a mill to do it is...is...not rational."

She sat again just as suddenly as she'd stood.

Many-Doves raised her head from her work and looked around the circle of faces. She said, "My daughter has spoken. I will consider what she says."

"And you, my sister's daughter?" Strong-Words asked Hannah directly. "You are of all of us the one who lives most in the O'seronni world. What must you keep?"

Hannah thought of the medicines in her own workroom and in Richard Todd's office that had come to them from all over the world; she saw in her mind's eye the fine scalpels and instruments that Hakim Ibrahim had given her as a gift. She thought of the smooth paper in her daybook, and the words she wrote on those pages.

"Maybe there's nothing at all," Strong-Words said hopefully.

She said, "The microscope." Then she found that she needed to explain exactly what a microscope was to Strong-Words and Strikes-the-Sky, who had never heard of such a thing or seen one.

"I can take you there to see for yourself," she finally volunteered. "A simple drop of pond water will convince you that there is more to life in this world than your eye can see."

Many-Doves looked up from her sewing. "My brother has promised me to stay away from the doctor and from all the Todds," she said.

Lily sent a significant look in her brother's direction that was lost on nobody at all. The children were always digging for information about the old feud between Strong-Words and Richard Todd, and this newest piece of information would keep them busy for a good while.

"What about you, Strikes-the-Sky?" Hawkeye said. "You got anything of the white man you'd rather not give back, if they packed up bag and baggage and went back across the water tomorrow?"

Hannah did not raise her head, but it was a struggle. She could almost hear him thinking, just as she could hear all the others in the room turning their attention to him.

"Kissing," he said finally, and surprised laughter echoed up to the rafters. Hannah would not raise her eyes but she suspected that everyone was looking at her.

"Are you claiming the white man thought up kissing?" demanded Runs-from-Bears, still laughing.

"I am," said Strikes-the-Sky. "My mother says that it's unnatural, the way whites press mouths together. She says the old ones never did such a thing until they saw the whites doing it. And old Fish-Carrier says the real people will never be good at kissing."

Elizabeth had put down her knitting. "Whoever this Fish-Carrier person is, I must challenge his wisdom. This can't be true. Why, I would have thought that kissing is as universally known as..." She broke off abruptly.

This time the laughter went on for so long that Hannah ventured a glance up from the needlework. Strikes-the-Sky was not laughing at all; he was looking at her. She stared back at him defiantly and got nothing more than a grin for her trouble.

Then Hawkeye said, "To tell the truth, there didn't seem to be much kissing back when I was a boy."

"Maybe not where you could see it," suggested Lily. "Maybe just in private." She sent a meaningful look to her parents, and Nathaniel reached over and tousled her hair.

"Wait till you're old enough and the right man comes along," he said. "You won't care so much about private anymore when you've got kissing on your mind."

"No, Nathaniel, she is right," Elizabeth said firmly. "Some things should remain private, between two people."

"Then why are you and Uncle always kissing?" piped up Kateri.

"A reasonable question. I suppose I must admit to a certain lack of—" She faltered, and Nathaniel leaned over to run a hand down her back.

"Never mind, Boots," he said. "It's all my fault anyway, I'll admit it. I've led you astray, but I can't say I'm sorry about it."

Elizabeth sent Strong-Words a firm look. "I would say that this conversation has gone astray."

Strong-Words cleared his throat and tried to calm his expression.

"Thank you, brother," he said to Strikes-the-Sky in his most solemn voice. "For all the years we've been talking about this no one had ever managed to come up with something the whites brought that I want to keep, until tonight. I think this is one thing we can finally all agree on. What do you think, Hannah?"

They were all looking at her, the women sympathetic and amused; the men more cautious and curious. Lily looked as if she might explode with anticipation; Daniel turned his face away, disgusted.

Hannah said, "I will have to reserve judgment on this particular matter." And wondered where the words came from inside herself.

By all rights Elizabeth should have fallen asleep easily and without dreams after such a long and eventful day, but deep in the night she gave up the struggle and slipped out of bed.

Her skin was damp with sweat and she was glad of the night breeze from the open window. From their spot by the hearth the dogs raised their heads and looked in her direction before they fell back into an effortless sleep. A banked coal fell in on itself with a sigh and whisper.

In the middle of the cabin she stopped to listen to the sounds from the sleeping loft. Daniel muttered and turned, a restless and reluctant sleeper from the day he was born, wrestling with blanket and pillow and sleep itself. Lily was made of different stuff: she slept with a furious concentration, curled tight into herself, her fists tucked under her chin. Always ready to do battle.

Elizabeth knew that if she climbed the ladder she would find that the twins were in the same bed, sleeping back to back. She could go up there now and separate them, but in the morning

she would find them together again. They might bicker and
wrangle endlessly during the day, but in sleep they could not
deny the bond that had been forged in the warm dark waters of
the womb. One day circumstance or age or both would separate them for good, but they were in no hurry for that day to
come, and neither was Elizabeth.

Tonight it was not the twins who had robbed her of sleep
but Hannah. She made her way to the workroom, where she
hesitated with one hand on the door. Over the last years the
room that had once been dedicated entirely to storage and
workspace had become more and more Hannah's, given over
to her medicines and books and journals, her narrow bed
tucked into a corner like an afterthought.

Cora Munro had followed Hawkeye into the endless forests
to take up housekeeping, but she had not done so without some
conditions of her own. This cabin was a copy of that first one,
larger than most with planked floors, but what distinguished it
from every other cabin was the abundance of windows. The
workroom was long and narrow and very light in the day. Even
in the night it was never completely dark, unless there was no
moon at all.

Elizabeth pushed the door open and saw Hannah sitting on
the edge of her bed with her hands folded in her lap.

"I heard you coming," she said. "I can't sleep either." She
moved over to make room for Elizabeth on the edge of the bed.

There were many things they could have talked about, but
neither of them seemed willing or able to begin. Elizabeth did
not have to close her eyes to see Cookie's face, Curiosity's,
Ambrose Dye's. The coffin of green wood; the circle of faces
overfull with anger, distorted with sorrow, changed forever.
Strikes-the-Sky, with his black eyes and bright purpose.

Instead she looked at Hannah, whose skin glowed like dark
opal in the moonlight: high brow, cheekbones like raised
wings, the planes beneath, the strong line of her jaw, the curve
of her mouth. With no trouble at all Elizabeth could blink and
call forth Hannah as a little girl, but that child was gone.

When Strikes-the-Sky looked at Hannah he saw a young
woman with a straight back and strong hands, a keen intelligence in the dark eyes, a simple and undeniable beauty.

"It might have been better if my uncle had come home
alone." She said it clearly but it was not true; they both knew it.

Elizabeth covered Hannah's hands with her own. She said, "I have never known you to be unfair."

Hannah stiffened as if it were her duty to protest. She started to speak and stopped herself. Started again, her voice rough. "It is not rational to make so much of a stranger who will go away so soon."

"Then you must ignore him, if that is the way you feel."

"That's the only reasonable plan." Hannah said this as if it were the least reasonable plan in the world.

Elizabeth patted Hannah's hand again, and when she spoke again she had to work very hard to keep her tone even.

"You know, when I came here from England I had a plan too. A very carefully constructed plan. I was going to start a school in the wilderness and devote my life to education. Especially to the education of girls. I wanted nothing else, and I was determined not to be distracted from that goal. But then I met your father. At first I was very angry at him for the way he complicated my plans."

Hannah did not get up or turn her face away, but her whole body hummed with denial.

"I should not have interfered," Elizabeth said finally. "Forgive me."

All Hannah's fury left her just that simply, her expression softening. She said, "It is happening too fast."

Elizabeth paused. "Fast or slow, it is up to you. If something is happening."

"Of course something is happening," Hannah said. "What did you think?"

Nathaniel was awake when Elizabeth came back to bed, and waiting for her. She saw it in the curve of his back and the set of his shoulders. She slipped under the covers and rubbed her face against his hair where it pooled behind him.

Nathaniel said, "My father told me it would come like this for her, but I didn't believe him. I guess I didn't want to believe him."

"Strikes-the-Sky may not be the right one. It's far too early to say."

He turned to her, and Elizabeth was relieved to see that he could smile. "If not Strikes-the-Sky, then someone else. And it won't be long. Nicholas Wilde will offer for her before the summer's out. She's ready, even if she doesn't know it yet."

"She does know it," Elizabeth said. "I think...I think that Strikes-the-Sky may be the one, and I think she knows that herself. But she's frightened."

"I hope she's more than frightened."

"Oh yes," Elizabeth said softly. "Of course she is, but she doesn't have the words for what she's feeling. Or rather she's not ready to use them. Not yet."

"I just hate the idea of her going off so far."

Elizabeth put a hand on his chest. "I imagine that's what your mother thought just before you went north and ended up living in Sarah's longhouse."

"Maybe so. So what did you tell her?"

"I told her about how it was for me, back then. How you managed to confuse all my well-laid plans when I first came to Paradise, and how irritating that was to me."

A hand snaked out from under the covers and around her waist, pulled her up against him. "At first," he prompted.

"At first," Elizabeth agreed, biting back a laugh. She struck away his other hand, busy wiggling its way under her night-dress; strong fingers on the curve of her hip.

"Then you saw the light," he said sternly.

"Then I saw—Nathaniel."

She tried to squirm away, and for her trouble he rolled, pinning her down beneath him. Took her hands to hold them still over her head as he kissed her hard.

"Then you saw the light," he prompted again.

"Then I saw the light," she whispered.

"You couldn't resist me."

She couldn't hold back a strangled laugh. "Oh, please. Really."

Her laugh gave way to a gasp, and then, eventually, a sigh.

A long time later when he had kissed her into boneless sub-mission he said, "You might as well give in, Boots. One way or another I'll have a full confession out of you by morning."

"Will you now?" she said. "Go on then, sir. Do your worst."

Because she could not sleep after Elizabeth's visit, Hannah went out to sit by the falls. Because she could not sleep, and because she knew that she would not sleep well again until she went to see what she knew in her heart was true: Strikes-the-Sky was sitting there in the light of a waning moon, alone. Waiting for her. He had been swimming; the water pearled on his back and scalp and ran down his chest.

She walked up to him and said nothing until he unfolded his legs and stood.

"Tell me what you want," she said.

There was a long silence, but it was an easy one. Strikes-the-Sky said, "I want peace for my people. I want the whites to stop pushing us west."

"Those are good things," Hannah said. She did not look up at him but she could feel the heat of him, as if he were in the grip of a terrible fever. "Now tell me why you are here. What do you want from me?"

She felt him shrug. An unexpected flush of anger and embarrassment rose up from deep in her gut and shot through her, tingling sharp and hot. Hannah started to turn away and Strikes-the-Sky caught her upper arm and used the force of her anger to swing her toward him.

And she saw that he was smiling, an honest and open smile with nothing of derision in it. Such a kind smile on such a frightening face; it still took her by surprise, and robbed her of her temper.

He said, "It is for you to say what you want, Walks-Ahead. What I want must wait until the time is right."

"I am tired," she said fitfully. "I want to sleep."

"And still you stand here with me."

He tugged at her arm with his strong fingers until she followed him down to sit. She stemmed her hands on the cool, moss-covered rocks and thought of swimming under the falls. If she had come a little earlier she could have watched him. He would be a good swimmer, strong and sure. If she went into the water now, he would follow her.

She said, "I will not lie down with you." The words felt strong and true as they left her mouth and still she wanted to call them back.

He was so quiet that she finally looked at him. His expression was neither closed nor open; he had been waiting patiently for her to look at him.

He said, "Not ever?"

The laughter came up out of her without any warning, slow

and deep, and she clasped a hand to her mouth. When she took it away again she said, "Not now. Not tonight. Maybe not ever."

"Ah," he said slowly. "That is good, that maybe. So why did you come out here to me? Was it all the talk of kissing?"

He had moved close enough so that their arms were touching. It was strangely comforting and unsettling at the same time: the feel of him, warm and smooth and hard through the fabric of her overdress. Sweat trickled at her throat and she shivered.

She said, "You were teasing me. Trying to get me to . . . re-act to you."

"You were so serious, Walks-Ahead. But my plan worked. Here you sit."

"It hasn't worked. The fact that I am sitting here does not mean you will do any kissing tonight, Strikes-the-Sky."

"A man can hope." He leaned against her a little harder and she could smell him faintly: lake water, pine sap, bear grease; other things she couldn't name. "And anyway, maybe it is you who will do the kissing."

All the discomfort and strange, unwanted longing that had followed Hannah throughout the last two days was simply gone, and between them now was a calm, a *knowing* that she had no name for. She did not understand it, but she was glad of the relief it brought her. *Like a patient who doesn't realize how bad a pain is until it is gone,* she thought. *But what strange medicine is this?*

Hannah said, "You think I have never kissed a man?"

"There is no right answer to that question. If I say you have never kissed a man, you will be angry at me for thinking of you as a child. If I say of course you have kissed many men, then you will be wounded that I might think you are too careless with yourself."

"I have kissed five men," Hannah said, too quickly. "Now what do you think of that?"

"Now that we have finally started, I think that this conversation will take many days to finish. I think you should go in to your bed and sleep—"

"Now that what has started?" she interrupted him.

He blinked at her, as if to reprove her for such a question.

"I think you should go to your bed and sleep. And I think

you should kiss me once or maybe twice before you go. Are you brave enough?"

She turned to him. "Now you ask questions that can't be answered. Either I must call myself a coward or kiss you. You tread very hard for a man who is supposed to be such a good hunter."

He inclined his head so that the hawk feather brushed against his shoulder, and smiled at her. "You do not look like a coward to me, Walks-Ahead."

"You are right, I am not afraid"—Hannah leaned forward until her mouth was very near his—". . . to be thought a coward." Then she hopped up before he could stop her.

Strikes-the-Sky craned his head to look at her over his shoulder. His back was perfectly straight, still wet in the moonlight. "Sleep well, Walks-Ahead."

Hannah looked down at him and thought suddenly of Lily's drawing.

"My little sister thinks you are the perfect man." *For me,* she might have added, but did not; her courage did not reach so far.

He smiled in surprise. "I have made one conquest, at least."

Hannah bent over and she pressed her mouth to his. His fingers caught in the dark veil of her hair and he cupped her face in his palms, hard and warm, and just that simply she came to know the taste of him: sweet and sharp. He made a welcoming sound deep in his throat.

She pulled away, her hair trailing through his hands.

"Good night," she said, and walked back to the cabin without looking back, not even once, because she was afraid that if she did she would go to him and make a liar of herself.

Chapter 37

There were two things that Lily and Daniel agreed on without hesitation: Jemima Kuick was plotting something bad, and Hannah needed to be protected from her. Lily's idea was this: they would take turns going on Hannah's rounds in the village with her.

Daniel said, "It's my responsibility to keep her safe, not yours. You're a girl. You can't even fire a gun." Not only was that a bald-faced lie—Lily was a good shot with a musket and would be a better one if she bothered to practice more; when she was tall enough, she would learn how to handle a rifle too—but all that was beside the point.

Her brother was doing his very best to start a fight that would end with him pinning her down on the floor, so he could remind her that he was bigger and stronger. It was an old trick of his, one Lily had discussed with their father. His advice had been simple and to the point, as it always was. He said, "You'll never best your brother for pure strength, Lily. You've got to use your mind. Pin him down with words first, that'll throw him off."

"I shouldn't have to fight my own brother," Lily had grumbled, and her father took her by the shoulders and looked her in the face.

"Where'd you get that idea?"

"From Mr. Gathercole. We were arguing about . . . something and he came up behind us and said we should be glad to have each other and that it was sinful for us to fight."

Her father got his most thoughtful look then. After a while he said, "Mr. Gathercole means well, but he don't always make sense. Listen here, daughter. You'll have to get along with all kinds of folks out there in the world when you go off on your own—don't argue with me now about staying here forever, just listen. Some'll play fair and some won't. What goes on between you and your brother, that's part of learning how to tell the difference. You know Daniel would never cause you real harm. You know he'd put his life on the line to keep you safe, and you'd do the same for him."

It wasn't a question, but Lily nodded anyway. The thought of Daniel's painted face that day at Eagle Rock came to her, and with it a rush of affection.

"Then pay no mind to Mr. Gathercole. You remember that your best weapon in any argument with your brother right now is your mind. Someday down the line he'll come around to realize that he needs to use his head before his muscles, but right now it's your advantage. You understand me?"

The funny part about advice was this: the better it was, the harder it was to remember when a person needed it most.

To her brother Lily said, "She'll be suspicious if it's always you. She's used to having me follow her around the village."

He frowned, because he didn't like the argument but he couldn't counter it either. "I could tell her I'm interested in medicine."

"Are you?"

Daniel lifted a shoulder in an absent way. "I could be."

Lily said, "I'm going with her today. I can't stop you if you want to come along but then it will look strange tomorrow when it's your turn. You decide for yourself."

It turned out that Lily didn't need to fool Hannah into letting her come along when she visited patients, because by the third day people had begun to ask for her. Word had traveled that Lily could draw a good likeness, and it seemed that everybody in Paradise wanted to see themselves on paper.

Her mother made her a new sketchbook, this one bound so that it could lie flat while she worked; her father gave her a penknife and spent time teaching her how to best whittle the pencils Gabriel Oak had left her without wasting any of the precious lead.

All of this combined with the fact that Hannah was spending more time every day talking to Strikes-the-Sky put Daniel in a bad mood that no words could counter. Then Runs-from-Bears decided to take the boys into the bush for a week of tracking.

"What about Jemima?" Lily asked him while he was getting ready to go. "I thought it was your job to protect Sister from Jemima Kuick."

The look on his face, confusion and guilt and anger, made Lily sorry to have spoken.

"Sister has Strikes-the-Sky," Daniel said crossly. "She doesn't need me now."

Which made Lily feel even worse, because there was some truth to it. Hannah was so busy with the doctoring and the vaccinations and with Strikes-the-Sky that she seemed to be moving away even when she stood at the hearth stirring soup and talking to the other women about the garden or work around the house or who was sick in the village.

Between her chores, going around the village with her sister, and Uncle Strong-Words, Lily shouldn't have had time to feel alone. But she hadn't thought about what it would be like to have the boys gone while Curiosity and Galileo were away in Albany too. She said as much to her father, who put down the trap he was fixing and pulled her onto his lap.

"Things have been mighty unsettled this summer," he said.

She snuggled closer to push her face against his buckskin shirt, better than any silk. As a little girl she had sometimes sat on his lap and chewed on the fringe on his shirt when her mother wasn't looking. Lily wished now she were not too old for such things.

He said, "It's no wonder you're anxious. I am too."

Her father made her no promises about everybody coming home soon safe and sound, but Lily felt better anyway.

"Yesterday I drew a likeness of Mrs. Cunningham that made her laugh out loud."

When her father was in a teasing mood his left eyebrow cocked up at an angle, as it did now. He leaned down to tickle her with his beard stubble until she shrieked. "Did you make her look like a queen with rubies and diamonds in her hair?"

"No." Lily struggled to get away, without success. "I drew her likeness, her real likeness, the way I see her."

"Including the wart on her chin, the one with three hairs as long as cat's whiskers?"

Lily narrowed her eyes. "Well, maybe I didn't make the hairs as long as they really are . . . but she liked it anyway. She said she didn't know she looked so much like her own mother, and she gave me a piece of maple sugar as big as your thumb."

"Well then," said her father. "I better have a look at this drawing of yours."

"Wait," Lily said, and he drew up. "I wanted to ask you something else." She gathered her words together and then let them out in a rush.

"Why does Hannah argue so much with Strikes-the-Sky? I thought she was starting to like him a little at least, but they do as much arguing as they do talking like normal people. One minute everything's fine and then she gets mad at him and he laughs and she stomps off."

"I don't suppose you heard what they were arguing about."

"Clothes."

"Ah."

"You see," Lily said with great seriousness, "Strikes-the-Sky believes that Sister shouldn't wear O'seronni clothes ever, not even when she goes to see people like the Gathercoles. He says if they want her help they should accept her for what she is."

"And your sister said?"

"She says that it's none of his business if she wears doeskin or calico or walks around buck naked—she said that, really—and that she wouldn't be shamed into or out of any kind of clothing at all. She said he was arguing for the sake of arguing and that if he *wasn't,* why then he was stupider than she thought not to see the obvious. Then she called him a name and slammed the door in his face."

"Did she? And what did she call him?"

Lily squinted. "She called him a pigheaded jackass. In *English.*"

"Oh ha." Her father gave her a sour smile and put her off his lap with a thump. "In your sister's case that kind of talk is called courting."

"That's what Mama said too, when I asked her."

"She's the expert," said Lily's father. "You can take your mother's word for it."

"Maybe I should be paying attention for when I'm older,"

Lily said. She paused once again. "Do you think that Sister was right, was he arguing just to argue? To get her mad?"

"I'd say that he's arguing for the sake of courting," her father said. "Now what about that sketch you were going to show me?"

Every other day Hannah's rounds took her to the Wildes' farm, so that she could check the progress of Nicholas's vaccination blisters and change his sister's dressing. Eulalia had caught her arm on a nail and the wound wasn't healing the way it should, something that worried Hannah enough to talk to Richard Todd about it.

While she recounted the treatments she had tried without success Hannah wondered how much the doctor was really taking in, as he was in the middle of making adjustments to the draw on the reverberating furnace.

Then he shot her an impatient glance. "Sounds like the wound might need cauterizing. I'll have a look at her tonight at the trading post."

It was the eighth day since the first batch of vaccinations—both the ones in the trading post and the ones she had done at home with virus material brought from the city—and tonight the village was supposed to gather for the next round. By Hannah's calculations, if everything went according to plan, she'd have virus from fifteen recently vaccinated patients, which meant that working with the doctor they might be able to do as many as sixty more today. If that many people showed up who were willing. Hannah wished again that Curiosity were home; her help would be much missed.

"Might as well look at Mrs. Gathercole's sore throat at the same time," Richard added, interrupting Hannah's calculations.

She thought of pointing out that Mrs. Gathercole, whose sensibilities were so easily upset, might not wish to be examined in a public place. The look on Richard's face as he crouched in front of the furnace made it clear that he wasn't interested in Mrs. Gathercole's sensibilities or any other kind of interruption, and so she simply gathered her things together and left.

Lily was waiting for her, her dark head bent over her sketchbook. One plait had come undone and the curls flew around her head in the breeze.

"Where are we going first?" She skipped along behind, putting her book and pencil into the pouch that hung from a string looped around her neck and shoulder. Many-Doves had sewn the pouch from moccasin leather and Pines-Rustling had done the beadwork, and Hannah had never seen a child more pleased with a gift.

"The Wildes' place," Hannah said.

"But I've drawn both of them," Lily said without any rancor at all. And then: "There's always that old dog of theirs, the one with the chewed-off tail and one eye. Maybe I can get him."

"Do you think you'll ever get tired of drawing?" Hannah asked, and then bit back a laugh at Lily's expression, both thoughtful and resentful.

"Do you think you'll get tired of medicine?"

"I hope not," Hannah said.

Lily nodded as if she had proved a point. "You won't, and neither will I. No more than Daniel will ever get tired of the endless forests and hunting and trapping and all of that."

At the Wildes' the door stood open, but there was no reply to Hannah's call.

"There they are." Lily pointed. "In the orchard."

With a few exceptions—the most obvious being the doctor, the preacher, and Axel Metzler, who kept the tavern—the men in Paradise made their living hunting and trapping, and left the crops and the raising of children and animals—pigs, chickens, goats, and the occasional cow—to their women. In this, Elizabeth sometimes pointed out quite sharply, men of all colors were equally stubborn. There was one way to divide things up on the frontier, and one way only: men's work was in the endless forests, in the marshes, or on the lakes; women planted corn and beans and squash, cabbage and kale in the rich soil near the river and tended it while their babies slept nearby in the shade.

But Nicholas Wilde seemed to be made of other stuff. He hunted for meat and he set a few traps for the furs they needed for their own use, but most of his effort went into the orchard he had started when he came to Paradise five years earlier on a wagon crowded with apple-tree saplings. The men of Paradise had laughed right out loud. Then the Wildes built a little cider mill and produced their first batch of applejack. Just that easily the jokes and comments and wonderings about Nicholas Wilde's manliness stopped.

Axel Metzler had said it for all of them: a man who could grow apples that produced such a strong and tasty jack deserved some respect.

After that, the men listened good-naturedly when Nicholas Wilde talked about being the one to come up with the perfect eating apple. Everybody knew that apples were for pressing, but if Wilde wanted to eat them too, that was all right with the men of Paradise, as long as he kept his priorities straight.

Hannah and Lily found Nicholas and his sister in the middle of the orchard with its neat rows of small trees, twisted branches heavy with fruit just beginning to move beyond green. They were both so involved in examining fruit on a tree just five feet tall that they didn't look up.

"What's this one called?" Lily asked straightaway.

"Come from seed off the graft of a Snow on the Seek-No-Further," said Nicholas. He was working with his sleeves rolled up and Hannah could see even from a few feet away that the vaccination blisters were at their peak. She just hoped that he didn't break one by accident, as happened more often than she liked.

He took no notice of her examination, as he was busy talking apples with Lily. "Don't have a name yet. Probably never will neither. Looks like another spitter to me."

"That's an apple too hard and sour to press or eat," Lily explained to Hannah with great seriousness. All the children spent a lot of time in the Wildes' orchard in the fall, and Nicholas would talk about his trees to anybody willing to listen.

Eulalia said, "If you can give us ten minutes we'd greatly appreciate it."

Her face was flushed and her upper lip and forehead were wet with perspiration. Hannah feared that it was not the sun but a fever that gave Eulalia such color, but she nodded. "We'll wait back at the cabin."

On the way Lily kept pausing to point out trees. "That one's called Spitzenburg, it's President Jefferson's favorite. Those there are Ribston Pippins. Nicholas grows those for cider. That's Maiden Blush, the earliest of them all. Tasty too."

"Are those the yellow ones—"

"Eulalia brought us some of those last fall, yup. You see that tree with a hump there? That's my favorite, Duchess. The apples are a greeny yellow color with red stripes. And all those trees over there—" She made a great sweep of her arm. "Those are the 'maybe trees.'"

They had reached the cabin, and Hannah sat down on the porch step with Lily just beside her. "I suppose I should ask what you mean by 'maybe trees.'"

Lily folded her arms around herself and rocked back and forth, pleased for once to know more than her formidable older sister, and to be able to share that knowledge.

"Did you know that an apple tree never ever breeds true? Every time you plant a seed you never know what's going to come of it except it won't be a copy of the tree it came from."

"Like people," Hannah said, and Lily tilted her head to one side in surprise. She let out a laugh. "Like people, yes. Maybe that tree there won't produce anything but tiny spitters no bigger than a knuckle, or maybe it'll put out big red apples better than the Duchess and the Spitzenburg both. That's why I call them 'maybe trees,' because maybe one of them will have that perfect apple that will make the Wildes a fortune. When they find that perfect apple they're going to call it Paradise. Look, here comes Eulalia. She looks sick."

"Yes," said Hannah, all thought of maybe trees and perfect apples banished instantly. "She does."

The wound on Eulalia Wilde's right forearm, four days old, was tender to the touch and inflamed all around with a bright red halo that was twice the size it had been two days ago. Worse still, red streaks reached out, moving toward her hand in one direction and her shoulder in the other.

"You should have sent for me," Hannah said mildly, because to show her alarm would only make things worse. "Or you might have gone to see Dr. Todd."

Eulalia had gone very pale under skin tanned dark from working in the sun. She said, "I washed it out with that medicine every day, the way you showed me. Didn't do much good though." She sucked in a breath as Hannah began to probe the wound with gentle fingers. Her brother put a hand on her other shoulder and cast Hannah a questioning glance.

Without looking Eulalia in the eye, Hannah said, "The doctor told me he was planning on checking your arm tonight at the trading post, but I'll ask him to come by here this afternoon.

You need to stay in bed, fevered as you are. I'm going to leave you willow bark tea; I want you to drink a cup every hour."

"There's so much work," Eulalia began, but her brother squeezed her shoulder to cut her off.

"She'll go to bed," he said firmly. "And wait for the doctor."

"Will you come with him?" Eulalia asked. "I'd feel better if you were here too."

"I'll be here," Hannah said. "I promise. Now let me do what I can for you."

When they were just out of hearing of the Wildes' cabin Lily said, "It's bad, isn't it. The smell means that the wound has gone bad."

"Yes," Hannah said. "It's very bad."

"Will Uncle Todd have to cut off her arm?"

Hannah let out a deep breath. "Maybe," she said slowly. "If it's a matter of saving her life. But he may want to cauterize it first." *But I doubt it,* she might have added. If it were her decision alone, Hannah would have told Eulalia that the arm would have to come off if they were to have any chance of saving her. If the infection hadn't settled in the blood already.

Just that suddenly she was very glad that she didn't practice medicine here on her own. As difficult as Richard Todd could be, he was an excellent surgeon and a confident one; thus far Hannah had never had to carry out an amputation by herself.

"I would rather die than lose my drawing hand," Lily said, with a sudden fierceness.

Sharp words rose in Hannah's throat. Then she saw the fear on her sister's face, and she swallowed them down again.

"I can't come with you when you go back to see her with the doctor, can I?" Lily said.

"No," said Hannah. "Not this visit."

Late in the afternoon Hannah dove into the lake under the falls and stayed submerged in the bone-cold, churning water until she began to feel clean again. By that time her lungs were screaming for mercy, and as she broke the surface a sound rose up deep from her belly, a rush of frustration and anger that sounded surprisingly like a scream.

Elizabeth was sitting on the rocks, barefoot, her arms

around her knees. She said, "I was starting to wonder. Come and sit with me, Squirrel."

Until she saw her stepmother sitting there Hannah didn't realize how much she had been wishing for her calm and trusted voice, the clear gray eyes that saw so much, the shy smile. She hiked herself up onto the rocks, warm with the sun, and lay down so that the doeskin of her overdress would have a chance to dry.

"You changed out of your village clothes," Elizabeth said.

With an arm over her eyes Hannah said, "This afternoon we . . . this afternoon I took Eulalia Wilde's left arm off above the elbow. Richard supervised."

The silence drew out for a long time, and while Hannah was glad to be with Elizabeth she was also very relieved that she had no questions to ask.

Finally she said, "It was easier than I expected, when I was in the middle of it. Then it was over and it was harder than I imagined."

"Because you know Eulalia?"

"Yes. And because it won't be enough," said Hannah, sitting up suddenly and wiping the lake water from her face. "Curiosity says you can tell about a wound sometimes if it's willing to give up or if it's nasty-minded. Richard doesn't like talk like that but Curiosity's right. And this wound is nasty."

Elizabeth struggled hard not to show the surprise and unease she was feeling. If she understood correctly, Hannah believed that Eulalia Wilde would not survive a simple scratch. Before she could think how to ask if she was correct, Hannah shook her head so that the water flew around her in a halo.

She said, "And then on the way home, Cookie stopped me."

"Cookie?" Elizabeth echoed. "From the mill house?"

"Yes. She took a great risk, I think. She was waiting for me in the trees just beyond the turnoff to Big Muddy. She thanked me for helping with Reuben's laying-out," Hannah said. "And then she asked me if I'd vaccinate her and the rest of the slaves. Behind the widow's back, of course."

Elizabeth realized she was holding her breath, and she let it go noisily. "And you said?"

Hannah shot her a sharp look, confusion and irritation. "I said of course I would vaccinate them if they wished. Should I turn them away? What other choice do I have?"

"None," Elizabeth said softly. "There is no other choice. Of course you must vaccinate them if they ask for it."

Hannah pressed the heels of her hands to her eyes. When she lowered them again she had managed to find a small and dismayed smile somewhere within herself.

She said, "You must forget that I told you about this, Elizabeth. I mustn't draw you into this new trouble. I don't know where it will end."

"Hannah Bonner," Elizabeth said, quite sharply. "Would you shut out your family when you need them most?" Then she put her arm around her stepdaughter's shoulder and drew her close. She was wet and shivering, and Elizabeth cared not at all.

Against Hannah's temple she said, "Just try to get rid of us. As single-minded as you are—and the Lord knows you came by that honestly—you wouldn't be able to shake us off. Whatever you do, wherever you go, Hannah, we are still your family. You must be very upset indeed if you need to be re minded of that."

They rocked together in the warm sun of the late afternoon for a few minutes. Then Hannah said, "I don't know what to do about Strikes-the-Sky."

Elizabeth made a soft sound and hoped it would be taken as encouragement. For many days now she had watched Hannah's face and seen so many new things there: exhilaration, confusion, longing, self-doubt. She had watched and waited for her to come and talk.

That Hannah had fallen—was still in the process of falling—in love, Elizabeth could see very well. What she did not know was how she could provide comfort when it was needed without intruding on something so perfectly personal. As Curiosity had done for her, in those first days of learning that she was capable of loving Nathaniel.

"If it were up to Strong-Words and Many-Doves I would go west with him," Hannah continued. "They both think he is a good match for me. Even Lily is convinced of it."

"Forgive me, daughter, but here the question is not what others think, but what you feel."

Hannah pulled away from her, shuddering a little in spite of the heat. "I don't want to go west."

It wasn't an answer to the question Elizabeth had asked, but she didn't point that out.

"My father likes him too," Hannah added.

"Yes," Elizabeth agreed. "He likes Strikes-the-Sky. Everyone here seems to."

"What do you think of him?"

Elizabeth hesitated. This was not the time for platitudes or empty comfort; Hannah needed the truth. "I think he has a courageous and kind heart," she said. "I think he needs help sometimes regulating his temper, but he will never direct that temper toward you. On his face I see that he loves you already, even after such a short time." She paused, but Hannah did not stop her.

"It will not be an easy life in the west but I think, if you decide you want to go with him, he will be a good husband."

In a tone that bordered on anger Hannah said, "That's what I think too."

This hung for a long minute in the air, as bright and untouchable as the dragonflies that played over the lake. Then a voice called down from the forest, a long *hiiii-eeeee!* of greeting.

"Otter," said Elizabeth. "And Strikes-the-Sky with him. I should go in now and see to supper if we have to be at the trading post by seven."

Strikes-the-Sky had a cut over his left eye that he had pressed closed with a handful of yarrow leaves. Sitting on a stool, he let Hannah examine the damage, his gaze fixed firmly on nothing at all, his hands resting on his knees. His breathing was deep and steady.

"To let yourself get caught in the face by a branch," she said grimly, pulling out the yarrow's delicate leaves. "You must have been daydreaming."

Strikes-the-Sky grunted and said nothing at all.

"You could have lost an eye."

"And yet I did not. I can see very well, Walks-Ahead, and what I see is that you're in a poor temper today. Trouble in the village?"

As she worked she told him about Eulalia Wilde, leaving nothing out. When she was finished he was quiet for a long time and then he said, "This evening I will burn some tobacco for her. To guide her to the shadowlands."

What a relief it was not to hear false hopes and the promise of healing through prayer. Hannah wanted to thank him, but she did not trust her own voice. Instead she said, "You will need three stitches, maybe four. It will hurt."

"You sound as if you like the idea," said Strikes-the-Sky, grinning without moving his head to look at her.

"Of course I don't like the idea. That would be—"

"Mean-spirited? Inappropriate? Wrong?"

She hushed him with an impatient look and got only a grin for her trouble.

Inappropriate. The word struck a nerve, because it made her nervous to stand so close to him bare-legged, in a damp doe-skin overdress. For the most part he had seen her only in O'seronni dress. What arguments they had had about calico and brocade and silk; how he had enjoyed goading her, and how little she had been able to resist that goading.

Now she stood next to him, for the first time in Kahnyen'kehàka dress and he said nothing at all. Which of course was what she wanted.

She was close enough to feel the warm hush of his breathing on her damp skin as she worked. Hannah understood very well what the fist in her gut meant; she knew that her body was responding even if her heart and mind were not yet ready. She looked around for Strong-Words, or for her father, but there was no sign of anyone who might have rescued her from her own feelings.

They were alone on the porch, although the door to the cabin stood open and they could hear Elizabeth moving from table to hearth and back again, the sounds of a knife on a cutting board and water being poured. From the cornfield where the rest of the women and children were at work voices and song drifted to them. Hannah thought briefly of calling for Lily to assist by passing the instruments she would need.

Coward, she whispered to herself.

Hannah focused on the contents of her medicine box and chose the bottle she needed. She took a curved suture needle and fine strong thread from the instrument case.

"Tilt back your head all the way, and don't move it until I tell you. I'm going to wash the wound out."

One corner of his mouth drew down sharply when the infusion of blackberry and winterbloom ran into the wound, but otherwise Strikes-the-Sky did exactly as she told him without complaint or question.

"There," she said as she tied the last stitch, and as if she had said *now,* he raised his hands and rested them on her hips. It was the first time he had touched her since the night by the side of the lake; it was the first time any man had touched her this way, and it made her catch her breath.

"Walks-Ahead," he said softly. "I have something important to tell you."

She was shaking; she knew he could feel it. Strikes-the-Sky drew her down to sit on the stool next to his own. His hands were back on his knees, and Hannah found that she could not look away from them.

He said, "Today we met a friend of yours deep in the forest. He cannot show himself, but he sends you a message."

Hannah blinked in surprise. "A friend of mine?"

"Almanzo Freeman."

"Manny?" Hannah repeated, her voice going hoarse and unfamiliar. "Manny is hiding in the forest? But why?"

Strikes-the-Sky said, "Here is the message. Tonight all of the blacks in the village, free or slave, will be in the trading post to be vaccinated. You must make sure that all of your people are there too. All of them. You must vaccinate the blacks first, and then keep them all there until you hear two gunshots, one after the other. Do whatever you have to do to make sure that none of the blacks and none of your people leave before they hear the shots. Anyone who is not in the trading post at the time the shots are fired might be accused of what is going to happen."

He recited this message in an easy tone, but his eyes never left hers.

"Do you understand, Walks-Ahead?"

"Yes. I understand. Is there any way to stop what is coming?"

"No," said Strikes-the-Sky. "And if there were I wouldn't tell you."

Hannah was quiet while she cleaned her suture needle and put her medicine box back in order. One part of her wanted to be angry with Strikes-the-Sky, but another part, the bigger part, was thankful for his watchful silence and for his help.

If Manny was nearby he knew about Selah and about Reuben both, and he would want the one thing that he would never be granted. Manny wanted justice, but he would have to settle for revenge. It was the kind of reasoning that would have shocked Elizabeth not so very long ago.

But not now; not after Selah.

Hannah looked up from her instrument case and found Strikes-the-Sky watching her. She said, "I will do what I can." And then: "You will be at the trading post this evening, I take it."

He tilted his head at her. "Yes. I'll be there to walk you home when you're done."

"I can walk myself home, thank you." She sounded prim and prissy to her own ears, but he did not laugh at her outright, as she expected him to.

"Not anymore," he said. "Tonight you must not walk alone, not anywhere."

"I need to talk to Manny," said Hannah. "You tell him that, tell him that I have to speak to him."

Strikes-the-Sky nodded and turned away, but not before Hannah saw the flicker of doubt that moved across his face.

Chapter 38

Neither Otter nor Strikes-the-Sky came to supper and so it fell to Hannah to tell the tale, something that she didn't much enjoy, as far as Nathaniel could see.

When she was done there was a small silence and then Lily spoke up, putting words to what everybody was thinking but didn't want to say.

"But how in the bejeezus—"

"Lily."

"Sorry, Mama—but how are you supposed to get everybody to the trading post in the first place, sister? Did anybody tell you that?"

"I expect that question's already been taken care of," said Nathaniel mildly. "Manny wouldn't leave something like that to chance. Not with the stakes so high."

Lily sat back suddenly, understanding crossing her face and worry following close behind. "Do you think—Strong-Words might be helping?"

"Maybe," Hannah said, too lightly. "It would make some sense."

Elizabeth tapped the table with one finger, looking from her husband to her father-in-law with narrowed eyes. "Why do I have the sense that this whole affair comes as no surprise to the two of you?"

Hawkeye grunted softly. "Manny's been in these parts three,

four days at least, judging by his tracks. We figured when he was ready he'd show himself."

"Why is he hiding?" asked Lily, looking from face to face. "Why doesn't he just come home?"

"There's a price on his head," said Hannah. "That's why."

"He is alone?"

It was the question Nathaniel had dreaded, and it came from Elizabeth. He looked her in the eye and lied.

"As far as I saw," he said.

Lily said, "I hate it when people won't say straight-out what's on their minds. Da, what's going on?"

Elizabeth shot Nathaniel an irritated look. "Yes, I have to agree. For our own safety we need to know exactly what it is you're planning."

Nathaniel pushed his empty plate away from him and leaned back in his chair. His wife and daughters were angry and scared, but there was no easy way to calm their fears—or his own.

He said, "Well, Boots, the plain truth is, I'm not planning anything at all except seeing that we all keep safe. So I want you to listen close. Once we leave for the trading post none of you is to move farther than three steps from me or Hawkeye. There's trouble afoot, but if you stick close you'll stay clear of it. Now before you take another chunk out of me, Elizabeth, I'll say this much: I don't know what it is that Manny's got planned, and I ain't about to sit here and guess either." He paused, and when Elizabeth had nothing to say, he cleared his throat and went on.

"We'll go down to the village like we said and we'll let Hannah here take the virus from these pretty blisters on our arms, and when she's done with the vaccinating, why, we'll come on home again. That's the plan, for the moment, or the best I can do, anyway."

Elizabeth looked only vaguely mollified, but she nodded anyway.

Nathaniel pushed back from the table. "I'll go have a word with Many-Doves and Pines-Rustling now. Be ready to leave in ten minutes."

Hannah's first worry was that nobody would show up to be vaccinated, but even before they came in view of the trading post the sound of voices put those fears to rest. The place was crowded, but whether that was good news or bad wasn't clear; some folks didn't seem to want to meet her eye, while others called out greetings in voices too loud and hearty. She threaded her way through the crowd, nodding at some and speaking a few words to others. There was a fine humming tension in the air, like swarming bees in the distance, but it wasn't until she was in the middle of the room that she saw the reason.

All of the blacks from the village stood there, slave or free, as Strikes-the-Sky had promised. All except Curiosity and Galileo. How strange it was to miss someone so fiercely and still to be glad they were safely somewhere else.

There was no talking or laughing among the blacks; their expressions ranged from fright to numb watchfulness. Cookie nodded at Hannah briskly, and the others followed her example.

Richard Todd was here already too, although there was no sign of Kitty or Ethan. He had his back to her as he made notations in the record book he had laid down on the top of a barrel of salt pork. The instruments they would need had been spread out neatly on a tray—by Bump, Hannah saw now—who was busy lining up ivory vaccinators. He paused to swing his head toward her and smile.

Richard straightened finally, grunted a greeting in Hannah's direction, and wiped his ink-stained fingers on a piece of linen he had draped over his shoulder.

"Time to get started!" he called out, loud enough to be heard on the porch and in the tavern too. "Those of you with eight-day blisters, step forward and roll up your sleeves. Those of you waiting to be vaccinated, you step back now until we need you. You too, Cookie, all of you. Just wait over there, it'll be a few minutes before we can start."

With the room so crowded it took a few minutes until the eight-day people could make their way to Richard: seven of Hannah's family from Lake in the Clouds, Jane McGarrity, Solange Hench, and Nicholas Wilde. Nicholas was pale and there were deep shadows beneath his eyes, but Hannah was surprised to see him here at all.

He caught her glance and said, "Mrs. Cunningham is sitting with my sister. I'd be thankful if you could take care of me first so I can get back to her, Miss Bonner." His tone as gentle and polite as ever; there was nothing of accusation in his tone or expression, but sorrow had already dug in deep. Richard didn't believe in giving families false hope, and he had told Nicholas Wilde straight-out how poor his sister's chances were.

Hannah did as he asked, listening as she worked to Richard as he answered a question Jed McGarrity had asked about the vaccinators. For once Hannah was thankful for Richard's gruff, efficient manner that made short work of gathering the virus from one person after another. Most of all she was thankful not to be alone just now in a room full of doubtful and worried people.

She was focused on catching the clear liquid from the blister on her father's right arm when Richard faced the room again. "We're just about ready here. Roll up your sleeves, both arms, as high as they'll go, and line up. Cookie, we'll start with your folks so you can get back to work."

An irritable voice rose from the back of the room.

"Dr. Todd! Are you planning on vaccinating them niggers without the widow's permission? And why in the hell ain't her man Dye here? Something ain't right."

Standing just beside her, Hannah's father put a hand on her shoulder and squeezed. "Steady now," he said softly. "Let Richard take care of it."

"That you talking, Tim Courtney?" Richard snapped.

A tall man as thin and knobby as old rope pushed forward from the crowd. "It is. And I ask again what right these slaves have to be here unless their rightful owner has sent them. Which don't seem likely, you'll have to agree."

"You here to be vaccinated, Courtney?"

The long face tightened. "May chance I am, may chance I ain't. What's that got to do with those slaves standing there?"

"I'll tell you. Anybody wanting to be vaccinated is welcome here. Anybody. If you're not planning on rolling up your sleeves, then you just shut your gob and get out. If you think it's your duty to go talk to the widow, why you do that.

"If you are here to get vaccinated, why then shut up anyway and mind your own business or I'll throw you out of here myself."

There was an uneasy murmuring in the room as people watched Tim Courtney for his reaction. He might take up the challenge just for the joy of it—he was a known brawler—but on the other hand he wasn't full drunk yet, and common sense might still prevail. Richard Todd had fifty pounds on him, and as mean as Courtney might be, the doctor in a fighting mood was worse, and everybody knew it.

Levi cleared his throat nervously. "Dr. Todd?"

"Yes?" Richard turned, still scowling.

He spoke with his gaze riveted on the floor. "It was Mr. Dye told us to come down and get vaccinated. Said he didn't want to lose valuable slaves to no pox and we was all to get scratched this evening. If Mr. Courtney wants to ask, Mr. Dye will tell him. Last we saw the overseer he was going into his quarters at the mill, like he do every evening after supper."

There was a moment's silence. Richard turned back to Courtney. "Does that satisfy you, or are you going up to the mill to ask?"

Courtney hesitated for three beats of Hannah's heart, and then he threw up a hand in surrender and shouldered his way to the back of the crowd.

"Let's get a move on, then," Richard said. "There must be forty people here."

Hannah turned in surprise. She hadn't bothered to count, but there were that many people here and maybe more, a third of them children. All of them rolling up their sleeves, all of them waiting to be vaccinated.

Just behind her Elizabeth said, "You see, you won them over."

And her father: "They're here because they trust you, daughter. Best get started."

Hannah gestured to Cookie, and picked up a lancet.

The first lesson Jemima Southern Kuick learned that evening while most of Paradise was filing into the trading post was a simple but bitter one: no matter how carefully a person might plan and scheme, something was bound to get in the way, or as her mother had been fond of saying: man proposes and God disposes.

She had come so far and managed so much and still here she sat on her mother-in-law's confounded Turkey carpet, bound hand and foot. It was only her anger that kept fear from getting the upper hand; that, and her pride. Mother Kuick might snivel and howl, but she would not.

To Jemima's right was her husband, pale, his hair disheveled and a cut over his cheekbone bleeding freely; to her left her mother-in-law rocked and moaned and sang snatches of bible verse. Just beyond her were Becca and Georgia, both of them as still and cold as stone.

And in front of them, sitting in the widow's own rocker with a primed musket in one hand and a tomahawk in the other, was a tar-black man Jemima had never seen before. He was young, tall, broad of shoulder, well armed, and dressed from his moc-casined feet to the crown of his shaved scalp like a Mohawk on the warpath. Streaks of red gleamed under each eye.

"Speak to him in French," the widow hissed at her son. "Try *French*. Offer him anything he wants." She sent a skittery sidelong glance in Jemima's direction, and licked her lips. "Tell him you'll show him the strongbox." This last came out in a hoarse whisper, and Jemima knew exactly why: every penny that belonged to the Kuicks was in that strongbox, hidden someplace that even Jemima had never been able to find.

"Mother," Isaiah said with a calm weariness. "I tried French. I tried English and German. If he speaks any of those languages he will not speak them to me."

The black eyes watched them without a hint of interest in the conversation, and still Jemima wasn't convinced that he didn't understand every word.

The widow said, "Then you must try to rush him, Isaiah. The Lord will guide your hand."

A shiver ran up Jemima's back, as wide and cold as a river. "Don't be foolish, old woman. Don't you see he's tied up just like the rest of us? You're only making things worse."

The widow made a noise deep in her throat and in re-sponse the black Indian inclined his head, lifted the cocked musket, and pointed it directly at her small white face. After a count of three he lowered it again.

"You see?" Jemima said, and her mother-in-law sobbed.

"What does he want?" Georgia asked, as she had asked every few minutes without pause or fail. "What does he *want*?" Her voice spiraled up and broke like a child's. "Why doesn't he just take what he wants and go?"

By the clock on the mantelpiece they had been asking each other and themselves that question for almost two hours.

They had just been finishing supper when the black Mohawk had walked into the dining room herding the servants in front of him with the musket tucked neatly into the niche under Georgia's shoulder blade. The widow had taken one look at him and fainted dead away. When she woke again they were all in the parlor, and her precious son was tying her wrists together under the close supervision of a creature she had hoped never to see outside her nightmares.

While the others wept and prayed and rocked, Jemima considered. To start with there had been very little in the room that might serve as a weapon—knitting needles, the poker that stood against the hearth, a heavy crystal bowl that had survived more than one of the widow's throwing fits, but each of those things was gone now; the black Indian had pointed at Becca, pointed at each potential weapon in turn, and then pointed out into the hall. When she had removed them all, he closed the door, turned the key, and put it in a pouch that hung around his neck.

Because there was no way to fight him, Jemima did the only thing she could: she made a study of his person. She memorized the angle where the broad nose met his brow, the shape of his skull, the line of the wide, full-lipped mouth; she counted the stripes painted on his face and upper arms, studied the tattoo of three dots below his left eye, and continued row by row down his face, his neck, his chest, and disappeared into his breechclout.

There was quillwork on his bullet pouch and his moccasins, an earring in one ear, and ornaments hung on rawhide strings around his neck: a leather pouch, a clutch of what looked like bear teeth, some wampum beads, a silver coin with a hole punched in it, a disk of wood with a stone lodged at its center, its edges carved in a geometric pattern.

"I have to use the necessary," Georgia hissed, her fear giving way in the face of desperation. "Don't you understand, you godless savage? The *necessary*."

"He doesn't care," Jemima snapped. "Piss your pants and shut up."

"Why doesn't anybody come?" Becca whispered. "Why doesn't Mr. Dye come? Where is Cookie? Do you think he killed them? Do you think everyone in the village is dead? Oh, my mother."

Isaiah was rocking slightly, his bound hands on his knees and his head bowed, but he stilled at Becca's words. Worried for his lover; more worried for Ambrose Dye than he was for his mother or wife—his pregnant wife—or even himself. A bitter taste filled Jemima's mouth; words that she could not say.

A scratching at the door and they all stilled.

"Help!" screeched the widow. "Help me! Help me!"

The Indian got up slowly from his chair and came over to the widow, who ducked her head and cowered and whimpered, her bound hands raised as if to ward him off. His face was contorted with fury and disgust.

Go ahead, Jemima thought. *Kill her. Start with her; grant me that much.*

Instead he spat on the widow's bowed head.

She screamed to feel his spittle on the back of her neck, jerked convulsively, and fainted.

The black Indian tucked the musket into the wide leather belt next to a knife sheath and touched the pouch around his neck. At the door he looked back at them, his face with the broad flat nose and wide mouth completely and utterly blank of anything that might be called human.

"Stay here until you hear two shots," he said. His English was accented like any Indian's, blunt sounds and chopped-off words. "If you try to leave this room before you hear those shots, the men keeping watch outside will kill you and set fire to the house. If you do as I say no harm will come to you."

When he had closed the door behind himself Becca let out a long and wavering sigh and then burst into noisy tears.

"Calm yourself," said Isaiah. "You must calm yourself."

Jemima sent him a disdainful look and began to inch her way to the windows on her knees.

"Don't!" Georgia cried out. "Don't! They'll kill us sure!"

"Be quiet, you cow," Jemima snapped. "Somebody get over there and blow out the candles so I can see."

It was Becca who did as she said, moving in odd little hops. When the light was extinguished Jemima put her face to the window and concentrated. The sun had set not a half hour ago, but there was no moon and she could see very little.

He was there, just below the house, looking toward the village where the trading post blazed with light and people moved about on the porch. He was there, and not alone; that much had been true.

There were two men with him, but she could make out little about them except that they were Indian. *Bonner's Mohawks,* she whispered to herself. Maybe something good would come of this night after all, if it drove the Mohawks off Hidden Wolf once and for all. That pleasant thought was interrupted by another one, less welcome.

What had happened in the two hours they had spent captive in this room?

Two of the men below the window raised arms above their heads and single shots rang out, one after the other, the flash from the muzzles almost enough to blind. Almost enough, and still Jemima saw so clearly: three men, two of them black. The third white, with hair such a deep and true red that it could never be forgotten or mistaken.

Jemima blinked, and Liam Kirby and the Indians were gone.

Hannah had just used the last of the fresh virus to vaccinate Anna McGarrity when two shots rang out in the night.

"Christ Almighty, what was that?" shouted Axel Metzler.

The vaccinator slipped from Hannah's fingers, spraying the precious clear liquid over the floor but it didn't matter: Anna was already gone, running with the rest of the crowd, a hand fluttering over her shoulder as if in apology.

"One arm's better than none!"

Hannah caught her father's eye, her grandfather's, and then Strikes-the-Sky, who stood near the door with Strong-Words while the others pushed out into the night. He gave her an almost imperceptible nod. *Yes, this is right.*

Lily sidled up next to her. She was trembling a little, and Hannah took her hand and squeezed it, just as Elizabeth, Many-Doves, and Pines-Rustling came up on Lily's other side. The women standing together, and the men with weapons at the ready. This was right too, but the comfort it gave was thin and cold.

"Miss Bonner? Dr. Todd?" Ezekiel spoke quietly. He had stepped to the front of the small group of blacks. "Is it all right if we go on back to the mill now?"

Richard Todd cast a suspicious glance from Ezekiel to Hannah and then to Strikes-the-Sky.

"You can go, Zeke. All of you can go."

"We thank you kindly for your help, Dr. Todd, Miss Bonner." Cookie smiled, a fierce smile. A triumphant smile, thought Hannah.

Cookie said, "Don't recall when I passed a more pleasant evening."

"What do we do now?" Lily wanted to know.

"We set right here and wait until we get some news," said Nathaniel. Elizabeth caught his eye and he pointed with his chin to the rocking chairs and stools by the cold hearth. "Might as well be comfortable, Boots."

What he wanted, Elizabeth could see very well, was for them to remove themselves to the back of the room where they would be better protected from whatever was about to come through the door. She had seen Nathaniel in every kind of situation outside of direct battle, and the uneasy thought came to Elizabeth that she was finally seeing that now.

A preternatural calm had come over him; when he moved his whole being seemed to shimmer with a focused energy as cold and hard as gunmetal. The others—Hawkeye, Strong-Words, Strikes-the-Sky—were just the same. For once even Richard Todd seemed to be paying attention, jolted finally out of the shell of boredom and irritation that he used to keep himself separate from everyone.

"What's this about, Bonner?" he asked.

It was Hawkeye who answered him. "We don't know, exactly. From the sound of it something's going on up at the mill. If they ain't calling for you I don't expect any blood's been spilled."

Beside Elizabeth, Hannah tensed almost imperceptibly.

Elizabeth took Lily on her lap and thought of Daniel, safe away in the endless forests with Runs-from-Bears and Blue-Jay.

"Maybe it's a good thing that Curiosity and Galileo have stayed away so long," Lily said softly. "Curiosity is always telling me she's getting too old for such excitement."

Elizabeth looked down at her daughter in surprise. In her arms Lily was strumming with an energy that seemed too large and bright for such a small being; she would not have been surprised to see her glowing like a star. The child wasn't afraid, and why should she be? Here in her mother's arms with these good men standing between them and whatever was out there in the dark, she was perfectly safe. Elizabeth pulled her closer.

From far away the sound of men's voices raised not in anger but alarm, agitation, rough laughter.

Some of the edginess went out of the room. Another five minutes passed, and then ten. They heard the tavern door open and shut.

"Axel?" called Hawkeye. "That you?"

Charlie LeBlanc stuck his head in the adjoining door. "He's still up at the mill. Nathaniel, Hawkeye, what are you boys still hanging around here for? You missed all the fun. Some Indians tied the widow Kuick up and left her trussed like a hog on her own parlor floor."

All the men let out a sigh, the tension running away from them like rainwater.

"What Indians?" asked Hawkeye.

Charlie had a tankard in his hand and he paused to take a good swallow. "Black skinned, or so say the Kuicks. Jemima says she never saw any of them before, and Becca didn't recognize them either. The widow's giving the details to Jed McGarrity right now."

"How many?" asked Richard Todd, looking more interested now.

"Three or four, but nobody got a real look. One of them stayed in the parlor while the others went through the house. Looks like all they took is the strongbox and a carving knife with an ivory grip." A thoughtful look passed over his otherwise guileless expression.

"Bad luck for the widow that the slaves was all down here getting vaccinated."

"Bad luck indeed," said Richard Todd grimly, shooting Nathaniel a sharp glance. "And where was Mr. Dye while all of this was happening?"

"That's the other strange thing," Charlie said, scratching his chin. "No sign of him anywheres. They searched the house and the mill and some of the men took torches and are still looking around outside but there's no trail. No blood or sign of a struggle either. Like he just disappeared. Say . . ."

He looked at each of the men in turn. "You don't think he could've been scheming with those Indians, do you? Maybe it was Dye who took the strongbox."

Elizabeth's mind raced. She hadn't thought of Jode for days and now he stood before her as she had last seen him, on the day that Selah died. A black-skinned Mohawk. It must be Jode, but how? Were the rest of the Red Rock people here with Manny? Why? She scrambled so hard to make sense of these strange pieces of information that Lily had to pinch her cheek before she realized her daughter had been asking her a question.

With her mouth against her mother's ear, Lily said, "They took Dye, didn't they, Mama? We'll never see him again."

Chapter 39

Cookie was at the hearth in the morning as if nothing had happened. For a few long minutes Jemima watched the old woman stir pots and check the biscuits as they browned. She was devious, and Jemima had underestimated her. That much she must admit, at least to herself.

All the work fell on Cookie alone this morning. Georgia had left at first light with her things tied in a sheet, willing to walk back to Johnstown if that's what it took to get away from Paradise; Becca was sitting with the widow, who had taken to her bed with a bottle of laudanum clutched in one trembling hand. But Cookie didn't seem to mind the extra work and in fact she looked tired, but satisfied. She hummed to herself, a melody Jemima didn't recognize.

Isaiah had been out all night with the search party that was tracking the thieves, except of course he wasn't. All that interested him was finding Ambrose Dye, who had disappeared so completely and quietly.

Down at the mill the slaves sat idle; they would sit that way all day until Dye came back, or Isaiah collected himself and remembered that they needed direction. Jemima imagined them sitting around grinning at one another. How sweet revenge must be, doubly sweet to have been bought so cheaply. Dye gone; the Kuicks robbed of every penny, and not one of them would hang.

When Jemima thought of the strongbox her insides clutched so hard that a wave of nausea rose up in her throat. All night long she had stared at the ceiling and asked herself how they had managed it. The answer came back every time like an echo: *with Liam Kirby's help.* How she would like to see him hang, but that would never happen, not unless the search party caught up with him. And then what would he say to save himself, what stories would he tell?

Sick with rage, Jemima had turned her face to the pillow and torn a hole in the linen with her teeth.

Now, standing in the doorway she said, "What are you planning to do with all that money, Cookie? Going to buy yourself a new headscarf or two?"

There wasn't even a ripple of response; it was as if the woman had gone deaf overnight. Jemima had promised herself that she'd hold her temper, and so she wound her hands in her skirt and stayed where she was.

"I'll say this much, it was a masterful plan. I think the part I like best is all of you going down to the trading post on Dye's orders. Everybody saw you there so nobody can say you had any hand in what happened, and Dye's not here to call you liars. I don't suppose they'll ever find him—" She paused, and thought of Liam Kirby, felt herself flushing.

Cookie glanced over her shoulder, her expression blank but a flashing behind her eyes. Bitter triumph; sour satisfaction. Pity.

"Glad to be rid of Dye, ain't you?"

Jemima's heart rabbited under her bodice, so fast that it echoed at her wrists and at the base of her throat where sweat trickled. Cookie's expression, white hot and knowing.

Her own voice coming from far away, "I wondered—" And she stopped.

"You wondered if I knew?" For a long time there was no reply at all, and then Cookie straightened. She wiped her hands on her apron as she studied Jemima.

"I been with the widow since she was sixteen years old and I was just a few years younger," she said, her voice strong and steady. "Every day for near fifty years I been cooking for the woman and looking after her. When Isaiah was born it was me that put him to the breast, right alongside my Ezekiel. I stood by and listened to her bargain for a better price when she sold my man away from me and our boys. Reuben wasn't a month old. You know why she sold Samuel? Because she didn't want me having no more children. I was too old, she said. Wasn't seemly. She said that to my face.

"It was me that nursed old Mr. Kuick through the gout and washed his skinny backside every day while he lay there dying of the Frenchman's disease, whispering things. Oh, he hated her even worse than I did, but he hid it good. Old Kuick and me, we had that in common.

"I watched Isaiah grow to a man, I watched him *hard*. Let me tell you something, Mrs. Jemima Kuick. There ain't nothing about this family I don't know. Nothing."

Her large eyes, perfectly black, blinked once and again and then they settled on Jemima's waist.

"Now I got something to say, and then I'll be quiet. Mr. Dye sent all us slaves down to the trading post to be vaccinated against the pox. We did as we was told, good niggers every one of us. What happened here while we was gone, where the overseer went, who those Indians were, who took the strongbox—I don't know nothing about any of that."

She turned her back on Jemima and picked up a spoon.

Jemima could not help the trembling in her voice, but neither could she walk away. She said, "Maybe the law says we can't hang you without proof, and maybe we can't even sell you south the way you deserve, but we can sell you. There are worse places to be in New-York State, and I guarantee you're going to find that out firsthand."

Cookie's smile was cold when she looked over her shoulder at Jemima. "My, my," she said softly. "Ain't you got a lot to learn. Don't you try to make the widow choose between me and you. You won't like what comes of it." Another glance at Jemima's thickening waist. "You won't like it at all."

Her head throbbed as if somebody had hit her with a rock, but Jemima did not go to her bed. Instead she went to the office and stood on the threshold of an open door that had always been locked to her.

The walls were lined with shelves laden with ledgers, file boxes marked: correspondence, lumber, bills payable, mill purchase.

She spread the papers from this last one over the desk, moving a stand of quills, a bottle of ink, tightly corked, a stick of sealing wax on a square of glass, a candle box, a flint box. A half-empty bottle of brandy, with a dirty glass beside it. A sprinkling of tobacco; slanting light laced with dust motes.

Jemima wasn't allowed in this room, not even to clean. Grime on the doorjamb; an inch of dust on the shelves; the stink of a dead mouse.

Letters, contracts, old John Glove's signature, wavering across the bottom of a deed. Cut neatly from the Albany newspaper:

> **FOR SALE in the Village of Paradise on the West Bank of the Sacandaga. On three acres, one wooded, a house and gristmill with outbuildings. The mill built of wood with stone foundation, two overshot oaken waterwheels on a strong and fast-moving mountain stream, three pair burr-stones. Millworks in good repair; new stone corn-kiln adjoining. Excellent business opportunity in a growing village. Inquire Mr. Glove, Paradise Millworks.**

The rug on the floor had been pushed to one side. Beneath it was a square of floorboards cleverly made that had been lifted out and set aside to reveal a hole the size and shape of a strongbox. An empty hole.

Ambrose Dye had sat in the straight-backed chair next to the desk many times. Oh yes. Invited, welcomed at the door; the key turned in the lock to keep others out. The clink of coin, the rustle of folding money. Down in the village the men who drank in the tavern never tired of calculating the widow's riches. How much money she had hid away, how much the mill brought in, the labor of the slaves she sent away over the winter. Was she as rich as old Judge Middleton had been? As rich as Dr. Todd? Was she as rich as the governor, the president, bloody King George? They couldn't agree on any of it, but they never let it go. And the hottest argument: what to call a woman with so much money who didn't believe in banks. Was it wisdom or foolery?

That question was answered now. The money was all gone, everything was gone. Everything except the house, the mill, and the land they stood on; a little lumber, some tarnishing silver, and the widow's tapestry pillows and pockets and bell pulls in colors too bright for this darkening house.

And the slaves, of course.

"Thief," the widow was muttering in her sleep in the next room. *"Viper."*

The widow had declared Dye guilty. She would accept no other explanation, and no one argued with her. Who else knew about the strongbox hidden under the floorboards, after all. But Jemima knew that it wasn't Dye and so did Isaiah, who stumbled about white-faced, empty-eyed. He was out there on the mountain looking for a man not to hang him, but to bury him.

Isaiah knew as his mother could not that Ambrose Dye had no cause to steal from the widow: he had the best of her already, and would have the rest, in time. While Jemima stood aside he would carry the key to the strongbox around his neck. One day she would have found herself asking Ambrose Dye for pocket money.

She wondered if they had killed him straightaway, or marched him to some spot deep in the forests where they could take their time with him. The Indians knew how to get the most out of a man, and for once that idea was a pleasant one.

Liam's image flashed in front of her throbbing eyes: Liam below the window. Liam shoulder to shoulder with the black Indian. Liam's face white with fury as he emptied himself into her. Liam and Nathaniel Bonner, plotting together. Liam and Hannah. *The most beautiful thing Paradise has to offer.*

Jemima blinked it all away in a rage of tears, drew a deep breath, and sat down at the desk. Took a piece of paper, opened the bottle of ink, and began to compose a letter.

The Bonner men were out with the search party and neither Strikes-the-Sky nor Strong-Words could show themselves in the village for fear that a jumpy trapper would shoot without looking. But Hannah refused to stay at home, and so Elizabeth went with her stepdaughter on her daily rounds. They left a furious Lily behind, and warned the men that she would slip away to follow if they did not watch her.

When Elizabeth looked back from the edge of the clearing she saw Lily and Kateri leading Strikes-the-Sky up the mountain. The girls had been promising to show him the caves under the falls since he came. Elizabeth felt a rush of gratitude that she kept to herself; she would not praise Strikes-the-Sky to Hannah, not because she did not like the man—she liked him very much—but because she could see how close her stepdaughter was to making a decision that she did not want to influence. On the way to the village they spoke of unimportant things until an uneasy silence fell between them.

Finally Elizabeth said, "It is so long since I have spent any time with Manny. You know him much better than I do. Do you think him capable—" She paused to gather her thoughts.

Hannah said, "You're wondering if he's turned into a renegade, like that Marauder of the Swamps we read about in the city papers."

"I was thinking more of Robert Hude, the Earl of Huntington," Elizabeth said. "If you remember the poem we read."

"I do," Hannah said. "So you can't imagine him killing innocent people, but you can see him stealing from the rich. You think he took the widow's strongbox to buy weapons and provisions for his band of outlaws?"

In spite of the seriousness of the situation, Hannah was smiling and Elizabeth had to smile too.

"If you put it that way it does sound ridiculous. And I must admit your father was just as dismissive when I suggested the idea to him yesterday. But certainly they did not go to so much trouble only to make sure that the slaves could be vaccinated."

"No, that was just a coincidence," Hannah said. "A fortunate one, but still a coincidence. What happened last night was blood vengeance, but of a carefully planned and thoughtful kind. As you would expect of Manny."

"The theft of the strongbox was just to divert people's attention from their real purpose, is that what you're saying?"

Hannah shrugged. "They will find some use for the money, I'm sure."

After a long time Elizabeth said something she had not been able to say to Nathaniel, for simple fear of hearing the words spoken. "They will never find Dye's body."

"No," Hannah said slowly. "Of that much you can be sure."

"And the...others, with Manny?" She thought again of Jode, and again she pushed the idea away. Jode was safe in Canada; she would entertain no other possibility. For what else had they gone so far and lost so much?

Hannah stopped, and in her face Elizabeth saw many things: cautiousness, worry, resignation. Hannah said, "I don't know all of it but I will tell you what Strikes-the-Sky told me. If you really want to know."

Elizabeth had an image of Hannah sitting on the rocks under the falls in the heat of a summer night, deep in conversation with Strikes-the-Sky. Last night he had left the trading post first and when they came home he had been waiting for her. She had gone to him without a backward glance, without apology or explanation.

An hour later Elizabeth had come out on the porch and they were still there in exactly the same position, talking. They did not touch, or even look at each other, but still it was clear to see how strong the attachment between them had grown.

Then Hannah went to her bed alone and Strikes-the-Sky and Strong-Words had kept watch all night while Nathaniel and Hawkeye were away, tracking the men who had robbed the widow. That those men would never be found was something no one said aloud, but it was true nonetheless.

She shook her head. "No," she said finally. "I don't need to hear the details. At least not for the time being." .

When Hannah opened the kitchen door she found Richard waiting, something that happened so rarely that it must cause alarm.

He looked as if he hadn't slept at all: his hair stood up in a wild halo around his head, and his eyes were rimmed red. It looked as though a dirty thumb had been pressed into the soft flesh under his eyes, as a child played with bread dough. He cradled a cup in his hands, and a bottle stood at his elbow.

"I was just going to send after you."

Elizabeth was tense with surprise, but Hannah kept her own voice dispassionate. "How is Miss Wilde?"

He emptied his cup in one long swallow. "Not good. I'd take the rest of the arm off if I thought she'd live through the operation."

"I'll go straight to her."

"No," Richard said, more quietly. He ran a hand over his face and fought back a yawn. "I'll go back there as soon as I've cleaned up. Come by at midday, that'll be soon enough. There's other calls to make. Gathercole was here an hour ago waking up the house looking for me to come tend to his wife's sore throat . . . Elizabeth."

His head turned suddenly, as if he had just noticed that Hannah was not alone. Like a dog getting wind of a cat, Hannah thought. The simple truth was that when these two came face-to-face, neither of them could control the way old animosities came surging to the surface. Richard, abrupt at the best of times, veered toward rude and stayed there; Elizabeth went as sharp and brittle as flint. Only when the children were present did they make any effort to hold back.

He said, "Kitty's been asking for you. You might as well go see her now while I go over this call list with Hannah. You're no use to me here."

Elizabeth's brow lowered ominously. "Dr. Todd. Once again I do not know whether to be affronted by your rude manner, or to submit to the inevitable and simply admire your consistency. It is your one virtue, after all. That must count for something."

"Whatever suits you best, Elizabeth," he said, and turned away. Sometimes Hannah had the feeling that he was holding back a laugh when he and Elizabeth were sparring, but not today.

Kitty was still in bed with a breakfast tray to one side and the baby Meg on the other. At the sight of Elizabeth she sat up against the pillows, her face breaking into a great smile.

"I was starting to wonder if you were angry with me, it's been so long since you've come to call."

Elizabeth drew up a chair to the side of the bed and took the hand that Kitty held out. "Are you unwell?"

"Oh no. Not in the least, but Richard insists that I stay abed until ten or until I finish my breakfast, whichever comes first. I'm so glad you're here; there's a question I've been meaning to ask—"

"If you want to know when Runs-from-Bears will bring the boys home, I expect that you'll see Ethan toward the end of the week."

Kitty looked slightly confused, and then she laughed. "I'm not concerned about Ethan. I'm sure that Runs-from-Bears is looking after him, and after all, he's never happier than when he can be running around in the forest with the other boys. What I wanted to ask you was this."

She scooped the baby into her arms and held her up for inspection.

In the middle of a vast expanse of lace, dimity, and linen a small face peered out, as pink as a spring rose with great round eyes.

"Is she not the prettiest baby?"

"She is beautiful," Elizabeth agreed. "And she has done miracles for you. You look so much better, Kitty, it does my heart good to see you."

Kitty wrinkled her nose. "People were making such a fuss about me, I just don't understand it. Dr. Ehrlich cured me, as I knew he would."

Elizabeth had heard a great deal about Dr. Ehrlich from Hannah, but to open up that conversation with Kitty would bring nothing good at all. She searched for something to say while concern flitted across Kitty's face.

In a conspiratorial whisper she said, "You needn't say as much to Hannah. She was so kind and helpful and she brought my Meg to me." She looked down at the baby in her arms and smiled. "I am thankful to Hannah, you know that I wouldn't hurt her feelings for the world. Such a good creature. If it will do her good to take credit for my recovery, why then she shall have credit, here in Paradise at least." Her tone lowered a little further.

"I will admit to you, Elizabeth, I do think Hannah is not quite rational about Dr. Ehrlich. Perhaps it is professional jealousy; that is often a problem between practioners of medicine."

Elizabeth said, "And how is the nurse you brought with you from the city? Are you satisfied with her?"

Another wrinkle of the nose. "She's not very friendly, but

she looks after Meg very well for the most part. Except of course she's very quick to complain, as are most Germans as you no doubt have noticed yourself. Her English is never so good as when she's got a pain or she thinks herself insulted. Such a thin-skinned people in spite of their gruff manners. She's been complaining about a sore throat in spite of the fact that Richard treated her himself." She paused.

"I do wish Curiosity would come back home, she deals with the nursemaid far better than I ever could. I wonder what can be keeping her so long in Albany."

Ten minutes in Kitty's company was usually enough to set Elizabeth's teeth on edge, but today she had managed it in just five. She said, "It has been a long time since they've seen their Polly, after all. You mustn't begrudge them a few days' visit." *And some time with their new grandson,* she added to herself.

But Kitty had already turned her mind to other things "Look," she said, holding the baby closer. "Look at how she clasps my finger so tightly. Such a strong little girl, so vigorous."

A scratching at the door and it opened far enough for Daisy to peep in. "You just about done with that breakfast, Mrs. Todd? And Hannah's waiting for you downstairs, Elizabeth. She says if you don't mind it's time she got started."

Kitty straightened. "But I thought you would spend the morning here with me, Elizabeth. It is very boring here with Curiosity away and Richard so busy with the vaccinations and his research. Won't you stay a while at least? You haven't even seen the new gowns I brought back from the city, oh and the beautiful India shawl."

"I promised Hannah my help," Elizabeth said, rising. "You'll have to spare me this morning at least."

"Help Hannah? Why would Hannah need your help?" Kitty's expression smoothed suddenly. "I suppose it's that business about the Indians stealing the widow Kuick's strongbox, isn't it. You are compelled to put yourself in the middle of whatever trouble comes along. That is your one real failing."

"Perhaps one day I will learn from your excellent example," Elizabeth said, leaning over to press a kiss to Kitty's forehead. "Don't despair of me yet."

*   *   *

It turned out that Mrs. Gathercole's sore throat was much less severe than her husband had given the doctor to believe, Hannah was relieved to see.

From her bed she said, "Mr. Gathercole does worry so, Miss Bonner. Thank you for coming by to check on me; it will put his mind to rest. Perhaps while you are here you could look at his throat. I've noticed he has some trouble swallowing these past two days, although he will not admit it unless he is pressed."

Mrs. Gathercole was from a family with money in Boston and she had never lost her way of talking, swallowed *r* sounds like an Englishwoman. There was a Yankee singsong to her voice, overly mannered and timid at the same time. She was comfortable with very few of the people in the village, but Elizabeth was one of them.

While Elizabeth related the news that Mrs. Gathercole really wanted but would not ask for directly—the little they knew about the trouble at the mill—Hannah examined Mr. Gathercole in the kitchen with the housekeeper looking on. Missy Parker, a woman of uncertain age but exacting opinions, hunched over the churn but never took her eyes off her master, who had given himself over to the care of a red Indian.

Hannah's relief at finding Mrs. Gathercole on the mend left as soon as she looked into her husband's throat. The symptoms he admitted to were alarming enough, but the things she could see for herself were even worse. She could hardly keep herself from starting at the sight of his tongue, swollen and bright red.

In response to her gentle questioning he admitted to an aching head, a feverish night, a sore throat. There was only one more question to ask, and Hannah knew what he would answer before she put it to him.

"Sir, I am sorry to have to bother you with a private matter, but is there any rash on your person?"

Mr. Gathercole peeked at her from under a fringe of thinning blond hair, his face rosy with embarrassment. He touched his neck, hidden under a snowy white stock. "Yes. On my throat, and . . . under my arms."

"Father brought up his dinner last night," Mary volunteered, and Mr. Gathercole flushed an even deeper shade. Gentlemen, it seemed, did not suffer from indigestion.

"What is it?" he asked. "Something dangerous?" And he cast a glance at his daughter.

"Canker rash is what most folks call it," said Missy Parker, looking up from the churn. "Although my mam called it 'strawberry tongue.'"

To Mr. Gathercole's confused and dismayed expression Hannah said, "There is no need for alarm. You see that Mrs. Gathercole is already recovering, and so shall you. It is your turn to take on the role of patient. Mrs. Parker, can you stay a while when you're finished there? He should take a mouthful of the tea I'm leaving every hour."

Mary Gathercole, blond and sincere as her parents, came forward to sniff at the open jar. "What's in it?"

"Mostly licorice root and slippery elm," Hannah said, putting a casual hand on the child's overwarm forehead. "Some hyssop and sage, and willow bark for the fever."

"No molasses?" Mary asked.

"I can add molasses," Hannah said. "But you must promise me that you'll take the tea too, every hour. And as long as your father is in his bed, you will stay in yours."

Mr. Gathercole put his hands over his face and let out a low sound.

"Hope you've got a lot of fixings for that tea in that bag of yours," said Missy Parker with grim satisfaction. "When canker rash gets legs under it it'll run away with half the village."

By midday Hannah could no longer hope that the Gathercoles would be an isolated case. They visited six patients, two with infected wounds and four with fever and sore throats. At the LeBlancs' Missy Parker's prediction had already come true and Hannah sent the oldest boy back to Dr. Todd's dispensary to ask Daisy for more of the ingredients for the sore throat tea.

He came back with the unsettling news that Daisy wasn't at the Todds' at all, she was at home tending to her own children, who were poorly. Margit Hindle sent her apologies but she couldn't find the slippery elm or the licorice root and neither could Dolly. Elizabeth went off with the boy the second time with exact instructions on where to find the things Hannah needed.

Just as well, because she needed time to study the LeBlanc

boys. There was no time to take notes but she made them in her head, as she had been taught to do.

The two youngest had the rash on their necks and cheeks, under their arms, and on the backs of their knees. Bright-eyed with fever and whimpering with headache, they let her run gentle fingers over the rash. It felt like fine sand, slightly rough to the touch. Both boys had swollen tongues, though Peter's was more strawberry in color while Simon's was coated white. From both boys Hannah scraped a little matter from their tongues and rashes in folds of paper, to look at under the microscope later.

The scarlet fever hit children hardest, but there was cause to worry about Molly too. She had climbed out of childbed to tend the boys, wobbling about the cabin on unsteady legs and wrapped in all the quilts and shawls she could find. When Hannah insisted on examining her, she found that Molly's belly was tender, which was by far the most alarming thing she had seen so far this day. For one brief moment Hannah wished fervently that she would look up and see Curiosity at the door.

"I will send Willy for his grandmother Kaes," said Elizabeth when Hannah took her aside to confide her fears. "Charlie cannot cope with this alone."

Before they left Hannah boiled a cup of water over the hearth and added some of her precious store of powdered black cohosh root, bought at considerable expense in the city. To this she added a great deal of maple syrup to disguise the bitter taste.

Charlie saw them out onto the porch, his new daughter tucked into the crook of his arm.

He said, "Once Matilda gets here she'll set things straight. She's a hellion, is my mother-in-law and the boys are feared of her but it'll give Molly some rest."

There was a question Charlie wanted to ask but did not dare; Hannah saw that clearly on his troubled face. Charlie was afraid to hear what Hannah might say; Elizabeth was biding her time. She was afraid too, but she would come looking for the truth, no matter how it frightened her.

When they were out of Charlie LeBlanc's hearing Hannah stopped, put down her bag and basket, and placed both hands on her stepmother's shoulders to look into her eyes. Elizabeth was far away in her thoughts, with Robbie on the summer evening that he died. *Malignant quinsy*, Richard Todd had written in the record book he kept for the village. *Robert Middleton Bonner, age two years.* And below that: *Falling-Day of the Wolf longhouse at Good Pasture, age sixty-two years.*

"It is not quinsy."

Elizabeth's complexion, always pale, lightened to the shade of thin milk. She looked away, and back again. "You are sure?"

Hannah said, "You know that quinsy comes with swelling in the neck—" Elizabeth flinched, but Hannah pushed on anyway. "And we saw no such swelling in any of the sick we saw today. The symptoms we have seen are fever, headache, sore throat, a bright red tongue, and rash. You saw the rash yourself; it looked like a sunburn. The doctors at the Almshouse called it scarlet fever. Not quinsy," she added firmly.

Elizabeth nodded. "Yes, I saw the rash." There was a tic in the muscles of her jaw, as if her fear of the disease that had killed her youngest child lived just beneath her own skin.

After a moment Hannah took up her things and they began to walk again.

"You have seen this scarlet fever before?" Elizabeth's voice was slightly hoarse and Hannah understood that she had forced herself to ask the question.

"I saw three cases in the city."

Little girls, she might have added. *All dead now, and no doubt their brothers with them.* Dr. Savard had requested her help and she had followed, winding through the narrow lanes to the tumbledown houses near the East River where many immigrants lived. A cellar damp with river water and sweat and urine, so crowded that many slept sitting upright. The sick children had been shunted off to a dark corner, two girls and a boy, grimy faces streaked clean by fever sweats. A mother huddled nearby with the rest of her children pressing into her. Dr. Savard spoke to her in a combination of French and German and English, but there was no way to make her understand what he had to say.

Hannah hadn't thought of those children for so long, and that bothered her almost as much as the certainty that none of them had survived. What did it mean that she could put those faces out of her mind so completely?

After a long time Elizabeth said, "None of the sick we've seen today have been vaccinated against the smallpox, did you note that?"

"Yes," Hannah said. "I did notice."

Neither of them said aloud what they were thinking. If any of the villagers got the idea that the vaccinations to prevent smallpox had caused canker rash, there would be panic—and worse—to deal with. Hannah should have been reassured by the fact that thus far scarlet fever had shown itself only in those who were not vaccinated, but instead she felt only a deep unease.

"The two things are completely unrelated to each other," she said, to comfort Elizabeth and herself too. "But I suppose that won't be obvious until someone who has been vaccinated comes down with scarlet fever too. It is a very strange thing to hope for."

They had come to the orchard that surrounded the Wildes' cabin. As they passed through neat rows of trees, a small herd of sheep shied away, stumbling away to graze at a safe distance. Bees hummed lazily around their heads, and Hannah would have liked to sit down right where she was and sleep.

But she could see Nicholas sitting on the porch waiting for them. As they got closer she catalogued the things that could not be denied: a face flushed with fever, a rash that covered the wide neck where it rose from the collar of his shirt, and sorrow too heavy to bear.

When they stood in front of him, he swallowed and the muscles in his neck spasmed.

"Your sister?" Elizabeth asked softly.

He blinked hard. "The doctor said for you to come right in, Miss Bonner." His voice was rough with the effort of speaking. "He said he can't start the autopsy without you."

Thank God, Elizabeth repeated to herself again and again. *Thank God Lily stayed on the mountain. Thank God the boys are safe away. I must get word to Many-Doves.*

To Nicholas Wilde, newly bereaved and in the first stages of scarlet fever, she said other things; she asked him questions about Eulalia's last hours, and listened as he wept and talked and wept again. She thought of giving him willow bark for his fever; she knew where it was in Hannah's bag, and it would allow him some relief, but she stopped herself because she understood that what he wanted from her at this moment was nothing more than her willingness to listen.

What Elizabeth wanted was Nathaniel. The urge to get up and begin walking until she found him was so strong that her legs trembled, and it took a conscious effort to make herself stay seated on the neat porch, recently swept. Eulalia had planted lavender along the walkway, reported Nicholas; she took such pleasure in the lambs; she had never thought of herself.

When the first furious tears had been shed he wiped his face on his sleeve and looked at her with bloodshot eyes. "How long will it take?"

Out in the orchard his apple trees bent and flexed under a rising wind.

I have children, Elizabeth wanted to say. *I cannot comfort you as you need to be comforted. I should not even sit here with you.*

Instead she said, "An hour, or a little more." And then: "You should be in bed, you are fevered. There is a tea you should take for your throat. I can get that ready for you while the others are—" She broke off. "Come, we must see to your needs. When did you last eat?"

He looked at her in surprise, raised a hand to his own brow and touched it thoughtfully. "Bump gave me some broth. He told me to go lie down in the barn and wait until he came for me." He stood, and steadied himself on the post. "But I have to dig her grave. My sister's grave."

Elizabeth stood too, ready to support him if he should fall and hoping fervently that he would not. She said, "You have neighbors to help you, Mr. Wilde. What you must do now is to follow Dr. Todd's orders and take your rest."

Nicholas Wilde could not be left alone, and Hannah knew without asking that Elizabeth could not be prevailed upon to stay with him. As soon as she was able, she would fly away up the mountain to warn Many-Doves to keep the children at Lake in the Clouds.

Maybe Bump understood too, because he offered to stay behind and nurse Nicholas. Hannah would have hesitated to accept without explaining to him first what it meant to say that scarlet fever was contagious, but Richard Todd was not concerned.

"I'll send somebody down to dig the grave," he told Bump. "And most probably Anna McGarrity will see to the laying-out." He turned to Elizabeth. "You won't be any help here, and Hannah and I have work to do. Go home to your family."

Even Richard understood, but Elizabeth's expression was equal parts frantic need to be away and concern for the situation at hand.

To Hannah Elizabeth said, "Send for one of us when you are ready to come home to Lake in the Clouds. Do you understand me?"

It took a moment for Hannah to make sense of the warning. *The mill,* she remembered suddenly. *The robbery. Manny Freeman. Ambrose Dye.* It seemed very long ago and very unimportant. But she nodded anyway, because it made no sense to give Elizabeth new cause for worry. "I will send word."

With an impatient toss of his head Richard said, "We have to visit every family in Paradise. God knows how far it's spread already. It may be full dark before we're done. She'll sleep at the house where I can call on her if I need her."

Irritation and indignation flickered in Elizabeth's eyes, and Hannah was almost glad to see evidence that she was not completely overwhelmed by her fear.

"Hannah will come home to her family to sleep in her own bed," she said, looking Richard Todd directly in the eye. "Or, if she chooses, she will stay here in the village. She is not an indentured servant to jump at your bidding, and I will thank you to remember that."

"Christ save me from the Bonner women," Richard muttered, turning away. "How Nathaniel lives with more than one of you I'll never know."

When Elizabeth came home, breathless and so overwrought that it seemed she would never be able to speak again, the men were gathered around the cold fire pit between the cabins. All the men: Strong-Words, Strikes-the-Sky. Hawkeye with Lily in his lap. Runs-from-Bears with his two youngest. Ethan, Blue-Jay. Daniel. Nathaniel.

With such elation and fear all at once, Elizabeth wondered

if it was possible for a heart to shatter like cold glass dropped
into boiling water. What she wanted more than anything else
in the world and what she feared: all her people together here
while in the village sickness took hold. Again. Like a snake un-
coiling itself from a winter's rest. This time it called itself by
another name (different *names,* she corrected herself: scarlet
fever and canker rash and strawberry tongue), but she was not
fooled.

Daniel reached her first, his joyous expression replaced by
hurt when she stepped away from his reaching arms. She had
spent the day comforting sick children, wiping their faces,
spooning tea and broth onto tongues swollen red and rough;
how could she embrace her son? But he did not hear her
warnings or did not want to understand them. He was enough
of a boy to want his mother's arms, and something small and
tender broke in Elizabeth when she had to refuse him.

Nathaniel came running to scoop him up, a boy too tall to
be held like the child he was and would always be to them.

"Let your mother get cleaned up," he said. "And then we'll
sit together and talk."

Nathaniel followed his wife into the cabin while the boys
went to draw water for the bath she must have. She paced up
and down while the buckets came and went and the cold water rose in the hip bath, refusing to wait for it to heat, refusing
to speak at all until the task was finished and the door had
closed behind them.

"Whatever it is, Boots, spit it out before you burst."

Generally Elizabeth tended to underplay her worries,
maybe because she thought if she could convince other people
things weren't so bad she'd start to believe it herself. But she
was scared to the bone and whatever tricks she had to calm
herself were no good at all: the story poured out of her while
she stripped to the skin and climbed into the cold water.
Young Eulalia Wilde dead, Molly LeBlanc down with
childbed fever, the names of the children sick with canker
rash: Joseph, Solange, Emmanuel, Lucy, Peter, Simon, Mary,
Faith.

Not quinsy. She said it so often that he wondered if she
even heard herself.

In the full heat of a summer afternoon she shivered and

shook, gooseflesh rising across her chest and arms. She asked for the common soap but he gave her one of the fine bars scented with lavender that her cousin had sent from the city. It slipped from her fingers once and then again until Nathaniel took it from her.

While he washed her back and rubbed soap into the sodden masses of her hair she talked and talked through chattering teeth and he listened.

When she had finally used all the words she had and he had finished rinsing her—more cold water—he helped her up, wrapped her in a blanket, and carried her to their bed.

The last thing she murmured to him before she fell asleep was the thing he feared most. She said, "We have to go away from here. We have to take the children away from here. I'm so sorry, Nathaniel, I'm so sorry but I can't, I can't, I can't."

For all the years since Elizabeth had agreed to be his wife and raise a family at Lake in the Clouds, Nathaniel had waited for the day she would have enough of such a rough life. There had been times when he could not keep this to himself and she had always laughed at him, hushed his worries with kisses or gentle ridicule or irritation. She missed nothing at all about England or the grand house where she had been raised; she wanted no finery or carriages; her books were better than theater or opera. She had her family, her friends, her school, more than she had ever imagined. What place had more to offer? she demanded to know. The only person in all of Paradise who would argue this point with her was Kitty Todd.

And still sometimes he saw something in her expression that he could not explain away. A yearning, a curiosity about the world. When Hawkeye spoke of going west she listened with eager eyes; when she read the papers from the city to them at night a new light came into her face. Nathaniel was not the only one to see this or even to point it out to her, but her shock was always genuine. The endless forests were enough of a frontier for her; she had no urge to take her children west, or anyplace else for that matter. All of them had been born at Lake in the Clouds and here their youngest child was buried; this was where they belonged.

Now Hannah stood on the cusp of leaving them, and Hawkeye would take that opportunity to leave them too. He would follow his granddaughter west but when she settled with the Seneca he would walk on, walk west until he came to the end of the world. *An itch deep in the bone* was how he put it when they talked about it in the last few days. *Walk or die,* he had said in the language of his childhood, a language he spoke now only when he had things of the greatest importance to share.

Nathaniel had gone to Many-Doves with this, as he had gone to her mother before her when he needed that particular kind of wisdom. Many-Doves had once been his sister-in-law, but she would always be the daughter of Falling-Day and the granddaughter of Made-of-Bones; had she chosen to leave this place and go live among the Kahnyen'kehàka who had made a new home for themselves in Canada, she would be a clan mother by now, a woman with the sight, his mother would have said. A dream-walker.

At thirty she was beautiful still, so much like Nathaniel's first wife that sometimes when he caught sight of her unexpectedly he felt a twist in his gut. *If Sarah had lived.* Sometimes the sentence presented itself to him, but he could not think beyond those few words. Could not think away the life he had now, because he wanted no other.

Many-Doves had listened to his worries, and when he was done she had taken some tobacco from the pouch around her neck and thrown it into the fire. While she watched it burn she said, "They will go, and you do not want to stop them, not in your heart. The time has come."

A truth as hard as a hickory nut. And now another: sickness in the village, and Elizabeth in a restless sleep where she searched for a safe place to raise her children. A place that must exist, because she would have it so. Because she had such faith in him, that he could find that place.

Elizabeth woke to the sound of children laughing in the dusk.

She pulled a dress over her head and went bare-legged out to the porch to watch them under the falls. The heat of the day had begun to give way, and she was glad of the breeze on her bare skin.

The children—her own, Many-Doves', Ethan—were shouting above the noise of the water, calling out dares to each other in English and Kahnyen'kehàka. Their joy was as clear and palpable as the cool air that came off the falling water.

The men crouched around a new fire, deep in conversation. All of them turned watchful eyes to the children, calling out easy words of encouragement now and then. Other men—white men, Elizabeth corrected herself—would shout warnings, directions, commands. She herself had called out such things. Over time she had come to understand that her fear prevented nothing, achieved nothing useful.

Ethan climbed up on the boulder the children called Hump Nose, the highest point from which they were allowed to dive. From there he waggled both hands frantically in her direction until she raised her own hand in response.

He went into the water as naked and slink as mink, browned skin glistening and his water-darkened hair streaming behind him. Blue-Jay followed with a screeching whoop with his little sister close behind. Then Lily, her hair a wild fury trailing around her head, over her shoulders to the small of her back. Daniel stepped into place and paused to look out, naked but for a breechclout, fists on his hips. Surveying his kingdom.

What Elizabeth saw was this: Nathaniel's face raised to watch his son, as he might watch the moon rising, unable to hide his wonder.

As if he heard her thoughts he got up from the fire and came to sit behind her on the porch, wrapped his arms around her and rested his chin on her shoulder. She could not see his face like this but she didn't mind, as long as she had his voice at her ear, low and sure.

"Feeling rested, Boots?"

"Nathaniel, about before—"

He hushed her with a shake of his head. "Look at Lily, she's determined to make the biggest splash." Their tiny daughter had rolled herself into a human cannonball, hurling toward the water with her arms wrapped around her raised knees. Water rose in a halo around her and the boys let out an approving holler.

Elizabeth leaned back and let out a sigh. "Why must she make a battle of everything?"

"Because she's your daughter." Nathaniel rocked a little, pulling her with him. "It's in her nature."

"I wanted to say about earlier—"

He shook his head again, more forcefully. "Wait, Boots. Listen." He rubbed his face against her head.

"I know you're afraid. I am too. I wish I could promise you that no harm will ever come to them, but I can't. Here or any-place else, I can't promise you that. But I'm willing to leave Hidden Wolf, if that's what it'll take to make you rest easy. We could move deeper into the forests, or out onto the Mohawk. We could probably scrape together enough money to buy a little farmstead, maybe near German Flats or downriver from Albany a ways. No matter what we do, Many-Doves and Bears will stay here at Lake in the Clouds so it's not like we couldn't come back if you decide you don't like it wherever we end up."

His arms hummed with a fine tension, as if he feared she might try to pull away. Elizabeth opened her mouth but no words came to her. Because she could not make sense of any of it, not of his calm or his meaning.

"Nathaniel—"

"Hush for now, Boots. You think it over and when you know what you want, you let me know." He started to pull away, but she wrapped her hands around his lower arm.

"Nathaniel. What about Manny? Is he safe?"

"For the moment," Nathaniel said, and she knew from his expression that no matter what question she thought to ask him, he would give her no information. Because he was hid-ing the worst of it. What had happened to Ambrose Dye and what exactly Manny was up to, those were things he didn't want to tell her.

But she did have something to ask, and she surprised herself with it. "You don't trust me, do you?"

"I trust you with my life, Boots. You know that."

"You think I'm too unstable to trust with the truth about Manny."

Irritation moved across his expression. "Don't put words in my mouth, Elizabeth."

She said, "Tell me about Jode."

"Ah, Christ." He ran a hand over his eyes. "What's there to tell that you haven't guessed already?"

"What's there to *tell*? To begin, let me ask: How is it that Jode is here in the first place? Manny must have gone north looking for the Red Rock group, that's the only way I can explain it to myself."

"Well then you did guess it," Nathaniel said flatly. "Manny went all the way to Good Pasture looking for his wife. It was Elijah who gave him the news about Selah. When he headed back this way, Jode followed him."

"You've actually spoken to them then."

Nathaniel said, "I spoke to them all. They'll be headed west soon so we can all stop worrying." He pulled away suddenly, and raised his voice over the rush of the falls.

"Children! There's chores to do before dark."

He left her to go back to the men around the fire, without even looking back. Afraid to look at her, in case she saw in his face what he thought he must keep from her; the rest of this business. The thought came to Elizabeth and ran up her spine in a shudder, as true as ice.

Most of the men were still out with the search party, Hannah discovered as they went from family to family, and all the women wanted news of what had happened at the mill. Richard, concerned only with examining everyone for symptoms of scarlet fever, grew more impatient with every visit.

"For God's sake, woman," he roared at Mrs. Hindle when she asked one question too many about the search party. "We've got eight cases of scarlet fever in this village and that boy sitting on your lap burning up with fever is one of 'em!"

Laura Hindle, ordinarily a plainspoken woman, first colored with indignation and then burst into tears, hugging her boy so hard that Hannah had to extract him before his mother caused some new harm.

When they left the Hindles' small cabin, Hannah waited until she could be sure of her voice and then she said, "You'll forgive me the observation, Dr. Todd, but you've got all the delicacy of an ox. Mrs. Hindle can hardly breathe for fear that Jock is lying out there in the bush scalped and his throat slit—don't interrupt me, you know I'm right. In every one of those cabins the women and boys are listening to the wind in the trees and wondering if they can prime a rifle fast enough if the next war party comes for them. My uncle can't come down the mountain for fear that somebody will shoot him in a panic."

"There is no war party within five hundred miles of here, Hannah Bonner, and you know it!"

"Of course there is not. But *they* won't believe that until their men are home safe. To shout at them because they are frightened and distracted is foolish and, worse, it will only panic them more."

Richard stopped in his tracks and turned on her. "So we let fevered children fend for themselves while their mothers are pointing muskets at shadows? I have no patience with such foolishness."

"Then let me deal with the mothers," Hannah said, and she saw how he twitched at her tone. "Because you are doing more harm than good."

"Next you'll send me off into the bush to join the search party," Richard blustered, but with far less energy.

"That is an excellent idea," Hannah said. "Why don't you do just that?"

"Maybe I will," Richard shot back. "But the last call we've got to make is at the mill, and if anybody's going to take a shot at you it's bound to be one of the Kuicks. And right at this moment I'm tempted to stand aside and watch it happen."

Given all the stories that Hannah had heard about the widow Kuick's household, she stepped into the kitchen expecting to find servants and slaves working frantically, light burning in every room, halls seething with shouts and wailed outrage. Instead the house seemed deserted, oddly cool for a summer evening, empty enough that she could hear Becca's mild voice echoing in the halls. The doctor was asking her about her mistress, and Becca was doing her best to answer.

There was no sign of Cookie. Anna McGarrity had put out the word that the new maid had left at first light without giving notice. A stack of dirty dishes on the table, the hearth smoldering down to its last cinder, a cat rubbed up against Hannah's skirt and trilled a question.

"I don't know where they've all gone," she told him, a tomcat the size of a fat raccoon, the color of dirty linen. "Maybe they're all down at the slave quarters. Shall we go have a look?"

The truth was, she was eager to be out of the house and the

tom seemed to have no objection. He trotted alongside her like a dog, his tail pointing straight up to the sky.

The sound of the stream that fed the mill grew louder and then Hannah came around a corner and it stood before her, as still and dark as the house. The cat ran ahead around the corner and it was her turn to follow, more reluctantly now.

The building that served as both warehouse and slave quarters stood on a small clearing between the millworks and the overseer's house, low and squat and still alive with light. Once on the porch Hannah hesitated, hearing voices raised in conversation: *more of those greens* and *would you give me my* and *how long you think the doctor going to* and *White Tom where you been boy*. The air was heavy with good smells: trout frying, cornbread, hot milk.

Suddenly Hannah couldn't remember why she had thought to come here, unless it was simply to get away from the cold kitchen at the mill house. She thought of going back again, of knocking on doors until she found Richard or Becca or Jemima. She thought of going home, just walking away into the forest and making her way alone, as she had promised Elizabeth she would not.

The door opened and Cookie stood there, a cautious expression giving way to a smile.

"Miss Bonner," she said, stepping backward and opening the door wider. "Now ain't it good to see you. Come on in and set down to supper with us. We got plenty."

"No sore throats here," Levi said when Hannah had finished telling them about the events of the day. The cheerful mood around the table had sombered, but not gone completely.

Ezekiel winked at Hannah. "No strawberry tongue neither, but Moses here was complaining yesterday about a headache."

"Because Malachi stepped on his head getting out of bed," said Shadrach, a very large man with an exceedingly soft voice.

The widow's seven slaves were sitting around a rough plank set atop barrels that served as a table, and each of them looked at Hannah with open curiosity and goodwill. If they were concerned about the scarlet fever they were hiding it well.

"It would be best if you stayed out of the village then," Hannah said. "What we're dealing with here is a catching sickness. I'll leave some sore throat tea just in case, and some willow bark, too, for fever."

"That's kind of you," said Cookie. "But you know that generally Curiosity or Daisy come up here to see to us when we need doctoring."

"Daisy's likely to be very busy for the next few days with the sickness in the village," Hannah said. "And Curiosity's not back yet. If you think you're coming down with the canker, you send for me." As soon as she said it, Hannah realized that she had offered them help that they could not accept; that the widow would not let them accept.

"That's Mr. Kuick's horse I hear." Cookie turned toward the window. Her tone was mild but her expression gave away more. "He ain't stopping at the house."

"He's headed this way, and in a hurry," added Levi.

All the men got up from the table together and went to the windows.

"Look like the whole search party is back," somebody murmured. "Lot of commotion down in the village."

"Is there anybody with Mr. Kuick?" Hannah must ask the question that no one else seemed willing to voice.

Cookie turned. "He's alone," she said, not even trying to hide her relief. "And empty-handed."

Isaiah Kuick's horse stood in front of the mill, dripping lather, its head hung low. For the first time Hannah saw something of concern on Cookie's face, but whether it was for the animal or for the man who had left it here in such condition she could not say.

"Mr. Isaiah?" Cookie called from the open door. "Mr. Isaiah? Come on out here, will you please?"

The doorstep was wet, and Hannah crouched down to convince herself that it was water and not blood that Isaiah Kuick was trailing behind him.

The building was full of echoing sounds: the rush of the stream on its way down the mountain to the Sacandaga, the rhythmic rattle of the water flume against its braces, the creak and moan of timber walls and wooden gears, the whistle of the wind in the air vents.

"Mr. Isaiah? We don't got no light with us, so you come on

out here now. You say something, Miss Bonner. Maybe he'll listen to you."

Hannah said, "Mr. Kuick, this is Hannah Bonner. Are you injured?"

The pale oval of his face came toward them out of the dark, swaying as if he were full drunk.

"I'll look again," he answered in a hoarse voice. "One more time." And he turned and disappeared back into the shadows.

"Are you looking for the overseer?" Hannah called after him. "There's been no sign of Mr. Dye here today, isn't that right, Cookie?"

The older woman had crossed her arms across her waist. She nodded. "No sign of him at all."

Hannah called, "You are unwell, Mr. Kuick, won't you come and let Dr. Todd see to your needs? He's at the house with your mother."

The only reply was a harsh laugh, so close that Hannah jumped.

He had come out of the building on the other side and circled around to stand behind them. His cloak was sodden, and his hair trailed wet over unshaved cheeks. In the evening light his face seemed to glow, his eyes red-rimmed and glassy. He stood there swaying slightly, all his attention on Cookie.

Very suddenly he stepped forward and slung his arms around her to bury his face in the curve of her shoulder. His whole body heaved and shuddered. "He's gone, Cookie," he whispered. "He's gone for good."

Cookie patted his back and rocked. "It's all right, Mr. Isaiah," she said softly. "It's all going to be all right now. We got to get you some dry clothes and something hot to drink. You chilled right through to the bone."

She looked at Hannah over Isaiah Kuick's trembling shoulders, her eyes as cool and cold as the water that dripped from his hair onto her face.

She said, "They'll find Mr. Dye and he'll come home, wait and see, just as good as ever. You just wait and see."

Well past midnight, Hannah found her way into the kitchen at the mill house and stood disoriented and disheartened and unable to remember what she needed.

Becca Kaes sat up suddenly from a pallet by the banked hearth, and Hannah let out a small cry of shock and surprise, stepping back.

"Becca," she hiccuped, pressing a hand to her throat. "You put a fright into me."

She had gone to school with Becca Kaes, a good-hearted girl with her mother's kindly ways and her father's laugh. On her face now there was nothing but worry and fearfulness.

"Hannah," she said, coming forward in a tangle of blanket. "Is it true about Eulalia Wilde?"

How strange, to have forgotten Eulalia Wilde in such a short time. Hannah blinked and blinked again, but the gritty feeling behind her eyelids stayed.

She nodded. "Yes. She had a bad infection that passed into her blood."

Becca drew in a breath and let it out in a sigh. "Lord rest her. She was my good friend. And Nicholas?"

"He has the canker rash," Hannah said. "But he's strong, and I think he'll survive."

Becca sat down heavily on a stool by the trestle table. After a moment she seemed to collect herself and she smoothed her hair away from her face.

"I'm afraid to ask about my sister and her boys."

Hannah sat down next to her. "Molly's in a bad way. The boys are strong and I think they'll all pull through."

"I would go to her if the widow would—" Becca began and Hannah cut her off with a shake of the head.

"Of course you would. But your mother is with her."

Becca pulled a handkerchief out of her sleeve and rubbed her nose with it.

"I suppose I should go look in on the widow," she said in the same voice she might have proposed cleaning out the stable.

"The doctor said that she should sleep until morning," Hannah said. "I don't think you need bother."

At that Becca looked directly relieved. "Would you like some tea, or something to eat? It is such a long time since you and I have talked. The widow..." Her voice trailed away. "You know how the widow is."

"Yes," said Hannah. "I know about the widow. Thank you for the offer of tea but what I really want is to go home. Do you think I could ask one of the men from the mill to walk with me up the mountain?"

Becca jumped up so suddenly that the dirty dishes on the table rattled. "Oh my, I clear forgot to tell you. There's somebody waiting for you, it must be hours now. An Indian. Not the Indian who—" She paused. Her tone was apologetic and slightly irritated, as if she resented even having to think about what had happened in the parlor the night before. "A friend of your family's, and I forgot to tell you," she finished.

A new wakefulness sparked in Hannah and she realized that she had been hoping for exactly this news. "I'll say good night then."

"Wait!" Becca stepped forward. "What about Mr. Kuick?"

"Cookie is with him," Hannah said.

"Is it the canker rash? Is he very ill?"

Hannah said, "It is the canker rash and a lung fever both. He is very ill indeed."

Hannah was too tired to be startled, and she barely glanced at Strikes-the-Sky when he stepped out of the shadows behind the stable and fell into step beside her. She was glad of the dark, and glad of the fact that there was just enough light from the moon to make a lantern unnecessary. She was glad of Strikes-the-Sky, too, for giving her the things she needed most: comfort and companionship and protection without explanations or questions.

As they walked she felt the day begin to peel away from her, layer by layer. Fevered children, frightened mothers. Isaac Cameron sputtering wild-eyed about Indian ambushes while Hannah cut the festering flesh from a burn on his hand gone bad. The slender shell that had once been Eulalia Wilde. Bump's kind face and the doctor's furious one, a bloody scalpel in his hand. That death should dare so much. Nicholas Wilde, torn in two by grief. Daisy Hench squeezing out a cool rag to ease the fever that burned in three of her four children, her eyes fixed on the healthy one, waiting. All of them, waiting.

Sometimes Strikes-the-Sky walked beside her and sometimes, when the path was narrow, before her. She watched him, tall and strong and everything that she was taught to admire in a man. His skin a deep copper shade, deeper and truer than her own.

As if she had called his name he looked at her over his shoulder, the egret feathers laced into his scalp lock lifting and turning in the breeze.

She asked the question that she feared most. "Is there sickness at Lake in the Clouds?"

"No," he said.

He might have said *not yet,* but he had not. Somehow he knew that those words would displease her. Satisfaction and irritation fought for the upper hand: that he would know her so well after such a short time. That he should know her so well.

She said, "You should go away from here while you are still healthy. Back to your people."

As soon as the words left her mouth she regretted them, but then he smiled at her and anger rose up hot and hard and filled her throat.

"Tomorrow you should go," she said. "Tonight."

She pushed ahead, but no matter how fast she walked he was behind her. By the time they came to the clearing at Lake in the Clouds they were trotting, both of them. At the sound of the waterfall Hannah broke into a run, dropped her basket, kicked off the summer moccasins she wore under her O'seronni dress, and without thought or pause she dove into the water.

Her mother's people dipped newborns in the waters of the great river so they would never forget who they were and who they would always be. She felt it in the pit of her stomach, the basin of her skull, in the long curve of her spine, in the very muscles of her heart: cold so intense that the sorrow and anger that had begun to etch itself in untouchable places must give way. And in their place a new understanding.

When she was born her father had brought her here and dipped her in the Lake in the Clouds; this was where she belonged.

When she climbed out of the lake, water and weariness streaming off her, Strikes-the-Sky was sitting there, where they had sat together for so many nights now. He had not kissed her or tried to kiss her or even spoken of kissing, and now Hannah was glad of that; it made everything easier.

As she walked past him he said her name, "Walks-Ahead." And then, in English the one word she had been waiting to hear from him; had thought never to hear him say: "Hannah."

She stopped, wrapped her arms around herself, turned.

He was standing, but she could not make out his face.

He said, "I see you."

"Yes," she answered him, clutching at the certainty that had come so suddenly and now left her again. "I understand that you do."

Chapter 40

Hannah dreamed of trees hung with plums and pears and clutches of cherries the color of blood, peaches as heavy and soft as she had imagined the moon to be when she was a child. As far as her dream self could see there were trees heavy with fruit.

In the way of dreams Eulalia Wilde was suddenly walking beside her, pointing to one tree after another.

Under a pear tree your cousin Isabel, under a quince your grandmother Falling-Day, for Selah Voyager sweet plums.

They came to the apple trees and Eulalia stopped, her arms wound around herself. *Here I lay me down to sleep,* she said with a smile. *Under the Snow.*

Beyond that a hundred trees or a thousand, branches swaying low with apples.

What of those trees? Hannah asked. *Who will rest under those trees?*

Eulalia raised her hands and chanted: *Grabenstein, Children-Waiting-in-a-Line, Seek-No-Further.*

Hannah woke with a start.

An epidemic in the village. Richard would need her help, but she had the urge to go out into Elizabeth's garden first.

When the Bonners came home from an unexpected and unwelcome trip to Scotland when the twins were just infants, they had brought with them a number of fruit trees in tubs, a gift from the Earl of Carryck's greenhouse. The idea of plums and pears and cherries at Lake in the Clouds had so appealed to Elizabeth that she had declared herself ready to take on the challenge. If Carryck could manage to grow peaches in Scotland, certainly she could nurse a few hardier trees through the winter at Lake in the Clouds.

In spite of Elizabeth's best will, consultations with every farmer in the village, letters back and forth from Scotland, the best manure, careful watering, and many layers of sacking through the winter, three of the trees had not survived the first January. The next winter had killed two more, but a single cherry tree had survived. Into this tree, planted in a sunny spot between cabin and stable where it was protected from the wind, Elizabeth put all her effort, and every midsummer since it had paid her back in kind.

The tree was like a gnarled old woman, bent of back and crusty, clutching her finery in spindly claws. Hannah filled a small basket and went into the barn to sort them.

It smelled of drying grass and damp sawdust and of old Toby, who snored softly in his stall, and would wake only when someone remembered to put him out to graze. Hannah left the double doors open for the breeze and the rumble of the waterfalls, a familiar and comforting melody.

When a shadow fell across the table she drew in a breath and held it.

Strikes-the-Sky stood in the open doorway; she knew it without raising her head. She knew him by his size and shape, by the way he breathed, and by the way her own heart disobeyed her, racing forward toward something she did not want. Not today, not now. Not yet.

She worked on, her fingers picking through the fruit of their own accord while he watched her. Hannah vowed to herself that she would not speak first, even though some part of her protested that she was being childish.

But he had called her by her English name and unsettled her. It was as if he saw the secret she had kept so long written plain on her forehead: she thought of herself as *Hannah,* first and always. The woman-name her grandmother had given her, Walks-Ahead, that name had never taken hold in her mind. It was a good name and one she had earned, but she answered to it as she might answer to *girl.*

You change when Strikes-the-Sky comes into the room, Daniel had said. She could not convince anyone, not even herself, that she felt only friendship for the man who stood in the doorway watching her.

Hannah looked up, as flushed and agitated as if she had run a mile.

"Why do you stand there staring? Have you forgotten what I look like in these few hours?"

Her tone did not seem to worry him. "I like the look of you, Walks-Ahead."

He came into the cool shadows. With the sun at his back she could not see his expression, and she was glad of it. All the things to say went through her mind in a muddle, and in the end she spoke only to hear the sound of her own voice.

"I am very busy here, as you can see. And I need to go to the village; the doctor will be waiting for me."

"Your hands are busy, yes. Your mouth is not."

She itched with the impulse to throw something at his head, but she forced herself to breathe deeply until the urge had passed.

"Have you no work to do?"

"Nothing as important as what I am doing now."

Those words ran up her spine like a fever chill. "Enough of your teasing. What do you want?"

His look was so direct and honest and so easily read that Hannah could not bear it; she dropped her head. Because she did not trust her own expression; because she did not want to see his. Most of all she did not want him to answer the question she had asked. *What do you want?* It hung in the air between them as full and ripe as the fruit in her hands. She wanted to snatch it back and swallow it whole.

"These cherries are ripe," she said without looking up. "If you are hungry."

When enough time had passed that she could trust herself she straightened her back and looked him in the eye, held out a clutch of cherries on the flat of her palm. Cherries of such a dark and deep color that all the other colors of the world were hidden in its depths. Not black or red, but both and neither. A color as deep and complex as the color of his eyes, looking at her with frank and unapologetic wanting.

He put out his hand to take what she offered and hesitated, his palm hovering over hers. Then his fingers curved over the fruit and they brushed against her wrist.

"I make you tremble, Walks-Ahead."

"You distract me from my work, nothing more."

"That is not the first lie I have heard from you, but it is the one that wounds."

She could pull away but instead she stood there while he trailed his fingers over her wrist, more purposefully this time so that the cherries rolled between their palms. His touch was light, his fingers strong and rough and cool.

When she raised her eyes to his he was smiling. He took his hand away, and the fruit with it.

He said, "You ran away from me last night."

"I was tired."

How odd, that the things they said could be true and false at the same time. Hannah thought he would go then, but he only turned to the side so that he could look out into the morning light while he ate. Juice ran down from the corner of his mouth like blood and she started at that, wound her fingers in her skirt to keep herself from touching him.

He caught the juice with the back of his hand, wiped it away.

Without looking at her he said, "Come west with me, Walks-Ahead. Come live with me among my people. There is work for you there, among the Seneca."

A sound escaped her, as if all the air had been caught up inside her belly and suddenly forced its way out. She leaned against the rough table with both her hands to keep them from shaking.

"You have nothing to say?" He was watching her again, impassively, as if he had asked her about the weather and was only waiting to hear if it would rain.

"You want me to come west because the Seneca need another healer." It was not so much a question as a demand; she heard that in her own voice, and so did he.

When he smiled the long grooves in his cheeks made him look like a boy with nothing to worry about, sure of himself and his place in the world.

He said, "In the old days our mothers would settle this for us, but now we must act for ourselves. Walks-Ahead, listen. If you will take me, I will be a good husband to you. We will stand together, side by side, among the real people."

Hannah blinked, struck by an unbidden memory as sharp as ice. Long ago, her girl-self had stood right on this very spot in the deep of winter, with Liam Kirby. He had looked at her like Strikes-the-Sky looked at her now. He had asked her for a promise she could not make.

She could see him still, snow caught in his eyebrows and in the deep red of his hair where it stuck out from his cap, his skin so pale that she could watch the pulsing of his blood in the veins at his temple.

To me you are white. He had said those words to her, and with them he put up the first barrier between them. The first of many barriers, although she had not imagined that then; when she was a child Liam had been as much a part of her life as Hidden Wolf, and as permanent. But he was gone, for now and ever.

On that day she had wanted to strike out at Liam, to spit out the denial that sat bitter on her tongue—*I am not white.* But those words could not be said, because they were only partly true. She was white, and she was red, and she was everything and nothing in between. But she had been a girl then, and now she was a woman and she had other words, better words, that she was not afraid to use, that she must say or choke.

"My people are real people," she said to Strikes-the-Sky, and she had to swallow hard to make her voice obey her. "All my people, white or Mohawk, they are all real people."

He raised his head and found her gaze, steady and sure and so focused, as if he had nothing else to see in the world. He studied her as he had studied the map of the mountain that Daniel had drawn for him, to win its secrets. To make it his own.

"Your people are all real people," he echoed. "You are right to correct me."

It was the single thing that he could say to open the door between them. Hannah was so surprised to hear those words that she could not think of any response that did not sound dull.

Strikes-the-Sky did not seem to be bothered by her silence. He said, "In my village, there would be time. We would dance with the others, every night by the great fire. We would dance with your scarf caught between our hands, and one night when you were ready you would put the scarf around my shoulders. And then I would leave my mother's fire and come to live in your longhouse."

He came no closer, but Hannah could feel him, the strength of him, his will, as strong as any she had ever known. *As strong as my own.* She closed her eyes and when she opened them he was there still, Strikes-the-Sky. She wondered if his skin would taste as sweet as his mouth had tasted for that short moment; Hannah looked away, and back again.

A good man, her uncle would say if she should ask. *He was a good husband to my wife's sister. Any woman should be glad of such a husband.*

"Is that how your first marriage was arranged with Tall-Woman?"

She saw the grief flicker in his eyes when she spoke the name of a wife dead three years. *That is good,* she said to herself, *to see that his heart is so true.* And just then it occurred to Hannah to wonder if her uncle Strong-Words had spoken to Strikes-the-Sky about her. If he had taken his friend aside and said *my sister's daughter is a good woman* or *she will make a good wife,* or *it is time now for you to take another woman.*

"No," Strikes-the-Sky said. "There was sickness in the village, and many of the elders and youngest died. Her mother died three days after mine. It was not a time of dancing." He paused, but he did not look away. "Tall-Woman came to me in the night, to give comfort. To take it."

There was a long silence between them, while he remembered and she imagined.

Finally Hannah said, "There is war, in the west."

"Yes. And there is war here too, of a different kind. You fight every day in that war. In a few minutes you will go fight again."

An image rose up before her of the widow Kuick, her face contorted in disgust. Her son, his eyes wild with fever and loss.

Shall I call your wife to you? she had asked him.

I have no wife, he had answered her.

She said, "Why did you make Tall-Woman come to you?"

Strikes-the-Sky blinked at her, as if she had spoken a language he did not recognize. "It was her choice, Walks-Ahead. As it is your choice now."

Very slowly she said, "We do not have to abandon all the old ways. You could leave your mother's fire and come to live among my people."

Such a stillness came over him that Hannah was struck with fear: he would turn and walk away. She knew then that she did not want him to go, but neither could she take back the words she had spoken. They were true words, and she would not be ashamed of them.

Strikes-the-Sky said, "I must go back to my people."

Her blood rushed so that Hannah felt light-headed. She swayed a little with it, and steadied herself against the table. "I would not try to convince you otherwise."

"Walks-Ahead." His tone was suddenly urgent. "Make no mistake, the choice is yours but you must *choose*."

Hannah looked him directly in the eye, and while he did not flinch his detached manner had gone, and in its place was an urgency and wanting that she had been waiting for.

"I am not ready to choose."

Strikes-the-Sky stepped toward her, reached out and took her hand. His breath came as fast and hard as her own, but he only took her hand in his.

"You are not ready to choose yet, Walks-Ahead," he said. "But soon."

She surprised herself by holding on to his hand when he would take it away. She said, "Sometimes you will call me Hannah, because that is my name too."

"Sometimes I will call you Hannah." He smiled then, a true smile. "But mostly I hope to call you wife."

It was a great relief to have Daniel home again, and still by morning Lily's worries were too big for even the two of them to carry.

He had wanted a report on Jemima Kuick straightaway, and when she told him the truth—Jemima seemed to have forgot the whole matter of what happened at Eagle Rock—he looked at her as if she had suddenly sprouted horns.

"More likely you've had your nose stuck in that sketchbook and you just didn't pay atention." And then seeing the look on her face Daniel's eyes filled with water, and Lily knew how worried he was, as worried as a boy could be.

Together they went to find Hannah in her workroom.

She was putting together the things she needed to take into the village. There was a line between her eyebrows that meant she was very worried or distracted or both, and so they waited.

Lily didn't know anyway what she wanted to say, but it was good to be here, the three of them together.

Hannah glanced at Daniel and said, "Can you hand me that pile of rags, please? Did the two of you come to ask me about Eulalia Wilde?"

Lily most definitely did not want to hear any more about Eulalia, who had been her friend and was gone now to the shadowlands without warning. To lose an arm did not seem so very terrible now, at least for Eulalia; she could have still tended trees and danced with Obediah Cameron, who would have to marry somebody else now.

Daniel said, "Her brother doesn't have anyone to look after him now."

Right then Hannah put down what she had in her hands and came over to put her arms around Daniel, who was not much shorter than she was but still put his head on her shoulder and stayed that way for a long minute.

When Hannah stepped away she said, "You needn't worry about me, Daniel. I am careful."

Lily said, "How can you be careful when there's sickness everywhere you go?"

"This sickness is not like last summer," Hannah said.

"It's not quinsy, yes. Ma told us. But it could be just as bad."

The real question was made of bolder words: *How many will die will I get it too what if we all get sick? Why can't you just stay here with us?*

Hannah understood, as she always did, and she paused in what she was doing to sit down on her bed and draw her sister down on one side and her brother on the other. Lily liked being in the workroom with Hannah, for the comforting smells and the closeness of it, but she was so afraid of what her sister would say that she had the urge to jump up and run away.

"Some will die," Hannah said. "How many depends on how strong the sickness is and how fast it spreads."

"Our mother is scared. Because of Robbie." Daniel said their little brother's name only seldom, and Lily knew what it cost him.

"Of course," Hannah said. "It was less than a year ago that we lost him. We are all scared, I think. It shows good common sense, as long as we do not let our fear get in the way of doing what must be done."

Hannah saw the thoughts moving behind her little sister's eyes, a fluttering like moths against a candlelit window at dusk. Daniel's worry showed itself in the way he would not meet her eye. They did not understand and nothing Hannah had to say could make them understand, because it was all a mystery. Where the sickness came from, how it moved from person to person, why it killed some and not others. How she could promise them that she would not come down with it and die.

Last night, sleepless, she had sat up to look through all her notes and extracts and books by candlelight. Hoping for some hint that would make a difference. What she found was not much more than she knew from Richard, who had seen scarlet fever when he was an army surgeon and again in Albany as well.

She could look in every book ever written, speak to every doctor or healer, and no one could tell her the one thing that these children—that everyone—wanted to know: how to stop it.

Hannah would spend the day in the village doing what she could to soothe fears and lessen fevers and fortify those who were still healthy, but she did not doubt that some would die. Most of them would be children. She could not even promise that the sickness would stay away from Lake in the Clouds, even if they quarantined themselves.

Lily sighed as if Hannah had said all this out loud.

Strikes-the-Sky was on the porch when Lily and Daniel came out. He had been eating cherries, and his mouth was red with juice.

Daniel said, "You could talk her out of going to the village."

Lily poked her brother in the arm. "You know that isn't true, why do you say such things?"

Daniel scowled and jerked away, but he had no words to

answer her. Then he looked Strikes-the-Sky up and down and said, "We aren't allowed to go with her because of the sickness."

Strikes-the-Sky made a sound deep in his throat. "I will keep watch over your sister when you cannot."

"She won't like that," Lily said.

"If I were you I'd keep my distance," added Daniel.

He looked down at them both with one corner of his mouth turned up and one eyebrow—the opposite one—cocked at an angle. It was meant to be a smile but there was more to it, and Daniel took it as a sign of something else entirely.

"Is it settled between the two of you then?"

Lily saw that he wanted to hear both answers: yes, because after long discussions with Father and Grandfather Daniel had decided that the Seneca from the western edge of Hodenoshaunee lands was almost good enough for their sister; and no, because he would never knowingly agree to any plan that took her away from them, no matter how reasonable or necessary to her happiness.

"Not yet," said Strikes-the-Sky. "But soon."

"With the sickness in the village she won't have any time for you." Lily heard her own peevishness and was embarrassed, but Strikes-the-Sky did not seem to mind.

He said, "We have many years before us. A few more days will not matter at all."

Daniel had chores still to do and he went off reluctantly, maybe, Lily thought, because he knew that she was determined to ask Strikes-the-Sky some very specific questions about his plans for their sister. She had just got up the courage to start when Joshua Hench came riding into the clearing on Uncle Todd's great gray stallion, the one that he didn't let anybody else saddle, much less ride.

That was the first hint that something was amiss, but if Lily wanted another one she need look no farther than the black-smith's expression. Joshua Hench was the quietest man Lily knew, quieter even than her grandfather, and it must mean something for him to look so unsettled.

Hannah heard him too, because she came out on the porch just as he pulled up in front of the cabin.

"The doctor sent me. Jupiter, you mind me now!" The stal-lion was dancing in a circle and Joshua Hench reined him in sharply while he spoke to them over his shoulder. "That German nursemaid is come down with the canker rash, and the little baby too. Got it bad, he says, and would you come straightaway? I'll take you down on Jupiter if you dare, he's right peevish today."

"The new baby," Lily said aloud to nobody in particular. "Aunt Todd will be sad."

Hannah didn't have anything to say to that, but she put her hand on the back of Lily's head and then in three steps she left the porch and launched herself up to the spot behind Joshua Hench on Jupiter's broad back.

Strikes-the-Sky handed up her bag, and Joshua hung it over his shoulder. Hannah stuck out her hand for her basket, and he handed that up too.

For once Hannah was taller than Strikes-the-Sky and he had to tilt his head back to look into her face. Strangest of all was the way Hannah was looking at him, as if there were too many things to say and she didn't know what words to use for any of them.

It wasn't until they were gone in a flurry of kicking hooves that Lily could put a name to it, and then it frightened her so badly that she had to say it out loud.

"Sister's not sure she'll ever come home again."

Strikes-the-Sky put a hand on her shoulder. "I will see to it that she does," he said. "I make you that promise."

"I did everything Dr. Todd told me," Dolly Smythe said to Hannah. "But none of it made any difference. Oh, I wish Curiosity would come home. How will I tell Mrs. Todd?"

They were standing beside a bed in the little chamber off the nursery where the nursemaid—*Esther,* Hannah had to remind herself, *her name was Esther*—had slept. A moody girl, less than friendly, and why not? She had come so far, losing both husband and child along the way to live and die on the edge of the wilderness.

Hannah sat down heavily. She shifted Meg in her arms but there was little reaction on the small, rash-covered face. The simple heat of the baby—it was like holding a bundle of live coals—told Hannah that if there was to be any hope for her the fever must be brought down.

"Don't worry about Kitty right now, I will talk to her. Tell me again what happened at the end."

Dolly nodded, willing but shaken. The story was simply told: Esther had been in a fevered and uneasy sleep. She woke suddenly, sat up, and complained of a terrible pain in her head. Or at least Dolly thought that must have been what she was saying, for while she spoke German, she held her head between her hands. Then she fell back against her pillow, dead. That was not a half hour ago.

There was other news from the doctor, which Dolly related in a breathless voice. While she spoke Hannah held the baby on her lap and dribbled water onto a tongue as red as the sunrise. The baby's throat worked, and she swallowed.

One good sign and there was another: none of the cases of scarlet fever in the village—twelve total—seemed as bad as these two right in the doctor's home, with the exception of Isaiah Kuick. The doctor was with Molly LeBlanc, who was in a bad way with childbed fever, and when he could get away he would go see Isaac Cameron, who looked to be developing gangrene.

"Is gangrene catching?" Dolly asked her. "I never thought it was but yesterday poor Eulalia and now Mr. Cameron—"

"It is a sad coincidence," Hannah said softly. Truth be told, she had been having the same thoughts herself. It would not do for the village to start worrying about some new kind of contagious gangrene when they were already struggling with the scarlet fever, and so she said nothing.

"The doctor asked that you go straight to the Kuicks' when you are done here." Before Hannah could show any surprise at such a strange order—she was the last person the widow would want to see—Dolly turned away.

"If you can excuse me for a little—" She hesitated, looking almost reluctantly at Meg and then Hannah understood. She had already decided the child could not live. It was something she had seen before: a woman who forced herself to turn away from the living to save herself the pain of another loss.

"I need to bathe her in cool water, and then I'll bring her to you in the kitchen before I leave. Is Mrs. Todd still asleep?"

"I am right here." From just beyond the door came Kitty's voice, ripe with impatience. She pushed past Dolly, her morning coat billowing around her, and came to a stop in front of the bed. For a long moment she looked at the nursemaid, and then she touched her throat with one finger.

"Dolly, you must call Anna Hauptmann or one of the other women to see to her laying-out. And ask Bump to please dig another grave. I hope Elizabeth has enough German to write to this poor girl's family." Her head came up suddenly and she held out her arms for Meg, her fingers jerking.

"I can tend to her, if you tell me what she needs."

"Kitty—" Hannah began slowly, and from Dolly a low wail: "The doctor said—"

It was not often Hannah had seen Kitty truly angry, but it was impossible to mistake in the way the bones of her face seemed to shine with light. "If my husband has any objection I will deal with him directly when he comes home. Now give me the child so that I can tend to her. And do not speak to me of my own health, Hannah. I have never felt better in my life."

There were two spots of color high on the thin cheeks, but the look in Kitty's eyes dared Hannah to mention them.

Hannah nodded. "Let's go into your chamber and I'll explain what needs to be done."

"No," Kitty said, folding the child against her chest very gently. "Leave her to me. You have another call to make. I understand that Mr. Kuick asked for you to attend him personally."

This time Cookie was in the kitchen. Hannah was glad to see her, and even happier to hear that she need not worry about dealing with Jemima.

"When she ain't in the office she's down at the mill," Cookie said dryly. "Trying to run things in the overseer's place." The small mouth puckered as if she had something sweet-sour on her tongue.

"And Mr. Kuick?"

Cookie hesitated. "Becca's in there with him now. He's in a bad way, but you'll see that yourself."

"The doctor said he asked for me."

"He did." Cookie flicked floury fingers over the dough on the table. "If you're going to ask me why, I really don' know."

"And his mother?"

Cookie smiled. "You don't have to worry about the widow none, she's so full of laudanum she wouldn't care if another Indian come to lay hisself down right next to her."

Becca met her at the chamber door with such relief in her expression that Hannah was sorry she had delayed so long.

"He is a little improved," she whispered. "At least, it seems to me that his fever has let up a bit. He's sweat through the linen again, I have to go fetch more." And she slipped away down the hall at a trot.

From the bed Isaiah Kuick said, "Miss Bonner. Thank you very much for coming." His voice was raw and hoarse with fever, but he made an effort to smile at her.

Hannah sat down beside him on a small chair with a curved back. Under a heavy load of blankets Jemima Kuick's husband shivered so that the bed frame shook. His hair was wet through with sweat, and when she put her hand on his forehead she had to stop herself from pulling away in surprise.

"Didn't know a human being could get so hot," he croaked. His breath came shallow, with a wheezing sound that meant his lungs could not do their work. *Pneumonia right and left,* Richard Todd had reported and Hannah knew what she would hear should she put her ear to his chest.

"It would be better if you saved your voice," she said, taking a rag from the bowl of water on the table to wipe his face.

"Save my voice?" The pale eyes blinked at her. "But I must talk, Miss Bonner. I called you here to hear my confession. You are a Catholic, are you not? I understand that Catholics believe that confession is good for the soul."

Hannah was so surprised that for a moment she did not know how to answer him.

"I was baptized by a Catholic priest," she said. "But I have never practiced that faith. What I *can* do for you—"

"You can do nothing for me," he interrupted her in a hoarse whisper. "I will be dead within a day. Sooner, if God has any mercy."

Hannah folded back the blanket to wipe his neck, grainy with the canker rash; she lifted his head from the pillow and turned it while she studied his face: eyes red-rimmed and already a little sunken from having lost so much fluid. She helped him drink some water before she turned to her things to get what she would need.

"What is that you're doing?"

"Making a tea that will give you some ease."

"Do not waste your medicines on me, Miss Bonner."

Hannah sat down again, and the bottles in her hands clinked together softly. She said, "I will not sit by idly and watch you die, Mr. Kuick. If you will not let me treat you, then I must go elsewhere. There are many sick in the village; maybe nobody has told you."

He looked at her very hard, and then, quite slowly, his eyes rolled back in his head and he began to convulse.

Fever convulsions were not uncommon, but Hannah had never dealt with them on her own. By the time they had passed she was drenched in her own sweat.

He fell into so deep a sleep that she had to convince herself at first that he still lived. His chest rose and fell in an uneasy rhythm, and Hannah watched him for a while, counting his respiration and his pulse, counting her own.

When Becca finally returned with the fresh linen they changed the bed together, not speaking at all.

Isaiah Kuick came to himself quite unexpectedly. He said, "Becca, you had best go sit with my mother. I have things to discuss with Miss Bonner."

"How many are sick in the village?"

Hannah studied him for a moment. The sound of his breathing was by far the worst sign, watery and wheezing. He was not a robust man, but healthy enough; if not for the inflammation in his lungs he would have every chance of surviving scarlet fever.

Hannah said, "Twelve, with the canker rash. There are other patients to see as well. Take some of this now."

She lifted his head to help him swallow the thin tea. When he was finished he wiped his mouth with his hand and grimaced. "Foul stuff."

"But effective, for the most part."

"So now that I've taken your tea, will you listen to my confession?"

Hannah bit back an impatient reply. "You should not

overextend yourself," she said. "You need all your strength to fight your fever."

Without warning he reached up to take her wrist in a circle of fingers as hot as iron off the fire. "What I need is for you to listen to me. It is in your own best interest, Miss Bonner. Will you not give me my last wish?"

Hannah had begun to think he had fallen asleep again when he began in his wheezing voice.

"You know my wife fears you above all people."

Hannah nodded warily. "I would say she hates me. Yes, I know that."

"Watch out for her, Miss Bonner. Once I am gone there will be no one to hold her back. I fear she has already started."

"Started? Started what?" The skin rose all along Hannah's spine. "I don't understand."

"Early this morning she sent Becca down to the village with two letters to go to Johnstown. Addressed to the circuit judge and the county magistrate. They will have the letters tomorrow, no doubt."

Hannah sat back in the chair, unable to hide her surprise.

He said, "Becca has been a good friend to me. Sometimes she tells me stories of her family and a grandmother—I forget the name—"

"They called her Froma Anje," Hannah supplied.

"Becca was fortunate, to have such a family."

"She still is," Hannah said, thinking too late of Becca's sister.

"Becca is a good soul, if a simple one." His breath came harder, and Hannah helped him sit up against the pillows.

"You were saying about the letters—"

He nodded. "I don't know what she wrote, but I fear it will be more trouble for you."

"But what—"

"Let me talk, I don't know how long my strength will last. You heard that the strongbox is gone, and with it all the money. When I'm dead Jemima will be left here with my mother and no way to get away from her." Something of real humor passed over his face. "You can see why she would be desperate."

"She will have her child," Hannah added. "Your child."

He turned his face away from her for a long moment. When he spoke again his voice was very low.

"You know only the worst of Ambrose Dye," he said. "There is no reason for you to believe me given what you saw, but once he was not so hard-hearted."

There was a longer silence. Finally Hannah said, "He was a friend to you."

Isaiah let out a rough sound, something that might have been a laugh. "Yes, he was that. Listen now, and mark me. It was my fault, what happened to Reuben and I must take responsibility for it before I die."

He had turned to look at her, his eyes moving over her face as if he would find some answer there. Forgiveness or understanding; even curiosity, something, now that he had said the words. Hannah could see what he wanted from her but she could not give it.

"Go on," she said quietly.

He took a deep breath that caused his whole body to shake. "It happened in a fit of rage. Ambrose threw the sack and it broke all over the boy— " He hesitated, and raising a hand, he pressed it to his eyes.

"It all happened so fast—that is not meant to be an excuse. There is no excuse," he added wearily. "And then I made it worse. I should have called the constable in. It was an accident, after all. But I was afraid."

Hannah kept herself very still while he wept like a tired child. She had the sense that if she made any noise at all, reached out to him in any way, he would not be able to go on. And she needed to hear what he had to say. For Cookie's sake, for everyone's.

"You must think I was worried about Ambrose, what might have happened to him. But I was worried for myself. Always for myself, first and last."

He shook his head suddenly as if to clear it, pulled himself up higher on the pillow and pointed toward a small ivory box that sat on the dresser. "There's a letter there that I wrote on the day of Reuben's burial."

"What does it say?"

"Many things, but the most important is this. Whatever rough justice Ambrose met he deserved. They should not hang for it."

"Hang." Hannah echoed the word, hollow-sounding and harsh. "You think Jemima would—"

"Probably not," he said, laying his head down again. "She would not throw away so much capital, not even to get back at you. Miss Bonner, I am feeling very faint so please listen. I did Cookie and the others a great wrong, but this way perhaps I can redeem myself a little, in their eyes at least. No harm should come to any of them. You will use the letter, if it comes to that?"

"Yes." Hannah nodded. "If I must I will use it."

There was so much Hannah didn't understand, but another part of her, the part that was a healer first saw the tripping pulse in his throat and knew that he would not stand any more strain.

And still he crooked a finger until she bent her head closer and took in the smell of him: hot sweat, sweet decay.

"You still don't know why I am asking this of you," he whispered. "Cookie was not the only person wronged by Ambrose Dye," he said, his voice trailing away. "You will find out soon enough, if my guess is right."

The letter was two sheets folded and sealed with wax, under which he had written in a neat hand: "I, Isaiah Simple Kuick, sound of mind and body, do hereby swear by the Almighty God and all that is Holy that what I have put down on these pages is true. Witness to my signature: Rebecca Kaes, of Paradise on this 24th day of April 1802."

Becca had signed in a round hand. On the other side, where an address would have been written, he had copied out some lines:

Light hath no tongue, but is all eye;
If it could speak as well as spy,
This were the worst, that it could say,
That being well, I fain would stay,
And that I loved my heart and honour so,
That I would not from him, that had them, go.

When Hannah left Isaiah's chamber an hour later with the unopened letter in her pocket, her patient had fallen into a sleep so deep and pure that Hannah took Becca aside to warn her what was to come.

Becca's face filled with a terrible sadness. Her eyes reddened, and Hannah felt a great warmth toward the girl, who had found a way to be a friend and comfort to a difficult and tormented man.

"Should I wake the widow?" She plucked nervously at her sleeve. "She'll want to take leave of him. Won't she?"

"You must do as you see fit," Hannah said. "But I would be surprised if he woke again. If you know where his wife might be . . ." She let the sentence drift away.

Becca blinked like a confused child, as if she had forgotten that her master had a wife.

"His wife, Jemima," Hannah said. "Jemima should be with him."

Becca nodded, and left her there on the doorstep.

Chapter 41

A summer storm drew itself around the village of Paradise and swaddled it as tightly as a fussy newborn. Rain, warm and soft, washed the dust from the leaves of the apple trees in Nicholas Wilde's orchard and wet the heads of the mourners gathered around his sister's grave. Rain turned the footpaths to mud that clung to shoework and made hems drag heavy. All over the village doors that would normally stand open in the summer were closed tight against the rain.

Even indulgent mothers who sent the youngest out to play in warm rain to save the trouble of a weekly wash closed their ears and ignored the complaints of bored children. Every parent in the village divided their nightmares between Indian raids and canker rash, and took the rain as a sign from God that they were meant to keep their children close.

In the households where the rash had already struck, mothers tended feverish children and waited for the next visit from Dr. Todd or Hannah Bonner, starting up at the sound of human footsteps as if they were angel wings. By the third day of the fever, when it was clear who would survive and who might not, the rhythm of the visits changed. The two doctors divided their time among four households: the Camerons, where old Isaac scrabbled for a hold on life and his grown sons drank away their fear, and the families where scarlet fever had put down taproots: LeBlanc, Ratz, and Hindle.

The LeBlancs were the family in the most trouble. The

newborn daughter had died on her second day but Molly, ever persistent and reluctant to leave her boys, rallied once and then fell into a last delirium that seemed to take no end. The little cabin filled up with the stink of childbed fever and the boys— even the two youngest still feverish with the canker rash— could not be kept inside. They climbed out windows to stand crying in the rain, and ignored their grandmother's threats and pleas alike.

A fine mist settled and stayed at Lake in the Clouds, threading through trees and turning familiar corners into caves to be explored. It seemed as if Elizabeth had used some witching spell to call down the rain and mist to bind them all to the mountain. Isolated as they were from the village, the only news came to them when Hannah returned home on a rare visit. It was from Hannah they heard the names of the dead: Isaiah Kuick, Esther Greber, Prudence Ratz, Isaac Cameron.

Lily followed Elizabeth around, talking and drawing and taking lessons in arithmetic and history without complaint when it could not be avoided. She even practiced her knitting and pretended to enjoy it, and still her mother didn't seem to take note of how unusually cooperative and good she was being. It was aggravating, but it also frightened Lily, the way her mother seemed to dream-walk her way through the day. Lily went to her father and was comforted, but it was Many-Doves who seemed to understand best of all what was wrong and could quiet Lily's fears.

"Your little brother sits heavy on her lap just now," Many-Doves told her. "She doesn't know what to do with her sorrow, and she has let her anger turn inward, where it festers."

The question Lily asked was the one Daniel would ask when she related all this to him. "Will she get better when the epidemic is past?"

"No," Many-Doves said, pausing in her work to look Lily directly in the eye. "That will be no more than a beginning."

Nathaniel spent the wet dark days of the epidemic mending broken tools and making a new stretching frame for Many-Doves, keeping a watchful and worried eye on his wife, and waiting for his eldest daughter's next visit.

At night he held a sleepless Elizabeth in his arms. They

spoke of many things, all of them unimportant. When he tried to turn the conversation to other matters she stiffened.

"A quarantine is nothing unusual, Nathaniel," she said to him. "Even a self-imposed quarantine. It is the sensible thing to do."

"You know, Boots," he said in a conversational tone that he hoped would hide his frustration. "You know, just to use the word 'sensible' doesn't make a thing true."

She sat up in the dark. He could just make out the shape of her face and back, but when he reached out she moved away.

"Once again," she said firmly. "Let me say this. From everything Hannah has told us this is not a very bad outbreak. It is a matter of days, nothing more, and then we can go on in our normal fashion."

Nathaniel said, "Why do you send the children to their beds when their sister comes home? You know she wouldn't come near us if she had any thought it might be dangerous."

"It's merely a precaution," Elizabeth said wearily. "Nothing more."

On the morning of the fourth day Jed McGarrity came up the mountain just as the sun showed itself. Elizabeth went very still when they heard the sound of his hello from out front, but this time she was not alone. Nathaniel went out to greet Jed sure in his gut that the man was here to tell them that Hannah was sick with the canker rash. But the sight of McGarrity's easy smile eased his fears. Nathaniel drew in a deep breath and let it out again.

"You come with news, Jed, or you just out for a walk?"

"I got some news," McGarrity said, blinking up at Nathaniel. "But mostly it's another matter. It might be best if we sat down with Hawkeye and Runs-from-Bears to have us this talk. So I don't have to tell the story more than once."

"A messenger come late yesterday evening from Johnstown," Jed began when they had gathered around the table. "With word from the circuit judge."

Of all the things Jed might have come to say, this was the last thing Nathaniel had imagined. The men looked at each other, and then Hawkeye spoke up.

"It ain't time for O'Brien to come through yet, is it? What does he want, Jed?"

McGarrity was a man with a long face that always looked worried, even when he was smiling. Dour, Nathaniel's mother would have called him. A true Scot. She would have said it with a wink, good Scotswoman that she was.

"You're not going to like it much. Seems like the Kuick widows have sworn a complaint against your Hannah, serious enough to bring him here out of rotation. He'll be arriving today sometime, and he's looking to hold an inquiry before he goes ahead and charges her."

Elizabeth gasped softly. She was listening from the doorway, her arms wrapped around herself.

"Charges her with what?" Hawkeye said, calm as ever but with a flash of fire in his eye that nobody at this table could overlook.

"Didn't say exactly." Jed studied his hands where he had spread them out on the table. "But I expect it's got something to do with the robbery at the mill."

"Being it was Indians that did it," Runs-from-Bears said to nobody in particular. "I suppose that means we'll all be hauled up in front of O'Brien. Don't matter that every one of us was in that trading post while the whole thing happened."

"Right now it's just Hannah," Jed said. "Now don't take this the wrong way, Bears, but I've been meaning to ask—"

"The men who broke into the mill house weren't Mohawk," Runs-from-Bears said. "And I can't tell you what tribe they are from their tracks. It's a reasonable question, Jed. I ain't about to take offense."

McGarrity looked confused, as if he liked the answer Runs-from-Bears had given him, but wasn't sure it matched the question he asked.

Nathaniel said, "Did O'Brien tell you to take Hannah into custody?"

Jed met his eye, and nodded.

"What're you planning to do?"

"Why, nothing," said Jed, leaning back in his chair so far that it creaked. "I figure the messenger got that part of it wrong, is how I'll tell it. Given we're all caught up in the canker rash and all, and Hannah's running from sickbed to sickbed. And if O'Brien don't like it, why then he can find hisself another constable. I never wanted the damn job in the first place."

There was a longer silence, and then Runs-from-Bears said, "What do you think is behind all this, Jed?"

McGarrity pushed his hands through his hair in a rough gesture. "I been asking myself that question all night. To tell the truth, looks to me like this is all Jemima in a temper. The widow let herself be dragged in gladly enough—Lord knows the woman would pick a fight with a polecat—but this is Jemima's work. I never have understood what she's got against your Hannah but whatever it is, it finally came to a boil."

In the sleeping loft the children began to argue in a whisper that could be heard in every corner of the cabin.

Elizabeth called up to them. "Lily. Daniel. Ethan. You must keep silent if you will listen, or I'll send you to Many-Doves."

Daniel's head appeared over the banister, his cheeks bright with color. "Sorry, Ma, but we can't keep quiet anymore. There's something we got to tell you about Jemima Southern."

"Jemima Kuick," Lily said, standing up next to her brother.

The men looked at each other, and then Nathaniel said, "Come on down here, then, and say what you got to say."

Ethan hung back with Elizabeth while the twins told the story, standing at attention in front of the gathered men. More than once a sigh escaped Elizabeth. When she met Nathaniel's gaze he saw the question there he was asking himself: their two youngest had been carrying this burden for weeks, how was it that they hadn't known something was wrong?

"Now let me get this straight," Hawkeye said when they had finished, and the twins went very still. "Jemima threatened to go after your sister if you told what you saw at Eagle Rock that day."

They nodded.

"And did you tell anybody?"

"No," Lily said, biting her lip. "We never did. I know we should have told about the trespassing—"

Hawkeye held up a hand to stop her. "I'm not worried about that right now. What I'm wondering is, what set Jemima off if it wasn't the two of you talking. Just a robbery don't seem like enough, unless it was Hannah who did it and we know that ain't the case."

From the doorway Elizabeth said, "It's the loss of the money. The loss of the money and her husband all at—" She faltered, and Nathaniel saw some understanding come into her face. "No," she corrected herself. "It is the money, it will always be that for Jemima. But this doesn't have to do with Isaiah Kuick."

"Then what?" said McGarrity.

Elizabeth lifted a shoulder. "I couldn't say how, but I wonder if this doesn't have something to do with Liam Kirby."

Jed threw an uneasy look in the twins' direction. "Jemima got what she wanted from Liam Kirby, it seems to me." His voice trailed away to a rough cough. "I suppose he could be hanging around these parts, keeping himself out of sight. Hannah hasn't said anything about seeing him, has she?"

Elizabeth sent Nathaniel a questioning look, but he had turned his attention to a callus on the heel of his hand, his mouth set in a deep frown. In fact, none of the men seemed eager to comment on Liam Kirby.

"No," Elizabeth said. "I can tell you for a certainty that Hannah has not seen or heard from Liam since your wedding party back in the spring. I must be mistaken about Liam. We will find out soon enough what moved Jemima to file that complaint, I suppose."

Jed McGarrity stood up slowly. "I don't like this," he said. "Not any of it, but O'Brien's on his way, and your Hannah will have to answer his questions. Don't see any way around that. And before I forget, there's one more thing I come to say. Mrs. Bonner, if I could have a word with you alone, I'd appreciate it."

Nathaniel went looking for Elizabeth expecting an argument, or at the very least, some hard questions about Liam Kirby. She was already on the verge of figuring out for herself what Nathaniel and his father had agreed not to tell her, quite yet: Liam Kirby was in hiding on the mountain again, but he wasn't looking for runaways; just the opposite. Somehow or another he and Manny had hooked up and decided to take the matter of Ambrose Dye into their own hands.

The question she would ask first was the hardest one: Why

would Manny be working together with the man who was re-sponsible—at least in part—for his wife's death? The answer was, of course, that Liam hadn't been responsible and, in fact, the opposite might just be true. He hadn't been able to save Selah but he had saved the rest of the runaways by simply keeping his mouth shut when Cobb was examining their papers.

If Nathaniel laid all this out for Elizabeth, she was likely to take a musket and go off in search of Liam to get the answers she'd want. He could only hope she didn't figure things out for herself before he could find a way to open up the subject with her.

The sight of Ethan standing white-faced by the window put all thought of Liam Kirby out of Nathaniel's head.

"It is your choice," Elizabeth was saying. "You may go if you need to be with her, Ethan, but for your own well-being I hope you will stay here with us."

"What's this about?"

Elizabeth jumped at the sound of his voice and sent him a flustered and embarrassed look.

"Kitty is come down with the scarlet fever," she said. "Richard sent word with Mr. McGarrity." On her face he could see what she did not want to say in front of Ethan: that Richard feared for her life, and thought her son should be with her.

"I'll take you home."

"But—" Elizabeth began.

"Get your things together and go wait for me on the porch," Nathaniel said to Ethan in as gentle a voice as he could manage.

When Ethan had left them Nathaniel said, "You go too far, Elizabeth. You can't keep the boy away from his mother when she asked for him."

She stood suddenly, bright anger flashing across her face. "It is for his own good that I tried," she said. "And I might have succeeded, if you hadn't interfered."

Nathaniel forced himself to take a deep breath, and then another. Elizabeth was trembling as if she feared he might raise a hand to her, and in some part of his mind Nathaniel knew that the anger on his face had given her that idea.

She said, "Let me go in his place. He is my brother's son, Nathaniel. I can't let him expose himself to such danger."

"It ain't your choice, Boots," Nathaniel said, and walked away before he said anything else.

She came running to the door just as he was about to close it behind himself, her face streaked with tears, and watched from the porch as he walked away with Ethan at his side.

Hannah had gone with so little sleep for so long that she was not surprised to find that she had lost the habit. Richard might order her to get a few hours' rest, and she might even lie down on the workroom cot and feel the room reel around her from exhaustion, but sleep still evaded her.

Upstairs Ethan was sitting by Kitty's bedside. He stayed through fever convulsions and delirium that would have scared most children away. He stayed because every now and then Kitty was clearheaded enough to recognize him and to say a few words before she fell away again into her fever dreams.

Hannah wanted to go home to Lake in the Clouds. It was a simple thing, really. She would go out to the stable where Strikes-the-Sky kept watch and waited for her, and she would ask him to take her home. The urge was so strong that Hannah found herself standing by the door before she remembered that she was alone in this house with a dead infant, a dying woman, and a little boy.

Richard was at the LeBlancs' or the Hindles', or maybe, if things had taken a turn for the worse, at some new bedside. Bump would be with him, keeping a watch on the doctor while the doctor watched the sick. Dolly Smythe, pressed into service by Richard, was gone to whatever family needed nursing.

Hannah stood with a hand on the door frame, looking at the cot where she was meant to be sleeping, and then at the kitchen table. A mouse sat right in its middle working diligently at a scrap of bacon rind. It occurred to Hannah that her own stomach was rumbling, and that she couldn't remember the last time she had eaten, or somebody had offered to feed her.

Then the kitchen door opened with a creak and Curiosity

stood there. She looked at the mouse on the kitchen table and then at Hannah, her face slack with surprise and something else, something like fear or dread.

Curiosity Freeman afraid of a mouse. A waking dream, then. Hannah went back to the cot, lay down, and the sleep that she had been looking for found her.

"Hannah." Ethan's voice, close to her ear. "Hannah, wake up. Please. Mama is asking for you."

Sleep left her as quickly as it had come, and Hannah started up so suddenly that Ethan jumped back.

"I didn't mean to startle you," he said, his breath hitching. "But Mama is asking for you and Curiosity said I should come tell you so."

Hannah rubbed her eyes, and rubbed them again, unsure for the moment what time of day it was or even where she found herself. Then she realized what Ethan had said.

"Curiosity is here?"

He nodded. "Hours ago. She said to let you sleep, but now Mama is asking for you."

"And Galileo?" Hannah asked as they made their way upstairs.

"He's here too, and Daisy." There was new color in Ethan's face, and a hopefulness that made Hannah wonder, just for that moment, if perhaps Kitty had taken a turn for the better simply because she had Curiosity with her.

She said, "I thought I dreamed you," and walked directly into Curiosity's arms, thin and wiry and fierce, and such a comfort that tears rose to Hannah's eyes and spilled over in a sudden quick burst.

Curiosity pulled away to look at her. Her mouth pressed hard, she ran a hand over Hannah's brow. With one long finger she tapped on Hannah's chin. "Open up now."

When she had studied Hannah's tongue she stepped back, and taking her by the upper arms she squeezed. "No canker, thank the Lord, but Hannah, child. Tell me, what help are you going to be to sick folks if you run yourself half to death?"

"It's not as bad as it could be. Curiosity, your Daisy—"

Curiosity hushed her with an upheld hand. "I sent Galileo straight over there soon as I seen the lay of the land. The children all on the mend and like to drive Daisy to drink with complaining about having to stay abed."

"Kitty—" Hannah began, and Curiosity shook her head sharply. In that one motion Hannah knew the worst.

"You best go straight in," she said. "There ain't a lot of time to waste."

The figure in the bed was so slight and insubstantial that she seemed more likely to be a sister than a mother to the boy sitting at her side. Kitty's breath hitched and caught, hitched and caught. Ethan leaned over her and put a light hand on her shoulder.

"Mama," he said softly. "Mama, Hannah is come."

She opened her eyes immediately, red-rimmed and glassy, and she drew a deeper breath.

Hannah came to sit where she could see Kitty's face without forcing her to turn her head. For her trouble she got a small smile, no more than a flickering at the corner of the mouth, fever-blistered and raw.

"Curiosity is come home," Kitty whispered.

"Yes," Hannah said. "And Galileo."

Kitty blinked once, and then again. She opened her mouth and her voice caught.

"Would you like some water?" Hannah started to stand, and Kitty shook her head.

"Hannah," she said. "I am worried for Richard."

In her surprise Hannah could only nod.

"When I am gone Elizabeth will want to take Ethan to raise, and Richard will be alone."

In her discomfort Hannah shifted on the chair. She met Curiosity's eye where she stood on the far side of the bed.

"Will you take her a message?" Kitty asked, her eyelids flickering as if she were about to lose the struggle to keep them open.

"Of course."

"I know she will not come into the village now, with the sickness about—" She paused, her throat working. "But this is so important, Hannah, please promise me you will make her understand."

"I promise," Hannah said. "Go on, Kitty."

"Tell her that I wish Ethan to stay here, to be raised by

Richard. With Curiosity's help and Galileo's. Elizabeth is not to take him away from Richard. He couldn't stand to lose us both at once."

"I will tell her," Hannah said, and wondered to herself how she could make Elizabeth understand something that she herself did not. Kitty wanted Ethan to stay in this house with a stepfather who would have little time or interest in raising him, for Richard's sake.

Kitty's hand moved across the covers toward Hannah.

"You think him hard-hearted and unfeeling," she said. "But you are wrong, Hannah, and so is Elizabeth. He needs to have Ethan with him, and Ethan needs Richard."

"Yes." Hannah met Kitty's eye. She said, "I understand."

"Curiosity, you are my witness," Kitty said, so softly now that Hannah had to lean forward to hear her.

Hannah said, "I'll go to Lake in the Clouds now, Kitty, and deliver your message."

Kitty's eyes opened again. "Will you come back? Do you promise to come back? I would rest easier if I knew you were nearby."

"I'll come back this evening," Hannah said. "I promise. Is there anything else you want right now?"

Kitty smiled dreamily. "All I want now is Richard," she said. "I want Richard to come to me."

"If that girl wasn't already dying I fear I'd have to wring her sorry neck," Curiosity said, dashing tears from her face with an impatient hand. Hannah had never seen her so furious or sad, and she had to work to swallow down her own tears.

"Worried about Richard Todd being lonely while that boy sitting right there with his soul on his face, just waiting for a few words from her. I swear—" Her voice went hoarse and broke, and Hannah watched the older woman struggle to control her tears. She straightened her shoulders with a visible effort.

"Hannah, you made a promise and I know I can't talk you out of it, so you best get on your way. Take that worthless message to Elizabeth."

"If I can bring Elizabeth back with me, I will," Hannah

said. "She of all people might be able to speak some sense to Kitty."

Curiosity drew in a long shuddering breath. "Not much chance of that. I expect Elizabeth sitting up on that mountain just about worrying herself to death. You go home now and sit with your folks for an hour, get your breath. Eat something that ain't been mouse nibbled." She cast a disgusted glance at the kitchen table. "When you ready come back here and set with her. I need one sane woman with me at a time like this." She laughed then, a harsh sound, and shook her head. When she looked at Hannah again she seemed more herself.

"I saw that Strikes-the-Sky fellow when we come up," she said. "Seem to me we got a lot to talk about, you and me, but it'll wait till you get back."

Strikes-the-Sky and Strong-Words were both waiting for her, and by their expressions Hannah saw immediately that the day's trouble had not yet ended.

"I have to go home," she said.

The two of them exchanged a glance. "A man is come from Johnstown," said Strikes-the-Sky. "His name is O'Brien. He's on his way now to Lake in the Clouds with a summons. For you."

Hannah thought at first she must have misunderstood. She looked them each in the eye, and knew that she had not. The day's anger and frustration and sorrow came together into something hot and sharp that started in her belly and flowed up to make her hands tingle and her voice shake.

"You two warriors stay here if you are afraid of an old white man with a piece of paper in his hand."

She gave them a furious look and set off at a trot. By the time she had passed the stable they had gathered their wits and had caught up to her. Strong-Words pulled ahead and Strikes-the-Sky brought up the rear so that Hannah found herself both following and leading, and unsure how she felt about either.

She pushed herself hard and harder until the breath burned in her lungs and she thought they would burst, and still Hannah could not shake the words out of her head. Judge O'Brien with a summons, for her. She wiped the sweat from her eyes, pulled her skirt more tightly through her belt to free her legs, and dug into the mountain. Who had sworn a summons against her but Jemima Kuick? She didn't need to be told what was so obvious to see.

Fury is the hottest fuel, her grandmother Falling-Day would have told her, and she was learning that lesson now.

A flickering in the branches of a maple tree and a squirrel scolded in a high voice. Hannah pulled up as if someone had called her name, knowing what she would see before it came: the shape of a man.

Manny Freeman stepped out in front of them, behind him a young black man Hannah had never seen before. Both of them wore buckskin and moccasins and carried muskets, and both of them had wary smiles on their faces. Instead of surprise she felt only another flush of anger, that they should choose now to draw her into their plot.

"Manny Freeman," she said breathlessly. "I was wondering when you'd show yourself. I've got just three things to say to you. I'm sorry about Selah—"

He nodded and looked away.

"—I'm glad you're safe, and your timing stinks. I can't stay around here and exchange news with you."

Manny laughed out in surprise, bowed from the shoulders, and touched his forehead with two fingers. "Good to see you too, Walks-Ahead."

"Do Curiosity and Galileo know you're here?"

He nodded. "They know."

Behind her Strong-Words said, "We would have told you if you had given us a chance, Walks-Ahead."

Hannah ignored him and looked at the boy. "You're Jode. My father and stepmother told me about you. Why aren't you in Canada?"

"There is work to do here," the boy said in perfect Kahnyen'kehàka.

"There's trouble here," she corrected him. "And it's your doing." She wiped the sweat from her forehead and drew in a deep breath. "If you've got business with me you'd best state it quick. I need to get home."

Manny said, "You can't go home. You can't go anywhere in Paradise right now. It's too dangerous with O'Brien looking for you."

She laughed, an odd harsh sound. "It's dangerous for every-one in Paradise. If you've been watching you know we've got scarlet fever in a third of the cabins."

Her uncle said, "O'Brien is here to arrest you."

"He's got no cause," Hannah said.

"Do you think he needs cause?" Manny said. "You know better than that, Hannah. You saw what happened in the city."

She stepped closer to him in her anger, but he held his ground. "Maybe if you returned the strongbox you stole, the widow would drop those charges, whatever they are," she said sharply. "That would be a better solution to all this than me running off and leaving sick children untended to."

They exchanged glances. "We can't return the strongbox," Manny said. "We got better use for the money than they do."

"Is that so?" Hannah could barely govern her temper. "What use would that be?"

Manny reached into a sack hanging around his neck and, pulling out a coin, he thrust it in her direction. "A good half of it never belonged to them in the first place. We're on our way to return it to the rightful owners."

Hannah looked at the coin in his hand and froze, just as he meant her to. In his hand Manny held a five-guinea gold piece with old King George in profile. "The Tory gold," she said, her voice catching. "The widow had the Tory gold?"

"A good lot of it anyway," said Manny. "About eight hun-dred coins."

"But—" Hannah shook her head to clear it. "How... Dye?"

Manny nodded. "You know Dye was here when you got back from Scotland in ninety-four, that summer Liam ran off. I expect it was the rumors about the gold that brought Dye here in the first place. So he went looking around Hidden Wolf while he had the chance and he found what he was look-ing for. Then he cut himself a deal with the widow. A silent partner, was the way he put it. Seems like she spent her last penny on the mill and didn't have any capital of her own."

"And how is it you know all this? My God," Hannah breathed. "Have you told my grandfather?"

"We had a chance to talk a few days back. I expect he was waiting until the time was right to tell you."

"You took the strongbox to make it look like Dye was a thief."

Jode smiled then, the first smile she had seen from him. All of them were smiling, pleased with how well their plan had worked.

Manny said, "It seemed like the only way to settle the score with him without somebody hanging for it."

"And the rest of the money in the strongbox?"

Manny said, "You'll have to take my word for it that we don't plan to spend it on fancy women and liquor, and we sure as hell ain't about to hand it to the Kuicks. Which brings us back around again to O'Brien."

"You think he's going to charge me with robbery when I was in the trading post while it happened? Maybe he's going to charge me with witchcraft too, being in more than one place at a time."

"I wouldn't put it past him," said Manny. "He's done worse. Which is why we think you should leave with us right now, before he gets the chance to put you in leg irons."

Strong-Words said, "You'll go with us now to save your life."

Hannah ignored him. To Strikes-the-Sky she said, "You think I should run scared from a man like O'Brien?"

He inclined his head. "I think you have to know your own mind, Walks-Ahead."

"You would make a good diplomat," she said dryly. For a moment she stared into the trees, trying to order her thoughts. Scarlet fever in the village, Kitty on her deathbed, O'Brien's warrant. The anger that had moved her up the mountain was still there when she thought of it, that she should let a man like O'Brien drive her away from sick children. That the widow Kuick, a thief herself, should drive her from her home.

"I'm going home to Lake in the Clouds," Hannah said. "And then I'm going back to the village. You run west if you want to. Unless you intend to take me by force, like you took Dye."

A flicker of uneasiness passed over Manny's face. For a moment the men looked at each other, and then Manny and Strong-Words both took steps backward.

When Hannah set off again, all four men followed her.

*   *   *

They waited in the cover of the forest until they saw O'Brien leave in a hurry, yelling threats back over his shoulder toward the men standing on the porch.

"She'll answer the summons or I'll put a price on her head!"

The rifle shot rang clear and then echoed along the cliffs, drowning out O'Brien's curses.

"You see," Hannah said to the men around her. "My grandfather knows how to handle O'Brien. You could take a lesson from him."

While Hannah sat with Elizabeth and the children and spoke of Kitty she listened with one ear to the argument going on in the common room, where the men were gathered.

Elizabeth was quiet for a very long time when Hannah had finished.

"Will you send a message back for Aunt Kitty?" Daniel asked softly, and Elizabeth looked at him as if she had forgotten he was sitting there.

"Yes," she said. "Of course."

Lily, on the verge of tears, put her head in her mother's lap and shuddered. Elizabeth stroked her head. "We will say a prayer for your aunt this evening."

"But can't we go down to her?" Lily wailed suddenly, pulling herself into an upright position. "Shouldn't we be there with them?"

Elizabeth closed her eyes and shook her head. "Hannah, tell Kitty that of course I will do as she asks."

Lily launched herself into her sister's lap and wept as if her heart had shattered. Hannah rocked her silently, and reached out a hand to put on Elizabeth's shoulder. In her own way she was as fragile right now as Kitty.

"I will tell her," she said.

"What about O'Brien?" asked Daniel. "What about the summons? O'Brien will be waiting for you in the village. Uncle wants you to leave here tonight."

"I'm not ready to go just yet," Hannah said. "And most of all I'm not worried about Baldy O'Brien. Most likely he's already knee-deep in Axel Metzler's ale." She flicked her fingers in a careless gesture. "I will run circles around him and his summons."

Daniel managed a grin at that, and even Lily's sobbing lessened. Elizabeth was looking out the window, and seemed not to have heard any of it at all.

"We will leave now, tonight," said Strong-Words. "We will leave this minute rather than let O'Brien arrest her."

Hannah walked into the circle of men and stopped. "Why do you talk about me as if I were a child?" she said in her strongest voice. "I can make decisions for myself, and I will not run in fear from O'Brien, or anyone else."

Hawkeye inclined his head so that his hair fell forward over his shoulder, and Hannah noticed with some unease how white it was now, with no trace of black. He said, "We know you are not afraid, granddaughter. No one here is questioning your courage."

His gaze shifted from Nathaniel to Strong-Words and then, for a longer time, to Strikes-the-Sky. "She is a grown woman, and she must speak for herself."

Hannah drew in a deep and shuddering breath. She looked at each of them in turn: Strong-Words and Manny and Jode all wore the same expression, their faces so full of fear and anger that there was no room for anything else. She looked at Runs-from-Bears and her father, watchful and quiet and patient above all things. They were concerned for her safety, but they held that concern in tight fists and would not let it go until she called on them to do so.

And she looked at Strikes-the-Sky, who held back because she had not made her choice and his role here was unclear. Finally she turned to her grandfather.

"I am going to sit with Kitty as I promised I would." Hannah wished that she could banish the tremor from her voice, but she held her head up and spoke clearly. "I promised her and I promised Curiosity, who is as close to me as my own mother or grandmother or stepmother. I will stay with Kitty until she needs me no more."

Until she is dead. She could not yet say those words out loud, but the men around her understood what was to come. "No one will interfere with me while I am attending her, not even O'Brien."

Strong-Words' frustration burst out of him. "You are putting all of us in danger."

"I will stay with Kitty until she needs me no longer," Hannah said calmly. "As my grandmother Falling-Day, your mother, taught me to do."

He threw up his hands in disgust. "Strikes-the-Sky," he said. "Speak to her. Tell her what it is like for a red woman in a white man's gaol—"

"Uncle!" Her anger flashed so sharp that even Strong-Words must falter, and stop.

She said, "Your temper has got the best of you. Now, do you have something to say to me, Strikes-the-Sky?"

He said, "I have nothing to say. You have made yourself clear, Hannah Bonner."

It was at that moment that she knew she was ready to make her choice.

Hannah heard no discussion of who would see her down to the village, but when she came out on the porch Strikes-the-Sky was waiting for her with his rifle resting in his crossed arms. In the light from the door he looked like something carved from stone, as immovable as the mountain itself.

Because they did not know for sure where O'Brien was, they carried neither torch nor lantern. But the sky was clear, and in a few days the moon would be full.

Strikes-the-Sky moved so silently that he might have been a ghost and she his shadow, trailing behind. When he stopped she must stop; he turned his head to listen and so did she, but the difference was this: he threw all his senses out into the night to whatever threats might be waiting for them in the dark, while she strained only to hear the sound of his breathing. They moved down the mountain like this, stopping now and then to listen and look before they moved on.

Where the forest paused at the beginning of the strawberry fields, Strikes-the-Sky stopped again, his eyes scanning the open expanse. The smell of the last of the berries hung over-sweet in the night air. And another smell, sharper and salty: spilled blood.

"Panther." He pointed to the other side of the field where the cat lay in among the strawberries, tawny gold and flexing muscle in the moonlight. The white leg of a deer jutted up, jittered, and jerked.

"A sign," said Strikes-the-Sky.

A sign, yes, but how to read it? Hannah rubbed her hands over her arms to calm the gooseflesh, and they set off again. He moved faster now, and did not stop again until they came into the village and stopped in the shadows behind the church. The call of a nightjar, and then a wolf trotted up from the riverbank, stopped to put his nose in the air and sniff, and moved back into the trees just as the mill house dog began to bark fiercely from up on the hill.

In the village the only light came from the lantern hanging at the tavern door.

"That is good," said Strikes-the-Sky. "O'Brien will drink as long as Metzler lets him."

"Then he will drink all night," said Hannah. She turned her head up to look at him, and found he was much closer than she had imagined.

He made a sound deep in his throat, that rough sound she recognized already as doubt, and at the same moment he put his hand on her shoulder and turned her toward him.

As if we were dancing, Hannah thought as she followed the gentle pressure of his hand. His fingers threaded through her hair and she had to tilt her head to look at him. His eyes moved over her face and then his finger, tracing the line of her lower lip and her jaw while his other hand covered her back.

He said, "You are trembling. Are you cold?"

"No." She shook her head. "I am not cold." And then: "I have no scarf to put around your shoulders, Strikes-the-Sky." How strange those words sounded in her own whispered voice, loud enough to echo over the mountain and down the river valley. Loud enough to fill the world.

"But you have arms," he said, smiling now. "They will serve the same purpose."

It should have been awkward to stand like this with him in the dark as she put her arms around his neck. All her uncertainty was gone, and in its place a calm acceptance and more than that, the beginning of something she thought might be joy.

The smell of him was already familiar, high and sharp; his voice reached inside of her, left his mouth and slid down her throat, sweet and heavy so that deep inside her body, in places still unknown and unknowing, a pulsing began.

She put her face to the curve of his neck and inhaled, and in response he drew her closer.

"The last time you tricked me into kissing you." Her own voice, high and far away.

His hands tightened across her back, drew her up on tiptoe and brought her mouth to his.

"The way I see it, you made me work hard for that kiss."

She made a fist and thumped him on the shoulder, but his mouth came no closer.

"Does that mean you intend to make me work hard for this one?"

"No," he said, his breath moving on her skin. "This time I'm going to do all the work myself. I'll work until you ask me to stop."

He meant to make her laugh, to shock, to draw her in, and he did all those things with his words and mouth, with the heat of his kiss and his hands that cradled her head. He kissed her until she gasped with it and then before she could catch her breath he kissed her again, drawing her closer to him and closer still until her body had softened to something strange and pliable to be wound around him, a vine around an oak reaching up and up.

Strikes-the-Sky broke off the kiss, held her away from him with an expression so fierce that it should have frightened her. He said, "Will you come with me, will you come west?"

And kissed her again, before she could answer, kissed her until she would have agreed to live in a cloud with him or at the bottom of a lake, anywhere as long as she could have this, have him and his mouth and the way he looked at her, the feel of him. He held her as if she were the earth itself, and the sky and all the stars, and he must draw her inside his skin to be complete. Her body ached.

"Will you?" His hands on her shoulders, fingers spread as he pulled her up to look into her face. She blinked at him, struck dumb by the things he was calling forth out of her, shocked at how simple it was, the truth of it.

"Will you come west with me and be my wife?"

The answer he wanted was pushing up from her belly, filling her throat, and it spilled out of her in a whisper. "Yes, I will come with you."

He went very still for a moment, and then he pressed his

mouth against her forehead. Then he stepped back, held her steady while she found her balance again.

He said, "When your work is done there will be time enough to make plans."

She said, "You don't think I should run?"

The smile he gave her was only half-serious. "Then you would not be the woman you are."

When Hannah came into the room they were all asleep: Ethan curled into a ball at his mother's feet, Richard with his head thrown back and his hands gripping the arms of a lady's chair far too small for him, Curiosity with her cheek bedded on her shoulder.

To see Curiosity idle was strange and somehow comforting too, to know that even she must take her rest. Her hands were folded in her lap with fingers intertwined, as if they must be restrained, even in sleep. Her head wrap had slipped to reveal hair that gleamed silver and black in the lamplight. In the last few months the soft wrinkles around her eyes and mouth had deepened, so that it seemed to Hannah that her age had finally caught up with her. In repose she looked her age, and more.

Kitty slept too, so quietly and deeply that Hannah waited, motionless, to see the hesitant rise and fall of her chest. Her skin was transparent in the soft light of the lamp, as tender and dry as silk. Veins like faint blue rivers etched their way across her forehead and over cheekbones, along the column of her throat. The same blue that tinged lips and eyelids and the fingernails of the hand that lay curled on the top of the blanket.

Ubi est morbus? She whispered the question.

Kitty's breath hitched and paused, caught and hitched.

Curiosity and Richard woke at once. Ethan stirred more slowly, and then bolted upright to roll off the foot of the bed, landing on his feet. To Hannah his eyes seemed as large and round as a rabbit's in that moment it feels the wolf's breath: the time for fear had passed, and in its place a placid acceptance.

Kitty's eyelids fluttered once and then opened.

"Curiosity." Her voice came remarkably clear, but very soft.

"I'm right here, little girl."

"Richard?"

"Here, my love." He sat on the edge of the bed and took her hand.

Kitty was trying to raise her head, and Curiosity bent down to support her neck with one long hand.

"There you are," Kitty said. "Come here to me, Ethan, come."

The boy sent a questioning look to Richard, who nodded his encouragement.

When the boy had climbed up beside his mother and laid his head down beside hers she sighed, a welcoming and content sigh. She lifted an arm and put it around him.

Her gaze drifted from one face to the next.

"Hannah, you came back."

"I told you that I would."

"No sickness at Lake in the Clouds?"

"No," Hannah said. "They are all well."

"Good. You gave Elizabeth my message?"

"Yes."

"Good," Kitty echoed, and then, "I am so tired, Richard."

"Yes," he said gruffly. "I know you are." He put a hand on her chest very gently and closed his eyes.

Hannah saw it all reflected on his face: the fluttering of muscle underneath the curve of his palm, the last beats of a tender and imperfect heart.

"My sweet good boy," Kitty murmured, her fingers trailing over Ethan's face. "Stay with me while I fall asleep."

Almost dawn, and Hannah and Curiosity sat at the kitchen table, silent in a silent house where Richard Todd kept watch over his wife's still form.

Hannah rested her head on her arms and tried to order the thoughts that presented themselves to her in a random jumble. Bump would be digging two graves today, one for Molly LeBlanc and one for Kitty. Tomorrow he might dig one more or two, but it seemed as if the scarlet fever was done with Paradise, for now at least. Either way she would not be here to see any more of her neighbors into their graves. She would be walking west with Strikes-the-Sky, leaving her father and family and home.

Or, if Jemima Kuick and Judge O'Brien had their way, she would be on her way to Johnstown and the gallows.

Curiosity put a hand on her head and Hannah started up. The older woman smiled at her, such a kind smile, a beloved face. Hannah realized she had been weeping when Curiosity wiped her cheeks with a gentle thumb.

"You know I ain't ever really met your Strikes-the-Sky," she said. "He's been waiting outside all night. Why don't you call him in here and let me feed the man? I'd be thankful for the distraction, to tell the truth."

"I'm going with him," Hannah said. "I'm going west with Strikes-the-Sky. I'm—I'm going to marry him."

"I know you are," Curiosity said, sitting down and leaning across the table to grasp both of Hannah's hands in her own. "I know that, child. I will surely miss your shining face, but it's time, ain't it. He's a good man?"

"Yes," Hannah whispered.

"Well, then. You'll come back here to show us your babies someday, I expect. Won't that be a homecoming."

Tears slid down Hannah's face and dropped on their intertwined fingers. "I don't know," she said, bowing her head. "I don't know how to go away from you."

"Why, of course you do," Curiosity said. "You do it just like you do all the other hard things that come your way. One foot ahead of the other, and looking ahead. You know you can."

After a while Hannah nodded.

"Now you can call me a selfish old woman, but there's one reason I'm glad to see you go. I won't worry about our Manny half so much knowing Hannah Bonner's nearby to keep an eye on him."

Hannah managed a smile. "I'll do my best, but he is a willful sort."

Curiosity rocked forward, laughing softly, and kissed Hannah on the top of her head.

Bump came in with Strikes-the-Sky and they sat around the table, the four of them, eating Curiosity's cornbread and drinking strong coffee laced with good cone sugar. Bump gave them the news they needed to hear: no new cases of the fever, no deaths except the one they had witnessed themselves.

"Bless her soul," Bump said. "Bless her weary soul."

"What about that Baldy O'Brien?" Curiosity asked, pouring more coffee into Bump's cup. "Any news of him?"

Strikes-the-Sky shook his head. "Slept in the tavern, as far as I can see."

It was a revelation to Hannah, how well Strikes-the-Sky spoke English when he cared to. She wondered what other talents he had kept a secret from her.

Curiosity ran her hands over the tabletop thoughtfully, and then she looked at Hannah, her mouth set hard.

"You going to run from that little no-account man, girl, or stand and fight?"

"I'm not running from him," Hannah said, drawing back in surprise.

"That's what it look like to me. You don't even know what lies Jemima been telling, and you ready to bolt. From Jemima Southern, of all people. From Baldy O'Brien." She looked as if she wanted to spit.

Hannah sent Strikes-the-Sky a questioning look, but his expression was unreadable.

"I am not running from Jemima Southern," Hannah said. "Or from anybody else. I have no reason to run, I have done nothing wrong. I never thought of running away. It's your son who came up with that idea." She cast a glance in Bump's direction, but if he was surprised by this revelation he showed no sign of it.

Neither did it slow Curiosity down. "Just 'cause Manny is my son don't mean he cain't be pure stupid at times. Look at all the trouble he stirred up while I was gone, sneaking around and tying people up and poking at Jemima Southern until she lost what little bit she had left of her mind. If he was here I'd be mighty tempted to turn him over my knee. Don't you listen to those hotheaded men, girl. You stand and fight."

Hannah had intended just that, but Curiosity's sudden insistence made her hackles rise. "Why should I?" Hannah shot back. "Why should I give O'Brien the satisfaction? I might as well leave now."

"Lordy, you can be slow at times, child. Don't you see? If you run then you giving Jemima what she want. You will never be able to come back home without sneaking around, hoping she don't call the law out on you again. You going to give her that kind of power over you?" She reached out and took Hannah's hand. More softly she said, "Don't you give her that, Hannah Bonner. Don't you run."

There was a persistent rapping at the door.

"I'll bet that's O'Brien now," said Curiosity, jumping up with all the energy of a sixteen-year-old girl. "Come to a house in mourning to do Jemima Southern's dirty business."

Strikes-the-Sky got up to follow her as she marched down the hall but Hannah stopped him with a hand on his forearm. "Don't make this worse than it already is," she said to him in her own language. "Don't give him an excuse to arrest you too. Let Curiosity talk."

He cupped her face in his hand. "Walks-Ahead," he said. "I know not to get in the way of a bear protecting her young."

To prove his point the sound of Curiosity's voice rose in the hall, sharp as claws.

"We better go rescue poor Mr. O'Brien," said Bump. "Before she really gets started."

Judge O'Brien was a soft lump of a man with a small pink circle of a face stuck dead center in a maze of hair. It radiated out from his scalp in a white halo and from his chin in a grizzled gray fan, interrupted only by two very pink earlobes that peeked out when he tilted his head a certain way. His head was tilted now, and his face flushed red with indignation. From what Hannah knew of him he did not like to be challenged, most especially not by a woman. A little man with a big picture of himself, tenacious as a mule and inflexible as rock.

A rock who seemed to be encountering Curiosity Freeman in a temper for the first time.

"You got no business here," she was saying to him in a harsh whisper. "If you want to speak to Miss Bonner you will just have to wait till she got time to come see you."

"I will see Hannah Bonner now," huffed O'Brien, stepping back from an advancing Curiosity and clutching his hat to his chest. "And if I feel it's necessary I will take her with me to Johnstown to be tried there. You cannot thwart the law because you don't like what it says, missus."

Just then he caught sight of Hannah and Strikes-the-Sky standing behind her. Hannah might have laughed at his expression—satisfaction followed quickly by shock and plain fear—if the situation had not been so dire.

"Miss Bonner," he said, drawing himself up to his full height. He cast Curiosity a triumphant look. "As duly appointed circuit judge——"

"She's not going anywhere, O'Brien." Richard's voice boomed down the stairs so unexpectedly that they all jumped.

"Dr. Todd," said the little man, thrusting out his chest as far as it would go, but then glancing nervously first at Curiosity and then at Strikes-the-Sky. "I'm here on official business, but I sure didn't mean to disturb you, sir."

"Then why the hell are you pounding on my door at sunrise!" Richard thundered.

O'Brien's cheeks paled while his nose turned a deeper shade of red. "Doctor, this young woman is evading the law." He nodded in Hannah's direction. "A complaint has been sworn out against her. She can't just ignore it."

Richard came down the stairs slowly, his expression so deadly calm that Hannah felt the hair rise on the nape of her neck. O'Brien seemed to feel just the same way, because he took another step back and bumped into the door.

"She's been evading you?" Richard said softly. "Evading you?"

O'Brien swallowed visibly and nodded. "She knows I was looking for her. Didn't I issue a notice, right and proper? Took it to her door too, but would she show herself? And on top of that I almost got shot for my trouble. Nobody is above the law, Dr. Todd."

"You miserable worm," Richard began in a conversational tone. Bump drew in a harsh breath and Curiosity put a hand to her mouth to cover a smile, but O'Brien's gaze was fixed on Richard and he took in nothing else.

"You smug, insignificant, nearsighted fool. Did you think she was out dancing? Did no one tell you that there's an epidemic in this village?"

O'Brien winced. "Well, yes."

"And you're aware that Miss Bonner is a doctor?"

The little man frowned. "I know she claims that title for herself."

Richard said, "Are you challenging my word and opinion on a matter of medicine, Mr. O'Brien?"

"I guess not," he said slowly.

"You guess not."

"No, then. I won't challenge you on that."

"At last, some hope. Now listen to me. Scarlet fever has killed five people in the last five days. Without proper medical attention it would have killed more. It still may. And you stand there and claim that in your learned opinion a *summons*"—his mouth worked as if he wanted very much to spit—"is more important than the lives of the people of Paradise. Do I understand you correctly?"

The color flooded back into O'Brien's face. "Last night—" And he stopped cold as Richard took another step toward him.

"Last night while you were emptying tankards at the tavern Miss Bonner was upstairs, keeping watch—" For the first time Richard's voice broke as cleanly and simply as an eggshell. "At my wife's deathbed."

His shoulders slumped as he turned away. "Get out," he said. "Get out now."

O'Brien blinked convulsively, but he didn't move until the sound of a door closing came to them. Then he slumped, his eyes darting nervously from Strikes-the-Sky to Curiosity.

Curiosity said, "Judge O'Brien, let me give you some advice. Don't come around here talking about dragging our Hannah off to Johnstown. There's other ways to get your business taken care of." She glanced at Hannah. "Ain't that so?"

Will you stand and fight?

They were looking at her, all of them. Judge O'Brien with a doubtful expression, and Curiosity with a hopeful one. Hannah felt Strikes-the-Sky's hand on her shoulder, the simple strength in him.

She said, "I will come to the village tonight at seven to answer the charges against me. You have my word."

"There," said Curiosity with a grim smile. "Now that's my girl."

Curiosity sent Bump to Lake in the Clouds with the news of Kitty's death and Hannah's appointment with Judge O'Brien, and then she put together a bundle of food and pressed it into Strikes-the-Sky's hands.

"You make sure she eats," she said solemnly, holding on to him longer than was necessary. "That's your job now, looking after her. She surely won't look after herself."

Hannah said, "You needn't grin at each other as if you're keeping some great secret from me. I am standing right here, and I see very well what you're up to."

"You hush," Curiosity said, flapping a hand at her. "This is between your man and me. Now this is what I want you to do, Strikes-the-Sky. You take Hannah and you go find a place where she can rest. Don't take her home to Lake in the Clouds, you hear me? I don't want my Manny or the rest of them bothering her none. Best she stay away from Elizabeth for a while too, or she'll worry the hair right off her head, you know she won't be able to help herself."

As much as Hannah wanted to protest she had to smile at that picture.

"It's going to be a fine day. Take her up the mountain someplace pretty and see to it she don't go running off to tend to nobody else for one day at least. You know what I'm telling you?"

"Yes," Strikes-the-Sky said. "I know."

"Good. The girl got to rest so she'll be ready to settle things with Jemima Southern once and for all. And then you two got a long journey in front of you."

Hannah went to Curiosity and put her head on the old woman's thin shoulder. "Not today," she said, her voice muffled. "Not yet."

"Not yet," Curiosity agreed, patting her back.

Hannah was taken by the sudden need to sit down here in the familiar kitchen and never go anywhere again.

"What about Richard and Ethan?"

"We got to let them sit with her a while," Curiosity said. "You know that. It'll be tomorrow before they can leave her go."

"The LeBlancs," Hannah said, close to tears and furious with herself for it. "And the Ratz girls. I said I'd call."

"There ain't nobody at death's door right now." Curiosity held her away so that she could look into her face. "Let me look after things, child. You got your own life to tend to."

On a high meadow that gave them the whole world, weariness and sorrow came over Hannah. She sat down heavily on an outcropping of stone and lay back with an arm over her eyes. Hot tears sprang up and ran over her face like rain.

Strikes-the-Sky sat nearby. He had no words to offer but Hannah was glad of his presence and mortified too, that she should lose control of herself so completely.

When there were no more tears left she drew in a shuddering breath and held it as long as she could, until her body quieted and she could hear the world around her. In the pines nearby siskins squabbled, and just below that the faraway sound of the falls. Strikes-the-Sky made no noise at all and Hannah was convinced, very suddenly, that he had left her here to weep.

She sat up, ready to be furious or hurt or both, and found him sitting cross-legged in front of her.

"Food," he said, holding out some of Curiosity's bread.

Hannah hadn't realized she was hungry, or how good fresh bread could taste on a hot summer's day. She ate the things he passed her, cold meat and new radishes from the garden, sharp on her tongue.

"What is this?" He was looking at a bundle of parsley with a doubtful expression.

"Chew on it," Hannah said. "It cleans your mouth and makes your breath sweet." And she blushed, realizing as she spoke that sending parsley along was Curiosity's way of teasing her. Strikes-the-Sky didn't understand or chose not to, but he did as she suggested.

"There's a stream," Hannah said, pointing. "And shade, to sleep." And ran ahead, uneasy with him suddenly, this stranger, this man she had promised herself to. He followed her, quick and silent, winding through the pines until they found the stream where they both drank. It was a cool place where the light came through the firs and pines to play on the water. Moss-covered rocks and deep beds of old pine needles, and overhead the chittering call of squirrels.

"A good place," Strikes-the-Sky said. He slipped the rifle sling off around his head and put it down carefully. Next to that he piled his powder horn and bullet sack, the pouch he wore around his neck and his knife sheath, until he stood there unarmed.

When he began to pull his hunting shirt over his head

Hannah said, "What are you doing?" in a voice so sharp that he paused and looked at her.

"I'm going to sleep, right here." He pointed with his chin to the ground. "I kept watch all night. You should sleep too, unless you had something else in mind."

His grin infuriated her. She turned her back on him and lay down, brought her knees up to her chin, and wrapped her arms around herself.

She would teach him, someday, that she was not to be trifled with. Hannah made that vow to herself, and then she fell asleep.

He woke her when the sun was high above them and the forest shimmered with heat, even here by the water.

"Your people will want to see you before it is time to go meet O'Brien." He was crouched next to her, his hunting shirt in one hand and his bare chest damp with sweat. She made herself look away, but she couldn't ignore the smell of him or the feelings that rose up from deep in her belly.

She sat up. "Yes. All right."

And still they stayed just like that, close enough to touch and not touching until he reached out with two fingers and brushed her hair. "Pine needles," he said, and she watched the muscles flex in his throat when he swallowed.

With a low sound he came closer, using his whole hand now to brush her hair free of dirt and needles, and she let him. She might have taken his wrist and pushed him away but she didn't want to, not really. What she wanted to do, wanted so much that the urge was almost impossible to resist, was to put her face to the curve where his shoulder met his neck so that she could draw in his smells.

"Walks-Ahead," he said, so close now that she felt his breath stir her hair.

She turned her face to him and opened her mouth to ask him *What?* and he kissed her, as she knew he would, as she wanted him to. A gentle kiss, soft and softer still. Nothing like the rough kisses of last night but with a power of their own. She put her hands on his chest, smooth and hard, the muscles fluttering under her palms. He pulled her to him and closed his arms around her.

For a long time they knelt together on the forest floor

while he cradled her to him and kissed her mouth and she kissed him back, learning the shape of him and the taste and the touch of his tongue. She had not imagined that a kiss could be something so potent, to draw her out of herself this way. To make her want so furiously that no matter how hard she pressed herself to him it was not enough.

She ran her fingers over his face, traced his ears, cupped his scalp in her hands. In between kisses she said, "Your hair is growing back. I want to see what you look like with hair. Will you let it grow?"

"Yes," he said, smiling against her mouth. "If you want it so, wife."

She pulled away again. "Am I your wife now?" And felt the tightening in her chest to even say such a thing out loud.

He tilted his head and one corner of his mouth tilted too. "That is a question only you can answer, Walks-Ahead. Hannah. Are you my wife?"

To tremble in the heat of the day, as if a fever had taken hold of her so completely that she would never recover. He was watching her, waiting. A stranger still, and no stranger at all. She had never been more frightened or happier, more sure of what she wanted.

"Yes," she said. "I am your wife."

His smile was enough to calm the trembling in her, but then he started all over again, his hands and mouth and the simple strength in his arms, all for her. When he drew her down to the forest floor she went willingly, and when he touched her breast she arched up into his hand.

"Is there time?" she asked him, her voice breathless and hoarse in her ears. "Is there enough time?"

His mouth at her ear, warm and soft.

"There is time. If you want me, there is time." His tongue moved against the pulse below her ear, along the line of her jaw to her mouth. A new kind of kiss, a promise of what was to come. His hand under her skirt, fingers trailing along her thigh to touch the aching place between her legs. A light touch, a question without words.

"Yes," Hannah whispered. "Yes."

Chapter 42

In the morning Elizabeth woke thinking of Kitty, but went to find Manny and Jode, determined to have a frank conversation with them about their recent activities and their plans for the immediate future. If Curiosity was too busy to come up the mountain to speak sensible words to her son, then Elizabeth would do it for her. And there was the mystery of Liam Kirby to be solved, and Elizabeth was virtually certain that Manny could solve it, too, once she had him cornered.

But they were gone. They had eaten at Many-Doves' hearth, thanked her politely, and melted away into the forest again.

"They'll wait until the others are ready to travel west," Blue-Jay informed her. He had that look of little boys who wanted to be included in an adventure and knew that it could not be: forlorn and wishful.

Many-Doves said, "They are afraid of your anger, and rightly so."

Elizabeth went back to her own cabin and found Bump sitting on the porch with Nathaniel. He brought them hard news and Curiosity's good bread to swallow along with it.

In the strong light of a perfect summer morning they sat and listened. Outwardly calm, Elizabeth wanted most of all to run away, to close her ears like a child in a temper, to shut out the words that she feared.

But for all his misshapen back and odd dress Bump was the

gentlest and kindest of creatures, and he told the story of Kitty's last hours in such a forthright and simple manner that Elizabeth could take some comfort in it. Kitty had been an unhappy girl when Elizabeth first met her, love-struck and lonely, but she had died with her son in her arms and her husband beside her.

"She went easy," Bump finished. "Curiosity said to tell you she was smiling."

Nathaniel rubbed Elizabeth's back and pulled her closer. In the very way he caught his breath she could hear how close he was to tears. Inside herself she could find none at all.

"And the rest of it?" Nathaniel's voice hoarse with sorrow, for the girl he had grown up with and the woman she had become.

Bump twisted his shoulders right and left as if to relieve a cramping in his back. He told this story more quickly, his eyes scanning Nathaniel's face as he spoke.

"Between the doctor and Curiosity, O'Brien didn't stand a chance," Bump said with a satisfied expression. And then, more cautiously, "He's a rough sort, the doctor, and tightfisted with praise. Many times have I seen him drive Miss Hannah to distraction with his demanding and overharsh ways. But this morning he stood up for her like she was one of his own, though he was shaking with grief like a sapling in a storm. I thought you should know that."

"Yes," Nathaniel said. "I'm glad you told us." He saw Elizabeth's expression, the struggle there to give Richard Todd the credit that was his due. Whatever trouble he had been to them in the past, they would have to put that aside now. With his loyalty and service to their daughter Richard Todd had earned their respect, and Elizabeth must trust him to raise her nephew, because she had made that promise to Kitty.

Bump said, "Now I know you've been keeping away from the village for fear of the canker rash—"

"Nathaniel will be there at seven to hear O'Brien's charges," Elizabeth interrupted him, as near to rude as she ever came. Her color had risen, and her jaw set itself hard. It was the fear that did it, and still for that small moment, for one second that lasted far too long, Nathaniel hated his wife for letting her fear get the best of her.

"What I was going to say," Bump continued evenly, "was

this. Young Ethan sends word. He hopes that you'll come to-morrow to see his mam buried, and he asked me to say that while he hasn't got the rash or any sign of it, he'll stay away if you'll only come, as Kitty would have wanted you there."

The color left Elizabeth's face so suddenly that Nathaniel feared she would faint. Then a shudder moved through her and she pressed both hands to her face. As she rocked forward a sob tore up from her throat.

Bump caught Nathaniel's eye. There was something know-ing in his expression, an understanding beyond judgment. He said, "I have messages for young Lily and Daniel as well."

Nathaniel nodded, and drew Elizabeth up to him. "I'll send them out to you."

When she had wept as much as a woman can weep, Elizabeth looked to Nathaniel as she had just after giving birth: emptied of everything, reduced to her very essence.

She said, "Is he still here?"

"Out on the porch with Lily."

For a moment he thought she might start again after all, but when a deep shuddering breath had left her she got to her feet.

"I regret that I did not go to Kitty," she said, her face turned away from him. "But most of all I am ashamed."

"Elizabeth."

"Let me finish. I am ashamed that it took a little boy's sor-row to make me understand what I have done. To you, most of all. I am sorry, Nathaniel. I am truly sorry."

Tears pooled in her swollen eyes, but she pushed away his hand when he reached for her.

"I have let fear make too many decisions for me. For us. I hope that I find a way to make amends—"

"Elizabeth." He lunged forward to grasp her by both wrists and drew her down to sit beside him on the bed. When she struggled he wrapped his arms around her and held her until she gave in to him.

He said, "Listen, listen to me. This is me, Elizabeth. Me. You don't owe me any apologies or explanations. There's noth-ing you're feeling that I don't feel. Every time one of the chil-dren walks around a corner there's a fist in my gut until they come back again. When one of them sneezes or coughs, when they sleep too soundly or wake up too slow, I think of Robbie and it seems I'll choke on the fear."

Her fingers curled into the fabric of his shirt and then relaxed.

"He was my son too. I miss him every day but I won't let the missing of him get in the way of what I owe the living, and neither should you."

"I want to talk to Bump," Elizabeth said against his shirt. "I want to send Ethan a message."

He was still sitting on the porch, but now Lily was with him and they had opened the book Gabriel Oak gave her across their laps. From the doorway Elizabeth listened and watched as they turned the pages.

"And this, A. Montgomery? Who is that?"

"Ah," he said with a grin. "Friend Gabriel drew that down South Carolina way. That's old Archie, a colonel do you see, by his uniform."

"It says 1760," Lily offered.

"Hmmm. So it would have been. When the Cherokee made short work of the militia at Echoe. That was just before Gabriel decided he'd had enough of the wars and got it into his head to strike out north."

"When you came here?"

"For the first time, yes. That following spring. I expect you'll come across some drawings of people you know in the next pages. And see, there's Half Moon Lake, as ever was. When your grandfather and the rest of the settlers lived right on the shore."

"Before the Kahnyen'kehàka burned the village," Lily said. "And see here in the margin, he wrote 'Alfred M.' I think that must be my grandfather Middleton."

"May I see?" Elizabeth's voice broke as they turned to her, the old man and the little girl, both smiling in welcome.

They made room for her between them and Lily fussed with the old book until she was satisfied with the way it sat on her mother's lap.

"Yes," Elizabeth said. "That is your grandfather. He looks very young there. And Axel Metzler, my goodness." She had to hold back a laugh. "I almost didn't recognize him. I never knew his wife, but I expect that must be her?"

She had directed the question to Bump, and he nodded. "So it is."

"Look," Lily said, with growing excitement. "Uncle Todd's mother and father, it says so."

"You must show him, Lily, he'll be very interested."

But the girl barely heard her in her growing excitement. She turned the page and stopped. "Oh," she breathed softly. "Oh, Ma. Look."

"Yes," Elizabeth said, blinking in the sunlight. "I see. My mother."

The likeness seemed to glow on the page. Dark hair covered by a plain Quaker cap, a heart-shaped face with wide-set eyes, a dimpled chin, and a shy smile. Just seventeen years old, by the date, newly married and separated from her family to follow her husband into the wilderness.

"You look so much like her," Lily said. "Doesn't she look like her mother, Bump?"

He made a whispery sound. "She does indeed, and so do you favor her."

"Were you there when Gabriel drew this?" Lily asked, leaning across the book to look at him very earnestly. "Do you remember my grandmother Middleton?"

"Of course I do," Bump said. "I could no more forget Maddy than I could forget my own mam's face. She was a fiery spirit, full of life. Paradise was a different place once she went away."

"Why *did* you go to England?" Lily asked, touching the curve of her grandmother's lip as if she might somehow get an answer from the likeness on the page. And then to Bump: "Did she tell you?"

He looked a little startled at the idea. "Oh no. We came back to Paradise one spring and heard that she was gone, and so we never saw her again. I've wondered now and then what it was that made her go."

"What's this that Gabriel wrote beneath her name?" Lily put her nose right to the page and read aloud. " 'McB 4, 2, 1, 3.' "

"A quotation," Elizabeth said. "I would suppose from *MacBeth*."

Lily leapt up from the stair and dashed into the house, calling

behind her: "Wait! I know where it is!" And came back again
before either Elizabeth or Bump could stop her.

She thrust the volume into her mother's hands and stood
jiggling with impatience until Elizabeth had found the passage.

> *His flight was madness: when our actions do not,*
> *Our fears do make us traitors.*

Lily's face was such a study in thoughtfulness and earnest
concern that Elizabeth could not look away from her.

"Do you understand what it means?" Lily demanded, looking back and forth between them.

"I'm not sure," Elizabeth said, although she had some uneasy sense that its meaning was there on the page if she only
would study her mother's image long enough. "But I will
think about it."

Bump smiled at her, his bright blue eyes lost in a sea of
folds. "That would please Friend Gabriel," he said. "I'm sure
of it."

For the rest of the day Elizabeth could think of little else beyond the drawing Gabriel Oak had done of her mother. With
one part of her mind she recognized that the conversation on
the porch was no coincidence: Bump had arranged it just exactly that way, to give her something to distract her. With her
head so full of her mother, Elizabeth had little time to reflect
on Kitty or Hannah's troubles with Judge O'Brien, on Manny
and Jode, or even the scarlet fever.

When she told Nathaniel the story he was only vaguely interested. "I wouldn't go trying to read something into a drawing more than forty years old," he said, stopping to kiss her in
case she took his common sense for a lack of interest. "But
you fret away at that quote, Boots, if it makes you happy."
Next she went to Many-Doves in the hope that another
woman would see what she saw: the questions raised that must
be answered.

She found her in the cornfield, and so Elizabeth picked up
a hoe and told the story while they cut weeds out from among
the corn plants.

Many-Doves listened in her usual thoughtful way and said,
"Gabriel Oak was one of the quiet ones, the Quakers. So was

your mother. It might have been some conversation between them that he wrote down, as your Lily does now. When she makes a drawing she writes odd words and sayings beneath it."

This was true, and it gave Elizabeth pause.

"What were you hoping?" Many-Doves asked her.

"I'm not sure," Elizabeth said. "Some understanding of my mother. I was so young when she died, I never thought to ask her any of the questions I ask myself now."

Many-Doves stopped to smile at her, and then she held a hand to shield her eyes from the sun. "Walks-Ahead is bringing her new husband home to us, look."

Elizabeth was almost afraid to turn, but she could not resist, and then she stood motionless among the swaying cornstalks, struck by the sight.

"When she is gone from us this is how I will remember her." She said it aloud, and Many-Doves nodded in agreement.

"He will be a good husband," Elizabeth said, because it was the thing she needed to hear, the only way to make the coming separation bearable.

Many-Doves was silent for a moment, only her eyes moving as she watched them come closer. "He is strong enough for her," she said finally, touching on the truth that Elizabeth had not been able to find words for. Strikes-the-Sky was indeed strong in body and spirit and force of will, strong enough to be a husband to Walks-Ahead.

Hannah caught sight of them then and raised a hand in greeting, all the joy in the world shining there in her beloved face.

"This is how we'll handle it," Nathaniel said over supper. He looked at each of them in turn. "O'Brien is going to read out the complaint. No comments of any kind, not even a burp. You understand me, Lily? Daniel?"

The twins nodded, staring fixedly at their plates.

"No doubt Jemima will have something to say then, and the widow, too, for all I know. O'Brien is likely to ask them questions. This ain't a trial, you understand, and he's under no obligation to give each side a turn. It's an inquiry, is the way Jed explained it to me. Which means O'Brien can pretty much do what he damn well pleases."

Hawkeye's expression was calm, mostly, Elizabeth thought, because he must have a plan of his own. If things did not go well he would kill O'Brien before he let him lay a hand on Hannah. To protect his granddaughter he would do that and more, without hesitation or apology.

Nathaniel was taking another approach. He said, "When it comes your turn to talk, daughter, you say what you've got to say with as few words as possible. Answer his questions just as simply as you can." He paused, and stared down at his plate. When he raised his head again, there was a still anger in his eyes.

"We don't know exactly what Jemima has been telling him, but whatever it is you'll have Richard there to back you up."

Elizabeth had been watching Hannah all evening. She looked for some sign of worry or confusion but found nothing there but calm acceptance and a faraway thoughtfulness that Elizabeth recognized for what it must be. The way Strikes-the-Sky looked at her and she looked at him left no doubt how things stood between them.

"Hannah, have you heard anything I said?" Nathaniel frowned at her, and got a smile for his trouble.

"I heard every word," she said.

"Well, I'm glad to see you're keeping your wits about you," Nathaniel said dryly. "Let's hope the rest of us can do the same."

Jed McGarrity had never wanted to be constable but somehow he ended up with the title and the trouble too, shortly after Judge Middleton died. Since that day all his worst fears had come to find him and more. There was just nothing worse than having to knock on a man's door to ask hard questions when you knew most of the answers anyway. He couldn't look the other way anymore when a trapper helped himself to somebody else's lines, nor could he cluck a few sympathetic sounds in Axel's direction when Ben Cameron got so drunk that he broke the tavern door in looking for a lost shoe. When old Dubonnet, a man as mean as God ever put on the earth, set out to beat his wife's head in with a wood stave and took a knife in the gut instead it was Jed who had to sort things out. For the first year it had been bad, and then it got worse when Sam Beck—a man with a sense of humor and an understand-

ing of the way things worked on the frontier—gave up the
post of circuit judge to move west. Then Baldy O'Brien, who
had been the tax collector for long enough to make himself
universally hated, gave up that line of work and bought himself into the judgeship just about the same time the widow
Kuick settled down in Paradise. That was the end of whatever
claim Jed McGarrity had to a quiet life.

If the widow wasn't writing to Johnstown about property
lines or timber or some other trespass she dreamed up in the
night she was spying on folks from her window and making
trouble. Up to now it had never been anything very serious, at
least nothing Jed had to bring to the attention of the real law.
As Sam Beck had told the widow to her face when she complained to him about one of the Cameron boys' more raucous
benders, if the New-York courts started prosecuting fornica-
tors and drunkards the very first thing they'd have to do was to
throw all the judges in gaol.

As much as Jed wanted to believe that this newest complaint would go the way of the others, he was uneasy in his
bones. The widow had Jemima Southern egging her on, and
in his mind the two of them together were worse than all the
hounds of hell. On top of that he couldn't ignore what they
had to say, for the simple fact that at least one crime had been
committed. The strongbox was gone, and so was the overseer.
Ever since word had come that O'Brien was on his way, Jed
had lain awake nights wondering how in the hell the two
Kuick widows were planning to hang those crimes on Hannah
Bonner, but no matter how many times he and Anna talked it
through they came up empty.

On top of all that, word had got out about the inquest and
pretty much all of Paradise had crowded into the church.
Charlie LeBlanc wasn't here but Molly's folks were, he was surprised to see. Nicholas Wilde, looking as wobbly as a man could
look and still walk upright, holding on to Dolly Smythe's arm
for all the world. Even the doctor had left a house in mourning
to come sit up front across from the Kuicks.

Baldy O'Brien was standing there in a full bluster, pleased
as pie to have a real audience for once. He had hooked his
thumbs in the band of his breeches while he walked up and
down and nodded to folks, like he was an old Dutch patroon

who had called all his tenants in to read them a long-overdue sermon.

Then all the Bonners came in. Elizabeth was as pale as new snow but to look at the men a person might think they had come to hear a musicale. Hawkeye touched his brow in greeting and smiled when Axel Metzler called a question after him. Nathaniel met Jed's eye and nodded. The Mohawks hung back near the door, the big Seneca who had been courting Hannah with them. It would make some folks here jumpy to see them standing there but Jed was glad of the backup, should the need arise.

Then Hannah came in last, and even the children went quiet. Not out of fear or worry or bad feelings of any kind, but just because Hannah Bonner in the gold light of eventide would rob anybody of words. And in spite of the reason she was here and the fact Baldy O'Brien was looking at her with his mouth curled, Hannah seemed as easy and happy as ever she was, talking to folks as she went up the aisle and smiling.

Jemima Kuick turned her head to watch her and gooseflesh ran up Jed's back at the look on her face. For no good reason he could name she reminded him just then of Jamie McGregor, dead some years now. He had been a veteran of King George's war and spent the rest of his days talking about who still needed killing, and how pleased he'd be to do the honors.

When the Bonners were settled, Hannah with her father to one side and her grandfather to the other and the rest of the family close alongside, O'Brien cleared his throat and raised his voice.

"I'm going to read out this complaint in parts because there are two different charges here." He bellowed so loud that the few folks who hadn't made it to the church were likely to hear him anyway.

"Anybody interrupts me or makes trouble I'll ask the constable here to throw them out. When I'm done I'll be asking some questions of the complainants—that's Missus Kuick sitting there. Then I'll question the defendant." He cleared his throat, rattled the piece of paper in his hand, and held it at arm's length.

" 'For some months or perhaps longer, Hannah Bonner of this village, a half-breed woman eighteen years of age, has been involved in the illegal traffic of runaways, whereby slaves from the cities to the South are encouraged and helped to run from their rightful owners. Hannah Bonner's part in this conspiracy is to guide them into the woods, where they are met by her Mohawk relatives and taken north to Canada, where they may pose as free blacks and evade justice.

" 'Witness to all this is one Liam Kirby of Manhattan, who tracked the runaway onto Bonner lands but was obstructed by Hannah Bonner in his pursuit. Further, when a certain Ambrose Dye, employed at our mill, took steps to stop this lawlessness, Hannah Bonner used deceit and lies to rouse our slaves into a state of savage anger against Mr. Dye. The slaves, together with Hannah Bonner and other members of her Mohawk family, contrived to have Mr. Dye abducted. We believe, as our husband and son believed, that our slaves, together with Hannah Bonner, were responsible for the overseer's death.

" 'During the abduction of Mr. Dye, our persons were taken prisoner by the Mohawk and the house was ransacked. A strongbox containing a great deal of money was taken by the Indian abductors, no doubt to finance further illegal activities.' "

O'Brien looked up from the paper into a crowd of almost a hundred people, and every face blank with shock. Jed himself was shaking, wondering if his hearing could be playing tricks on him and if he had heard right and the Kuick women had really accused Hannah Bonner of everything from slave running to murder, wondering why neither Nathaniel nor Hawkeye had got up yet when he himself had to fight the urge to walk up to O'Brien and punch him right in the face.

The judge had started to lose some of his self-satisfied look, maybe because he was as surprised at the reaction he was seeing as Jed was. He cleared his throat. "This first set of charges are slave running, theft, assault, and conspiracy to murder. Now the second set of charges—"

A voice rose up from a shadowy corner at the back of the church. "Before you move on, Judge O'Brien, I'd like to speak to those first charges."

Every head in the church swiveled toward the voice as Liam Kirby stepped forward into a shaft of light. A woman's strangled cry cut through the murmuring: Jemima Southern, the last woman on earth Jed would have thought capable of fainting, had come to her feet and stood there swaying.

"Who is that?" blustered O'Brien. "Who are you, sir, to interrupt these proceedings?"

"You've got a church full of folks who can tell you my name. I'm the Liam Kirby the Kuicks name as a witness in that complaint you've got in your hand."

O'Brien could have looked no more surprised if Liam Kirby had called himself Tom Jefferson. "Mr. Kirby, I understood you to be in the city."

"Don't know where you'd get that idea. Unless it's from the same people who told you that pack of lies you just read out."

Jemima Southern sat down hard and leaned forward like a woman ready to spill her supper all over her shoes.

Liam Kirby.

The very last person Hannah expected or wanted to see, and there he stood with his cap in his hands as if he belonged. As if he had never been away. Just behind him Strong-Words and Strikes-the-Sky stood near the open door, both of them with their rifles in their hands. There was a rushing in Hannah's ears but she pinched the web of flesh between thumb and finger until her vision cleared and she could hear again.

O'Brien's face was blotched with color, and he fairly danced in place in his agitation.

"Explain yourself, sir."

Liam stepped forward, and looked around himself. Hannah felt her father's hand on her shoulder and she leaned against him.

Liam said, "If there was any slave running going on in Paradise I couldn't find any trace of it, on Hidden Wolf or anywhere else. I cain't deny that I came here tracking a runaway, and it may even be true that the woman I was after passed through the village. My dogs thought she did. I never did pick up her trail again, but it wasn't Hannah Bonner who stopped me."

The widow rose to her feet as if she were being pulled up by strings, jerking and trembling. Her color was very bad, and her eyes so bloodshot that the part of Hannah that was a doctor first and would always be a doctor imagined the nest of veins and arteries that throbbed deep in the cradle of her skull.

"Judge O'Brien," she said. "Even if that should prove true, we are still left with the matter of Ambrose Dye's abduction and murder."

Liam barked out a laugh that made Hannah jump.

"I saw Ambrose Dye two days ago up Canada way. He was alive then and I'd guess he's still alive now, spending money hand over fist. If you've got other charges against Miss Bonner you'd best read 'em out, Judge—"

A wavering howl rose up, so much like a war cry that the hair rose all along Hannah's arms. Jemima was on her feet again, pointing with one finger toward Liam Kirby.

"He was there too," she screamed. "He was under the window with the Mohawks who robbed us. I saw him plain as day. I saw you, Liam Kirby. Ambrose Dye is dead and you killed him, it's you that took the strongbox."

Hannah turned to look up into her father's face and saw two things there: what Jemima said was true—inexplicably, astoundingly true—and that it came as no surprise to him. His fingers tightened on her shoulder and he blinked at her.

"Later," he said to her in her mother's language. "Save your questions for later."

A roaring of voices filled the church, people shouting at Jemima and Liam and no one in particular, fists waved in the air. O'Brien picked up a bible from the table in front of him and thumped it down three times with such force that the room went quiet.

"Sir," Mr. Gathercole said in an apologetic tone. "That is the Good Book."

"And I'll put it to good use!" O'Brien bellowed.

Jed hid his smile behind his hand and ducked his head.

"Now you listen to me, you rabble," O'Brien huffed. "You'll show respect or you'll all get out!"

"Mrs. Kuick," he said when he had caught his breath. "You saw Mr. Kirby under the window after you were assaulted in your home?"

She nodded, clutching both hands to her throat. "I did, he was there with the black Mohawks."

"But then you must explain why," said O'Brien in a weary

tone. "Why would you put Kirby down in your complaint as somebody who could testify against Hannah Bonner for that very same crime?"

"And why didn't you say nothing about him being there when it happened?" yelled Axel Metzler. "Not a word did you say about Liam Kirby, missy, and you know it."

The crowd had begun to mutter and stir again, and O'Brien sent a fiery look over their heads. "I'll have silence or I'll take my stick to you!" He looked in Jed's direction.

"Constable McGarrity, did either Missus Kuick say anything to you about Mr. Liam Kirby being in the vicinity of the mill house at any time on the night of the robbery and abduction?"

Jed felt Hawkeye's gaze on him, nothing of anger there but simple interest, as if he knew just what Jed would say but not how he might say it.

"Neither of them said a word about Kirby. Nor did any of the others present at the time. I see Becca Kaes sitting right over there, you can ask her."

O'Brien turned on his heel. "Miss Kaes?"

Becca stood, and sent a trembling look in the direction of her employer. "Yes, sir."

"You were present at the mill house when the intruder arrived?"

"I was, sir."

"You sat in the room with the intruder along with the Missus Kuicks and the others?"

"I did, sir."

"And the intruder himself, you saw him clearly?"

"Oh yes, sir."

"How would you describe him?"

"Well, he sure as sugar wasn't Liam Kirby, Your Honor, sir. He was as black as January molasses and Liam's red as the devil, as anybody can see."

In the back pew a derisive snort was followed by a ripple of laughter. The Cameron boys, drunk but not too drunk, not yet.

"And did you see Mr. Kirby that evening, at any time?"

"No, sir. Nor did I hear any mention of him. Mrs. Kuick never said his name in my hearing."

O'Brien turned a sharp eye toward the pew where the Kuick widows sat, as still and white as stone.

"Miss Bonner."

Hannah stood, her hands folded in front of herself. "Yes, sir."

"Did you conspire with Liam Kirby to abduct Mr. Ambrose Dye and steal the Kuicks' strongbox?"

"No," she said calmly. "I did not."

"Ask her about those heathens standing back there!" Lucy Kuick's voice rose in a wavering screech. "Ask her if she conspired with them!"

"Mrs. Kuick," said O'Brien sharply. "I'll conduct the hearing in my own fashion." He tugged at his neckcloth as if it were suddenly too tight.

"Did you conspire with Liam Kirby or with anyone else to abduct Ambrose Dye and steal the strongbox?"

"I did not," Hannah said.

"What is your relationship to Mr. Kirby?"

Hannah glanced down at her hands. "We were childhood friends," she said. "Nothing more or less."

"Did you conspire with anybody else who might *resemble* Liam Kirby?"

She shook her head. "I did not."

"Do you know where Mr. Dye is now?"

"I do not. Nor do I particularly care, sir, except to say that he was a cruel man and I hope he never returns."

Jed stirred uneasily, but O'Brien wasn't concerned with Hannah's boldly stated opinion. "As there are no witnesses, conflicting testimony from the persons filing the complaint, and no evidence at hand, I see no grounds for filing charges on these counts."

The widow Kuick let out a strangled noise, but it was Jemima who worried Jed. She looked to him like a woman who could do murder with her bare hands, and he was glad to see that she'd have to get through Hawkeye and Nathaniel both to get to Hannah.

"To the second set of charges." O'Brien lifted up the complaint, now much rumpled, and raised his voice.

" 'The same Hannah Bonner, a female and half-breed, having the temerity to fashion herself a doctor, convinced a good number of the citizens of Paradise to submit to her so-called kine-pox vaccination. Only days later an epidemic came down upon us. The symptoms are fever, headache, and a rash upon the body. Further, when our son and husband, Isaiah Kuick, returned home from searching for the intruders who assaulted and robbed us in a frightful state of ill health, Hannah Bonner intruded herself into our home without cause or permission. While she was in his chamber alone with him, Isaiah Kuick's condition worsened and he died only a few hours later. We charge Hannah Bonner with the murder of Isaiah Kuick, her motive being the removal of all persons who might have testified against her.'"

O'Brien sent a nervous look over the crowd, which had begun to seethe again and looked ready to come to a violent boil. He said, "This complaint charges Hannah Bonner with practicing medicine without proper training or experience, malicious and knowing mistreatment of the ill to her own personal gain, and murder by methods as yet undetermined." He stepped back, and clutched the complaint to his chest. In a smaller voice he said, "Dr. Todd, you have something to say?"

Richard Todd seemed to tower over the crowd like Moses coming off the mountain when he found the Hebrews worshiping the Golden Calf. If Moses had looked half as angry as Richard Todd did as this moment, Jed wondered that any of them had stayed around long enough to take their punishment.

He strode up the church aisle with his fists swinging at his sides and stopped in front of the Kuick widows, where he did nothing more than stare. Jemima, fool that she had always been, drew herself up as tall as she could and stared right back as if she were the one wronged.

Todd's great shaggy head swung up and looked over the crowd. In a voice so big he put O'Brien to shame he said, "I want you to stand up now if Hannah Bonner has ever come to your home when you or yours was sick or hurt."

With a quick shuffle every person in the church stood, the Bonners included, leaving the Kuicks as the only two people sitting in the whole church.

Richard fixed Jemima with a stare. "I believe you should be on your feet, missus."

"I don't care to stand," Jemima hissed back at him.

"Now," he continued. "If anybody here has any complaint about the care they got from Hannah Bonner, at any time, I'll ask them to sit down."

No feet shuffled, there were no snickers or snorts, no murmuring or whispers, and no one sat down.

He said, "Ratz, you lost a girl to the scarlet fever. I believe Hannah Bonner sat by her bedside for a whole night, ain't that right?"

Horace Ratz cleared his throat. "It is."

"Then why are you still standing, man? Seems to me you got grounds to complain about Hannah Bonner's care."

The man swallowed so hard that every person in the church heard it. "She nursed the other seven right through," he said. "Four girls and my three boys all on the mend. It wouldn't be right to hold the one she couldn't save against her."

"Were any of those children of yours vaccinated against the smallpox by Hannah Bonner, or anybody else?"

"No, sir," Ratz said, hanging his head. "I'm sorry to say I doubted her word. That was my mistake. I'll apologize to her right now if the judge will allow it."

"Anybody else here care to speak to Hannah Bonner's skill as a doctor?"

"I will," called Nicholas Wilde, and the call repeated itself through the church until Richard had to hold up his hands to stop them.

He turned toward O'Brien. "I think that settles the question of Hannah Bonner's qualifications as a doctor, Judge O'Brien. Would you agree?"

O'Brien threw up his hands in surrender.

"Then there's only the matter of how Isaiah Kuick met his end. The rest of you can sit down now, all except Becca Kaes."

When the rustling and whispering had stopped and Becca stood alone in the church Richard said, "Becca, you work as a servant at the mill house, isn't that so?"

She bobbed her head in agreement. "Ever since the widow come to Paradise, yes, sir."

"Were you in the house the night Mr. Kuick died?"

Another bob of the head.

"And who was with him?"

She looked confused. "You mean, who was there with him before he died or when he died or after?"

Richard drew in a harsh breath. "All three, Becca. Start with the first."

She dropped her gaze and then raised it again. "First was Hannah Bonner. She came around sunset it was, after I sent word that Mr. Kuick was asking for her."

"So she came by invitation."

"Yes, sir. He asked for her particular and said I wasn't to tell his mother or his wife."

"And why was that?"

Becca shrugged. "I expect because he knew they wouldn't much like her being there. There's no love lost between Hannah and Jemima, everybody knows that."

"But you did as he asked."

"I did, sir. You yourself had told me earlier in the afternoon that he was dying, and I thought a dying man should have what he wants."

"How long was she with him?"

"Maybe an hour all told, sir. She made him a fever tea. I don't know all that was said as I was busy with the widow for most of the time."

Jemima turned, her face blazing with satisfaction, to look at Richard. "Did he drink that tea, Becca?"

"He did. I helped him to a few swallows myself."

Richard said: "And she left after an hour, and then who came to him?"

"I went in and out as I was able but he was alone a great deal. The widow kept calling me, complaining of an ache in her head, she was sure she had the canker rash coming on, you see, though she never did get sick. I sent Cookie to find Missus Kuick and she came to sit for a short while but then left again when he said he didn't want her."

"Then Mr. Kuick was alone? His mother didn't come in to see him?"

"No, sir, she was in such a state. I finally gave her the rest of the fever tea that Hannah left for Mr. Kuick, along with her laudanum, you see, and that settled her. She slept for the rest of the night." Becca's voice wavered. "I've been worried ever since that I should have roused her so she could sit with him at the end, but it went so fast."

"So let me understand, Becca. You gave the widow the last of the tea Hannah Bonner made—" He cast a significant look at the widow, who sat whey-faced in the first pew, and then a longer look at Jemima. "And then you sat with Mr. Kuick until he died."

"Yes, sir."

"Now the widow sits right there, isn't that so? Hale and hearty?"

"She's sitting there, sir."

"So the tea didn't kill her."

"Not as I could see, sir."

Muffled laughter, silenced by a thump of the bible.

"And there at the end, did Mr. Kuick have anything to say?"

"How do you mean, Dr. Todd?"

"Did he accuse anyone of his murder? His wife, say, or his mother?"

"Dr. Todd!" O'Brien thundered, and the church came to its feet. When O'Brien's thumping of the bible had quieted them he pointed a finger at the doctor. "How dare you, sir."

Richard frowned at him. "They had just as much opportunity to cause him harm as Hannah Bonner did, Judge. The innocent need fear no inquiry, isn't that so?"

Without waiting for an answer he turned back to Becca, who had begun to tremble. "Did he accuse anyone at all of murdering him?"

"No sir. At least not to me, not in words to me." She glanced nervously at her hands and back up again at Richard. "There was a letter, though."

Richard Todd looked unsure of himself for the first time since he had begun questioning Becca. Jemima Kuick looked as if somebody had punched her in the gut, and the widow perked up, her little head bobbing and turning.

"Letter?" The widow rose to her feet slowly. "What letter? My son left a letter, Becca? Why have you not given it to me?"

"Begging your pardon, Mrs. Kuick," Becca said, ducking her head. "But it wasn't a letter for you."

"And how do you know that?" The widow drew herself up, and something of her old tone came back to fill the church. "Did you steal that letter, girl?"

"No ma'am, no, I didn't." Becca looked as angry as Jed had ever seen her. "I know because he sealed it with wax and signed his name just under the seal, and then he asked me to sign too, as a . . . what did he call it . . . a . . ."

"A witness," suggested the judge.

"Yes, that it was really him that was signing it." Becca held up her chin. "There wasn't anybody's name on that letter but his and mine. And that's the last I ever saw of it. I don't know what was in it and I don't know where it's gone or who's got it. Ask Jemima, maybe she's got it."

"I have no letter," Jemima said stiffly. She started to say something and then stilled. "Can't we just get on with this?"

Richard Todd stood contemplating Jemima for a long minute, but she would not meet his eye.

"Very well," he said finally. "Since this mysterious letter is nowhere to be found, let us get on with it. A shame, though. My guess is that it would have cleared up many a mystery." He grinned suddenly and turned back to Becca.

"So you were telling us that Mr. Kuick said nothing to you of murder, made no accusations, mentioned no names."

"No, sir," Becca said.

"Not his mother or wife?"

"No, sir. Nor Hannah, nor you. Nobody. He just breathed in and never let it out again."

"And then?"

"Then I sent for you, Doctor, and you came."

"And what did I say to you?"

"You said that Mr. Kuick died of a lung fever and complications from the canker rash. And that my sister Molly was dead of the childbed fever."

"We're all sorry about Molly. Thank you, Becca, for your help."

Richard turned, and seeking out Hannah Bonner's gaze, he bowed briefly from the waist. Then he walked back down the church and out into the evening, never pausing or looking around him. It was then Jed realized that Liam Kirby was gone too.

There was a moment's silence, and then Axel Metzler stood, his white hair standing out in a cloud around his head and his eyes blazing. "I got something to say."

"What?"

"You heard me. Gold guineas. The Tory gold."

"The Tory gold?" Her voice spiraled and broke just as Nathaniel grabbed her and pinned her to the bed.

"Boots," he whispered against her mouth. "Listen to me now before this gets out of hand. The gold's back. Recovered. Found. As of yesterday. It's not like I've been sitting on it for eight years."

She stared into his eyes and he stared back. After a moment she blinked. "Came back? Walked in on little golden feet? Declared itself home again like so many prodigal sons?"

The corner of his mouth jerked in relief. "I thought you'd want to skin me alive. I don't suppose you'll ever stop surprising me."

"But why should I be angry?" She pulled out of his grip and sat up. "What I am is curious, and mightily confused."

He groaned. "That's why I was hoping to save this conversation until tomorrow," he said. "After I've had some sleep."

"Most of all," she continued as if he hadn't spoken at all. "Most of all I am relieved. I did so hate the idea of sending them off without any kind of gift."

Nathaniel laughed, a full-bodied laugh tinged with a kind of gleeful desperation. "Good. Now can we go to sleep?"

"Certainly," Elizabeth said. "Now that we have that problem settled. Of course there's still the matter of Liam Kirby."

He pulled her down next to him. "No," he said firmly. "Not now. Not tomorrow. Maybe not ever."

She was tense in his arms, every muscle vibrating. She would never be satisfied until she had worked out the mystery around Liam Kirby to her satisfaction, and that meant, Nathaniel admitted to himself, that she would simply never be satisfied. Liam was gone from Paradise and would not be back again, he felt that certainty in his gut.

Little by little she relaxed against him, tucked into the curve of his body. She wouldn't stay that way for long; independent Elizabeth, she would turn away in her sleep, flinging off the blankets and the protection of his arms to conquer the night hours on her own terms. By morning she would be back again, her head bedded on his shoulder.

The familiar sounds of the summer night rose up as if she had called to them: crickets and falling water and the comfortable

643

wore under his breath. "I wouldn't believe
   ...rn if she swore on a pile of bibles that pigs is
   ...ble McGarrity, I'll leave this to you."

...e smoothed the fabric of his coat and walked away, his
back ramrod straight.

Hannah knelt down. Elizabeth had already folded her cape
and put it under the widow's head. Their eyes met.

She said, "Did you know? About Liam?"

"No," Elizabeth said, her mouth pressed hard. "I didn't
know. I intend to have a talk with him, though. There are
some questions I will have answers to this very night."

Lily had been standing quietly by while they worked, but
now she spoke up. "But didn't you see him go?" she said.
"Liam Kirby's gone and your answers with him."

Chapter 43

"Boots," Nathaniel said sleepily, turning over and pulling the pillow up over his head. "We've been over this now twenty times at least. If I tell you that you're right and that you'll always be right about everything, forever more, will you let me go to sleep then?"

Elizabeth, sitting with her legs crossed in the light of a single candle, rocked forward to pinch him lightly. He jerked convulsively, sat up, and scowled at her. Then he yawned.

"I'll take that as a no."

"Perceptive man," she said. "Now we must settle this matter before morning. Apply yourself, Nathaniel Bonner, or you will end up sending your eldest daughter off to her new life empty-handed."

"Christ, Boots, you haven't had enough excitement for one day? A burial and a wedding should be enough for even you. And tomorrow we've got a leave-taking, I hate to remind you."

He watched the emotions chasing across Elizabeth's face: sorrow and resignation and then a softer joy. For Hannah, married this evening in a simple ceremony that took more from her mother's people than his own. At sunset she had gone off with her new husband to spend her last night at Lake in the Clouds in the caves under the falls—something Nathaniel didn't care to think about too closely.

"It was a lovely party, wasn't it? I think Kitty would have approved."

ᵗething she had repeated many times, mostly to con-
Nathaniel knew very well. He said, "I know she
When did she ever miss a chance to go dancing?"
Elizabeth nodded. "Very well, I will stop worrying about
that, at least. But there's still the matter of what to give
Hannah."

He yawned again. "You'll have every one of them laden down
like beasts of burden, Boots. She's already talked Strong-Words
into humping fifty pounds of books and medical supplies."

"Well then, perhaps we should give them Toby."

"That old horse wouldn't last as far as Canajoharee,"
Nathaniel said, and Elizabeth nodded in reluctant agreement.

"If only there was some money to give them. Are you not at
all concerned about this? Sending her off with nothing at all?"

Nathaniel leaned against the pillows and covered his eyes
with one arm for the simple reason that he was too tired to
hide what he was thinking from her, and he had hoped to
avoid the subject of money for a few days at least. He had yet
to tell her about the recovered Tory gold.

Then she poked him hard and he sat up again.

"Nathaniel Bonner, you look as guilty as your son when
he's been raiding the maple sugar. And do not sigh as if I were
beating you. I insist that you sit up now and explain yourself.
Why did you make such a face when I said we had no money
to give Hannah and Strikes-the-Sky?"

"Come and kiss me, Boots, and I'll tell you." He tugged on
the sleeve of her nightdress and she pulled her arm away.

"Why must you always change the subject?"

"Because after I'm finished talking you may not want to
kiss me for a good while."

"Will you please explain yourself? It is far too late for such
games, Nathaniel. Whatever it is that you want to say—"

"Boots."

"Yes?"

"We can."

"What do you mean, we can? We can give them Toby?"

"We can give them money," said Nathaniel wearily. "To be
exact, we can give them gold guineas, eight hundred of them
if you're feeling especially generous."

He watched the color drain from her face and then come
rushing back with growing understanding. She blinked at him.

"What?"

"You heard me. Gold guineas. The Tory gold."

"The Tory gold?" Her voice spiraled and broke just as Nathaniel grabbed her and pinned her to the bed.

"Boots," he whispered against her mouth. "Listen to me now before this gets out of hand. The gold's back. Recovered. Found. As of yesterday. It's not like I've been sitting on it for eight years."

She stared into his eyes and he stared back. After a moment she blinked. "Came back? Walked in on little golden feet? Declared itself home again like so many prodigal sons?"

The corner of his mouth jerked in relief. "I thought you'd want to skin me alive. I don't suppose you'll ever stop surprising me."

"But why should I be angry?" She pulled out of his grip and sat up. "What I am is curious, and mightily confused."

He groaned. "That's why I was hoping to save this conversation until tomorrow," he said. "After I've had some sleep."

"Most of all," she continued as if he hadn't spoken at all. "Most of all I am relieved. I did so hate the idea of sending them off without any kind of gift."

Nathaniel laughed, a full-bodied laugh tinged with a kind of gleeful desperation. "Good. Now can we go to sleep?"

"Certainly," Elizabeth said. "Now that we have that problem settled. Of course there's still the matter of Liam Kirby."

He pulled her down next to him. "No," he said firmly. "Not now. Not tomorrow. Maybe not ever."

She was tense in his arms, every muscle vibrating. She would never be satisfied until she had worked out the mystery around Liam Kirby to her satisfaction, and that meant, Nathaniel admitted to himself, that she would simply never be satisfied. Liam was gone from Paradise and would not be back again, he felt that certainty in his gut.

Little by little she relaxed against him, tucked into the curve of his body. She wouldn't stay that way for long; independent Elizabeth, she would turn away in her sleep, flinging off the blankets and the protection of his arms to conquer the night hours on her own terms. By morning she would be back again, her head bedded on his shoulder.

The familiar sounds of the summer night rose up as if she had called to them: crickets and falling water and the comfortable

mbers flexing like old bones. If he listened hard
ld hear his children sleeping, the sound of their
he very beats of their hearts. Two where last
ere had been three. His daughter was gone from him
now and still he could call her to him by closing his eyes.
Hannah as a newborn, as a laughing three-year-old, as a solemn
child of nine, as a young woman standing next to a man she now
called her husband.

"Nathaniel?" Elizabeth whispered against his ear.

"Hmmmm?"

"He'll take good care of her, and she of him."

"Boots," he said, running a hand up her arm to cup her
face. "I don't doubt it for a moment."

Epilogue

Our Dearest Daughter Hannah,

It is six weeks since you left us on your journey west, and we trust that you have arrived safely. We send this parcel to the trading post at Fort Erie to be held for you there, as agreed, and hope that it finds you in good health and spirits upon your arrival on the Grand River. Included you will find letters from Scotland, from the Spencers, and from your friend Hakim Ibrahim. We have a letter, too, from the president's secretary for you, something that caused great excitement in the village. Your father scruples to forward that particular letter to you while you are in Canada, for reasons that must be obvious in these unsettled times. Both your brother and sister write you letters of their own, a task they approach with great seriousness of purpose. I know this because Daniel inquired of me whether he must address you as "missus," now that you are a married woman. I reminded him that you are, as you have always been and will always be, his beloved sister, and he was very relieved to hear it.

The twins miss you tremendously, as do we all, but every night we sit together and imagine you walking along with your grandfather in the lead and Jode bringing up the rear. You have started out your marriage with a ready-made squadron of boys to look after, but if anyone is equal to that task, it is you. Curiosity bids me tell you that you have her leave to take a strap to any of them as you see fit. Dr. Todd sends his best

reminds you that you are to keep careful records
of vaccinations you undertake as you move west.
om the village is plentiful and varied in nature.
Doves has decreed that we will start the corn harvest
tomorrow, and that Lily must sing in your place. In response
your sister noted, quite rightly, that every time we do
something it is the first time we do it without you. To which
Many-Doves replied that like all things, this would pass too.

I have visited with Nicholas Wilde and bought from him
two saplings to plant on either side of my cherry tree, and hope
that by the time you come home to visit you will have apples
to make a cobbler for your husband.

We have had two weddings since your own. Dolly Smythe
married Nicholas Wilde, as you will have guessed, and Becca
Kaes, who did you such good service at the hearing in the
church, married Charlie LeBlanc to help him raise poor
Molly's children, her nephews. This leaves the widows Kuick
with no servants at all, and neither have they had any success
in hiring any, which can come as no surprise.

What was a surprise to us all was this: two weeks ago Mr.
Gathercole went to see the widow Kuick and brought with him
a bag full of money, close to a thousand dollars in cash. His
story, and we have no cause to doubt it, is that he found it on
the church doorstep with an unsigned note, instructing him to
use the money to buy the freedom of all the slaves in Paradise.

Whatever the widow might think of this cannot be said, as
she has shown no recovery of her speech since her stroke and
is quite unable to rouse herself. Jemima, on the other hand, let
her displeasure be known in such a loud voice that Anna
claims to have heard it at the trading post. Jemima's position is
that the money left on Mr. Gathercole's doorstep is in fact her
own money, from the stolen strongbox, and that she will not
be fooled into believing otherwise. To his credit, Mr.
Gathercole will not give in to her demands without some
credible proof, which does not seem to be forthcoming. Jemima
took her complaint to Mr. McGarrity as constable, but as you
can perhaps imagine, he was not very sympathetic and
suggested only that she might write to Judge O'Brien, as he
would certainly be glad to hear from her again.

Your father, who sits with me at the table, reminds me of
Curiosity's position that if Jemima keeps on giving vent to her

emotions in such a way, her baby will have a disposition like a mule with botflies, which is to say, much like her own. I fear I am become quite cruel in my advancing years, and I must laugh as I read these lines out loud to myself. I wonder sometimes what is to become of Jemima.

It is your father's belief that in the end she will indeed sell the slaves, not only because they need the money but also— and I must admit that this is true—because things do not go well for her at the mill, and the slaves seem quite content to let the business flounder. Charlie LeBlanc has offered to buy the millworks from the widow with the money her son left to Becca (another scandal of the highest order, of course), but Jemima says quite publicly that she'd sooner swallow the buhrstone. In the end that, too, may come to pass.

Because I know you will be wondering, I must report that there has been no word of or from Liam Kirby since he disappeared from the church that July night. To be truthful, I still do not know what to make of him. Sometimes it seems to me that his actions of those last weeks must have been calculated to purchase redemption for himself, or perhaps just some small measure of forgiveness for the role he played in the death of our mutual friend. Other times it seems that there was more to the story than we knew, or ever will know, unless you are someday able to get the entire tale from Manny. In any case I know not what to think, nor how to feel.

On a happier note, you should know that Ethan improves. Every day he is a little more himself and less weighed down by sorrow. Curiosity reports that Richard spends less time in his laboratory and more with the boy, and that they both seem the better for it. It seems to me that in the end Kitty did understand those she loved best in a way the rest of us do not, and never could.

I have not written yet in this long letter of your new husband, and in fact I find myself oddly unable to form any thoughts to put on paper that are not excessively sentimental. And so your father, who insists on leaving the writing of letters to me, will have the last word after all. He sends his love, and to Strikes-the-Sky this message: that he may endeavor to deserve you.

With all our fondest good wishes and loving affection,
Your stepmother, Elizabeth Middleton Bonner

Author's Notes and Acknowledgments

My relationship with New York City (and hence this story) begins with Theunis and Belitjegen Quick, some of my earliest known ancestors, who left Holland for New Amsterdam sometime before 1640 and lived on what is now Whitehall Street, where the Spencers make their (fictional) home in this novel. Almost three hundred years later my paternal grandfather came from Italy, passed through Ellis Island, and a few years later married a good Italian girl, an orphan who had been raised at the Mother Cabrini orphanage when it was still in Manhattan. For these and other reasons my curiosity about and affection for the city are endless.

The first job of any novelist is to tell a whopping good story, and I hope I have done that here. My secondary goal is that the unsuspecting reader caught up in the lives of these characters of mine will unwittingly absorb some history, along with a new awareness and appreciation for the city and its people in all their complexity.

Truth is stranger than fiction goes the old chestnut, and thus I sometimes found it necessary to tweak various facts behind this story to render them less incredible. For example: there was, in truth, a Mr. Cock who was the purveyor for New York City's almshouse in the early 1800s, just as there was a Dr. Valentine Seaman. In those cases where real names caused too great a distraction to the readers of early drafts, I have amended spelling. Thus Mr. Cock became Mr. Cox and Dr. Seaman became Dr. Simon. Like all the other historical personages I have borrowed in the telling of this story, I start with the available facts and then make up the rest. This is a novel, after all.

Many events described here happened, although I have

sometimes taken the outrageous liberty of rearranging them (very slightly!) in time. Dr. Seaman (or Simon) did found the city's Kine-Pox Institution in the Almshouse; there was a riot of free blacks outside the home of a wealthy French expatriate when she tried to evade the Gradual Manumission Act; two Irishmen did stand up to an alderman and land in jail for their trouble, causing a scandal that took place largely in the newspapers; and the Tammany Society's appropriation of Indian customs and costume to their own ends in their annual June 12 celebration went on for many years.

The Gradual Manumission Act was passed into law by the state legislature in 1799, and following that, the institution of slavery began to slowly give way in New York State. However, slaves continued to take the risk of running to freedom, and slaveholders tried to get them back, in part by paying bounties to blackbirders. The Red Rock community and Manny's work are based on documented "maroon societies" of the period.

The Manumission Society did in fact establish and oversee the African Free School, but the Libertas Society is a fiction. For those interested in the history of slavery, resistance to slavery, and black communities in the North, I recommend Shane White's excellent *Somewhat More Independent: The End of Slavery in New York City 1770–1810*, T. Stephen Whitman's *The Price of Freedom*, Joyce Hansen and Gary McGowan's *Breaking Ground Breaking Silence: The Story of New York's African Burial Ground*.

Michael Howe is a composite character based on James Cheetum (editor of the *American Citizen*) and James Keltetas, a lawyer who wrote anonymously for Thomas Greenleaf's *Journal*. Keltetas did indeed go to the bridewell for writing in defense of Irish ferrymen sentenced to hard labor for speaking back to an abusive alderman.

Most of the medical practices, treatments, and beliefs described in the story are based on documentation of the time. Debates about the cause and treatment of smallpox, yellow fever, tuberculosis, and other diseases are taken from a variety of historical sources. For example, medical practitioners were deep in a debate on the relationship between syphilis and gonorrhea, and many believed them to be different manifestations of the same disease. Just the opposite confusion reigned about the group of related illnesses caused by streptococcus bacteria. Medical practitioners of the period did not recognize the relationship between maternal postlabor/delivery infections, strep throat, scarlet fever, certain skin infections, focal infections such as pneumonia, sepsis, streptococcal toxic shock syndrome, and necrotizing fasciitis.

Information is not always easy to find, but among the more useful resources are Thacher's *New American Dispensatory,* Morgagni's *Seats and Causes of Disease Investigated by Anatomy,* and the excellent *Cambridge World History of Human Disease,* edited by Kenneth F. Kiple.

I have tried to be as true to the geography of Manhattan in 1802 as the record will allow. All institutions (Almshouse, theaters, shops, the New-York Dispensary, African Free School, taverns, churches, docks, etc.) have been left in their original locations, insofar as that information was available. Developments in what is now known as the Adirondack park are less documented for the same period, and much of that part of the story's location is based on approximation and guesswork. The village of Paradise is fictional, but it is situated on a site on the west bank of the Sacandaga with some ruins called "White House," which may have been a single homestead or a small village.

I am especially thankful to historians and librarians for their assistance. Dan Prosterman combed through the resources at the New York City Municipal Archives for hours, and the staff at the New-York Historical Society and the New York Public Library were tremendously helpful in locating information and documents. Steven Lopata provided information on chemical laboratories, Adrienne Mayor was helpful in tracking down information about fossils and related myths in the Hudson Valley, Jim and Janet Gilsdorf continue to provide excellent medical information.

To my perceptive, watchful, and ever dependable readers and friends, Suzanne Paola, Patricia Bolton, and S/He Who Must Not Be Named, my endless gratitude. I am also thankful to the UCross Foundation for a month's seclusion in the high desert of Wyoming in which to write, to Harmony and Loren Kellogg for support, friendship, and the gift of refuge and a house with a view. Tamar Groffman provided another kind of peaceful space and calm guidance that made all the difference in the hardest times.

As always I am thankful to my agent and friend, Jill Grinberg, to my splendid editor, Wendy McCurdy, and to Nita Taublib for their encouragement and enthusiasm.

And of course there's Tuck, Bill, and Beth—now and always.

About the Author

SARA DONATI lives with her husband and daughter in the Pacific Northwest, where she is at work on her next novel.